WARRIORS
OF THE
WAY

WARRIORS OF THE WAY

THE HAMMER AND THE CROSS

ONE KING'S WAY

HARRY HARRISON
JOHN HOLM

Published by arrangement with
Tor Books
Tom Doherty Associates, Inc.
175 Fifth Avenue
New York, New York 10010

Tor® is a registered trademark of
Tom Doherty Associates, Inc.

ISBN 1-56865-146-5

Printed in the United States of America

10/02
gift

CONTENTS

THE HAMMER
AND THE
CROSS

Qui credit in Filium, habet vitam aeternam; qui autem incredulus est Filio, non videbit vitam, sed ira Dei manet super eum.

He that believeth on the Son hath everlasting life: and he that believeth not the Son shall not see life; but the wrath of God abideth on him.

—John 3 : 36

Augusta est domus: utrosque tenere non poterit. Non vult rex celestis cum paganis et perditis nominetenus regibus communionem habere; quia rex ille aeternus regnat in caelis, ille paganus perditus plangit in inferno.

The house is narrow : it cannot hold both. The king of heaven has no wish to have fellowship with damned and heathen so-called kings; for the one eternal king reigns in Heaven, the other damned heathen groans in Hell.

—Alcuin, deacon of York, A.D. 797

The greatest disaster ever to befall the West was Christianity.

Gravissima calamitas umquam supra Occidentem accidens erat religio Christiana.

—Gore Vidal, A.D. 1987

THRALL

CHAPTER ONE

Spring. A spring dawn on Flamborough Head, where the rock of the Yorkshire Wolds juts out into the North Sea like a gigantic fishhook, millions of tons in weight. Pointing out to sea, pointing to the ever-present threat of the Vikings. Now the kings of the little kingdoms were uneasily beginning to draw together against this threat from the North. Uneasy and jealous, remembering the long hostilities and the trail of murder that had marked the history of the Angles and the Saxons ever since they came here centuries ago. Proud warsmiths who overcame the Welsh, noble warriors who—as the poets say —obtained the land.

Godwin the Thane cursed to himself as he paced the wooden palisade of the little fort erected on the very tip of Flamborough Head itself. Spring! Maybe in more fortunate parts the lengthening days and the light evenings meant greenery and buttercups and heavy-uddered cows trooping to the byres to be milked. Here on the Head it meant wind. It meant the equinoctial gales and the nor'easter blowing. Behind him the low, gnarled trees stood in line, one behind the other like men with their backs turned, each successive one a few inches higher than the one to windward, so that they formed natural wind-arrows or weathercocks, pointing out to the tormented sea. On three sides all round him the gray water heaved slowly like an immense animal, the waves starting to curl and then flattening out again as the wind tore at them, beating them down and levelling out even the massive surges of the ocean. Gray sea, gray sky, squalls blotting the horizon, no color in the world at all except when the rollers finally crashed into the striated walls of the cliffs, shattering and sending up great plumes of spray. Godwin had been there so long that he no longer heard the roar of the collision, noticed it only when the spray reached so high up the cliff that the water which soaked his cloak and hood and dripped onto his face turned salt instead of fresh.

Not that it made any difference, he thought numbly. It was all just as cold. He could go back into the shelter, kick the slaves aside, warm his frozen hands and feet by the fire. There was no chance of raiders on a day like this. The Vikings were seamen, the greatest seamen in the world, or so they said. You didn't have to be a great seaman to know that there was no point in putting out on a day like this. The wind was due east—no, he reflected, due east a point north. Fine for blowing you across from Denmark, but how could you keep a longship from broaching to in this sea? And how could you steer for a safe landing once you arrived? No, no chance at all. He might as well be by the fire.

Godwin looked longingly at the shelter with its little trail of smoke instantly whipped away by the wind, but turned his pace and began to shuffle along the palisade again. His lord had trained him well. "Don't think, Godwin," he had said. "Don't think maybe they'll come today and maybe they won't. Don't believe that it's worth keeping a lookout some of the time and it's not worth it the rest. While it's day, you stay on the Head. Look out all the time. Or one day you'll be thinking one thing and some Stein or Olaf'll think another and they'll be ashore and twenty miles inland before we can catch up with them—if we ever do. And that's a hundred lives lost and a hundred pounds in silver and cattle and burnt thatch. And the rents not paid for years after. So watch, Thane, or it's your estates that will suffer."

So his lord Ella had said. And behind him the black crow, Erkenbert, had crouched over his parchment, his quill squeaking as he traced out the mysterious black lines that Godwin feared more than he feared the Vikings. "Two months' service on Flamborough Head to Godwin the thane," he had pronounced. "He is to watch till the third Sunday after *Ramis Palmarum*." The alien syllables had nailed the orders down.

Watch they had said and watch he would. But he didn't have to do it as dry as a reluctant virgin. Godwin bellowed downwind to the slaves, for the hot spiced ale he had commanded half an hour before. Instantly one of them came running out, the leather mug in his hand. Godwin eyed him with deep disfavor as he trotted over to the palisade and up the ladder to the watchkeeper's walkway. A damned fool, this one. Godwin kept him because he had sharp eyes, but that was all. Merla, his name. He had been a fisherman once. Then there had been a hard winter, little to catch, he had fallen behind with the dues he owed to his landlords, the black monks of St. John's Minster at Beverley, twenty miles off. First he had sold his boat to pay his dues and feed his wife and bairns. Then, when he had no money and could not feed them any longer, he had had to sell his family to a richer man, and in the end had sold himself to his former landlords. And they had lent Merla to Godwin. Damned fool. If the slave had been a man of honor he would have sold himself first and given the money to his wife's kin, so at least they would have taken her in. If he had been a man of sense he would have sold his wife and the bairns first and kept the boat. Then maybe he would have had a chance to buy them back. But he was a man of neither sense nor honor. Godwin turned his back on the wind and the sea and took a firm swallow from the brimming mug. At least the slave hadn't been sipping from it. He could learn from a thrashing if from nothing else.

Now what was the wittol staring at? Staring past his master's shoulder, mouth agape, pointing out to sea.

"Ships," he yelled. "Viking ships, two mile out to sea. I see 'em again. Look, master, look!"

Godwin spun automatically, cursed as the hot liquid slopped over his sleeve, peered out into the cloud and rain along the pointing arm. Was that a dot there, out where the cloud met the waves? No, nothing. Or . . . maybe. He could see nothing steadily, but out there the waves would be running twenty feet high, high enough to shelter any ship trying to ride out a storm under bare poles.

"I see 'em," yelled Merla again. "Two ships, a cable apart."

"Longships?"

"No, master, knorrs."

Godwin hurled the mug over his shoulder, seized the slave's thin arm in an iron grasp, and slashed him viciously across the face, forehand, backhand, with a sodden leather gauntlet. Merla gasped and ducked but did not dare to try to shield himself.

"Talk English, you whore's get. And talk sense."

"A knorr, master. It's a merchant ship. Deep-bellied, for cargo." He hesitated, afraid to show further knowledge, afraid to conceal it. "I can recognize 'un by . . . by the shape of the prow. They must be Vikings, master. We don't use 'em."

Godwin stared out to sea again, anger fading, replaced by a cold, hard feeling at the base of his stomach. Doubt. Dread.

"Listen, Merla, to me," he whispered. "Be very sure. If those are Vikings I must call out the entire coast-watch, every man from here to Bridlington. They are only churls and slaves, when all is said and done. No harm if they are dragged from their greasy wives.

"But I must do something else. As soon as the watch is called I must also send riders in to the minster at Beverley, to the monks of good St. John— your masters, remember?"

He paused to note the terror and the old memories in Merla's eyes.

"And they will call out the mounted levy, the thanes of Ella. No good keeping them here, where the pirates could feint at Flamborough and then be twenty miles off round Spurn Head before they could get their horses out of the marsh. So they stay back, so they can ride in any direction once the threat is seen. But if I call them out, and they ride over here in the wind and the rain on a fool's errand . . . And especially if some Viking sneaks in through the Humber while their backs are turned . . .

"Well, it would be bad for me, Merla." His voice sharpened and he lifted the underfed slave off the ground. "But by almighty God in heaven I'll see you regret it till the last day you live. And after the thrashing you get that may not be long.

"But, Merla, if those are Viking ships out there and you let me *not* report them—I'll hand you back to the black monks and say I could do nothing with you.

"Now, what do you say? Viking ships, or no?"

The slave stared out again to sea, his face working. He would have been wiser, he thought, to say nothing. What was it to him if the Vikings sacked Flamborough, or Bridlington, or Beverley Minster itself? They could not enslave him any more than he was already. Maybe foreign heathens would be better masters than the people of Christ at home. Too late to think that now. The sky was clearing, momentarily. He could see, even if his weak-eyed landlubber of a master could not. He nodded.

"Two Viking ships, master. Two mile out to sea. Southeast."

Godwin was away, bellowing instructions, calling to his other slaves, shouting for his horse, his horn, his small, reluctant force of conscripted freemen. Merla straightened, walked slowly to the southwest angle of the palisade, looked out thoughtfully and carefully. The weather cleared momentarily, and for a few heartbeats he could see plain. He looked at the run of the waves—the turbid yellow line a hundred yards offshore which marked the long, long expanse of tidal sandbanks which ran the full length of this barest and most harborless, wind- and current-swept stretch of English shore—tossed a handful of moss from the palisade into the air and

studied the way it flew. Slowly a grim and humorless smile creased his careworn face.

Great sailors those Vikings might be. But they were in the wrong place, on a lee shore with a widow-maker blowing. Unless the wind dropped, or their heathen gods from Valhalla could help them, they stood no chance. They would never see Jutland or the Vik again.

Two hours later fivescore men stood clustered on the beach south of the Head, at the north end of the long, long, inlet-less stretch of coast that ran down to Spurn Head and the mouth of the Humber. They were armed: leather jackets and caps, spears, wooden shields, a scattering of the broadaxes they used to shape their boats and houses. Here and there a sax, the short chopping sword from which the Saxons to the south took their name. Only Godwin had a metal helmet and mail-shirt to pull on, a brass-hilted broadsword to buckle round his waist. In the normal way of things men like these, the coast-watch of Bridlington, would not hope or expect to stand on the shore and trade blows with the professional warriors of Denmark and Norway. Rather, they would fade away, taking as much as they could of their goods and wives with them. Waiting for the mounted levy, the thane-service of Northumbria, to come down and do the fighting for which they earned their estates and manor houses. Waiting hopefully for a chance to swarm forward and join in the harassing of a beaten enemy, the chance of taking loot. It was not a chance which had come to any Englishman since Oakley fourteen years before. And that had been in the south, in the foreign kingdom of Wessex, where all manner of strange things happened.

Nevertheless the mood of the men watching the knorrs out in the bay was unalarmed, even cheerful. Almost every man in the coast-watch was a fisherman, skilled in the ways of the North Sea. The worst water in the world, with its fogs and gales, its monstrous tides and unexpected currents. As the day strengthened and the Viking ships were blown remorselessly closer in, Merla's realization had come to everyone: The Vikings were doomed. It was just a matter of what they could try next. And whether they would try it, lose, and get the wreck over with before the mounted levy Godwin had summoned hours before could arrive, resplendent in its armor, colored cloaks and gold-mounted swords. After which, opinion among the fishermen felt, the chances of any worthwhile plunder for them were low. Unless they marked the spot and tried later, in secret, with grappling irons . . . Quiet conversations ran among the men at the rear, with an occasional low laugh.

"See," the town reeve was explaining to Godwin at the front, "the wind's east a point north. If they put up a scrap of sail they can run west, north or south." He drew briefly in the wet sand at their feet. "If he goes west he hits us. If he goes north he hits the Head. Mind you, if he could get past the Head he'd have a clear run northwest away up to Cleveland. That's why he was trying his sweeps an hour ago. A few hundred yards out to sea and he'd have been free. But what we knows, and what they doesn't, is there's a current. Hell of a current, rips down past the Head. They might as well stir the water with their . . ." He paused, not sure how far informality could go.

"Why doesn't he go south?" cut in Godwin.

"He will. He's tried the sweeps, tried the sea-anchor to check his drift. It's my guess the one in charge, the *jarl* what they call them, he knows his men are exhausted. A rare old night they must have had of it. And a shock in the morning when they saw where they were." The reeve shook his head with a kind of professional sympathy.

"They are not such great sailors," pronounced Godwin with satisfaction. "And God is against them, foul, heathen Church-defilers."

A stir of excitement behind them cut off the reply the reeve might have been incautious enough to make. The two men turned.

On the path that ran along behind high-water mark, a dozen men were dismounting. The levy? thought Godwin. The thanes from Beverley? No, they could not possibly have arrived in this time. They must only now be saddling up. Yet the man in front was a nobleman. Big, burly, fair hair, bright blue eyes, with the upright stance of a man who had never had to plough or hoe for a living. Gold shone beneath his expensive scarlet cape, on buckles and sword-pommel. Behind him strode a smaller, younger version of himself, surely his son. And on the other side of him another youth, tall, straight-backed like a warrior. But dark in complexion, poorly dressed in tunic and wool breeches. Grooms held the horses for half a dozen more armed, competent-looking men—a retinue, surely, a rich thane's hearth-troop.

The leading stranger held his empty hand up. "You do not know me," he said. "I am Wulfgar. I am a thane from King Edmund's country, from the East Angles."

A stir of interest from the crowd, the dawnings his message might be of hostility.

"You wonder what I am doing here. I will tell you." He gestured out at the shore. "I hate Vikings. I know more of them than most men. And, like most men, to my sorrow. In my own country, among the North-folk beyond the Wash, I am the coast-guard, set by King Edmund. But long ago I saw that we would never get rid of these vermin while we English fought only our own battles. I persuaded my king of this, and he sent messages to yours. They agreed that I should come north, to talk with the wise men in Beverley and in Eoforwich about what we might do. I took a wrong road last night, met your messengers riding to Beverley this morning. I have come to help." He paused. "Have I your leave?"

Godwin nodded slowly. Never mind what the lowborn fish-churl of a reeve said. Some of the bastards might come ashore. And if they did, this lot might well scatter. A dozen armed men just might be useful.

"Come and welcome," he said.

Wulfgar nodded with deliberate satisfaction. "I am only just in time," he remarked.

Out to sea the penultimate act of the wreck was about to take place. One of the two knorrs was fifty yards farther in than the other; her men more tired or maybe less driven by their skipper. Now she was about to pay the price. Her wallowing rolls in the waves changed angle, the bare mast rocking crazily. Suddenly the watching men could see that the yellow line of underwater sandbanks was the other side of the hull. Crewmen exploded from the deck and the planks where they had been lying, ran furiously up and down, grabbing sweeps, thrusting them over the side, trying to pole their ship off and gain a few extra moments of life.

Too late. A cry of despair rang thinly across the water as the Vikings saw it, echoed by a hum of excitement from the Englishmen on the shore: the wave, the big wave, the seventh wave that always rolls farthest up the beach. Suddenly the knorr was up on it, lifted and tilted sideways in a cascade of boxes and barrels and men sliding from the windward into the leeward scuppers. Then the wave was gone and the knorr smashed down, landing with a thump on the hard sand and gravel of the bank. Planks flew, the mast was over the side in a tangle of cordage; for an instant a man could be seen grasping desperately to the ornamented dragon-prow. Then another wave covered everything, and when it passed there were only bobbing fragments.

The fishermen nodded. A few crossed themselves. If the good God spared them from the Vikings, that was the way they expected to go one day—like men, with the cold salt in their mouths, and rings in their ears to pay kindly strangers to bury them. Now, there was one more thing for a skillful captain to try.

The remaining Viking was going to try it, to scud south with the wind abeam and all the easting he could get, rather than wait passively for death like his consort had. A man appeared suddenly at the steering oar. Even from two furlongs' distance the watchers could see his red beard wagging as he bellowed orders, could hear the echo of his urgency rolling across the water. There were men at the ropes, waiting, heaving together. A scrap of sail leapt free from the yard, caught instantly by the wind and tugged out. As the ship shot urgently towards shore another volley of orders swung the yard round and the boat heeled downwind. Within seconds she was steady on a new course, picking up speed, throwing water wide from her bow-wave as she raced away from the Head down toward the Spurn.

"They're getting away!" yelled Godwin. "Get the horses!" He cuffed his groom out of the way, scrambled astride, and set off at a gallop in pursuit, Wulfgar, the stranger thane, only a pace or two behind, and the rest of their retinues following in a strung-out, disorderly lines. Only the dark boy who had come with Wulfgar hesitated.

"You're not hurrying," he said to the motionless reeve. "Why not? Don't you want to catch up with them?"

The reeve grinned, stooped, picked a pinch of sand from the beach and threw it in the air. "They've got to try it," he remarked. "Nothing else to do. But they're not going to get far."

Turning on his heel he indicated a score of men to stay where they were and watch the beach for wreckage or survivors. Another score of mounted men set off along the path behind the thanes. The rest, bunched together, began to trot purposefully but deliberately along the beach after the racing ship.

As the minutes passed even the landsmen realized what the reeve had seen straight away. The Viking skipper was not going to win his gamble. Twice already he had tried to force his ship's head out to sea, two men joining the red-bearded one as he strained at the steering oar, the rest of the crew bracing the yard round till the ropes sang iron-hard in the wind. Both times the waves had heaved, heaved remorselessly at the prow till it wavered, swung back, the ship's hull shuddering with the forces contending on it. And again the skipper had tried, turning back parallel with the coastline and building up speed for another dash to the safety of the open sea.

But was he parallel with the coastline this time? Even to the inexperienced eyes of Godwin and Wulfgar it looked this time as if something was different: stronger wind, heavier sea, the grip of the inshore current dragging at the bottom. The red-bearded man was still by the oar, still shouting orders for some other maneuver, the ship was still racing along, as the poets said, like a foamy-necked floater, but her prow was turning in inch by inch or foot by foot; the yellow line was perilously close to her bow-wave, it was clear she was going to—

Strike. One instant the ship was running full tilt, the next her prow had slammed into unyielding gravel. The mast snapped off instantly and hurled itself forward, taking half the crew with it. The planks of the clinker-built boat sprang outward from their settings, letting in the on-rushing sea. In a heartbeat the whole ship had opened up like a flower. And then vanished, leaving only cordage streaming in the wind for a moment to show where she had been. And, once again, bobbing fragments in the water.

Bobbing fragments, the fishermen noticed interestedly as they panted up, this time rather closer to shore. One of them a head. A red head.

"Is he going to make it, do you think?" asked Wulfgar. They could see the man clearly now, fifty yards out in the water, hanging still and making no effort to swim farther as he eyed the great waves pounding in to destroy themselves on the shore.

"He's going to try," replied Godwin, motioning men forward to the watermark. "If he does, we'll grab him."

Redbeard had made his mind up and started to swim forward, hurling the water aside with great strokes of his arms. He had seen the great wave coming behind him. It lifted him, he was swept forward, straining to keep himself on top of the wave as if he could propel himself up the beach and land as weightlessly as the white foam that crawled almost to the soles of the thanes' leather shoes. For ten strokes he was there, the watchers turning their heads up to look at him as he swung to the crest of the wave. Then the wave in front, retreating, checked his progress in a great swirl of sand and stone, the crest broke, dissolved. Smashed him down with a grunt and a snap. Rolled him helplessly forward. Dragged him back with the undertow.

"Go in and get him," yelled Godwin. "Move, you hare-hearts! He can't hurt you."

Two of the fishermen darted forward between the waves, grabbed an arm each and hauled him back, for a moment waist-deep amid the smother but then out, the redbeard braced between them.

"He's still alive," muttered Wulfgar in astonishment. "I thought that wave was enough to break his spine."

The redbeard's feet touched the shore, he looked round at the eighty men confronting him, his teeth showed suddenly in a flashing grin.

"What welcome," he remarked.

He turned in the grip of his two rescuers, placed the outside of his foot on one man's shin, raked it down with full weight onto the instep. The man howled and let go the brawny arm he was clutching. Instantly the arm swept across, two fingers extended, driving deep into the eyes of the man still holding on. He, too, shrieked and fell to his knees, blood starting from between his fingers. The Viking plucked the gutting-knife from his belt, stepped forward, seized the nearest Englishman with one hand and stabbed savagely upwards with the other. As the fisherman's mates leapt back, shouting in alarm, he snatched a spear, whipped the knife back and hurled it, grabbed a sax from the hand of the fallen man. Ten heartbeats after his feet touched the shore he was the center of a semicircle of men, all backing away from him, except the two still lying at his feet.

His teeth showed again as he threw his head back in a wild guffaw. "Come now," he shouted gutturally. "I one, you many. Come to fight with Ragnar. Who is great one who comes first? You. Or you." He flourished his spear at Godwin and Wulfgar, now isolated, mouths gaping, by the fisher-men still drawing respectfully back.

"We'll have to take him," muttered Godwin, drawing his broadsword with a wheep. "I wish I had my shield."

Wulfgar followed suit, stepping sideways, pushing back the fair-haired boy who stood a pace behind him. "Go back, Alfgar. If we can disarm him the churls will finish it for us."

The two Englishmen edged forward, swords drawn, facing the bearlike figure which stood grinning, waiting for them, the blood and water still surging round his feet.

Then he was in motion, heading straight for Wulfgar, moving with the speed and ferocity of a charging boar. Wulfgar sprang back in shock, landed awkwardly, a foot twisting under him. The Viking missed with a lefthand slash, poised the right arm for a downward killing thrust.

Something jerked the redbeard off his feet, hurled him backward, strug-gling helplessly to free an arm, twisted him round and threw him heavily into the wet sand. A net. A fisherman's net. The reeve and two more jumped forward, seized handfuls of tarry cordage, jerked the net tighter. One twitched the sax from an enmeshed hand, another stamped savagely on the fingers holding the spear, breaking shaft and bones in the same movement. They rolled the helpless man quickly, expertly, like a danger-ous dogfish or herring-shark. They straightened, looking down, and waited for orders.

Wulfgar limped over, exchanging glances with Godwin. "What have we caught here?" he muttered. "Something tells me this is no two-ship chief-tain out of luck."

He eyed the garments of the netted man, reached down and felt them. "Goatskin," he said. "Goatskin with pitch on. He called himself Ragnar. We've caught Lothbrok himself. Ragnar Lothbrok. Ragnar Hairy-Breeks."

"We can't deal with him," said Godwin in the silence. "He'll have to go to King Ella."

Another voice broke in, the voice of the dark boy who had questioned the reeve.

"King Ella?" he said. "I thought Osbert was king of the Northumbrians."

Godwin turned to Wulfgar with weary politeness. "I don't know how you discipline your people in the North-folk," he remarked. "But if he were mine and said something like that I'd have his tongue torn out. Unless he's your kin, of course."

Wulfgar's knuckles whitened on his sword-hilt.

In the lightless stable no one could see him. The dark boy leaned his face on the saddle and let himself slump. His back was like fire, the wool tunic sticky with blood, rasping and pulling free at every movement. The beating had been the worst he had ever suffered, and he had suffered many, many thrashings from rope and leather, bent over the horse-trough in the yard of the place he called home.

It was that remark about kin that had done it, he knew. He hoped he had not cried out so that the strangers would hear him. Toward the end he hadn't been able to tell. Pained memories of dragging himself out into the daylight. Then the long ride across the Wolds, trying to hold himself straight. What would happen now they were in Eoforwich? Once upon a time the fabled city, home of the long-departed but mysterious Rome-folk and their legions, had stirred his fervent imagination more than the songs of glory of the minstrels. Now he was here, and he only wanted to escape.

When would he be free of his father's guilt? Of his stepfather's hate?

Shef pulled himself together and began to unbuckle the girth, dragging at the heavy leather. Wulfgar, he was sure, would soon formally enslave him, put the iron collar round his neck, ignore the faint protests of his mother, and sell him in the market at Thetford or Lincoln. He would get a good price. In childhood Shef had hung around the village forge, drawn by the fire, hiding from the abuse and the thrashings. Slowly he had come to help the smith, pumping the bellows, holding the tongs, beating out the iron blooms. Making his own tools. Making his own sword.

They would not let him keep it once he was a slave. Maybe he should run now. Slaves sometimes got away. Usually not.

He pulled off the saddle and groped round the unfamiliar stable for a place to stow it. The door opened, bringing in light, a candle, and the familiar cold, scornful voice of Alfgar.

"Not finished yet? Then drop it, I'll send a groom. My father is called to council with the king and the great ones. He must have a servant behind his chair to pour his ale. It is not fitting for me to do it and the companions are too proud. Go, now. The king's bower-thane waits to instruct you."

Shef plodded out into the courtyard of the king's great wooden hall, new-built within the square of the old Roman ramparts, into the dim light of the spring evening, almost too tired to walk straight. And yet, inside him, something stirred, something hot and excited. Council? Great ones? They would decide the fate of the prisoner, the mighty warrior. It would be a story to tell Godive, one that none of the wiseacres of Emneth could match.

"And keep your mouth *shut*," a voice hissed from inside the stable. "Or he *will* have your tongue torn out. And remember: Ella is king in Northumbria now. And you are no kin to my father."

CHAPTER TWO

"We think he's Ragnar Lothbrok," King Ella asked his council. "How do we know?"

He looked down a long table with a dozen men seated round it, all of them on low stools except for the king himself, who was on a great carven high seat. Most of them were dressed like the king, or like Wulfgar, who sat at Ella's left hand: in brightly colored cloaks, still pulled round them against the drafts that swirled in from every corner and closed shutter, making the tallow-dipped torches flare and eddy; gold and silver round wrists and brawny necks; clasps and buckles and heavy sword-belts. They were the military aristocracy of Northumbria, the petty rulers of great blocks of land in the south and east of the kingdom, the men who had put Ella on the throne and driven out his rival Osbert. They sat on their stools awkwardly, like men who spent their lives on foot or in the saddle.

Four other men stood out against them, grouped at the foot of the table as if in conscious isolation. Three wore the black gowns and cowls of the monks of St. Benedict, the fourth the purple and white of a bishop. They sat easily, bending forward over the table, wax tablets and styli ready to record what was said, or to pass their thoughts to one another in secret.

One man made ready to answer his king's question: Cuthred, captain of the bodyguard.

"We can't find anyone to recognize him," he admitted. "Everyone who ever stood face-to-face with Ragnar in battle is dead—except," he remarked courteously, "the gallant thane of King Edmund who has joined us. However, that doesn't prove this one is Ragnar Lothbrok.

"But I think he is. One, he won't talk. I reckon I'm good at getting people to talk, and anyone who won't is not a common pirate. This one for sure thinks he's somebody.

"Another, it fits. What were those ships doing? They were coming back from the south, they'd been blown off course, they hadn't seen sun nor stars for days. Otherwise skippers like that—and the Bridlington reeve says they were good—wouldn't have got into that state. And they were cargo ships. What cargo do you take south? Slaves. They don't want wool, they don't want furs, they don't want ale. Those were slavers on their way back from the countries down south. The man's a slaver who's a somebody, and that fits Ragnar. Doesn't prove it, though."

Cuthred took a heavy pull at his ale-mug, exhausted by eloquence.

"But there's one thing that makes me sure. What do we know about Ragnar?" He looked round the table. "Right, he's a bastard."

"Church-despoiler," agreed Archbishop Wulfhere from the end of the table. "Ravisher of nuns. Thief of the brides of Christ. Assuredly his sins shall find him out."

"I dare say," agreed Cuthred. "One thing I have heard about him is this, and I've only heard it about him, not all the other Church-despoilers and ravishers there are in the world. Ragnar is very big on information. He's like me. He's good at getting people to talk. The way he does it, I hear, is this"—A note of professional interest crept into the captain's voice.—"If he catches someone, first thing he does—no talk, no argument—is gouge one eye out. Then he still doesn't talk, he reaches round and gets the man's head ready for the next one. If the man thinks of something Ragnar really wants to know while he's getting ready, all right, he's in business. If he doesn't, well, too bad. They say Ragnar wastes a lot of people, but then churls aren't worth a lot on the block. They say he reckons it saves him a lot of time and breath."

"And our prisoner has told you this is his view too?" It was one of the black monks who spoke, his voice dripping condescension. "In the course of a friendly discussion on professional matters?"

"No." Cuthred took another pull at his ale. "But I looked at his nails. All clipped short. Except the right thumbnail. It's been grown an inch long. Hard as steel. I got it here." He tossed a bloody claw onto the table.

"So it's Ragnar," said King Ella in the silence. "So what do we do with him?"

The warriors exchanged puzzled looks. "Like you mean beheading's too good for him?" ventured Cuthred. "We should hang him instead?"

"Or something worse?" put in one of the other nobles. "Like a runaway slave or something? Maybe the monks—what was that story about Holy Saint . . . Saint . . . ? The one with the gridiron, or . . ." His imagination ran out; he fell into silence.

"I have another idea," said Ella. "We could let him go."

Consternation faced him. The king leaned forward from his high seat, his sharp, mobile face and keen eyes passing to each man in turn.

"Think. Why am I king? I'm king because Osbert"—the forbidden name sent a visible shudder through the listening men, and called an answering twinge from the lacerated back of the servant who stood listening behind Wulfgar's stool—"because Osbert could not defend this kingdom against the Viking raiders. He just did what we'd always done. Told everyone to keep a lookout and organize their own defense. So we had ten shiploads land on a town and do what they liked while the other towns and parishes pulled the blankets over their heads and thanked God it wasn't them. What did I do? You know what I did. I pulled everyone back except the lookout stations, I organized the rider teams, I set up the mounted levies at the vital places. Now, they come down on us, we have a chance of coming down on them before they get too far, of teaching them a lesson. New ideas.

"I think we need another new idea here. We can let him go. We can do a deal with him. He stays away from Northumbria, he gives us hostages, we treat him as an honored guest till the hostages come, we send him off with a pile of presents. Doesn't cost us too much. Could save us a lot. By the time he's exchanged he'll have got over Cuthred's conversation with him. All part of the game. What do you say?"

The warriors looked at each other, eyebrows rising, heads shaking in surprise.

"Might work," muttered Cuthred.

Wulfgar cleared his throat to speak, a look of displeasure crossing his reddened face. He was cut off by a voice from the black monks at the end of the table.

"You may not do that, my lord."

"May not?"

"Must not. You have other duties than those in this world. The archbishop, our reverend father and former brother, has reminded us of the foul deeds done by this Ragnar against Christ's Church. Deeds done against us as men and Christians—those we are commanded to forgive.

But deeds done against Holy Church—those we must avenge with all our heart and all our strength. How many churches has this Ragnar burned? How many Christian men and women carried off to sell to the pagans and worse, to the followers of Mohammed? How many precious relics destroyed? And the gifts of the faithful stolen?

"It would be a sin against your soul to forgive these deeds. It would imperil the salvation of every man around this table. No, King, give him to us. Let us show you what we have made for you, for those who molest Mother Church. And when the news of that reaches back to the pagans, the robbers from the sea, let them know that Mother Church's arm is as heavy as her mercy is long. Let us give him to the serpent-pit. Let us make men talk of the worm-yard of King Ella."

The king hesitated, fatally. Before he could speak, the sharp agreement of the other monks and of the archbishop was echoed by the rumble of surprise, curiosity, approval from his warriors.

"I have never seen a man given to the worms," said Wulfgar, his face beaming with pleasure. "It is what every Viking in the world deserves. And so I shall say when I return to my own king, and I shall praise the wisdom and the cunning of King Ella."

The black monk who had spoken rose to his feet: Erkenbert the dreaded archdeacon. "The worms are ready. Have the prisoner taken to them. And let all attend—councillors, warriors, servants—to see the wrake and the vengeance of King Ella and Mother Church."

The council rose, Ella among them, his face still clouded by doubt, but swept along by the agreement of his men. The nobles began to jostle out, calling already for their servants, friends, wives, women to join them, to see the new thing. Shef, turning to follow his stepfather, looked back at the last moment to see the black monks still clustered in a little knot at the end of the table.

"Why did you say that?" muttered Archbishop Wulfhere to his archdeacon. "We could pay a toll to the Vikings and still save our immortal souls. Why did you force the king to send this Ragnar to the serpents?"

The monk reached in his pouch and, like Cuthred, threw an object on the table. Then another.

"What are those, my lord?"

"This is a coin. A gold coin. With the script of the abominable worshippers of Mohammed on it!"

"It was taken from the prisoner."

"You mean—he is too evil to let live?"

"No, my lord. The other coin?"

"It is a penny. A penny from our own mint here in Eoforwich. It has my own name on it, see—Wulfhere. A silver penny."

The archdeacon picked up both coins and stowed them back in his pouch. "A very bad penny, my lord. Little silver, much lead. All the Church can afford in these days. Our slaves run away, our churls cheat on their tithes. Even the nobles give as little as they dare. Meanwhile the heathens' pouches drip with gold, stolen from believers.

"The Church is in danger, my lord. Not that she may be defeated and pillaged by the heathen, grievous though that is, for from that we may recover. It is that the heathens and the Christians may make common cause. For then they will find that they have no need of us. We must not let them deal."

Nods of agreement, even from the archbishop.

"So. To the serpents."

The serpent-pit was an old stone cistern from the time of the Rome-folk, with a light roof hastily erected over it to keep off the drizzle. The monks of St. Peter's Minster in Eoforwich were tender of their pets, the shining worms. All last summer the word had gone out to their many tenants scattered across the Church lands of Northumbria: Find the adders, seek them out in their basking places on the high fells, bring them in. So much remission of rent, so much remission of tithes for a foot-long worm; more for a foot and a half; more, disproportionately more for the old, the grand-father worms. Not a week had passed without a squirming bag being delivered to the *custos viperarum*—the keeper of the snakes—its contents to be lovingly tended, fed on frogs and mice, and on each other to promote their growth: "Dragon does not become dragon till it has tasted worm," the *custos* would say to his brothers. "Maybe the same is true of our adders."

Now lay brothers racked torches round the walls of the stone court to augment the evening twilight, carried in sacks of warm sand and straw and spread it on the floor of the pit to make the serpents fiery and active. And now the *custos* too appeared, smiling with satisfaction, waving along a gang of novices, each the proud—if careful—bearer of a leather sack that hissed and bulged disconcertingly. The *custos* took each bag in turn, held it up to the crowd now pushing and jostling round the low walls of the cistern, undid the lashings, and slowly poured the struggling inhabitants down into the pit. He moved a few paces as he did each one, to distribute his serpents evenly. His task done, he stepped back to the edge of the lane kept open for the great ones by brawny companions—the king's own hearth-troop.

They came at last: the king, his council, their body-servants, the prisoner pushed along in the middle of them. There was a saying among the warriors of the North: "A man should not limp while both his legs are the same length." And Ragnar did not limp now. Yet he found it hard to hold himself straight. Cuthred's ministrations had not been gentle.

The great ones fell back when they came to the edge of the pit, and let the prisoner see what he faced. He grinned through broken teeth, his hands tied behind him, a powerful guard holding each arm. He still wore the strange shaggy clothes of tarred goatskin which had brought him his name. Erkenbert the archdeacon pushed forward to face him.

"That is the worm-yard," he said.

"Orm-garth," corrected Ragnar.

The priest spoke again, in simple English, the trade-talk of the merchants. "Know this. You have a choice. If you become Christian, you live. As a slave. No orm-garth then for you. But you must become Christian."

The Viking's mouth twisted in contempt. He spoke in reply, still in the trade-tongue. "You priests. I know your talk. You say I live. How? As a slave, you say. What you not say, but I know, is how. No eyes, no tongue. Cut legs, cut hough-sinews, no walk."

His voice rose to a chant. "I fought in the front for thirty winters, always I struck with the sword. Four hundred men I killed, a thousand women I ravished, many minsters I burned, many men's bairns I sold. Many have wept for me, I never wept for them. Now I come to the orm-garth, like Gunnar the god-born. Do your worst, let the shining worm sting me to the heart. I shall not ask for mercy. Always I struck with the sword!"

"Get on with it," snarled Ella from behind the Viking. The guards began to hustle him forward.

"Stop!" Erkenbert called. "First bind his legs."

They tied the unresisting man roughly, pulled him to the edge, balanced him on the wall, then—he looking round at the pushing but silent crowd —shoved him over. He fell a few feet, landing with a thump on top of a pile of crawling snakes. Instantly they hissed, instantly they struck.

The man in the shaggy tunic and breeches laughed once from the ground.

"They cannot bite through," called a voice in disappointment. "His clothes are too thick."

"They may strike at his hands or face," called the serpent-keeper, jealous for the honor of his pets.

One of the largest adders indeed lay a few inches from Ragnar's face, the two staring almost eye-to-eye, the forked tongue of the one almost touching the chin of the other. A long moment of pause.

Then, suddenly, the man's head moved, shooting sideways, teeth agape. A threshing of coils, a mouth spitting blood, the snake lay headless. Again the Viking laughed. Slowly he began to roll, humping his body despite the bound arms and legs, trying to fall on the snakes with the full weight of hip or shoulder.

"He's killing them," cried the *custos* in mortal pain.

Ella moved forward in sudden disgust, clicking his fingers. "You and you. You've stout boots on. Go in and lift him out.

"I'll not forget this," he added in an undertone to the disconcerted Erkenbert. "You've made a damned fool of all of us.

"Now, you men, free his arms, free his legs, cut his clothes off, bind him again. You and you, go fetch hot water. Serpents desire heat. If we warm his skin they will be drawn to it.

"One more thing. He will lie still this time, to thwart us. Bind one arm to his body and tie the left wrist to a rope. Then we can make him move."

They lowered the prisoner again, still grinning, still unspeaking. This time the king himself steered the lowering to the spot where the snakes lay thickest. In a few moments they began to crawl to the warm body steaming in the chill air, writhing over it. Cries of disgust came from the women and servants in the crowd as they imagined the scales of the fat adders brushing over bare skin.

Then the king jerked his rope, again and again. The arm moved, the adders hissed, the disturbed ones struck, felt flesh, struck again and again, filling the man's body with their poison. Slowly, slowly, the awed watchers saw his face begin to change, to puff, to turn blue. As his eyes and tongue began to bulge, finally he called out once more.

"*Gnythja mundu grisir ef galtar hag vissi,*" he remarked.

"What did he say?" muttered the crowd. "What does that mean?"

I know no Norse, thought Shef from his vantage point. But I know that bodes no good.

"Gnythja mundu grisir ef galtar hag vissi." The words still rang in the mind of the massive man, weeks later and hundreds of miles to the east, who was standing in the prow of the longship easing gently up toward the Sjaelland shore. It was sheer chance that he had ever come to hear them. Had Ragnar been talking to himself alone? he mused. Or had he known someone would hear, would understand and remember? It must have been very long odds against anyone in an English court knowing Norse, or

anyway, enough Norse to understand what Ragnar had said. But dying men were supposed to have insight. Maybe they could tell the future. Maybe Ragnar had known, or had guessed, what his words would do.

But if those were the words of fate, which would always find someone to speak them, they had chosen a strange route to come to him! In the crowd pushing round the orm-garth there had been a woman, concubine to an English noble, a "lemman," as the English called such girls. But before she had been bought for her master in the slave-mart of London, she had plied the same trade in the court of King Maelsechnaill in Ireland, where much Norse was spoken. She had heard, she had understood. She had had the wit not to tell her master—lemmans without wit did not live to see their beauty fade—but she had whispered it to her secret lover, a trader going south. He had passed it on to the other members of his caravan. And among them there had been another slave, a former fisherman on the run, one who had taken special interest in it because he had seen the actual capture of Ragnar on the shore. In London, thinking himself safe, the slave had made a story of it to earn himself mugs of ale and hunks of bacon in the waterfront booths where all men were welcome, English or Frankish, Frisian or Dane, as long as their silver was good. And so the tale had come in the end to Northern ears.

The slave had been a fool, a man of no honor. He had seen in the tale of the death of Ragnar only excitement, strangeness, humor.

The massive man in the longship—Brand—saw in it much more. That was why he brought the news.

The boat was gliding in now along a long fjord, reaching into the flat, rich countryside of Sjaelland, easternmost of the Danish islands. There was no wind; the sail was furled up against the yard, the thirty oarsmen rowing a steady, unhurried, practiced stroke, the ripples of their progress fanning out across the flat, pondlike sea to caress the shore. Cows moved gently in rich meadows, fields of thickly shooting grain stretched into the distance.

The air of peace was totally deceptive, Brand knew. He was at the still center of the greatest storm in the North, its peace guaranteed only by hundreds of miles of war-torn sea and burning coastline. As they rowed in he had been challenged three times by naval patrols—heavy coastal warships never designed for the open sea, filled with men. They had let him through with increasing amusement, always keen to see a man try his luck. Even now two ships twice the size of his were cruising behind him, just to make certain there was no escape. He knew, his men knew, that worse lay ahead.

Behind him the helmsman passed the steering-oar to a crewman and strolled forward to the prow. For a few moments he stood behind his skipper, his head barely reaching the huge man's shoulder blade, and then spoke. He spoke softly, taking care not to be overheard even by the foremost rowers.

"You know I'm not one to question decisions," he murmured. "But since we're here, and we've all stuck our pizzles well and truly in the wasps' nest, maybe you won't mind me asking why?"

"Since you came so far without asking," replied Brand in the same low tones, "I'll give you three reasons and charge you for none of them.

"One: This is our chance to gain lasting glory. This will be a scene for sagamakers and for poets until the Last Day, when the gods fight the giants and the brood of Loki is loosed on the world."

The helmsman grinned. "You have enough glory already, champion of the men of Halogaland. And some men say the ones we are going to meet *are* the brood of Loki. Especially one of them."

"Two, then: That English slave, the runaway who told us the tale, the fisherman running from the Christ-monks—did you see his back? His masters deserve all the woe in the world, and I can send it to them."

This time the helmsman laughed aloud, but gently. "Did you ever see anyone after Ragnar had finished talking to him? And those we are going to visit are worse. Especially one of them. Maybe he and the Christ-monks deserve each other. But what of all the others?"

"So, then, Steinulf, it comes to three." Brand lifted gently the silver pendant which hung round his neck and lay on his chest, outside the tunic: a short-hafted, double-headed hammer. "I was asked to do this, as a service."

"By whom?"

"Someone we both know. In the name of the one who will come from the North."

"Ah. Well. That is good enough for both of us. Maybe for all of us. But I am going to do one thing before we get too close to the shore."

Deliberately, making certain his skipper saw what he was doing, the helmsman took the pendant which hung round his own neck and tucked it inside his tunic, pulling the collar so that no trace of the chain showed.

Slowly, Brand turned to face his crew and followed suit. At a word, the steady beat of the oars in the calm water checked. The oarsmen shuffled chains and pendants out of sight. Then the beat of oars resumed.

At the jetty ahead men could now be seen sitting or strolling, never looking at the approaching warboat, giving a perfect impression of total indifference. Behind them a vast dragon-hall lay like an upturned keel;

behind it and round it, a vast confusion of sheds, bunkhouses, rollers, boatyards on the edge of the fjord, smithies, stores, ropewalks, corrals, barracoons. This was the heart of a naval empire, the power center of men intent on challenging kingdoms, the home of the homeless warriors.

The man sitting on the very end of the jetty ahead of him stood up, yawned, stretched elaborately and looked in the other direction. Danger. Brand turned to shout orders. Two of his men standing by the halliards ran a shield up to the masthead, its new-painted white face a sign of peace. Two others ran forward and eased the gaping dragon-head off its pegs on the prow, turning it carefully away from the shore and wrapping it in a cloth.

More men onshore suddenly became visible, now prepared to look directly at the boat. They gave no sign of welcome, but Brand knew that if he had not observed proper ceremonial his welcome would have been very different. At the thought of what might have happened—might still happen—he felt his belly give an unaccustomed twinge, as if his manhood was trying to crawl back within him. He turned his face out to the far shore, to ensure no expression betrayed him. He had been taught since he could crawl, *Never show fear. Never show pain.* He valued this more than life itself.

He knew also that in the gamble he was about to take, nothing could be less safe than a show of insecurity. He meant to bait his deadly hosts, draw them into his story: appear as a challenger, not a suppliant.

He meant to offer them a dare so shocking and so public that they would have no choice but to take it. It was not a plan that allowed half measures.

As the boat nosed into the jetty ropes were thrown, caught, snubbed round bollards, still with the same elaborate air of carelessness. A man was looking down into the boat. If this had been a trading port he might have asked the sailors what cargo, what name, where from? Here the man raised one eyebrow.

"Brand. From England."

"There are many men called Brand."

At a sign two of the ship's crewmen swung a gangplank from ship to jetty. Brand strolled across it, thumbs in belt, and stood facing the dockmaster. On the level boards he was looking down. Far down. He noted with inner pleasure the slight shift of the eyes as the dockmaster, no stripling himself, weighed up Brand's bulk, realized that man-to-man, at least, he was outmatched.

"Some men call me Viga-Brand. I come from Halogaland, in Norway, where men grow bigger than Danes."

"Killer-Brand. I have heard of you. But there are many killers here. It needs more than a name to be welcome."

"I have news. News for the kinsmen."

"It had better be news worth hearing if you disturb the kinsmen, coming here without leave or passport."

"News worth hearing it is." Brand looked directly into the dockmaster's eyes. "Come to hear it yourself. Tell your men to come and hear it. Anyone who cannot be bothered to hear what I have to say will curse his laziness till the last day he lives. But of course if you all have an urgent appointment in the privy let me not ask you to keep your breeches up."

Brand brushed past the other and strode wordlessly toward the plume of smoke rising from the great longhouse, the hall of the noble kinsmen, the place no enemy had seen and left alive and free to tell the tale—the Braethraborg itself. His men trooped off the ship and silently began to follow him.

The dockmaster's lips twitched, finally, with amusement. He made a sign and his men, picking their spears and bows from concealment, began to straggle inland. A flag dipped in acknowledgement from the still-vigilant outpost on the headland two miles off.

Light shone into the hall from many open shutters, but Brand halted when he got inside to let his eyes adjust, to look around, to get the feel of his audience. In later years, he knew, this scene would be famous in song and saga—if he played it right. In the next few minutes he would gain either imperishable glory or unthinkable death.

Inside the hall many men were sitting, standing, loitering, playing at one game or another. None looked at him as he came in, or at the other men silently filtering in behind him, but he knew they had registered his presence. As his eyes cleared he saw slowly that though there was no apparent order in the hall, indeed a careful avoidance of it—a pretense that all warriors, all true *drengir,* were equal—still the groupings of the men were all subtly poised on one center. At the end of the hall, there was a little space no one ventured into. There four men were grouped, all seeming intent on their own concerns.

He walked toward them, the padding of his soft seaman's shoes audible in what had indiscernibly become silence.

He reached the four men. "Greetings!" he said, pitching his voice loud for the audience clustered around and behind him. "I have news. News for the sons of Ragnar."

One of the four glanced over his shoulder at him, went back to paring his fingernails with a knife. "Great news it must be, for a man to come to the Braethraborg without invitation or passport."

"Great news it is." Brand filled his lungs and controlled his breathing. "For it is news of the death of Ragnar."

Utter silence now. The man who had spoken continued his paring, intent on his left index finger, the knife slicing, slicing. Blood sprang out, the knife cut on down, down to the quick and the bone. The man made no sound and no movement.

A second one of the four spoke, picking up a stone piece from the checkerboard to make his move, a powerful, thick-shouldered man with grizzled hair. "Tell us," he remarked, his voice carefully unperturbed, deliberately refusing to show unmanly emotion. "How did our old father Ragnar die? For it is not to be surprised at, since he was getting on in years."

"It all began on the coast of England, where he was wrecked. According to the story I heard, he was caught by the men of King Ella." Brand changed his voice slightly, as if to match, or to mock, the second Ragnarsson's studied pretense of imperturbability. "I do not suppose they had much trouble, for, as you say, he was getting on in years. Maybe he offered no resistance."

The grizzled man still held his draughtsman, his fingers closing on it tighter, tighter. Blood spurted out from under his fingernails, splashed on the board. The man put the piece down, moved it once, twice, lifted the captured draughtsman to the side. "I take, Ivar," he remarked.

The man he was playing with spoke. He was a man with hair so fair it was almost white, swept back off his pale face and held with a linen headband. He looked at Brand with eyes as colorless as frozen water, under lashes that never blinked.

"What did they do once they had caught him?"

Brand looked carefully into the pale man's unblinking stare. He shrugged, still elaborately unconcerned.

"They took him to King Ella's court at Eoforwich. It was no great matter, for they thought him only a common pirate, of no importance. I believe they asked him some questions, had some little sport with him. But then, tiring of him, they decided they might as well put him to death."

In the dead silence Brand studied his fingernails, conscious that his baiting of the Ragnarssons had almost reached its climax of danger. He shrugged again.

"Well. They gave him to the Christ-priests in the end. I expect he did not seem worthy of death from the warriors."

A flush shot into the pale man's cheeks. He seemed to be holding his breath, almost choking. The flush deepened, deepened till his face was scarlet. He began to sway to and fro in his chair, a kind of coughing coming from deep in his throat. His eyes bulged, the scarlet deepened to purple—in the dim light of the hall, almost to black. Slowly the swaying stopped, the man seemed to win some deep internal battle within himself, the coughing died, the face ebbed back to a startling pallor.

The fourth man who stood by his three brothers, watching the draughts game, was leaning on a spear. He had not moved or spoken, had kept his eyes down. Slowly now he raised them to look at Brand. For the first time the tall messenger flinched. There was something in the eyes he had heard of but had never believed: the pupils astonishingly black, the iris around them as white as new-fallen snow—startlingly clear—and surrounding the black totally, like the paint around an iron shield-boss. The eyes glinted like moonlight on metal.

"How did King Ella and the Christ-priests decide to kill the old man, in the end?" asked the fourth of the Ragnarssons, his voice low, almost gentle. "I suppose you will be telling us it did not take much doing."

Brand answered bluntly and truthfully, taking no more risks. "They put him in the serpent-pit, the worm-yard, the orm-garth. I understand there was some little trouble, as to begin with the snakes would not bite and then—from what I heard—Ragnar bit them first. But in the end they bit him and he died. It was a slow death, and no weapon-mark on him. Not one to be proud of in Valhalla."

The man with the strange eyes did not move a muscle. There was a pause, a long pause, as the intently watching audience waited for him to make some sign that he had heard, for him to show some failure in self-control like his brothers. It did not come. The man straightened finally, tossed the spear he had been leaning on to a bystander, hooked his thumbs in his belt, prepared to speak.

A grunt from the bystander, a grunt of surprise, drawing all eyes to him. Silently he held up the tough ashwood spear he had been thrown. On it men could see indentations, marks where fingers had gripped. A slight hum of satisfaction ran round the hall.

Before the man with the strange eyes could speak, Brand interrupted, seizing the moment. Pulling his mustache thoughtfully, he remarked, "There was one other thing."

"Yes?"

"After the snakes had bitten him, as he lay dying, Ragnar spoke. They did not understand him, of course, for he spoke in our tongue, in the *norroent mal,* but someone heard, someone passed it on; in the end I was fortunate enough to come by it. I have no invitation and no passport, as you said just now, but it occurred to me you might be interested enough to want to know."

"What did he say, then, the old man dying?"

Brand lifted his voice loudly so that it filled the whole hall, like a herald issuing a challenge. "He said, *'Gnythja mundu grisir ef galtar hag vissi.'* "

This time there was no need to translate. The whole hall knew what Ragnar had said: "If they knew how the old boar died, how the little pigs would grunt."

"So that is why I came uninvited," called Brand, his voice still high and challenging. "Though some told me it might be dangerous. I am a man who likes to hear grunting. And so I came to tell the little pigs. And you must be the little pigs, from what men tell me. You, Halvdan Ragnarsson" —he nodded to the man with the knife. "You, Ubbi Ragnarsson"—the first draughts-player. "You, Ivar Ragnarsson, famous for your white hair. And you, Sigurth Ragnarsson. I see now why men call you Orm-i-auga, the Snake-eye.

"It is not likely that my news has pleased you. But I hope you will agree that it was news you should be told."

The four men were on their feet now, all facing him, the pretense of indifference gone. As they took in his words, they nodded. Slowly, they were beginning to grin, their expressions all the same, looking for the first time as if they were all a family, all brothers, all sons of the same man. Their teeth showed.

It was the prayer of the monks and minster-men in those days: *Domine, libera nos a furore normannorum*—"Lord, deliver us from the fury of the Northmen." If they had seen those faces, any sensible monk would have added immediately: *Sed praesepe, Domine, a humore eorum*—"But especially, Lord, from their mirth."

"It was news we should be told," said the Snake-eye, "and we thank you for bringing it. At the start we thought you might not be telling all the truth about this matter, and that was why we may have seemed displeased. But what you said at the end—ah, that was our father's voice. He knew someone would hear it. He knew someone would tell us. And he knew what we would do. Didn't he, boys?"

A gesture, and someone rolled forward a great round chopping block, an oak trunk sawn off. A heave from the four brothers together, and it crashed down firm on the floor. The sons of Ragnar clustered round it, facing their men, each raising one foot and placing it on the block. They spoke together, following the ritual:

"Now we stand on this block, and we make this boast, that we will—"

". . . invade England in vengeance for our father"—so Halvdan said.

". . . capture King Ella and kill him with torments for Ragnar's death" —so Ubbi.

". . . defeat all the kings of the English and bring the land into subjection to us"—so Sigurth the Snake-eye.

". . . wreak vengeance on the black crows, the Christ-priests who counseled the orm-garth"—so Ivar spoke. They ended again together:

". . . and if we go back on our words let the gods of Asgarth despise us and reject us, and may we never join our father and our ancestors in their dwellings."

As they ended, the smoke-blackened beams of the longhouse were filled with a roar of approval from four hundred throats, the jarls, the nobles, the skippers, and the helmsmen of the whole pirate fleet in unison. Outside, the rank and file gathering from their booths and bunkhouses nudged each other with excitement and anticipation, knowing that a decision had been made.

"And now," the Snake-eye yelled over the din, "pull out the tables, spread the boards. No man may inherit from his father till he has drunk the funeral ale. And so we shall drink the arval for Ragnar, drink like heroes. And in the morning we shall gather every man and every ship and take our way to England, so that they shall never forget us nor be quit of us!

"But now, drink. And, stranger, sit at our board and tell us more of our father. There will be a place for you in England once it is ours."

Far away, Shef, the dark boy, the stepson of Wulfgar, lay on a straw pallet. The mist was still rising from the dank ground of Emneth, and only a thin old blanket covered him from it. Inside the stout-timbered wooden hall, his stepfather Wulfgar lay in comfort, if not in love, with the boy's mother, the lady Thryth. Alfgar lay in a warm bed in a room by his parents, and so too did Godive, the concubine's child, Wulfgar's daughter. At Wulfgar's homecoming they had all eaten lavishly of the roasted and the boiled, the baked and the brewed—duck and goose from the fens, pike and lamprey from the rivers.

Shef had eaten rye porridge and gone out to his solitary hut by the smithy where he worked, to have his only friend dress his new-got scars. Now he was tossing in the grip of a dream. If dream it was.

*   *   *

He saw a dark field somewhere on the edge of the world, lit only by a purple sky. On the field lay shapeless huddles of rags and bone and skin, white skulls and rib cages showing through the remains of gorgeous garments. Round the huddles, everywhere on the field, hopped and swarmed a great army of birds— huge black birds with black beaks, stabbing savagely into eye sockets and pecking bone-joints for a morsel of flesh or marrow. But the bodies had been picked over many times, the bones were dry; the birds began to croak loudly and peck at each other instead.

They ceased, they grew quiet, they clustered together to where four black birds were standing. They listened as the four croaked and croaked in ever louder and more menacing tones. Then the whole flock rose as one into the purple sky, circled and closed formation, then banked slowly like a single organism and flew directly toward him, toward Shef, to where he was standing. The leader flew straight at him, he could see the remorseless unblinking golden eye, the black beak pointed at his face. It did not pull back, he could not move; something was holding his head firm and rigid; he felt the black beak driving deep into the soft jelly of his eye.

Shef woke with a shout and a start, leaping straight off the pallet, clutching his thin blanket round him as he stared out of the hole in his hut's wall into a marshy dawn. His friend Hund called from the other pallet.

"What is it, Shef? What frightened you?"

For a moment he could not reply. Then it came out as a croak—he did not know what he was saying.

"The ravens! The ravens are on the wing!"

CHAPTER THREE

"**A**re you certain it is the Great Army itself which has landed?" Wulfgar's voice was angry but unsure. It was news he did not want to believe. But he did not dare to challenge the messenger openly.

"There is no doubt," said Edrich, the king's thane, trusted servant of Edmund, king of the East Angles.

"And this army is led by the sons of Ragnar?"

Even more fearful news for Wulfgar, thought Shef as he listened to the debate from the back of the room. Every freeman in Emneth had crowded into their lord's hall, summoned by runners. For though a freeman in England could lose everything—land-right, folk-right, even kin-right—for failing to answer a lawful summons to arms, for that very reason it was also their right to hear all issues debated publicly before they answered any call.

Whether Shef had any right to join them was another matter. But he had not been collared as a slave yet, and the freeman standing by the door to verify presence and absence still owed Shef for his mended ploughshare. He had grunted doubtfully, looked at the sword and shabby scabbard at Shef's side, and decided not to press the point. Now Shef stood at the very back of the room among the poorest cottagers of Emneth, trying to hear without being seen.

"My men have spoken to many churls who have seen them," said

Edrich. "They say this army is led by four great warriors, the sons of Ragnar, all of equal status. Every day the warriors gather round a great banner with the sign of a black raven. It is the Raven Banner."

Which the daughters of Ragnar wove all in one night, which spreads its wings for victory and droops them for defeat. It was a familiar story, and a fearful one. The deeds of the sons of Ragnar were famous all over Northern Europe, wherever their ships had sailed: England, Ireland, France, Spain, and even the lands beyond in the Middle Sea, from which they had returned years before laden with booty. So why had they now turned their fury on the poor and puny kingdom of the East Angles? Anxiety grew on Wulfgar's face as he pulled his long mustache.

"And where are they camped?"

"In the meadows by the Stour, south of Bedricsward." Edrich the King's Thane was visibly beginning to lose his patience. He had been over this several times before, and in more than one place. It was the same with every petty landowner. They didn't want information, they wanted a way out of their duty. But he had expected better from this one, famous for his hatred of the Vikings, a man—so he told it—who had stood sword to sword with the famous Ragnar himself.

"So what are we to do?"

"The order of King Edmund is that every freeman of the East Angles capable of bearing arms is to muster at Norwich. Every man over fifteen winters and under fifty. We will match their host with ours."

"How many of them are there?" called one of the richer tenants from the front.

"Three hundred ships."

"How many men is that?"

"They row three dozen oars, mostly," said the king's thane, briefly and reluctantly. This was the sticking point. Once the yokels realized what they were up against, they might be hard to move. But it was his duty to tell them the truth.

There was a silence while every mind confronted the same problem. Shef, faster than the others, spoke aloud.

"Three hundred ships, and three dozen oars. That's nine hundred dozen. Ten dozen is a long hundred. More than ten thousand men. All of them warriors," he added, more in amazement than fear.

"We can't fight them," said Wulfgar decisively, turning his glare away from his stepson. "We must pay tribute instead."

Edrich's patience was at an end. "That is for King Edmund to decide. And he will pay less if the Great Army sees that it is matched by a host of equal size. But I am not here to listen to talk—I bring a summons to obey. You and the landholders of Upwell and Outwell and every village between Ely and Wisbech. The king's order is that we shall muster here and set out for Norwich tomorrow. Every man liable for military service from the village of Emneth must ride or be liable to penalty and punishment from the king. Those are my orders and they are your orders too." He turned on his heel, facing the room full of stirring, unhappy men. "Freemen of Emneth, what do you say?"

"Aye," said Shef compulsively.

"He's not a freeman," snarled Alfgar from his place by his father.

"Then he damned well should be. Or he shouldn't be here. Can't you people make your minds up about anything? You've heard your king's commands."

But Edrich's words were drowned by a slow, reluctant mutter of assent from sixty throats.

In the Viking camp by the Stour, things were very different. Here the four sons of Ragnar made the decisions. They knew each others' minds too well for more than the briefest discussion.

"They'll pay in the end," said Ubbi. He and Halvdan were very much like the rest of their army, in both physique and temperament. Halvdan ruddy, the other already grizzled, both of them powerful and dangerous fighters. Not men to be trifled with.

"We must decide now," grunted Halvdan.

"Who shall it be then?" asked Sigurth.

All four men considered for a few moments. Someone who could do the job, someone experienced. At the same time someone they could afford to lose.

"Sigvarth," said Ivar finally. His pale face did not move; his colorless eyes remained fixed on the sky; he spoke only the one word. What he said was not a suggestion, but the answer. He who was called the Boneless One, though never in his presence, did not make suggestions. His brothers considered, approved.

"Sigvarth!" called out Sigurth Snake-eye.

A few yards away the jarl of the Small Isles bent over his game at knucklebones. He finished his cast, to show a proper spirit of independence, but then straightened and walked hopefully over to the little group of leaders.

"You called out my name, Sigurth."

"You have five ships? Good. We think the English and their little King

Edmund are trying to play stupid games with us. Resisting, trying to bargain. No good. We want you to go out and show them who they're dealing with. Take your ships up the coast, then round to the west. Push inland, do as much damage as you can, burn some villages. Show them what could happen if they provoke us. You know what to do."

"Yes. Done it before." He hesitated. "But what about spoils?"

"Anything you get, it's yours. But loot isn't what this is about. Do something that they will remember. Do it as Ivar would do it."

The jarl grinned again, but more hesitantly, as most men did when the name of Ivar Ragnarsson the Boneless was mentioned.

"Where will you land?" asked Ubbi.

"Place called Emneth. I was there once before. Found me a nice little chicken." The jarl's grin was cut off this time by a sudden movement from Ivar.

Sigvarth had given a stupid reason. He was not going on this mission to repeat the escapades of his youth. It was unwarriorlike. It was also the kind of thing Ivar did not discuss.

The moment passed. Ivar leaned back in his chair and turned his attention elsewhere. They knew Sigvarth was not the best in the Army—one of the reasons they were letting him go.

"Do the job and never mind chickens," said Sigurth. He waved a hand in dismissal.

At least Sigvarth knew the mechanics of his profession. At dawn two days later his five ships were sweeping cautiously into the mouth of the river Ouse, with the tide still on the flow. An hour's rowing at high tide took them as far inland as the water would bear, until the boats' keels grated on the sand. The dragon-prows nuzzled in, the men poured ashore. Instantly the assigned ship-guards backed water, pulled their wave-coursers offshore to the mudbanks, and waited there for the ebb tide to ground them out of reach of any counterattack from the local levies.

The youngest and swiftest men of Sigvarth's command had already moved out. Finding a small stud of ponies they cut down the lad in charge and raced off to round up more. As they captured the horses they sent them back to the main body. By the time the sun struggled through the morning mists a hundred and twenty men were pounding along the twisted and muddy paths towards their goal.

They rode in a hard, disciplined group. Keeping together, without advance or flank guards, counting upon strength and surprise to drive through any resistance. When their path took them up to any inhabited place—farmhouse, garth, or hamlet—the main body halted for as long as it might take a man to piss. The lighter men on the better horses swept round to the flanks and rear and halted, to prevent any escapes that might raise the alarm. Then the main body attacked. Their orders were simple, so simple that Sigvarth had not even bothered to repeat them.

They killed every person they met—man, woman, child, or babe in cradle—immediately, without halting to ask questions or seek for entertainment. Then they remounted and drove on. No looting, not yet. And, on the strictest of instructions, no fire.

By midday a corridor of death was slashed through the peaceful English countryside. Not a single person was left alive. Far behind the attackers men were beginning to notice that their neighbors were not astir, were finding horses missing and corpses in fields, were ringing the church bells and lighting their alarm beacons. But ahead of the Vikings there was not the slightest suspicion of their deadly presence.

The party from Emneth had set out considerably later in the day than Sigvarth's men. They had had to wait for the reluctant contingents from Upwell, Outwell, and beyond. Then there was a long delay while the landholders of the area greeted each other and ponderously exchanged courtesies. Next Wulfgar decided that they could not start on empty bellies and generously called for mulled ale for the leaders and small beer for the men. It was hours after sunrise when the hundred and fifty armed men, the military service of four parishes, set off down the road through the marsh which would lead them across the Ouse and in the end to Norwich. Even at this early stage they were already trailed by stragglers whose girths had broken, or whose bowels had loosened, or who had slipped off to make their farewells to their own wives or to other men's. The troop rode without precautions and without suspicion. The first inkling they had of the Vikings' presence was as they came round a bend in the road and saw heading toward them a tight-packed column of armed men.

Shef was riding just behind the leaders, as close to Edrich the King's Thane as he dared to go. Speaking up at the council had got him Edrich's favor. No one would send him back while Edrich was watching. Yet he was still there, as Alfgar had taken pains to point out to him, as a smith, not as a freeman on military service. At least he still had his self-forged sword.

Shef saw them as soon as the others, and heard the startled cries of the leaders.

"Who are those men?"

"It's the Vikings!"

"No—it can't be! They're in Suffolk. We're still negotiating."

"It's the Vikings, you porridge-brains! Get your fat arses off your horses and form up for battle. You there, dismount, dismount! Horse-holders to the rear. Get your shields off your backs and form up."

Edrich the king's thane was by this time bellowing at the top of his voice, whirling his horse round and riding into the tangled confusion of the English column. Slowly men began to appreciate the situation, to drop from their saddles, to root desperately for weapons that they had stowed for comfortable riding. To edge toward the front or toward the rear, depending on personal inclination, boldness or cowardice.

Shef had few preparations to make—the poorest man in the column. He dropped the reins of his nag, a grudging loan from his stepfather, pulled the wooden shield from his back, and loosened his only weapon in its sheath. All the armor he had was a leather jacket with such studs as he had been able to collect sewn onto it. He took position immediately behind Edrich and stood ready, his heart beating fast and excitement clutching his throat—but all outweighed by a vast curiosity. How would the Vikings fight? What was the nature of battle?

On the Viking side, Sigvarth had grasped the situation as soon as he saw the first riders coming toward him. Dropping his heels from their tucked-up riding position, he rose in his saddle, turned, and bellowed a brief command to the men behind him. Instantly the Viking column dissolved in practiced disarray. In a moment they had all dismounted. One man in five, already told off for the task, seized horse-reins and led the mounts to the rear, bending down, as soon as they were clear of the throng, to drive pegs into the ground and knot the reins to them. As soon as this was done, the two dozen horse handlers clustered in the rear and formed a reserve.

Meanwhile the others halted for the space of twenty heartbeats. Some in grim silence, others swiftly reknotting their shoes, or gulping water or pissing as they stood. Then all simultaneously unslung shields, loosened swords, passed their axes to shield-hands, poised the long battle-spears in their casting-hands. Without further words they spread into a line two-deep, from edge to edge of the road, where it dissolved into swamp on either side. At a single shouted word from Sigvarth they stepped forward at a brisk walk, the flanks falling back until the line formed a broad shallow arrow pointing directly at the English levies. At its apex was Sigvarth himself. Behind him his son Hjörvarth led a picked dozen—the men who, when the English line was broken, would sweep through and round to the rear, cutting men down from behind and turning setback into rout.

* * *

Facing them, the English had formed into a rough line three- or four-deep, also extending from edge to edge of the road. They had solved their problem with the horses by abandoning them, dropping reins and leaving the animals to stand or trot away. Among the mob of ponies there were also a few men who had slunk quietly to the rear. Not many. After three generations of raid and war many of the English had personal grudges to pay off —while none wished to be exposed to the derision of his neighbors. Shouts of encouragement rose from all the men who thought their rank entitled them to do so. But no orders. Glancing round, Shef saw that he was very much alone, immediately behind the group of armored nobles. As the Viking arrow drove toward the English line, men had unconsciously edged to left or right. Only the most determined were there to take the first blow, where the weight would fall if Wulfgar and his colleagues were to fail. The wedge formation was said to be the invention of the Viking war-god. What would happen when it struck?

Spears began to fly from the English line, some falling short, some batted aside by the shields of the leaders. Suddenly, simultaneously, the Vikings began to trot forward. One, two, three paces, and the throwing arms of the leaders drew back and a shower of javelins whirred at the English center. In front of him, Shef saw Edrich adroitly twist his shield-boss so that one spear flew over his head and far to the back of the line, and smash another with the edge so that it fell at his feet. A few paces to one side, a noble dropped his shield to block a spear aimed at his belly, choked, and fell sideways as another ripped through his beard and throat. Another landholder cursed as three spears found his shield at once, tried to knock them free with his sword, then frenziedly struggled to pull the strap from his elbow and drop the now-clumsy encumbrance dragging down his arm. Before he could succeed the Viking wedge was on them.

In front of him Shef saw the Viking leader swing a mighty blow at Wulfgar. The Englishman caught it on his shield, tried to stab in reply with his sword. But the Viking had already recovered and swung again with all his force, backhand. Once more Wulfgar parried, with a mighty clang as his own blade met the Viking's, but he was already off balance. With a sudden thrust the Viking clubbed him in the face with his sword-pommel, thrust a shield-boss into his ribs, and hurled him aside by main force. As he stepped forward to stab, Shef sprang at him.

For all his size the Viking leader was amazingly fast on his feet. He jumped back a pace and slashed at the boy's unarmed head. Shef had realized two things already from his three heartbeats' observation of real battle: One, in battle everything must be done with full force, with none of the unconscious restraint of training or practice. He put all his smithy-hardened muscle into the parry. Two, in battle there could be no interval or pause between blows. As the Viking swung again, Shef was already braced for him. This time his parry caught the blow higher up. He felt a clang and a snap and the fragment of a blade whirred over his head. Not mine, thought Shef. Not mine! He stepped forward and stabbed exultantly for the groin.

Something knocked him sideways and backwards. He staggered, caught his balance, and found himself shoved aside again by the figure of Edrich, bellowing something in his ear. As he glanced round Shef realized that while he exchanged blows with their leader, the tip of the Viking wedge had broken through. Half a dozen English nobles lay on the ground. Wulfgar, still on his feet, was backing dazedly toward Shef, but a dozen Vikings were facing him, pouring through the broken line. Shef found himself shouting, brandishing his sword, daring the foremost of the Vikings to come on. For a heartbeat the man and the boy stared into each other's eyes. Then the man wheeled left, following his orders, moving through the gap to roll up the English line and drive the flankers into the swamp in disorder and confusion.

"Run for it!" shouted Edrich. "We're beat. Nothing to do now. Run now and we can get away."

"My father," shouted Shef, lunging forward to try to grasp Wulfgar by the belt and haul him back.

"Too late, he's down."

It was true. The dazed thane had taken another smashing blow on the helmet and staggered forward, to be enveloped by a wave of enemies. The Vikings were still fanning sideways, but at any moment some would press forward and overwhelm the few men left standing in the center. Shef found himself seized by the collar and hustled, half-choking to the rear.

"Damned fools. Half-trained levies. What can you expect? Grab a horse, boy."

In seconds Shef was cantering down the track the way he had come. His first battle was over.

And he had run from it within seconds of the first blow being struck.

CHAPTER FOUR

The reeds at the marsh's edge moved slightly in the morning breeze. They moved again and Shef peered out at the empty countryside. The Viking raiders were gone.

He turned and waded back through the reeds to the path he had found the previous evening. The small island was hidden by low trees. Edrich the king's thane was eating the cold remains of their dinner from the night before. He wiped greasy fingers on the grass and raised his eyebrows.

"Nothing in sight," Shef said. "Quiet. No smoke that I could see."

They had fled the battle, knowing it was lost, seeking only to save their own lives. There had been no sign of pursuit when they abandoned their horses and fled on foot into the marsh where they had spent the night—an oddly comfortable and pleasant night for Shef. He thought about it with mixed feelings of both pleasure and guilt. It had been an island of peace in a sea of anxiety and trouble. Just for one evening there had been no work to do, no duty that could possibly be performed. All they had to do was hide, protect themselves, and stay as comfortable as possible. Shef had splashed off into the marsh and quickly found them a dry island in the midst of the pathless fen, where it was certain that no stranger would ever penetrate. It had been easy to put up a shelter made out of the reed which the marsh-folk used for thatching. Eels had been snared in the sluggish water, and Edrich, after brief consideration, had seen no harm in making a fire. The Vikings had other things to do and weren't going to come splashing all the way over here just because of a bit of smoke.

In any case, before darkness fell, they could see smoke rising all around them. "The raiders on their way back," said Edrich. "They don't mind sending up signals when they're retreating."

Had he ever run from a battle before? Shef asked cautiously, nagged by the worry that kept on surfacing every time memory brought back the picture of his stepfather going down, engulfed by a tide of enemies. "Many times," Edrich replied, in the curious camaraderie of this day stolen out of time. "And don't think that was a battle. Just a skirmish. But I've run for it often. Too often. And if everybody did that we'd have a lot fewer dead men on our side. We never lose very many while we're standing and fighting, but once the Vikings break through it's just a slaughter. Just stop a moment and think of it—every man who gets off the field is saved for another stand-up fight on even terms another day.

"Trouble is," he smiled grimly, "the more often it happens the less likely most people are to be willing to try again. They lose heart. And there's no need for it. We lost yesterday because nobody was ready, not physically, not in their minds either. If they'd spend a tenth of the time they spend in whining afterwards in getting ready beforehand, we'd have no need ever to lose a battle. As the proverb says: 'Often the deed—late in doom diminishes, in all successes. Starves he later.' Now show me your blade."

Face unmoving, Shef drew it from its scuffed leather scabbard and passed it over. Edrich turned it thoughtfully in his hands.

"It looks like a hedger's tool," he remarked. "Or a reed-cutter's bill. Not a real weapon. Yet I saw the Viking jarl's sword snap on it. How did that happen?"

"It is a good blade," Shef replied. "Maybe the best in Emneth. I made it myself, forged in strips. Much of it is soft iron. I beat it out myself from the iron blooms they send us from the South. But there are layers too of hard steel. A thane from March gave me some good spearheads in payment for work I did for him. I melted and beat them out, and then I twisted the iron and steel strips round each other and forged the whole into a blade. The iron lets it bend, the steel gives it strength. In the end I welded on a cutting edge of the hardest steel I could find. Four man-loads of charcoal the whole work cost me."

"And with all that work you made it short and single-edged, like a work-tool. Put on a plain ox-bone handle, with no guard. And then you left it out in the wet and let it get rusty."

Shef shrugged. "If I swaggered round Emneth with a warrior's weapon on my hip and serpent-patterns glittering on the blade, how long would I have kept it? The rust is just enough to discolor the blade. I make sure it eats no further."

"That was the other question I meant to ask you. The young thane said you were not a freeman. You behave as if you were in hiding. Yet in the fight you called Wulfgar 'father.' There is some mystery here. The world is full of thanes' bastards, God knows. But no one tries to enslave them."

Shef had faced the same question many times, and in another time or place would not have answered. But in the island in the fen, speaking one to another, status forgotten, the words came.

"He is not my father, though I call him that. Eighteen summers ago the Vikings raided here. Wulfgar was away from Emneth then, but my mother, the lady Thryth, was here, with her baby son Alfgar—my half brother, her child and Wulfgar's. A servant got Alfgar away when the raiders came in the night, but my mother was taken."

Edrich nodded slowly. All this was familiar enough. But still his question was not answered. There was a system in these matters, at least for those of rank. After a while, surely, the husband might have expected to hear from the slave-marts of Hedeby or Kaupang, to tell him such and such a lady was ransomable, at a price. If he did not, then he could have considered himself a widower, free to marry again, to set his fine silver bracelets on another woman who would rear his son. Sometimes, it was true, such arrangements were disturbed by the arrival, twenty years later, of some withered crone who had managed to outlive her usefulness in the North and bribe her way, God knew how, onto a ship that would take her home. But not often. Neither case explained the young man sitting before him.

"My mother returned, only a few weeks later. Pregnant with me. She swore that my father was the jarl of the Vikings himself. When I was born she wanted me named Halfden, because I am half a Dane. But Wulfgar cursed her. He said that was a hero's name, the name of the king who founded the race of the Shieldings, from whom the kings of England and Denmark both claim descent. Too good for me. And so I was given a dog's name instead. Shef."

The young man dropped his eyes. "That is why my stepfather hates me and wants to make me a slave, why my half brother Alfgar has everything, and I nothing."

He had not told the full story: How Wulfgar had pressed and pressed his pregnant wife to take birthwort, to kill the rapist's child in her womb. How he himself had only been saved by the intervention of Father Andreas, who had denounced fiercely the sin of child-murder, even of a Viking's child. How Wulfgar in his rage and jealousy had taken a concubine, and bred on her Godive the beautiful, so that in the end there had been three children growing up in Emneth: Alfgar the trueborn; Godive, child of Wulfgar and his slave-lemman; Shef, child of Thryth and the Viking.

The king's thane passed back the hand-forged blade in silence. Still a mystery, he thought. How had the woman escaped? Viking slavers were not usually so careless.

"What was the name of this jarl?" he asked. "Of your . . ."

"Of my father? My mother says his name was Sigvarth. The jarl of the Small Isles. Wherever they are."

They sat for a while in silence, then stretched out for sleep.

It was late the next day when Shef and Edrich walked cautiously out of the reeds. Well-fed and unharmed, they approached what they could already see were the ruins of Emneth.

All the buildings were burnt, some mere heaps of ash, others with blackened timbers protruding. The thane's house and stockade were gone, the church, the smithy, the huddle of wattle-and-daub houses for the freemen, the lean-tos and sandpit-houses of the slaves. A few people still moved, stumbling haphazardly here and there, poking in the ashes or joining those already clustered round the well.

As they came into the village area, Shef called to one of the survivors, one of his mother's maids.

"Truda. Tell me what happened. Are there more . . . ?"

She was shaking, gaping up at him with horror and amazement, looking at him unharmed, his shield, sword. "You better . . . come see your mother."

"My mother's still here?" Shef felt a slight lift of hope at his heart. Maybe the others would be there too. Could Alfgar have got away? And Godive? What of Godive?

They followed the maid as she hobbled clumsily along.

"Why does she walk like that?" muttered Shef, looking at her painful limp.

"Been raped," said Edrich briefly.

"But . . . But Truda's no virgin."

Edrich answered the unspoken question. "Rape's different. If you have four men hauling at you while another does it, all of them excited, tear sinews, breaks bones sometimes. Even worse if the woman tries to fight them."

Shef thought of Godive again, and his knuckles whitened as he gripped the inside of his shield-boss. It was not only the menfolk who paid for lost battles.

They followed Truda in silence as she limped before them to a makeshift shelter, a collection of planks propped on half-burnt timbers and leaning against a fragment of stockade saved from the flames. She reached the shelter, looked inside, muttered a few words, and waved them in.

The lady Thryth lay inside, on a heap of old sacking. From the grim look of pain on her face and the awkward way she sprawled, it was obvious that she too had been through Truda's experience. Shef knelt beside her and felt for her hand.

Her voice was just a whisper, weakened by terrible memory. "We had no warning, no time to prepare. No one seemed to know what to do. The men rode straight here after the battle. They couldn't make up their minds. Those pigs caught us while they were still arguing. They were all round us before anyone knew that they had come."

She grew silent, writhed a bit in pain, looked up at her son with empty eyes.

"They are beasts. They killed everyone who showed fight. Then they gathered the rest of us together outside the church. It was beginning to rain by then. First they picked out the young girls and the pretty girls, and some of the boys. For the slave markets. And then . . . then they brought out their prisoners from the battle and then . . ."

Her voice began to quake and she pulled her stained apron up to her eyes.

"And then they made us watch . . ."

Her voice was drowned in tears. After a few moments she seemed to remember something and moved suddenly. She gripped Shef's hand and for the first time looked directly at him.

"But Shef. It was him. It was the same one as last time."

"Sigvarth Jarl?" asked Shef, his mouth thick.

"Yes. Your . . . your . . ."

"What did he look like? Was he a big man, dark hair, white teeth?"

"Yes. With gold bracelets all up his arm." Shef thought back to the moments of conflict, felt again the snap of the sword breaking and the moment of delight with which he had stepped forward to stab. Could it be that God had saved him from a terrible sin? But if that were the case— what had God been doing afterward?

"Couldn't he protect you, mother?"

"No. He didn't even try." Thryth's voice had gone hard and controlled again. "When they broke ranks after . . . after the show, he told them to loot and enjoy themselves till the warhorns blew. They kept their slaves, tied them together; but the rest of us, Truda and the ones they weren't keeping . . . We were just handed over.

"He recognized me, Shef! And he remembered me. But when I begged him just to keep me for himself he laughed. He said . . . he said I was a hen now, not a chicken, and hens must look after themselves. Especially hens who flew away. So they used me like Truda. They used me more because I was the lady, and some of them thought that this was something very funny." Her face twisted with anger and hatred, her pain forgotten for the moment.

"But I told him, Shef! I told him that he had a son. And that his son would one day seek him out and kill him!"

"I did my best, mother." Shef hesitated, another question forming on his lips. But Edrich, behind him, spoke first.

"What did they make you watch, lady?"

Again Thryth's eyes filled with tears. Unable to speak, she waved vaguely at the outside of the shelter.

"Come," said Truda. "I will show you the Vikings' mercy."

The two men followed her out, across the ashy remains of the village green, to where another makeshift shelter had been set up near the ruin of the thane's house. A small huddle of people stood outside it. Occasionally one would break away and walk inside, look, and come out again. Their expressions were unreadable. Grief? Anger? Mostly, thought Shef, it was just plain fear.

Inside the shelter stood a horse-trough, half filled with straw. Shef recognized at once Wulfgar's blond hair and beard, but the face between them was that of a corpse: white, waxy, the nose pinched and the bones sticking through the flesh. Yet the man was not dead.

For a moment Shef could make no sense of what he saw. How could Wulfgar lie in a horse-trough? He was too big. He was six feet tall, and the horse-trough—Shef knew it well from the beatings of his youth—was barely five feet long. . . . There was something missing.

Wulfgar had something wrong with his legs. His knees reached the bottom of the trough, but then there were only clumsy bandages, wrapped round and round the stumps, with dark blood and foul matter clotted in them. A smell of corruption, and of burning, drifted up to Shef.

With growing horror he saw that Wulfgar appeared to have no arms either. The bits that were left were crossed on his breast, the limbs ending in stumps and bandages just below the elbows.

A voice murmured behind them. "They brought him out in front of us all. Then they held him over a log and chopped off his arms and legs with an axe. Legs first. After each one they seared the stump with a red-hot iron, so that he would not die from loss of blood. First he cursed them and fought, but then he began to beg them to leave him just one hand, so that he could feed himself. They laughed. The big one, the jarl, said they would leave him everything else. Leave him his eyes so he could see fair women, and his balls, so he could desire them. But he would never be able to take down his own breeches, never again."

Never do anything for himself again, Shef realized. He would depend on others for every action of life, from eating to pissing.

"They've made him a *heimnar*," said Edrich, using the Norse word. "A living corpse. I've heard of this before. Never seen it. But don't trouble yourself, boy. Infection, pain, loss of blood. He won't live long."

Incredibly, the wasted eyes in front of them opened. They shone with pure malevolence on Shef and Edrich. The lips parted and a dry snakelike whisper came forth.

"The runaways. You ran and left me, boy. I will remember. And you, king's thane. You came, exhorted us, would have us fight. But where were you when the fighting ended? Have no fear, I will live yet, to be avenged on you both. And on your father, boy. I should never have reared his get. Or taken back his whore either."

The eyes closed, the voice was still. Shef and Edrich walked out into the thin drizzle that was beginning once again.

"I don't understand," said Shef. "What did they do it for?"

"That I do not know. But I can tell you one thing. When King Edmund hears of this he will be in a fury. Raid and murder under truce, that's normal enough, but this, done to one of his men, a former companion . . . He will be of two minds, perhaps feeling that he must spare his people more of the same. But then again he may decide he is honor-bound to seek vengeance. It will be a difficult decision for him." He turned to look at Shef.

"Will you come with me, lad, when I take him the news? You are not a freeman here, but it is plain to see that you are a fighter. There is nothing for you now in this place. Come with me and you will be my servant till we can get you proper equipment and armor. If you can fight well enough to stand up to a jarl of the heathens the king will make you his companion, no matter what you were here in Emneth."

The lady Thryth was walking toward them, leaning heavily on a stick.

Shef asked her the question that had been burning in his mind since first he saw the smoke from ravaged Emneth.

"Godive. What has happened to Godive?"

"Sigvarth took her. She has gone to the Vikings' camp."

Shef turned to Edrich. He spoke firmly, without apology.

"They say I am a runaway and a slave. Now I will be both." He unbuckled his shield and dropped it on the ground. "I shall make for the Viking camp down by the Stour. One more slave—they may take me in. I must do something to rescue Godive."

"You won't last a week," said Edrich, voice cold with anger. "And you will die a traitor. A traitor to your people and to King Edmund." He turned on his heel and walked away.

"And to the blessed Christ Himself," added Father Andreas, appearing from the shelter. "You have seen the pagans' deeds. Better to be a slave in Christendom than a king among such as they."

Shef realized that he had made the decision quickly—perhaps too quickly, without thinking. But having done this he was now committed. Thoughts tumbled in his head: I have tried to kill my father. I have lost my foster father to a living death. My mother now hates me for what my father did. I have lost my chance to be free and have lost one who would have been my friend.

Such thoughts would not help him now. He had done this all for Godive. Now he must finish what he had begun.

Godive woke with a splitting pain in her head, smoke in her nostrils and someone struggling beneath her. Terrified, she struck out and pushed herself away. The girl on whom she had been lying began to whimper.

As her eyes cleared, Godive realized she was in a wagon, a moving wagon creaking along a puddled road. Through its thin canvas tilt, light shown on its cramped interior packed with humanity, half the girls of Emneth lying one on top of another. A steady chorus of moans and sobbing rose from them. The small square of light at the back of the wagon suddenly darkened and a bearded face showed at it. The sobbing dissolved into shrieks and the girls clutched at each other or tried to hide themselves behind their companions. But the face only grinned—its white teeth gleaming brilliantly—shook a finger in warning, and withdrew.

The Vikings! Godive remembered it all in one instant, everything that had happened: the wave of men, the panic, her dart for the marsh, the man rising in front of her to catch her by the skirt, the overmastering terror she had felt at being held by a grown man for the first time in her uneventful life . . .

Her hand flew suddenly to her thighs. What had they done while she was unconscious? But though the pain in her head grew and grew, there was no throb, no soreness in her body. She was a virgin. She had been a virgin. Surely they could not have raped her and left her feeling nothing?

The girl next to her, a cottager's daughter—one of Alfgar's playmates—saw the movement and said, not without malice, "Don't be afraid. They did nothing to any of us. They're keeping us for sale. And you a maiden too. You have nothing to fear till they find you a buyer. Then you will be like the rest of us."

The memories kept arranging themselves. The square of people, with armed Vikings all round the outside. And inside the square her father being dragged forward, shouting and offering terms, to the log . . . The log. The horror when she realized what they were going to do as they had spread-eagled her father and the axeman had stepped forward. Yes. She had run forward, screaming and clawing at the big man. But the other, the one he had called "son," had caught her. Then what? She felt her head gingerly. A lump. A splitting pain on the other side from the lump. But—she looked at her fingers—no blood.

She was not the only one treated like that; the Viking had hit her with a sandbag. The pirates had been in the trade a long time and were used to dealing with human cattle. At the start of a raid, charge in with axe and sword, spear and shield, to kill the menfolk or the warriors. But after that even the flat of a sword or the back of an axe were unhandy weapons for stunning. Too easy to slip, to fracture a skull or slice an ear from some valuable piece of merchandise. Even a clenched fist was unsafe, given the oar-pulling strength of the man behind it. Who would buy a girl with a broken jaw, or one with her cheekbone smashed and set awry? The skin-flints of the outer isles, maybe, but never the buyers for Spain or the choosy kings of Dublin.

So, in Sigvarth's command and in many others, the men detailed for slave-taking carried in their belts or hooked inside their shields a "quietener"—a long sausage of canvas stoutly sewn and filled inside with dry sand collected carefully from the dunes of Jutland or of Skaane. A smart blow with that, and the merchandise lay still, and gave no further trouble. No risk of damage.

Slowly the girls began to whisper to each other, their voices trembling with fear. They told Godive what had happened to her father. Then what had happened to Truda, to Thryth, and to the rest. How they had finally been loaded into the wagon and pulled off down the track toward the coast. But what would happen next?

Late the next day, Sigvarth, jarl of the Small Isles, also felt an inner chill, though with far less apparent cause. He sat now at his ease in the great tent of the Army of the sons of Ragnar, at the jarls' table, comfortably full of best English beef, a horn of strong ale in his hand, listening to his son Hjörvarth tell the story of their raid. Though he was only a young warrior he spoke well. It was good also to let the other jarls, and the Ragnarssons, see that he had a strong young son who would, in the future, have to be taken account of.

What could be wrong? Sigvarth was not a man given to self-examination, but he had also lived a long time, and had learned not to ignore the prickles of oncoming danger.

There had been no trouble coming back from the raid. He had taken the column of wagons and booty, not back along the Ouse, but down the channel of the Nene. The ship-guards, meanwhile, had waited on their mudbank till an English force appeared, had traded jeers and stray arrows with them for a while, watched them slowly assemble a force of rowing-boats and fishercraft, and then at the appointed time had kedged themselves off on the tide and sailed gently upcoast to the rendezvous, leaving the English behind fuming.

And the march to the rendezvous had gone well. The most important thing was that Sigvarth had done exactly what the Snake-eye had said. Torches in every thatch and every field. Every well with a few corpses down it. Examples too, brutal ones. Nailed to trees or mutilated, not dead, to tell their tale to everyone they knew.

Do it like Ivar would do it, the Snake-eye had said. Well, Sigvarth had no illusions about being in the Boneless One's class when it came to brutality, but no one could say he hadn't tried. He had done well. That countryside would not recover for years.

No, it wasn't that disturbing him; that had been a good idea. If there was anything wrong it was further back. Reluctantly, Sigvarth realized that it was the memory of the skirmish that was troubling him. He had fought in the front for a quarter of a century, killed a hundred men, taken a score of battle-wounds. That skirmish should have been easy. It hadn't been. He had broken through the English front line like so many times before, brushed the fair-haired thane out of his way almost with contempt, and got through to the second line, as ragged and disorganized as ever.

And then that boy had come out of the ground. He hadn't even a helmet or a proper sword. Only a freedman, or the poorest of the cottagers' children. Yet two parries and Sigvarth's own sword was in pieces and he himself off balance with his guard too high. The fact was, Sigvarth concluded, if that had been single combat he would have been a dead man. It was the others coming up on each side who had saved him. He did not think anyone had noticed, but if they had—if they had, some one of the bolder heads, the frontmen or the duelers, might be thinking of calling him out even now.

Could he face them? Was his son Hjörvarth strong enough yet for his vengeance to be feared? Maybe he was getting too old for the business. If he couldn't settle a half-armed boy, and an English boy at that, then perhaps he was.

At least he was doing the right thing now. Getting the Ragnarssons on your side—that could never be a bad idea. Hjörvarth was coming to the end of his tale. Sigvarth turned in his chair and nodded at his two henchmen waiting near the entrance. They nodded back and hastened out.

". . . so we burned the wagons on the shore, threw in a couple of churls that my father in his wisdom had kept back, as sacrifice to Aegir and to Ran, boarded ship, ran down the coast to the rivermouth—and here we are! The men of the Small Isles, under famous Sigvarth Jarl—and I his lawful son Hjörvarth—at your service, sons of Ragnar, and ready for more!"

The tent erupted in applause, horns banged on tables, feet stamped, knives clashed. The men were in a good temper at this fair start to the campaign.

The Snake-eye rose to his feet and spoke.

"Well, Sigvarth, we said you could keep your plunder, and you have earned it, so you need have no fear of telling us your good luck. Tell us, how much did you take? Enough to retire and buy yourself a summer home in Sjaelland?"

"Little enough, little enough," called Sigvarth, to groans of disbelief. "Not enough to make me turn farmer. There are only poor pickings to be expected from country thanes. Wait till the great, the invincible Army sacks Norwich. Or York! Or London!" Cries of approval now, and a smile from the Snake-eye. "It is the minsters we must sack, full of gold which the Christ-priests have wrung from the fools of the South. No gold and little silver from the countryside.

"But some things we did take, and I am ready to share the best of it. Here, let me show you the finest thing that we found!"

He turned and waved his followers in. They pushed through the tables, leading with them a figure draped completely in sacking, a rope round its waist. The figure was pushed to the front of the center table, and then in two movements the rope was cut, the sacking whisked away.

Godive emerged blinking into the light, facing a horde of bearded faces, open mouths, clutching hands. She shrank back, tried to turn away, and found herself staring into the eyes of the tallest of the chieftains, a pale man, no expression on his face and eyes like ice, eyes that never blinked. She turned again, looking almost with relief at Sigvarth, the only face she could even recognize.

In this cruel company she was like a flower in a patch of dank undergrowth. Pale hair, fine skin, full lips more attractive now as they parted with fear. Sigvarth nodded again, and one of his men ripped down at the back of her gown. Tearing at it until the fabric tore, then stripping it from her despite screams and struggles until the young girl stood naked but for her shift, her youthful body clear for all to see. In an agony of fear and shame she crossed her hands over her breasts and hung her head, waiting for whatever they would do with her.

"I will not share her," called out Sigvarth. "She is too precious for sharing. So I will give her away! I give her to the man who chose me for this expedition, in thanks and in hope. May he use her well, and long, and vigorously. I give her to the man who chose me out, wisest of all the Army. It is to you I give her. You, Ivar!"

Sigvarth ended with a shout, and a raise of his horn. Slowly he realized that there was no answering shout, only a confused murmur, and that from the men farthest away from the center, the ones who, like him, knew the Ragnarssons least and were the latest comers to the Army. No horns were raised. Faces seemed suddenly troubled, or blank. Men looked away.

The chill at Sigvarth's heart came back. Maybe he should have asked first, he thought to himself. Maybe something was going on that he didn't know about. But where could the harm be in this? He was giving away a piece of plunder, one that any man would be glad to own, doing it publicly and honorably. Where could be the harm in making a gift of this girl, a maiden—a beautiful maiden—to Ivar? Ivar Ragnarsson. Nicknamed— Oh, Thor aid him, why was he so nicknamed? A terrible thought possessed Sigvarth. Was there meaning in that nickname?

The Boneless.

CHAPTER FIVE

Five days later, Shef and his companion lay in the slight shelter of a copse, staring across flat watermeadows to the earthworks of the Viking camp a long mile away. For the moment, at least, their nerve had failed.

They had had no trouble getting away from ruined Emneth, which normally might have been the most difficult task for the runaway slave. But Emneth had had troubles of its own. No one in any case considered himself Shef's master, and Edrich, who might have thought it his duty to keep anyone from going over to the Vikings, seemed to have washed his hands of the whole business. Without opposition, Shef had gathered his few possessions, quietly lifted a small store of food which he kept in an outlying shelter, and had made his preparations to leave.

Still, someone had noticed. As he had stood hesitating over whether to bid a farewell to his mother, he had become aware of a slight figure standing silently next to him. It was Hund, boyhood friend, child of slaves on both sides, perhaps the least important and lowest ranking person in the whole of Emneth. Yet Shef had learned to value him. There was no one who knew the marshes better, not even Shef. Hund could slide through the water and take moorhens on their nests. In the foul and crowded hut he shared with his parents and their litter of children there was often an otter cub playing. The very fish seemed to come to his hands to be caught without rod or line or net. As for the herbs of the countryside, Hund knew them all, their names, their uses. Already—though he was two winters younger than Shef—the humble folk were beginning to come to him for simples and for cures. In time to come he might be the cunning man of the district, respected and feared even by the mighty. Or action might be taken against him. Even the kindly Father Andreas, Shef's preserver, had several times been seen to look at him with doubt in his eyes. Mother Church had no love for competitors.

"I want to come," Hund had said.

"It will be dangerous," Shef had replied.

Hund had said nothing, as was his custom when he felt nothing more needed to be said. It was dangerous to stay in Emneth too. And Shef and Hund, in their different ways, increased each other's chances.

"If you are coming you will have to get that collar off," Shef had said, glancing at the iron collar which had been fitted round Hund's neck at puberty. "Now is the time. No one is interested in us. I'll get some tools."

They had sought shelter in the marsh, not wanting to draw attention. It had been a difficult business getting the collar off even so. Shef had filed through it, first putting rags inside the collar to save Hund's neck from rasps, but once broken through it had been hard to get the tongs inside the circlet to bend it open. In the end Shef had lost patience, wrapped the rags round his hands, and pulled the collar open by main strength.

Hund had rubbed the calluses and weals where the iron had worn his neck and stared at the U-shape of the bent collar. "Not many men could do that," he had observed.

"Need will make the old wife trot," Shef had answered dismissively. Yet secretly he was pleased. He was coming into his strength, he had faced a grown warrior in battle, he was free to go where he would. He did not yet know how he could do it, but there must be a way to free Godive, and then leave the disasters of his family behind.

They had set out without further words. But trouble had begun at once. Shef had expected to have to dodge a few inquisitive people, sentries, maybe levies heading for the muster. Yet from the first day of travel he had realized that the whole countryside was beginning to buzz like a wasps' nest stirred with a stick. Men cantered down every road. Outside every village groups waited, armed and hostile, suspicious of every stranger. After one such group had decided to hold them, ignoring their story of being sent to borrow cattle from a relative of Wulfgar's, they had had to break and run for it, dodging spears and outdistancing their pursuers. But clearly orders had gone out and the folk of East Anglia had for once decided to obey wholeheartedly. There was fury in the air.

For the last two days Shef and Hund had crept through the fields and hedges, going painfully slowly, often on their bellies in the mud. Even so, they had seen patrols out, some of them horsemen commanded by a thane or a king's companion, but others—and these the more dangerous ones—moved quietly on foot like themselves, armor and weapons padded to prevent jingle or clink; marshmen in the lead, carrying bows and hunters' slings for ambush or stalk. They meant, Shef realized, to keep the Vikings in, or at least to prevent them coming out in small parties for private plunder. But at the same time they would be only too happy to catch and hold, or kill, anyone they thought might have any intention of giving the Vikings aid, information, or reinforcement.

Only in the last couple of miles had the danger receded; and that, the pair soon understood, was only because they were now within the range of the Vikings' own patrols—these easier to avoid, but at the same time more menacing. They had spotted one group of men waiting silently within the borders of a small wood, maybe fifty of them, all mounted, all armored, great axes resting on shoulders, the man-killing battle-spears bristling above them like a gray-tipped thorn thicket. Easy to see, quite easy to avoid. But it would take a full-scale incursion by the English to drive them off or defeat them. The village patrols would stand no chance.

These were the men to whose mercy they now had to trust themselves. It did not seem as easy now as it had at Emneth. To begin with, Shef had had a vague idea of reaching the camp and declaring his relationship to Sigvarth. But there would be far too much chance of being recognized, even from the few seconds of contact they had had. It was terrible luck that had brought him into hand-to-hand combat with the one person in the camp who might—or might not—have accepted him. But now Sigvarth was one person they had to avoid at all costs.

Would the Vikings accept recruits? Shef had an uneasy feeling that much more would be needed than willingness and a hand-forged sword. But they could always use slaves. Again, Shef had an uneasy feeling that he himself might do for a laborer or galley-slave in some far-off country. But Hund had nothing visibly valuable about him. Might the Vikings just let him go, like a fish that was too small for the pan? Or would they take the easy way out of dealing with an encumbrance? The evening before, when they had first caught sight of the camp, the two youths' keen eyes saw a party come out of one of the gates and start digging a hole. A little later there had been no doubt about the contents of the cart that creaked out and emptied a dozen bodies unceremoniously down the pit. Pirates' camps had a high wastage rate.

Shef sighed. "It doesn't look any better than it did last night," he said. "But we'll have to move sometime."

Hund gripped his arm. "Wait. Listen. Can you hear something?"

The sound strengthened as the two youths turned their heads this way and that. Noise. Song. Many men singing together. The sound, they realized, was coming from the other side of a slight rise maybe a hundred yards to their left, where the watermeadows ran into a tangle of uncultivated common.

"It sounds like the monks singing at the great minster at Ely," murmured Shef. A foolish thought. There would be neither monk nor priest left within twenty miles of this place.

"Shall we look?" whispered Hund.

Shef made no reply, but began to crawl slowly and carefully toward the sound of deep-voiced singing. It could only be the pagans in this spot. But maybe a small group of them would be easier to approach than the whole army. Anything was better than simply walking out across that flat plain.

After they had covered half the distance on their bellies, Hund gripped Shef's wrist. Silently he pointed up a slight slope. Twenty yards away, beneath a huge old hawthorn, stood a man, motionless, his eyes scanning the ground. He leaned on an axe two-thirds his own height. A burly man, thick-necked, broad across paunch and hip.

At least he did not seem built for speed, Shef reflected. And he was standing in the wrong place if he wanted to be a sentry. The two youths exchanged a glance. The Vikings might be great seamen. They had much to learn about the art of stealth.

Gently Shef snaked forward, angling away from the sentry, round a thicket of bracken, between and beneath a tangle of gorse, Hund crawling immediately behind him. Ahead, the noise of singing had ceased. Replaced by a single voice talking. Not talking. Exhorting. Preaching. Could there be secret Christians even among the heathen? Shef wondered.

A few yards on, he parted the bracken stems and peered silently down into a little dell, hidden from view. There, forty or fifty men sat on the ground in a rough circle. All carried swords or axes, but their spears and shields were propped up or planted in the ground. They sat within a corded-off enclosure made of a dozen spears with a thread running between them. From the thread, at intervals, dangled clumps of the bright red berry that the English called "quickbeam," now in autumn brilliance. At the center of the enclosure, with the men seated round it, a fire burned. Next to it was planted a single spear, point up, its shaft gleaming silver.

One man stood by the fire and the spear, his back to the hidden watch-

ers, speaking to the men round him in tones of persuasion, of command. Unlike the others, and unlike anyone else Shef had ever seen, his tunic and breeches were neither natural homespun in color nor dyed green or brown or blue, but a brilliant white, white as the inside of an egg.

From his right hand there dangled a hammer, short-hafted, double-headed—a blacksmith's hammer. Shef's keen sight locked on the front row of sitting men. Round every neck, a chain. On every chain, a pendant displayed on the chest. They were of different kinds: He could see a sword, a horn, a phallus, a boat. But at least half the men wore the sign of a hammer.

Shef rose abruptly from his concealment and walked forward into the dell. As they saw him, fifty men leap simultaneously to their feet, swords coming out, voices raised in warning. A grunt of amazement behind him, a crashing of feet through the bracken. The sentry was behind him now, Shef knew. He did not turn to look.

Slowly the man in white turned to meet him, the two facing each other across the berry-fringed thread, looking each other up and down.

"And where are you come from?" said the man in white. He spoke English with a strong, burring accent.

What shall I say? thought Shef. From Emneth? From Norfolk? That will mean nothing to them.

"I come from the North," he said aloud.

The faces in front of him changed. Surprise? Recognition? Suspicion?

The man in white gestured his followers to hold still. "And what is your business with us, the followers of the *Asgarthsvegr,* the Asgarth Way?"

Shef pointed to the hammer in the other's hand, the hammer-pendant round his neck. "I am a smith, like you. My business is to learn."

Someone was translating his words now to the others. Shef realized Hund had materialized at his left, and there was a threatening presence just behind them both. He kept his eyes fixed on those of the man in white.

"Show me a sign of your craft."

Shef pulled his sword from its sheath and passed it over, as he had to Edrich. The hammer-bearer turned it over and over, looked at it intently, flexed it gently, noting the surprising play in the thick, single-edged blade, scratched with his thumbnail at the surface discoloration of old rust. Carefully, he shaved a patch of hair from his forearm.

"Your forge was not hot enough," he remarked. "Or you lost patience. Those steel strips were not even when you twisted them. But it is a good blade. It is not what it seems.

"And neither are you. Now tell me, young man—and remember, death is just behind you—what it is that you want? If you are just a runaway slave like your friend"—he gestured toward Hund's neck, with the telltale marks on it—"maybe we will let you go. If you are a coward who wants to join the winning side, maybe we will kill you. But maybe you are something else. Or someone else. Say then, what do you want?"

I want Godive back, thought Shef. He looked into the pagan priest's eyes and said, with all the sincerity he could muster, "You are a mastersmith. The Christians will let me learn no more. I want to be your apprentice. Your learning-knave."

The man in white grunted, handed back Shef's sword, bone hilt first. "Lower your axe, Kari," he said to the man behind the pair. "There is more here than meets the eye.

"I will take you as a knave, young man. And if your friend has any skill, he may join us too. Sit, both of you, to one side, till we have finished what we were doing. My name is Thorvin, which is to say, 'the friend of Thor,' the god of the smiths. What are yours?"

Shef flushed with shame, dropped his eyes.

"My friend's name is Hund," he said, "which is to say, 'dog.' And I too, I have only a dog's name. My father— No, I have no father. They call me Shef."

For the first time Thorvin's face showed surprise, and more. "Fatherless?" he muttered. "And your name is Shef. But that is not only a dog's name. Truly you are uninstructed."

Shef felt his spirits sinking as they moved toward the camp. He was not afraid for himself, but for Hund. Thorvin had told the pair of them to sit to one side while they finished their strange meeting: first him talking, then some kind of discussion in the burring Norse Shef could almost follow, and then a skin of some drink passed ceremoniously from hand to hand. At the end all the men had gathered in little groups and joined hands in silence on one object or another: Thorvin's hammer, a bow, a horn, a sword, what looked like a dried horse's penis. No one had touched the silver spear till Thorvin had gone over, pulled it briskly into two parts and rolled them up in a cloth bag. A few moments later the enclosure had been broken up, the fire put out, the spears reclaimed, the men of the group already drifting away in fours and fives, moving warily and taking different directions.

"We are followers of the Way," Thorvin had said in partial explanation to the two youths, still speaking his careful English. "Not everyone wishes to be known as such—not in the camp of the Ragnarssons. Me they accept." He tugged at the hammer pendant on his chest. "I have a skill. You have a skill, young smith-to-be. Maybe it will protect you.

"What of your friend? What can you do?"

"I can pull teeth," replied Hund unexpectedly.

The half dozen men still standing round had grunted in amusement. *"Tenn draga,"* remarked one of them. *"That er ithrott."*

"He says, 'To draw teeth, that is an accomplishment,' " Thorvin translated. "Is it true?"

"It is true," supplied Shef for his friend. "He says it is not strength you need. It is a twist of the wrist—that, and knowing how the teeth grow. He can cure fevers too."

"Tooth-drawing, bone-setting, fever-curing," said Thorvin. "There is always trade for a leech among women and warriors. He can go to my friend Ingulf. If we can get him there. See, you two, if we can get to our own places in the camp—my forge, Ingulf's booth—we may be safe. Till then—" He shook his head. "We have many ill-wishers. Some friends. Will you take the risk?"

They had followed him mutely. But wisely?

As they came toward it, the camp looked more and more formidable. It was enclosed by a high earth rampart, with a ditch outside it, each side at least a furlong in length. Lot of work in that, thought Shef. Lot of spadefuls. Did that mean they were going to stay a long time, that they thought it worth doing so much? Or was it a matter of course to the Vikings? A routine?

The rampart was crowned with a stockade of sharpened logs. A furlong. Two hundred and twenty yards. Four sides—No, from the lay of the land Shef realized suddenly that one side of the camp was bounded here by the river Stour. On that side he could even see prows projecting into the sluggish stream. He was puzzled—until he realized that the Vikings must have pulled their ships, their most precious possessions, up on the mudflats there, then grappled them together so that they themselves formed one wall of the enclosure. Big. How big? Three sides. Three times two hundred and twenty yards. Each log in the stockade maybe a foot wide. Three feet to a yard.

Shef's mind, as it so often did, tried to grapple with the problem of numbers. Three times three times two hundred and twenty. There must be a way to know the answer to that, but this time Shef could see no shortcut to finding it. It was a lot of logs, anyway, and big ones too, cut from trees hard to find down here on the flats. They must have brought the logs with them. Dimly, Shef began to discover an unfamiliar notion. He knew no word for it. Making plans, perhaps. Planning ahead. Thinking things out before they happened. No detail was too small for these men to trouble with. He suddenly realized that they did not think war was only a matter of the spirit, of glory and speeches and inherited swords. It was a trade, a matter of logs and spades, preparation and profit.

More and more men came into view as they trudged up to the ramparts, some of them simply lounging at ease, a group round a fire apparently cooking bacon, others throwing spears at a mark. They looked very much like Englishmen in their grubby woolens, Shef decided. But there was a difference. Every group of men Shef had ever seen before had had in it its proportion of casualties, men not fit to stand in the line of battle: men whose legs had broken and had been set awry; men undersized, deformed; men with bleared eyes from the marsh fever or with old head injuries that affected the way they talked. There were none like that here. Not all were of great stature, Shef was rather surprised to see, but all looked competent, hard-bitten, ready. Some adolescents, but no boys. Bald men and grizzled men, but no palsied elders.

Horses, too. The plain was covered with horses, all hobbled, all grazing. It must take a lot of horses for this army, Shef thought, and a lot of grazing for those horses. In a way that might be a weak point. Shef realized that he was thinking as an enemy, an enemy scouting for opportunities. He was not a king or a thane, but he knew from experience that there was no way to guard all those herds at night, whatever you did. A few true marshmen could reach them however many patrols you had out, could cut them loose and frighten them off. Maybe ambush the horse-guards in the night as well. Then how would the Vikings feel about going on guard duty—if the guards made a habit of never coming back?

Shef felt his spirits sink again as they came up to the entrance. There was no gate, and that was ominous in itself. The track led straight up to a gap in the rampart ten yards broad. It was as if the Vikings were saying, "Our walls protect our goods and keep in our slaves. But we don't need them to hide behind. If you want to fight, march up to us. See if you can get past our gate-guards. It is not these logs that protect us, but the axes that felled them."

Forty or fifty men stood or sprawled by the gap. They had an air of permanence. Unlike those outside, they all wore mail or leather. Spears were propped against each other in clumps, and shields were in easy reach. These men would be ready for battle within seconds—wherever an enemy might erupt from. They had been scanning Shef, Hund, Thorvin, and party—eight men all told—for minutes as they came into sight. Would they be challenged?

At the gate itself a big man in mail strolled forward and stared at them thoughtfully, making it clear he had noted the two newcomers and every-thing about them. After a few moments he nodded and jerked a thumb towards the inside. As they passed into the camp itself he called a few words after them.

"What does he say?" hissed Shef.

"He says, 'On your own head be it.' Something like that."

They walked on into the camp.

Inside, all appeared to be confusion; yet it was a confusion with an under-lying regularity, a sense of overriding purpose. Men were everywhere—cooking, talking, playing at knucklebones or squatting over game boards. Canvas tents stretched in all directions, their guy-ropes an inextricable tangle. Yet the path in front of them was never obscured or encroached on. It stretched straight forward, ten paces broad, even its puddles neatly filled with loads of gravel, and the signs of passing carts barely visible on the beaten earth. These men work hard, Shef thought again.

The little group pressed forward. After a hundred yards, when by Shef's calculation they must have been almost in the middle of the camp, Thorvin stopped and beckoned the other two up close.

"I whisper, for there is great danger. Many in this camp speak many languages. We are going to cross the main track that runs north to south. To the right, to the south, down by the river with the ships, is the encamp-ment of the Ragnarssons themselves and their personal followers. No wise man willingly goes there. We shall cross the track and go straight on to my forge near the gate opposite. We will walk straight forward, not even looking down to our right. When we reach the place we will go right into it. Now move. And take heart. Not far now."

Shef kept his eyes rigidly down as they crossed the broad track, but he wished he could have ventured a moment's gaze. He had come here be-cause of Godive—but where would she be? Did he dare ask for Sigvarth Jarl?

Slowly they moved through the crowds again, till they could see the east stockade almost in front of them. There, a little separated from the others, stood a roughly constructed shelter, open on the side facing them, inside it the familiar apparatus of the smithy: anvil, clay hearth, pipes and bellows. Round it all ran the threads, with the vivid scarlet splashes of quickbeam berries dangling from them.

"We are here," said Thorvin, turning with a sigh of relief. As he turned his eyes passed beyond Shef and the color drained suddenly from his face.

Shef turned with a sense of doom already on him. In front of him there stood a man, a tall man. Shef realized he was looking up at him—realized too how rarely he had done that in the last few months. But this was a man strange for reasons well beyond size.

He was wearing the same wide homespun breeches as everyone else, but no shirt or overtunic. Instead his upper body was wrapped in something like a wide blanket, of a plaid colored a startling yellow. It was pinned over his left shoulder, leaving his right arm bare. Projecting above his left shoulder was the handle of an enormous sword, so great it would have trailed along the ground if slung from a belt. In his left hand he carried a small round buckler with a central grip. An iron spike a foot long stuck out from the center of it. Behind him crowded a dozen others in the same garb.

"Who are these?" he snarled. "Who let they in?" The words were strangely accented but Shef could understand him.

"The gate-wards let them in," Thorvin replied. "They will do no harm."

"These two. They are English. *Enzkir.*"

"The camp is full of English."

"Aye. Wi' chains round their necks. Give them to me. I'll see they fettered."

Thorvin paced forward, between Shef and Hund. His five friends spread out, facing the dozen half-naked men in yellow plaids. He gripped Shef's shoulder.

"I have taken this one into the forge, to be my learning-knave."

The grim face, long-mustached, sneered. "A bonny weight. Maybe ye have other uses for him. The other?" He jerked a thumb at Hund.

"He goes to Ingulf."

"He's no' there yet. He's had a collar on his neck. Give him to me. I'll see he does no spying."

Shef felt himself taking a slow pace forward, stomach contracting with fear. He knew resistance was hopeless. There were a dozen of them, all fully armed. In a moment one of those mighty swords would be hacking the limbs from his body or the head from his neck. Yet he could not let his friend be taken. His hand crept to the hilt of his short sword.

The tall man leapt back, hand reaching over shoulder. Before Shef could draw, the longsword had wheeped free. All round, weapons flashed, men sprang on guard.

"Hold," cried a voice. An immense voice.

While Thorvin and the plaid-wearer had been talking, their group had become the focus of total attention for yards around. Sixty or eighty men now stood in a ring, watching and listening. From the ring now stepped the biggest man Shef had ever seen, taller than Shef by head and shoulders, taller than the man in the plaid, and broader, heavier by far.

"Thorvin," he said. "Muirtach," nodding to the strangely dressed one. "What's the stir?"

"I'm taking that thrall there."

"No." Thorvin seized Hund suddenly and pushed him through the gap in the enclosure, clenching his hand round the berries. "He is under the protection of Thor."

Muirtach strode forward, sword raised.

"Hold." The immense voice again, threatening this time. "You have no right, Muirtach."

"What's it to you?"

Slowly, reluctantly, the immense man reached inside his tunic, fumbled, brought out a silver emblem on a chain. A hammer.

Muirtach cursed, swept his sword back, spat on the ground. "Take him then. But you, boy—" His eye turned to Shef. "You touched yer hilt to me. I catch you on yer own before long. Then ye're dead, boy." He nodded to Thorvin. "And Thor is nothing to me. No more than Christ and his hoor of a mother. Ye'll not fool me like ye've done him." He jerked a thumb at the immense man, turned, and walked away down the track, head high, swaggering like one who has met a defeat and will not show it, his fellows straggling after.

Shef realized he had been holding his breath and let it out with careful and affected ease.

"Who are those?" he asked, looking at the retreating men.

Thorvin replied not in English, but in the Norse they had been using, speaking slowly, with stress on the many words the languages had in common. "They are the Gaddgedlar. Christian Irishmen who have left their god and their people and turned Viking. Ivar Ragnarsson has many in his following and hopes to use them to become king of England and Ireland as well. Before he and his brother Sigurth turn their minds back to their own country, to Denmark, and Norway beyond."

"And there may they never come," added the immense man who had saved them. He bobbed his head to Thorvin with odd respect, even deference, looked Shef up and down. "That was bold, young swain. But you have irked a mighty man. I too. But for me it has been long in the coming. If you need me again, Thorvin, call. You know that since I took the news to the Braethraborg the Ragnarssons have kept me with them. How long that will last now that I have shown my hammer, I do not know. But in any case I am growing tired of Ivar's hounds."

He strolled away.

"Who was that?" asked Shef.

"A great champion, from Halogaland in Norway. He is called Viga-Brand. Brand the Killer."

"And he is a friend of yours?"

"A friend of the Way. A friend of Thor. And so of smiths."

I do not know what I have got into, thought Shef to himself. But I must not forget why I am here. Unwillingly his eyes drifted away from the enclosure where Hund still stood, toward the danger-center, the southern river-wall of the Viking base, the encampment of the Ragnarssons. She must be there, he thought suddenly. Godive.

CHAPTER SIX

For many days Shef had no time to think of his quest for Godive—or anything else for that matter. The work was too hard. Thorvin rose at dawn and worked on sometimes into the night, hammering, reforging, filing, tempering. In an army of this size there seemed to be innumerable men whose axe-heads had come loose, whose shields needed a rivet, who had decided that their spears needed reshafting. Sometimes there would be a line of men twenty-long, stretched from the forge to the edge of the precinct and on down the lane that led to it. There were also harder and more complex jobs. Several times men brought in mail shirts, torn and bloody, asking for them to be repaired, let out, altered for a new owner. One at a time each link of the mail had to be laboriously fitted into four others, and each of the four others into four others. "Mail is easy to wear, and it gives freedom to the arms," Thorvin had remarked when Shef finally ventured to grumble. "But it does not give protection against a fierce stroke—and it is hell on earth for smiths."

As time went by Thorvin handed over the routine jobs more and more to Shef, and concentrated on the difficult or special items. Yet he was rarely far away. He talked continually in Norse, repeating himself as often as was necessary. Sometimes, in the beginning, using mime until he was sure Shef understood. He spoke English well enough, Shef knew, but he would never use it. He insisted too that his apprentice spoke back to him in Norse, even if all he did was repeat what had been said to him. In fact the languages were close to each other in vocabulary and in basic style. After a while Shef caught the trick of repronunciation, and began to think of Norse as a bizarre and aberrant dialect of English, which had only to be imitated, not really learned from the beginning. After that matters went well.

Thorvin's conversation was also a good cure for boredom or frustration. From him, and from the men who stood waiting their turn, Shef learned a great many things that he had never heard before. The Vikings all seemed enormously well-informed about everything that had been decided or intended by their leaders, and had no scruples about discussing it or criticizing it. One thing that soon became clear was that the Great Army of the pagans, feared throughout Christendom, was by no means a unit. At its heart were the Ragnarssons and their followers, maybe half the total. But to these were attached any number of separate contingents, joined to share the loot, of any size from the twenty ships brought down by the Orkney jarl to single crews from villages in Jutland or Skaane. Many of these were already dissatisfied. The campaign had started well enough, they said, with the descent on East Anglia and the establishment of the fortress as a base. Yet the idea had always been not to stay too long, but to gather horses, acquire guides, and then move suddenly from a firm base in the East Anglian kingdom against the true enemy and target, the kingdom of Northumbria.

"Why not land with the ships in Northumbria in the first place?" Shef had asked once, wiping the sweat from his forehead and signaling to the next customer. The stocky, balding Viking with the dented helmet had laughed, loudly but without malice. The really tricky part of a campaign, he had said, was always getting started. Getting the ships up river. Finding a place to beach them. Getting horses for thousands of men. Contingents turning up late and going down the wrong river. "If the Christians had the sense they were born with," he had said emphatically, spitting on the ground, "they would pick us off before we got started almost every time." "Not with the Snakeeye in charge," another man had remarked. "Maybe not," the first Viking had agreed. "Maybe not with the Snakeeye. But lesser commanders. Do you remember Ulfketil down in Frankland?"

So, better to get your feet planted before you tried to hit, they had agreed. Good idea. But this time it had gone wrong. Their feet were planted too long. It was that there King Edmund, most of the customers agreed—or "Jatmund" as they pronounced it—and the only question was, what was making him act so stupid? Easy to ravage his country till he gave in. But they didn't want to ravage East Anglia, the customers complained. Takes too long. Too thin pickings. Why in Hell didn't the king just pay up and come to a sensible deal? He'd had a warning.

Maybe too much of a warning, Shef thought, remembering the wasted face of Wulfgar in the horse-trough, and that indefinable buzz of rage which he had felt in the fields and woods on their journey. When he asked why the Vikings were so determined to march on Northumbria, largest but not by any means richest of the English kingdoms, the laughter at that question took a long time to die down. Eventually, when he unraveled the tale of Ragnar Lothbrok and King Ella, of the old boar and the little pigs who would grunt, of Viga-Brand and his taunting of the Ragnarssons themselves in the Braethraborg, a chill fell on him. He remembered the strange words he had heard from the blue-swelling face in the snake-pit of the archbishop, the sense of foreboding he had known at the time.

Now he understood the need for revenge—but there were other things about which he remained curious.

"Why do you say 'Hell'?" he asked Thorvin one night after they had put their gear away and were sitting mulling a tankard of ale on the cooling forge. "Do you believe there is a place where sins are punished after death? Christians believe in Hell—but you're no Christian."

"What makes you think Hell is a Christian word?" answered Thorvin. "What does heaven mean?" For once he used the English word, *heofon*.

"Well—it's the sky," answered Shef, startled.

"Also the Christian place of bliss after death. The word was there before the Christians came. They just borrowed it, gave it a new meaning. Same with Hell. What does *hulda* mean?" This time he used the Norse word.

"It means to cover, to hide something. Like *helian* in English."

"So. Hell is what is covered. What's underground. Simple word, just like heaven. You can put what meaning you like to it after that.

"But your other question: Yes, we do believe there is a place of punishment for your sins after death. Some of us have seen it."

Thorvin sat silent for a while, as if brooding, unsure how far to speak further. When he broke the silence it was in a half chant, slow and sonorous, like the monks of Ely Minster Shef had heard once, long ago, singing on the vigil of Christmas Eve.

"A hall stands, no sunlight on it,
On Dead Man's Strand: its doors face northward.
From its roof rain poison drops.
Its walls are made of woven serpents.

There men writhe in woe and anguish:
Murder-wolves and men forsworn,
Those who lie to lie with women."

Thorvin shook his head. "Yes, we believe in punishment for sins. Maybe we have a different idea from the Christians about what is a sin and what is not."

"Who are 'we'?"

"It is time I told you. It has come to me several times that you were meant to know." As they sipped their warm, herb-scented ale in the glow of the dying fire, the camp quietening around them, Thorvin, fingering his amulet, spoke. "This is how it was."

All this began, he said, many generations before, maybe a hundred and fifty years ago. At that time a great jarl of the Frisians—the people on the North Sea coast opposite England—had been a pagan. But because of the tales that had been told him by missionaries from Frankland and from England, and because of the old kinship felt between his people and the now-Christian English, he had decided to take baptism.

As was the custom, baptism was to take place publicly, in the open air, in a great tank that the missionaries had constructed for all to see. After the jarl Radbod had been immersed and baptized, the nobles of his court were to follow and soon after that the whole earldom, all the Frisians. Earldom, not kingdom, for the Frisians were too proud and independent to allow anyone the title of king.

So the jarl had stepped to the side of the tank, clad in his robes of ermine and scarlet over the white baptismal garment, and put one foot down onto the first step of the tank. He actually had his foot in the water, Thorvin asserted. But then he turned and asked the head of the missionaries—a Frank, whom the Franks called Wulfhramn, or Wolfraven—whether it was true that as soon as he, Radbod, accepted baptism, his ancestors, who now lurked in Hell along with the other damned, would be released and allowed to wait for their descendants' coming in the courts of heaven.

No, said the Wolfraven, they were pagans who had never been baptized, and they could not receive salvation. No salvation except in the Church, reinforcing what he said with the Latin words: *Nulla salvatio extra ecclesiam.* And for that matter no redemption once in hell. *De infernis nulla est redemptio.*

But my ancestors, said the jarl Radbod, never had anyone speak to them of baptism. They had not even the chance to refuse it. Why should they be tormented forever for something they knew nothing about?

Such is the will of God, said the Frankish missionary, perhaps shrugging his shoulders. At that Radbod took his foot out of the baptismal tank and declared with oaths that he would never become a Christian. If he had to choose, he said, he would rather live in Hell with his blameless ancestors than go to heaven with saints and bishops who had no sense of what was right. And he began a great persecution of Christians throughout all the jarldom of the Frisians, arousing the fury of the Frankish king.

Thorvin drank deep of the ale, then touched the small hammer that hung about his neck.

"Thus it began," he said. "Radbod Jarl was a man of great vision. He foresaw that as long as the Christians were the only ones with priests and books and writing, then what they said would come in the end to be accepted. And that is the strength and at the same time the sin of the Christians. They will not accept that anyone else has so much as a splinter of the truth. They will not deal. They will not go halfway. So to defeat them, or even to hold them at arm's length, Radbod decided that the lands of the North must have their own priests and their own tales of what is the truth. That was the foundation of the Way."

"The Way," prompted Shef, when Thorvin seemed disinclined to continue.

"That is who we are. We are the priests of the Way. And our duties are threefold, and ever have been since first the Way came to the lands of the North. One is to preach the worship of the old gods, the Aesir: Thor and Othin, Frey and Ull, Tyr and Njörth and Heimdall and Balder. Those who put full faith in these gods carry an amulet like mine, made in the sign of whichever god they love the best: a sword for Tyr, a bow for Ull, a horn for Heimdall. Or a hammer for Thor, such as I wear. Many men carry that sign.

"Our second duty is to support ourselves by some trade, as I support myself by smithcraft. For we are not permitted to be like the priests of the Christ-god, who do no work themselves but take tithes and offerings from those who do, and enrich themselves and their minsters till the land groans beneath their exactions.

"But our third duty is hard to explain. We must take thought for what is coming, what will happen in this world—not the next. The Christian priests, you see, believe that this world is only a resting place on the way to eternity, and that the true duty of mankind is to get through it with as little harm to the soul as possible. They do not believe that this world is in any way important. They are not curious about it. They do not want to know any more about it.

"But we of the Way, we believe that in the end a battle will be joined, so great that no man can conceive of it. Yet it will be fought in this world, and it is the duty of us all to make our side, the side of gods and men, stronger when that day comes.

"So the duty laid on us all, besides practicing our skill or art, is to make that skill or art the better for what we learn. Always we must try to think what we can do that is different, that is new. And the most honored among us are those who can think of a skill or art that is entirely new in itself, that no man has ever heard of or thought of before. I am far from the heights of such men as those. Yet many new things have been learned in the North since the time of Radbod the Jarl.

"Even in the South they have heard of us. In the cities of the Moors, in Córdoba and Cairo and the lands of the blue men, there is talk of the Way and what is happening in the North among the *majus,* the 'fire-worshippers' as they call us. They have sent emissaries to watch and learn.

"But the Christians do not send to us. They are still confident in their single truth. They alone know what is salvation and what is sin."

"Is it not a sin to make a man a *heimnar?*" asked Shef.

Thorvin looked up sharply. "That is not a word I have taught you. But I forgot—you know more of many things than I have thought fit to ask you.

"Yes, it is a sin to make a man a *heimnar,* whatever he has done. It is a work of Loki—the god in whose memory we burn the fire in our enclosures next to the spear of his father Othin. But few of us wear the sign of Othin, and none wear that of Loki.

"To make a man a *heimnar.* No. That has the mark of the Boneless One about it, whether he did it himself or not. There are more ways than one of defeating the Christians, and Ivar Ragnarsson's way is foolish. It would come to nothing in the end. But there—you have seen already for yourself that I have no love for the creatures and the hirelings of Ivar.

"Now. Go to sleep." And with that Thorvin swilled down his mug, retired to the sleeping tent, and left Shef to follow him thoughtfully.

Working for Thorvin had given Shef no chance at all to pursue his quest. Hund had been taken off almost immediately to the booth of Ingulf the Leech, also a priest of the Way, but one dedicated to Ithun the Healer, some distance away. After that the two had not seen each other. Shef was left to the routine duties of a smith's assistant, made more trying by being confined to the enclosure of Thor: the forge itself, near it a small sleeping tent and an outhouse with a deep-dug latrine, the whole surrounded by the cords and the quickbeam berries, which Thorvin called *rowan*. "Don't step outside the cords," Thorvin had told him. "Inside you are under the peace and protection of Thor, and killing you would bring down vengeance on the killers. Outside"—he shrugged—"Muirtach would think himself happy to find you wandering around on your own." Inside the precinct Shef had stayed.

It was the following morning when Hund came.

"I have seen her. I saw her this morning," he whispered as he slipped into place beside the squatting Shef. For once Shef was alone. Thorvin had gone off to see about their turn for baking bread in the communal ovens. He had left Shef grinding wheat kernels into flour in the hand quern.

Shef jumped to his feet, spilling flour and unground kernels all over the beaten earth. "Who? You mean—Godive! Where? How? Is she—"

"Sit down, I beg," Hund started to scrape hurriedly at the spilt mess. "We must look normal. There are always people watching in this place. Please listen. The bad news is this: She is the woman of Ivar Ragnarsson, the one they call the Boneless. But she has not been harmed. She is alive and well. I know because as a leech, Ingulf gets everywhere. Now he has seen what I can do, he often takes me with him. A few days ago he was called to see the Boneless One. They would not let me enter—there is a strong guard round all their tents—but while I was waiting outside for him I saw her pass. There could be no mistake. She was not five yards off, though she did not see me."

"How did she look?" asked Shef, painful memory of his mother and Truda forcing itself forward.

"She was laughing. She looked—happy." Both youths fell silent. From all that both had heard there was something ominous in anyone feeling or seeming happy anywhere within the range of Ivar Ragnarsson's power.

"But listen, Shef. She is in terrible danger. She does not understand. She thinks that because Ivar is courteous and speaks well and does not use her immediately as a whore, then she is safe. But there is something wrong with Ivar, maybe in his body, maybe in his head. He has ways of easing it. Maybe, one day, Godive will be one of them.

"You have to get her out, Shef, and soon. And the first thing is to let her see you. What we do after that I cannot guess, but if she knows you are near at least she will maybe be thinking of a chance of passing a message. Now I have heard another thing. All the women, of all the Ragnarssons and their highest chiefs, will be going out from the tents today. I have heard them complaining. They say they have not had a chance to wash

anywhere except in the filthy river for weeks. They mean to go out this
afternoon and wash their clothes and themselves. They are going out to a
backwater maybe a mile off."

"Could we get her away?"

"Don't even think about it. There are thousands of men in the army, all
of them desperate for women. There will be so many trusted guards on
that trip you won't be able to see between them. The best thing you can do
is make sure she sees you. Now this is where they are going to go." Hund
began to explain the lay of the land hastily, pointing to add emphasis to
his words.

"But how am I to get away from here? Thorvin—"

"I thought of that. As soon as the women start to leave I will come here
and say to Thorvin that my master needs him to come and put a final edge
on the tools he uses for opening men's bellies and heads. Ingulf can do
marvelous things," Hund added, shaking his head in admiration. "More
than any church-leech I have ever heard of.

"When Thorvin hears that, he will come with me. Then you must leave
here, slip over the wall, and get well ahead of the women and the guards
so you can meet them accidentally on the path."

Hund was right about Thorvin's reactions. As soon as Hund sidled up to
him with the request, and explanation of why he was needed, Thorvin had
agreed. "I will come," he said, putting down his hammer and searching for
whetstone, oilstone, sleekstone. He went off without further ado.

And then things went wrong. Two customers in line, and neither of
them ready to be put off, both of them knowing full well that Shef never
left the precinct. Those got rid of, a third wandered up full of inquiries and
surprise and desire to talk. When he finally stepped over the rowan-fes-
tooned cords for the first time, Shef realized that he was now bound to do
the most dangerous thing he could in this crowded campment full of eyes
and bored intelligences: hurry.

Yet hurry he did, loping through the crowded lanes with never a look at
the interested faces, cutting suddenly through the ropes of a few deserted
tents, up to the wall with its stockade of logs, two hands on the sharp,
man-high poles, and over them in one powerful vault. A shout from somewhere told him that he had been seen, but there was no hue and cry. He
was going out, not in, and no one had reason to call "Thief."

Now, he was out on the plain, still dotted with horses and exercising
men, with the tree-line of the backwater a mile away. The women would
make their way along the river, but it would be suicide to run up after
them. He had to get there first and had to be walking innocently back, or

better still, to be standing where they would pass. Nor could he go near the gateway where the guards stood noting all that went on. Heedless of the danger, Shef stretched his legs and began to run across the meadow.

Within ten minutes he had reached the backwater and was strolling along the muddy lane which led beside it. No one there yet. Now all he had to do was look like a member of the Army taking his ease. Difficult: There was one thing that set him off from the others. He was on his own. Outside the camp and even inside it, the Vikings went round in ship's crews, or at least with an oarmate to bear company.

He had no choice. Just walk by them. Hope that Godive had the eyes to see him and the wit to say nothing.

He could hear voices ahead, women calling out and laughing, men's voices among them. Shef stepped round a bank of hawthorn and saw Godive in front of him. Their eyes met.

At the same moment he saw a blaze of saffron plaids all round her. He looked convulsively to either side, and there was Muirtach, not five yards away, striding towards him, a cry of triumph on his lips. Before he could move, hard hands had him by each arm. The rest were crowding up behind their leader, their female charges for the moment forgotten.

"The little cock-sparrow," gloated Muirtach, thumbs in belt. "The one who showed his hilt to me. Come out for a look at the womenfolk, is it? And an expensive look it's bound to be. Here, boys, take him aside a few paces." He unsheathed his longsword with a chilling *wheep*. "We don't want the ladies to be dashed by the sight of blood."

"I'll fight you," said Shef.

"That you won't. Am I a chieftain of the Gaddgedlar and to be matched with a runaway with the collar hardly off his neck?"

"There's never been collar on my neck," snarled Shef. He could feel a heat rising within him from somewhere, driving out the chill of fear and panic. There was only one small chance here. If he could draw them into treating him as an equal he might live. Otherwise he would be a headless corpse in a bush within a minute. "My birth is as good as yours. And I speak the Danish tongue a deal better!"

"That is true," said a chilly voice from somewhere behind the plaids. "Muirtach, your men are all watching you. They should be watching the womenfolk. Or does it need all of you to deal with this lad?"

The crowd in front of Shef melted away, and he found himself staring into the eyes of the speaker. Almost white eyes. They were as pale, Shef thought, as pale as ice in a dish—a dish of the thinnest maplewood, carved so thin it was almost transparent. They did not blink, and they waited for

Shef's eyes to drop. Shef tore his own eyes away with an effort. Felt fear that instant, knew death was very close.

"You have a grudge, Muirtach?"

"Yes, lord." The Irishman's eyes too were dropped.

"Then fight him."

"*Och*, now, I said before—"

"Then if you won't—let one of your men fight him. Pick the youngest. Let a boy fight a boy. If your man wins I'll give him this." Ivar plucked a silver ring from his arm, threw it in the air, replaced it. "Step back and give them room. Let the women watch as well. No rules, no surrender," he added, teeth flashing in a chill and humorless smile. "To the death."

Seconds later Shef found himself staring once more into Godive's eyes, round now with terror. She stood at the front of a ring, two-deep, women's clothes intermixed with bright saffron plaids, and scattered through them also the scarlet cloaks and gold armrings of jarls and champions, the aristocracy of the Viking army. In the midst of them Shef caught sight of a familiar figure, the giant frame of Killer-Brand. On impulse Shef stepped over to him as the others prepared his opponent for battle on the far side of the ring.

"Sir. Lend me your amulet. I will return it—if I can."

Impassively the champion pulled it over his head and handed it over. "Kick your shoes off, lad. Ground's slippery."

Shef took the advice. He was beginning, consciously, to breathe hard. He had been in many wrestling matches and had learned that it would prevent that momentary stillness, the unreadiness to fight that looked like fear. He peeled his shirt off too, donned the hammer amulet, drew his sword and threw the sheath and belt aside. It was a big ring, he thought. Speed would have to do it.

His enemy was coming out of his corner, plaid also thrown aside, stripped like Shef to his breeches. In one hand he held the longsword of the Gaddgedlar, thinner than the usual broadsword but a foot longer. In the other hand he had the same spiked targe as his fellows. A helmet was pulled down over his braided hair. He did not look much older than Shef, and in a wrestle Shef would not have feared him. But he had the longsword, the shield, a weapon in each hand. He was a warrior who had seen battle, fought in a dozen skirmishes.

From somewhere outside him, an image formed in Shef's mind. He heard again the solemn voice of Thorvin chanting. He stooped, picked a twig from the ground, threw it over his adversary's head like a javelin. "I give you to Hell," he called. "I give you to Dead Man's Strand."

A buzz of interest rose from the crowd, cries of encouragement: "Go on, Flann boy!" "Get him with your buckler!"

No voice encouraged Shef.

The Irish Norseman padded forward—then attacked swiftly. He feinted a thrust at Shef's face, turned it into a sideways backhand slash, aimed at the neck. Shef ducked under it, stepped away to his right, dodged the thrust with the spiked buckler. The Viking paced forward, swung again, backhand up, forehand down. Again Shef stepped back, feinted to step right, stepped left again. For an instant he was to his adversary's side, with a thrust possible at the bare right shoulder. He leapt back instead and moved rapidly to the center of the ring. He had already decided what to do, and he felt his body answering perfectly, light as a feather, buoyed up by a force that swelled his lungs and raced the blood through his veins. He remembered for an instant the way that Sigvarth's sword had broken and the fierce joy that had filled him.

Flann the Irishman came in again, swinging the sword faster and faster, trying to box Shef in against the bodies of the ring. He was quick. But he was used to men standing up to him to trade blows and catching them on blade or buckler. He did not know how to deal with an opponent who simply tried to avoid him. Shef jumped a wide sweep at knee level and saw that the Irishman was beginning to pant already. The Viking Army was made of sailors and horsemen, strong in the arm and shoulder, but men who walked little, and ran even less.

The shouting in the background was getting angry as the watchers grasped Shef's tactic. They might start to close in and narrow the ring. As Flann tried his favorite backhand sweep downward—a little slower now, a little too predictable—Shef stepped forward for the first time and parried fiercely, aiming the base of his thick blade at the tip of the longsword. No snap. But as the Irishman hesitated, Shef slashed out of the parry at the back of the other man's arm—a quick spurt of blood.

Shef was out of reach again, refusing to follow up his advantage, circling to his right, changing step as the other man advanced and then moving to his left again. He had seen the momentary shock in the warrior's eyes. Now there was blood running down over Flann's sword-hand, quite a lot of it, enough to weaken him in a few minutes if he did not finish things quickly.

For a hundred heartbeats they stood close to the center of the ring, Flann trying now to thrust as well as cut, stabbing out with his buckler; Shef parrying as well as dodging, trying to knock the sword from his enemy's blood-smeared hand.

Then Shef felt, suddenly, the confidence draining from his enemy's blows. Shef began to move again, springing on tireless feet, circling his opponent, moving always to the left, trying to get behind the other's sword-arm, careless of the energy he expended.

Flann's breath came almost as a sob. He hurled the buckler at Shef's face and followed it with a ripping upward stab. But Shef was in a crouch, knuckles of his sword-hand on the ground. His parry deflected the thrust far over his left shoulder. In an instant Shef straightened and drove his own sword deep beneath the naked, sweating ribs. As the stricken man shuddered and staggered away, Shef seized him in a wrestler's grip round the neck and poised his sword again.

Shef heard through the yelling the voice of Killer-Brand. "You gave him to Naströnd," it shouted. "You must finish him."

Shef looked down at the pallid, terror-stricken, still-living face in the crook of his arm, and felt a surge of fury. He drove the sword deeply home through the chest and felt the pain of death leap through Flann's body. Slowly, he dropped the corpse, retrieved his sword. Saw Muirtach's face, pale with rage. He stepped over to Ivar, where he stood with Godive now at his side.

"Most instructive," said Ivar. "I like to see someone who can fight with his head as well as his sword-arm. You have saved me a silver ring too. But you have cost me a man. How are you going to pay me back?"

"I am a man as well, lord."

"Join my ships, then. You will do as a rower. But not with Muirtach. Come to my tent this evening and my marshal will find you a place."

Ivar looked down for a moment, considering. "There is a notch on your blade. I did not see Flann put it there. Whose blade was it?"

Shef hesitated an instant. But with these men the bold course was always wisest. He spoke loudly, challengingly. "It was the sword of Sigvarth Jarl!"

Ivar's face tightened. "Well," he said, "this is no way to wash women or sheets. Let us be on our way." He turned, pulling Godive with him, though for an instant her face remained fixed, looking agonizedly at Shef.

Shef found himself staring up at the bulk of Viga-Brand. He slowly pulled off the amulet.

Brand weighed it in his hand. "Normally I would say keep it, boy, you earned it. If you live you will be a champion one day; I say it, Brand, champion of the men of Halogaland.

"But something tells me the hammer of Thor is not the right sign for you, smith though you are. I think you are a man of Othin, who is called also Bileyg, and Baleyg, and Bölverk."

"Bölverk?" said Shef. "And am I a doer of evil, a bale-worker?"

"Not yet. But you may be the instrument of one who is. Bale follows you." The big man shook his head. "But you did well today, for a beginner. Your first kill, I believe, and I am talking like a spaewife. Look, they have taken his body, but they have left the sword and shield and helmet. They are yours. It is the custom."

He spoke like one setting a test.

Slowly Shef shook his head. "I cannot profit from one I gave to Naströnd, to Dead Man's Strand." He picked up the helmet, threw it into the muddy water of the stream, hurled the buckler up into a bush, put his foot on the long thin sword, bent it once, twice, into unusability, left it lying.

"You see," said Brand. "Thorvin never taught you to do that. That is the sign of Othin."

CHAPTER SEVEN

Thorvin showed no surprise when Shef returned to the smithy and told him what had happened. He grunted a little wearily when Shef finally told him that he would be joining the contingent of Ivar, but said only, "Well, you'd better not go looking like that. The others would laugh at you—then you'll lose your temper and worse will happen."

From the pile at the back of the smithy he dug out a spear, recently reshafted, and a leather-bound shield. "With these you'll look respectable."

"Are they yours?"

"Sometimes people leave things in for repair, don't come back for them."

Shef took the gifts and then stood awkwardly, his rolled blanket and few possessions on his shoulder.

"I must thank you for what you did for me."

"I did it because it was my duty to the Way. Or so I thought. Maybe I was wrong. But I'm not a fool, boy. I am sure that you're after something I don't know about. I just hope it doesn't get you into trouble. Maybe our paths will run together again another day."

They parted with no more words, Shef stepping for only the second time over the rowan-berry cords of the precinct and for the first time walking down the lane between the tents without fear, face forward, not looking furtively around him. He headed not for the encampment of Ivar and the other Ragnarssons, but for the tent of Ingulf the leech.

As usual there was a small crowd standing round it, watching something. It dispersed as Shef strolled up, the last few men to leave carrying a stretcher with a bandaged shape on it. Hund came to meet his friend, wiping his hands on a rag.

"What were you doing?" Shef asked.

"Helping Ingulf. It's amazing what he can do. That man there was wrestling, fell awkwardly—leg broken, just like that. What would you do with that if you were back at home?"

Shef shrugged. "Bandage it up. Nothing else you can do. In the end it would heal."

"But the man would never walk straight again. The bones would just join each other wherever they happened to be. The leg would be all lumps and twists—like Crubba, who was rolled on by his horse. Well, what Ingulf does is pull the leg out straight before he starts bandaging, squeezes hard to feel if the broken ends of the bone are together. Then he bandages the leg between two stakes, so that the whole thing stays straight while it is healing. But what is even more marvelous is what he does in cases like this one, when it's broken so badly that the bones are sticking up through the skin. If he has to he even cuts back the bone, and opens the leg so that he can push the bone back straight! I didn't think that anyone would live through being opened and cut like that. But he is so quick—and he knows exactly what to do."

"Could you learn to do it?" Shef asked, watching the glow of enthusiasm on his friend's normally sallow face.

"With enough practice. Enough instruction. And something else. Ingulf studies the bodies of the dead, you know, to see how bones fit together. What would Father Andreas say to that?"

"So you mean to stay with Ingulf?"

The runaway slave nodded slowly. He pulled from under his tunic a chain. On it was a small silver pendant, an apple.

"Ingulf gave it me. The apple of Ithun the Healer. I am a believer now. I believe in Ingulf and the Way. Maybe not in Ithun." Hund looked at his friend's neck. "Thorvin has not converted you. You are not wearing a hammer."

"I wore one for a bit." Shef spoke briefly about what had happened. "I may have a chance now of rescuing Godive and getting away. Maybe if I watch for long enough God will be good to me."

"God?"

"Or Thor. Or Othin. I'm beginning to think that it makes no difference to me. Maybe one of them is watching."

"Is there anything I can do?"

"No." Shef gripped his friend's arm. "We may not see each other again. But if you leave the Vikings I hope one day I will have a place for you. Even if it's just a hut in the fen."

He turned and headed for the place he had not dared even to look at when they first entered the Viking camp days before: the Vikings' command tents.

The domain of the four Ragnarsson brothers ran from east wall to west wall, a full furlong along the riverfront. At its heart, in the center, were the great meeting tent—with room in it for tables for a hundred men—and the decorated tents of the brothers themselves. Round each of these four clustered the tents of women, dependents, the most trusted immediate bodyguards. Further away ran the lines of bivouac tents of the soldiers, usually three or four tents for every ship's crew, sometimes with smaller ones scattered through for the captains, helmsmen, and champions. The retinues of the brothers for the most part kept separate, if close together.

The Snakeeye's men were mostly Danes: It was common knowledge throughout the army that in time Sigurth would return to Denmark to challenge for the kingdom in Sjaelland and Skaane which his father had owned, and would go on one day to challenge for the rule of Denmark from the Baltic to the North Sea—a kingdom no man had possessed since the days of that King Guthfrith who fought Charlemagne. Ubbi and Halvdan, men with no stake and no claim to any throne other than that which their strength might bring them, recruited from anywhere: Swedes, Gauts, Norwegians, men from Gotland and Bornholm and all the islands.

Ivar's men were mostly exiles of one sort or another. Many no doubt were mere murderers escaping vengeance or the rule of one law or another. But the bulk of his following came from the floating population of Norsemen who for generations had been moving into the Outer Isles of the Celtic regions: the Orkneys and Shetlands, then the Hebrides, the Scottish mainland. For years these men had been tempered in the constant skirmishes of Ireland and Man, Strathclyde and Galloway and Cumbria. Among themselves they boasted—but the claim was fiercely rejected by many, especially the Norwegians, who viewed Ireland as their own property to keep or dispose of—that one day Ivar Ragnarsson would rule the whole of Ireland from his castle by the black pool, the Dubh Linn itself, and would then lead his victorious navies in triumph against the feeble kingdoms of the Christian West. The Ui Niall might still have a say in that, muttered the Gaddgedlar among themselves, speaking Irish as none of the Hebridean or Scottish Norsemen would deign to. But they said it quietly.

For all their race pride they knew that they themselves were the most hated of all by their countrymen, apostates from Christ, accomplices of those who had brought fire and slaughter to every part of Ireland. Who had done it for pay and for power, not merely for joy and for glory, as had been the Irish custom since the days of Finn and Cuchulainn and the champions of Ulster.

Into this touchy and tinder-dry encampment, graded with differences and with excuses for quarrel, Shef walked as the cooking fires were lighting for the night meal.

He was met by a marshal who heard his name, listened to his story, ran a disapproving eye over his shabby equipment, and grunted. He called a young man from the throng to show Shef his tent, sleeping place and oar, and to introduce him to his duties. The man—Shef never caught his name, nor did he want to—told him that there were four jobs at which he would have to take his turn: ship-guard, gate-guard, pen-guard, and if necessary, guard on the tent of Ivar. Mostly they were assigned by crew.

"I thought the Gaddgedlar guarded Ivar," Shef said.

The young man spat. "When he's here. When he's not they go with him. But the treasure and the womenfolk stay behind. Someone has to look after them. Anyway, if the Gaddgedlar got too far from Ivar someone would take a dislike to them—Ketil Flatnose and his men have a spite against them, and Thorvald the Deaf too. And a dozen more."

"Would we be trusted to guard the tent of Ivar?"

The young man looked at him aslant. "Shouldn't we be? I tell you, *Enzkr*, if you are thinking of Ivar's treasure you had better cut your thoughts right out of your head. It will be less painful that way. Did you ever hear what Ivar did to the Irish king at Knowth?"

As they walked round, he told him in detail what Ivar had done to kings and lesser men who had displeased him. Shef took little notice, looking with great interest at the camp. The tales were clearly meant to frighten him.

The ships, he thought, were the weak point of the camp. Space had to be left clear for them to be drawn up on the muddy banks, so there could be no fortifications there. The ships themselves represented a sort of obstacle, but they were also the Vikings' most precious possession. If anyone got past the riverbank-guards, they could be in among the ships with torch and axe, and they would be difficult to dislodge.

The gate-guards were a different matter. Surprising them would be hard. Any fight would be on level ground and on even terms, where the Vikings' great axes and iron-shafted javelins would have easy play. Anyone who did manage to get through them would in any case only find himself fighting his way through rank after rank of warriors, in a tangle of tents and ropes.

The pens, now . . . They occupied an area of their own near the east wall: a sorry strip of posts hammered into the ground, leather ropes binding them together. Inside, men huddled under makeshift coverings of canvas against the rain. Iron fetters on their feet, iron manacles on their hands. Held together, though, Shef noted, only by leather. Chain was too dear. But by the time a man had chewed through the leather bonds, even the least alert guard should have noticed—and penalty for any disobedience in the slave-pens was fierce. As Shef's guide pointed out, if you marked up a slave too much you couldn't sell him anyway, so you might as well go ahead and finish the job to frighten the others.

As he peered over the logs into the pen, Shef noticed a familiar-looking head lying on the ground, its owner sunk in a depth of despair: a blond head, curls matted with grime. His half brother, son of the same mother. Alfgar. Part of the prey of Emneth. The head stirred as if sensing the eyes upon it, and Shef dropped his gaze instantly, as he would have done had he been stalking a doe or a wild pig of the marshes.

"You haven't sold any slaves since you arrived?"

"Nay. Too much trouble getting them out to sea, with the English ambushing all the time. Sigvarth owns that lot." The young man spat again, eloquently. "He's waiting for someone else to clear the road for him. Will, too."

"Clear the road?"

"Ivar's taking half the army out in two days, to make the kinglet Jatmund—Edmund, you English call him—fight, or destroy his country for him. We'd rather have done it the easy way, but we wasted too much time already. Be bad news for Jatmund when Ivar catches up with him, I tell you. . . ."

"Are we going out or staying here?"

"Our crew stays." Again, the young man looked half curiously, half angrily at Shef. "Why you think I'm telling you all this? We'll be providing guards all the time. I wish I was going. I'd like to see what they'll do to that king when he's caught. I told you about Knowth. Well, I was there at the Boyne when Ivar robbed the tombs of the dead kings and this Christ-priest tried to stop us. What Ivar did, he . . ."

The subject occupied the young man and his mates all through the dinner of broth, salt pork and cabbage. There was a barrel of ale, someone had taken a hatchet or an axe to its top, and they all dipped into it liberally. Shef drank more than he realized, the day's events circling in his head. His mind was revolving what he had learned, trying to put together the rudiments of a plan. He lay down that night exhausted. The Irishman leaping in death in his arms was a detail, a matter of the past.

Then exhaustion seized him, drove him into sleep, into something more than sleep.

He was looking out from a building, through a half-shuttered window. It was night. A bright moonlit night, so bright that the racing clouds above threw dim shadows even in the dark. And out there something had flashed. Something had flashed.

There was a man standing next to him, gabbling out explanations of what the something might be. But he did not need them. He knew. A dull feeling of doom grew within him. Against it, a rising tide of fury. He cut the explanations short.

"That is not dawn from the east," said the Shef-who-was-not-Shef. "Nor is it a dragon flying, nor the gables of this hall burning. That is the flashing of drawn weapons, of secret foes coming to take us in our sleep. For now war awakens, war that will bring about disaster for all the people. So rise now, my warriors, think of courage, guard the doors, fight heroically."

In the dream, a stirring behind him as the warriors rose, gripped their shields, buckled their sword-belts.

But in the dream and over the dream, not in the hall, not part of the hero-tale that was unfolding before his eyes, he heard a mighty voice, too mighty to come from a human throat. It was a god's voice, Shef knew. But not the voice anyone would have imagined of a god. Not dignified, not honorable. An amused, chuckling, sardonic voice.

"Oh half-Dane who is not of the Half-Danes," it said. "Do not listen to the warrior, the brave one. When trouble comes, do not rise to fight. Seek the ground. Seek the ground."

Shef woke with a start, the smell of burning in his nostrils. For several seconds, half-drugged with fatigue, his mind circled around that: strange smell, something acrid, like tar—what could be burning tar? Then there was a confusion of movement all around him, a foot stamping on his guts jerked him into full wakefulness. The tent was abroil with men scrambling for breeches, boots, weapons, all in full darkness; there was a glare of fire on one side of the tent. Shef realized suddenly that there was a continuous roar in the background. Voices shouting, timber crackling, and over it all a deafening metallic clanging, the impact of blade on blade and blade on shield. The noise of full-scale battle.

The men in the tent were shouting, crowding past each other. Voices outside shouting, yelling in English, voices suddenly only yards away. Shef understood suddenly, the mighty voice still ringing in his ears. He hurled himself back to the ground again, fighting his way to the middle of the floor, away from the walls. As he did so the whole side of the tent caved in and through it there flashed a spear-blade. The young man who had guided him turned half toward it, his feet still trapped in folds of blanket, met the spear full in the chest. Shef grabbed the falling body and pulled it on top of him, feeling for the second time in a dozen hours the convulsive leap and start of a heart bursting.

As he did so, the whole tent collapsed and a wave of trampling feet ran over it, spears stabbing down into the trapped pile of struggling men. The body in his arms jerked again and again; in the darkness inches away there came screams of pain and fear; a blade plunged into the dirt, scraping against Shef's sprawling knee. Then suddenly the feet were gone, a rush of bodies and voices swarmed past in the lane outside, a new hubbub of clanging and shrieking broke out ten yards toward the center of the camp.

Shef knew what had happened. The English king had taken the Vikings' dare, had attacked their camp in the night, and by some miracle of organization and his enemies' overconfidence, had broken through or over the stockade, driving for the ships and the tents of the leaders, killing as many trapped in their blankets as they could. The English were pouring on, driving toward the center of the river-line. Shef seized his breeches, his boots and his sword-belt and wriggled past the corpses of his temporary fellows into the open. Pulled the gear on, ran, keeping low to the ground.

There was no one standing within twenty yards. Between himself and the stockade was a swathe of leveled tents with bodies sprawled among them, some calling feebly for help or trying to struggle to their feet. The English raiders had charged through the camp hacking frenziedly at anything that moved. They had left few survivors.

Before the Vikings could recover, join together, the raiders would be deep in the heart of their enemies' fortress, the battle irrecoverably won or lost.

All along the river-line there was glare and smoke, leaping up as sails caught or the fire took hold of some new-tarred timber hull; against the blaze a frieze of capering demons, hurling spears, swinging swords and axes. The English must have met little resistance down by the ships in their first charge. But the Vikings closest to the ships had rallied swiftly and fiercely to defend their wave-stallions. What was going on by the tents of the Ragnarssons? Was this the moment? Shef thought with a calm and intent calculation which left no room for self-doubt. Was this the moment to try to get Godive out?

No. Clearly there was battle and fierce resistance on all sides. If the Vikings beat off the assault, then she would remain as she was: a slave, the bedslave of Ivar. But if the attack succeeded—and if he were there to save her . . .

He ran, heading not toward the fighting, where one more half-armed man would find nothing but quick death; but in the opposite direction, toward the stockade walls, still dark, still quiet. Not completely. Shef realized now that there was battle not only close to him but also far away, in all directions round the further walls of the stockade. Spears were flying in the blackness, firebrands coming looping over the logs of the stockade. King Edmund had sent in simultaneous assaults from all sides at once. Each Viking had rushed to the nearest point of danger. By the time they realized where help was needed most, again Edmund would have won or lost.

Like a shadow Shef ran towards the slave-pens. As he neared them a figure lurched towards him in the fire-lit dark, its thigh black with blood, a longsword drooping in its hand. *"Fraendi,"* it said, "help me a moment, stop the bleeding—" Shef stabbed once from below, twisted the sword, withdrew.

One, he thought, grabbing up the sword.

The pen-guards were still there, clustered in tight formation in front of the pen's gates, clearly determined to resist any attempt to break through. All along the logs of the slave-stockade heads were bobbing as the tethered slaves tried to peer over, to see what was happening. Shef lobbed the longsword over the nearest wall, followed it in one surge of motion. There was a yell as the guards spotted him, but no movement. Undecided whether to guard the gate or to follow him.

Figures all round him, stinking, clutching. Shef snarled abuse in English, pushed them away. With the longsword he slashed the leather bonds between one pair of hand manacles, did the same for the man's foot fetters, pushed the sword into the freed hands.

"Start cutting them free," he hissed, turning instantly to the next man and drawing his own sword from its scabbard. The slaves saw what was happening, thrust their hands out, then snatched their leg-bonds, held them up for an easy cut. In twenty heartbeats half a score of slaves were free.

The palisade gate creaked open, the guards deciding to come in and catch the intruder. As the first Viking came through, hands caught his arms and legs, a fist slammed into his face. In seconds he was on the ground, his axe and spear snatched away, blows swinging at his fellows who crowded after him from the light into the darkness of the pen. Shef slashed furiously at leather, then saw suddenly the hands of his half brother Alfgar, a face staring at him in amazement and twisted rage.

"We have to get Godive."

The face nodded.

"Come with me. You others, there's weapons at the gate, cut yourselves free. Those with weapons, who want to strike a blow for Edmund, over the wall and follow me."

Shef's voice rose to a bellow. He sheathed sword, stepped to the wall, caught the top of the logs and heaved himself over in a second powerful roll. Alfgar was with him a moment later, staggering from the shock of release, a score of half-naked figures swarming after him and more pouring over the wall. Some ran instantly into the friendly dark, others turned in rage toward their guards, still embroiled in their struggle round the gate. Shef ran back through the leveled tents with a dozen men behind him.

Weapons lay everywhere for the snatching, dropped where their owners had died or still lying where they had been piled for the night. Shef hauled aside a tent flap, rolled over a corpse, seized a spear and a shield. For a long, hard-breathing pause he studied the men who had followed him as they armed themselves too. Peasants mostly, he judged. But angry and desperate ones, maddened by what had happened to them in the pens. The one in the front, though, staring at him intently, rolls of muscle on arm and shoulder, he carried himself like a warrior.

Shef pointed ahead, to the struggle still going on round the untouched command tents of the Viking Army. "There is King Edmund," he said, "trying to kill the Ragnarssons. If he succeeds the Vikings will break and flee and never recover. If he fails they will hunt us all down again and no village of any shire will be safe. We are fresh, and armed. Let us join them, break through together."

The released slaves surged as one toward the fighting.

Alfgar held back. "You did not come with Edmund, half-armed and half-naked. How do you know where to find Godive?"

"Shut up and follow." Shef sprinted ahead again, hurdling through the confusion towards the tents of the women of Ivar.

CHAPTER EIGHT

Edmund—son of Edwold, descendant of Raedwald the Great, last of the Wuffingas, and now by God's grace king of the East Angles—glared through the eyeholes of his war-mask in frustration and rage.

They had to break through! One more thrust and the desperate resistance of the Viking chiefs would crumble, the Ragnarssons would all die together in blood and fire, the rest of the Great Army would fall back in doubt and confusion. . . . But if they held . . . If they held, he knew, in a few more minutes the war-wise Vikings would realize that the assaults on their perimeter were no more than angry peasants with torches, that the real attack was here, here. . . . And then they would be down on the struggle by the riverbank with their overwhelming numbers, and it would be the English who were caught like rats in the last unmown square of the hayfield. He, Edmund, had no sons. The whole future of his dynasty and his kingdom had now narrowed down to this yelling, clanging tumult, maybe one hundred men on each side, as the picked champions of the East English and the last hard core of the Ragnarssons' personal forces fought it out: the one side straining every nerve in their bodies to break into the three-sided square of the Ragnarssons' tents down by the river; the other, standing poised and confident among the tangle of their guy-ropes, bracing themselves to hold out for five minutes more after the unimaginable shock of the English assault.

And they were doing it too. Edmund's hand tensed on the bloody

sword-hilt and he swayed as if to move forward. Instantly the brawny
shadows on either side of him, the captains of his bodyguard, edged
slightly forward, blocking him in with shield and body. They would not let
him throw himself into the melee. As soon as the initial slaughter of
sleeping men had stopped and the fight had begun, they had been in front
of him.

"Easy, lord," muttered Wigga. "See Totta and the boys there. They'll get
through these bastards yet."

As he spoke the battle surged in front of them, first a few feet forward as
a Viking went down and the English rushed at the momentary gap. Then
back, back. Above the helmets and the raised shields a battle-axe whirled,
the thuds as it struck lindenwood turning to a crash of steel on mail. The
swaying mob ejected a body, cleft through its mail from neck to breastbone. For an instant Edmund saw a giant figure twirling its axe in one
hand like a boy's ox-goad, daring the English to come on. They did,
fiercely, and all he could see was straining backs.

"We must have killed a thousand of the bastards already," said Eddi on
his other hand. In a moment, Edmund knew, one or the other of them
would say "Time to get out of here, lord," and he would be hustled away.
If they could get away. Most of his army, the country thanes and their
levies, were already making for the rear. They had done their job: burst
over the stockade behind the king and his picked strikers, massacred the
sleepers, overwhelmed the ship-guards and set fire to as many beached
longships as they could. But they had never expected to stand in line and
exchange blows with the professional champions of the North, nor did
they mean to. Catch them asleep and unarmored, yes. Fight them awake
and enraged, man to man, toe to toe—that was the duty of their betters.

One break, Edmund prayed. Almighty God eternal, one break in this
square and we will be through and attacking them from all sides. The war
will be over and the pagans destroyed. No more dead boys in meadows
and children's corpses tossed down wells. But if they stand another minute, long enough for a mower to whet his scythe . . . Then it is we who
will break and, for me, it will be the fate of Wulfgar.

The thought of his tormented thane swelled his heart till it seemed the
links of his mail must snap. The king shoved Wigga aside and strode
forward, sword raised, looking for a gap in the fighters where he could
thrust forward. He shouted full-throatedly, so that his voice echoed inside
the metal of his ancient visor:

"Break through! Break through! The hoard of Raedwald, I swear it, to the man who breaks their ranks. And five hundreds to the man who brings me the head of Ivar!"

Twenty paces away, Shef gathered his little band of rescued prisoners in the night. Many of the tarred longships along the river were now blazing furiously, throwing lurid light on the battle. All around them, the Vikings' bivouac tents were down, flattened by the English charge, their occupants dead or wounded. Only in one place, in front of them, eight or ten pavilions still stood: the homes of the Ragnarssons, their chieftains, their guards —and their women. Round these the battle raged.

Shef turned to Alfgar and to the heavily-muscled thane beside him, standing a pace in front of the little knot of half-armed, heavy-breathing peasants.

"We have to break into those tents there. That's where the Ragnarssons are." And Godive, he thought silently. But only Alfgar would care about that.

In the firelight the thane's teeth showed, a mirthless smile.

"Look," he pointed.

For an instant again, as the battle cleared, two warriors showed in black silhouette, each leap of flame seeming to catch them in another contorted pose. The swords whirled, each blow parried *forte à forte,* the strokes coming forehand, backhand, at all angles, each one meeting a precisely timed counter. The warriors twisted and stamped, raising their shields, leaping over low strokes, moving with each blow into position for the next, trying to gain leverage even from the strokes of their enemy for a tiny advantage on the next counter, a weakened wrist, a strain, a hesitation.

The thane's voice was almost affectionate. "Look at them, both sides. Those are the king's warmen and the best of the pirates. They are the *drengir,* the hard *here-chempan.* How long would we last against them? Me —maybe I could give one a little trouble for half a minute. You—I don't know. These—" He gestured with his thumb at the peasants behind him. "Make sausage meat of them."

"Let's get out of here," said Alfgar abruptly. The peasants stirred and muttered.

Suddenly the thane had Alfgar by the arm, fingers sinking deep.

"No. Listen. That is the king's voice. He is calling on his true men. Hear what he wants."

"He wants the head of Ivar," snarled a peasant.

Suddenly they were all moving forward, raising spears, bracing shields, the thane among them.

He knows it won't work, Shef realized—but I know what will!

He leapt in front of them, pointing, gesturing. Slowly the men caught his meaning, turned away, dropped their weapons, headed for the nearest of the blazing longships.

Over the clash of steel the Vikings too heard the king's voice calling, and understood him—many of them had had English bedslaves for years, and their fathers before them.

"King Jatmund wants your head," cried one of the jarls.

"I don't want Jatmund's head," Ivar called back. "He must be taken alive."

"What do you want him for?"

"I will give that much thought. Something new. Something instructive."

Something to put heart back into the men. This had all been much too close for comfort, Ivar reflected, edging from side to side to keep a clear view of the action. He would never have thought that the king of a little kingdom like this would have had the guts to challenge the Great Army in its own base.

"All right," he said quietly to the Gaddgedlar, waiting behind the battle-line as his personal reserve. "No need to wait much longer. They aren't going to break through. Over here, between the tents. Now, when I give the word we are going to charge. Go right through them, don't bother to fight. I want you to catch the kinglet, King Jatmund. See him. There. The little man, the one with the war-mask over his face."

Ivar filled his lungs to shout, over the din of battle, in mockery of the cry of Edmund. "Twenty ounces, twenty ounces of gold to the man who brings me the English king. But don't kill him. He must be taken alive."

But before he could speak he felt Muirtach and the Irish gasp and stiffen around him.

"Will you look at that!"

"It's a fiery cross coming for us!"

"Mac na hoige slan."

"Mother of God be merciful."

"What in the name of Othin is it?"

Over the heads of the struggling men a giant shape rushed toward them like a cross, a monstrous, blazing cross. The ranks of the English parted, Killer-Brand leapt forward with his axe raised. Then the huge timber fell forward, half hurled by the capering furies who grasped it.

Brand sprang aside, tripped over a rope and fell with a clang to the ground. Something struck Ivar a numbing blow on the shoulder. The

Gaddgedlar scattered in all directions as the waxed flax walls of the tents started to blaze. The shrieking of women rose to add itself to all the other noises of the battle.

And instantly, running along the blazing timber itself, his face contorted with rage and delight, there came a half-naked churl, the slave manacles still on his wrist, hurtling through the scattered ranks of his captors. A spear stabbed at Ivar's face. Without thought he parried it, slicing the point from its shaft at the same moment his shoulder shrieked protest. The peasant raced on, reversing his clumsy weapon and smashing it at the side of Ivar's head.

The blow, the ground rising up, the fall into burning wax and skin. Struck by a peasant, Ivar's brain thought in the last instant of consciousness, darkness embracing him. But I am the champion of the North.

Through the flames other figures came leaping. It's that boy, thought Ivan, the one who fought the duel by the washing-place. But I thought he was one of mine. . . .

A bare foot landed in his testicles, and his body gave up the fight.

Shef raced along the still-smoldering timber of the longship's mast. He was aware that his hands were burned, swelling, puffy already with blisters. There was no time for that. He and the thane and Alfgar had seized the smoldering timber, its yard still attached, as soon as the peasants had pulled it from the flame, had grasped the upper end and had run toward the fighting battle-line, struggling desperately to keep it upright till they could throw it into the warriors. But the instant they hurled it a wave of furious peasants had run straight past them and over them. And behind him, he knew, came King Edmund's champions, all beside themselves with rage and fear and the passion to kill. He had to reach Godive first.

In front of him a churl rained blows on an amazed Viking with a broken spear-staff. Something groaned and squirmed under his feet. Another peasant was down with a slash from the side. Yellow plaids seemed to be scattering in flight everywhere—the Gaddgedlar, in superstitious panic and fear of the fiery cross that had come to avenge their apostasy. And women shrieking.

Shef swerved instantly to the left round a tent. Bulging sides, the screaming just beyond it. He drew his sword, bent, and scored it open at knee level, instantly catching the flap and hauling at it with all his strength.

A wail of women erupted from it like water from a broken milldam, in their shifts, in their gowns, at least one still naked from her sleep. Godive

—where! That one, there, the scarf over her head. Shef seized her shoulder, hauling her round to him, dragging the scarf down. A blaze of yellow hair, turned copper by the flames in the sky, and furious pale eyes, nothing like Godive's gray ones. A fist caught him full in the face and he staggered back, full of shock and incongruous pain: all around him heroes were dying and he had just been punched on the nose!

Then the woman was away, and Shef glimpsed a familiar body-shape, not scuttling like the other women but running full stride like a young deer. Straight into disaster. The English were everywhere now, inside the Viking square, taking their enemies from front and rear simultaneously, determined to wipe out the pirates' leadership and aristocracy in the scant seconds they had before rescue and revenge came down from the main camp. They were cutting at everything that moved, carried away with fear and triumph and long frustration.

Shef was on her, throwing himself forward, catching her round the hips and bowling her over just as a furious warrior, seeing something moving behind him, swung round and launched a body-severing blow at waist level. The two rolled sideways in a tangle of legs and dress and nails as new combat clashed above them. Then he had a grip round her waist and was hauling her by main force into the shadow of a pavilion, tenanted only by corpses.

"Shef!"

"Me." He put his hand over her mouth. "Listen. We have to get away now. There won't be another chance. Go back to where I broke in. Everyone there is dead now. If we can just get through the fight we'll be out there, by the river. Understood? Now, let's go."

Sword in one hand, clutching Godive tightly with the other, Shef stepped crouching into the night, eyes darting for a route through the fifty single combats that raged around him.

The battle was over, Edmund thought. And he had lost. He had broken the Vikings' last ring, sure enough, thanks to that rabble of churls that had sprung from nowhere with the half-naked youth in their midst. In the last few minutes he had done crippling execution among the Great Army's hardest of hard cores, so much that the Army would never be quite the same again. Or remember the camp on the Stour without a shudder. But he had not yet seen a Ragnarsson dead. There were little knots of men still fighting back-to-back and the Ragnarssons must be among them. Only if he held this place of slaughter, defeated and killed every one of them, could he be sure of lasting victory.

He would not get the chance to do it. Edmund felt the blood-rage inside him cooling, cooling to a slow and wary calculation. Ominously, the noise from the main camp above the Ragnarssons' tents by the river had lessened. Stung by arrows from the palisades, harassed by mock assaults and parties of running knifemen in their rear, the Vikings had let the Ragnarssons deal with their own troubles in their own way. But you could not fool these veterans for long; they would not stand by forever while their leaders were destroyed.

Edmund sensed that men were gathering beyond the reach of the flames. Those were orders being given. Someone was getting ready to come down like a warhammer on a hazelnut, with a thousand men together. How many had he left on their feet and not escaped into the night? Fifty?

"Time to go, lord," muttered Wigga.

Edmund nodded, knowing that he had reached the absolute last instant. His escape route was still clear, and he had a handful of champions round him to brush aside any scattered interceptors there might be between him and the east stockade.

"Back," he ordered. "Back to where we broke in. We'll run for the stockade from there. But kill everyone, everyone on the ground, ours as well as theirs. Don't leave them for Ivar. And make certain every single one is dead!"

Ivar felt consciousness returning. Yet it would not come back all at once; it was there and not there. He had to grasp it, grasp it quickly. Something terrible was coming toward him. He could feel the thump, thump, thump of heavy footsteps. It was a *draugr*—giant, swollen, blue as a three-day corpse, strong as ten men, with all the strength of those who live in the Halls of the Mighty, but come back to earth to vex their descendants. Or to avenge their deaths.

Ivar remembered who he was. In the same instant he realized who the *draugr* must be. It was the Irish king Maelguala, whom he had killed years before. Ivar remembered still his contorted face, glistening with sweat from rage and pain, but still cursing Ivar steadily and fearlessly as the wheels turned and the strongest men of the Army threw their weight on the levers. They had bent him back and back over the stone till suddenly—

As his mind registered the snap of broken spine, Ivar awoke fully. Something over his face; skin, cloth—had they wrapped him in his cloak already for burial? An instinctive movement checked a stab of agony from the right shoulder, but the pain burned away the mist from his head. He sat up instantly, more pain from his head, not the right side, the left side, the side opposite from where he had been hit. Concussion, then. He had felt that before. Get down and stay down. No time to do that now. He could tell where he was.

Ivar lurched slowly to his feet, the effort sending a wave of nausea and giddiness through him. His sword was still in his hand, and he tried to lift it. No strength there. He dropped the blade and leaned heavily on it, feeling the point sink into the close-packed earth. He stared to the west, between the ripped-open tents, toward an arena where still threescore of men fought desperately to buy time, or to annihilate their enemies, and saw doom approaching him.

No *draugr,* but a king. Heading straight toward him, evidently bent on escape, was the short, broad-shouldered figure in the war-mask. The English kinglet. Jatmund. Flanking and following him were a half dozen enormous men, big as Vikings, big as Viga-Brand, obviously the king's own personal bodyguard—the very heart and soul of the king's warriors, the *chempan* as the English called them. As they came they were stabbing carefully, economically, professionally, at every figure that still lay on the ground. They were doing it just right. One of them he would have squared off to, if he had been fighting fit and unwounded and the men had needed to be encouraged. Six. And he could hardly hold a weapon, still less could he wield it. Ivar tried to shuffle his feet round to face them, so that no one could say afterward that Ivar Ragnarsson, the champion of the North, had been caught unawares or trying to flee. As he did so, the war-mask turned toward him.

A cry of recognition broke from it, a wave, a pointing arm. All the English together broke into a run, charging toward him, swords raised, the bodyguards striving vainly to outstrip their king.

As Edmund attacked, Shef, dodging from dark space to dark space round the edges of the conflict, saw the gap between the tangled tents, pushed Godive violently into it, and tensed his muscles for the final dart to liberty.

Without warning she had torn free of his grasp, was rushing ahead of him. She had seized a man by the arm, a wounded man, was holding him up. By Christ, it was Ivar! Hurt, done for, staggering as he stood.

Shef's lips pulled back in a killing snarl, and he paced forward like a leopard—one step, two, three—sword dropped to hip level, already aiming the fierce thrust upward beneath the chin where no armor covered.

Then Godive was in front of him, clutching at his sword-hand. He tried to throw her off but Godive clung on, pounding his naked chest with her free hand. Shrieking.

"Behind you! Behind you!"

Shef flung her off and spun to see a sword already slicing at his neck. His own sword met it with a clang, driving it up; a second blow came instantly after the first. He ducked under it and heard the whizz as it slashed the air. Realized in the same instant that Godive was behind him and that he had to keep his own body between the swords and her.

Then he was backing between a maze of guy-ropes, half a dozen men crowding toward him behind the short figure in the fantastically molded and gilded war-mask. It was the king. But no matter who it was or how many supporters he had, for just this one moment it was Shef the slave, Shef the dog and the king of the East Angles facing each other.

"Get out of the way," said Edmund, pacing forward. "You are an Englishman. You brought the ship's timber, you broke the line. I saw you. That is Ivar behind you. Kill him, let me kill him, and you will have the reward I promised."

"The woman," Shef stammered. He had meant to say "Just leave me the woman." But he had no time.

Too late. As the gap between the tents widened, the champions of Edmund saw their chance. One was by the side of his king in an instant, stabbing furiously upward at the unarmored youth in front of him, converting the stab instantly into a slash, jerking his shield forward as the slash missed, to break a rib or smash a wrist. Shef stepped back, ducked, twisted, as he had against the Irishman Flann, making no attempt to strike back or parry.

"You can have him," he yelled.

He beat a thrust aside, ducked into a shield-boss, and with the strength of desperation grappled a wrist as thick as a horse's fetlock, twisted, and hurled Wigga the champion over his thigh in a village-green cross-buttock throw.

He was on the ground and legs were all around him; cries and blows and the clang of metal. A dozen Vikings had appeared, Viga-Brand at their head, to protect their chief. Now it was the English king whose men had to close round him, to die one by one while all the time Ivar called out for Jatmund to be spared, for the kinglet not to be killed.

Taking no notice of the fray Shef wriggled clear, saw Godive standing a few yards away from the edge of the battle, staring round in panic. He seized her by the arm and dragged her at full speed toward the dying fires of the longships and the muddy waters of the Stour. The English kingdom lay in ruins behind him, and if the pirates ever caught him again his fate would be terrible. But Godive was unhurt. He had saved her.

Though she had saved Ivar.

CHAPTER NINE

The stars were paling in the eastern sky behind them as the young man and the girl stole carefully and cautiously through the depths of the wood. If he looked back Shef could see the topmost branches now silhouetted against the sky, moving slightly in the breeze, the little wind that comes before dawn. Down at ground level nothing of it could be felt. Where the two crossed the occasional clearing created by the fall of oak or ash, the dew soaked their feet. It would be a hot day, Shef thought, one of the last of the late, event-filled summer.

It could not come soon enough for him. Both were cold. Shef wore only the boots and woolen breeches which he had snatched up when the English attack came in. Godive had only her shift. She had stripped off her long dress before slipping into the water by the fired ships. She could swim like a fish, like an otter; and like otters they had swum out, underwater for as many strokes as they could, concentrating on noiselessness and cutting out both splash and gasp. A hundred slow strokes and ten breaths up the river, against the slow, weedy current; eyes alert every time they came up for watchers on the bank. Then a careful filling of the lungs while Shef warily eyed the stockade edge, where surely guards might still be posted. Then the deep dive and the long swim underwater, till it was time to come up and repeat the otter stroke, on, on, for another quarter mile before he decided it might be safe to creep ashore.

He had felt no chill while they were escaping, only a momentary prickle on his burned hands and body as he dashed into the water the first time. But now he was beginning to shiver uncontrollably, the great shudders wracking his body. Shef knew that he was close to collapse. He would have to let go soon, lie down, let his muscles relax. And let his mind come to terms with the events of the last twenty-four hours. He had killed a man; no, two men. He had seen the king, something he might have expected to do once or twice in a lifetime. But this time the king had seen him, had even spoken to him! And he had stood toe to toe with Ivar the Boneless, champion of the North. Shef knew he would have killed him if it had not been for Godive. He could have been the hero of all England, of all Christianity.

But she had stopped him. And then he had betrayed his king, delayed him, all but handed him over to the power of the pagans. If anyone were ever to know about that . . . But his mind shied away from the thought. They had escaped. He would ask Godive about her and Ivar when he could.

As the light strengthened, Shef's eye caught the faint trace of a trail. It was overgrown, had not been used for weeks. That was good. Used last to flee from the Viking landing. But at the end of the trail there might be something: a hut, a shed. Anything left behind would now be worth its weight in silver.

Now, the trees were thinning, there was something in front of him: not a hut, he realized, but a shelter, a lean-to made of branches. The coppicers must have made it to store their gear in as they worked through the forest cutting the poles that all farmers relied on for hurdles and fencing, for handles, and for the centerpieces for their flimsy wattle-and-daub walls.

There was no one there. Shef led Godive over. Turning her toward him, he held her hands in his own and looked down into her eyes.

"What we have here," he said, "is nothing. One day, I hope we will have a real house of our own, somewhere we can live together untroubled. That is why I came to take you back from the Vikings. It will not be safe to travel in the day. Let us rest as well as we can till evening."

The coppicers had rigged up a bark gutter beneath the roof of rough shingles. It led to a large broken crock, full to overflowing with clear rainwater: one more proof that no one had been there for weeks. The boughs inside were covered with old, torn strips of blanket. Stiffly the pair wrapped themselves, lay down huddled together, fell immediately into an exhausted slumber.

* * *

Shef woke as the sun began to pierce through the branches. He rose, careful not to disturb the still-sleeping girl, and crawled out of the shelter. Concealed beneath the boughs he found flint and steel. Should he risk a fire? he wondered. Better not. They had water and warmth, but there was no food to cook. He would take what he had found with them when they left. Slowly, Shef was beginning to think of the future. He owned nothing now, save his breeches, so every single possession he accumulated would be precious.

He did not think they would be disturbed, not this day. They were still well within range of the Viking fighting patrols he had seen on his way into the camp, but the Vikings would have other things to think about for a while. Everyone would be at the camp, counting casualties, deciding what to do—probably fighting among themselves for control of the Army. Had Sigurth the Snakeeye survived? Shef wondered. If he had, even he might have trouble in reimposing his authority on a shaken army.

As for the English, Shef knew that as he and Godive had left the river and started to make their way into the woods there had been other folk about. The refugees from King Edmund's army, the ones who had fled, or at any rate decided to retreat before the crisis of the battle. They were all making their way to their respective homes as fast as ever they could. Shef doubted if there would be an Englishman within five miles of the Viking encampment by now. They had guessed that their lord's attack had failed, and that he was dead.

Shef hoped so, remembering what his pirate guide had told him about Ivar's ways with defeated kings.

He lay in the sun on the blanket, feeling his body relax. A muscle jumped irregularly in his thigh. He waited for it to stop, looking at the puffed blisters on both hands.

"Will it be better if I prick them?" Godive was at his side, kneeling in her shift, holding up a long thorn. He nodded.

As she began to work on his left hand and he felt the slow tears rolling down his arm, he held her warm shoulder with his right.

"Tell me," he said. "Why did you stand between me and Ivar? How was it with you and him?"

Her eyes lowered, Godive seemed unsure what to say. "You know I was given to him? By—by Sigvarth."

"By my father. Yes. I know. What happened then?"

She kept her eyes down, studying his blisters attentively.

"They gave me to him at a banquet, with everyone watching. I—I only had this to wear. Some of them do terrible things to their women, you know, like Ubbi. They say he takes them in front of his men, and if things do not go to his liking he hands them over to the men then and there, to be used by all. You know I was a virgin—I am a virgin. I was very frightened."

"You are virgin still?"

She nodded. "Ivar said nothing to me then, but he had me brought to him in his tent that night, and he talked to me. He told me—he told me that he was not like other men.

"He is not a gelding, you know. He has sired children, or so he says. But he told me where other men can feel desire just at the sight of flesh, he needs—something else."

"Do you know what that something is?" asked Shef sharply, remembering the hints Hund had given.

Godive shook her head. "I do not know. I do not understand. But he says that if men were to know how it is with him, they would mock him. In his youth the other young men called him the Boneless One because he could not do as they do. But, he says, he killed many men for mocking him and discovered it was a pleasure to him. Now all those who laughed are dead, and only the closest suspect how it is with him. If everyone had known, Sigvarth would not have dared to hand me over to him openly and publicly, as he did. Now, he says, men call him the Boneless because they fear him. They say that at night he turns—not into a wolf or a bear, like other skin-changers—but into a dragon, a great long-worm, that creeps out in the night for its prey. Anyway, that is what they think now."

"And what do you think?" asked Shef. "Do you remember what they did to your father? He is your father, not mine, but even I felt sorrow for him. And though Ivar did not do that, he gave the orders. That is the kind of thing he does. He may have spared you rape, but who knows what else he had in mind for you. You say he has children. Has anyone seen the mothers?"

Godive turned over Shef's palm and began to lance the blisters that covered it.

"I don't know. He is hateful and cruel to men, but that is because he fears them. He fears they are more manly than he is. But how do they show it, this manliness? By violating those who are too weak, by taking their pleasure from pain. Maybe Ivar has been sent by God—as a punishment for men's sins."

"Do you wish I had left you with him?" Hardness edged Shef's voice.

Slowly Godive bent over him, abandoning her thorn. He felt her cheek against his naked chest, her hands sliding along his sides. As he pulled her up next to him, her loose shift slid from one bare shoulder. Shef found himself staring at a naked breast, its nipple girlish pink. The only woman he had seen before like this was the slut Truda—heavy, sallow, coarse-fleshed. His roughened hands began to stroke Godive's skin with disbelieving tenderness. If he had thought of this happening—and he had, often, lying by himself in fisherman's hut or deserted forge—it was years in the future, after they had found a place, after he had deserved her and made a home where they could be safe. Now, in the wood, in the clearing, in the sunlight, without blessing of priest or consent from parents . . .

"You are a better man than Ivar or Sigvarth or any other man I have ever met," sobbed Godive, her face still buried in his shoulder. "I knew you would come for me. I only feared they would kill you for it."

He pulled at her shift, her legs squirming beneath him as she turned onto her back.

"We should both be dead by now. It is so good to be alive, with you—"

"There is no blood between us, we have different fathers, different mothers—"

In the sunlight he entered her. Eyes watched from a bush; breath drew in, in envy.

An hour later, Shef lay on the soft grass, in the sunshine where the rays of the now-hot sun came through the upper branches of the oak trees. He was torpid, completely relaxed. He was not asleep. Or he was, but at some dim level he remained awake, conscious that Godive had slipped away. He had been thinking of the future, of where they could go: into the marshes, he thought, remembering his night spent with the king's thane Edrich. He was still conscious of the sun on his skin, of the soft turf beneath his body, but they seemed further away. This had happened before—in the Viking camp. His mind was rising from the forest clearing, traveling out beyond the body, beyond the heart's confines. . . .

A voice spoke to him—rough, gravelly, laden with authority.

"Of mighty men," it said, "the maid you have taken."

Shef knew he was somewhere else. He was at a forge. Everything was familiar: the hiss as he wound the wet rags round the scorching handles of the tongs, the heft in his back and shoulder muscles as he lifted the red-hot metal out of the heart of the fire, the scrape and scratch of the top of his leather apron across his chest, the automatic duck and shake of the head as the sparks flew up toward his hair. But it was not his forge, back in Emneth, nor Thorvin's forge within the enclosure of the rowan berries. He sensed round him an enormous space, a gigantic open hall so high he could not see the top, just mighty pillars and columns leading away to the top where the smoke clung.

He took the heavy hammer and began to beat out a shape from the formless mass glowing on his anvil. What that shape should be he did not know. Yet his hands knew, for they moved expertly and without hesitation, shifting the tongs, turning the bloom, striking from one direction and then another. It was no spear-blade or axe-head, no ploughshare or coulter. It seemed to be a wheel, but a wheel with many teeth, sharp-pointed ones, like a dog's. Shef watched with fascination as the thing came to life beneath his blows. He knew, in his heart, that what he was doing was impossible. No one could make a shape like that straight from a forge. And yet—he could see how it might be done, if you made the teeth separately and then fitted them all together on the wheel you had originally made. But what would the point of it all be? Maybe, if you had one wheel like that, turning one way, up and down like a wall, and another wheel, turning the other way, flat and level with the ground, then, if the teeth on the one wheel matched with the teeth on the other, the first could drive the second round.

But what would be the point of that? There was a point. It had something to do with the object, the giant construction, twice man-height over by one wall, just beyond his vision in the dimness.

Shef realized as his senses cleared that there were other figures looking at him, figures on the same enormous scale as the hall. He could not see them clearly, and he did not dare look up for more than moments from his work, but he caught their presence unmistakably. They were standing together and watching him, even discussing him, he thought. They were Thorvin's gods, the gods of the Way.

Nearest to him was a broad and powerful shape, an immensely scaled-up Viga-Brand, giant biceps muscles rolling beneath a short-sleeved tunic. That must be Thor, thought Shef. His expression was scornful, hostile, faintly anxious. Behind the shape was another god—keen-eyed, sharp-faced, thumbs stuck into a silver belt, eyeing Shef with a kind of concealed approval, as if he were a horse to be bought, a thoroughbred going at a bargain price from a foolish owner.

That one is on my side, thought Shef. *Or maybe he thinks I am on his.*

Others clustered behind the two: tallest of them, and furthest away, a god leaning on a mighty spear with a triangular head.

Shef became aware of two other things. He was hamstrung. As he moved around the forge, his legs trailed behind him uselessly, making him take the weight on his arms and pull himself from one place to another. High stools, stocks of wood and benches were littered around in seemingly random fashion, but actually, he realized, to support him as he went from one workplace to another. He could prop himself on his legs, stand, like a man balancing on two stout props, but there was no spring, no movement at all from the thigh muscles to the calf. A dull ache spread upward from his knees.

And there was someone else watching him, not one of the mighty figures, but a tiny one, down in the shadows of the smoke-filled hall, like an ant, or a mouse peering out from the wainscoting. It was Thorvin! No, it was not Thorvin, but a smaller and a slighter man with a long face and sharp expression, both accentuated by the thinning hair falling back from the high forehead. But it was someone dressed like Thorvin, all in white, with the rowan berries round his neck. He had something of the same expression too, thoughtful, intensely interested, but here also, cautious and fearful. The small figure was trying to speak to him.

"Who are you, boy? Are you a wanderer from the realms of men, set for a while in Völund's place? How have you come here, and by what fortune did you find the Way?"

Shef shook his head, pretending it was just a toss to keep the sparks out of his eyes. He tossed the wheel aside into a bucket of water and began to set to another piece of work. The three quick raps, the turn, the three raps again, and a glowing something flying through the air into the cold water, to be instantly replaced on the anvil by another. What he was doing Shef did not know, but it filled him with wild excitement and a furious impatient glee, like a man who would one day be free and did not want his jailer to know the joy inside him.

Shef realized that one of the giant figures was coming toward him—the tallest of them, the one with the spear. The mouse-man saw too and ducked back into the shadows, now visible only as the palest of blurs in the gloom.

A finger like the trunk of an ash turned Shef's chin upward. One eye looked down at him, from a face like the blade of an axe: straight nose, jutting chin, sharp gray beard, wide, wide cheekbones. It was a face that would have made Ivar's seem a relief, as something at least comprehensible, ravaged only by human passions like envy, hate and cruelty. This was far different: One touch of the thoughts behind that mask, Shef knew, and any human mind would go insane.

Yet it did not seem entirely hostile, more thoughtful, considering.

"You have far to go, mannikin," it said. "Yet you have begun well. Pray that I do not call you to me too soon."

"Why would you call me, High One?" said Shef, amazing himself with his own temerity.

The face smiled like a glacier calving. "Do not ask," it said. "The wise man does not pry or peek like a maiden searching for a lover. He looks even now, the gray fierce wolf, into Asgarth's doors."

The finger dropped, the great hand came sweeping across, over forge and *anvil and tools, over benches and buckets and the smith all together, brushing them all away like a man sweeping nutshells from a blanket. Shef felt himself hurled into the air, spinning end over end, apron flying away from him, his last memory the little face-shaped blur in the shadows, watching and marking him.*

In a heartbeat he was back on the grass, back beneath the open sky of England in the forest clearing. But the sun had moved off him, leaving him in shadow, cold and suddenly afraid.

Where was Godive? She had crept from his side for a moment, but then—

Shef was on his feet, wide awake, staring round for an enemy. Tumult in the bushes, thrashing and fighting and the sound of a woman trying to scream with a hand over her mouth and an arm round her throat.

As Shef sprang toward the struggle, men rose from their cover behind the tree-trunks, and closed on him like the fingers of doom. Leading them came Muirtach the Gaddgedil, a newly livid weal across his face and an expression of bitter, contained, contented fury twisting it.

"Nearly you got away, boy," he said. "You should have kept running, not stopped to try out Ivar's woman. But a hot prick knows no sense. It will be cold soon enough."

Hard hands closed on Shef's shoulders as he lunged towards the bushes, desperate to reach Godive. Had they seized her already? How had they found them? Had they left some trail?

A jeering laugh rose above the babble of Gaddgedlar voices. Shef recognized it, even as he writhed and fought, drawing all the Vikings to him. It was the laugh of an Englishman. Of his half brother. Alfgar.

CHAPTER TEN

When Muirtach and the others had dragged him back inside the stockade, Shef had been close to collapse. He had been exhausted in the first place. The shock of recapture had also bitten deep into him. The Vikings had been rough with him as well as they pulled him back, punching and cuffing him repeatedly as they hustled him through the woods, eyes alert all the time for any fringe of scattered Englishmen still lurking in the trees. Then, as they came out onto the meadows and sighted their comrades rounding up such horses as remained, jerking their captive off his feet again and again in rough triumph. They had been badly scared. Having one trophy to take back to Ivar was not much of a set off against all they had lost. Dimly, through weariness and horror, Shef realized that they were in the mood now to work out all their earlier fears on such little satisfaction as they could find. But before he could take in much of that thought, they dragged him to the pen, beat him unconscious.

He only wished he had not had to come round. They had thrown him inside the stockade at mid-morning. He had been unconscious the whole of the long, warm late-summer day. When he finally blinked his blood-sealed eyelids open he was sore, stiff, bruised—but no longer dizzy or bone weary. But he was also chilled to the bone, dry-mouthed with thirst, weak from hunger—in a state of deadly fear. At nightfall he looked round to try to see some prospect of escape or rescue. There was none. Iron anklets on his feet were lashed to stout pegs. His hands were bound in front of him. In time he might have worked the pegs out or chewed through the rawhide lashings on his wrists, but the slightest movement in either direction brought a growl and a kick from the nearby guard. They had, Shef realized, almost no prisoners to watch. In the confusion of the night attack almost all the accumulated slave-booty of the campaign had fought itself free and vanished, taking the Vikings' profits with them. Only a few other figures, newly captured prisoners secured like himself, dotted the floor space of the pen.

What they said brought Shef no comfort. They were the very few survivors of King Edmund's picked men, who had fought to the last in the final attempt to destroy the Ragnarssons and cripple the Viking army's leadership. All were wounded, usually badly. They expected to die, and talked quietly among themselves as they waited. Mostly, they regretted their failure to make a clean sweep of their enemies in the first few minutes of their attack. But then, they said, it could never have been expected that they could get to the heart of the Great Army without resistance. They had done well: burned the ships, killed the crews. "We have gained great glory," said one. "We stand like eagles on the bodies of the slain. Let us not repent, whether we die now or later."

"I wish they had not taken the king," said one of the warrior's comrades after a silence, speaking with difficulty through the wheezing of his pierced lung. At that they nodded soberly, and their eyes moved together toward a corner of the pen.

Shef shivered. He had no wish to face the aggrieved King Edmund. He remembered the moments when the king had come toward him, pleading with him—the gadderling, the thrall, the child of no father—to stand out of the way. If he had done so, the English would be counting the night still as a victory. And he would not have to face the wrath of Ivar. Dazed as he had been, Shef had heard the taunts of his captors about what their chief would do with him. He remembered the fool of a boy who had shown him round these selfsame pens only the evening before, and his stories of how Ivar dealt with those who crossed him. And he, Shef, had taken his woman. Taken her away, taken her carnally, taken her so that she would not be returned. What had happened to her? Shef wondered detachedly. She had not been dragged back with him. Someone had taken her off. But he could hardly worry about her anymore. His own fate was too all-encompassing. Above the fear of death, the shame of treachery, there loomed the fear of Ivar. If only, Shef thought again and again during the night, if only he could die now of cold. He did not wish to see the morning.

The thump of a boot in the back stirred him from torpor in the growing light of the next day. Shef sat up, conscious above all of the dry, swollen stick of his tongue. Round him the guards were cutting lashings, hauling bodies away; some had been granted Shef's wish in the night. But in front of him squatted a small, slight figure in a stained and dirty tunic, drawn lines of fatigue on the sallow face. It was Hund. He was holding a crock of water. For some minutes Shef thought of nothing else, while Hund carefully, and with many agonizing pauses, allowed him to drink a mouthful at a time. Only when he felt the blessed fullness under his breastbone, and knew the luxury of being able to roll an excess mouthful round his tongue and spit it onto the grass, did Shef realize that Hund was trying to speak to him.

"Shef, Shef, try to take this in. We have to know some things. Where is Godive?"

"I don't know. I got her away. Then I think someone else snatched her. But they had me before I could do anything about it."

"Who do you think took her?"

Shef remembered the laugh in the thickets, the sense he had had, and had dismissed, that there were other fugitives in the wood. "Alfgar. He was always a good tracker. He must have followed us."

Shef paused again for thought, dispelling the lethargy of cold and weariness. "I think he must have gone back, led Muirtach and the others to us. Maybe they did a deal. They got me, he got her. Or maybe he just snatched her while they were busy with me. There weren't enough of them to risk following very far. Not after the fright they'd had."

"So. Ivar is more concerned about you than about her. But he knows you got her away from the camp. That's bad." Hund passed a hand worriedly across his sparse, scanty beard. "Shef, think back. Did anyone see you actually kill any of the Vikings with your own hands?"

"I only killed one. That was in the dark and no one saw. It was no great deed. But someone may have seen me get into the pen and start freeing the prisoners—freeing Alfgar." Shef's mouth twisted. "And do you know, I broke the Viking shield-wall with a burning timber when all the king's comrades could not do it." Shef turned his palms and looked mutely at the pads of white skin, the tiny thorn holes where the blisters had been.

"Yes. Still, that might not be a cause for blood-vengeance. Ingulf and I have done a lot of favors during this last day and a night. There are many chieftains who would be dead or crippled for life if it had not been for us. You know, he will even stitch together entrails, and sometimes the man will live, if he is strong enough to stand the pain and there is no poison inside the body."

Shef looked more attentively at the stains on his friend's tunic.

"You are trying to beg me off? From Ivar?"

"Yes."

"You and Ingulf? But what do I matter to him?"

Hund dipped a lump of hard bread in the remaining water and passed it over.

"It's Thorvin. He says it is business of the Way. He says you have to be saved. I don't know why, but he is totally set on it. Someone spoke to him yesterday and he came running over to see us at once. Have you done something I don't know about?"

Shef lay back in his bonds. "A lot of things, Hund. But I'm sure of one thing. Nothing is going to get me away from Ivar. I took his woman. How can I pay boot for that?"

"When bale is highest, boot is nighest." Hund filled the crock with water once again from a skin, placed a handful of bread beside it on the ground, and passed over the length of dirty homespun he had been carrying over his arm. "Food is short in the camp, and half the blankets are being used for shrouds. That's all I can find for now. Make it last. If you want to pay boot—see what the king can do."

Hund jerked a chin toward the corner of the pen, beyond where the dying warriors had sat, called something to the watching guards, rose, and left.

The king, thought Shef. What boot will Ivar take for him?

"Is there any hope?" hissed Thorvin across the table.

Killer-Brand looked at him with mild surprise. "What sort of language is that from a priest of the Way? Hope? Hope is the spittle that runs from the jaws of Fenris Wolf, chained till the day of Ragnarök. If we start only doing things because we think there may be some hope—why, we will end up no better than Christians, singing hymns to their God because they think he may give them a better bargain after death. You are forgetting yourself, Thorvin."

Brand looked with interest at his own right hand, spread out on the rough table next to Thorvin's forge. It had been split open by a sword-blade between second and third fingers, cut clean open almost down to the wrist. Ingulf the leech was bending over it, washing the wound with warm water from which a faint scent of herbs drifted. Then he slowly, carefully, pulled the lips of the gash apart. White bone showed for an instant before the oozing blood covered it in the track of Ingulf's fingers.

"This would have been easier if you had come to me straight away, instead of waiting a day and a half," said the leech. "Then I could have treated it while it was fresh. Now the wound has started to clot together, and I have to do this. I could take a chance and stitch it up as it is. But we do not know what was on the blade of the man who struck you."

A trickle of sweat broke out on Brand's eyebrow, but his voice remained mild, contemplative. "You go ahead, Ingulf. I have seen too many wounds go bad to take that risk. This is just pain. The flesh-rot is certain death."

"Still, you should have come earlier."

"I was lying among the corpses for half a day, till some clever warrior noticed they had all gone cold and I hadn't. And when I came round and decided that this was really the worst wound I had, you were busy with more difficult tasks. Is it true you pulled old Bjor's entrails out, stitched them together and pushed them back in again?"

Ingulf nodded, pulling with sudden decision at a bone splinter with a pair of tweezers. "They tell me he calls himself 'Grind-Bjor' now, because he swears he saw the gates of Hell itself."

Thorvin sighed gustily, and pushed a tankard closer to Brand's left hand. "Very well. You have punished me enough with your chatter. Tell me, then. Is there any chance?"

Brand's face was paling now, but he answered with the same even tone. "I don't think so. You know how it is with Ivar."

"I know," said Thorvin.

"That makes it hard for him to be sensible over some things. I do not say 'forgive'—we are none of us Christians to pass over an injury or an insult. But he will not even listen, or think about where his interest lies. The boy took his woman. Took a woman that Ivar—had plans for. If that fool Muirtach had brought her back, then maybe—But even then I don't think so. Because the girl went willingly. That means the boy did something Ivar could not. He must have blood."

"There has to be something that would make him change his mind, accept compensation."

Ingulf was stitching now, needle rising high over his right shoulder as he pierced and pulled, pierced and pulled again.

Thorvin placed his hand on the silver hammer that hung on his chest. "I swear, this may be the greatest service you or I may ever do for the Way, Brand. You know there are some among us who have the Sight?"

"I have heard you talk of it," admitted Brand.

"They travel into the realms of the Mighty, of the gods themselves, and return, to report what they saw. Some think these are just visions, no better than dreams, a kind of poetry only.

"But they see the same things. Or sometimes they do. More often it is as if they all saw different parts of the same thing, as there might be many reports of the battle the other night, and some would say the English had the best of it, and some would say we did, and yet all would be telling the truth and all would have been at the same place. If they confirm each other, that means it must be true."

Brand grunted. Perhaps in disbelief, perhaps in pain.

"We are sure that there is a world out there, and that people can go into it. Well, something very odd happened only yesterday. Farman came to see me, Farman who is priest of Frey in this Army as I am priest of Thor, or Ingulf of Ithun. He has been in the Otherworld many times, as I have not. He says—he says he was in the Great Hall itself, the place where the gods meet to decide the affairs of the nine worlds. He was down on the floor, a tiny creature, like a mouse in the wainscoting of one of our own halls. He saw the gods in conclave.

"And he saw my apprentice Shef. He is in no doubt. He had seen him at the forge; he saw him in the vision. He was dressed oddly, like a hunter in our own forests in Rogaland or Halogaland, and he stood badly, like one who has been—crippled. But there was no mistaking the face. And the Father of gods and men himself—he spoke to him. If Shef can remember what he said . . .

"It is rare," Thorvin concluded, "for any wanderer in the Otherworld to see another one. It is rare for the gods to speak to or notice a wanderer. For both to happen . . .

"And there is another thing. Whoever gave that boy a name did not know what he was doing. It is a dog's name now. But that was not always so. You have heard of Skiold?"

"Founder of the Skioldungs, the old Danish kings. The ones whom Ragnar and his sons would drive out if they could."

"The English call him Scyld Sceafing—Shield with the Sheaf—and they tell a foolish tale of how he drifted over the ocean on a shield with a sheaf beside him, and that was how he got his name. But anyone can tell that Sceafing means 'the son of Sheaf,' not 'with a sheaf.' So who, then, is Sheaf? Whoever he was, he was the one who sent the mightiest king of all over the waves, and taught him all that he knew to make the lives of men better and more glorious. It is a name of great good luck. Especially if given in ignorance. Shef is only the way the English in these parts say 'Sheaf.'

"We have to save that boy from Ivar. Ivar the Boneless. People have seen him on the other side too, you know. But he did not have the shape of a human being."

"He is not a man of one skin," agreed Brand.

"He is one of the brood of Loki, sent to bring destruction on the world. We have to get my apprentice away from him. How can we do it? If he will not do it on your urging, Brand, or on mine, can we bribe him? Is there something he wants more than vengeance?"

"I do not know how to take this talk of other worlds and wanderers," said Brand. "You know I am with the Way because of the skills it teaches, like Ingulf's here, and because I have no love either for the Christians or for the madmen like Ivar. But the boy did a brave deed to come into this camp for a girl. It took guts to do that. I know. I went into the Braethraborg to bait the Ragnarssons into this venture, as your colleagues told me to, Thorvin.

"So I wish the boy well. Now I do not know what Ivar wants—who does? But I can tell you what he needs. Ivar may see that too, even if he is mad. But if he does not, then the Snakeeye will make him."

As he spoke on, the other two nodded, thoughtfully.

They were not Ivar's men who came for him, Shef noticed as soon as they appeared. Just from his few days in the Viking camp he had come to be able to discriminate at least in an elementary way between the various grades of heathen. These were not the Gaddgedlar, nor did they have the somehow non-Norse or half-Norse air of the Hebrideans and Manxmen whom Ivar recruited in such numbers, nor did they even have that vaguely footloose and less-than-respectable look that so many of even his Norse followers had. Younger sons and outlaws, the bulk of them, detached from their parent communities and with no homes to go to and no lives outside the camp. The men who came into the stockade now were heavily built, mature in years, almost middle-aged; their hair was grizzled. Their belts were silver, gold armlets and neck-rings shone on them, to prove years or decades of success. When the warden of the pen blocked their self-assured way, ordering them back, Shef could not hear the reply. It was given in a low voice, as if the speaker no longer expected to have to shout. The warden replied again, crying out and pointing down the ruined campsite, as if to the burned tents of Ivar. But before his sentence had ended there was a thud and a groan. The leader of the newcomers looked down for a moment, as if to see if there was any chance of further resistance, slid the sandbag back up his sleeve, and marched on without deigning to look round again.

In a moment Shef found the lashings on his ankles cut and himself jerked to his feet. His heart leapt suddenly and uncontrollably. Was this death? Were they dragging him out of the pen to a clear patch of ground, where in an instant they could force him to his knees and behead him? He bit his lip savagely for an instant. He would not speak or plead for mercy. Then the savages would have the chance to laugh, to mock the way an Englishman died. He stumbled along in grim silence.

Only a few yards. Outside the gate, along the fence-posts of the pen, and then, jerked to a stop in front of another gate. Shef realized that the leader of the newcomers was staring hard at him, deep into his eyes, as if trying to burn an understanding into the tough hide of Shef's face.

"You understand Norse?"

Shef nodded.

"Then understand this. If you talk—doesn't matter. But if he in there talks—maybe you live. Maybe. Lot to be answered for. But there's something in there that could mean life for you. Could mean more for me. Whether you live or die, you may need a friend pretty soon. Friend in court. Friend on the execution ground. There's more than one way to die. All right. Throw him in. Rivet him good."

Shef found himself hauled inside a shelter propped up against the side of the pen. An iron ring hung from a stout post; a chain from it to another ring. In an instant the collar was being fitted round his neck, a bolt of soft iron forced through its two holes. A couple of blows with a hammer, a quick inspection, another blow. The men turned and tramped out. Shef's legs were free, but his hands still bound. The collar and chain round his neck gave him only a few feet of space to walk.

There was another man in the shelter, Shef realized, secured as he was; he could see the chain running down from a post into the half-darkness. Something about the figure sprawled there on the ground filled him with unease, with shame and fear.

"Lord," he said doubtfully. "Lord. Are you the king?"

The figure stirred. "King Edmund I am, son of Edwold, king of the East Angles. But who are you, that talk like a Norfolk man? You are not one of my warriors. Did you come with the levies? Did they catch you in the woods? Move, so I can see your face."

Shef moved round. The sun, now westering, streamed in through the open door of the shelter and caught his face as he stood at the limit of his chain. He waited in dread for what the king would say.

"So. You are the one who stood between me and Ivar. I remember you. You had no armor and no weapon, but you stood before Wigga my champion, and held him for ten heartbeats. If it had not been for you those would have been the last heartbeats of the Boneless One's life. Why would an Englishman wish to save Ivar? You ran from your master? Were you a slave to the Church?"

"My master was your thane Wulfgar," Shef said. "When the pirates came —you know what they did to him?"

The king nodded. With his eyes adjusting to the light Shef could see the face that turned to him. It was pitiless, resolute.

"They took his daughter, my—my foster sister. I came to try to get her back. I was not trying to protect Ivar, but your men were going to kill both of them, all of them. I just wanted you to let me pull her aside! Then I would have joined you. I am no Viking, I killed two of them myself. And I did one thing for you, king, when you had need of it. I . . ."

"So you did. I called out for someone to break the ring, and you did it. You and a gang of churls from nowhere, with a ship's timber. If Wigga had thought of that, or Totta, or Eddi, or any of the others, I would have made him the richest man in the kingdom. What did I promise?"

He shook his head in silence, then looked up at Shef.

"You know what they are going to do to me? They are building an altar now, to their heathen gods. Tomorrow sometime they will take me out and lay me on it. Then Ivar will get to work. Killing kings is his trade. One of the men who guarded me told me he was standing by when Ivar killed the Irish king of Munster, told me how he stood there while Ivar's men twisted the rope and twisted the rope and the veins stood out on the king's neck and he called out curses by all the saints on Ivar's name. And then the crack as his back broke over the stone. They all remember that.

"But tomorrow Ivar prepares a new fate. They tell me that he meant to save this for the man who killed their father, for Ella of Northumbria. But they have decided I merit it just as much.

"They will take me out, and lay me on their altar, face down. In the hollow of my back, Ivar will place a sword. Then—you have felt how your ribs make a house of bone, and how each of the ribs fits into its place on the backbone? Ivar will cut each of them away, working up from the lowest to the highest. They say he will use a sword only for the first cut. After that he will use hammer and chisel. When he has cut them all away, he will cut the flesh free, and then he will put his hands in and pull the ribs up and out.

"I expect I will die then. They say he can keep a man alive to that point, if he is careful not to cut deep. But when they pull the ribs out, your heart must burst. When it is done, they pull your lungs out of your back, and then turn the ribs out so they look like a raven's wings, or an eagle's. They call it 'cutting the blood-eagle.'

"I wonder what it will feel like when he first puts the sword in the hollow of my back. You know, young churl, I think that if I can hold my courage at that point, the rest will be easier. But the feel of the cold steel on skin, before the pain begins . . .

"I never thought that I would come to this. I have defended my people, kept all my oaths, been charitable to orphans.

"Do you know, churl, what the Christ said when he hung dying on the cross?"

Father Andreas's lessons had been confined usually to the merits of chastity or the importance of paying contributions duly to the Church. Shef shook his head dumbly.

"My God, my God, why hast thou forsaken me?"

The king paused for a long while.

"I know why he means to do it, though. After all, I am a king too. I know what his men need. These few months have been bad ones for the Army. They thought they would have an easy start here for their real march on York. And so they might have—if they had not done what they did to your foster father. But since then they have made no gains, caught few slaves, had to fight for every few beeves. And now—say what anyone wishes, there are many fewer of them than there were two nights ago. They have seen their friends die of wounds, and more of them are sitting waiting for the flesh-rot. If there is nothing grand for them to see, then they will lose heart. Ships will row off in the night.

"Ivar needs a display. A triumph. An execution. Or . . ."

Shef remembered the warning of the man who had pushed him into the pen.

"Do not speak too freely, lord. They want you to speak. And me to listen."

Edmund laughed, in one sharp bark. The light had almost gone by now, the sun well down, though the long English twilight lingered.

"Then listen. I promised you a half of Raedwald's hoard if you broke the Viking line, and break it you did. So I will give you the whole of it, and you may make your own bargain. The man who gives them this can have his life and more. If I gave it to them, I could be a Viking jarl. But Wigga and all the others died rather than speak. It would not be fitting for a king, one of the line of Wuffa, to give way out of fear.

"But you, boy. Who knows? You may gain something.

"Now listen and do not forget. I will tell you the secret of the hoard of the Wuffingas, and from that I swear by God a wise man can find the hoard.

"Listen and I will tell you."

The king's voice dropped to a hoarse murmur and Shef strained to hear.

"In willow-ford,   by woody bridge,
The old kings lie,   keels beneath them.
On down they sleep,   deep home guarding.
Four fingers push   in flattest line,
From underground,   Grave the northmost.
There lies Wuffa,   Wehha's offspring.
On secret hoard.   Seek who dares it."

The voice tailed away. "My last night, young churl. Maybe yours too. You must think what you will do to save yourself tomorrow. But I do not think the riddle of an Englishman will prove easy to the Vikings.

"And, if churl you are, the riddle of the kings will do you no good either."

The king spoke no more, though after a while Shef tried faintly and despondently to rouse him. After an age Shef's battered body too began to drift off into uneasy dozing. In his sleep the king's words repeated themselves, twining round and round and running into each other like the dragon-shapes carved on a burning stem-post.

CHAPTER ELEVEN

This time the Great Army was troubled and unsure. So much King Edmund had foreseen. It had been taken in its own base, by a small state and a petty kinglet of whom no one had ever heard, and while they knew the matter had ended well enough, too many also knew in their hearts that for a time they had been outfought. The dead had been buried, the irreparable ships dragged onshore, the wounded had been treated. Arrangements had been made between this chieftain and that to sell or trade ships, to transfer or exchange men to bring contingents up to the mark. But the warriors, the rank-and-file oar-pullers and axe-wielders, still needed reassurance. Something that would show their leaders still had confidence. Some ritual to demonstrate that they were still the Great Army, the terror of the Christians, the invincibles of the North.

From the early morning, men were crowding down to the marked-out space outside the camp, which would be the site of the wapentake: the meeting where men could show their assent by *vapna takr*, the clashing of weapons, of blade on shield. Or, on rare occasions, under careless leaders, their dissent. From even earlier in the morning, from well before day, the Viking leaders had been making their plan, and considering the balance of forces, the sentiments that might swing their dangerous and unpredictable followers one way or the other.

When they came for him, Shef was ready, at least physically. His hunger was a hole inside him, thirst once more drying his tongue and his lips, but he was awake, alert and fully conscious. Edmund too was awake, he knew, but made no sign. Shef was ashamed to disturb him.

The Snakeeye's men arrived with the same brisk certainty as the day before. In a moment one had Shef's iron collar in his tongs and was forcing the rivet out. It came free, the collar jerked off, and brawny hands were pulling Shef out into the cold murk of an early-autumn morning. Fog still clung to the river, condensed in drops on the bracken roof of the shelter. Shef stared at it for a moment, wondering if he might lick it off.

"You were talking yesterday. What did he tell you?"

Shef shook his head and gestured with bound hands to the leather bottle at a man's belt. Silently the man passed it over. It was full of beer—muddy, thick with barley husks, drawn all too obviously from the bottom of a cask; Shef drank it down in steady gulps, till he could tilt his head back and drain out the last drops. He finished, wiped his mouth, feeling as if the beer had swollen him out like an empty skin, handed the bottle back. There was a grunt of amusement as the pirates watched his face.

"Good, eh? Beer is good. Life is good. If you want more of both, you'd better tell us. Tell us everything he said."

Dolgfinn the Viking watched Shef's face with his usual, unblinking intensity. He saw on it doubt, but no fear. Also, stubbornness, knowledge. The lad would do a deal, he reflected. It would have to be the right one. He turned away and beckoned, a preconcerted signal. From a group a little way off, a large man came walking, gold round his neck, left hand resting on the silver pommel of a sword. Shef recognized him instantly. It was the big man he had fought in the skirmish on the causeway. Sigvarth, jarl of the Small Isles. His father.

As he strolled forward, the others drew back a few paces, leaving the two face-to-face. They studied one another for a few seconds, each staring the other up and down, the older man looking at the younger's physique, the younger staring intently into his father's face. He's looking at me the same way I'm looking at him, thought Shef. He's looking to see if he can recognize himself in me, just as I am at him. He knows.

"We've met before," remarked Sigvarth. "On the causeway in the marsh. Muirtach told me there was a young Englishman walking round claiming he'd fought me. Now they tell me you're my son. The leech's assistant, the boy who came with you. He says so. Is that true?"

Shef nodded.

"Good. You're a burly lad, and you fought well that day. See here, son" —Sigvarth stepped forward and put a broad hand round Shef's biceps, squeezing gently—"You're on the wrong side. I know your mother's En-

glish. That's true of half the men in the Army. English, or Irish, or Frankish, or Finnish or Lapp for that matter. But blood goes with the father. And
I know you were brought up by the English—by that fool you were trying
to rescue. But what have they ever done for you? If they knew you were
my son I dare say you had a hard life of it. Eh?"

He looked into Shef's eyes, conscious that he had scored a point.

"Now, you may be thinking that I just ditched you, and that's true, I
did. But then I didn't know you were there. I didn't know how you'd
grown up. But now you're here, and I see how you've turned out, well, I
reckon you'll be a credit to me. And to all our kin.

"So, say the word. I'm offering to recognize you as my true son. You'll
have the same rights you'd have had if you'd been born on Falster. Leave
the English. Leave the Christians. Forget your mother.

"And, as my son, I'll speak for you to Ivar. And what I say, the Snakeeye
will back up. You're in trouble here. Let's get you out of it."

Shef looked over his father's shoulder, considering. He remembered the
horse-trough and the beatings. He remembered the curse his stepfather
had laid on him, and the accusation of cowardice. He remembered the
incompetence, the dillydallying, the exasperation of Edrich at the way the
English thanes preened and hesitated. How could anyone be victorious
with people like that on one's side? Over his father's shoulder he could
see, in the front of the group that Sigvarth had left, a young man gazing at
them—a young man with decorated armor, a pale face, strong, projecting
front teeth like a horse. He too is a son of Sigvarth, Shef thought. Another
half brother for me. And he does not like what is going on.

Shef remembered the laugh of Alfgar from the thickets. "What do I have
to do?" he asked.

"Say what the king Jatmund told you. Or find out from him what we
need to know."

Deliberately, Shef took aim, blessing the draft of beer that had moistened his mouth, and spat on his father's leather shoe.

"You cut Wulfgar's arms and legs off while men held him. You let the
men rape my mother, after she had borne you a son. You are no *drengr*.
You are nothing. I curse the blood I had from you."

In an instant the Snakeeye's men were between them, hustling Sigvarth
away, holding his arms down as he struggled to draw his sword. He did
not struggle very hard, Shef thought. As they forced him back he was still
staring at his son with a kind of baffled longing. He still thinks there is
more to be said, thought Shef. The fool.

"You've done it now," remarked Dolgfinn, the Snakeeye's emissary, jerking his captive along by the rawhide round his wrists. "All right. Take him along to the wapentake. And get the kinglet out of there and let's see if he's decided to be reasonable before the assembly sees him."

"No chance," remarked one of his henchmen. "These English can't fight, but they haven't the sense to give in. He's for Ivar now, and Othin before nightfall."

The Viking army was drawn up outside the east stockade, not far from the place where Shef had vaulted over to intercept Godive and kill Flann the Gaddgedil barely three days before. It filled three sides of a hollow square; the fourth, nearest the stockade, occupied only by the jarls, the chieftains, the Ragnarssons and their immediate followers. Elsewhere, the men crowded together behind their skippers and helmsmen, talking to each other, calling out to men from other crews, offering advice and opinion without reproof and without control. The army was a democracy, in its way: Status and hierarchy were important, especially when it came to taking shares. But no man could be entirely silenced, if he cared to take the risk of giving offense.

As they shoved their way into the square with Shef, a great yell went up, and a simultaneous clash of metal. Vikings were hustling a tall man away toward a block in the corner of the square, the man's face standing out even from thirty yards away in a crowd. All the rest had the usual wind-burned faces of men who spend their time out-of-doors, even in an English summer. The tall one was deathly pale. Without ceremony they thrust him over the block, one Viking seizing his hair and pulling it forward over the nape of his neck. A flash, a thud, and the head rolling free. Shef stared at it for an instant. He had seen several corpses in Emneth, and many in the last few days. But hardly one in broad daylight, and with a moment to look. There will be no time once they give their decision, he thought. I must be ready as soon as they clash their weapons.

"What was that?" he asked, nodding towards the head being thrown into a pile.

"One of the English warriors. Someone said he had fought well and truly for his lord and we should take ransom. But the Ragnarssons say now is not the time for ransoms, it is time to give a lesson. Now you."

The warriors pushed him forward and left him standing ten feet in front of the chieftains.

"Who wishes to press this case?" called one of the chieftains, in a voice that could compete with a North Sea gale. Slowly, the hubbub faded to a buzz. Ivar Ragnarsson stepped forward from the ranks of the leaders. His right arm was bound in front of him in a sling. Broken collarbone, thought Shef, noting the angle at which the arm was slung. That's why he could not wield a weapon against Edmund's warriors.

"I present the case," said Ivar. "This is not an enemy, but a traitor, a truth-breaker. He was not one of Jatmund's men, he was one of my men. I took him into my band, I fed and lodged him. When the English came, he did not fight for me. He did not fight at all. He ran in while the warriors fought and took a girl from my quarters. He stole her away, and she has never been returned. She is lost to me, though she was lawfully mine, given to me by Sigvarth Jarl in the sight of all men.

"I claim ransom for the girl, and he cannot pay it. Even if he could pay it, I would still kill him for the insult done me. But even more than that, the whole Army has a claim against him for treachery. Who supports me?"

"I support you," called another voice: a burly, grizzled man standing close to Ivar. Ubbi, perhaps, or Halvdan? One of the Ragnarssons, at any rate, but not the leader, not Sigurth, who still stood aloof in the middle of the line of men. "I support you. He has had a chance to show his true loyalty, he has refused it. He came to our camp as a spy and a thief and a stealer of women."

"What penalty do you assess?" called the herald's voice again.

"Death is too easy," cried Ivar. "I claim his eyes for the insult put on me. I claim his balls as compensation for the woman. I claim his hands for the treachery against the Army. After that he may keep his life."

Shef felt the shudder running through him. His spine seemed to have turned to ice. In an instant, he thought, the cry would go up, and the clash of arms, and then in ten heartbeats he would be facing the block and the knife.

A figure strolled slowly forward from the ranks—a massive, bearded, leather-jacketed figure. His hand was in a great white bandage, with spots of dark blood showing through it.

"I am Brand. Many men know me." A yell of approval and agreement came from the men behind him.

"I have two things to say. First, Ivar, where did you get the girl? Or where did Sigvarth get her? If Sigvarth stole her, and the lad here stole her back, where is the wrong in that? You should have killed him when he tried it. But since you did not, it is too late to start calling for vengeance now.

"And there is a second thing, Ivar. I was coming to help you when the warriors of Jatmund advanced on you—I, Brand, champion of the men of Halogaland. I have stood in the front for twenty years. Who can say that I

ever held back when the spearmen were fighting? I got this wound there, right by you, when you yourself were hurt. And I challenge you to tell me I lie; when the fight was nearly over, and the English king was breaking out, he came straight toward you with his men. You were hurt and could not raise a sword. Your men were dead, and I had only my left hand, and no other man stood by you. Who stood in front of you with his sword but this youth here? He held them off—till I and Arnketil came down with his band and trapped the king. Tell me, Arnketil, do I lie?"

A voice from the other side of the square. "As you say, Brand. I saw Ivar, I saw the Englishmen, I saw the boy. I thought they had killed him in the stir, and was sorry. He stood bravely."

"So, Ivar, the claim for the woman falls. The claim for treachery cannot be true. You owe him your life. I do not know what he has to do with Jatmund, but I say this: If he is good at stealing women, I have a place for him in my crew. We need some new ones. And if you cannot look after your women, Ivar—well, what is that to do with the Army?"

Shef saw Ivar stepping forward towards Brand, his eyes fixed on him, a pale tongue flickering on his lips like a snake. A hum of interest came from the crowd, not a hostile sound. The warriors of the Army liked entertainment, and here some was promised.

Brand did not move, but thrust his left hand into his broad sword-belt. As Ivar got to three paces of him, he held up his bandaged hand for the crowd to see.

"When your hand is mended, I will remember what you say, Brand," remarked Ivar.

"When your shoulder is whole, I will remind you of it."

A voice called out behind them, cold as stone—the voice of Sigurth Ragnarsson, the Snakeeye.

"The Army has more important things to do than talk of boys. I say this: My brother Ivar must pursue his own claim for the stolen woman. In payment for his life, Ivar must give the boy his own life, and not cripple him so that he cannot live it. But the boy came into this camp as one of us. He did not behave as a true comrade when we were attacked, but thought first of his own advantage. If he is to join the crew of Killer-Brand we must teach him a lesson. Not a hand, or he cannot fight. Not a testicle, for no woman-theft is involved. But the Army will take an eye."

With great effort Shef stood firm as he heard the beginnings of the cry of assent.

"Not both eyes. One. What does the Army say?"

A roar of approval. A clash of weapons. Hands dragging him, not to the block, but to the opposite corner of the square. Men parting, pushing each other aside to reveal a brazier, coals glowing red, Thorvin pumping at a bellows. From a bench rose Hund, face pale with emotion.

"Hold still," he muttered in English, as the men kicked Shef's legs from beneath him and thrust his head back. Dimly, Shef realized that the brawny arms holding his head in a grip like a clamp were Thorvin's. He tried to struggle, to call out, to accuse them of treachery. A cloth thrust into his mouth, pushing the tongue back from his teeth. The white-hot needle coming closer, closer, a thumb pushing his eyelid back while he tried to scream, to twist his head, to clench his eyes tight shut.

Inexorable pressure. Only the searing point coming closer and closer to his right eye. Pain, agony, the white fire running from the eyeball into every corner of his brain, tears and blood streaming down his face. Through it all, dimly, the sound of sizzling, of steel being tempered in the tub.

He was hanging in the air. There was a spike through his eye, a continuous burning pain that made him twist his face and clench the muscles in his neck to try to reduce it. But the pain never went away or grew less; it was there all the time. Yet it did not seem to matter. His mind was unaffected, continuing to think and to ponder without distraction from the screaming pain.

Nor was his other eye affected. It remained open all the time, never even blinking. Through it, and from wherever in all the worlds he was, he could see out across a vast panorama. He was high up, very high up. Below him he could see mountains, plains, rivers, and here and there on the seas little collections of colored sails that were Viking fleets. On the plains scattered dust clouds that were giant armies marching, the Christian kings of Europe and the pagan nomads of the steppe permanently mustering for war. He felt that if he narrowed his eyes—his eye—a certain way, just so, he could focus in on anything he wanted to: read the lips of the commanders and the cavalrymen, see the words of the emperor of the Greeks or the khakhan of the Tartars even as they formed them.

Between himself and the world below, he realized, birds were floating—giant ones keeping station with never a flap or a flutter, just the little tremor along the trailing feathers of the wings. Close to him two passed by, staring at him with brilliant and intelligent yellow dots of eyes. Their feathers were glossy black, their beaks threatening, stained: ravens. The ravens that came to peck out the eyes of hanged men. He stared at them as unblinkingly as they at him; they slanted their wings hastily and swooped away.

The spike through his eye. Was that all that was holding him? So it seemed.

But then he must be dead, no one could survive a spike through the brain and the skull, into the wood behind. Through the feel of the bark he could sense a bursting of sap, a steady pumping of fluid, up from roots unimaginably deep to branches far above him, so high that no man could ever climb them.

His eye stabbed him again and he twisted, his hands still hanging loose below him like a dead man's. There were the ravens again—curious, greedy, cowardly, clever, alert for any sign of weakness. They drifted in toward him, flapped their wings, came suddenly closer, landed heavily on his shoulders. Yet this time, he knew, he need not fear their beaks. They clung to him for reassurance. A king was coming.

The figure appeared in front of him, moving upward from a spot on Earth from which he had averted his eye. It was a terrible shape, naked, blood running from it down its ruined loins, an expression of ghastly pain on its face. Its back lifted up behind its shoulders in a parody of the ravens' wings; its chest was shrunken and twisted in; gobbets of spongy matter hung over its nipples. It carried its own backbone in its hand.

For a moment the two figures hung there, eye to eye. The creature recognized him, the hanged one thought. It pitied him. But it was going beyond the nine worlds now, to some other destiny where few if any would follow. Its blackened mouth twisted.

"Remember," it said. "Remember the verse I taught you."

The pain in Shef's eye redoubled, and he shrieked out loud, shrieked and twisted against the spike that restrained him, the bonds that held him down, the soft, gentle, immovable hands. He opened his eye and stared out, not at the panorama of the nine worlds from the great ashtree, but into the face of Hund. Hund with the needle. He shrieked again and threw up a hand to fend him off, and the hand clutched Hund's arm with desperate force.

"Easy, easy," said Hund. "It's all over now. No one can touch you. You are a carl of the army, in the crew of Brand of Halogaland, and the past is forgotten."

"But I must remember," cried Shef.

"Remember what?"

Water filled both his eyes, the good one and the ruined socket. "I don't remember it," he whispered.

"I have forgotten the king's message."

CARL

CHAPTER ONE

For many miles the track had run over flat, well-drained land —the southern half of the great Vale of York, rolling up from the marshes of the Humber. Even so, it had been hard going for the Great Army: eight thousand men, as many horses, hundreds of camp-followers and bedfellows and slaves for the market, all trampling along together. Behind them even the great stone-laid roads built by the Rome-folk of old turned into muddy tracks splashing as high as the horses' bellies. Where the Army marched along English lanes or drover roads it left nothing but a morass behind.

Brand the Champion lifted his still-bandaged hand and the troop of men behind him—three ships' crews, a long hundred and five—eased their reins. The ones at the very rear, the last men in the Army, immediately faced about, peering at the gray, wet landscape behind them, from which the autumn light was already beginning to seep.

The two men at the very point of the troop stared closely at what lay in front of them: a deeply mudded track, four arm-spans wide, descending down and round a bend to what must be the bed of another small stream. A few hundred yards ahead the men could see the land rising again and the unhedged track running across it. But in between, along the bed of the stream, ran a belt of tangled forest, large oak and chestnut trees swaying their brown leaves in the rising wind, crowding up to the very edge of the road.

"What do you think, young marshal?" asked Brand, pulling at his beard with his left hand. "It may be that with your one eye you can see further than most men with two."

"I can see one thing with half an eye, old kay-handed one," replied Shef equably. "Which is that that horse-turd by the side of the road there has stopped steaming. The main body is getting further away from us. We're too slow. Plenty of time for the Yorkshiremen to get in behind them and in front of us."

"And how would you deal with that, young defier-of-Ivar?"

"I would get us all off the road and all go down the right-hand side. The right hand, because they might expect us to go down the left, with our shields toward the trees and the ambush. Get down to the stream. When we get to it, blow all our horns and charge it as if it were the gap in an enemy stockade. If there's no one there, we look stupid. If there's an ambush there we'll flush them out. But if we're going to do it—let's do it fast."

Brand shook his massive head with a kind of exasperation. "You are not a fool, young man. That is the right answer. But it is the answer of a follower of your one-eyed patron, Othin the Betrayer of Warriors. Not of a carl of the Great Army. What we are here for is to pick up the stragglers, to see that no one falls into the hands of the English. The Snakeeye does not care for heads thrown into the encampment every morning. It makes the men restless. They like to think every one of them is important, and that anyone who gets killed gets killed for a good reason, not just by accident. If we went off the road we might miss someone, and then his mates would come round asking for him sooner or later. We will take the risk and go down the track."

Shef nodded, and swung his shield off his back, pushing his arm through the elbow-strap to grip the handle behind the boss. Behind him there was a clanking and rustling as a hundred and twenty-five men moved their weapons to a ready position and urged their horses forward. Shef realized that Brand had these conversations in a way to train him, to teach him to think like a leader. He bore no grudge when his advice was overruled.

Yet deep down he struggled with the thought that these wise men, these great and experienced warriors—Brand the Champion, Ivar the Boneless, even the matchless Snakeeye himself—were wrong. They were doing things the wrong way. Their wrong way had smashed every kingdom they had ventured against, not just the tiny and petty kingdom of the East Anglians. Even so, he, Shef—once thrall, slayer of two men, a man who had never stood in a battle line for ten heartbeats together—he was sure that he knew better how to array an army than did they.

Had he seen it in his visions? Was the knowledge sent to him by his father-god in Valhalla—Othin the Traitor, God of the Hanged, Betrayer of Warriors—as Brand obliquely continued to suggest?

Whatever the cause, Shef thought, if I were the marshal of the Army, I would call a halt six times a day, and blow the trumpets, so the flank-guards and the rear-guard would know where I was. And I would move no further till I heard the trumpets in reply.

It would be better if everyone knew the time when the trumpets would blow. But how could that be, once we are all out of sight of each other? How do the black monks in the minsters know when it is time for their services? Shef chewed on the problem as his horse took him down between the trees and shadows began to fall across the path. Again and again these days his head swam with thoughts, with ideas, with difficulties to which there seemed to be no solution in the wisdom of his time. Shef's fingers itched to hold a hammer again, to work in the forge. He felt he could beat out a solution on an anvil instead of restlessly brooding in his own brain.

There was a figure on the road ahead of them. He spun about when he heard the horses—then let his sword slide back down when he recognized them.

"I am Stuf," the man said. "One of the band of Humli, out of Ribe."

Brand nodded. A small band, not very well organized. The sort of group that would let a man slip out of line and not think to inquire what had happened to him till too late.

"My horse went lame and I dropped behind. Then I decided to turn him loose and go on with just my own pack."

Brand nodded again. "We have spare horses here. I will let you have one. It will cost you a mark of silver."

Stuf opened his mouth to protest, to start the automatic haggling expected of any deal in horseflesh, but then closed it suddenly as Brand waved his men on. He grabbed the reins of the horse Brand was leading.

"Your price is high," he said. "But maybe now is not the time to be arguing. There are Englishmen around. I can smell them."

As he said the words Shef saw a flicker of movement out of the corner of his eye. A branch moving. No, the whole tree sweeping downward in a stately arc, the ropes tied to its top suddenly visible as they tightened into a straight line. An instant later, movement all along the left-hand edge of the track.

Shef threw his shield up. A thump, an arrow-point just protruding through the soft lindenwood an inch from his hand. Shouts and screams behind him, horses rearing and kicking. Already he had hurled himself off the horse and was crouching below its neck, its body between him and the ambush. His mind registered a dozen facts as if in one flash of lightning, far quicker than any words.

That tree had been cut through after the Great Army had passed through. The rear-guard was even further behind than they had thought. The attack would be coming from the left; they wanted to drive their enemies into the wood to the right. No escape forward over the felled tree, none back through the confusion of shot horses and startled men. Do what they least suspected!

Shef ran round the front of his horse, shield up, and hurled himself straight at the steep left bank of the track, his spear gripped underhand. One leap, two, three—not pausing lest the muddy bank give way. A make-shift barricade of branches and a face glaring over it at him, an Englishman fumbling an arrow out of his quiver. Shef drove the spear through the barricade at groin level and saw the face contort in agony. Twist, wrench backward, reach over and drag the man forward through his own barri-cade. Shef drove his spear-point into the ground and vaulted over body and branches, turning instantly and stabbing at the ambushers, first one side then the other.

He realized suddenly that his throat was raw with shouting. A much bigger voice was bellowing in unison: Brand down on the track, not fit to fight one-handed but directing the startled Vikings up the bank and into the breach he had made. One instant a dozen figures were closing on Shef, with him stabbing furiously in all directions to keep them off. The next there was an elbow in his back, he was stumbling forward, there were mailed men on either side, and the English were backing hastily, turning suddenly in open flight.

Churls, Shef realized. Leather jackets, hunting bows and billhooks. Used to driving boar, not to fighting men. If the Vikings had fled into the woods as they had been expected to, no doubt they would have been in a killing ground of nets and pits, where they would have wallowed helpless till speared. But these Englishmen were not warriors to stand and hew at each other over the war-linden.

No point, certainly, in trying to pursue them through their own woods. The Vikings looked down, stabbed or cut thoughtfully at the few men their charge had caught, making sure none would live to boast of the day. Shef felt a hard hand slap him on the back.

"You did right, boy. Never stand still in an ambush. Always run away—or else run straight toward it. But how do you know these things? Maybe Thorvin is right about you."

Brand clasped the hammer pendant round his neck, and then began once more to bellow orders, hustling his men off the track and round the felled tree-trunk, stripping gear off dead or crippled horses, looking briefly at the ten or twelve men wounded in the skirmish.

"At this range," he said, "these short bows will send an arrow through mail. But only just. Not enough punch in them to get through the ribs or into the belly. Bows and arrows never won a battle yet."

The cortege wound its way up the slope on the other side of the little stream, out of the woods and into the last of the autumn light.

Something lay on the track in front of them. No, some things. As the Vikings crowded forward again, Shef realized that they were warriors of the Army—two of them, stragglers like Stuf, dressed in the grubby wadmal of the long-service campaigner. But there was something else about them, something horrifying, something he had seen before. . . .

With the same shock of recognition he had experienced in Emneth, Shef realized the men were too small. Their arms were hacked off at the elbow, their legs at the knee; a reek of seared flesh told how they had lived. For they were still alive. One of them lifted his head from the ground as the riders came toward him, saw the shocked and angry faces.

"Bersi," he called. "Skuli the Bald's crew. *Fraendir, vinir,* do what you must. Give us the warrior's death."

Brand swung from his horse, his face gray, drawing his dagger left-handed. Gently he patted the living corpse's face with his bandaged right hand, steadied it, drove the dagger home with one hard thrust behind the ear. Did the same for the other man, lying mercifully unconscious.

"Pull them out of the road," he said, "and let's get on. Heimnars," he added to Shef. "Now I wonder who has taught them to do that."

Shef made no reply. Far off, but caught in the last rays of the sun now streaming almost horizontally through a breach in the clouds, he could see yellow stone walls, a thicket of distant houses on a slight hill in front of them, smoke streaming away from a thousand chimneys. He had seen them before. Another moment of recognition.

"Eoforwich," he said.

"*Yovrvik,*" repeated the Viking standing next to him, struggling with the unfamiliar consonants and diphthongs.

"To Hell with that," said Brand. "Just call it York."

* * *

After dark the men on the city walls looked down on the innumerable twinkling points of the Great Army's cooking fires. They were on the round bastion of the southeast corner of the old and impressive square Roman fortress, once home of the Sixth Legion, placed there to hold the North in awe. Behind them, inside the three-hundred-and-twenty-acre defended site, bulked St. Peter's Minster, once the most famous home of learning and scholarship in the whole Northern world. Inside the walls, too, lay the king's quarters, the houses of a hundred noble families, the jammed-together barracks of their thanes and companions and hired swords. And the forges, the arsenals, the weapon-shops, the tanneries, the sinews of power. Outside there lay a sprawling town with its warehouses and jetties down on the Ouse. But this was dispensable. What mattered lay inside the walls: those of the old legionary fortress or its matching walled site across the river, centered on St. Mary's—once the Roman *colonia* where the time-expired legionaries had settled and had walled themselves in as was their custom, against the turmoil or resentment of the natives.

King Ella stared down grimly at the countless fires, the burly captain of his guard, Cuthred, at his side. Close by stood the archbishop of York, Wulfhere, still in his purple and white, and flanked by the black figure of Erkenbert the deacon.

"They have not been much delayed," said Ella. "I thought they might be held up by the Humber marshes, but they slipped across. I hoped they might run out of supplies, but they seem to have managed well enough."

He might have added that he hoped they might have been discouraged by the desperate assault of King Edmund and the East Anglians, of which so many tales already were told. But that thought sent a chill to his heart. All the tales that were told ended with a description of the death by torment of the king. And Ella knew—he had known ever since the Ragnarssons were identified in England—that they had the same or worse in store for him. The eight thousand men camped round the cooking fires out there had come for him. If he fled, they would come after him. If he hid, they would offer money for his body. Wulfhere, even Cuthred, could hope to survive a defeat. Ella knew he must beat the Army or die.

"They have lost many men!" Erkenbert the deacon said. "Even the churls are out, to delay them, to cut off their rear-guards and their forage parties. They must have lost hundreds of men already, maybe thousands. All our people are rallying to the defense."

"That's true," agreed Cuthred. "But you know to whose credit that is."

The group turned together to look at the strange contrivance a few yards from them. It was like a shallow box, on long handles so that it could be carried like a stretcher. Between one pair of handles ran an axle with wheels on it, so that it could be trundled on level ground. Inside the box lay the trunk of a man, though now that the box was tipped forward he was upright, able to see over the battlements like the rest. Most of his weight was taken by a broad strap round his chest and under his armpits. His groin rested on a padded projection. He braced himself on the bandaged stumps of his knees.

"I serve as a warning," rumbled Wulfgar, his voice shockingly deep-toned coming from such a seemingly small man. "One day I will serve as vengeance. For this and all the heathens have done to me."

The other men did not reply. They knew the effect the mutilated East Anglian thane had had, the almost triumphal progress he had made from his home, ahead of the Army, halting in every village to tell the churls what lay in store for them and for their womenfolk.

"What good has all the rallying done?" King Ella asked bitterly.

Cuthred screwed up his face in calculation. "Not slowed them. Not lost them many. Made them keep together. May even have tightened them up. Still around eight thousand of them."

"We can put half as many again in the field," said Arch Deacon Erkenbert. "We are not the East Anglians. Two thousand men of military age live in Eoforwich itself. And we are strong in the strength of the Lord of Hosts."

"I don't think we've got enough," said Cuthred slowly. "Not even counting the Lord of Hosts. It sounds good to say you're three-to-two. But if it's a fight on level ground it's always one to one. We've got champions as good as theirs, but not enough of them. If we marched out to fight them we would lose."

"Then we will not march out against them?"

"We stay here. They have to come to us, try and climb the walls."

"They will destroy our properties," cried Erkenbert. "Kill the stock, carry off the young people, cut down the fruit trees. Burn the harvest. And there is worse. The rents on Church properties are not due till Michaelmas, none have yet been paid. The churls still have their money in their pouches, or hidden in the ground, but if they see their lands ravaged and their lords penned inside a wall, will they pay?"

He threw his hands up theatrically. "It would be a disaster! All over Northumbria the houses of God would fall into ruin, the servants of God would starve."

"They won't starve for loss of a year's rents," said Cuthred. "How much of last year's have you got set aside in the minster?"

"There is another solution," said Ella. "I have proposed it before. We could make peace with them. Offer them tribute—we could call it wergild for their father. It would need to be a mighty tribute to attract them. But there must be ten households in Northumbria for every man out there in the Army. Ten households of churls can buy off a carl. Ten households of thanes can buy off one of their nobles. Some of them will not want to accept, but if we make the offer publicly, the rest may argue them round. What we would ask for from them is a year's peace. And in that year—for they will come again—we will train every man of military age in the kingdom till he can stand against Ivar the Boneless or the devil himself. Then we can fight them three to two, eh, Cuthred? Or one to one if we have to."

The burly captain snorted in amusement. "Brave words, lord, and a good plan. I'd like to do it. Problem is . . ." He pulled the laces on the pouch at his belt and tipped the contents into his palm. "Look at this stuff. A few good silver pennies that I got from selling a horse when I was down South. The rest is imitations from the archbishop's mint here—mostly lead, if it's not copper. I don't know where all the silver's gone—we used to have plenty of it. But there's been less and less of it all over the North for twenty years now. We use the archbishop's money, but the Southerners won't take it; you have to have something to trade to deal with them. You can be damned sure the Army out there won't take it. And it's no good offering them grain or honeycombs."

"But they're here," said Ella. "We must have something they want. The Church must have reserves of gold and silver. . . ."

"You mean to give Church treasures to the Vikings, to buy them off?" gasped Erkenbert. "Instead of marching out to fight them, as is your Christian duty? What you say is sacrilege, Church-breach! If a churl steals a silver plate from the least of God's houses, he is flayed and his hide nailed to the church door. What you suggest is a thousand times worse."

"You imperil your immortal soul even to think of it," cried the archbishop.

Erkenbert's voice hissed like an adder. "It was not for this that we made you king."

The *heimnar* Wulfgar's voice cut across them both. "And you forget, besides, who you are dealing with. These are not men. They are spawn from the pit—all of them. We cannot deal with them. We cannot have them out there for months—we must destroy them. . . ." Spittle began to show round his pale lips, and he lifted an arm for an instant as if to wipe it away before the truncated limb fell back. "Lord king, *heathens are not men.* They have no souls."

Six months ago, Ella thought, I would have led the host of the Northumbrians out to fight. It's what they expect. If I order anything else there is the risk of being called a coward. No one will follow a coward. Erkenbert has as good as told me: If I do not fight they will bring that simpleton Osbert back. He is still hiding up there in the North somewhere. He would march out to fight like a gallant fool.

But Edmund has shown what happens if you fight on even ground, even when you catch them by surprise. If we march out in the old style, I know we will lose. I *know* we will lose, and I will die. I must do something else. Something Erkenbert will accept. But he will not accept an open payment of tribute.

Ella spoke with sudden decision, the weight of kingship in his voice.

"We will stand a siege and hope to weaken them. Cuthred, check defenses and provisioning, send away all useless mouths. Lord archbishop, men have told me that in your library there are learned books by the old Rome-folk who wrote on matters of war, especially of siegecraft. See what aid they can give us in destroying the Vikings."

He turned away, left the wall, Cuthred and a trail of lesser nobles following; Wulfgar was tipped back on his stretcher and carried off by two stout thralls down the stone steps.

"The East Anglian thane is right," whispered Erkenbert to his archbishop. "We must get these people away before they destroy our rents and seduce our thralls. Even our nobles. I can think of some who might be tempted into thinking they can do without us."

"Look it out—Vegetius," Wulfhere replied. "The book called *De Re Militari.* I had not known our lord was so learned."

"He has been in the forge four days now," observed Brand. He and Thorvin, with Hund and Hund's master Ingulf, stood in a little knot a few yards away from the glowing fire of a smithy. The Vikings had found it, still stocked with charcoal, in the village of Osbaldwich a few miles outside York. Shef had taken it over immediately, called urgently for men, iron and fuel. The four stared at him through the wide-flung doors of the smithy.

"Four days," repeated Brand. "He has hardly eaten. He would not have slept except the men told him if he did not sleep, they still had to, and made him cease the din of hammering a few hours a night."

"It doesn't seem to have done him much harm," said Hund.

Indeed his friend, who he still thought of as a boy, a youth, seemed to have changed totally in the course of the past summer. His frame was not massive by the demanding standards of the Army, full of giants. But there seemed to be no excess flesh on it. Shef had stripped to the waist in spite of the gusts of an English October. As he moved round the forge, pecking now at something small and delicate, shifting the red-hot metal with tongs, barking quickly at his iron-collared English assistant to pump harder at the bellows, his muscles moved under the skin as if they lay directly beneath it, without blurring fat or tissue. A quick jerk, metal sizzling into a tub, another piece snatched from the fire. Each time he moved, separate muscles slid smoothly over each other. In the red light of the forge he might have seemed a bronze statue of the ancient days.

Except that he had not their beauty. Even in the light of the forge the sunken right eye seemed a crater of decay. On his back the thrall-marks of flogging showed vividly. Few men in the Army would have been so careless as to display such shame.

"No harm in the body, maybe," replied Thorvin. "I cannot speak for the mind. You know what it says in the *Völund-lay*:

"He sat, he did not sleep, he struck with the hammer.
Always he beat out the baleful work for Nithhad."

"I do not know what cunning thing our friend is beating out in his mind. Or who he is doing it for. I hope he will be more successful than Völund—more successful at gaining the desire of his heart."

Ingulf turned the questioning. "What has he been making these four days?"

"This, to begin with." Thorvin held a helmet up for the others to scrutinize.

What Thorvin held up was like no helmet they had ever seen. It was too big, bulbous as the head of a giant insect. A rim had been welded round it, filed to bright razor-sharpness in the front. A nose-guard ran down in front, ending in bars running back to cheek-protectors. A flared skirt of solid metal covered the nape of the neck.

More surprising to the watchers was the inside. A leather lining had been fitted to the helmet, suspended by straps. Once the helmet was on, the lining would fit the head snugly but the metal would not touch it. A broad strap and a buckle fitted under the jaw, to hold all firm.

"Never seen the likes," said Brand. "A blow on the metal will not crash into the skull. Still, it's better not to get hit, I say."

As they talked, the racket at the forge had ceased, and Shef had been seen diligently fitting small pieces together. Now he walked over to them, smiling and sweating.

Brand raised his voice. "I say, young waker-of-warriors-untimely, if you avoid the blow you don't need the helmet. And what in the name of Thor is that you are holding?"

Shef grinned again, and held up the strange weapon from the forge. He held it out horizontally, balancing it after an instant on the edge of one hand, just where wood joined metal.

"And what do you call that?" asked Thorvin. "A hewing-spear? A haft-axe?"

"A beard-axe that's had bastards by a ploughshare?" suggested Brand. "I don't see the use of it."

Shef picked up Brand's still-bandaged hand and gently rolled back the sleeve. He put his own forearm next to his friend's.

"How good a swordsman am I?" he asked.

"Poor. No training. Some talent."

"If I had the training, would I ever be fit to stand against a man like you? Never. Look at our arms. Is yours twice as thick round as mine? Or just half as thick again? And I am not a weak man. But I am a different shape from you, and yours is the shape for a swordsman, even more, an axeman. You swing a weapon as if it were a stick for a boy to slash thistles. I cannot do that. So if I were ever to face a champion like you . . . And one day I will have to face a champion like you. Muirtach maybe. Or worse."

All five men nodded silently.

"So I have to even things up. With this, you see . . ." Shef began to twirl the weapon slowly. "I can thrust. I can cut forehand. I can strike backhand without reversing the weapon. I can change grip and strike with the butt. I can block a blow from any direction. I can use two hands. I need no shield. Most of all—a blow from this, even in my hands, is like a blow from Brand, which few survive."

"But your hands are exposed," said Brand.

Shef beckoned, and the Englishman in the forge nervously moved over. He held two more metal objects. Shef took them and passed them over.

They were gauntlets: leather-lined, leather-palmed, with long metal projections designed to fit halfway up the forearm. Yet the striking thing about them, the men saw as they peered more closely, was the way the metal moved. Each finger had five plates, each plate fitted to the next on small rivets. Larger plates fitted over the knuckles and the backs of the hands, but they too moved. Shef pulled them on, and slowly flexed his hands, opening and closing them round the shaft of his weapon.

"They are like the scales of Fafnir the dragon," said Thorvin.

"Fafnir was stabbed in the belly, from below. I hope to be harder to murder." Shef turned away. "I have another task to do. I could not have done all this in time without Halfi here. He is a good leather-worker, though he is slow with the bellows."

Motioning the Englishman to kneel before him he began to file at the iron collar. "You will say there is not much point in freeing him, since someone will enslave him again immediately. But I will see him outside the Army's watch fires in the night, and his master is shut up tight in York. If he has any sense or luck he will run away, run far away, and never be caught again."

The Englishman looked up as Shef began gently to pry the soft iron from his throat. "You are heathens," the slave said, not understanding. "Priest said you're men with no mercy. You cut the arms and legs from the thane—I saw him! How can it be that you set a man free where the Christ-priests hold him a slave?"

Shef lifted him to his feet. He replied in English, not in the Norse they had been using before. "The men who crippled the thane should not have done what they did. Yet I say nothing of Christians and heathens, except that there are evil men everywhere. I can give you only one rede. If you do not know who to trust, try a man who wears one of those." He gestured at the four men watching, who, following the speech, silently raised their silver pendants: hammers for Brand and Thorvin, the apples of Ithun for the two leeches, Hund and Ingulf.

"Or others like them. It may be a boat for Njörth, a hammer for Thor, a penis for Frey. I do not say they will help you. But they will treat you as a man, not as a horse or a heifer."

"You do not wear one," said Halfi.

"I do not know what to wear."

Around them, the normal noise of the camp was turning to hubbub as news spread; voices were raised, warriors shouted to each other. The men in the smithy looked up as one of Brand's men appeared, a broad grin splitting the tangle of his beard.

"We're off!" he cried. "The jarls and the Ragnarssons and the Snakeeye have all stopped riding round and round and pondering and scratching their arses. We take the wall tomorrow! Let the women and girls there beware!"

Shef looked darkly at the man, finding no humor in his words. "My girl was called Godive," he said. "That is, 'God's gift.' " He pulled on his gauntlets, swung his halberd thoughtfully. "I shall call this 'Thrall's-wreak'—the vengeance of the slave. One day it will do vengeance for Godive. And other girls as well."

CHAPTER TWO

In the gray morning light the Army began to filter through the narrow, hovel-lined streets of the outer town of York. All three main bridges over the Ouse were commanded by the walls of the old *colonia,* on the south bank of the river, but this had caused no difficulty for the skilled shipwrights and axemen who filled the Viking ranks. They had torn down a few houses and an outlying church for some bigger timbers, and had thrown a wide bridge over the Ouse close to their own encampment. The Army had crossed, and were now lapping their way up, like the tide, toward the yellow stone walls at the heart of the town. There was no sense of hurry, no shouting of commands, just eight thousand men, less the crews detailed to guard the camp, pressing forward toward their obvious goal.

As they tramped up through the narrow streets, men turned aside in small groups to kick down doors or break open shutters. Shef turned his head, stiff and clumsy with the unaccustomed weight of the helmet, and raised brows in silent inquiry at Brand, strolling peacefully by his side, flexing the scarred hand just unwrapped from its bandages.

"There are fools everywhere," remarked Brand. "The runaways say the king here ordered the place cleared days ago, the men inside the fortress, all the others off into the hills somewhere. But there's always someone who knows better, thinks it won't happen."

Commotion broke out ahead of them to lend force to his words: voices shouting, a woman shrieking, the sound of a sudden blow. Out from a shattered doorway squeezed four men, grins splitting their faces, a grubby, slatternly young woman writhing and twisting in their grip. The other men pushing up the hill stopped to exchange jokes.

"Make you too weak to fight, Tosti! You'd be better off with another pancake, keep your strength up."

One of the men pulled the girl's gown up over her head like a sack, pinning her arms and muffling her shrieks. Two others seized her bare legs and pulled them roughly apart. The mood of the crowd passing by changed. Men began to stop and watch.

"Room for more when you're finished, Skakul?"

Shef's gauntleted hands clenched on the shaft of "Thrall's-wreak," and he too turned toward the writhing, grunting group. Brand's enormous fist closed gently over Shef's biceps.

"Leave it, boy. If there's a fight she'll be killed for sure. Easy targets always are. Leave them to it, and maybe they'll let her go at the end. They've a battle to fight, so they can't take too long."

Reluctantly Shef turned his eyes and walked on, trying not to hear the sounds coming from behind—and, as they walked further, from other sides as well. The town, he realized, was like a cornfield in autumn. It seemed to be empty, but as the scythemen walked through it, cutting the wheat down into a smaller and smaller square, so its inhabitants became more and more visible, anxious, terrified, finally running anywhere to get away from the voices and the blades. They should have gone when they were told, he told himself. The king should have made sure. Why can no one see sense in this world?

The buildings ended and before them was a cleared zone of mud and rubble with the yellow stone wall some eighty yards off, the wall the Rome-folk had made. Brand and his crew emerged from the alley, looked up at the top of the wall where figures moved and called jeeringly. A zip in the air, and an arrow thumped into the wattle and daub of a house wall. Another, and a Viking swore in anger as he looked at the shaft sticking from his hip. Brand reached over and pulled it out, glanced at it, tossed it over his shoulder.

"Hurt, Arnthor?"

"Just got through the leather. Six inches higher and it would have bounced off my jacket."

"No punch," remarked Brand again. "Don't look at those fellows. Someone gets one in the eye now and then."

Shef plodded forward, trying to ignore the zips and thuds like the others. "Have you done this kind of thing before?" he asked.

Brand halted, called to his crews to halt as well, turned toward the wall and promptly hunkered down on his heels.

"Can't say I have. Not on this scale. But today we just do what we're told. The Ragnarssons say they've a plan and they will take the city if everybody stands by to lend their weight where needed. So we watch and wait.

"Mind you, if anyone knows what they're doing it should be them. Do you know, their old man, their father Ragnar, tried to take the city of the Franks—oh, it must be twenty years ago. Paris, it's called. So the Ragnarssons have thought a lot about stone walls and cities ever since. Though it's a far cry from some rath in Kilkenny or Meath to this. I'd like to see how they go about it."

Shef leaned on his halberd and stared around him. To his front ran the stone wall, topped with battlements, men loosely scattered along it, no longer wasting arrows on the mass of the Army drawn up on the fringe of the cleared zone facing them, but clearly ready to shoot at any forward movement. Surprising, Shef thought, how little range even a great stone wall could give you. The men on top of their walls thirty feet were impregnable, unreachable. Yet the archers on the wall could do virtually nothing to the men standing watching them. At fifty yards' range you were in danger, at ten you might well be dead. At eighty you could stand in the open and make your preparations at leisure.

He looked more closely at the wall. To the left, two hundred yards away, it ended in a round, jutting tower, from which men could shoot along the line of the wall, at least for as far as their bows would carry. Beyond the tower the ground dropped toward the brown and muddy Ouse, immediately beyond it on the other bank, the wooden stockade that guarded the river fringe of the *colonia*—Marystown, as the locals called it. It too carried a frieze of men, watching anxiously the preparations of the heathen so close, so out of range.

The Army waited, six- and eight-deep, facing the wall on a five-hundred-yard front; more packed into the mouths of the streets and alleyways, the steam of their breath rising into the air. Dull metal, grubby wool and leather were picked out only here and there by the bright paint on shields. The warriors looked calm, patient, like farmhands waiting for the owner.

There came a blare of horns from the center of the waiting ranks, maybe fifty or sixty yards to Shef's right. Shef realized suddenly that he should have been studying the gate in the center of the wall. A wide street ran out from it, no longer prominent in the waste of mud and trampled wattle where houses had been, but clearly the main road out to the east. The gate itself was new, not work of the Rome-folk, but massively formidable for that. Its timbers were seasoned oak tree-trunks, fully as high as the towers on either side of it. Its hinges were the heaviest iron that English smiths could make.

Yet it was weaker than stone. Opposite it now, the four Ragnarssons strode forward. Shef picked out the tallest of them, looking almost frail beside his mighty brothers. Ivar the Boneless. Clad for the occasion in flaring scarlet cloak, grass-green breeches beneath his long mail-coat, shield and helmet silver-painted. He paused and waved to his nearest supporters, to a roar of recognition. The horns blew again, and the English on the wall responded with a cloud of arrows, to hiss by, thud into shields, bounce away from mail.

This time the Snakeeye waved, and suddenly hundreds of men were trotting forward, the Ragnarssons' own picked followers. The first line of them carried shields, not the usual round ones for combat, but large rectangles, capable of covering the body from ankle to neck. They ran forward through the arrow-sleet and halted, forming a V aimed at the gate. The second and third line were bowmen. They too ran forward, crouched behind the shields and began to shoot up. Now men began to fall on both sides, shot through throat or brain. Shef could see others crouching, struggling with arrows this time deeply embedded through mail and flesh. A trickle of wounded men was already beginning to walk back from the Viking ranks.

But the job of these first attackers was only to sweep the battlements clear.

Crawling forward from the mouth of the street up which it had been towed came the Ragnarssons' pride. Shef, looking at it as it emerged from the ranks of men, saw it for a moment as a monstrous boar. The legs of the men who pushed it from inside could not be seen. Twenty feet long, it was armored on either side with heavy, overlapping shields, roofed over with more.

Inside was an oak-trunk ram which swung on iron chains from its frame. Fifty men picked for strength heaved it along, pushing it on eight double-size cartwheels. From its front poked the iron snout of the ram. As it rolled ponderously forward, the warriors on either side of it cheered and began to surge forward with it, ignoring the English arrows. The Ragnarssons were on either side of the ram, waving their men back and trying to get them into some sort of column. Shef looked grimly at the flurry of saffron plaids. Muirtach was there, his longsword still not drawn, also waving and cursing.

"Well, that's the plan," said Brand—he had still not bothered to stand up. "The ram bashes the door down and then we all walk in."

"Will it work?"

"That's what we're fighting the battle to find out."

The ram was only twenty yards from the gate now, level with the foremost archers, accelerating to a rapid walk as the men pushing saw their goal through the frontal slit. On the battlement men appeared suddenly, drawing an instant hail of shot from the Viking archers. They leveled their bows, and fire-arrows shot down from wall to ram, thumping into the heavy timbers.

"Won't work," Brand said. "Somewhere else maybe, but in England? After harvest? You'd have to dry that wood for a day at your forge before you could get it to take light."

The fires fizzled and guttered. The ram was at the gate, still accelerating till it stopped with a crash. A pause, as the champions left their drag-ropes and stepped across to the handles on the ram itself. The whole structure shifted as they swung it back on the iron chains hanging from the roof of the frame. Then a heave forward, propelled by a hundred arms and the massive weight of the tree-trunk itself. The gate shook.

Shef realized suddenly that the excitement of battle was beginning to take hold. Even Brand was on his feet now, and everyone was beginning to edge forward. He himself was ten yards further forward than he had been. No reply from the battlements, no harassing fire hoping to take its toll.

Now all attention on both sides was fixed on the gate. The ponderous frame of the boar was shifting again as the men heaved the trunk back. Another drive forward, a crash which carried even over the noise of thousands of voices, another tremor from the massive gate. What were the English doing? If they let the boar carry on its routing, their gate would soon be in splinters and the Army surging through.

Heads began to appear at the gate towers, bobbing up in spite of the waves of shafts directed at them. Each man—they must be strong men up there—held a boulder, heaved it over his head, hurled it over and down at the overlapped shields of the ram. It was a target that could not be missed. Shields cracked and broke. But they were nailed firmly in place, and sloping. The boulders fell, rolled to one side.

Something else was happening. He was closer now, just behind the line of the Ragnarsson archers, men behind him darting forward with bundles of retrieved arrows. What was it? Ropes. They had ropes in the gate towers, both of them, lots of ropes, and the men in the towers, still out of arrowshot, were heaving mightily at them. A Ragnarsson ran across his view—Ubbi, it seemed to be—shouting at the men pressing forward. He was telling them to throw javelins up over the battlements, to come down where the men seemed to be pulling. A few men ran forward to cast; not many. It was blind shooting, and a costly throwing spear was not something to waste idly. The ropes tightened.

Up over the edge of the gate came a round object, a great roller teetering slowly toward the edge. It was a pillar: a stone pillar from the Roman days, sawn off at both ends. Falling from thirty feet no frame could stop it.

Shef passed "Thrall's-wreak" to Brand and ran forward, yelling inarticulately. The men inside the boar could see nothing of what was happening above their heads, but others could. The trouble was, no one had a clear idea of what to do. As Shef reached the frame several men were clustered at its rear, urging its crew to drop the handles, turn back to the drag-ropes, and haul the whole contrivance back to safety. Others were calling to Muirtach and his stormers to come to the outside and add their weight to the withdrawal. As they did so, the English archers rallied again and the air was once more full of the zip and thud of missiles, this time coming at killing range.

Shef pushed a man aside, another, and ducked into the rear entrance of the ram. Inside there was an immediate reeking fog of sweat and steaming breath, fifty heroes gasping with exertion and confusion, some already at the drag-ropes, others turning away from the massive swinging trunk.

"No," Shef bellowed at the top of his lungs. "Get back to the handles."

Faces gaped at him, men began to throw their weight on the ropes.

"You don't need to push the whole thing back, just swing back the ram—"

An arm caught him in the back, he was hurled forward, other bodies charged past him, he found a rope thrust in his hand.

"Pull, ye useless bodach, or I'll cut yer liver out," screamed Muirtach in his ear.

Shef felt the frame tremble, the wheel behind him start to turn. He threw his weight on the rope—two feet would do it, maybe three—they couldn't throw that great thing right out from the gate. . . .

A ground-trembling crash, another violent blow in the back, his head making contact with a timber, a sudden terrible shrieking like a woman's that this time went on and on . . .

Shef stumbled to his feet and looked around. The Vikings had been too slow. The stone pillar, finally hauled over the edge by a hundred arms, had come down squarely on the iron snout of the ram, driving it into the ground, snapping chains and tearing out their fixing bolts. It had also smashed the front of the frame, and come down finally across the hips of one of the crew. He was the one—a massive grizzled man in his forties—who was shrieking. His mates backed away—frightened, shamed, ignoring the three or four silent bodies caught by flailing chain or smashing timber. At least, apart from the one man, no one was making any noise. They would begin to babble in a moment, but for a moment, Shef knew, he could bend them to his will. He knew what must be done.

"Muirtach. Stop that noise." The cruel dark face gaped at him, seemingly without recognition, then stepped forward, pulling a dirk from his hose-top.

"The rest of you. Roll the ram back. Not far. Six feet. Stop. Now—" He was at the timbers at the front, examining the damage. "Ten of you, outside; take broken wood, spear-shafts, anything, roll that column right hard up against the gate. It's only a few feet wide—if we get the front wheel right up to it we can still swing the ram.

"Now, rerig these chains. I need a hammer, two hammers. Start pulling the ram back, right back on its slings . . ."

Time passed in a frenzy. Shef was aware of faces staring at him, of a silver helmet pushing in and out of the rear entrance, of Muirtach wiping a dirk. He paid no attention. For him, the chains and posts, the nails and broken timbers, were glowing lines in his head, shifting as he thought how they should be. He had no doubt what to do.

A roar of excitement outside as the Army tried a sudden escalade with makeshift ladders against a seemingly undefended wall. Only to be hurled back and off as the English rallied in defense.

Inside, gasps of effort, mutters: "It's the smith, the one-eyed smith. Do as he says."

Ready. Shuffling to the back, Shef waved the champions to their ropes again, saw the ram rumble forward till its wheels lay against the column and its head; the shattered iron snout, chopped off and discarded, was once again flush with the gate, oak against oak. The champions seized their handles once more, waited for the word, swung back all together, and forward. And forward. They were singing now, a rowing song, putting their bodies into the stroke, heaving mindlessly and without direction. Shef ducked out of the frame once more and into the daylight.

Round him the aimless muddy waste of the morning had taken on the look of a battlefield. Bodies on the ground, hurt men walking or being carried away, spent shafts littering the earth or being picked up by scavenging archers. Anxious faces turning first toward him. Then toward the gate.

It was beginning to split. Movement ran across it now as the ram struck; one post was slightly out of line with the other. The men inside were inching the ram forward, to get a better stroke. In fifty breaths, maybe a hundred, it would go. The champions of Northumbria would surge out, waving their gold-handled swords, to meet the champions of Denmark and the Vik and the apostates of Ireland. It was the turning point of the battle.

Shef found himself staring into the face of Ivar the Boneless, only a few feet away, the pale eyes fixed on him, full of hatred and suspicion. Then Ivar's attention changed. He too knew the battle had reached its crisis. Turning, he waved both arms in prearranged signal. From the houses down toward the Ouse a horde of figures trotted. They carried long ladders, not makeshifts like those of the last escalade, but carefully made and concealed ones. Fresh men, who knew what they were doing. If the champions were at the gate, Ivar would send a wave in at the corner tower, which all the bravest and the best of the English would have left, to join the climactic struggle at the gate.

The English are finished, Shef thought. Their defenses are down in two places. Now the Army will go through.

Why did I do this to them? Why have I helped Ivar and the Army—the ones who burned out my eye?

From the other side of the quaking gate there came a curious dull twang, like a harp-string snapping, but immensely louder, fit to be heard above the din of battle. Up into the air there rose a mass, a mighty mass, a boulder bigger than ten men could lift. That's impossible, Shef thought. Impossible.

But the boulder continued to rise, up and up till Shef had to tilt his head back to look at it. It appeared to hang for an instant.

Then down.

It landed square on the center of the ram, smashing through shields and frame and supports as if they were a child's house of bark. The ram's head kicked up in the air and jerked sideways like a dying fish. From inside, hoarse cries of pain.

The scaling parties now had ladders up against the wall; they were scrambling up; one ladder had been pushed away, the rest were standing firm. Two hundred yards further off, across the Ouse, something was happening on top of the wooden stockade of Marystown: men crouched round some kind of machine.

Not a boulder this time, a line, rising as it streaked across the river, then falling as it headed for the ladders. The hero on top of the one nearest them had his hand on the stone battlement, and was just reaching over to scramble across. The streak intersected with his body.

He smashed forward as if struck in the back by a giant, smashed so hard the ladder broke under him with the impact. As the ladder fell beneath him and he turned, arms flung wide, Shef saw the giant bolt projecting from the man's spine. He folded over backward as if in two pieces and fell slowly onto the heap of his mates scrambling beneath him.

An arrow. But not an arrow. No human being could have shot it, nor heaved the boulder. Yet these things had happened. Shef walked forward slowly and considered the rock lying amid the ruins of the ram, ignoring the pitiful struggles and cries for help beneath it.

These things had been done by machines. And such machines! Somewhere inside the fort, maybe among the black monks, there must be a machine-master such as he had never imagined. He must find out. But now, anyway, he knew why he had helped the Army. Because he could not bear to see a machine mishandled. But now there were machines on both sides.

Brand had seized him, thrust "Thrall's-wreak" into his hands, was hustling him away, snarling angrily at him.

". . . standing there like a wittol, they'll have a war-band out any moment!"

Shef saw they were almost the last men left on the cleared ground, the place of slaughter. The rest had filtered back down the hill as they had filtered up.

The Ragnarssons' assault on York had failed.

Very carefully, tongue protruding between his teeth, Shef laid the keen blade of his meat-knife to the thread. It snapped. The weight on the end of the wooden arm dropped, the other end flew up. A pebble arced lazily across the forge.

Shef sat up with a sigh. "That is how it works," he said to Thorvin. "A short arm, a heavy weight; a long arm, a lighter weight. There it is."

"I am glad you are satisfied at last," replied Thorvin. "Two days you have been playing with bits of wood and string, while I do all the work. Now maybe you can bear a hand."

"I will, yes, but this is important too. This is the new knowledge that those of the Way must seek."

"It is. And important. But there is the day's work to be done as well."

Thorvin was as keenly interested as Shef in the experiments, but, after a few attempts to help, had realized that he was merely standing in the way of the excited imagination of his former apprentice, and had gone back to the enormous pile of work an army, in being, created for its armorers.

"But is it *new* knowledge?" Hund asked. "Ingulf can do things no Englishman has ever been able to. And he learns how to do them by trial, and by taking to pieces the bodies of the dead. You are learning by trial, but you are only trying to learn what the black monks already know. And they are not playing with models."

Shef nodded. "I know. I am wasting my time. I understand now how it can be done, but there are all kinds of things I do not understand. If I had a real weight here, like the one they really shot, then what kind of a weight would I need to put in the other arm? It would be far greater than a dozen men could lift. And if it was as heavy as that, how could I wind down the long arm, the shooting arm? It would need some sort of a windlass. But I know now what the sound was that I heard just before the rock came over. It was the sound of someone cutting the rope, to release the rock.

"And there is another thing that bothers me even more. They shot one rock—that smashed the ram. If they had not hit with that one shot, the gate would have been down and all the machine-masters would be dead. They must have been very sure they could hit with the first shot."

He swept suddenly at the lines he had been drawing in the dirt. "It is a waste of time. Do you see what I mean, Thorvin? There must be some sort of skill, some sort of craft, which would tell men where it would go without me having to try again and again. When I first saw the stockade round your camp by the Stour, I was amazed. I thought, how do the leaders know how many logs to bring with them to build a stockade that will hold all their men? But now I know how even the Ragnarssons do it. They notch a stick for each ship, ten notches to a stick, and then they throw the sticks down in turn in separate piles, one pile for each one of the three walls, or the four walls, or however many there are, and when there are no more sticks they pick the piles up and count them. And that is the reckoning of the greatest leaders and captains in the world. A pile of sticks. But what they have over there in the city is the knowledge of the Rome-folk, who could write in numbers as easily as they could write in letters. If I could learn to write in Roman numbers, then I would build a machine!"

Thorvin laid down the tongs and looked thoughtfully at the silver hammer displayed on his chest.

"You should not think the Rome-folk had the answers to everything," he remarked. "If they had they would still be ruling England from York. And they were only Christians, when all is said and done."

Shef jumped impatiently to his feet. "Hah! How do you explain the

other instrument then? The one that shot the great arrow. I have thought
and thought about that. Nothing will do. You could not make a bow big
enough. The wood would break. But what can shoot except a bow?"

"What you need," said Hund, "is a runaway from the city, or from
Marystown. One who has seen the machines work."

"Maybe one will come," said Thorvin.

A silence fell, broken only by the renewed pounding of Thorvin's hammer and the puffing of the bellows as Shef blew angrily at the forge.
Runaways were a subject better avoided. After the failure of the assault the
Ragnarssons, in rage, had turned on the countryside around the city of
York—a defenseless countryside, since its armed men and nobles, its
thanes and champions, were shut up with King Ella inside the city. "If we
cannot take the town," Ivar had cried, "we will ravage the shire." Ravage it
they had.

"I'm getting sick of it," Brand had confided to Shef after the last sweep of
an already-gutted countryside, all crews taking their turn. "Don't think I'm
a milksop, or a Christian. I want to get rich and there are few things I
won't do for money. But there's no money in what we're doing. Not much
sport either, to my eye, in what the Ragnarssons and the Gaddgedlar and
the riffraff are doing. No fun going through a village after they've been
through. They're only Christians, I know, and maybe they deserve what
they get for cringing to the Christ-god and his priests.

"It still won't do. We're picking up slaves by the hundred, good quality
stuff. But where to sell them. Down South? If you do that you need to go
with a strong fleet and a sharp eye open. We aren't popular down there—
and I blame Ragnar and his brood for that. Round in Ireland? A long way,
and a long time before you get your cash. And slaves apart, there's nothing. The churches got their gold and silver into York before we arrived.
What money the peasants have got, or the thanes—it's poor stuff. Very
poor stuff. Strange. It's a rich land, anyone can see. Where's all their silver
gone? We'll never get rich the way we're going. Sometimes I wish I had not
taken the news of Ragnar's death to the Braethraborg, no matter what the
priests of the Way said to me. It's little enough I have got out of it."

But Brand had taken the crews out again, probing up across the shire to
the shrine of Strenshall, hoping for a haul of gold or silver. Shef had asked
not to accompany him, sickened with the sights and sounds of a land
crisscrossed by the Ragnarssons and their followers, each one intent on
showing to the others his skill on racking secrets and information and
buried treasure out of churls and thralls who had no information, and
certainly no treasure, to yield. Brand had hesitated, scowling.

"We are all in the Army together," he had said. "What we decide together, all must do, even if some of us don't like it. If we don't like it we have to talk the others round, in open meeting. But I don't like the way you think you can take some bits of the Army and leave the others, young man. You are a carl now. Carls do what is best for each other. That is why we are all given a voice."

"I did what was best when the ram broke."

Brand had grunted, doubtfully, and had muttered, "For your own reasons." But he had left Shef behind, with Thorvin and a mountain of smithy-work, in the guarded camp that watched York, ever alert for a sally. Shef had begun immediately to play with models, to imagine giant bows, sling-stones, mallets. One problem at least he had solved—if not in practice or even in theory.

Outside the smithy there was a pad of running feet, a gasping of exhaustion. The three men inside moved as one to the wide, open doors. A few feet beyond them Thorvin had set up a line of poles, connected with yarn, from which he had hung the rowan berries that indicated the limits of his precinct, the holy place. To one of the posts clung a panting figure, dressed in rough sacking. The iron collar round his neck indicated his status. Desperately his eyes moved from one to the other of the three faces staring at him, then brightened with relief as he saw, finally, the hammer round Thorvin's burly neck.

"Sanctuary," he gasped, "give me sanctuary." He spoke in English, but used the Latin word.

"What is 'sanctuarium'?" asked Thorvin.

"Safe-keeping. He wants to come under your protection. Among the Christians, a runaway may grasp a church door in some churches, and then he is under the protection of the bishop till his case is tried."

Thorvin shook his head slowly. He could see now the pursuers coming into view—half a dozen of them, Hebrideans by the look of them, among the most ardent of the slave-takers, not hurrying now that they could see their quarry.

"We don't have that custom here," he said.

The slave wailed with fear as he saw the gesture and felt the presences behind him, and clung tighter to the fragile poles. Shef remembered the moment when he too had walked forward to Thorvin inside his enclosure, not knowing if he was walking to his death or not. But he had been able to call himself a smith, a fellow of the craft. This man looked as if he was just extra labor, knowing nothing of any value.

"Come along, you." The leader of the Hebrideans said, clouting the cringing figure round one ear, and began to pry his fingers from the pole.

"How much do you want for him?" said Shef impulsively. "I'll buy him off you."

Guffaws of laughter. "What for, One-eye? You want a bum-boy? I've got better down in the pen."

"I said I'll buy him. Look, I've got money." Shef turned towards "Thrall's-wreak," stuck in the ground at the entrance to the precinct. From it he had hung his purse with the few coins in it that Brand had doled out as his share of the meager plunder so far.

"No chance. Come down to the pens if you want a slave, sell you one anytime. I've got to take this one back, make an example of him. Too many down there run from one master, think they might run from another. Got to show them it doesn't pay."

The slave had caught something of the dialogue, and wailed with fear again, this time more desperately. As the men gripped his arms and hands and began to pull him off, trying as they did so not to damage the precinct-markers, he thrashed and fought. "The pendants," he cried. "They said the pendant-men were safe."

"We cannot help you," Shef replied, speaking again in English. "You should have stayed with your English master."

"My masters were the black monks. You know what they are like to their slaves. And my master was the worst of all—Erkenbert the deacon, who makes the machines. . . ."

An angry Hebridean lost patience with the man's struggles, whipped a sandbag from his belt, and struck out. He missed his blow, caught the slave along the jaw instead of on the temple. A crack, the jaw lolling forward, blood trickling from the corner of the mouth.

"Er'en'ert. He' a de'il. Ma' 'e de'il-'chines."

Shef seized his gauntlets, pulled them on, ready to jerk his halberd out of the ground. The knot of struggling men swayed back a few paces.

"Hold on," he said. "The man's valuable. Don't hit him again." Ten words, he thought, ten words might be all I need. Then I will know the principle of the great bow.

The slave, fighting now with the frenzy of a tormented weasel, got a foot free, kicked out. A Hebridean grunted, bent forward cursing.

"That's enough," snapped the head of the gang. As Shef leapt forward in entreaty he whipped a knife from his belt, stepped forward and drove upward, backhand. The slave, still held, arched and contorted, went limp.

"You blockhead!" yelled Shef. "You killed one of the machine-men!"

The Hebridean turned back to him, mouth twisting with anger. As he started to speak, Shef punched him full in the face with his armored glove. He sprawled backward, landed on the ground. A dead silence fell.

The Hebridean climbed slowly to his feet, spat one tooth, then another, into his hand. He looked at his men, shrugged. They dropped the slave's corpse, turned, walked off together toward their camp.

"You've done it now, boy," said Thorvin.

"What do you mean?"

"Only one thing can happen now."

"What's that?"

"*Holmgang.*"

CHAPTER THREE

Shef lay on the straw pallet close to the banked fire of the forge, moving uneasily in his sleep. Thorvin had forced a heavy dinner on him, which should have been welcome after days of increasingly short commons in a camp dependent entirely on foraging for its food. But the rye bread and fried bullock lay heavy on his stomach. Heavier still were his thoughts. They had explained the rules of *holmgang* to him, far different from the impromptu brawl in which he had killed the Irishman Flann months before. He knew he was at terrible disadvantage. But there was no getting out of this. The whole Army knew, looked forward to the morning's duel as a major distraction. He was trapped.

And he still thought about the machines. How were they built? How could better ones be built? How could the walls of York be breached? Slowly, he slipped into heavier slumber.

He was on some distant plain. In front of him loomed monstrous walls. On a scale to dwarf the walls of York, or any other walls that had ever been built by mortal man. High above were the figures he had seen before in his dreams, his "visions" as Thorvin called them—the massive figures with the faces like axeblades and the expressions of severe gravity. But now their expressions were also of concern, alarm. In the foreground, moving up to the walls, he saw there was a figure even more gigantic than those of the gods, so enormous that it towered up even to the height of the walls on which the gods were standing. But it did not have the proportions of a human being: stumpy-legged, fat-armed, swollen-bellied and gap-toothed, it looked like an immense clown. A wittol, one of the children born deformed, who, if Father Andreas were not on hand very swiftly, would quietly have found their way into the fen in Emneth. The giant was urging on an immense horse, fully built to his own scale, and drawing a cart, on it a block of stone large as a mountain.

Shef realized the block was to fill a gap in the great wall. The wall was not complete—but nearly so. The sun in this strange world was setting, and he knew that if the wall were finished before the sunset, something appalling, something incurably dreadful would take place. That was why the gods looked their alarm, and why the giant was urging on his horse—his stallion, Shef saw—with whoops of glee and anticipation.

A whicker from behind. Another horse, this time a more normally propor-tioned one. A mare, too, with chestnut hair and mane blowing around her eyes. She whickered again, then turned coyly as if unaware of the effect her call had had. But the stallion had heard. His head rose. He shook in his traces. His member started to slide out of its sheath.

The giant shouted, beat the stallion round the head, tried to cover its eyes. Its nostrils flared, a whinny of rage, yet another encouraging whicker from the mare, now close by, heels kicking skittishly. The stallion reared, lashed out with mighty hooves at the giant, at the traces. Over went the cart, out tipped the stone, the giant dancing with vexation. The stallion was free, lunging towards the mare to sheathe his erect, chain-long penis. But she was coy, prancing away, provoking him to follow, then darting sideways. The two horses gyrated, sud-denly dashed off at full gallop, the stallion slowly gaining on the mare but both rapidly out of sight. Behind them, the giant cursed and leapt in comic panto-mime. The sun set. One of the figures on the wall strode forward grimly, pulling on a pair of metal gloves.

There is a forfeit to be paid, thought Shef.

Again he was on a plain, facing a walled city. It too was mighty, the walls rising far above the heights of those at York, but this time it was at least on a human scale, as were the thousands of figures milling about within the walls and outside the walls. Outside the walls the figures were heaving at a monstrous image—not a boar, like the Ragnarssons' battering ram, but a giant horse. A wooden horse. What is the point of a wooden horse? thought Shef. Surely no one could be deceived by it.

Nor were they. Arrows and missiles flew out against the horse from the walls, or flew at the men heaving at its mighty wheels. They bounced away, scattered haulers, did not dislodge or discourage the hundreds of new hands rushing to take the place of the fallen. The horse edged up to the walls, overtopping them.

What would take place now, Shef knew, was the crisis of something that had gone on for many years, that had swallowed thousands of lives and would yet swallow thousands more. Something told him also that what happened here would fascinate men for generation upon generation—but that few men would ever understand it, preferring instead to make up their own stories.

A voice Shef had heard before spoke suddenly in his mind. The voice that had warned him before the night battle by the Stour—still with the same note of deep, interested amusement.

"Now watch this," it said. "Watch this."

The horse's mouth opened, its tongue slid out to rest on the walls. From the mouth . . .

Thorvin was shaking him, dragging relentlessly at his shoulder. Shef sat up, still groping for the meaning of his dream.

"Time to rise," said Thorvin. "You have a hard day ahead of you. I only hope you live to see the end of it."

Erkenbert the archdeacon sat in his tower room high above the great hall of the minster and pulled the candlestick closer to him. There were three candles in it, each of best beeswax, not stinking tallow, and the light they gave was clear. He viewed them with satisfaction as he took the goosefeather from its inkpot. What he was about to do was difficult, was laborious, and its results might be sad.

In front of him lay a confusion of scraps of vellum, written on, crossed out, written on again. Now he took his quill and a fresh, large, handsome piece. On it he wrote:

De parochia quae dicitur	*Schirlam desunt nummi*	*XLVIII*
" " " "	*Fulford* " "	*XXXVI*
" " " "	*Haddinatunus* " "	*LIX*

The list crept on and on. At the end he drew a line beneath the record of the minster's unpaid rents, drew a deep breath, and began the mind-wrenching toil of adding the numbers up. *"Octo et sex,"* he muttered to himself, *"quattuordecim. Et novo, sunt . . . viginta tres. Et septem."* To assist himself he began to draw little lines on a discarded sheet, hatching them through when he completed a ten. He began also, as his finger crawled down the list, to put a little mark between the *XL* and the *VIII*, the *L* and the *IX*, to remind himself which bits were to be added and which were to be left. Finally he came to the end of his first calculation, wrote down

firmly *CDXLIX*, and began to work his way down again with the figures he
had omitted before. *"Quaranta et triginta sunt septuaginta. Et quinquaginta.
Centum et viginta."* The novice who decorously moved an eye round the
doorway a few minutes later to see if anything was required returned in
awe to his fellows.

"He is saying numbers of which I have never heard," he reported.

"He is a marvelous man," said one of the black monks. "God send there
may be no harm in the learning of such black arts."

"Duo milia quattuor centa nonaginta," pronounced Erkenbert, writing it
down: *MMCDXC*. The two figures now lay next to each other: *MMCDXC*
and *CDXLIX*. After another interval of crossing and hatching, he had the
answer: *MMCMXXXIX*. And now the real toil began. That was the sum of
the failed rents for one quarter. What would this represent for a full year, if
by divine punishment the scourges of God, the Vikings, were permitted to
lie so long upon the backs of the suffering people of God? Many, even
among *arithmetici*, would have taken the easier route and added the same
figure up four times. But Erkenbert knew himself superior to such subter-
fuges. Painstakingly, he set up the complex procedure for the most difficult of all diabolic skills: multiplication in Roman numerals.

When all was done he stared at the figure, disbelievingly. Never in all
his experience had he come upon such a sum. Slowly, with shaking fingers, he snuffed the candles in recognition of the growing gray light of
dawn. After matins he would have to seek out the Archbishop.

It was too great. Such losses could not be borne.

Far away, a hundred and fifty miles to the south, the same growing light
reached the eyes of a woman, snuggled deep in a nest of down mattress
and woolen rugs piled high against the cold. She stirred, shifted. Her hand
touched the warm, naked thigh of the man next to her. Recoiled as if it
had touched the scales of a mighty adder.

He is my half brother, she thought for the thousandth time. Son of my
own father. We are in mortal sin. But how could I tell them? I could not
tell even the priest who married us. Alfgar told him we had sinned carnally
while fleeing from the Vikings and now prayed God's forgiveness and
blessing on our union. They think he is a saint. And the kings, the kings of
Mercia and of Wessex, they listen to all he says of the menace of the
Vikings, of what they did to his father, of how he fought at the Viking
camp to set me free. They think he is a hero. They say they will make him
an alderman and set him over a shire, they will bring his poor, tormented
father home from York, where he is defying the heathens still.

But what will happen when our father sees us together? If only Shef had lived . . .

As she thought the name, Godive's tears started to leak slowly, as they did every morning, through closed eyelids onto the pillow.

Shef marched down the muddy street, between the lines of booths which the Vikings had set up to keep out the winter weather. His halberd rested on his shoulder, and he wore his metal gloves, but the helmet remained at Thorvin's forge. Mail and helmets may not be worn in *holmgang,* they had told him. The duel was fought as a matter of honor, so mere expediencies, like surviving and killing your enemy, were not the point.

That did not mean you would not be killed.

And a *holmgang* was a four-man affair. Each of the two principals took turns to strike at the other. But each principal was covered from the blows of the other by his second, the shieldbearer, who carried a shield for him and intercepted the strokes. Your life depended on the skill of your second.

Shef had no second. Brand and all his crews were still away. Thorvin had pulled his beard frantically, thumping his hammer again and again into the ground with frustration, but as a priest of the Way he could take no part. If he offered, his offer would be refused by the umpires. The same went for Ingulf, Hund's master. The only person he might have asked was Hund, and as soon as Shef framed the thought, he knew that Hund—once he realized the situation—would surely volunteer. But he had immediately told his friend he must not think of helping. All other considerations apart, he was sure that at the critical moment, with a sword-blow descending, Hund would stop to observe a heron in the marsh or a newt in the fen, and would probably kill them both.

"I will see it through myself," he told the priests of the Way, who had gathered together from the whole Army to advise him, much to Shef's surprise.

"This is not why we spoke for you to the Snakeeye, and saved you from the vengeance of Ivar," said Farman sharply—Farman the priest of Frey, famous for his wanderings in the other worlds.

"Are you then so sure of the ways of fate?" Shef had replied, and the priests had fallen silent.

But in truth, as he walked toward the place of the *holmgang,* it was not the duel itself which bothered him. What bothered him was whether the umpires would let him fight on his own. If they did not, then he would stand for the second time in his life at the mercy of the Army's collective judgement, the *vapna takr*. At the thought of the roar and the clash of weapons that accompanied a decision, his guts knotted within him.

He marched through the gates of the stockade and out onto the trampled meadow by the river where the Army was assembled. As he walked forward, a buzz of comment rose, and the watching crowd parted to let him through. At their center stood a ring of willow wands, only ten feet across. "The *holmgang* should strictly be fought on an island in a stream," Thorvin had told him, "but where there was no eyot suitable, a symbolic one was marked out instead. In a *holmgang* there was to be no maneuvering: The participants stood and cut at each other till one was dead. Or could fight no more, or ransomed himself off, or threw down his weapons, or stepped outside the marked area. To do either of the two last meant submitting yourself to the mercy of your opponent, who could demand death or mutilation. If a fighter showed cowardice, the judges would certainly order either, or both.

Shef saw his enemies already standing by the willows: the Hebridean whose teeth he had knocked out, whose name he now knew was Magnus. He held a naked broadsword in his hand, burnished so that the serpent-markings on its blade wriggled and crawled in the dull, gray light. By him stood his second: a tall, scarred, powerful-looking man of middle age. He held an oversized shield of painted wood, with metal rim and boss. Shef looked at them for a moment, and then looked deliberately round for the umpires.

His heart checked as he recognized instantly, in a little group of four, the unmistakable figure of the Boneless One. Still wearing scarlet and green, but the silver helmet put aside; the pale eyes with their invisible eyebrows and lashes stared straight into his own. But this time, instead of suspicion they held assurance, amusement, contempt, as they recognized Shef's uncontrollable start of fear and the immediate attempt to replace it with impassivity.

Ivar yawned, stretched, turned away. "I disqualify myself from judgement in this case," he said. "This barnyard cock and I have another score to settle. I will not have him say that I took advantage to judge unfairly. I leave his death to Magnus."

A rumble of agreement came from the nearest watchers, and a buzz as the information was passed to those further back. Everything in the Army, Shef realized again, was subject to public agreement. It was always best to have public opinion on your side.

Ivar's withdrawal left three men there, all obviously senior warriors, well armed, necks, belts and arms flashing with silver to show their status. The middle one, he recognized, was Halvdan Ragnarsson, the eldest of the brothers: a man with a reputation for ferocity, for fighting when there was no need—not as wise as his brother Sigurth nor as dreadful as his brother Ivar, but not a man to show mercy on the unwarlike.

"Where is your second?" said Halvdan, frowning.

"I do not need one," replied Shef.

"You must have one. You cannot fight a *holmgang* with no shield or shield-bearer. If you present yourself without one, then that is as good as surrendering to the mercy of your enemy. Magnus, what do you want to do with him?"

"I do not need one!" This time Shef shouted, stepped forward, jammed the butt of his halberd upright in the earth. "I have a shield." He raised his left forearm, on which he had strapped a square buckler, a foot across, fastened firmly at wrist and at elbow, made entirely of iron. "I do not fight with board and broadsword, but with this and this. I do not need a second. I am an Englishman, not a Dane!"

A growl rose from the audience as they heard him—a growl with a note of amusement in it. The Army liked a drama, Shef knew. They might bend the rules if there was something to bet on. They would support a man who was in the wrong, if he showed enough daring.

"We cannot accept this proposal," said Halvdan to the other two judges. "What do you say?"

A disturbance behind, someone forcing his way through the ring, stepping forward to join Shef as he stood before his judges. Another large and powerful figure, laden with silver. The Hebrideans stood frowning a little way apart. Shef saw with shock that it was his father Sigvarth. Sigvarth looked across at his son, then turned to the judges. He spread his burly arms with a cunning air of conciliation.

"I wish to act as this man's shield-bearer."

"Has he asked you to?"

"No."

"Then what standing do you have in this affair?"

"I am his father."

Another growl from the audience, with a rising note of excitement. Life in a winter camp was cold and boring. This was easily the best entertainment anyone had had since the failed assault. Like children, the warriors of the Army were anxious not to see the show end too early. They pressed closer, straining to hear and to pass on the news to those further back. Their presence affected the umpires: They had to judge correctly, but also gauge the mood of the crowd.

As they began to mutter quietly among themselves, Sigvarth turned quickly toward Shef. He stepped close, bent the inch or two needed to be on a level, and spoke with a note of entreaty.

"Look, boy, you turned me down once before when you were in a fix. That showed guts, I've got to say. Look what it cost you. Cost you an eye. Don't do it again. I'm sorry—what happened to your mother. If I'd known she'd had a son like you I wouldn't have done it. Many men have told me what you did at the siege, with the ram—the Army's full of it. I'm proud of you.

"Now, let me carry this shield for you. I've done it before. I'm better than Magnus, better than his mate Kolbein. With me as shield-bearer nothing will get through to you. And you—you've knocked that Hebridean fool as dizzy as a dog once already. Do it again! We'll finish the pair of them."

He gripped his son's shoulder hard. His eyes shone with emotion, a mixture of pride, embarrassment, and something else—it was the lust for glory, Shef decided. No one could be a successful warrior for twenty years, a jarl, the leader of warbands, without the urge to be at the front, to have all eyes fixed on one, to break down destiny by sheer violence. Shef felt suddenly calm, composed, even able to think of how to save his father's face while rejecting him. He knew now that his worst fear would not be realized. The umpires would let him fight on his own. It would be too much of an anticlimax to decide anything different.

Shef stepped clear of his father's near embrace.

"I thank Sigvarth Jarl for his offer to bear my shield in this *holmgang*. But there is blood between us—he knows whose it is. I believe that he would support me loyally in this affair, and his help would mean much to a young man like myself. But I would not show *drengskapr* in accepting the offer."

Shef used the word for warriorhood, for honor—the word one used to show that you were above trifles, that you did not care for your own advantage. The word was a challenge. If one man laid claim to *drengskapr,* his opponent would be ashamed to show less.

"I say again: I have a shield, I have a weapon. If this is less than I should have, so much the better for Magnus. I say it is more. If I am wrong, then that is what we are fighting to see."

Halvdan Ragnarsson looked at his two co-arbiters, saw their nods of assent, and added his own. The two Hebrideans walked immediately inside the round of withies and took up their stations one beside the other: they knew any hesitation or further argument would look ill to the Army.

Shef walked over to face them, saw the two junior umpires taking their places to either hand, while Halvdan, in the middle, repeated the rules of the combat. Out of the corner of his eye he saw Sigvarth still standing well to the front of the others, joined now by the young man he had seen before, the one with a horse's projecting teeth. Hjörvarth Jarlsson, he thought detachedly. His half brother. Just behind the pair of them stood a rank of men with Thorvin in their center. Even though he strove to keep his mind on Halvdan's exposition he saw that each was wearing a silver pendant, prominently displayed. Thorvin had at least mustered a body of opinion, in case it could have an effect.

". . . combatants must strike alternately. If you try to strike twice, even if your enemy is off guard, you forfeit the *holmgang* and become liable to the judgement of the umpires. And it will not be light! So, begin. Magnus, as injured party, shall be the first to strike."

Halvdan stepped back, eyes wary, sword drawn to strike up any illegal blow. Shef found himself in the midst of a great silence, face-to-face with his two enemies.

He swung his halberd forward and trained the point on Magnus's face, left hand gripping the weapon just below its massive and complex head. His right hand down by his right side, ready to seize the haft to block or parry in any direction. Magnus frowned, realizing he must now step to one side or the other and signal his direction. He stepped forward and right, to the very edge of the line Halvdan had drawn in the mud to separate the combatants. His sword swung down, forehand, aimed at the head, the most elementary stroke possible. He wants to get this over with, thought Shef. The blow was merciless and lightning-quick. He swung up his left arm to catch it squarely in the center of the iron buckler.

A clang, a recoil. The blow left a dull line and a dent the length of the buckler. What it had done to the edge of the sword-blade, Shef, as a smith, did not like to think.

Magnus was back behind his line now, Kolbein stepping forward with the shield to cover him. Shef raised the halberd with both hands over his right shoulder, stepped forward to the edge of the line and stabbed point-first straight forward at Magnus's heart, ignoring the covering of the shield. The triangular lance-head drove through the lindenwood as if it were cheese, but as it did so, Kolbein jerked it up, so that the point stabbed past Magnus's cheek. Shef jerked back, twisted, jerked again, freeing the weapon with a crunch of broken wood. Now there was a gaping hole in the gay blue paint of the shield, and Kolbein and Magnus looked at each other with grave expressions.

Magnus came forward again, and realized that he must not strike on the buckler side. He swung backhand, but still at the head, still thinking that a man without proper sword and shield must needs be at a disadvantage. Without shifting grip, Shef swung the head of his halberd eighteen inches sideways at the descending sword, catching it not with the axe-side but with the reverse, the thumb-wide iron spike.

The sword flew out of Magnus's grasp, to land well on Shef's side of the line. All eyes flew to the umpires. Shef stepped back a pace, two paces, looked firmly at the sky. A buzz as the audience realized what was happening, a low growl of approval—a growl that went on as the keenly intent audience began to realize the potentialities of Shef's weapon and the problem the two Hebrideans were facing. Stone-faced, Magnus stepped forward, recovered his blade, hesitated, then saluted briefly with it and returned to his side of the line.

This time Shef swung the weapon over his left shoulder, and struck like a woodsman felling a tree, left hand sliding down the weapon as it swung, concentrating all his force and all the weight of the seven feet of metal behind the slicing half-yard of blade. Kolbein leapt quickly and decisively to save his partner, and got the shield well up above head height. The axe slashed through its edge and swung on, turned only slightly by the resistance of the metal rim, shore through two feet of lindenwood, and embedded itself with a thunk in the muddy ground. Shef jerked it free and stood once more on guard.

Kolbein looked at the half-shield still strapped to his arm and muttered something to Magnus. Impassive, Halvdan Ragnarsson stepped forward, picked up the severed oval of wood and tossed it to one side.

"Shields may only be replaced at the agreement of both parties," he observed. "Strike."

Magnus stepped forward with something like desperation in his eyes now, and swung a wicked blow with no warning, just above knee height. A swordsman would have jumped it, or tried to—it was just above the height a man might be expected to manage. Shef moved his right hand slightly and stopped the blow dead with his weapon's metal-reinforced shaft. Almost before Magnus could regain the shelter of his partner's shield, he was stepping forward, this time swinging upward, with the spike side foremost. A thump as it met the remnants of the shield, a resistance which this time was not one of wood alone, Kolbein staring at the foot-long spike which had driven through shield and forearm, splitting ulna and humerus bones.

Stone-faced, Shef slid his hand high up the head of the halberd, gripped tight, and jerked back. Kolbein staggered forward, put a foot over the line, recovered himself and straightened up, face white with shock and pain. There was a simultaneous yell as his foot went down, and then a confusion of cries.

"Fight's over, past the mark!"

"He struck at the shield-bearer!"

"He struck at the man. If the shield-bearer puts his arm in the way . . ."

"First blood to the smith, settle all bets!"

"Stop it now, stop it now," Thorvin called out. But over him an even louder voice, that of Sigvarth: "Let them fight it out! These are warriors, not girls to snivel at a scratch."

Shef looked sideways, saw Halvdan, grave but fascinated, wave the opponents on.

Kolbein was shaking, starting to fumble with the buckles of the useless shield, clearly unable to hold it up much longer. Magnus too had gone white. Each strike with the halberd had come close to killing him. Now he had no protection left. Yet there was no escape, no chance to run or surrender.

White-lipped, he stepped forward with the resolution of despair, raised the sword and swung straight down. It was a blow any active man could dodge without thinking; but in a *holmgang* you had to stand still. For the first time in the contest, Shef twisted his left hand and swung a parry, full force, with the axe edge of the halberd. It met the descending broadsword halfway down the blade and battered it aside, knocking Magnus off balance. As he recovered, he glanced at his weapon. It had not snapped off, but was cut halfway through, and bent out of line.

"Swords may only be replaced," intoned Halvdan, "by the agreement of both parties."

Magnus's face sagged with despair. He tried to pull himself together, to stand straight for the deathblow that must come. Kolbein shuffled a little forward and tried to pull his shield-arm up into place with his other hand.

Shef looked at the blade of his halberd, running a thumb over the nick that he had just put in it. Some careful work with a file, he reflected. The weapon was called "Thrall's-wreak." He was fighting because the man over there had murdered a thrall. Now was the time for vengeance, for that thrall and no doubt for many others.

But he had not knocked the Hebridean down because he had murdered a slave, but because he, Shef, had wanted the slave. Wanted to know about the machines the slave had made. Killing Magnus would not bring the knowledge back. Besides, he had more knowledge now.

In the utter silence Shef stepped back, drove his halberd point-first into the mud, unstrapped his buckler, threw it down. He turned to Halvdan and called out in a loud voice, making sure the whole Army could hear him.

"I give up this *holmgang,* and ask for the judgement of the umpires. I regret that I struck Magnus Ragnaldsson in anger, knocking out two of his front teeth, and if he will release me from the *holmgang* I offer him self-doom for that injury, and for the injury just inflicted on Kolbein his partner, and I ask for his friendship and support in the future."

A groan of disappointment mingled with shouts of approval. Yelling and pushing in the crowd as the two points of view found expression. Halvdan and the umpires pushed together to confer, after a few moments calling over the two Hebrideans to join their discussion. Then an agreement, slow quietening as the crowd waited to hear the decision and to ratify it. Shef felt no fear, no memory of the last time he had stood to hear a Ragnarsson pronounce. He knew he had judged the mood of the crowd rightly, and that the umpires would not dare to go against that.

"It is the judgement of all us three umpires that this *holmgang* has been fought well and fairly, with no discredit to any participant, and that you, Shef . . ." He struggled with the English name, could not pronounce it. ". . . *Skjef,* son of Sigvarth, had the right to offer to submit to judgement while it was your turn to strike." Halvdan stared round and repeated the point. "While it was your turn to strike. Accordingly, since Magnus Ragnaldsson is also prepared to accept a judgement, we declare that this contest may be ceased without penalty to either side."

Magnus the Hebridean stepped forward. "And I declare that I accept the offer of Skjef Sigvarthsson to self-doom for the injuries inflicted on me and on Kolbein Kolbrandsson, and we value them at half a mark of silver for each of us . . ." Whistles and hoots at the low rate set by the proverbially grasping islanders. ". . . on one condition:

"That Skjef Sigvarthsson, in his smithy, makes weapons for both of us similar to the one he wields, at the price of half a mark of silver each. And with this we admit him to our full friendship and support."

Magnus walked forward, grinning, clasped hands with Shef as Kolbein too shambled forward. Hund was inside the ring as well, seizing Kolbein's bleeding and already-swollen arm, clucking over the filthy state of the sleeve. Sigvarth was there also, hovering behind the duellers, trying to say something. An icy voice cut through the babble.

"Well, you are all agreed on one thing and another. If you had meant to stop fighting as soon as two drops of blood were shed, you could have done it all behind the privy and not wasted the whole Army's time.

"But tell me this, little dunghill cock—" The Boneless One's voice fell now into a pool of silence as he stalked forward, eyes blazing. "What do you think you can do to get my full friendship and support? Eh? For there is blood between us too. What can you offer me in exchange for it?"

Shef turned and pitched his voice high, allowing once again the note of challenge and contempt to brazen it, so that the Army would know Ivar had been dared.

"I can give you something, Ivar Ragnarsson, that I already tried to get for you once, but that we know you cannot get for yourself. No, I do not mean a woman's skirts . . ." Ivar swayed back, eyes never leaving Shef's face, and Shef knew that now Ivar would never leave him, never forget him till one or the other was dead. "No. Give me five hundred men and I will give you something to share with all of us. I will give you machines stronger than the Christians'. Weapons greater than the one I used here. And when I have all those I will give you something else.

"I will give you York!"

He ended with a shout, and the Army shouted with him, clashing their weapons in tumult and approval.

"It is a good brag," replied Ivar, glaring round at Sigvarth, at the Hebrideans, at Thorvin and his group of pendant-wearers, all clustered in support of Shef. "But it will be a sad one for the boy if he fails to carry it out."

CHAPTER FOUR

Hard to tell when dawn comes in an English winter, Shef thought. The clouds come down to the ground, the showers of rain or sleet come sweeping across—wherever the sun may be, it has to cut through layer after layer before the light gets through. He needed light for his own men, he needed light to see the English. Till he had it, they could all wait.

He moved his aching body beneath the layer of sweat-sodden wool that was his tunic and the layer of stiff boiled leather that was still the only armor he had had time to acquire. The sweat was chilling now, after the hours of gasping, whispering labor. More than anything he would like to strip everything off and rub himself dry on a cloak. The men in the darkness behind him must feel the same.

But each of them now had only one thing to think about, one duty to carry out, and that duty something painfully and repetitively drilled into them. Only Shef had the image in his mind of all the things that had to happen, all the parts that had to fit. Only he could see all the hundreds of things that could go wrong. Shef was not afraid of death or maiming, of pain or shame or disgrace—the usual terrors of the battlefield, to be dispersed by action and excitement and battle-fury. He was afraid of the unpredicted, the unexpected, the broken spoke, the slippery leaves, the unknown machine.

To an experienced jarl of the pirates, Shef would already have done everything wrong. His men were formed-up, but cold, tired, stiff and uncertain as to what was happening.

But this was going to be a new kind of battle. This one did not depend on how men felt or how well they fought. If everyone did as he was supposed to, nothing needed to be done well. It just needed to be done. This would be battle like ploughing a field, or tearing out tree-stumps. No valor, no heroic deeds.

Shef's eyes caught a spark of flame. Yes. More sparks, a growing bush of flame, more flames further away, all from separate sources. The shapes of buildings could be seen now, and smoke was beginning to pour from them, blown by the wind. The flames lit up the long line of wall with the gate that the Ragnarssons' ram had assaulted two weeks before. All along the line facing that eastern wall, men were setting fire to the houses. Long trails of smoke billowing out, men rushing forward through it with ladders raised—a sudden assault, arrows flying, the blast of warhorns, more men coming forward as the first ones withdrew. The noise and flames and rushes were harmless. Soon enough the English leaders would realize this was a feint attack, would turn their attention elsewhere. But Shef remembered the desperate slowness and confusion of the Emneth levies; with the English what the leaders thought hardly mattered much. By the time they persuaded their men not to believe the evidence of their eyes he sincerely hoped that he would have the battle won.

The flame, the smoke. Warhorns on the ramparts blowing an alarm, faint signs of activity on the walls he could now see in front of him. Time to start.

Shef turned to his right and began deliberately to walk along the long line of houses above the north wall, his halberd swinging easily. Four hundred double-paces to count. As he reached forty he saw the great square bulk of the first war-machine, its crew clustered round it in the mouth of the alleyway where they had heaved it up with such immense labor. He nodded to them, reached out the butt of his halberd and tapped the man in front—Egil the hersir, from Skaane. Egil nodded solemnly and began to tramp his feet up and down, laboriously counting under his breath every time his left foot touched ground.

Nothing in the whole job had been harder than making them do that. It was not warlike. It was not the way drengir should behave. Their men might laugh at them. Anyway, how could a man keep count of so many? Five white pebbles Shef had given Egil, one for each hundred, and a black one for the final sixty. At five hundred and sixty paces Egil would move off —if he did not lose the count, if his men did not laugh. By then Shef

would have reached the far end of his line, turned, and paced back to his own station in the middle. He did not think Egil's men would laugh. The ten counters he had picked were all famous warriors. Dignity was something they defined.

That was a leader's job in the new kind of battle, Shef thought as he paced on. Picking men the way a carpenter picked pieces of wood for a house-frame. He counted eighty, saw the second war-machine, tapped Skuli the Bald, saw him grip his pebbles and start his count, paced on. And fitting together the pieces of the plan the way a carpenter would.

There had to be an easier way to do it all, he told himself as he passed the third and fourth machines. This would be easy for the Rome-folk, with their numbercraft. But he knew no forge hot enough to beat out this skill for him.

Brand's three crews manned the next three machines in the line. The Hebrideans came next, half a dozen of them clutching their newly forged halberds.

Strange, the volunteers he had got. After the *holmgang* he had asked Sigurth Snakeeye for five hundred men. He had needed more like two thousand in the end, not only to man the machines and make up the diversion squads, but above all else to form the labor gangs to forage for wood, to cut it into shape, to find or forge the massive nails he needed, to manhandle the great contrivances up the muddy slope from the Foss. But the men who had done the work had not been provided by Sigurth, Ivar, or any of the Ragnarssons, who after a few days had held aloof. They had been the men from the small crews, the uncommitted, the fringes of the Army. A high proportion of them wore the pendants of the Way.

Shef was uneasily aware that Thorvin's and Brand's beliefs about him were beginning to leak out into the ranks. People were beginning to tell stories about him.

If all went well they would have another to tell soon enough.

He reached the last machine at the count of four hundred and twelve, turned on his heel, striding out more briskly now as he realized his count was over. The light was strengthening all the time; the din was at its peak over by the eastern wall, smoke still rising in the murky air.

Unbidden, a verse came into his mind, a little English verse from his childhood:

In willow-ford, by woody bridge,
The old kings lie, keels beneath them . . .

No, that was wrong! It was *"Dust rose to heaven, dew fell to earth, night went forth"*—that was the verse . . . So what was the other verse . . . ?

He stopped, doubled over as if stricken by cramp. Something horrible, in his head, just when he had no time to deal with it. He struggled to rise. Saw Brand approaching, concern on his face.

"I lost my count."

"No matter. We can see forty paces now. We'll move when Gummi does. Just one thing . . ." Brand bent and muttered in Shef's ear. "A man's come up from the rear. He says the Ragnarssons aren't behind us. They're not following our lead."

"We'll do this ourselves, then. But I tell you: the Ragnarssons, anyone—those who don't fight, don't share!"

"They're moving."

Shef was back by his own machine, in the comforting smell of sawdust. He ducked inside its shell, hooked the axe-blade of his halberd over a broken nail he had hammered in himself last night, stepped to his appointed place at the rearmost push-bar, and hurled his weight forward. Slowly, the machine began to creak along the level ground toward the waiting wall.

To the English sentries, it seemed as if the houses moved. But not the little, squat wattle-and-daub houses they knew were there. Rather, it seemed to them as if thane's halls, church towers, belfries, were rolling toward them out of the rising mist. For weeks they had looked down from their wall at everything the eye could see. Now things were coming toward them at their own level. Were they rams? Disguised ladders? Screens for some other kind of devil-work? A hundred bows bent, loosed arrows. Useless. Anyone could see the constructions coming toward them would take no heed of bolts from a breast-bow.

But they had better weapons than that. Snarling, the thane of the northern gate hurled a white-faced fyrdman, a conscript in the service of some petty lord, back to his place on the battlements, seized one of his slave errand-runners, and barked at him.

"Go to the eastern tower! Tell the machine-folk there to shoot. You! Same tale, western tower. You! Back to the square, tell the men with the stone-hurler that there are machines coming up to the northern wall. Tell them *machines!* Definitely! Whatever is going on over there, this is not a feint attack. Go on, all of you, move!"

As they scattered he turned his attentions to his own troops, the ones off

guard pounding up the ladders to their places, the ones who had seen already shouting and pointing at the shapes rolling closer.

"Keep your minds on what you're doing," he bellowed. "Look down, for God's sake! Whatever these things are, they can't come up to the wall. And once they get close enough the priests' weapons will destroy them!"

If the Rome-soldiers still had been in the fortress, Shef had realized, there would have been a deep ditch at the base of the wall, which any stormer would have had to cross before trying any kind of escalade. Centuries of neglect and refuse-tipping had filled this in, had created a swelling, turf-grown mound five feet high and as many broad. A man who ran up it would still be a dozen feet below the often-patched battlements. It had not seemed dangerous to the defenders. Indeed, without their knowing it, it had become one more hindrance to the enemy.

As the siege-tower rolled up to the wall the men at the front raised a yell, the push-teams stepped up their pace to a half-trot. The machine rolled forward, met resistance from the swelling mound, shuddered to a halt. Immediately a dozen men ran forward from their positions behind the tower. Half of them held up heavy square shields to block the arrow-shower. The others carried picks and shovels. Without words they set instantly to cutting a track along the marks of the front wheels, throwing the earth aside like badgers.

Shef walked forward between the sweating push-teams and peered through the light planking across the machine's front. Weight, that had been the problem. In essence the tower was simply a square frame eight feet wide, twelve feet long, thirty feet high, running on six cartwheels. It was unstable and unwieldly, and the whole of both lower sides were made of the heaviest beams the houses and churches of Northumbria could provide. As defense against the English bolt-throwers. They had had to save weight somewhere, and Shef had decided to skimp at the front. The wood there was only shield-thickness. As he looked out, arrows thumped into it, driving their points through. Only inches away the diggers shoveled frantically to gain the extra two feet to advance the wheels.

That was it. As he turned to call to the push-teams there was a tumult of yells behind him, and a great crash. Shef spun round, heart leaping. A bolt? One of the giant boulders? No, not so bad. Some burly Englishman on the wall had hurled down a rock, weighing fifty pounds at least. It had crashed through the shielding and bounced into the front of the machine, splintering the planks. No matter. But there was a man down, too—Eystein, lying with his leg crooked right under the left-hand wheel, gaping up at the engine towering over him.

"Hold it!" The men checked as they gathered their muscles for the final heave that would have gone straight over Eystein's smashed leg.

"Hold it. Drag him clear, Stubbi. All right. Pick-and-shovel party back into cover. Heave now, boys, and make it a good one. There—she's home! Hammer in the piles, Brand, so she doesn't roll back. Drop the ladders. Archers to the top platform. Storming party, after me."

One pair of ladders took the heavily armed and armored men up twelve feet, all of them gasping now with exertion but swept along with excitement. More ladders, another twelve feet. A hand passed Shef his halberd, forgotten in the rush. He seized it, watched the men jamming close together on the top platform. Were they level with the wall?

Yes! He could see the battlements below him, not much more than knee height. There was an Englishman shooting upward. The point found a gap between the planks, whirred through till the shaft caught and snapped, ended an inch from his good eye. Shef broke it off and dropped it. The men were ready now, all waiting for the signal.

Shef laid the razor edge of his halberd to the rope and cut.

Immediately the drawbridge began to fall forward, slowly for a moment, then hurtling forward like a great hammer, its front edge weighted with sandbags. A thump, a cloud of sand blowing in the wind as a bag burst, bowstrings twanging just above him as the archers tried to keep the battlements clear.

Then a great grunt as Brand propelled his massive frame onto the drawbridge and hurled himself across, beard-axe raised. As Shef leapt to follow, arms closed round him from behind. He found himself staring over his shoulder at Ulf, the ship's cook, the biggest man in three crews, after Brand.

"Brand said not you. He said keep you out of trouble for a few minutes."

The men poured by, first the detailed storming party, then the rest of the machine's crew, flinging themselves up the ladders and across the drawbridge without a pause. Then the men from the pick-and-shovel teams followed the rest of Brand's crew. Shef struggled in Ulf's grip, feet off the ground, hearing the clash of weapons, the screaming and shouting of the battle.

As complete strangers from other crews began to haul themselves up the ladder, Ulf released his grip. Shef leapt out onto the drawbridge, out into the open air, and for the first time could see how his plan had worked.

In the gray light, the cleared ground between wall and outer city was dotted with immense bulks, giant animals of some unknown species that had crawled there to die. That one must have shed a wheel or broken an axle on a bit of uneven ground, maybe an old cesspit. The one beyond them, the Hebridean one, seemed to have reached the wall successfully. The drawbridge was still in place from tower to battlements, and as he watched, another group of men trotted over it. Another, not as successful. They had cut the rope and then the drawbridge had fallen just feet short of the wall. It hung limply, like an enormous tongue from an eyeless face. Mailed bodies lay at the base of the wall beneath it.

Shef stepped off the drawbridge to let another wave of stormers pass by, then began to count. Three towers had not reached the wall, two had failed to get their men over the wall once they had reached it. That meant at most, five successful breaches. That had been enough. But they would have lost more if they had been slower, Shef thought. Or if they had not all come at once.

There must be a rule there. How would you say it? Maybe, in Norse, "Höggva ekki hyggiask." Hit 'em, don't think about it. One heavy blow, not a string of little ones. Brand would think that a good rule, once it was explained to him.

He looked up and saw in the sky what for weeks he had seen in his dreams, in his nightmares: the gigantic boulder rising with superhuman ease, still rising after all sense demanded that it must stop, reaching a peak. Starting to come down. Not on him. On the tower.

Shef cringed in terror—not for his own skin but for the appalling crash that must come, the ripping and rending as all the timbers and wheels and axles he had sweated over sprang apart. The Viking on the bridge cringed too and threw up a useless shield.

A thud, a ripple of loose earth. Hardly believing, Shef gaped at the boulder now embedded in the earth twenty feet from the side of his tower, looking as if it had been there since the dawn of creation. They had missed. Missed by yards. He had not thought they could.

The man in front of him, a burly figure in mail, was hurled aside.

Blood in the air, a thrum like the bottom note of a giant's harp, a line in the air that came too fast to be seen and drove in and through the warrior's body.

The bolt-machine as well as the boulder-machine. Shef stepped to the edge of the wall and looked down at the broken body now sprawled at its foot. Well, they might be in action now—but one had missed and both were too late. They must still be captured.

"Come on, don't stand there like young maidens who've just seen the bull!" Shef gestured angrily at the men clustered in the tower's exit. "It will take them an hour to wind their machines again. Follow me now and we'll see they don't get the chance."

He turned and loped along the walkway behind the battlements, Ulf striding like an enormous nursemaid a pace behind.

They found Brand just inside the now-opened gates, in an open space scattered with the familiar debris of battle: split shields, bent weapons, bodies, incongruously, a torn shoe somehow parted from its owner. Brand was breathing hard, and sucking a scratch on his bare arm above his gauntlets, but otherwise was unhurt. Men were still pushing through the gates, being hailed and directed by the skippers according to some plan already agreed upon, all done with an air of frantic haste. As they approached, Brand called two senior warriors over to him and gave brief instructions.

"Sumarrfugl, take six men, go round all the bodies here, strip all the Englishmen and pile what you find over by that house there. Mail, weapons, chains, jewelry, purses. Don't forget to check under their armpits. Thorstein, take another six and go do the same job up along the walls. Don't get cut off and don't take any risks. Bring back all the stuff you find and pile it with Sumarrfugl's. When you've done that you can sort out our own dead and wounded. Now—you there, Thorvin!"

The priest appeared through the gates, leading a laden packhorse.

"You've got your gear? I want you to stay here till we've secured the

Minster and then come right along as soon as I send a squad for you. Then you can set your forge up and start melting down the take.

"The take!" Brand's eyes gleamed with delight. "I can smell that farm in Halogaland already. Estate! County! All right, let's get going."

Shef stepped forward as he swung on his heel and grabbed an elbow.

"Brand, I need twenty men."

"What for?"

"To secure the shooting-machine up in the corner tower, and then go on to the throwing one."

The champion turned, still eying the confusion around him. He grasped Shef's shoulder in enormous metal fingers, squeezed gently.

"Young madman. Young snotnose. You have done great things today. But remember—men fight to rake together money. Money!" He used the Norse word fe, which meant every form of property together, money and metal and goods and livestock. "So forget your machines for a day, young hammerer, and let's all go get rich!"

"But if we have—"

Shef felt the fingers tighten crushingly on his collarbone.

"Now I have told you. And remember, you are still a carl in the Army, like all of us. We fight together, we share together. And by the shining tits of Gerth the Maiden, we are going to loot together. Now get in the ranks!"

Moments later, five hundred men were tramping in dense column into the mouth of one of the streets of the inner city, heading firmly in the direction of the minster. Shef, at the rear, stared at a mail-clad back, hefted his halberd, looked longingly over his shoulder at the little groups left behind.

"Come along," urged Ulf. "Don't worry, Brand left enough men there to guard the loot. It's share and share alike in the Army, and everyone knows it. They're only there to keep off any stragglers from the English."

The advancing column had speeded up almost to a trot and at the same time had shaken out into the familiar wedge-shape Shef remembered from his first skirmish. Twice it met resistance: makeshift barricades across the narrow street, desperate Northumbrian thanes hacking at their enemies across the war-linden while their churls and followers hurled javelins and stones from the houses above them. The Vikings stormed up, exchanged blows, poured into the houses, dislodged the archers and spear-throwers, broke down interior walls to take the English from flank and rear, acting all the time without orders and without pause, with a dreadful killing urgency. Each time there was a check, Shef seized his chance to struggle closer to the front, aiming for the broad back of Brand. He had to let them take the minster, he realized. But maybe once the loot had been secured, the precious relics of centuries, he could be spared some men to seize the machines. And above all, he must be near the leaders to save prisoners' lives—the lives of the skilled men, the number-workers.

The Vikings were up to a trot again, Brand only a couple of ranks in front of him. A turn in the narrow street, the men on the inside slowing fractionally to let their mates on the outside keep up—and there was the minster, looming suddenly above them like the work of giants, not sixty paces off, set back in its own precinct from the lesser buildings huddled round it.

And there too were the Northumbrians again, coming on one last time with the valor of desperation and the house of their God behind them.

The Vikings checked their rush, heaved shields high again. Shef, still thrusting forward, found himself suddenly level with Brand, saw a Northumbrian broadsword swinging like a meteor at his neck.

Without thought he parried, felt the familiar clang of a breaking blade, stabbed forward with the lance-head of the halberd, twisted and jerked to tear his enemy's shield aside. His back to Brand's, he lashed out blindly with a full-armed sweep. Space round him, enemies to all sides. He swung again, the axe-blade of the halberd hissing in the air, changed grip, and swept back as his enemies tried to dart in beneath the blows. A miss and another miss, but in those instants the Vikings had re-formed. Their wedge surged forward, the broadswords cutting from all angles, Brand leading them, swinging his axe with a joiner's precision.

As one wave the storming column broke over the English defenders, trampling them down. Shef found himself propelled forward at a run into open space, clear ground all around him, the minster in front, whoops of exultation in his ears.

Dazzled by the sudden gleam of sunshine he saw in front of him— saffron cloaks. Unbelievably, the familiar grinning face of Muirtach, driving a spike into the ground. A line of spikes, roped together, like the rowan-berry line that guarded Thorvin's forge. The whoops died uncertainly.

"Well-run, boys. But ye're off limits here. No one over the rope, d'ye hear?"

Muirtach backed away, spreading his arms, as Brand stepped forward. "Now take it easy, lads. Ye'll get yer share, I make no doubt. But it's all been fixed over yer heads. Ye'd have got yer share even if yer attack had failed, now."

"They came in the back," shouted Shef. "They never followed us this morning at all. They broke in the west gate while we attacked the north!"

"Broke in, nothing," snarled a furious voice. "They were let in. Look!"

Out from the minster door, as composed as ever, still dressed in scarlet and grass-green, strolled Ivar. By his side paced a figure in a garb Shef had not seen since the death of Ragnar a year before: a man in purple and white, a strange, tall hat on his head, a gold-decorated crook of ivory in his hand. As if automatically, he raised his other hand in benediction. The Archbishop of the Metropolitan Province of Eoforwich himself, Wulfhere *Eboracensis*.

"We've done a deal," said Ivar. "The Christ-folk offered to let us into the town on condition the minster itself was spared. I gave my word on it. We can have everything else: the town, the shire, the king's property, everything. But not the minster or the belongings of the Church. And the Christ-folk will be our friends and show us just how to wring this land dry."

"But you are a jarl of the Army," bellowed Brand. "You have no right to make deals for yourself and leave the rest of us out."

Theatrically, Ivar moved one shoulder, rotating it and grimacing with exaggerated pain.

"I see your hand is recovered, Brand. When I too am fit we will have several matters to talk over. But keep your side of the rope! And keep your men in hand or they'll suffer for it.

"Boys too," he added, his eyes falling on Shef.

From behind the minster men had been pouring, the Ragnarssons' personal followers in hundreds—fully armed, fresh, confident, eyeing their scattered and weary comrades coldly. The Snakeeye stepped out from among them, his two other brothers flanking him—Halvdan looking grim, Ubbi for once shamefaced, eyes on the ground as he spoke.

"You did well to get here. Sorry you got a surprise. It will all be explained in full meeting. But what Ivar says is right. Stay outside this rope. Keep away from the minster. Apart from that you can get as rich as you like."

"Small chance of that," shouted an anonymous voice. "What gold do the Christ-priests leave for anyone else?"

The Snakeeye made no reply. His brother Ivar turned, gestured. Behind the Ragnarssons a pole rose into the sky, was driven firmly into the packed earth in front of the minster doors. A jerk on a rope and from it spread— fluttering limply in the damp wind—the famous Raven Banner, the brothers' personal ensign, wings spread wide for victory.

Slowly, the once-united group who had stormed the wall and fought their way through the city lost cohesion, began to break up, mutter among themselves, count their losses.

"Well, they may have the minster," muttered Shef to himself. "But we can still get at the machines."

"Brand," he called. "Brand. *Now* can I have those twenty men?"

CHAPTER FIVE

A group of men sat together in pale winter sunlight in a leafless copse outside the walls of York. Cords encircled them, rowan berries dangling scarlet between the spears. It was a conclave of priests, all the priests of the Asgarth Way who had accompanied the Army of the Ragnarssons: Thorvin for Thor, Ingulf for Ithun, but others too—Vestmund the navigator, charter of the stars, priest of Njörth the sea-god; Geirulf the chronicler of battles, priest of Tyr; Skaldfinn the interpreter, priest of Heimdall. Most respected of all for his visions and his travels in the other worlds, Farman, priest of Frey.

Within their circle was planted the silver spear of Othin, next to it the sacred fire of Loki. But no priest in the Army cared to take the great responsibility of the spear of Othin. There had never been a priest of Loki —though that he existed was never forgotten.

Inside the roped circle, but sitting apart and silent, were two laymen, Brand the champion and Hund the apprentice of Ithun. There to give evidence and, if asked, advice.

Farman spoke, looking round the group. "It is time to consider our position."

Silent nods of agreement. These were not men to talk without need.

"We all know that the history of the world, *heimsins kringla*, the circle of the earth, is not foreordained. But many of us have seen for many years a vision of the world as it seems it must be.

"A world where the Christ-god is supreme. Where for a thousand years and more men are subject to him alone and to his priests. Then, at the end of that thousand years—the burning and the famine. And all through the thousand years, the fight to keep men as they are, to tell them to forget this world and think only of the next. As if Ragnarök—the battle of gods and men and giants—were already decided and men were sure of victory." His face was as stern as stone as he looked at the circle of priests.

"It is against that world that we have set our faces, and it is that future which we mean to avert. You will remember that by chance I heard in London of the death of Ragnar Hairy-Breeks. Then it came to me in my sleep that this was one of those moments when the history of the world may take a different turn. And so I called on Brand"—he waved a hand at the massive figure hunkered down a few feet away—"to take the news to the sons of Ragnar, and to take it in such a way that they could not refuse the challenge. Few men might have survived that errand. Yet Brand did it, as a duty to us, in the name of the one who will come from the North. Come from the North, we believe, to set the world on its true path."

The men in the circle touched their pendants respectfully.

Farman went on. "It was in my mind that the sons of Ragnar, falling on the Christian kingdoms of England, might break their power and be a mighty force for us, for the Way. I was a fool to guess at the meaning of the gods. A fool, too, to think that good might come from the evil of the Ragnarssons. They are not Christians, but what they do gives the Christians strength. Torture. Violation. The making of *heimnars*."

Ingulf, Hund's master, cut in. "Ivar—he is of the brood of Loki, sent to afflict the earth. He has been seen on the other side—and not as man. He is not one to be used for any good purpose."

"As now we see," replied Farman. "For far from breaking the power of the Christ-god church, he has made alliance with it. For his own ends—and only that fool of an archbishop would trust him. Yet for the moment both are stronger."

"And we are poorer!" growled Brand, driven beyond respect.

"But is Ivar richer?" asked Vestmund. "I cannot see what Ivar and his brothers have from this deal they have made. Except entry into York."

"I can tell you that," said Thorvin. "For I have looked well into this matter. We have all seen how poor their money is here. Little silver, much lead, much copper. Where has all the silver gone? Even the English ask each other that. I can tell you. The Church has taken it.

"We do not understand—even Ivar cannot know—how rich the Church in Northumbria is. They have been here two hundred years and all that time they have taken gifts of silver, and of gold, and of land. And from the land they wring more silver, and from the land they do not own they wring yet more. To splash a child with water, to make her wedding holy, in the end to bury them in holy soil and take away the threat of eternal torment—not for their sins, but for failure to pay the toll."

"But what do they do with this silver?" Farman asked.

"They make ornaments for their god. It all lies now in the minster, as useless as when it was first in the soil. The silver and the gold in their chalices, in their great roods and rood-screens, in the plates for the altar and the boxes for the bodies of their saints—it comes out of the money. The richer the Church, the poorer the coinage." He shook his head in disgust.

"The Church will hand nothing over—and Ivar does not even know what lies in his hand. The priests have told him that they will call in all the coins of the realm and melt them down. Purge out the base metal and leave him only the silver. And then with that they will make him a new coinage. A coinage for Ivar the Victorious, king of York. And Dublin too.

"The Ragnarssons may not be richer. They will be more powerful."

"And Brand, son of Barn, will be poorer!" snarled an angry voice.

"So what we have done," summed up Skaldfinn, "is to bring the Ragnarssons and the Christ-priests together. How sure are you now of your dream, Farman? And what of the world's history and of its future?"

"There is one thing I did not dream then," replied Farman. "But I have dreamed him since. And that is the boy Skjef."

"His name is Shef," put in Hund.

Farman nodded agreement. "Think of it. He defied Ivar. He fought the *holmgang*. He broke the walls of York. And he walked up to Thorvin's meeting months ago and said he was one who came from the North."

"He only meant he came from the north part of the kingdom, from the Northfolk," protested Hund.

"What he meant is one thing, what the gods mean is another," said Farman. "Do not forget also: I saw him on the other side. In the home of the gods itself.

"And there is another strange thing about him. Who is his father? Sigvarth Jarl thinks he is. But for that we have only his mother's word. It comes to me that perhaps this boy is the beginning of the great change, the center of the circle, though no one could have guessed it. And so I have to ask his friends and those who know him a question:

"Is the boy mad?"

Slowly, eyes turned to Ingulf. He raised his eyebrows.

"Mad? That is not a word to be used by a leech. But since you put it to me in that way, I will tell you. Yes, of course the boy Shef is mad. Consider . . ." Hund found his friend, as he had known he would, standing amid a litter of charred wood and iron at the northeast tower, above the Aldwark, surrounded by a knot of interested pendant-wearers. He slipped between them like an eel.

"Have you worked it out yet?" he asked.

Shef looked up. "I think I have the answer now. There was a monk with each machine, whose duty was to see it destroyed instead of captured. They started the job, then scuttled back to the Minster. The men they left behind had no great desire to see the burning finished. This slave was captured," he nodded at a collared Englishman inside the ring of Vikings. "He told me how it worked. I haven't tried to rebuild the machine, but I understand it now."

He indicated the pile of charred timbers and iron devices.

"This is the machine that fires the bolts."

Shef pointed. "See, the spring is not in the wood, it is in the rope. Twisted rope. This axle is turned and twists the rope which puts more and more force on each bow-arm and the bowstring. Then, at the right moment, you release the bowstring . . ."

"Wham," said one of the Vikings. "And there goes old Tonni."

A grunt of laughter. Shef pointed at the toothed wheels on the frame. "See the rust on them? They are as old as time. I do not know how long it is since the Rome-folk left, or if these things have been lying round in some armory ever since. But anyway, they were not made by the minster-folk. It is all they can do to use them."

"What of the great boulder-machine?"

"They burnt that better. But I already knew how they were made before we got over the wall. The minster-folk had all that in a book, and the parts of the machine also, left over from olden times, so the slave says. I am sorry they burnt it all, for that alone. And I should like to see the book that tells how to build machines. That and the book of numbercraft!"

"Erkenbert has the numbercraft," said the slave suddenly, catching the Norse word in Shef's still faintly English pronunciation. "He is the *arithmeticus.*"

Several Vikings clutched their pendants protectively. Shef laughed.

"*Arithmeticus* or no *arithmeticus,* I can build a better machine than him. Many machines. The thrall says he heard a minster-man say once, of themselves and the Rome-folk, that the Christians now are as dwarves on the shoulders of giants. Well, they may have the giants to ride on, with their books and their old machines and old walls left over from time past. But they are dwarves just the same. And we, we are—"

"Do not say it," cut in a Viking, stepping forward. "Do not say the ill-luck word, Skjef Sigvarthsson. We are not giants, and the giants—the *iötnar*—are the foes of gods and men. I think you know that. Have you not seen them?"

Shef nodded slowly, thinking of his dream of the uncompleted walls and the gigantic, clumsy stallion-master. His audience stirred again, looking at each other.

Shef threw the iron parts he was holding onto the floor. "Let the slave go, Steinulf, in payment for what he has told us. Show him how to get well away from here, so the Ragnarssons do not catch him. We can make our own machine without him now."

"Have we time to do it?" asked a Viking.

"All we need is wood. And a little work in the forge. There are still two days till the Army meeting."

"It is new knowledge," added one of the listeners. "Thorvin would tell us to do it."

"Meet here tomorrow, in the morning," said Shef decisively.

As they turned away, one of the Vikings said, "They will be a long two days for King Ella. It was a dog's deed of the Christian archbishop to hand him over to Ivar. Ivar has much in store for him."

Shef stared at the departing backs and turned again to his friend.

"What is that you have there?"

"A potion from Ingulf. For you."

"I need no potion. What is it for?"

Hund hesitated. "He says it is to ease your mind. And—and to bring back your memory."

"What is wrong with my memory?"

"Shef, Ingulf and Thorvin say—they say you have forgotten even that we blinded your eye. That Thorvin held you and Ingulf heated the needle, and I, I held it in position. We only did it so it would not be done by some butcher of Ivar's. But they say that it is not natural for you never to speak of it. They believe you have forgotten your blinding. And forgotten Godive, for whom you went into the camp."

Shef stared down at the little leech with his silver apple pendant.

"You can tell them, I have never forgotten either for a moment.

"But still." He stretched out his hand. "I will take your potion."

"He took the potion," Ingulf said.

"Shef is like the bird in the old story," Thorvin said. "The one the Christians tell of how the English in the North became Christian. They say that when the king Edwin called a council to debate whether he and his kingdom should leave the faith of their fathers and take a new one, a priest of the Aesir had said they might as well, for following the old gods had brought him no profit. But then another councillor said, and this is a truer tale, that to him the world seemed like a king's hall on a winter evening— warm and brightly lit inside, but outside dark and cold, and a world no one could see. 'And into that hall,' said the councillor, 'flies a bird, and for a moment it is in the light and the warm, and then flies out into the dark and cold again. If the Christ-god can tell us more surely about what happens before man's life and after man's life,' said the councillor, 'we should seek to learn more of his teaching.' "

"A good story, with some truth," Ingulf said. "I see why you think Shef could be like that bird."

"He could—or he could be something else. When Farman saw him in his vision, in Asgarth, he says he had taken the place of the smith of the gods, Völund. You do not know that story, Hund. Völund was caught and enslaved by the wicked king Nithhad, and hamstrung so that he could work, but not run away. But Völund enticed the king's sons to his forge, killed them, made brooches of their eyeballs and necklaces of their teeth, gave them to their father, his master. Enticed the king's daughter to his forge, stupefied her with beer, raped her."

"Why would he do that if he was still a prisoner?" asked Hund. "If he was too lame to run away?"

"He was the master-smith," said Thorvin. "When the king's daughter awoke, and ran to her father and told him the tale, and he came to kill the slave-smith with torments—then Völund put on the wings he had made secretly in his forge. And flew away, laughing at those who thought him crippled."

"So why is Shef like Völund?"

"He can see up and down. In a direction other men cannot see. It is a great gift, but I fear it is the gift of Othin. Othin Allfather. Othin Bölverk, Othin Bale-worker. Your potion will make him dream, Ingulf. But what will be in those dreams?"

Shef's sinking mind was brooding on taste. The potion Ingulf had sent him had tasted of honey, which was a change from the foul brews he and Hund usually concocted. Yet beneath the sweetness there had been another taste: of mold? of fungus? He did not know, but something dry and rotten beneath the mask. He had known as soon as he drank it that there would be something to be endured.

And yet his dream started sweetly, like one he had had many times before any of his troubles began, before even he had known that they meant him for a thrall.

He was swimming, in the fen. But as he swam on and on the power of his strokes doubled and redoubled, so that the bank seemed to fall away behind him and he was swimming faster than a horse could run. Now his strokes took him clear from the water and he was lifting in the air, no longer striking with his arms, but first climbing, and then, as fear left him, sweeping forward again, rising higher and higher in the air, like a bird. The country beneath him was green and sunny, with the new leaves of spring breaking out everywhere, and meadow rolling higher and higher to sunlit uplands. Suddenly dark. In front of him now there was an immense column of darkness. He had, he knew, been there before. But then he had been in the column, or on the column, looking out: he did not want to see again what he had seen then. The king, the king Edmund, with his sad and tortured face and his backbone in his hand. If he flew in carefully, and did not look out or back, he might not see him this time.

Slowly, cautiously, the wandering soul closed on the enormous darkened tree-trunk. To it was nailed, as he had known there would be, a figure with a spike projecting from its eye. He looked at the face with care—was it his own?

It was not. Its one whole eye was closed. It appeared to take no interest in him.

By the figure's head there hovered two black birds, with black beaks: ravens. They turned bright eyes on him, cocking their heads curiously. The flight pinions of their wings ruffled and shifted slightly as they maintained their positions without strain or effort. The figure was Othin, or Woden, and the ravens were his constant companions.

What were their names? That was the important thing. He had heard them somewhere. In Norse they were— That was right, Hugin and Munin. In English that would be Hyge and Myne. Hugin/Hyge. That meant "mind." That was not the one he wanted. As if dismissed, the one raven spiraled down, perched on its master's shoulder.

Munin/Myne. That meant "memory." That was what he wanted. But he would have to pay for it. He had a friend, a protector among the gods, so much he realized already. But it was not Othin, whatever Brand might think. So a price must be paid. He knew what the price must be. Again unbidden, another scrap of verse came to him, again in English. It described the hanged man, on the gallows, who swayed there creaking for the birds, unable to raise a hand to protect himself, while the black ravens came. . . .

Came for his eyes. For his eye. The bird was there suddenly, so close that it blocked out all other sight, its black beak like an arrow only an inch from his eye. Not his good eye, though. His bad eye. The one he had already lost. But this was memory, back in a time when he still had it. His hands were down, he could not move them. That was because Thorvin was holding them. No, he could move them this time, but he must not. He would not.

The bird realized he would not move. It came forward with a shriek of triumph, driving its nail of a beak deep through his eye and into his brain. As the white-hot pain stabbed through him, the words shot into his head: the words of the doomed king.

In willow ford, by woody bridge
The old kings lie, keels beneath them.
On down they sleep, deep home guarding.
Four fingers push in flattest line,
From underground. Grave the northmost.
There lies Wuffa, Wehha's offspring,
On secret hoard. Seek who dares it.

He had done his duty. The bird released him. He fell instantly from the tree-trunk, tumbling without control, hands still locked, toward the ground miles below. Plenty of time to think what to do. No need for hands. He could just turn his body whichever way was needed, turn and roll till he was heading out into the sun once more, turn and dip till he was spiraling down gently to the place where he should be, where his body lay on straw.

Strange to see the land from here, and the people and the armies and the merchants coming and going, many of them spurring furiously, but not moving at all beneath his enormous twenty-mile circuits. He could see the fen, he could see the sea, he could see the great tumuli, the barrows swelling up beneath green turf. He would remember that, think of it another time. Now he had only one duty, and he would carry it out as soon as his spirit was back in its right place, in the body he could now see on its mattress, in the body he was entering. . . .

Shef jerked from sleep in one motion. "I must remember, but I cannot write," he called in dismay.

"I can," said Thorvin, on his stool six feet away, dimly visible by the banked fire.

"Can you? Write like a Christian?"

"I can write like a Christian. But I can write like a Norseman too, or a priest of the Way. I can write in runes. What do you want me to write?"

"Write it quickly," said Shef. "I bought this from Munin with pain."

Thorvin kept his eyes down as he took a beech board and a knife and prepared to cut.

" *'In willow ford, by woody bridge*
The old kings lie, keels beneath them. . . .' "

"It is hard to write English in runes," Thorvin muttered. But he muttered it beneath his breath.

The Army mustered—in distrust and ill humor, three weeks before the day the Christians celebrated the birth of their God—on the open space outside the city's east wall. Seven thousand men take up a good deal of space, especially when all are both fully armed and heavily wrapped against the wind and intermittent sleet. But since Shef had fired the remaining houses on that side there was room enough to spread everyone in a rough half-circle from wall to wall.

In the midst of the semicircle stood the Ragnarssons and their supporters, the Raven Banner behind them. A few paces away, gripped and encircled by a flutter of saffron plaids, waited the black-haired figure of the king —of the ex-king Ella. His face was as white, Shef reflected from his place in the semicircle thirty yards away, as white as the white of a cooked egg.

For Ella was doomed. The Army had not pronounced yet, but it was certain as fate. Soon Ella would hear the clash of weapons by which the Army signaled assent. And then they would start on him, as they had on

Shef, as they had on King Edmund, on King Maelguala and all the other Irish kinglets on whom Ivar had sharpened his teeth and his techniques. There was no hope for Ella. He had put Ragnar in the orm-garth. Even Brand, even Thorvin accepted that a man's sons had a right to take revenge in kind. More than a right, a duty. The Army watched judiciously, to see that the job was done well and warriorlike.

But it sat, or rather stood, also in judgement on its own leaders. It was not only Ella who was at risk here. Not even Ivar Ragnarsson, not even Sigurth the Snakeeye himself, could this time be absolutely sure of walking from the meeting with a whole skin, or with an undamaged reputation. There was tension in the air.

As the sun reached what passed for midday in the English winter, Sigurth called the Army to business.

"We are the Great Army," he called out. "We are met to talk over what has been done and what should be done next. I have things to say. But first I hear that there are men in the Army who are not content with how this city was taken. Will one of them speak openly before us all?"

A man stepped forward from the ring, walked into the open space in the middle, and turned so that both his own supporters and the Ragnarssons could hear him. It was Skuli the Bald, who had led the second tower up to the wall, but had wrecked it without getting over.

"Put-up job," muttered Brand. "Been paid to speak, but not too hard."

"I am not content," called out Skuli. "I led my crews to attack the wall of this city. I lost a dozen men, including my brother-in-law, a good man. We got over the wall just the same and fought our way up to the minster. But then we were prevented from sacking the minster, as was our right. And we found that we did not need to lose the men, because the city was already taken. We got neither plunder nor compensation. Why did you let us attack the wall like fools, Sigurth, when you knew we had no need to?"

A rumble of agreement, some catcalls from Ragnarsson crews. Sigurth stepped forward in his turn, silencing the noise with a wave.

"I thank Skuli for saying this, and I admit that he has right on his side. But I want to say two things. First, I did not know he had no need to. We could not be sure that we would get in. The priests could have been lying to us. Or if the king had found it, he might have put his own men on the gate that was opened. If we had told the whole Army about it, some slave might have heard and passed the news. So we kept it to ourselves.

"The other thing I have to say is this: I did not think Skuli and his men would get over the wall. I did not think they would even get to the wall. These machines, these towers, they are something we have never seen before. I thought they were a toy, and that everything would be finished with just some arrowshot and wasted sweat. If I had known different I would have told Skuli not to risk his life and waste his men. I was wrong, and I am sorry."

Skuli nodded in a dignified way and walked back to his place.

"Not enough!" yelled a voice from the crowd. "What about compensation? Wergild for our losses!"

"How much did you get from the priests?" yelled another. "And why don't we all share?"

Sigurth raised a hand again. "That's more like it. I ask the Army: what are we here for?"

Brand stepped out, waving his axe, back of his neck purpling instantly with the effort in his shout. "Money!"

But even his voice was drowned in the chorus: "Money! Wealth! Gold and silver! Tribute!"

As the tumult died down, Sigurth shouted back. He had the meeting well in hand, Shef realized. All this was going according to a plan, and even Brand was going along with it.

"And what do you want the money *for?*" called Sigurth. Confusion, doubt, shouts of different answers—some ribald.

The Snakeeye drove on over them. "I'll tell you. You want to buy a place back home, with people to till it for you, and to never touch a plough again. Now I'm telling you this: there's not enough money here to get you what you want. Not good money." He threw a handful of coins derisively on the ground. The men recognized the useless low-alloy coinage they had found so often already.

"But that isn't to say we can't get it. Just that it's going to take time."

"Time for what, Sigurth? Time for you to hide your take?"

The Snakeeye stepped a little forward, his strange white-rimmed eyes searching the crowd for the man who had accused him. His hand reached for his sword-pommel.

"I know this is open meeting," he called, "where all may speak freely. But if anyone accuses me or my brothers of not acting like warriors, then we will call him to account for it outside the meeting!

"Now I tell you. We took a ransom from the minster, right enough. Those of you who stormed the wall took loot as well, from the dead and from the houses inside the wall. All of us profited from what was taken outside the minster."

"But all the gold was inside the minster!" That was Brand shouting, still incensed, and well forward so that he could not be mistaken.

A cold look from Sigurth, but no check. "I tell you. We will all pool all that we took—ransom, loot, whatever—and divide it up crew by crew as has always been the custom of the Army.

"And then we will lay a further tribute on this shire and this kingdom, to be delivered before the end of the winter. They will pay in bad metal, sure enough. But we will take that metal and melt the silver out of it and coin it again ourselves. And *that* we will divide up so that everyone gets his share.

"Only one thing. To do that we need the mint." A buzz as the unfamiliar word was repeated. "We need the men to make the coins and the tools to make them with. And they are in the minster. They are the Christian priests. I have never said this before, but I say it now.

"We have to make the priests work with us."

This time the dissension in the Army went on a long time, with many men stepping forward and speaking confusedly. Shef realized slowly that Sigurth's point was being carried, had a certain appeal to men tired of profitless harrying. Yet there was determined resistance—from adherents of the Way, from men who simply disliked and distrusted Christians, from those who still resented losing the sack of the minster.

And the resistance was not dying down. Violence at a meeting was almost unheard-of, for the penalties were so severe. Yet the crowd was fully armed, even to mail, shields and helmets, and every man in it used to striking out. There was always the chance of an outburst. The Snakeeye was going to have to do something, Shef thought, to get the crowd back under control. Just at the moment one man—it was Egil from Skaane, who had taken a tower to the wall—had got the attention of the Army with a furious diatribe about the treachery of the Christians.

"And one more thing," he shouted. "We know the Christians never keep their word to us, because they think that only the followers of their god will live after death. But I tell you what is more dangerous. They make other men start to forget their word as well. Start to think a man may say one thing one day and another another, and tell the priest and ask for forgiveness, and wipe away the past like a housewife wiping shit off a baby's bottom. And I say this for you! For you, the sons of Ragnar!"

He turned to face the cluster of brothers, stepping closer to them in defiance—a brave man, thought Shef, and an angry one. He threw back his cloak deliberately to reveal the silver horn of Heimdall gleaming on his tunic.

"How have you remembered your father, who went to his death in the orm-garth here, inside this city? How have you remembered the boasts you made in the hall at Roskilde, when you stood on the stock and made your vows to Bragi?

"What happens to the oath-breakers in the world we believe in? Have you forgotten?"

A voice supported him from the throng: a deep voice, a solemn one. Thorvin's, Shef realized, quoting the holy poems.

"There men writhe in woe and anguish,
Murder-wolves and men forsworn.
Nithhögg sucks blood from naked bodies,
The wolf tears them. Do you wish more?"

"Men forsworn!" shouted Egil. He turned and walked to his place, showing the Ragnarssons his back. Yet they seemed pleased, almost relieved. They had known someone would say it.

"We have been challenged," called Halvdan Ragnarsson, speaking for the first time. "Let us reply. We know well what we said in the hall at Roskilde, and this was it: I swore that I would invade England in vengeance for my father . . ." All four brothers, bunching together, began to call out the words in unison.

"And so I have. And Sigurth, he swore . . ."

". . . to defeat all the kings of the English and bring them into subjection to us."

"Two I have defeated, and the rest will follow."

Yells of approval from the Ragnarsson followers.

"And Ivar, he swore . . ."

". . . to wreak vengeance on the black crows, the Christ-priests who counseled the orm-garth."

Dead silence, for Ivar to speak.

"And this I have not done. But it is unfinished, not forgotten. Remember: the black crows are now in my hand. I shall decide when to close it."

Still dead silence. Ivar went on. "But Ubbi, my brother, he swore . . ."

The brothers in unison again. ". . . to capture King Ella and kill him with torments for Ragnar's death."

"And this we shall do," called Ivar. "So two of our boasts will be completed, and two of us free before Bragi, the oath-god. And the other two we shall yet complete."

"Bring out the prisoner!"

Muirtach and his gang were hustling him forward instantly. The Ragnarssons were counting on this, Shef realized, to alter the mood of the crowd. He remembered the youth who had shown him round the slave-pens back at the camp on the Stour, with his tales of the cruelty of Ivar. There were always some who would be impressed. Yet it was not clear that this crowd was.

They had Ella well out in front now, and were hammering a thick pole into the earth. The king was even whiter than before, the black hair and beard showing it even more clearly. He was not gagged, his mouth was open, but no sound came out. There was blood on the side of his neck.

"Ivar's cut his voice-cords," said Brand suddenly. "They do it with pigs so they can't squeal. What's the brazier for?"

The Gaddgedlar, hands padded, were lifting forward a brazier full of glowing coal. Irons projected from it ominously, already shining red-hot. The crowd surged and muttered, some pushing forward for a closer look, others sensing, apparently, that this was a distraction from their real business, but unsure how to reject it.

Muirtach whisked the cloak suddenly from the doomed man so that he stood naked before them, not even a loincloth to cover him. Some laughter, some jeers, some groans of disapproval. Four Gaddgedlar gripped him and spread-eagled him upright between them. Ivar stepped in front, a knife glinting in his hand. He bent towards Ella's belly, between the king and Shef's horrified gaze, not a dozen yards off. A mighty contortion, a thrashing of limbs, held mercilessly by the four apostates.

Ivar stepped back, a coil of something blue-gray and slippery in his hand.

"He's opened his belly and pulled his gut out," commented Brand.

Ivar stepped over to the pole, pulling gently but remorselessly on the uncoiling intestine, watching the look of despair and agony on the king's face with a half-smile. He reached the pole, took a hammer, nailed in the free end he had extracted.

"Now," he called out. "King Ella will walk round the pole till he pulls his own heart out and dies. Come, Englishman. The quicker you walk, the quicker it will be over. But it may take a few turns before you reach that. You have ten yards to walk, by my count. Is that so much to ask? Start him, Muirtach."

The henchman stepped forward, brand glowing, thrust it against the doomed king's buttock. A convulsive start, a face turning gray, a slow shuffle.

This was the worst death a man could face, thought Shef. No pride, no dignity. The only way out, to do what your enemies wanted, and to be jeered for it. Knowing you must do it and come to an end, and yet not able to do it quickly. The hot irons behind so you could not even choose your own pace. Not even a voice to scream. And all the time your bowels pulling out from inside.

He passed his halberd silently to Brand, and slipped back through the shoving, craning crowd. There were faces looking down from the tower where he had left his helpers to keep an eye on their machine. A rope snaking down as they realized what he wanted. A scramble up the wall to the familiar clean smell of new-sawn wood and new-forged iron.

"He has walked round the pole three times," said one of the Vikings on the tower, a man with the phallus of Frey round his neck. "That is no way for any man to go."

Bolt in place, the machine swiveled round—they had thought, yesterday, to rest the bottom frame on a pair of stout wheels. Barb upright between the vanes, three hundred yards, it would still shoot a little high.

Shef aimed the tip of the barb on the wound at the base of the king's belly as he hobbled round to face the wall a fourth time, red-hot brands urging him on. Shef squeezed the release slowly.

The thump, the line rising and falling—clear through the center of Ella's chest and straining heart, and on into the ground behind him, almost between Muirtach's feet. As the king was hurled backward by the force of the blow, Shef saw his face change. Relax in peace.

Slowly the crowd rippled, every face in it turning to face the tower from which the shot had come. Ivar bent over the corpse, but then straightened, turning too, hands clenched.

Shef took one of the new halberds and went down the wall toward the throng, wanting to be recognized. At the edge of the semicircle he stopped, vaulted onto the battlement.

"I am only a carl," he called out, "not a jarl. But I have three things to say to the Army:

"First, the sons of Ragnar fulfilled this bit of their Bragi boast because they had no heart to fulfill the rest.

"And second, whatever the Snakeeye says, when he sneaked into York by the back door with the priest holding it open for him, he was not thinking of the Army's good, but of his own and of his brothers'. He had no mind to fight and no mind to share."

Shouts of anger, the Gaddgedlar whirling, looking for the gate into the city and the steps up to where Shef stood. Others obstructing them, grabbing at their plaids. Shef raised his voice even more above the din.

"And third: to treat a man and a warrior the way they treated King Ella has no *drengskapr*. I call it *nithingsverk*."

The work of a *nithing,* a man beneath honor, a man with no legal rights, worse than an outlaw. To be proclaimed *nithing* before the Army was the worst shame a carl—or a jarl—could endure. If the Army agreed.

Some people were shouting agreement. Shef could see Brand down there, axe raised now and ready to strike, his men clustering behind him, thrusting off Ragnarsson followers with their shields. A stream of men coming from the other side of the circle to join him—Egil the Heimdall-worshipper at their head. Who was that moving out? Sigvarth, face flushed as he shouted reply to some insult. Skuli the Bald wavering by Ella's corpse as Ubbi bellowed something at him.

The whole Army was moving. Dividing. After a hundred heartbeats there was space between the two groups and both were edging further away from each other. The Ragnarssons in front of the furthest group; in front of the nearer one, Brand, Thorvin, a handful of others.

"It is the Way against the rest," muttered the Frey-worshiper behind Shef. "And some of your friends thrown in. Two to one against us, I reckon."

"You have split the Army," said a Hebridean, one of Magnus's crew. "It is a great deed, but a rash one."

"The machine was wound," replied Shef. "All I had to do was shoot it."

CHAPTER SIX

As the army marched away from the walls of York, snowflakes started to drift out of the windless sky. Not the Great Army. The Great Army would never exist again. That part of the once-great army which now refused the command of the Ragnarssons and could no longer live in fellowship with them—perhaps twenty long hundreds of men, two thousand four hundred by the Roman count. With them were a host of horses, pack-horses, pack-mules and fifty wooden carts creaking along with their burden of heavy loot: bronze and iron, smith-tools and grindstones—along with the chests of poor coinage and a meager handful of true silver from the division. Their burden, too, of wounded men not fit to march or straddle a pony.

From the city walls, the rest of the army watched them go. Some of the younger and wilder members had whooped and jeered, even launched a few arrows at the ground behind their former messmates. But the silence of the marching column, and of their own leaders on the wall, cast down their spirits. They pulled their cloaks tighter about them, and looked up at the sky, the lowering horizon, the frostbitten grass on the slopes outside the city. Grateful for their own billets, stored firewood, shuttered windows and draftless walls.

"It will snow harder before tomorrow's dawn," muttered Brand from his position at the rear of the column, the main point of danger till they were well past the Ragnarssons' reach.

"You are Norsemen," replied Shef. "I thought snow would not bother you."

"All right while the frost stays hard," said Brand. "If it snows and then thaws, like it does in this country, we'll be marching through mud. Tires the men out, tires the beasts out, slows the carts even more. And when you're marching in those conditions, you need food. You know how long it takes an ox-team to eat its own weight? But we must put some distance between us and those behind. No telling what they'll do now."

"Where are we making for?" asked Shef.

"I don't know. Who's leading this army anyway? Everybody else thinks you are."

Shef fell silent, in consternation.

As the last bundled figures of the rear-guard disappeared from view among the ruined houses of outer York, the Ragnarssons on the wall turned and looked at each other.

"Good riddance," said Ubbi. "Fewer mouths to feed, fewer hands to share. What are a few hundred Way-folk anyway? Soft hands, weak stomachs."

"No one ever called Viga-Brand soft-handed," replied Halvdan. Since the holmgang he had been slow to join in his brothers' attacks on Shef and his faction. "They're not all Way-folk, either."

"It doesn't matter what they are," said Sigurth. "They're enemies now. That's all you ever need to know about anyone. But we can't afford to fight them just yet. We have to keep our hold on . . ."

He jerked his thumb at the little cluster a few yards away from them on the wall: Wulfhere the archbishop with a knot of black monks, among them the scrawny pallor of Erkenbert the deacon, now master of the mint.

Ivar laughed, suddenly. His three brothers looked at him with unease.

"We don't need to fight them," he said. "Their own bane marches with them. For some it does."

Wulfhere too scowled at the retreating column. "Some of the blood-wolves gone," he said. "If they had gone earlier we might never have needed to treat with the rest. But now they are within our gates." He spoke in Latin, to make sure hostile ears did not overhear.

"We must, in these days of strife, live by the wisdom of the serpent," replied Erkenbert in the same language, "and by the cunning of the dove. But both our foes without the gates and those within may yet be overcome."

"Those within I understand. There are fewer of them now, and they may be fought again. Not by us in Northumbria. But by the kings of the South —Burgred of Mercia, Ethelred of Wessex. That is why we sent south the crippled thane of East Anglia, slung between his ponies. He will show the southern kings the nature of the Vikings and wake their drowsy spirits to war.

"But what, Erkenbert, is your plan for those now marching away? What can we do in dead of winter?"

The little deacon smiled. "Those marching in winter need food, and the ravagers of the North are accustomed to take it. But every mouthful they steal now is one less for a man's children before spring comes. Even churls will fight with that incentive.

"I have seen to it that the word of their coming will run before them."

The attacks began as the short winter daylight seeped from the sky. At first they were little more than scuffles: a churl appearing from behind a tree, launching a stone or an arrow downwind, and then fleeing hastily, not even waiting to see if he hit the mark. Then a little knot of them coming in closer. The marching Vikings unslung bows if they had them, tried to keep the bowstrings dry, shot back. Otherwise they ducked heads behind shields, let the missiles bounce off, shouted derisively to their foes to stand and fight. Then one, irritated, launched a spear at a darting figure who seemed to come too close, missed and plunged off the track with a curse to recover it. For an instant a snow-flurry hid him. When it cleared he was nowhere to be seen. With difficulty his crewmates halted the column, plodding, head-down, and set off grimly to rescue him, a group thirty strong. As they lurched back with the body, already stripped and muti-lated, the arrows came whipping from behind them again, out of the murk of the dying day.

The column was now spread over almost a mile of road. Skippers and helmsmen pushed and cursed the men into a thicker, shorter line, bow-men on both flanks, carts in the center. "They can't hurt you," Brand bellowed repeatedly. "Not with hunting bows. Just shout and bang your shields; they'll wet themselves and run. Anyone gets hit in the leg, sling him on a packhorse. Dump some of that junk in the carts if you have to. But keep moving forward."

Soon the English churls began to recognize what they could do. Their enemies were laden with gear, heavily wrapped and muffled. They did not know the country. The churls knew every tree, bush, path and patch of mud. They could strip to tunics and hose, rush in light-footed, strike and

slash and be away before an arm was free of its cloak. No Viking would
pursue more than a few feet into the gloom.

After a while some village war-leader organized the growing number of
men. Forty or fifty of the churls came in together on the west flank of the
column, beat down the few men they faced with clubs and billhooks,
started to drag off the bodies like wolves with their prey. Furious, the
Vikings rallied and charged after them, shields up, axes raised. As they
straggled back, snarling, having caught no one, they saw the halted carts,
the ox-teams poleaxed where they stood. The wagon tilts pulled open,
their cargo of wounded men a burden no longer, the snow already blotting
out the stains.

Prowling up and down the column like an ice-troll, Brand turned to
Shef at his side. "They think they've got us now," he snarled. "But come
daylight I'll teach them a lesson for this if it's the last thing I ever do."

Shef stared at him, blinking the snow from his eyes. "No," he said. "You
are thinking like a carl, a carl of the Army. There is no Army anymore. So
now we must forget to think like carls. Instead we must think as you say I
do, like a follower of Othin, orderer of battle."

"And what are your orders, little man? Little man who has never stood
in a battle-line?"

"Call over the skippers, as many as are within earshot." Shef began to
draw swiftly in the snow.

"We marched through Eskrick, here, before the snow got bad. We must
be a short mile north of Riccall." Nods, understanding. The area around
York was well known from much foraging.

"I want one hundred picked men, young men, quick on their feet, not
yet tired, to push ahead now and secure Riccall. Take some prisoners—
we'll need them—chase the others out. We will stay there the night. Not
much, fifty huts and a church of wattles. But they will shelter a lot of us if
we pack in close.

"Another long hundred in four small groups to keep moving up and
down on our flanks. The English won't rush in if they even think there
might be someone out there to cut them off. Without their cloaks they'll
keep warm running. Everyone else, just keep going and keep the carts
going. As soon as we reach Riccall, use the carts to block all the gaps
between the huts. Oxen and all of us on the inside of the ring. We'll make
fires and rig up shelters. Brand, pick the men, get everyone moving."

Two crowded hours later, Shef sat on a stool in the thane's longhouse of
Riccall, staring at a grizzled elderly Englishman. The house was packed

with Vikings, stretched out or squatting on their heels, already steaming as massed body heat dried the sodden clothes on their backs. As ordered, none paid any attention to what was going on.

Between the two men, on the rough table, stood a leather mug of beer. Shef took a pull at it, looked closely at the man facing him; he seemed to still have his wits about him. There was an iron collar round his neck.

Shef pushed the mug toward him. "You saw me drink, you know there is no poison. Go on, drink. If I wanted to harm you there are easier ways."

The thrall's eyes widened at the fluent English. He took the mug, drank deeply.

"Who is the lord you pay your rents to?"

The man finished the beer before he spoke. "Thane Ednoth holds much of the land, from King Ella. Killed in the battle. The rest belongs to the black monks."

"Did you pay your rents last Michaelmas? If you did not, I hope you hid the money. The monks are severe with defaulters."

A flash of fear when Shef spoke of the monks and their retribution.

"If you wear a collar, you know what the monks do with runaways. Hund, show him your neck."

Silently Hund unslung his Ithun pendant and handed it to Shef, pulled back his tunic to reveal the calluses and weals worn into his neck by years of the collar.

"Have any runaways been here? Men who spoke to you of these." Shef bounced the Ithun pendant in his hand, passed it back to Hund. "Or those." He pointed to Thorvin, Vestmund, Farman and the other priests, clustered nearby. Following the gesture, they too silently displayed their insignia.

"If they did, maybe they told you such men might be trusted."

The slave lowered his eyes, trembled. "I'm a good Christian. I don't know about no pagan things. . . ."

"I'm talking about trust—not pagan or Christian."

"You Vikings are men who take slaves, not men who set them free."

Shef reached forward and tapped the iron collar. "It was not the Vikings who put that on you. Anyway, I am an Englishman. Can you not tell from my speech? Now listen closely. I am going to let you go. Tell those out there in the night to stop the attacks, because we are not their enemies— they are still in York. If your fellows let us pass, no one will get hurt. Then tell your friends about this banner."

Shef pointed across the smoky, steaming room to a clutch of the army's drabs, who rose from the floor and stretched out the great banner at which they had been frantically stitching. There, on a background of red silk, taken from the carts of plunder, a double-headed smith's hammer in white linen was picked out with silver thread.

"The other army, the one we have left, marches behind the black raven, the carrion bird. I say that the sign of the Christians is for torture and death. Our sign is the sign of a maker. Tell them that. And I will give you an earnest of what the hammer can do for you. We're taking off your collar."

The slave was shaking with fear. "No, the black monks, when they return . . ."

"They will kill you most horribly. Remember this and tell the others. We offered to free you, we pagans. But fear of the Christians is keeping you a slave. Now go."

"One thing I ask. In fear. Do not kill me for speaking of it but—your men are emptying the meal-bins, taking our winter store. There'll be empty bellies and dead bairns before spring comes if you do that."

Shef sighed. This was going to be the hard bit. "Brand. Pay the thrall. Pay him something. Pay him in good silver, mind, not the archbishop's dross."

"Me pay him! He should pay me. What about the wergild for the men we have lost? And since when did the Army pay for its supplies?"

"There is no Army now. And he owes you no wergild. You trespassed on his land. Pay him. I'll see you don't lose by it."

Brand muttered under his breath as he untied his purse and began to count out six silver Wessex pennies.

The slave could scarcely believe what was happening, staring at the shining coins as though he had never seen money like this before; perhaps he hadn't.

"I will tell them," he said, almost shouting the words. "About the banner too."

"If you do that, and return here tonight, I will pay you six more—for you alone, not to share."

Brand, Thorvin and the others looked doubtfully at Shef as the slave went out, with an escort to see him outside the sentry-fires.

"You'll never see money nor slave again," Brand said.

"We'll see. Now I want two long hundreds of men, with our best horses, all with a good meal inside them, ready to move as soon as the slave returns."

Brand pushed a shutter open a crack and looked at the night and the whirling snow. "What for?" he grunted.

"I need to get your twelve pennies back. And I have another idea." Slowly, intense concentration furrowing his brow, Shef began to scratch lines into the table in front of him with the point of his knife.

The black monks of St. John's Minster at Beverley, unlike those of St. Peter's at York, did not have the safe walls of a legionary fortress round them. Instead, their tenants and the men of the flatlands east of the Yorkshire Wolds could easily put two thousand stout warriors into the field, with many more half-armed spearmen and bowmen to back them. All through the autumn of raids of York, they had known themselves safe against anything but a move by a major detachment of the Great Army. They had known it must come. The sacristan had disappeared months since with all the minster's most precious relics, reappearing days later with word only for the abbot himself. They had kept half their fighting force mobilized, the rest dispersed among their holdings to oversee the harvest and the preparations for winter. Tonight they felt secure. Their watchers had seen the Great Army split, one detachment even marching away to the South.

But a midwinter night in England is sixteen hours long between sunset and dawn: more than time enough for determined men to ride forty miles. Guided on their way through muddy, meandering farm-tracks for the first few miles, then picking up speed as they walked or trotted their horses along the better roads of the Wolds. They had lost a little time circumventing each village they came to. The slave, Tida, had guided them well, abandoning them only as the first paling sky had shown them the steeple of Beverley Minster itself. The guard-huts just beginning to disgorge sleepy female quern-slaves, to light the fires and grind the grain for the breakfast porridge. At the sight of the Vikings they ran shrieking and wailing, to drag incredulous warriors from their blankets. To be called fools for their pains and to become part of the utter confusion which was the English way of taking surprise.

Shef pushed open the great wooden doors of the minster and walked in, his companions jostling behind.

From inside the minster came the antiphonal song of the choirmonks, facing each other across the nave and singing sweetly the anthems which called the Christ-child to be born. There were no other worshippers, though the doors were unbolted for them. The monks sang lauds every day, whether they were joined or not. At dawn on a winter morning they would not expect to be.

As the Vikings paced down the aisle which led to the high altar—still wrapped in sodden cloaks, no weapons showing except for the halberd over Shef's shoulder—the abbot looked at them in shocked horror from his great seat in the choir. For a moment Shef's nerve and wit faltered in the face of the majesty of the Church he had grown up in, worshipped in.

He cleared his throat, unsure how to begin.

Guthmund behind him, a skipper from the Swedish shore of the Kattegat, had no such doubts or scruples. All his life he had wanted to be at the sack of a really first-class church or abbey, and he had no intention of letting a beginner's nerves spoil it. Courteously he picked his young leader up and put him to one side, seized the nearest choir-monk by his black robe and hurled him into the aisle, dragged his axe from under his cloak and embedded it with a thunk into the altar-rail.

"Grab the blackrobes," he bellowed. "Search 'em, put 'em in that corner there. Tofi, get those candlesticks. Frani, I want all that plate. Snok and Uggi, you're lightweights, see that statue there . . ." He waved at the great crucifix, high above the altar, looking down at them with sorrowing eyes. "Shin up it and see if you can get that crown off, looks genuine from here. The rest of you, turn everything over and shake it, grab everything that looks as if it might gleam. I want this place clear before those bastards behind us have got their boots on. Now, you . . ." He advanced on the abbot shrinking back in his throne.

Shef forced his way between them. "Now, father," he began, speaking again in English. The familiar language drew a basilisk stare from the abbot, terrified but at the same time mortally offended. Shef wavered a moment—then remembered the inside of the minster door, covered, like many, with skin on the inside. Human skin, flayed from a living body for the sin of sacrilege, of laying hands on Church property. He hardened his heart.

"Your guards will be here soon. If you want to stay alive you will have to keep your men off."

"No!"

"Then you die now." The point of his halberd pushed at the priest's throat.

"For how long?" The abbot's shaking hands were on the halberd, could not move it back.

"Not long. Then you may hunt us, recover your stolen goods. So do as I say . . ."

Crashes of destruction behind, a monk being dragged forward by Guthmund. "I think this is the sacristan. He says the hoard is empty."

"True," the abbot admitted. "All was hidden months ago."

"What's hidden can be found again," said Guthmund. "I'll start on the youngest, just to show I mean it. One, two dead, the hoard-keeper will speak."

"You will not," Shef ordered. "We'll take them with us. There will be no torture among those who follow the Way. The Asa-gods forbid it. And we have taken a fair haul. Now get them out where the minster-guards can see them. We still have a long ride ahead."

In the growing light, Shef noticed something hanging on the wall: a flattened roll of vellum with no image on it that he could recognize.

"What's that?" he asked the abbot.

"It has no value to one like you. No gold, no silver on the frame. It is a *mappamundi*. A map of the world."

Shef tore it down, rolled it, thrust it deep inside his tunic as they hustled the abbot and the choirmonks out to face the ragged battle-line of Englishmen at last roused from bed.

"We'll never make it back," muttered Guthmund again as he clutched a clanking sack.

"Not going back," answered Shef. "You'll see."

CHAPTER SEVEN

Burgred, king of Mercia, one of the two great kingdoms of England still unconquered by the Vikings, paused at the entrance to his private chambers, dismissed the crowd of attendants and hangers-on, doffed his mantle of marten-fur, allowed his snow-soaked boots to be removed and replaced by slippers of soft whittawed leather, and prepared to enjoy the moment. By command, the young man and his father were waiting for him, as was the atheling Alfred, there to represent his brother Ethelred, king of Wessex —the other surviving great English kingdom.

The issue before them was the fate of East Anglia. Its king dead with no successor, its people demoralized and uncertain. Yet Burgred knew well that if he marched an army to take it over, to add it to Mercia by force, the East Angles might well fight, Englishmen against Englishmen, as they had so often before. But if he sent them a man of their own, he calculated—one of noble blood, one who nevertheless owed absolutely everything, including the army he led with him, to King Burgred—well, that they might swallow.

Especially as this particular noble and grateful young man had such a very useful father. One who, so to speak—Burgred allowed himself a grim smile—carried his anti-Viking credentials with him. Who could fail to rally to such a figurehead? A figure-head and -trunk, indeed. Burgred blessed, silently, the day the two ponies with their leaders and their slung stretcher had brought him in from York.

And the beautiful young woman too. How affecting it had been. The young man, fair hair swept back, kneeling at his father's feet before ever they had unstrapped him from his litter, and begging forgiveness for having married without his father's consent. The pair might have been forgiven for more than that after all they had been through, but no, young Alfgar had been the essence of propriety all through. It was the spirit that would one day make the English the greatest of all nations. Decency, mused Burgred: *gedafenlicnis*.

What Alfgar had really muttered as he knelt at his father's feet had been: "I married Godive, father. I know she's my half sister, but don't say anything of it, or I'll tell everyone you're mad. And then an accident could happen to you. Men with no arms smother easily. And don't forget, we're both your children. If we succeed, your grandsons could still be princes. Or better."

And after the first shock, it had seemed well enough to Wulfgar. True, they had committed incest, "sibb-laying," as the English called it. But what did a trifle like that matter? Thryth, his own lady, had committed fornication with a heathen Viking, and who had done anything about that? If Alfgar and Godive had an incest child like Sigemund and his sister in the legends, it could be no worse than that gadderling brat he, Wulfgar, had been fool enough to rear.

As the king of the Mercians strode into the room, the men in it rose and bowed. The one woman, the East Anglian beauty with the sad face and the brilliant eyes, rose and made her courtesy in the new style of the Franks. Two attendants—they had been arguing quietly about the right thing to do —lifted Wulfgar's padded box to the vertical before leaning it back against the wall. At a gesture they resumed their seats: stools for all but the king and the heimnar. Wulfgar too was lifted into a high seat with wooden arms. He could not have balanced himself to sit on a stool.

"I have news from Eoforwich," began the king. "Later news than you brought," with a nod to Wulfgar. "And better news. Still, it has decided me to act.

"It seems that after the surrender by the Church of the town and of King Ella—"

"Say, rather," cut in the young atheling from Wessex, "the disgraceful betrayal of King Ella by those he had protected."

Burgred frowned. The young man, he had noticed, had little sense of respect to kings, and none at all for senior members of the Church.

"After the surrender of King Ella, he was unhappily put to death in vile manner by the heathen Ragnarssons, and especially the one called the

Boneless. Just as happened to your master, the noble Edmund," he added, nodding again to Wulfgar.

"But it seems that this caused dissension among the heathens. Indeed there is a strange story that the execution was put to an end by a *machine* of some kind. Everything at Eoforwich seems to have something about machines attached to it.

"Yet the important news is the dissension. For after it the Viking army split."

Mutters of surprise and pleasure.

"Some of them have now left Eoforwich and are marching south. A lesser part of the Army, but still formidable. Where, I must ask myself, are they heading? And I say, they are heading back to East Anglia, from where they came."

"Back to their ships," snapped Alfgar.

"That could well be. Now, I do not think the East Anglians will fight them again. They lost their king and too many leaders, thanes and warriors in the battle by the Stour, from which you, young man, so valiantly fought your way. Yet, as you have all been telling me," Burgred glanced sarcastically at Alfred, "the Vikings must be fought.

"So I shall send East Anglia a war-leader, with a strong force of my men to support him till he can rally his own.

"You, young man. Alfgar, son of Wulfgar. You are of the North-folk. Your father was a thane of King Edmund. Your family has lost more, suffered more and dared more than any other. You will put the kingdom back on its feet.

"Only it can no longer be a kingdom."

Burgred locked eyes with the young atheling, Alfred of Wessex: eyes as blue and hair as blond as Alfgar's, a true prince of a royal line. But something queer, cross-grained about him. A clever look. They both knew that this was the sticking point. Burgred of Mercia had no more claim to East Anglia than Ethelred of Wessex. Yet the one who filled the gap would clearly become the mightier of the two.

"What would my title be?" asked Alfgar carefully.

"Alderman. Of the North-folk and the South-folk."

"Those are two shires," objected Alfred. "A man cannot be alderman of two shires at once."

"New times, new things," replied Burgred. "But what you say is true. In time, Alfgar, you may win a new title. You may be what the priests call *subregulus*. You may be my under-king. Say, will you be loyal to me and to Mercia? to the Mark?"

Alfgar knelt silently at the king's feet and put his hands between the king's knees in token of subjection. The king patted his shoulder and lifted him up.

"We will do this more formally by and by. I just wanted to know we are all agreed." He turned to Alfred. "And yes, young atheling, I know you have not agreed. But tell your king and brother the way of it is now this. Let him stay his side of the Thames and I'll stay mine. But north of the Thames and south of the Humber: that belongs to me. All of it."

Burgred let the tense silence hang a moment and then thought to disperse it. "One strange piece of news they told me. The Ragnarssons have always led the Great Army, but they have all stayed in Eoforwich. Those who marched away are said to have no leaders, or many. But one report is that among their leaders, or their main leader, is an Englishman. A man of the East Angles by his speech, the messenger said. But he could only give me what the Vikings call him, and they speak English so badly I could not make it out as a man's name at all. They call him Skjef Sigvarthsson. Now what could that be in English? Even in East Anglian?"

"Shef!" It was the silent woman who had spoken. Or gasped. Her eyes, her brilliant liquid eyes, blazed with life. Her husband stared at her like one who measures a back for the birch, while her father-in-law goggled and reddened.

"I thought you saw him dead," snarled the heimnar accusingly at his son.

"I will yet," muttered Alfgar. "Just give me the men."

Nearly two hundred miles to the north, Shef turned once again in his saddle to see if the rear-guard was keeping up. Important to have everyone well closed up, all within earshot of each other. Shef knew that four times his own number were pounding the filthy road behind him, unable to attack while Shef held his thirty hostages, the choirmonks of St. John's and their abbot Saxwulf. It was important too to keep up the pace, even after their long night's ride, to outrun the news of their coming and prevent any arrangement being made for their reception.

The smell of the sea led them on—and there, as they came trampling over a slight rise, there as an unmistakable landmark was Flamborough Head itself. Shef urged the vanguard on with a yell and a wave.

Guthmund dropped back a yard or two, hand still clutching the bridle of the abbot's horse. Shef waved him over. "Keep up—and keep the abbot close to me."

With a whoop he spurred his tiring gelding forward, catching up just as the whole cavalcade, a hundred and twenty raiders and thirty hostages, stormed down the long slope into the squalid huddle of Bridlington.

Instant confusion. Women running, snatching up blue-legged ragged children, men seizing spears, dropping them again, some racing for shelter down to the beach and the boats drawn up on the dirty snow-covered sand. Shef wheeled his horse and thrust the abbot forward like a trophy, instantly recognizable in his black robes.

"Peace," he shouted. "Peace. I want Ordlaf."

But Ordlaf was already there, the reeve of Bridlington, the capturer—though no one had ever credited him with it—of Ragnar. He stepped forward from his people, eyeing the Vikings and the monks with amazement, reluctantly taking responsibility.

"Show them the abbot," Shef snapped to Guthmund. "Make those behind keep their distance." He pointed at Ordlaf the reeve. "You and I have met before. The day you netted Ragnar."

Dismounting, he drove his halberd-spike deep into the sandy soil. Putting his hand on the reeve's shoulder, he drew him a little away, out of earshot of the wrathfully glaring abbot, began to speak in urgent tones.

"It's impossible," said Ordlaf a minute later. "Can't be done."

"Why not? It's a high sea, and cold, but the wind is from the west."

"Southwest a point west," corrected Ordlaf automatically.

"You can run downcoast with it on your beam. To the Spurn. Twenty-five miles, no more. Be there by dark. Never out of sight of land. I'm not asking for a sea-crossing. If the weather changes we can drop sea-anchor and ride it out."

"We'd be pulling into the teeth of it once we got to the Spurn."

Shef jerked a thumb over his shoulder. "Best rowers in the world, right with you. You can set them to it and stand back at the steering oar like lords."

"Well . . . What happens when I get back and the abbot sends his men down to burn me out?"

"You did it to save the abbot's life."

"I doubt he'll be grateful."

"You can take your time coming back. Time enough to hide what we'll pay you. Silver from the minster. Your silver. Your rents for many a year. Hide it, melt it down. They'll never trace it."

"Well . . . How do I know you won't just cut my throat? And my men's?"

"You don't—but you have little choice. Decide."

The reeve hesitated a moment longer. Remembered Merla, his wife's cousin, whom the abbot behind him had enslaved for debt. Thought of Merla's own wife and bairns, living still on charity with their man fled in terror.

"All right. But make it look as if you're treating me rough."

Shef exploded with feigned rage, swung a blow at the reeve's head, whipped a dirk from its scabbard. The reeve turned away, shouting orders at the little knot of men who had collected at a few yards' distance. Slowly men began to push beached fishing boats towards the tide, to step masts, haul sailcloth from sheds. In a tight huddle the Vikings pressed down to the water's edge, hustling their captives. Fifty yards away, five hundred English riders pressed forward, ready to charge sooner than see the hostages taken off, held back by the bright weapons waving over tonsured heads.

"Keep them back," snapped Shef to the abbot. "I'll let half your men go when we board. You and the rest go in a dinghy once we're afloat."

"I suppose you realize this means we lose the horses," said Guthmund gloomily.

"You stole them in the first place. You can steal some more."

"So we pulled into the mouth of the Humber under oars just at dusk, beached for the night when we were sure no one could see us, then rowed upriver in the morning to meet the rest of you. With the take."

"How much is it?" asked Brand, sitting with the other members of the impromptu council.

"I've weighed it out," said Thorvin. "Altar-plate, candlesticks, those little boxes the Christians keep saints' finger-bones in, box for the holy wafers, those things for burning incense, some coins—a lot of coins. I thought monks weren't supposed to have property of their own, but Guthmund says they all had purses if you shook them hard enough. Well, after what he gave the fishermen we still have ninety-two pounds weight of silver.

"Better than that is the gold. The crown you took off the Christ-image was pure gold, and heavy. So was some of the plate. That's another fourteen pounds. And we reckon gold as outvaluing silver eight for one. So that counts as eight stone of silver: a hundredweight to add to your ninety-two pounds."

"Two hundred pounds, all told," said Brand thoughtfully. "We will have to divide it all between crews and let the crews make their own division."

"No," said Shef.

"You say that a lot these days," Brand said.

"That is because I know what to do—others don't. The money is not to be divided. It is the war chest of the army. That was why I went for it. If we divide it up everyone will be a little richer. I want to use it so that everyone becomes a lot richer."

"If it's put like that," said Thorvin, "I think the army will accept it. You got it. You have a right to say how you think it should be used. But how are we all going to get a lot richer?"

Shef pulled from the front of his tunic the *mappamundi* he had taken from the minister wall. "Look at this," he said. A dozen heads bent over the vast vellum sheet, faces wearing different degrees of puzzlement at the scrawled, inked marks.

"Can you read the writing?" asked Shef.

"In the middle there," said Skaldfinn the Heimdall-priest. "Where the little picture is. It says 'Hierusalem.' That is the holy city of the Christians."

"Lies, as usual," commented Thorvin. "That black border is supposed to be Ocean, the great sea that runs round Mithgarth, the world. They are saying their holy city is the center of everything, just as you would expect."

"Look round the edges," rumbled Brand. "See what it has to tell us of places we know. If it is lying about them, then we can guess it is all lies, as Thorvin says."

" '*Dacia et Gothia,*' " read Skaldfinn. " 'Gothia.' That must be the land of the Gautar, south of the Swedes. Unless they mean Gotland. But Gotland is an island, and this is marked as being mainland. Next to it—next to it they have 'Bulgaria.' "

The council broke into laughter. "The Bulgars are the enemies of the emperor of the Greeks, in Miklagarth," said Brand. "It is two months' travel from the nearest of the Gautar to the Bulgars."

"On the other side of Gothia they have 'Slesvic.' Well, at least that is clear enough. We all know Slesvik of the Danes. There is some more writing by it. '*Hic abundant leones.*' That means 'There are many lions here.' "

Again a roar of laughter. "I have been to Slesvik market a dozen times," said Brand. "And I have met men who have spoken of lions. They are like very large cats, and they live in the hot country south of Sarkland. But there has never been one lion in Slesvik, let alone many. You wasted your time bringing back this—what do you call it?—this *mappa*. It is just nonsense, like everything the Christians count as wisdom."

Shef's finger continued to trace lettering, while he muttered to himself the letters that Father Andreas had half-successfully taught him.

"There is some English writing here," he said. "In a different hand from the rest. It says '*Suth-Bryttas,*' that is, 'South British.' "

"He means the Bretons," Brand said. "They live on a large peninsula the other side of the English Sea."

"So that is not so far wrong. You can find truth on a *mappa*. If you put it there."

"I still don't see how it is going to make us rich," replied Brand. "That is what you said it was going to do."

"This won't." Shef rolled the vellum up, thrust it aside. "But the idea of it may. We need to know more important things. Remember—if we had not known where Riccall was, that day in the snow, we might have been cut off and destroyed in the end by the churls. When I set off for Beverley, I knew the direction, but I would never have found the minster if we had not had a guide who knew the roads. The only way I found Bridlington and the man who could sail us out of a trap was because I had traveled the road already.

"You see what I mean? We have plenty of knowledge, but it all depends on people. But no one person knows enough for all the things we need. What a *mappa* should be is a store of knowledge from many people. Now if we had that we could find our way to places we had not been before. We could tell directions, work out distances."

"So we make a knowledge *mappa*," said Brand firmly. "Now tell me about rich."

"We have one other precious possession," said Shef. "And this we did not get from the Christians. Thorvin will tell you. I bought it myself. From Munin, the raven of Othin. I bought it with pain. Show them, Thorvin."

From inside his tunic Thorvin pulled a thin square board. On it were lines of small runic letters, each one scratched with a knife and then marked out with red dye.

"It is a riddle. The one who solves the riddle will find the hoard of Raedwald, king of the East Angles. That is what Ivar was searching for last autumn. But the secret died with King Edmund."

"A *royal* hoard," said Brand. "Now that could be worth something, all right. But first we have to solve the riddle."

"That is what a *mappa* can do," said Shef firmly. "If we write down every piece of knowledge we can find, in the end we will have the right number of pieces to solve the riddle. But if we do not write them down, by the time we come on the last piece we need we will have forgotten the first.

"And there is another thing." Shef struggled with an image in his mind, a trace of memory from somewhere, of looking down—down on the land in a way no man could ever in reality see it. "Even this *mappa*. It has one idea. It is as if we were looking down on the world from above. Seeing it all spread out below us. Like an eagle would see it. Now that is the way to find things."

Guthmund the skipper broke the considering silence. "But before we see or find anything, we have to decide where we go now."

"More important even than that," said Brand, "we must decide how this army is led, and under what law it shall live. While we were men of the Great Army we lived under the old *hermanna lög* of our ancestors—the warriors' law. But Ivar the Boneless broke that and I have no wish to return to it. Now I know that not everyone in this army wears the pendant." He looked significantly at Shef and Guthmund in the group around the table. "But it is in my mind that we should now agree to live under a new law. *Vegmanna lög*, I would call it. The law of the Way-folk. The first stage to that, though, is for the army to agree in open assembly to whom it will give the powers to make the laws."

While they worked it out, Shef's mind drifted away, as it often did, from the wrangling debate that immediately broke out. He knew what the army would now have to do. March out of Northumbria to get away from the Ragnarssons, cross the shires of Burgred, the powerful king of the Mark, as fast as possible. Establish themselves in the kingless realm of the East Angles, and take toll of the population in return for protection. Protection from kings, protection from abbots and bishops. In a short while, toll on that scale would make even Brand feel contented.

Meanwhile he would work on the *mappa*. And on the riddle. And most important of all, if the Army of the Way was to protect its shires from other predators, he would have to give them new weapons. New machines.

As he began to draw, in his mind's eye, the lines of the new catapult, a voice broke through to his half-attention, arguing violently for a place in the council for all hereditary jarls.

That would include Sigvarth, his father, whose crews had joined the column leaving York almost at the last moment. He wished Sigvarth had remained behind. And his horse-toothed son, Hjörvarth. Still, maybe they need not meet. Maybe the Army would not make the rule about jarls.

Shef went back to wondering how he could replace the power of the slow and clumsy counterweight. His fingers itched again to hold a hammer.

CHAPTER EIGHT

our weeks later the itch in Shef's fingers had been eased. Outside the makeshift camp where the Wayman army had halted for the winter, he stood on the catapult range. But the machine he stood behind was not one the Rome-folk would have recognized.

"Lower away," he shouted to his eight-man team.

The long boom creaked down towards his waiting hands, the ten-pound rock in its leather sling dangling from two hooks, one fixed, one free.

"Take the strain." The eight brawny Vikings on the other end of the catapult's arm put their weight on the ropes and braced themselves for a pull. Shef felt the arm—it was the top sixteen feet of a longship's mast, sawn off a little above deck level—flex between their weight and his, felt himself beginning to lift off the sodden ground.

"Pull!" The Vikings heaved as one, each man putting his full body-weight and back strength into it, as beautifully coordinated as if they had been heaving up a longship's yard in an Atlantic swell. The short arm of the catapult jerked down. The long arm whipped up. The sling, whirling round with sudden, vicious force, reached the point where the free hook was pulled off its ring, and swung loose.

Up into the murky sky soared the boulder. For a long moment it seemed to pause at the top of its arc, then began the long descent to splash into the Fenland soil two hundred and fifty paces off. Already a half-score of ragged figures were racing forward at the other end of the practice range, jealously competing to seize the ball and run back with it.

"Lower away!" bellowed Shef at the top of his lungs. His crew, as always, took not the slightest notice. They whooped and cheered, beating each other on the back, watching for the fall of the shot.

"A furlong if it's an inch!" shouted Steinulf, Brand's helmsman.

"Lower away! This is a speed test!" bellowed Shef again. His team slowly remembered his existence. One of them, Ulf the cook, ambled round and patted Shef tenderly on the back.

"Speed test be buggered," he said companionably. "If we ever have to shoot it fast, we will. Now—it's time to get the food on."

His mates nodded agreement, picked up their jackets from where they had draped them over the catapult's gallowslike frame.

"Good fun, good shooting," said Kolbein the Hebridean, newly sporting his Wayman pendant, the phallus of Frey. "We'll come down again tomorrow. Time to eat."

Shef watched them trail back toward the palisade, the cluster of tents and roughly roofed booths which were the winter camp of the Wayman army, wrath and frustration at his heart.

He had got the idea for this new-model catapult while watching Ordlaf's fishermen hauling on their mast-ropes. The giant boulder-thrower of the monks at York, the machine that had destroyed the Ragnarssons' ram three months before, had got its power from a counterweight. The counterweight itself was hauled into the air by men heaving at a windlass. All the counterweight really did was to store up the power the men had put into heaving on the windlass handles.

So why store the power? he had asked himself. Why not just have men attach ropes to the short arm and heave down on it directly? For small stones, like those they had roughly chipped into spheres, the new machine, the "pull-thrower" as the Vikings called it, was magnificent.

It threw in a perfectly straight line and could be aimed for direction within a couple of feet. The effect of the missile it hurled was literally pulverizing, turning rock to powder and smashing through shields like paper. As they learned how to shoot the weapon with maximum efficiency, its range steadily increased out to an eighth of a mile. And he was sure, if only they would do as they were told, that he could launch ten rocks while a man counted to a hundred.

But his team had no notion of the catapult as a weapon. To them, it was just a toy. Maybe useful one day against a stockade or a wall. Otherwise, a diversion during the tedium of a winter camp in the Fens, with even the traditional Viking amusements of raiding the surrounding countryside for girls and money severely forbidden.

But these throwers would work against anything, Shef thought. Ships. Armies. How would a drawn-up battle-line fare against a rain of boulders from men well out of bowshot, each one sure to kill or cripple?

He became aware that a cluster of excited, grinning faces was staring at him. The slaves. Runaways from the North-folk or from the lands of the king of the Mark, drawn to the camp here in the flat, soggy borderland between the streams of Nene and Welland by the astonishing rumor that here their collars would be removed. That food was to be had in return for services. They had been told, though they didn't believe it yet, that they would not be re-enslaved once their masters moved on.

Each of the ragged figures was clutching one of the ten-pound stones, which they had spent the last day or so chipping into shape with a couple of Thorvin's least-valued chisels.

"All right," said Shef. "Take the pegs out, dismantle the machine, take the beams back and wrap them in their tarpaulins."

The men shuffled and looked at each other. One of them, nudged forward by the rest, spoke haltingly, eyes on the ground.

"We was thinking, master. You being from Emneth and that. And talking like us and all. So . . ."

"Get on with it."

"We was wondering, you being one of us and all, if you would let us have a shot."

"We know how to do it!" cried one of his supporters. "We watched. We ain't got the beef they got, but we can pull."

Shef stared at the excited faces. The scrawny, underfed physiques. Why not? he thought. He had always assumed that what you needed most for this task was raw strength and weight. But coordination was even more important. Maybe twelve lightweight Englishmen would be as good as eight heavyweight Vikings. It would never have been true with swords or axes. But at least these ex-slaves would do what they were told.

"All right," he said. "We'll shoot five for practice. Then we'll see how many you can loose while I count fivescore."

The freedmen cheered and capered, pushing for the ropes.

"Hold on. This is going to be a speed test. So, first thing. Put the stones close there in a pile so you won't have to move more than a step to get them. Now, pay attention . . ."

An hour later, his new team dismissed to store what they now called their machine, Shef walked thoughtfully towards the booth of Hund and Ingulf, where the sick and injured lay. Hund met him coming out of the booth, wiping bloody hands.

"How are they?" Shef asked. He meant the casualties from his other machine, the torsion-catapult or "twist-shooter" as the Vikings called it, the dart-machine which had released King Ella into death.

"They'll live. One lost three fingers. Could as easily have been his hand, or arm for that matter. The other has most of his rib cage stove in. Ingulf had to cut him to get a piece out of his lung. But it's healing well. I've just smelt his stitches. No sign of the flesh-rot. That's two men badly hurt by that machine in four days. What's the matter with it?"

"Nothing wrong with the machine. It's these Norsemen. Strong men, proud of their strength. They twist the cogwheels tight—then one of them will throw his weight on the lever just to wring an extra turn out of it. The bow-arm snaps—and someone gets hurt."

"Then it's not the machine at fault, but the men who use it?"

"Exactly. What I need are men who will take so many counted turns and no more, who will do what they're told."

"Not many of those in this camp."

Shef stared at his friend. "Not speaking Norse, certainly." The seed of an idea had been planted.

The winter dark upon them now, he would take a candle and continue to work on the new *mappa*—the map of England as it really was.

"Nothing left to eat, I suppose, but the rye porridge?"
Silently Hund passed him his bowl.

Sigvarth looked round with a trace of uncertainty. The priests of the Way
had formed the holy circle, within the rowan-hung cords, spear planted
and fire burning. Once again the laymen of the Way were excluded: no
one was present in the dim, sail-roofed shed except the six white-clad
priests and Sigvarth Jarl of the Small Isles.

"It is time we came to a clearer understanding, Sigvarth," said Farman
the priest, "and that is, how sure are you that you are the father of the boy
Shef?"

"He says so," replied Sigvarth. "Everyone thinks he is. And his mother
claims him—and she should know. Of course she might have done anything once she escaped from me—a girl on the loose for the first time. She
might have enjoyed herself." Yellow teeth flashed. "But I don't think so.
She was a lady."

"I think I know the main story," said Farman. "You took her from her
husband. But a thing I cannot understand is this: She escaped from you, or
so we hear. Are you usually as careless as that with your captives? How did
she escape? And how could she have got back to her husband?"

Sigvarth rubbed his jaw reflectively. "This is twenty years back now.
Still, it was funny. I remember pretty well.

"What happened was this: We were coming back from a trip down
South. Hadn't gone very well. As we came back I decided, just for luck, to
look into the Wash and see what we could find. Usual stuff. Pushed
ashore. English all over the place, as always. Came down on this little
village, Emneth, grabbed everyone we could. One of them was the thane's
lady—I forget her name now.

"But I don't forget her. She was good. I took her for myself. I was thirty
then, she was maybe twenty. That's often a good combination. She'd had a
child, she was broken in all right. But I got the impression she had not had
much joy from her husband. She fought me fiercely to start with, but I'm
used to that—they have to do it to show they aren't whores. Once she
knew there was no choice, though, she buckled down to it. Had a trick, a
way to her—she used to lift herself right off the ground, me too, when she
reached her moment."

Thorvin grunted disapprovingly. Farman, one hand clutching the dried
stallion-penis that was his badge of office, as the hammer was Thorvin's,
hushed him with a gesture.

"But it's not so much fun in a rolling longship. After we pushed up the coast a bit, I looked out for a good place. Bit of *strandhögg*, I thought. Light fires, warm up, roast some beef, get out a couple of barrels of ale, have some sport for an evening. Put the boys in good heart for the ocean crossing. But not take any risks, mind, not even with the English.

"So, I picked a spot. Stretch of beach backed by good, high cliffs. One stream leading down to it through a gully. I put half a dozen men there just to make sure none of the girls we'd caught escaped. I put one man on each of the cliffs to either side, with a horn to blow if he saw any sign of a rescue party turning up. And because of the cliffs, I gave each of them a rope tied to a stake. If we were surprised, they blew the horns, the party in the gully ran back, and the ones on the cliffs slid down the ropes. We had the boats, three of them, tethered bow and stern—bow to the beach, stern to an anchor well out to sea. In a hurry all we had to do was pile in, loose the bow-ropes, haul ourselves off on the stern-rope and set sail. But the main thing is, I had the beach sealed off tight as a nun."

"You would know," said Thorvin.

Sigvarth's teeth flashed again. "None better, unless he's a bishop."

"But she got away," Farman prompted.

"Right. We had our fun. I did it with her, on the sand, twice. It got dark. Now, I wasn't passing her round, but the men had a dozen girls they were sharing, and I felt like joining in—hah, I was thirty then! So I hauled in my boat, I left my clothes on the sand and got in it with her. I pulled out on the stern-rope, maybe thirty yards out, and made fast. I left her there, dived in the sea and swam back. Fine, big blonde girl there I fancied. She'd been making a lot of noise.

"But after a while—I'd got a roast rib in one hand and a mug of ale in the other—the men started shouting. Just outside the light of our fires there was a shape on the sand, a big shape. Beached whale, we thought, but when we ran over, it wheezed and came at the first man there. He backed off, we looked for our weapons. I thought it might be a hross-whale. *Whaleross*, some say.

"And right that moment there was a lot of shouting from the top of one cliff. The lad up there, Stig was his name, shouting for help. Not blowing his horn, mind, but wanting help. Sounded as if he was fighting something. So I climbed up the rope to see what it was."

"And what it was it?"

"Nothing, when I got there. But he said, near in tears, he'd been attacked by a skoffin."

"A skoffin?" said Vigleik. "What's that?"

Skaldfinn laughed. "You must talk more to old wives, Vigleik. A skoffin is the opposite of a skuggabaldur. The one is the get of a male fox and a she-cat, the other of a tom and a vixen."

"Well," Sigvarth concluded, "by this time everyone was getting unsettled. So I left Stig up there, told him not to be a fool, slid back down the rope and told everyone to get back on board.

"But when we hauled the boat in, the woman was gone. We searched the beach. I checked the party in the gully—they hadn't moved an inch while we were getting ready, swore no one had passed. I went up both ropes to both cliffs. No one had seen anything. In the end I was so angry, what with one thing and another, that I threw Stig down the cliff for sniveling. He broke his neck and died. I had to pay wergild for him when I got home. But I never saw the woman again till last year. And then I was too busy to ask for her story."

"Aye. We know what you were busy with," said Thorvin. "The business of the Boneless One."

"Are you a Christian to whine about it?"

"What it comes to," said Farman, "is that she could have swum away in the confusion. You swam to shore."

"She would have had to do it fully dressed, for her clothes were gone too. And not just to shore. A long way, in the dark sea, to get round the cliffs. For she was not on the beach, I am sure of that."

"A whaleross. A skoffin. A woman who vanishes and reappears carrying a child," mused Farman. "All this could be explained. Yet there are more ways than one of explaining it."

"You think he is not my son," challenged Sigvarth. "You think he is the son of one of your gods. Well, I tell you: I honor no god save Ran the goddess who lives in the deep, whom drowned sailors go to. And the other world you talk of, the visions you boast of—I have heard them speak of it in camp about this Way of yours—I think them all born of drink and sour food, and one man's blather infecting another, till everyone must tell his tale of visions to keep in with the rest. There is no more sense in it than there is in skoffins. The boy is my son. He looks like me. He acts like me—like I did when I was young."

"He acts like a man," snarled Thorvin. "You act like a rutting beast. I tell you that though you have gone many years without regret and without punishment; still there is fate for such as you. Our poet said it when he saw the Hel-world:

" '*Many men I saw moan in pain,*
Walk in woe the ways of Hel.

Streaming red their wretched faces,
Punishment for the pain of women.'"

Sigvarth rose to his feet, left hand on sword. "And I will tell you a better poem. The Boneless One's skald made it last year, of the death of Ragnar:

" '*We struck with the sword. I say it is good*
For swain to meet swain in the sway of brands.
Not flinch from fighting. The friend of warriors
Shall earn women by war, by the way of the drengr.

"That is poetry for a warrior. For one who knows how to live and how to die. There will be a place for such a one among the halls of Othin, no matter how many women he has made weep. Poetry for a Viking. Not a milksop."

In the silence Farman said mildly, "Well, Sigvarth. We thank you for your tale. We will remember you are a jarl and one of our council. You will remember you live by the law of the Waymen now, no matter what you think of our beliefs."

He pulled open the ropes of the precinct, to let Sigvarth out. As the jarl left, the priests began to talk in low tones.

Shef-who-was-not-Shef knew that the darkness round him had not been breached by light for twice a hundred years. For a while the stone chamber and the earth round it had glowed with the phosphorescence of corruption, lighting up the silent, heaving struggle of the maggots as they consumed the bodies, the eyes and livers and flesh and marrow of all that had been placed there. But the maggots were gone now, the many corpses reduced to white bone, as hard and inert as the whetstone lying under his own fleshless hand. They were nothing but possessions now, without life of their own, as unchallengeably his as the chests and coffers round his feet and under his chair, as the chair itself—the massive wooden high seat in which he had settled himself seven generations ago, for eternity. The chair had rotted underground with the owner—the two had grown into one another. Yet still the figure sat unmoving, the empty eye-sockets staring out into the earth and beyond.

He, the figure in the chair, remembered how they had placed him there. The men had dug the great trench, slid into it the longship on its rollers, placed the high seat as he had directed on the poop, by the steering oar. He had settled himself in it, placed the whetstone with its carved savage faces on one armrest, laid his long broadsword on the other. He had nodded to the men to continue.

First they brought in his war-stallion, held it facing him, and poleaxed it where it stood. Then his four best hounds, each one pierced to the heart. He watched carefully to see that each one was quite dead. He had no mind to share his everlasting tomb with a trapped meat-eater. Then the hawks, each one quickly strangled. Then the women, a pair of beauties, weeping and calling out in spite of the poppy forced upon them; the men strangled them quickly.

Then they brought in the chests, two men to each one, grunting with the weight of them. He watched carefully again to see there was no delay, no reluctance. They would have kept his wealth if they dared. They would dig it up again if they dared. They would not dare. For a year to come the barrow would glow blue with the light of corruption beneath it; a man with a torch would ignite the bale-fires of the reek coming out of the ground. Tales would spread, till all feared and dreaded the grave-mound of Kar the Old. If grave it was for Kar.

The chests stacked, the men began to deck over the belly of the longship with its freight of corpses. Others piled stones around and behind him till they reached the height of the top of his seat with its silken canopy. Over them they laid stout beams, and over them in turn a sheet of lead. Around his feet and over his chests they tucked tarred canvas. In time the wood would rot, the earth fall in on the longship's hold, the dead women and beasts would lie mingled in confusion. Still he would sit here, looking out over them, the earth held at bay. They had been buried dead. He would not be.

When all was done a man came to stand in front of the seat: Kol the Niggard, men would call him, son of Kar the Old. "It is done, Father," he said, face twisting between fear and hate.

Kar nodded, eyes unblinking. He would not wish his son luck or farewell. If he had had the black blood of his ancestors, he would have joined his father in the mound, preferring to sit with his treasures for eternity than to hand them over to the new king pushing up from the South, to enjoy life with dishonor, to be an under-king.

The trusted warriors, six of them, began to slaughter the slave-laborers and stack them round the ship. Then they and his son scrambled out. A few moments later the loose earth of the digging began to fall in clods on the deck, covering it quickly, mounting up over the planks and the canvas and the sheet of lead. Slowly he saw it rise, to his knees, to his chest. He sat unmoving, even when earth began to trickle into the stone chamber itself, to cover his hand on the whetstone.

Still a glimmer of light. More earth raining down. The glimmer gone, the dark deepening. Kar settled back finally, sighing with relief and contentment. Now he had things as they should be. And so they would stay forever. His.

He wondered if he would die down here. What could kill him? It did not matter. Whether he died or lived he would always be the same. The hogboy, the haugbui. *The dweller in the mound.*

Shef woke with a start and a gasp. Underneath the coarse blankets his body streamed sweat. Reluctantly he pulled them back, rolled with a grunt from the string-bed to the wet, tramped-earth floor. He seized his hemp shirt as the freezing air hit him, pulled it on, groped for the heavy wool tunic and trousers.

Thorvin says these visions are sent by the gods for my instruction. But what did that tell me? There was no machine in it this time.

The canvas flap over the booth-door pulled back and Padda the freedman shuffled in. Outside, the late January dawn showed only thick mist rising from the waterlogged ground. The Army would frowst late in its blankets today.

The names of the men in the dream: Kar and Kol. They did not sound English. Nor Norse, altogether. But then the Norsemen were great ones for shortening names. Guthmund was Gummi to his friends, Thormoth became Tommi. The English did it too. Those names in King Edmund's riddle: ". . . Wuffa, Wehha's offspring . . ."

"What's your long name, Padda?" he asked.

"Paldriht, master. Haven't been called that since my mother died."

"What would Wuffa be short for?"

"Don't know. Wulfstan, maybe. Could be anything. I knew a man once called Wiglaf. Very noble name. We called him Wuffa."

Shef pondered as Padda began to blow carefully on the embers of last night's fire.

Wuffa, son of Wehha. Wulfstan or Wiglaf, son of—Weohstan, it might be, or Weohward. He did not know those names—he must find out more.

As Padda fiddled with wood and water, his pans and the everlasting porridge, Shef unrolled the vellum *mappamundi* from its waxcloth wrapping, spread it out, corners weighted, on his trestle table. He no longer looked at the completed side, the side with the map of Christian learning. On the reverse he had begun to draw a different map. A map of England, putting down all the information he could uncover. He would sketch in rough outlines, names, distances, on birchbark. Only after information had been checked and proved consistent with what he knew already would he ink it in on the vellum itself. Yet the map still grew with every day, dense and accurate for Norfolk and the Fens, doubtful and patchy for Northumbria away from York, completely blank down in the South, apart from London on the Thames and the vague mention of Wessex to the west of it.

Padda had found a Suffolk man among the freedmen, though. In return for his breakfast he would tell Shef all he knew about the shire.

"Call him in," said Shef, unrolling fresh birchbark and testing the point of his scratching-tool as the man entered.

"I want you to tell me all you can about places in your shire. Begin with the rivers. I know already of the Yare and the Waverly."

"Ah," said the Suffolk man reflectively. "Well, below that you've got the Alde, which reaches the coast at Aldeburgh. The Deben next. That comes into the coast ten mile south of Aldeburgh at Woodbridge, near where they say the old kings lie. We had our own kings in Suffolk once, you know, before the Christians came. . . ."

Minutes later Shef pounded into the forge where Thorvin was preparing for another day of forging iron cogwheels for the twist-shooters.

"I want you to call the army council together," he demanded.

"Why?"

"I think I know how to make Brand rich."

CHAPTER NINE

The expedition set out a week later, under a lowering sky, an hour after dawn. The council of the Wayman army had refused to sanction abandoning the base and marching out in full force. There were still the ships to be guarded, hauled up on the banks of the Welland. The camp held not only warmth for the remaining weeks and months of the winter but also a laboriously gathered food supply. And it could not be denied that many of the councillors were reluctant to believe Shef's passionate conviction that his *mappa* held the secret of generations of wealth.

Yet it was obvious that more than a few crews were needed. The kingdom of the East Angles was a kingdom no more, and all its mightiest warriors and noblest thanes were dead. Still, there was the chance that they might rally if provoked. A small party of Vikings could be cut off and massacred by overwhelming numbers. Brand had rumbled that foolish as he thought the whole expedition might be, he had no wish to be woken one morning by the heads of his messmates being thrown into the camp. In the end Shef had been allowed to call for volunteers. In the tedium of winter encampment, there had been no trouble in finding them.

A thousand Vikings rode out on their ponies, eight long hundreds and forty, riding crew by crew as was their custom. Hundreds of pack-ponies carried tents and bedding, food and ale, led in strings by English thralls. At the center of the column, though, was something new: a string of carts, carrying ropes and beams, wheels and levers—all the beams carefully notched and marked for reassembly. A dozen pull-throwers, eight twist-shooters. Every machine Shef and Thorvin had been able to construct in their weeks at the base was here. If he had left them behind they would have been forgotten, dispersed, used for firewood. Too much work had gone into them for that to happen.

Round the carts there clustered a mob of thralls, the runaways of the region, each catapult crew stepping by its cart and its machine, each crew captained by one of Shef's original dozen. The Vikings did not like this. Yes, every army needed a gang of thralls to dig latrines, light fires, groom horses. But gangs this size? All eating their share of the supplies? And starting to think they might not be thralls after all? Even the followers of the Way had never considered admitting men who did not speak Norse to full fellowship. Nor did Shef dare to suggest it.

He had made clear to Padda and the rest of the machine-captains that they had better tell their men to keep their heads down. "If someone wants you to grind his meal or pitch his tent, just do it," he had told them. "Otherwise keep out of the way."

Yet he wanted his recruits to feel different. To take pride in the speed and dexterity with which they leapt to their places, turned the levers or whirled the beams.

To mark them out, every catapult-man now wore an identical jerkin, made only of rough sackcloth, hodden gray, over the rags they had been wearing when they arrived. On it each man had carefully stitched a white linen double-headed hammer, front and back. Each man, too, had a belt or at least a rope round his middle, and all those who owned them bore knives.

Maybe it would work, thought Shef, watching the carts creak forward, Vikings in front and behind, jerkined freedmen in the middle. Certainly they were much better already with the catapults than the Vikings they had replaced. And even on a winter day in the raw cold, they looked cheerful.

A strange noise split the sky. At the front of the train of carts, Cwicca, a thrall who had come in a few days before, escaped from the shrine of St. Guthlac at Crowland, had brought with him his treasured bagpipe. Now he led the carts along, cheeks puffed, fingers skipping briskly on the bone pipe. His mates cheered and stepped out harder, some of them whistling in unison.

A Viking from the vanguard turned his horse, scowling angrily, front teeth sticking out. It was Hjörvarth Sigvarthsson, Shef saw. His half brother. Sigvarth had volunteered instantly to join the expedition with all his crews, too quickly to be turned down, quicker even than Thorvin or the Hebrideans or the still-doubting Brand. Now Hjörvarth trotted back menacingly towards the piper, sword half-drawn. The music wailed discordantly and died.

Shef turned his pony between them, slipped off it and handed the reins to Padda.

"Walking keeps you warm," he said to Hjörvarth, staring up at the angry face. "Music makes the miles go faster. Let him play."

Hjörvarth hesitated, jerked his pony's head round. "Suit yourself," he flung over one shoulder. "But harps are for warriors. Only a *hornung* would listen to a pipe."

Hornung, gadderling, thought Shef. How many words there are for bastard. It doesn't stop men putting them in women's bellies. Maybe Godive has one by now.

"Keep playing," he shouted to the bagpiper. "Play 'The Quickbeam Dance.' Play it for Thunor, son of Woden, and to Hell with the monks."

The piper started again to play the jerky quickstep tune, louder this time, backed by united defiant whistling. The carts rolled forward behind the patient oxen.

"You're sure King Burgred means to take over the East Angles?" King Ethelred asked. His question ended in a fit of coughing—sharp, high-pitched, going on again after it had seemed to stop.

Ethelred's younger brother, Alfred the atheling, looked at him with concern. Also, a reluctant calculation. Alfred's father, Ethelwulf—king of Wessex, conqueror of the Vikings at Oakley—had had four strong sons: Ethelstan, Ethelbald, Ethelbert, Ethelred. By the time the fifth came along it had seemed so unlikely that he would ever be called upon to rule that the royal mark of the house of Wessex, the Ethel-name, had seemed unnecessary. He had been called Alfred after his mother's people.

But now the father and three of the strong sons were dead. None killed in battle, but all killed by the Vikings. For years they had marched in all weathers, lain in damp cloaks, drunk water from streams that flowed through the camps of armies careless of where they dumped their waste or relieved themselves. They died of the bowel-cramps, of the lung-sickness. Now Ethelred had contracted the wasting-cough. How long might it be, Alfred thought, till he was the last atheling of the royal house of Wessex? Till then, though, he must serve.

"Quite sure," he replied. "He said so openly. He was mustering his men when I left. But he's not making it too obvious. He has an under-king, an

East Angle, to put in charge. That will make it easier for the East Angles to accept his rule. Especially as he has a totem. The man with no limbs, the one I told you of."

"Does it matter?" Ethelred dabbed wearily at spittle-slimed lips.

"The East Angles have twenty thousand hides. That, added to what Burgred has already, will make him stronger than us, far stronger than the Northumbrians. If we could trust him to fight the heathens only . . . But he may prefer easier prey. He could say it was his duty to unite all the kingdoms of the English. Ours included."

"So?"

"We must put in a claim. See, Essex is ours already. Now the border of Essex and the South-folk runs . . ."

The two men, the king and the prince, began slowly to thrash out a claim to territory, a likely dividing line. They had no image of the territory they were discussing, only knowledge that this river was north of that one, this town in this or that shire. The debate took even more toll of Ethelred's waning strength.

"You're sure they've split?" said Ivar Ragnarsson sharply.

The messenger nodded. "Almost half of them marched south. Maybe twelve long hundreds left behind."

"But no quarrel?"

"No. The word in the camp was they had some scheme for getting the wealth of King Jatmund, whom you killed with the blood-eagle."

"Nonsense," snarled Ivar.

"You heard what they got from the raid on the minster at Beverley?" asked Halvdan Ragnarsson. "A hundred pounds of silver and the same again in gold. That's more than we've taken anywhere. The boy is good at new schemes. You should have settled with him after the holmgang. He is a better friend than enemy."

Ivar turned on his brother, eyes pale, face whitening in one of his celebrated rages. Halvdan stared back at him placidly. The Ragnarssons never fought each other. This was the secret of their power, even Ivar in his madness knew it. He would take his rage out on someone else in some other way. Another matter to keep secret. But they had done it before.

"Only now he is an enemy," said Sigurth decisively. "We have to decide if he is our main one at this moment. And if he is . . . Messenger, you can go."

The brothers put their heads together in the little room off the drafty hall of King Ella in Eoforwich, and began to reckon numbers, rations, distances, possibilities.

"The wisdom of the serpent, the cunning of the dove," said Erkenbert the archdeacon with satisfaction. "Already our enemies destroy themselves and each other."

"Indeed," agreed Wulfhere. "The heathen make much ado and the kingdoms are moved. But God hath showed his voice and the earth shall melt away."

They spoke over the clanging of the dies, as each of the lay brothers in the monastic mint put his silver blank in place, struck it firmly with his hammer to drive the embossed design into one side. Moved it to the other die, struck again, First the spread-winged raven for the Ragnarssons. Then the letters *S.P.M.—Sancti Petri Moneta*. Collared slaves shuffled by, carrying man-loads of charcoal, rolling out carts of rejected lead, copper, slag. Only choirmonks touched the silver. They shared in the wealth of the minster. And any who thought for a moment of his own advantage could reflect on the Rule of Saint Benedict and the archbishop's power of chastisement written into it. It was long since a choirmonk had been flogged to death in chapter, or bricked alive into the vaults. But such cases had been known.

"They are in God's hand," concluded the archbishop. "Surely a divine vengeance will fall upon those who stole the goods of St. John's at Beverley."

"But God's hand shows itself through the hands of others," said Erkenbert. "And we must call for help from those."

"The kings of the Mark and of Wessex?"

"A mightier power than they."

Wulfhere looked down with surprise, doubt, comprehension. Erkenbert nodded.

"I have drafted a letter, for your seal. To Rome."

Pleasure showed on Wulfhere's face, perhaps anticipation of the much-rumored pleasures of the Holy City. "A vital matter," he announced. "I shall take the letter to Rome myself. In person."

Shef stared thoughtfully at the reverse side of his *mappa,* the map of England. Halfway through his work he had discovered the concept of scale, too late to apply consistently. Suffolk now bulked incongruously large, taking up a whole quadrant of the vellum. At one edge was his detailed drawing of all the information he had been able to wring out about the north bank of the Deben.

It fits, he thought. There is the town Woodbridge. That is in the first line of the poem, and the line must mean the town, because otherwise it would make no sense: all bridges are wood bridges. But more important is what the thrall says about this place, with no name, downstream of the bridge and the ford. That is where the barrows are, the resting place of the old kings. And who are the old kings? The slave knew no names, but the thane of Helmingham, who sold us mead, listed the ancestors of Raedwald the Great, and among them were Wiglaf and his father Weohstan: Wuffa, then, Wehha's offspring.

If the slave had remembered well, then there were four barrows together in a line running roughly south to north. The northmost of those. That was the place of the hoard.

Why had it not been plundered? If King Edmund had known it was the secret hiding place of the treasures of his realm, why was it not guarded?

Or maybe it was guarded. But not by men. That was what the slave had thought. When he had realized what Shef intended to do he had grown silent. Now no one could find him. He had preferred to take his chances of recapture than go to rob the grave.

Shef turned his attention to practicalities. Diggers, guards. Spades, ropes, boxes and slings for hauling up earth from deep down. Lights—he had no intention of digging in daylight with an interested county watching.

"Tell me, Thorvin," he said. "What do you think we might find inside this barrow? Other than gold, we hope."

"A ship," said Thorvin briefly.

"Close on a mile from the water?"

"See on your map. You could carry it up the slope there. The barrows are ship-shaped. And the thane told us Wiglaf was a sea-king, from the shores of Sweden, if he told us true. In my country even rich farmers, if they can afford it, will have themselves buried sitting upright in their boats. They think that this way they can sail over the seas to Odainsakr— to the Undying Shore—where they will join their ancestors and the Asa-gods. I do not say they are wrong."

"Well, we will soon know." Shef looked at the setting sun, glanced through the tent flap at the picked men—fifty Viking guards, a score of English diggers—quietly making ready. They would move only after dark.

As he rose to make his own preparations, Thorvin caught his arm. "Do not take this too lightly, young man. I do not believe—much—in *draugar* or in hogboys, the living dead or dragons made from corpses' backbones. Yet you are going to rob the dead. There are many tales of that, and all say the same. The dead will give up their goods, but only after a struggle. And only for a price. You should let a priest come with you. Or Brand."

Shef shook his head. They had argued this out before. He had made excuses, given reasons. None of them true. In his heart Shef felt he alone had the right to the hoard, bequeathed him by the dying king. He went out into the falling dusk.

Many, many hours later, Shef heard a mattock strike on wood. He straightened from his crouch over the black hole. It had been a night to forget so far. They had found the site without trouble, guided by the map. They had encountered no one. But where to begin digging? The guards and the diggers had clustered together in silence, waiting for orders. He had had torches lit, to see if he could discover signs of soil disturbance. But the moment the first resinous bundle had crackled to life a sudden blue flare of flame had run up the barrow and into the sky. Shef had lost half his diggers in that moment; they had simply bolted into the night. The Viking escort had held together much better, instantly drawing weapons and facing about them as if expecting to be attacked any moment by the vengeful dead. Yet even Guthmund the Greedy, keenest treasure-hunter of all, had suddenly lost enthusiasm. "We'll spread out a bit," he had muttered. "Not let anyone get too close." Since then no Viking had been seen. They must be out there in the dark somewhere, in little knots, backs together. Shef had been left with ten English freedmen, teeth chattering with fear. Lacking knowledge or plan he had simply taken them all to the top of the barrow and told them to dig straight down, as near to the center as he could measure.

At last they had hit something. "Is it a box?" he called hopefully down the shaft.

The only response was frantic tugs on the ropes that led down into the eight-foot-deep hole. "They want to come up," muttered one of the men standing round it.

"Haul away, then."

Slowly the mud-stained men were dragged up out of the earth. Shef waited with what patience he could for a report.

"Not a box, master. It's a boat. The bottom of a boat. They must have buried 'un upside down."

"So break through it."

Heads shook. Silently, one of the ex-slaves held out his mattock. Another passed a faintly glowing fir-brand. Shef took both. There was no point now, he realized, in asking for further volunteers. He drove the halberd in his hand deep into the ground by its spike, took a rope, tested its anchor-stake, glanced round at the dark figures, only their eyeballs showing in the night.

"Stay by the rope." Heads nodded. He lowered himself awkwardly, torch and mattock in one hand, into the dark.

At the bottom he found himself standing on gently sloping wood, obviously near the keel. He ran his hand over the planks in the faint torchlight. Overlapping, clinker-built. And, he could feel, heavily tarred. How long might that have lasted in this dry, sandy soil? He lifted the mattock and struck—struck again more firmly, heard the sound of splintering wood.

A rush of air and a foul stench enveloped him. His torch glowed with sudden force. Cries of alarm and scamperings from above. Yet this was not a stench of corruption. More, he felt, like the smell of a cow-byre at winter's end. He struck again and again, widening the hole. Beneath it, he realized, there was vacancy, not earth. The barrow-builders had succeeded in creating a chamber for the dead, and for the hoard, had not merely left it buried in the ground for him to sift through a shovel at a time.

Shef dropped the rope through the hole he had made and swung himself after it, torch in hand.

His feet crunched on bones. Human bones. He looked down, and felt a wave of pity. The ribs he had snapped were not those of the master of the hoard. They were a woman's bones. He could see her cloak-brooch glinting below the skull. But she lay facedown, one of a pair, stretched out lengthwise along the floor of the burial chamber. Both women's spines, he could see now, were snapped, by the great quernstones that must have been hurled down upon them. Their hands had been tied, they had been lowered into the tomb, their backs had been broken and then they had been left to die in the dark. The quernstones showed what they had been and what they were there for: they were the master's grinding slaves. Here to grind his meal and prepare his porridge into eternity.

Where the slaves were, there the master would be. He lifted his torch and turned toward the stern of the ship.

There, on his high seat, sat the king. Gazing out over hounds and horse and women. His teeth grinning out through shriveled skin. A gold circlet still lay on the bald skull. Stepping closer, Shef stared into the half-preserved face, as if looking for the secret of majesty. He remembered the urge of Kar the Old, to keep things his, to have them under his hand forever rather than live without them. Beneath this king's hand there was the regal whetstone, the ensign of the warrior-king who lived by sharpened weapons alone. Shef's torch suddenly went out.

Shef stood stock-still, skin crawling. In front of him there was a creak, a shifting of weight. The old king lifting himself out of his chair to settle with the invader who had come to take what he had hoarded. Shef braced for the touch of bony fingers, the awful teeth in the dried leather face.

He turned from his place and in the pitch-black walked back four, five, six paces, hopefully to the point where he had first descended. Was the blackness just perceptibly reduced? Why was he shaking like a common slave? He had faced death above—he would face death here in the darkness.

"You have no right to the gold now," he said into the blackness, groping his way back to the high seat. "Your children's children's child gave it to me. For a purpose."

He groped till his fingers found the torch, then bent over while he worked his flint and steel and tinder out of their pouch, strove to catch a spark.

"Anyway, Old Bones, you should be glad to give your wealth to an Englishman. There are worse than me who would take it from you."

Torch alight again, he propped it against a rotting timber, stepped up to the seat with its grisly occupant, put his arms round the body and lifted it carefully, hoping the remains of flesh and skin and cloth would hold the crumbling bones together. Turning, he laid it down to face the women's bodies in the well of the boat.

"Now you three must fight your own battles down here."

He took the gold circlet from the skull and pressed it down on his own head. Turning back to the empty chair, he picked up the whetstone, the scepter that had lain under the king's right hand and tapped its solid two-foot weight meditatively into one palm.

"One thing I will give you for your gold," he added. "And that is vengeance for your descendant. Vengeance on the Boneless One."

As he spoke, something rustled in the dim darkness behind him. For the first time Shef recoiled with shock. Had the Boneless One heard his name and come? Was he trapped in the tomb with some monstrous serpent?

Mastering himself, Shef stepped towards the noise, torch high. It was the rope by which he had climbed down. The end of it had been cut.

From above, dimly, he heard grunts of effort. Earth began, as it had done in his dream of Kar the Old, to patter down through the hole.

* * *

It took all his effort of will to reason this out. It was not a nightmare, not something to destroy one's wits. Call it a puzzle, something to work out and solve.

There are enemies up there. Padda and his men might have become frightened and run off, but they would not have cut the rope or thrown earth down on me. Nor would Guthmund. So someone has driven them off while I was down here, maybe the English, come to defend their king's mound. But they do not seem to want to come down after me. Still, I will never get out this way.

But is there another way? King Edmund had spoken of this as Raedwald's hoard, but this is the mound of Wuffa. Could he and his ancestors have been using this as a hiding place for wealth? If so, there might be a way to add to it—or to withdraw it. But the mound was solid above. Is there another way? If there is, it will be close to the gold. And the gold will be as close as it can be to the guardian.

Stepping over the bodies he walked to the chair and pulled it to one side to reveal four stout wooden boxes with leather handles. Sound leather handles, he noted, fingering one. Behind them, cut neatly out of the planking where the bow of the boat curved down, a square black hole, hardly bigger than a man's shoulders.

That is the tunnel! He felt immense relief, an invisible weight lifted from him. It was possible. A man from outside could crawl along that, open a box, close a box, do what he needed. He would not even have to face the old king he knew was there.

The tunnel must be faced. He pushed the circlet down on his head again, gripped the torch, now burned almost to its end. Should he take whetstone or mattock? I could dig myself out with the mattock, he thought. But now I have taken his scepter from the old king, I have no right to put it down.

Torch in one hand, whetstone in the other, he stooped and crawled into the blackness.

As he inched forward the tunnel narrowed. He had to thrust first with one shoulder, then with the other. The torch burned down, scorching his hand. He crushed it out against the earth wall and crawled on, trying to believe that the walls were not closing on him. Sweat sprang out on his head and ran into his eyes; he could not free a hand to wipe them. Nor could he crawl back now; the tunnel was too low for him to raise his hips and edge backward.

His hand before him met not earth floor but vacancy. A push and his head and shoulders were over a gap. Cautiously, he reached forward again.

Solid earth, two feet ahead, leading only downward. The builders did not want to make this too easy, he thought.

But I know what must be there. I know this is not a trap, but an entrance. So I must crawl down, round the bend. My face will be in the soil for a foot or two, but I can hold my breath for long enough.

If I am wrong, I will die smothered, face down. The worst thing will be if I struggle. That I will not do. If I cannot get through I will push my face in the earth and die.

Shef crawled over the edge and twisted his body down. For a moment he could not make his muscles force him on, as his legs retained a lingering grip on the level floor he had left. Then he pushed himself down, slid a foot or two, and stuck. He was jammed upside down in the tunnel in the pitch-black.

Not a nightmare, no panic. I must think of this as a puzzle. This cannot be a blind alley, no sense to it. Thorvin always said that no man bears a better burden than sense.

Shef groped round him. A gap. Behind his neck. Like a snake he slid into it. And there was level floor again, with this time a gap leading upward. He heaved himself into it, and for the first time in what seemed an age, stood upright. Beneath his fingers he found a wooden ladder.

He climbed unsteadily upward. His head bumped against a trapdoor. But a door designed to be approached from outside would not open so readily from within. There could be feet of earth heaped on top of it.

Pulling the whetstone from his belt he braced himself against the shaft-wall and stabbed upward with the sharpened end. The wood splintered, creaked. He struck again and again. When he could get a hand through broken wood he wrenched more free. Sandy soil began to patter down into the tunnel, rushing faster and faster as the hole widened and the pale sky of dawn appeared above.

Shef hauled himself exhaustedly from the tunnel, emerging inside a copse of dense hawthorns, no more than a hundred paces from the barrow he had entered so long ago. On the barrow-top stood a knot of figures, staring down. He would not hide nor crawl away from them. He straightened up, settled the circlet, hefted the whetstone and walked quietly over toward them.

It was Hjörvarth, his half brother, as he had almost expected. Someone saw him in the growing light, cried out, fell back. The clump of men drew away from him, leaving Hjörvarth in the middle, by the still-unfilled hole. Shef stepped over the body of one of his English diggers, cut from shoulder to chest by a broadsword. He was aware now that Guthmund had a group of men drawn up fifty yards off, weapons drawn but unready to interfere.

Shef looked wearily at the horse-toothed face of his half brother.

"Well, brother," he said. "It seems you want more than your share. Or are you maybe doing this for someone who is not here?"

The face in front of him tightened. Hjörvarth pulled his broadsword free, thrust his shield forward and paced down the slope of the barrow.

"You are no son to my father," he snarled, and swung his broadsword. Shef lifted the wrist-thick whetstone into its path. "Stone blunts scissors," he said as the sword snapped. "And stone crushes skull." He whipped the stone round backhand and felt the crunch as one of the carved, savage faces at one end sank into Hjörvarth's temple.

The Viking staggered, fell on one knee, propping himself for a moment with his broken sword. Shef stepped sideways, measured the blow and swung with all his strength. Another crunch of bone, and his brother toppled forward, blood streaming from mouth and ears. Slowly, Shef wiped the gray matter from the stone and looked round at the gaping men from Hjörvarth's crew.

"Family business," he said. "None of you need be concerned."

CHAPTER TEN

His appeal to the Viking council was not going Sigvarth's way. His face, white and strained, stared across the table.

"He killed my son—and for that I demand compensation."

Brand lifted a great hand to silence him. "We will hear Guthmund out. Continue."

"My men were spread out in the darkness around the mound. Hjörvarth's men came on us suddenly. We heard their voices, knew they weren't Englishmen, but were not sure what to do. They pushed aside those who challenged them. No lives lost. Then Hjörvarth tried to kill his brother Skjef, first by burying him alive in the barrow, then by attacking him with a sword. We all saw it. Skjef was armed only with a stone rod."

"He killed Padda and five of my diggers," said Shef. The council ignored him.

Brand's voice rumbled gently but decisively. "As I see it there can be no claim for compensation, Sigvarth. Not even for a son. He tried to kill a fellow member of the Army, protected under our Wayman-law. If he had succeeded I would have hanged him. He tried, too, to bury his brother in the barrow. And if he had succeeded in that, think what we would have lost!" He shook his head with disbelieving wonder.

At least two hundred pounds' weight of gold. Much of it of workmanship far exceeding the value of the raw metal. Carved bowls from the

Rome-folk. Great torques of pale gold from the land of the Irish. Coins with the heads of unknown Rome-folk rulers. Work of Córdoba and Miklagarth, of Rome and Germany. And added to it, sackloads of silver wedged into the tunnel mouth where the kings' depositors had put them over the generations. Enough there, all told, for every man of the whole Wayman army to be rich for life. If they lived to spend it. Secrecy had vanished with the dawn.

Sigvarth shook his head, his expression unchanging. "They were brothers," he muttered. "One man's sons."

"So there must be no question of vengeance," Brand said. "You cannot avenge one son on another, Sigvarth. You must swear to that." He paused. "It was the doom of the Norns. An ill doom, maybe. But not to be averted by mortals."

Sigvarth nodded this time. "Aye. The Norns. I will swear, Brand. Hjörvarth will lie unavenged. For me."

"Good. Because I tell you all." Brand looked round the table. "With all this wealth in hand I have grown nervous as a virgin at an orgy. The countryside must be buzzing with tales of what we have found. Shef's freedmen talk to the churls and the thralls. News goes both ways. They have heard that a new army has marched into this kingdom. An English army, from the Mark, come to reestablish the kingdom. You can be sure they have already heard of us. If they have any sense they will be marching already to cut us off from our ships, or to pursue us there if they are too late.

"I want camp struck and the men marching before the sun sets. March through the night and the next day. No halt before sunset tomorrow. Tell the skippers, get the beasts fed and the men in ranks."

As the group broke up and Shef moved to see to his carts, Brand caught him by the shoulder.

"Not you," he said. "If I had a polished steel I would make you look in it. Do you know you have white hairs on your temples? Guthmund will take care of the carts. You travel in the back of a cart, with my cloak over you as well as your own." He passed over a flask.

"Drink this. I saved it. Call it a gift from Othin, for the man who found the greatest hoard since Gunnar hid the gold of the Niflungs." Shef caught the odor of fermented honey: Othin's mead.

Brand looked down at the ghastly, ruined face—one eye sunk and shriveled, cheekbones standing out over tight-drawn muscles. I wonder, he thought. What price did the *draugr* in the mound take for his treasure? He clapped Shef again on the shoulder and hurried away, shouting for Steinulf and his skippers.

They marched with Shef in the back of a cart, flask drained now, lulled to half-sleep by the rocking motion. Wedged in between two treasure-chests and a catapult-beam. Close beside each treasure-cart marched a dozen men of Brand's own crews, now detailed as close escort. Round them clustered the freedmen catapulteers, spurred on by the rumor that they too might earn a small share, hold money for the first time in their lives. To front and rear and on the flanks rode strong squads of Vikings, alert for ambush or pursuit. Brand rode the length of the column, changing horses as often as one flagged beneath his weight, continually cursing all to greater effort.

Someone else's job now, thought Shef. He slid again into a deeper slumber.

He was riding across a plain. More than riding—spurring frantically. His horse groaned under him as he raked the rowels again across its bleeding ribs, fought against the bit, was mastered and driven on. Shef rose in his saddle and looked behind. Over the brow of a low hill, a horde of riders pouring after him, one well out in front on a mighty gray. Athils, king of Sweden.

And who was he, the rider? The Shef-mind could not tell what body it occupied. But it was a man strikingly tall, so tall that even from the great horse he rode his long legs brushed the ground. The tall man had companions, the Shef-mind noted. Strange ones too. Nearest him was a man so broad in the shoulder that it seemed he had a milkmaid's yoke under his leather jacket. His face was broad also, his nose snub, his expression one of animal resource. His horse, too, was laboring, unable to bear the weight at the speed they were traveling. By him was a man unusually handsome—tall, fair, eyelashes like a girl's. Nine or ten other riders pounded along at the same killing pace in front of the tall man and his two nearest companions.

"They will catch us!" called the broad man. He detached a short axe from his saddle-bow and shook it cheerfully.

"Not yet, Böthvar," said the tall one. He halted his horse, pulled a sack from his own saddlebag, reached inside, pulled out handfuls of gold. He scattered them on the ground, wheeled the horse again, rode on. Minutes later, turning on the brow of a hill again, he saw the pursuing horde check, fragment, break into a cluster of men pushing and thrusting their horses against each other while they groped on the ground. The gray horse detached itself, came on, other riders spurring to catch up in its wake.

Twice more the tall man did the same thing as the pursuit continued, each time losing more of the pursuers. But the spurs were having no effect now, the ridden horses moving at hardly a walk. Yet there was not far to go, to reach safety—what the safety was the Shef-mind did not know. A ship? A boundary? It did not matter. All that had to be done was reach it.

Böthvar's horse collapsed suddenly, rolling over in a flurry of foam and blood from its nostrils. The broad man leapt nimbly free, clutched his axe, turned eagerly to face the riders now a bare hundred yards off. Still too many riders, and the king in front—Athils of Sweden on the gray horse Hrafn.

"Drag him, Hjalti," said the tall man. He reached in the sack once again. Nothing there for his fingers to draw out. Except one thing. The ring Sviagris. Even as death rode toward him, with safety a final spurt away, the tall man hesitated. Then, with an effort, he raised it and flung it far back down the muddy trail toward Athils, slipping instantly from his horse and running with all his might towards the safe haven across the ridge.

At the ridge, he turned. Athils had reached the ring. He slowed his horse, reached down with a spear, trying to pick the ring off the ground with its point and ride on without check. Failure. He wheeled his horse, confusing the men behind him, tried again. Again a miss.

In hatred and indecision Athils looked at his enemy there on the brink of escape, looked down again at the ring sinking in the muck. Suddenly he lunged from his horse, bent down, groped for his treasure. Lost his chance.

The tall man cawed with laughter, ran on after his fellows. As the broad one, Böthvar, turned questioningly towards him, he cried out in triumph: "Now I have made he who is greatest among the Swedes root like a swine!"

Shef sat up violently in the cart, mouthing the word *svinbeygt*. He found himself staring into Thorvin's face.

" 'Swine-bowed,' is it? That is the word that King Hrolf spoke on Fyris-vellir Plain. I am glad to see you rested. But now I think it is time you stepped out like all of us."

He helped Shef scramble over the side of the cart, jumped down beside him. Spoke in a low whisper. "There is an army behind us. At every hamlet your thralls manage to get more news. They say there are three thousand men behind us, the army of the Mark. They left Ipswich as we left Woodbridge, and they have heard now about the gold. Brand has sent riders ahead to the camp at Crowland and told the rest of our army to meet us ready for battle—at March. If we join with them we are safe. Twenty long hundreds of Vikings, twenty-five of Englishmen. But they will break as usual. If they catch us before March it will be another story.

"They say a strange thing, too. The army, they say, is led by a heimnar. A heimnar and his son."

Shef felt a chill sweep through him. A volley of shouted orders rang out from ahead, with carts pulling aside and men suddenly unslinging packs.

"Brand halts the column every two hours to water the beasts and feed the men," said Thorvin. "Even in haste he says it saves time."

An army behind us, thought Shef. And us marching in haste for safety. That is what I saw in my dream. I was meant to learn from the ring, the ring Sviagris.

But *who* meant it? One of the gods, but not Thor, not Othin. Thor is against me, and Othin only watches. How many gods are there? I wish I could ask Thorvin. But I do not think my protector—the one who sends the warnings—I do not think he likes inquiries.

As Shef strode toward the head of the column, brooding on Sviagris, he saw Sigvarth by the side of the road, slumped on a folding canvas stool his men had placed for him. His father's eyes followed him as he passed.

It was just dawn when Shef's weary eyes picked out through the February murk the bulk of Ely Minster, to the right of their line of march. It had been gutted already by the Great Army, but the spire was still there.

"Are we safe now?" he asked Thorvin.

"The thralls seem to think so. Look at them laughing. But why? It is a day's tramp yet to March, and the Mark-men are close behind."

"It is the fens beyond Ely," said Shef. "This time of year, the road to March is a causeway for many miles, built up above the mud and water. If we needed to, we could turn and block the road with a few men and a barricade. There is no way round. Not for strangers."

There was a stillness spreading down the column, a stillness in the wake of Brand. He suddenly stood before Shef and Thorvin, his cloak black with mud, face white and shocked.

"Halt!" he yelled. "All of you. Feed, water, loosen girths." In a much lower voice he muttered to the two councillors, "Bad trouble. Meeting up ahead. Don't let it show on your face."

Shef and Thorvin looked at each other. Silently they followed him.

A dozen men, the Viking leaders, stood to one side of the track, boots already sinking in the mire. Unspeaking in the midst of them, left hand always on sword-pommel, was Sigvarth Jarl.

"It's Ivar," said Brand without preamble. "He hit the main camp at Crowland last night. Killed some, scattered the rest. Certainly caught some of our people. They must have talked by now. He'll know where we're supposed to meet. He'll know about the gold.

"We have to figure that he's already marching to intercept us. So we've got him to the north and the English a couple of miles to the south."

"How many men?" asked Guthmund.

"They thought—the ones who escaped and rode to meet us—about two thousand. Not the whole York army. None of the other Ragnarssons there. Only Ivar and his lot."

"We could take them if we were at full strength," said Guthmund. "Bunch of criminals. Gaddgedlar. Broken men." He spat.

"We aren't at full strength."

"But we will be soon," went on Guthmund. "If Ivar knows about the gold, I bet everyone in that camp knew about it first. They were probably all pissed drunk celebrating when he turned up. As soon as their heads clear, the ones who got away will head straight for the meeting ground at March. We meet them there, we're at full strength, or damn near. Then we'll settle Ivar's lot. You can have Ivar yourself, Brand. You have a score to pay."

Brand grinned. It was hard, Shef reflected, to scare these people. They had to be killed, one at a time, till they were all dead, to defeat them. Unfortunately that was what was likely to happen.

"What about the English behind us?" he asked.

Brand sobered again, drawn from his dream of single combat.

"They should be a lot less of a problem. We've always beaten them. But if they come up on us from behind while we're engaged with Ivar . . . We need time. Time to pick up the rest of the army at March. Time to settle Ivar's hash."

Shef thought of his vision. We have to throw them something they want, he reflected. Not treasure. Brand would never let go of it.

The old king's whetstone from the barrow was still in his belt. He pulled it out, stared at the bearded, crowned faces carved on each end. Savage faces, full of the awareness of power. Kings have to do things other men would not. So do leaders. So do jarls. They had said there would be a price to be paid for the hoard. Maybe this was it. When he looked up he saw Sigvarth was staring round-eyed at the weapon that had beaten out the brains of his son.

"The causeway," said Shef hoarsely. "A few men can block it against the English for a long time."

"They could," Brand agreed. "But they will have to be led by one of us.

A leader. One who is used to independent command. One who can rely on his own men. Maybe a long hundred of them."

For long moments the silence was unbroken. Whoever stayed behind was as good as dead. This was asking a lot—even of these Vikings.

Sigvarth stared at Shef coldly, waiting for him to speak. But it was Brand's voice that broke the silence.

"There is one here who has a full crew to back him. One who made the heimnar that now is carried toward us by the English. . . ."

"Do you speak of me, Brand? Do you ask me to set my feet and those of my men on the path to Hell?"

"Yes, Sigvarth, I speak of you."

Sigvarth started to answer, then turned and looked towards Shef. "Yes, I will do it. I feel that the runes are already cut that tell of this. You said my son's death was the will of the Norns. I think the Norns are weaving fates together on this causeway too. And not the Norns alone."

He raised his eyes to meet his son's.

The front ranks of the army of the Mark, hurrying on through the night in pursuit of their fleeing enemies, fell into Sigvarth's trap an hour after sunset. In twenty heartbeats of slaughter the Englishmen, packed ten abreast on the narrow causeway through the marsh, lost half a hundred picked champions. The rest—weary, wet, hungry, furious with their leaders—fell back in confusion, not even coming on again to recover the bodies and their armor. For an hour Sigvarth's men, standing tensely ready, heard them shouting and haranguing each other. Then, slowly, the noise of men retreating. Not frightened. Unsure. Wondering if there was a way round. Waiting for orders. Leaving it to the next man. Ready for a night's sleep, even in a sodden blanket on the ground, before risking precious life against something unknown.

Twelve hours gained already, thought Sigvarth, standing his men down. Though not for me. I may as well watch as anything else. I shall not sleep again after the death of my son. My one son. I wonder if the other is my son. If he is, he is his father's bane.

With dawn, the English returned, three thousand men, to see the nature of the barrier that blocked their way.

The Vikings had dug into the sodden February soil on both sides of the track through the fens. A foot down they had reached water. Two feet down and only mud came up. Instead of their normal earthwork they had dug a water-filled ditch ten feet broad. On their side of it they had jammed into the ground such bits of timber as they could break up from the cart

Shef had left behind. A flimsy obstacle to be cleared in a few moments by a gang of churls. If there had been no men behind it.

There was room on the causeway for only ten to stand. For only five to wield weapons. The warriors of the Mark, coming forward cautiously, shields raised, found themselves floundering thigh-deep in freezing water before they were in sword-range of an enemy. Their leather shoes skidded on the bottom. As they edged on, bearded faces glared at them, two-handed axes resting on shoulders. Strike at the men? A man had to struggle up a muddy slope to get in a blow. While he did, the axemen could pick their spot.

Strike at the timbers then, at the breastwork. But take your eyes off the man above you and he would cut arm from shoulder or head from neck.

Gingerly, striving desperately for balance, the Mercian champions probed crabwise into battle, urged on by cries of encouragement from those not yet engaged.

As the short day drew on, the fighting gathered momentum. Cwichelm, the Mercian captain, deputed by his king to advise and support the new alderman, lost patience with the tentative assaults, pulled his men back, ordered forward a score of bowmen with unlimited arrows to line the track. "Shoot at head level," he told them. "Doesn't matter if you miss. Just keep them down."

Other men kept up a barrage with javelins, just over the heads of their fighting fellows. Cwichelm's best swordsmen, spurred on with appeals to their pride, were told to go forward and fence—to not rush forward. Tire them out for a while, then change places with the next rank. Meanwhile a thousand men had been sent miles to the rear, to cut brushwood, bring it forward, throw it under the feet of the fighters, let them trample it under to make, in time, a solid platform.

Alfgar, watching from twenty paces back, pulled his fair beard with vexation.

"How many men do you need?" he asked. "It's only a ditch and a fence. One good push and we'll be through it. It doesn't matter if we lose a few."

The captain eyed his master-by-title sardonically. "Try telling that to the few," he said. "Or maybe you'd care to try it yourself? Just take out that big fellow in the middle. The one laughing. With the yellow teeth."

In the dim light, Alfgar stared across the cold water and the struggling men at Sigvarth, padding from side to side as he beat aside sword-strokes, sparred to get in a blow. Alfgar thrust his hand into his belt as it began to tremble.

"Bring my father forward," he muttered to his attendants. "There is something for him to see."

"The English are bringing up a coffin," observed one of the Viking front-rankers to Sigvarth. "I would have thought they needed more than just one by now."

Sigvarth stared at the padded box, held almost upright by its bearers, its occupant held in place by chest- and waist-straps. Across the water, his eyes met those of the man he had maimed. After a moment, he threw his head back in a wild cry of laughter, raised his shield, shook his axe, called out in Norse.

"What does he say?" muttered Alfgar.

"He is calling to your father," translated Cwichelm. "Does he recognize the axe? Does he think it forgot something? Drop his breeches and he will do his best to remember."

Wulfgar's mouth moved. His son bent to hear the hoarse mumble.

"He says he will give his whole estate to the man who takes that one alive."

Cwichelm pursed his lips. "Easier said than done. One thing about these devils. You can beat them, sometimes. But it's never easy. Never, never easy."

From the sky above them came a shrill whistling, dropping closer.

"Lower away!" barked the leader of catapult team one. The twelve freed thralls on the ropes thrust right hand over left hand over right hand, shouting hoarsely as they did so. "One—two—three." The sling dropped into the leader's hands. As it came down, the loader sprang from his kneeling position, shoved a ten-pound rock into position, leapt instantly back into his place, reaching for the next one.

"Take the strain!" Backs bent, the machine's arm flexed, the leader felt himself pulled up on to his toes.

"Pull!" A simultaneous grunt, the lash of the sling, a rock whirling into the air. As it went, it span, the chipped grooves on its surface setting up an ominous whistling. In the same moment, the crew heard the cry from behind them of the leader of catapult two.

"Take the strain!"

Traction-catapults were strange beasts in that they had most power at maximum range. They lobbed their missiles up in the sky. The higher they went, the harder they hit. The two teams of ex-slaves Shef had left behind with their cart and their machines had accordingly set up their pull-throwers a carefully paced two hundred yards behind Sigvarth's breastwork on the causeway; their missiles would strike twenty-five yards further on.

The narrow causeway was the ideal killing-ground for the machines. They threw perfectly straight, never deviating more than a few feet either side of the center. The English freedmen had perfected a drill designed to ensure that everyone did everything exactly the same way every time, and as fast as possible. For three minutes they shot. Then stood easy, panting.

The boulders dropped death from the sky on the Mercian column. The first one struck a tall warrior on the head as he stood unmoving, beating his skull almost into his shoulders. The second hit an automatically raised shield, shattering the arm behind it, caroming off to smash in a rib cage. The third hit a turned back, crushing the spine. In instants the causeway was jammed with struggling men, attempting to get back and away from a death they still could not see or understand. On the packed mass the stones continued to fall, varying a few yards forward or back as the launchers' heaves fluctuated, but never missing the causeway itself. Only those who crowded forward into the ditch closest to the Vikings remained safe.

At the end of the three minutes the warriors leading the attack saw only chaos and ruin behind them. Those who fled to the rear saw now that at a certain distance they were safe.

Cwichelm, in the fore, waved his broadsword, yelled out in rage to Sigvarth, "Come out! Come out from your ditch and fight like men. With swords, not stones."

Sigvarth's yellow teeth showed again in a grin. "Come and make me," he called, in an approximation of English. "You so brave. How many of you you need?"

More hours gained, he thought. How long does it take an Englishman to learn sense?

Not quite long enough, he reflected as the short February day drew toward its end in rain and sleet. The ditch and the stone-throwers had shocked them. But very, very slowly, maybe not quite slowly enough, they had got over their shock and worked out what they should have done in the first place.

Which was everything—and all at once. Frontal assault to keep Sigvarth busy. Spears and arrows launched overhead, to harass. Brushwood under the feet of the fighters, to build up a platform. Men coming up in thin lines, eyes alert, to give poor targets for the stone-throwers. Others floundering through the marsh in small bodies, to try to climb the causeway behind his block, splitting his meager force. Commandeered boats poling along to get behind him and threaten to cut off his retreat. Sigvarth's men were looking behind them now. One solid push by the English, regardless of casualties, and they really would be through.

One of the slaves from the stone-throwers was tugging at Sigvarth's sleeve, talking in broken Norse.

"We go now," he said. "No more rocks. Master Shef, he said, shoot till rocks gone, then go. Cut ropes, throw machines in swamp. Go now!"

Sigvarth nodded, watched the puny figure scamper away. Now he had his own honor to think of. His own destiny to fulfill. He walked forward toward the front line of the fighters, clapping men on the shoulder. "Move," he said to each one. "Get your horse. Get out of this now. Ride straight for March and they won't catch you."

His helmsman Vestlithi hesitated as Sigvarth tapped him. "Who's bringing your horse, jarl? You'll have to move quick."

"I have something to do yet. Go, Vestlithi. This is my fate, not yours."

As the feet splashed away behind him, Sigvarth faced the five leading champions of the Mark, probing suspiciously forward, made wary of every opportunity by a long day of slaughter.

"Come on," he called to them. "Only me!"

As the foot of the center man slipped, he leapt forward with appalling speed, slashed, countered, thrust sword through beard, leapt back again, feinting from one side to the other as the enraged Englishmen closed in.

"Come on!" he shouted, yelling again the words of Ragnar's death-song, which Ivar Ragnarsson's skald had made:

" 'We struck with the sword. Sixty times and one
I have fought in the front when foemen clashed.
Never yet have I met—young though I started
To mar the mailcoats—my match in battle.
The gods will greet me. I grieve not for death.' "

Over the clash of combat, one man against an army, Wulfgar's deep tones carried.

"Take him alive! Pin him with shields! Take him alive!"

I must let them do it, thought Sigvarth as he whirled and slashed. I have not bought my son quite enough time. But there is a way to buy him yet one more night.

It will be a long one for me.

CHAPTER ELEVEN

Shef and Brand, standing close together, watched the battle-line, two-hundred-men wide, tramping slowly toward them across the level meadowland turf. Over the advancing line battle-standards waved, the personal flags of jarls and champions. Not the Raven Banner of the Ragnarssons, which flew only when all four brothers consented to it. But above the central reserve a gust puffed out one long ensign: the Coiling Worm of Ivar Ragnarsson himself. Even at this distance Shef thought he could catch the glint of the silver helmet, the scarlet cloak.

"Going to be a killing-ground today. We're too evenly matched," Brand muttered. "Even the side that wins is going to take very heavy losses. Takes guts to walk forward in the front rank, knowing that. Ivar's not in the front, pity. I was hoping he would be; I could have a go at him myself. The only cheap way for us to win this will be to kill a leader and take the heart out of the rest."

"Is there a cheap way for them?"

"I doubt it. Our lads have seen the money. They've only heard about it."

"But you still think we're going to lose?"

Brand patted Shef reassuringly. "Heroes never think things like that. But everybody loses some time. And we're outnumbered."

"You haven't counted my thralls."

"I've never known thralls to win battles."

"Wait and see."

Shef ran back a few paces from where he and Brand had been standing, beneath the Flag of the Hammer, at the rear center of their own—the Wayman line. It was drawn up in exactly the same style as Ivar's force, but only five-deep, with fewer reserves. Shef had placed his wheeled torsion-catapults—the dart-shooters—in the line, screened only by a single rank of men and shields. Well back behind the line stood the traction-catapults —the stone-throwers—all of them except for the pair he had left with Sigvarth, their half-crews clutching the flapping ropes.

But it was the twist-shooters that would do the work now. Using his halberd, Shef vaulted onto the central cart of the nine he had left, still drawn up, oxen still hitched. He looked up and down the line of men, seeing the faces of his catapult-crews turned toward him.

"Clear your line!"

The Vikings masking the line of fire shuffled sideways. The ropes were wound tight; loaders stood ready with bundles of javelins; they were aimed and ready. The slowly advancing line of men was a target impossible to miss. Over the turf came the hoarse chanting of the Ragnarsson army: "Ver thik," they shouted again and again. "Ver thik, her ek kom."— "Guard yourself, here I come."

Shef dropped the head of his halberd forward as he shouted, "Shoot!"

Black streaks, rising at the launch, falling as they flashed through the air. Plunging into the lines of advancing men.

The lever-men were rewinding furiously, javelins dropped into place. Shef waited until the last one was reloaded, the last hand up to signal readiness.

"Shoot!"

Again the thrums, the streaks, the swirls. A hum of excitement rose from the Wayman army. And there was something happening with the Ragnarsson line as well. They had abandoned their steady walk, their chanting wavered and died. Now they were trotting forward, anxious to close before they were impaled like roast pigs—without a blow struck. Running half a mile in armor would tire them nicely. The shooters had done one job already.

But they could not shoot much longer. Shef calculated that he could shoot twice more before the attackers reached the line. Kill a few more men, unsettle the rest.

As the machines leapt back on their wheels for the last time he ordered them back.

The crews lifted the trails, ran their machines back out of the line toward the carts, calling out with triumph.

"Shut up! Man the throwers."

In seconds the ex-thralls were loading and aiming the machines. Vikings would never have done that, thought Shef. They would have needed time to tell each other what deeds they had done. He raised his halberd up and ten boulders were hurled simultaneously into the air.

They reloaded as quickly as they could, inched the clumsy frames round as the captains lined them up. A rain of boulders whistled out of the sky, no longer in volleys, each machine shooting as fast as its crew could lower and load.

Harassed and shaken, the Ragnarsson line broke into all-out charge. Already stones were flying high, landing behind the charging men. Still Shef saw with satisfaction a long trail of smashed bodies and writhing injured, like a snailtrack behind the oncoming army.

The two battle-lines met with a roar and a crash of metal, instantly swaying back and then forward as the impetus of the Ragnarsson rush was felt, held, returned. In moments the battle had become a line of single combats, men beating swords and axes on shields, trying to drag an arm down, stab under a guard, crush face or rib with shield-boss.

In unison the white-clad priests of the Way, grouped behind their men round the sacred silver spear of Othin, god of battles, began a deep chant.

Shef hefted his halberd in indecision. He had done the job he meant to do. Should he now thrust forward to stand amid the fighters? One man amid four thousand?

No. There was still a way to bring his machines to bear. He ran to the thralls round their throwers, shouting and gesturing. Slowly, they took his meaning, ran back to the dart-shooters, began to run the wheeled machines up onto the waiting carts.

"Around their flank—follow me! They battle face-to-face. We can get behind them."

As the ox-carts creaked with agonizing slowness round behind the Way-man position, Shef saw faces turning. Wondering whether he was fleeing from battle. Fleeing in ox-carts? Some of them he recognized: Magnus, Kolbein and the other Hebrideans, clustered at the rear in reserve. Brand had put them there, saying their weapons would be difficult to fence with in a packed mass.

"Magnus! I want six of your men with each cart for close defense."

"If we do that there'll be no reserve left."

"Do it and we won't need a reserve."

Halberdiers closed round the carts as Shef led them in a long sweep round the flanks of both battling armies, first the Waymen, then the Ragnarsson troops gaping in surprise. But with battle joined, unable to see the lumbering carts as anything but a distraction. At last they were in a position well to the rear right flank of the Ragnarsson army.

"Stop. Wheel the carts left. Chock the wheels. No! Don't unload the machines. We'll shoot from inside the carts.

"Now. Drop the tilts." Halberdiers whipped out the pins, let the wagon tilts fall forward. The wound and loaded catapults trained round.

Shef stared carefully at the scene in front of him. The two battle-lines were locked along a two-hundred-yard front, making no attempt to outmaneuver each other. But at the center of the Ragnarsson line Ivar had bunched a mass of men, twenty-deep, pushing steadily forward, aiming to break their outnumbered enemy by sheer weight. Above the central mass flew his standard. There was the place to aim—not at the front, where Shef might hit his own men.

"Aim for the center. Aim for the Coiling Worm. Shoot!"

The catapults leapt in the air as they shot, their recoil on hard planks instead of soft ground sending them skidding. The thralls seized them and ran them back again, lever-men struggling to fit the winders back in place.

Round the Worm Standard of Ivar there was chaos. In the throng of milling men Shef saw for an instant a long spike with two bodies threaded on it like larks on a spit. There was another man threshing desperately to free a snapped javelin-head from his arm. Faces were turning, and not just faces. He could see shields as well, as men realized the attack had come somehow from their rear and turned bodily to meet it. The Worm Standard still waved, its bearer still protected by the ranks of bodies that had been behind it. Reloading complete, Shef screamed the command.

"Shoot!"

This time the Worm went down, to a roar of delight from the Wayman center. Someone seized it, heaved it defiantly up once more, but the Ragnarsson center had yielded five blood-soaked yards, the men in it trying to keep their footing as they stumbled back over wet soil and their own dead. But there were men running now toward the carts.

"Change target?" shouted a captain, pointing at the advancing men.

"No! The Worm again! Shoot."

Another hail of darts into the tight-packed throng, and again the Worm went down. No time to see if it would come up again, or if Brand would now finish the job. The lever-men were still winding desperately but they would not get in another shot.

Shef reached down with his armored gloves, seized "Thrall's-Wreak" and the helmet he had never yet worn in battle.

"Halberdiers in the carts," he shouted. "Just fend them off. Catapulteers, use your levers, use your mattocks."

"What about us, master?" Fifty unarmed freedmen still clustered behind the carts, hammer-emblems on their jerkins. "Shall us run?"

"Get under the carts. Use your knives."

Moments later the Ragnarsson wave reached them in a turmoil of glaring faces and slashing blades. Shef felt a weight roll from him. There was no need for thought now. No responsibility for others. The battle would be won or lost elsewhere. All he had to do now was swing his halberd as if he were still beating out metal at the forge: ward and cut, lunge overhand and stab downward.

On level ground the Ragnarsson followers would have rolled over Shef's outnumbered and half-armed force in instants. But they had no idea of how to fight men in farm wagons. Their enemies were feet higher than themselves, behind oak planks. The halberds Shef had made for them gave Magnus and his Hebrideans extra feet of reach. Vikings lunging under the halberds and trying to haul themselves into the carts were simple targets for the clubs and mattocks of the English thralls. Knives in skinny hands ripped upward at thigh and groin from behind sheltering wheels.

After a few desperate trials the Vikings fell back. Orders barked from the more level-headed among them. Men slashed the oxen free, seized the drag-poles, prepared to haul the carts off the thralls underneath. Javelins poised, ready for a united volley against the exposed halberdiers.

Shef found himself staring suddenly into the eyes of Muirtach. The big man paced forward, his own ranks parting for him, like a great wolf. He wore no mail, only the saffron plaid which left his right arm and torso bare. He had thrown away his targe, and carried only the dagger-pointed longsword of the Gaddgedlar in two hands.

"You and me now, boy," he said. "I'm going to keep yer scalp and use it for a bum-wipe."

In answer Shef jerked the pin free and kicked the wagon tilt down once more.

Muirtach charged before he could straighten up, faster than Shef had ever seen a human being move. Reflex alone hurled Shef backward, stumbling on the wheel of the machine behind him. But Muirtach was already in the cart, swordpoint down for the thrust. Shef leapt back again, cannoning off Magnus, unable to drop his halberd enough to stab or guard.

Muirtach was swinging already. A lunging lever from Cwicca deflected his stroke, guided it onto the bowstring of the fully wound but unloosed catapult.

A deep twang, a thwack louder than a whale-fluke on water.

"Son of the Virgin," said Muirtach, staring down.

One arm of the catapult, released, had slammed forward the six inches which were all that it could travel. In those six inches it had expended all the stored energy that could drive a barb a mile. The whole side of Muirtach's bare chest was crushed in as if from the hammer-blow of a giant. Blood ran from the Irishman's mouth. He stepped back, sat down, slumped back against the wagon wall.

"I see you have turned Christian again," said Shef. "So you will remember, 'an eye for an eye.'" Reversing his halberd, he drove its butt-spike deep through Muirtach's eye and into the brain.

In the brief seconds of the confrontation everything had changed. Shef looked up and saw only backs. The Ragnarsson attackers had turned away, were throwing down their weapons, unbuckling their shields. "Brother," they shouted, "fellow, messmate." One, incongruously, was pulling open his tunic, hauling out a silver emblem. A Wayman, maybe, who had decided to stay with a father or a chief rather than march out of York. Behind them hundreds of men were moving forward in a bristling wedge, the giant figure of Brand at its apex. In front of the wedge the plain was covered only with men running, men limping, men standing in knots with their hands raised. The Ragnarsson army had broken. Its survivors had the choice only of running for their lives in heavy mail or hoping for immediate mercy.

Shef lowered "Thrall's-Wreak," suddenly weary. As he started to clamber from the wagon a flash of movement caught his eye. Two horses, one with a rider with a scarlet cloak, grass-green trousers.

For an instant Ivar Ragnarsson stared from his saddle across the lost battlefield at Shef standing on the cart. Then he and his horse-swain were away, clods flying in the air from the trampling hooves.

Brand strode over, clasped Shef's hand.

"You had me worried there, thought you were running away. But toward battle, not from it. A good day's work done."

"The day's not done yet. There is still an army behind us," said Shef. "And Sigvarth. The Mercians should have been at our backs this dawn. He has held them twelve hours longer than I thought possible."

"But maybe not long enough," said Magnus Gaptooth from his place on the wagon. He stretched out an arm, pointed. Far away across the level plain, a stray shaft of winter sunlight sent up a prickle of darting reflections: the spear-points of an army, deployed and advancing.

"I need more time," said Brand gruffly in Shef's ear. "Go talk, bargain, buy me some."

He had no choice. Thorvin and Guthmund joined him as he walked toward the advancing Mercian battle-line, different from the one they had just broken, only—to outward appearance—by the three great crosses towering above it.

Behind them the Wayman army struggled to regroup. Perhaps a third of them were dead or gravely injured. Now even the walking wounded were furiously busy: stripping the surrendered Ragnarsson warriors of weapons and armor, scavenging the battlefield for whatever was usable or valuable —with the enthusiastic assistance of Shef's freedmen—herding the enemy wounded off in the direction of their ships still under guard by the Wash, carrying such few as had survived the attentions of the body-strippers off to the leeches.

The "army" was a mere front. A few hundred of the fittest men in line to make a show. Behind them, rank on rank of captives, hands loosely roped, told to stand there and be counted in return for their lives. Half a mile behind them, thralls and warriors were hastily digging a ditch, setting up the machines—and rounding up horses and wagons ready for the next retreat. The Wayman army was not yet fit to fight—the heart had not gone out of it, not yet. But all tradition dictated a pause for celebration and relief after surviving a pitched battle against superior forces. Being asked to do the same again immediately was too much.

The next few minutes, Shef thought, would be very dangerous. Men were coming to meet him and his small party: three men walking together, one a priest. Two more pushing a strange, upright box on wheels. The thing in it, he realized an instant later, could only be his stepfather Wulfgar.

The two groups halted ten paces apart, surveyed each other. Shef broke the deep, hating silence.

"Well, Alfgar," he said to his half brother, "I see you have risen in the world. Is our mother pleased?"

"Our mother never recovered from what your father did. Your late father. He told us much about you before he died. He had plenty of time."

"Did you capture him, then? Or did you stand back as you did in the fight by the Stour?"

Alfgar stepped forward, hand reaching for his sword. The grim-faced man beside him, the one who was not a priest, caught his arm quickly.

"I am Cwichelm, marshal of King Burgred of the Mark," he said, "charged to restore the shires of Norfolk and Suffolk to their new alderman and to make them subject to my king. And who are you?"

Slowly, mindful of the frantic preparations still going on behind, Shef introduced the others on his side, let Cwichelm do the same. Disclaimed hostile intention. Declared intention to withdraw. Hinted at compensation for damage.

"You're fencing with me, young man," broke in Cwichelm. "If you were strong enough to fight, you wouldn't be talking. So I'll tell you what you have to do if you want to see tomorrow's dawn. First, we know you took treasure from the mound by Woodbridge. I must have it all, for my king. It comes from his realm."

"Second," cut in the black-robed priest, staring fixedly at Thorvin, "there are Christians among you who have deserted their faith and betrayed their masters. They must be handed over for punishment."

"You included," said Alfgar. "Whatever happens to the others, my father and I will not see you march away. I will put the collar on you with my own hands. Think yourself lucky we do not treat you as we did your father."

Shef did not bother to translate for Guthmund.

"What did you to my father?"

Wulfgar had not spoken till then. He sprawled in his box, held by the straps. Shef remembered the yellow, pain-racked face he had last seen in the trough. Now Wulfgar's face was ruddy, his lips showing red in the white-streaked beard.

"What he did to me," he said, "I did to him. Only more skillfully. First we took the fingers, then the toes. Ears, lips. Not his eyes, so he could see what we did, nor his tongue, so he could still call out. Hands, feet. Knees and elbows. And never allowed to bleed. I whittled him like a boy whittling a stick. In the end there was nothing left but the core.

"Here, boy. A memorial of your father."

He nodded and a servant threw a leather pouch in Shef's direction. Shef loosed the strings, glanced inside, hurled it at Cwichelm's feet.

"You are in poor company, warrior," he remarked.

"Time to go," said Guthmund.

The two sides backed away from each other, turned at safe distance. As they stepped briskly toward their own lines, Shef heard the Mercian warhorns bellow, heard a roar and a clash of mail as the English army came on.

Instantly, as prearranged, the Wayman line turned tail and ran. The first stage of its long, planned retreat.

*   *   *

Hours later, as the long winter twilight faded into dark, Brand muttered dry-throated to Shef, "I think we may have done it."

"For the day," Shef agreed. "I see no hope for the morning."

Brand shrugged massively, called the orders to stand down, light fires, heat water, make food.

All day the Waymen had fallen back, screening Shef's machines, shooting as the Mercians deployed, making them check, loading the carts and pack-horses hastily and then falling back in sections to another line. The Mercians had followed them like men anxious to tether a savage dog, closing in, drawing back from the snarls and snaps, pressing forward again. At least three times the two armies had clashed hand to hand, each time when the Waymen had had some obstacle to defend: the ditch they had cut, a dyke along the edge of the fen, the shallow muddy stream of the Nene. Each time, after half an hour's slashing and hewing, the Mercians had fallen sullenly back, unable to force the crossing—and in doing so, exposed themselves again to the lash of the boulders and the barbs.

The Waymen had fought better as their spirits rose, thought Shef. The trouble was, the Mercians were learning too. At the start they had flinched from the first whistle in the sky, the first displayed twist-shooter in a battle-line. Each ditch in the boggy soil made them hesitate. Sigvarth must have taught them a bitter lesson in the fen.

But as the day wore on they grew bolder, seeing the true weakness of the Wayman numbers.

Still holding a half-eaten bowl of porridge, Shef sank back on a pack-saddle and fell into instant sleep.

He woke, stiff, clammy and bitterly cold, as the horns blew for first light. All round him men clambered to their feet, drank water or the last hoarded remains of ale or mead. They shuffled to the crude breastwork they had made in the hamlet Brand had selected for their last stand.

As the light grew they looked out on a sight to daunt the boldest. The army they had fought the day before, like themselves, had grown steadily more ragged—clothes sodden, shields defaced with muck, its men grimed up to their eyebrows, weakened by a steady trickle of casualties and deserters—down to the point where it was barely half again their own size.

It had gone. In its place, drawn up in front of them, rank on rank, horns blasting a continual challenge, stood a new army, as fresh as if it had never marched a mile. Shields blazed with new paint, mail and weapons glinted red in the dawn. Crosses towered over the ranks, but the banners—the banners were different. Next to the crosses, a golden dragon.

From the line in front of them trotted a rider on a gray horse, his saddle and trappings bright scarlet, shield turned outward in sign of truce.

"He wants a parley," Shef said.

Silently the Waymen shifted an upturned cart to one side, allowed their leaders to edge out: Brand, Shef, Thorvin and Farman, Guthmund and Steinulf. Still silent, they tramped behind the horseman to a long trestle-table, set up incongruously in the midst of the standing men.

To one side of it sat Cwichelm and Alfgar, faces set. Wulfgar in his vertical box a pace behind them. The herald waved the six councillors of the Way to stools opposite.

Between the two groups sat one man—young, fair-haired, blue-eyed, a golden circle on his head like the old king in the mound. He had a strange, intense look, thought Shef. As he sat down, their eyes met. The young man smiled.

"I am Alfred, atheling of Wessex, brother of King Ethelred," he said. "I understand that my brother's fellow-king, Burgred of the Mark, has appointed an alderman for the shires once belonging to the king of the East Angles." He paused. "That cannot be allowed." Sour looks, silence from Alfgar and Cwichelm. They must have heard this already.

"At the same time I will not allow any Viking army from the North to base itself within any English shire, to rob and kill as has been your custom. Rather than do that I will destroy you all."

Another pause. "But I do not know what to do with you. From what I hear, you fought and beat Ivar Ragnarsson yesterday. Him, I will have no peace with, for he killed my brother's fellow-king Edmund. Who killed King Ella?"

"I did," said Shef. "But he would have thanked me for it if he could. I told Ivar that what he did to the king was *nithingsverk*."

"On so much we agree, then. The thing is, can I have peace with you? Or must we fight?"

"Have you asked your priests?" said Thorvin in his slow, careful English.

The young man smiled. "My brother and I have found that whenever we ask them anything, they demand money. Nor will they aid us even to keep off the likes of Ivar. But I am a Christian still. I believe in the faith of my fathers. I hope one day even you warriors of the North will take baptism and submit to our law. But I am not a Churchman."

"Some of us are Christians," said Shef. "Some of us are English."

"Are they full fellows of your army? With full rights to share?"

Brand, Guthmund and Steinulf looked at each other as they grasped the sense of the question.

"If you say they must be, then they are," said Shef.

"So. You are English and Norse. You are Christian and heathen."

"Not heathen," said Thorvin. "Wayman."

"But you can get along together. Maybe that is a model for us all. Listen, all of you. We can work out a treaty: shares and taxation, rights and duties, rules about wergilds and freedmen. All details. But the center of it must be this:

"I will give you Norfolk, to rule under your own law. But you must rule fairly. Never let in invaders. And the one who becomes alderman, he must swear on my relics and on your holy things to be the good friend of King Ethelred and his brother. Now, if that is to happen, who shall the alderman be?"

Brand's scarred hand reached out, tapped Shef. "He it must be, king's brother. He speaks two languages. He lives in two worlds. See, he has not the mark of the Way on him. He has been baptized. But he is our friend. Choose him."

"He is a runaway," yelled Alfgar suddenly. "He is a thrall. He has the marks of the whip on his back!"

"And of the torturer on his face," said Alfred. "Maybe he will see to it there is less of both in England. But console yourself, young man. I shall not send you back to King Burgred alone."

He waved a hand. From somewhere behind them came a flutter of skirts. A group of women were led into view.

"I found this party left behind and wandering, so I brought them along lest worse befall. I hear one of them is your wife, young noble. Take her back to King Burgred and be grateful."

His wife, thought Shef, staring deeply into Godive's gray eyes. She looked more beautiful than ever. What could she possibly think of him, covered in mire, stinking of sweat and worse, eye sunk in its socket? Her face showed utter horror. He felt a cold fist close round his heart.

Then she was in his arms, weeping. He held her tight with one hand, looked round. Alfgar was on his feet, struggling in the grip of two guards, Wulfgar bellowing from his box, Alfred rising with alarm on his face.

As the tumult ceased, Shef spoke. "She is mine."

"She is my wife," shouted Alfgar.

She is his half sister too, thought Shef. If I said that the Church would intervene, take her away from him. But then I would be letting the rule of the Church shape me and the law of the Way. The land of the Way.

This is the price the old *draugr* demands for his gold. Last time it was an eye. This time it is a heart.

He stood still as the attendants pulled Godive from him, drew her back to incest—her husband—and the bloodstained birch.

To be a king, to be a leader, demands things that cannot be asked of an ordinary man.

"If you are prepared to return the woman as a sign of good faith," said Alfred clearly, "I will take Suffolk into my brother's realm, but recognize you, Shef Sigwardsson, as alderman of Norfolk. What do you say?"

"Do not say 'alderman,'" said Brand, cutting in. "Use our word. Say he will be our jarl."

JARL

CHAPTER ONE

Shef sat facing the crowd of supplicants on a plain, three-legged stool. He still wore a hemp tunic and woolen breeches, with no signs of rank. But in the crook of his left arm rested the whetstone-scepter taken from the mound of the old king. From time to time Shef ran a thumb gently over one of its cruel carved, bearded faces as he listened to the witnesses.

". . . and so we took the case to King Edmund at Norwich. And he judged it in his private chamber—he had just returned from hunting and was washing his hands, God strike me blind if I lie—and he decided that the land should come to me for ten years and then be returned."

The speaker, a middle-aged thane of Norfolk, years of good living swelling his gold-mounted belt, hesitated for a moment in his tirade, unsure whether the mention of God might not count against him in a Wayman court of doom.

"Have you any witnesses to this agreement?" Shef asked.

The thane, Leofwin, puffed out his cheeks with grotesque pomposity. Not used to being questioned, or contradicted, evidently.

"Yes, certainly. Many men were in the king's chamber then. Wulfhun and Wihthelm. And Edrich the king's thane. But Edrich was killed by the pagan—was killed in the great battle, and so was Wulfhun. And Wihthelm has since died of the lung-sickness. Nevertheless, things are as I say!" Leofwin ended defiantly, glaring round him at the others in the court:

guards, attendants, his accuser, others waiting for their cases to be heard and decided.

Shef closed his one eye for a moment, remembering a far-off evening of peace in the fen with Edrich, not so very far from here in space. So that was what had happened to him. It might have been guessed.

He opened it again and stared fixedly at Leofwin's accuser. "Why," he said gently, "why does what King Edmund decided seem to you unjust in this case? Or do you deny that what this man says is what the king decided?"

The accuser, another middle-aged thane of the same stamp as his opponent, blanched visibly as the jarl's piercing gaze fell on him. This was the man, all Norfolk knew, who had begun as a thrall in Emneth. Who had been the last Englishman ever to speak to the martyred king. Who had appeared—God only knew how—as leader of the pagans. Had dug up the hoard of Raedwald. Defeated the Boneless One himself. And somehow had gained the friendship and support of Wessex as well. Who could tell how all that had come about? Dog's name or no, he was a man too strange to lie to.

"No," said the second thane. "I do not deny that was what the king decided, and I agreed to it as well. But when it was agreed, the understanding behind the decision was this: That after ten years' time the land in question should revert from Leofwin to my grandson, whose father was also killed by the pagans. That is to say, by the—by the men from the North. In the state in which it was in the beginning! But what this man has done"—indignation replaced caution in his voice—"what Leofwin has done ever since is to ruin it! He has cut the timber and planted no more, he has let the dykes and the drains go to ruin, he has turned ploughland into a watermeadow for hay. The land will be worth nothing at the end of his lease."

"Nothing?"

The complainant hesitated. "Not as much as before, lord jarl."

Somewhere outside a bell rang, a sign that the dooms-giving was over for the day. But this case must be decided. It was a hard one, as the court had heard already at tedious length, with debts and evasions of them going back for generations, and all the parties in the case related to each other. Neither of the men present today was of much consequence. Neither had seemed of special note to King Edmund, which was why they had been allowed to live on their estates when better men, like Edrich, had been called to service and to death. Still, they were Englishmen of rank, whose families had lived in Norfolk for generations: the sort of people who had to be won over. It was a good sign that they had come to the new jarl's court for judgement.

"This is my doom," said Shef. "The land shall remain with Leofwin for the rest of his ten-year lease." Leofwin's red face brightened into a beam of triumph.

"But he shall render an account of his gains each year to my thane at Lynn, whose name is—"

"Bald," said a black-robed figure standing by a writing-desk to Shef's right.

"Whose name is Bald. At the end of the ten years, if the gain on the property seems more than is reasonable to Bald, Leofwin shall either pay the extra gain for the whole ten years to the grandson in this case, or else he shall pay a sum to be fixed by Bald, equal in value to the worth the land has lost during his stewardship. And the choice shall be made by the grandfather, here present today."

One face lost its beam, the other brightened. Then both faces took on an identical expression of anxious calculation. Good, thought Shef. Neither is altogether happy. So they will respect my decision.

He rose. "The bell has struck. The dooms-giving is over for today." A babble of protest, men and women pushing forward from the waiting ranks.

"It will begin again tomorrow. You have your tally-sticks? Show them as you enter and cases will be heard in proper order." Shef's voice rose strongly above the babble.

"And all mark this! In the court of the Way there is neither Christian nor pagan, neither Wayman nor Englishman. See—I bear no pendant. And Father Boniface here"—he pointed to the black-robed scribe—"priest though he is, he bears no cross. Justice here does not depend on faith. Mark it and tell it. Now go. The hearing is over."

The doors at the back of the room swung open. Attendants began to urge the disappointed litigants outside into the spring sunshine. Another, the hammer-sign stitched neatly onto his gray tunic, waved the two disputants of the last case over toward Father Boniface, to see the jarl's doom written out twice and witnessed, one copy to remain in the jarl's scriptorium, the other to be torn carefully in two and divided between the litigants, so that neither could present a forgery at some future court.

Through the rear doors there stalked a massive figure, head and shoulders above the people pushing out, in mail and cloak, but unarmed. Shef felt the lonely gloom of judgement suddenly lighten.

"Brand! You are back! You come just at the right moment, when I am free to talk."

Shef felt his hand gripped in one the size of a quart tankard, saw his own beaming smile answered.

"Not quite, lord jarl. I came two good hours ago. Your guards would not let me through, and with all those halberds waving and never a word of Norse among the lot of them I had not the heart to argue."

"Hah! They should—No. My orders are to let no one interrupt court of doom except for news of war. They did right. But I am sorry I did not think to make an exception for you. I would have liked you to attend the court and say what you thought of it."

"I heard." Brand jerked a thumb behind him. "The head of your guards there was a catapulteer and knew me, though I did not know him. He brought me good ale—excellent ale, after a sea-voyage, to wash out the salt —and told me to listen through the door."

"And what did you think?" Shef turned Brand about and strolled with him through the now-cleared doorway into the courtyard outside. "What did you think of the jarl's assembly?"

"I am impressed. When I think of what this place was like four months ago—mud everywhere, warriors snoring on the floor for lack of beds, never a kitchen in sight and no food to cook in it. And now. Guards. Chamberlains. Bakeries and brewhouses. Wood-wrights fixing shutters and gangs painting everything that doesn't move. Men to ask your name and business. And *writing it down* when you tell them."

Then Brand frowned and looked about, lowered his enormous voice to an unpracticed whisper. "Shef—lord jarl, I should say. One thing. Why all these blackrobes? Can you trust them? And what in the name of Thor is a jarl doing, a lord of warriors, listening to a couple of muttonheads arguing about drains? You'd be better off shooting catapults. Or in the forge even."

Shef laughed, looking across at the massive silver buckle holding together his friend's cloak, the bulging purse on his sword-belt, the ornamental waist-chain of linked silver coins.

"Tell me, Brand, how did your trip home go? Were you able to buy all you meant to?"

Brand's face took on a hucksterish look of caution. "I put some money in safe hands. Prices are high in Halogaland, and folk are mean. Still, when I hang up my axe for good, it may be there is some small farm for me to retire to in my old age."

Shef laughed again. "With your share of all our winnings, in good silver, you must have bought up half the county for your relatives to look after."

This time Brand grinned too. "I did pretty well, I admit. Better than ever in my life before."

"Well, let me tell you about the blackrobes. What none of us has ever realized is the money the stay-at-homes have. The wealth in a whole county, a rich county of England, not a poor stony one in Norway where you come from. Tens of thousands of men, all tilling the soil and raising sheep and trimming wool and keeping bees and cutting timber and smelting iron and raising horses. More than a thousand square miles. Maybe a thousand thousand acres. All those acres must pay something to me, to the jarl, if it is only the war-tax, or bridge-and-road money.

"Some of them pay everything. I took all Church land into my own possession. Some of it I gave at once to the freed slaves who fought for us, twenty acres a man. Wealth to them—but a fleabite compared to the whole. Much I leased out straightaway, to the rich men of Norfolk, at low rates, for ready money. Those who got it will not want to see the Church come back. Much I kept in my own hand, for the jarldom. In future it will make money for me, to hire workers and warriors.

"But I could not have done it without the blackrobes, as you call them. Who could keep all this land, all these goods, all these leases, in his head? Thorvin knows how to write in our letters, but few others. Suddenly there were many lettered men, men of the Church, with no land and no income all of a sudden. Some now work for me."

"But can you trust them, Shef?"

"The ones who hate me and will never forgive me, or you, or the Way— they have gone off to King Burgred, or to Wulfhere the Archbishop, to stir up war."

"You should have just killed them all."

Shef hefted his stone scepter. "They say, the Christians, that the blood of martyrs is the seed of the Church. I believe them. I make no martyrs. But I made sure that the angriest of those who left knew the names of those who stayed. The ones who work for me will never be forgiven. Like the rich thanes, their fate now depends on mine."

They had come to a low building within the stockade that ran round the jarl's *burg,* its shutters open to the sun. Shef pointed inside to the writing-desks, the men conferring quietly, writing on parchment. On one wall Brand could see hung a great *mappa:* a newly made one, devoid of ornament, full of detail.

"By the winter I shall have a book of every piece of land in Norfolk, and a picture of the whole shire on my wall. By next summer not a penny will be paid for land without my knowledge. And then there will be wealth such as even the Church has never seen. We can do things with it that have never been done before."

"If the silver is good," said Brand dubiously.

"It is better than up North. I have been thinking this: It seems to me that there is only so much silver in this country, in all the kingdoms of the English put together. And there is always the same amount of work for it to do—land to buy, things to trade. Now, the more that there is locked up in the coffers of the Church, or traded for gold, or made into precious things that do not move, the more the less that is left—No, the harder the less that is left . . ."

Shef floundered to a halt, neither English nor Norse adequate to explain what he meant.

"What I mean is, the Church took too much out of the Northern kingdom and put nothing back. That is why their coins were so bad. King Edmund was less kind to the Church, and so money here was better. Soon it will be the best.

"And not only the money will be the best, Brand." The young man turned to face his massive colleague, his one eye glittering. "I mean this shire of Norfolk to be the best and the happiest land in the whole of the Northern world. A place where everyone can grow from child to graybeard in safety. Where we can live like people, not like animals scratching for a living. Where we can help each other.

"Because I have learned another thing, Brand, from Ordlaf the reeve of Bridlington, from the slaves who made my *mappa* and led us to the riddle of Edmund. It is something the Way needs to know. What is the most precious thing to the Way, the Way of Asgarth?"

"New knowledge," said Brand, automatically clutching his hammer-pendant.

"New knowledge is good. Not everyone has it. But this is just as good, and it can come from anywhere: *old knowledge that no one has recognized.* It is something I have seen more clearly since I became the jarl. There is always someone who knows the answer to your question, the cure for your need. But usually no one has asked him. Or her. It may be a slave, a poor miner. An old woman, a fisher-reeve, a priest.

"When I have all the knowledge in the county written down, as well as all the land and the silver, then we shall show the world a new thing!"

Brand, on Shef's blind side, glanced down at the taut tendons in the neck, the young man's trimmed beard now sprinkled with gray.

What he needs, he thought, is a fine, active woman to keep him busy. But even I, Brand the Champion, even I dare not offer to buy him one.

*   *   *

That evening, as the woodsmoke from the chimneys began to mix with the gray twilight, the priests of the Way met within their corded circle. They sat in the wort-yard, the garden of a cottage outside the jarl's stockade, in a pleasant smell of apple-sap and green growth. Thrushes and blackbirds trilled vigorously about them.

"He has no idea of the real purpose of your sea-trip?" asked Thorvin.

Brand shook his head. "None."

"But you passed the news?"

"I passed the news and I got the news. The word of what has happened here has gone to every Way-priest in the Northern lands, and they will tell their followers. It has gone to Birko and to Kaupang, to Skiringssal and to the Tronds."

"So, we can expect reinforcements," said Geirulf, Tyr's priest.

"With the money that has been taken home, and the tales every skald is telling, you can be sure that every warrior of the Way who can raise a ship will be here looking for work. And every priest who can free himself as well. There will be many who take the pendant in hope, also. Liars, some of them. Not believers. But they can be dealt with. There is a more important matter."

Brand paused, looking round the circle of intent faces. "In Kaupang, as I came home, I met the priest Vigleik."

"Vigleik of the many visions?" asked Farman tensely.

"Even so. He had called a conclave of priests from Norway and from the South Swedes. He told them—and me—that he was disturbed."

"What about?"

"Many things. He is sure now, as we are, that the boy Shef is the center of the change. He has even thought, as we have, that he may be what he said he was when first he met you, Thorvin: the one who will come from the North."

Brand looked round the table to meet the eyes fixed on him. "And yet, if that is true, the story is not what any of us expected, not even the wisest. Vigleik says, for one thing, he is not a Norseman. He has an English mother."

Shrugs. "Who hasn't?" asked Vestmund. "English, Irish. My grandmother was a Lapp."

"He was brought up a Christian, too. He has been baptized."

This time, grunts of amusement. "We've all seen the scars on his back," said Thorvin. "He hates the Christians, just as we do. No. He doesn't even hate them. He thinks they are fools."

"All right. But this is the sticking point: He has not taken the pendant. He has no belief in us. He sees the visions, Thorvin, or so he has told you. But he does not think they are visions of another world. He is not a believer."

This time the men sat silent, eyes turning slowly to Thorvin. The Thor-priest rubbed his beard.

"Well. He is not an unbeliever, either. If we asked him, he would say that a man with a pendant of a heathen god, as the Christians call them, could not rule Christians, not even for as long as it will take for them to stop being Christians. He would say that wearing a pendant is not a matter of belief, it would just be a mistake, like starting to hammer before the iron was hot. And he does not know which pendant he should wear."

"I do," said Brand. "I saw it and said it last year, when he killed his first man."

"I think so too," agreed Thorvin. "He should wear the spear of Othin, God of the Hanged, Betrayer of Warriors. Only such a one would have sent his own father to death. But he would say, if he were here, that it was the only thing to do at that time."

"Is Vigleik only talking of probabilities?" asked Farman suddenly. "Or did he have some particular message? Some message a god sent him?"

Silently Brand pulled a packet of thin boards wrapped round with seal-skin from inside his tunic and passed it over. Runes were cut on the wood, and inked in. Slowly Thorvin scanned them, Geirulf and Skaldfinn leaning close to look also. The faces of all three darkened as they read on.

"Vigleik has seen something," said Thorvin at length. "Brand, do you know the tale of Frodi's mill?"

The champion shook his head.

"Three hundred years ago there was a king in Denmark called Frodi. He had, they say, a magic mill, which did not grind corn, but instead ground out peace and wealth and fertility. We believe it was the mill of new knowledge. To grind the mill he had two slaves, two giant-maidens called Fenja and Menja. But so anxious was Frodi to have continuing peace and wealth for his people that no matter how much the giantesses begged for rest, he denied it to them."

Thorvin's deep voice broke into sonorous chant:

" 'You shall not sleep,' said Frodi the king,
'Longer than the time it takes a cuckoo
To answer another, or an errand-lad
To sing a song as he steps on his way.'

"So the slaves grew angry and remembered their giant-blood, and instead of grinding peace and wealth and fertility, they began to grind out flame and blood and warriors. And his enemies came on Frodi in the night and destroyed him and his kingdom, and the magic mill was lost forever.

"That is what Vigleik has seen. He means one can go too far, even in hunting new knowledge, if the world is not ready for it. One must strike while the iron is hot. But one can also blow the bellows too long and too furiously."

A long pause. Reluctantly, Brand got ready to reply. "I had better tell you," he said, "what the jarl, what Skjef Sigvarthsson told me this morning of his intentions. Then you must decide how this fits Vigleik's visions."

A few days later, Brand stood staring at the great stone now sunk into the meadow, near the spot where the muddy causeway from Ely debouched into the fields outside March.

On it was carved a curling ribbon of runes, their edges still sharp from the chisel. Shef touched them lightly with his fingertips.

"What they say is this. I composed it myself, in verse in your language as Geirulf taught me. The runes read:

" *'Well he left life, though ill he lived it.*
All scores are settled by death.'

At the top is his name: *'Sigvarth Jarl.'* "

Brand grunted doubtfully. He had not liked Sigvarth. And yet the man had taken the death of his one son well. And there was no doubt he had saved his other son, and the Army of the Way, by enduring his last night of torture.

"Well," he said at last. "He has his *bautasteinn,* right enough. It is an old saying: 'Few stones would stand by the way, if sons did not set them up.' But this is not where he was killed?"

"No," said Shef. "They killed him back in the mire. It seems my other father, Wulfgar, could not wait even till he reached firm ground." His mouth twisted, and he spat on the grass. "But if we had set it up there it would have been out of sight in the marsh in six weeks.

"Besides, I wanted you here to see this."

He grinned, turned, and waved an arm in the direction of the almost imperceptible rise that led toward March. From somewhere out of sight there came a noise like the squealing of a dozen pigs being butchered simultaneously. Brand's axe flicked from the ground as his eyes darted round for a lurking enemy, an attacker.

Into sight, from down the deeply rutted track, came a column of bag-pipers, four abreast, cheeks puffed. As his alarm receded Brand recognized the familiar face of Cwicca, the former slave of St. Guthlac's at Crowland, in the front rank.

"They are all playing the same tune," he bellowed over the din. "Was that your idea?"

Shef shook his head and jerked a thumb at the pipers. "Theirs. It's a tune they made up. They call it 'The Boneless Boned.' "

Brand shook his head in disbelief. English slaves mocking the champion of the North himself. He had never thought . . .

Behind the pipers, a score of them, stepped a longer column of men clutching halberds, their heads hidden in shining, sharp-rimmed helmets, each man wearing a leather coat with metal plates stitched onto it, and a small round targe strapped to his left forearm. They must be English too, Brand thought as they marched on. How could he tell? Mainly, it was their size—not a man much above five and a half feet. And yet many of the English ran to size and strength as well, to look at the hulks whom Brand had seen fighting to the last round their lord King Edmund. No, these were not only Englishmen, but poor Englishmen. Not thanes of the En-glish, not carls of the Army, but churls. Or slaves. Slaves with arms and armor.

Brand looked at them in skepticism and disbelief. All his life he had known the weight of mail, known the effort needed to swing an axe or a broadsword. A fully armed warrior might need to carry—and not just to carry, to wield—forty or fifty pounds' weight of metal. How long could a man do that? For the first man whose arm weakened in a battle-line would be dead. In Brand's language, to call a man "the stout" was a valued compliment. He knew seventeen words for "man of small size," and all of them were insults.

He watched the pygmies tramp by, two hundred of them. All held their halberds the same way, he noticed, straight up above the right shoulder. Men marching close together could not afford the luxury of individual decision. But a Viking army would have straggled and held its weapons any way that seemed good, to show proper independence of spirit.

Behind the halberdiers came team after team of horses, he noticed with surprise. Not the slow, dogged ox-teams that had dragged Shef's catapults round the flank of Ivar's army. The first ten pairs of horses dragged the carts with the disassembled beams he had seen before, the pull-throwers, the traction-catapults that lobbed stones. By each cart walked its crew, a dozen men with the same gray jerkins and white hammer-insignia as the pipers and halberdiers. In each crew, a familiar face. Shef's paid-off veterans of the winter campaign had seen their land, had left men to till it, and had returned to their master, the wealth-giver. Each one now captained a crew of his own, recruited from the slaves of the vanished Church.

The next ten pairs were something new again. Behind the horses came a thing on broad cart-wheels, a long trail on each lifted high so that the other end bowed like a chicken scratching for worms in the mud. A twist-shooter, the torsion-catapults that shot the great darts. Not disassembled, but ready for action, the high wheels marking the only difference from the one that had killed King Ella: the ones that had brought down the Coiling Worm standard of Ivar. Again, a dozen men crewed each, marching with their winding-levers sloped and bundles of darts over their shoulders.

As they too tramped by, Brand realized that the bagpipe music, though changed, had not moved into the distance. The five hundred men he had seen already were filing past and then turning back on themselves, lining up in ranks behind him.

But here at last was something like an army approaching, scores and scores of men, not in ranks, not marching, but slouched on ponies and flooding forward down the track like a gray tide. Mail-shirts, broadswords, helmets, familiar faces. Brand waved cheerfully as he recognized Guthmund—still known as the Greedy—in front of his ship's crew. Others waved back, calling out as the English had not done: Magnus Gaptooth and his friend Kolbein, clutching halberds as well as the rest of their armament, Vestlithi, who had been the helmsman of Sigvarth Jarl; and a dozen others he knew for followers of the Way.

"Some went off to spend their winnings, like you," said Shef in Brand's ear. "Others sent the money off or kept it, and stayed on here. Many have bought land. It is their own country they are defending now."

The pipers ceased their din simultaneously, and Brand realized he was surrounded by a ring of men. He stared round, counting, calculating.

"Ten long hundreds?" he said at last. "Half English, half Norse?"

Shef nodded. "What do you think of them?"

Brand shook his head. "The horses to pull the teams," he said. "Twice the speed of ox-teams. But I did not know the English knew how to harness them properly. I have seen them try, and they harness them as if they were oxen, pushing against a pole. Cuts their wind off and they cannot use their strength. How did you realize that?"

"I told you," said Shef. "There is always someone who knows better.

This time it was one of your men, one of your own crew—Gauti, who walks with a limp. The first time I tried to harness horses he walked by and told me what a fool I was. Then he showed me how you do it in Halogaland, where you always plough with horses. Not new knowledge— old knowledge. Old knowledge not everyone knows. But we worked out how to hitch up the catapults ourselves."

"Well and good," said Brand. "But answer me this: Catapults or no catapults, horse-teams or no horse-teams: how many of your English are fit to stand in a battle-line against trained warriors? Warriors half their weight again and twice their strength? You cannot make front-fighters out of kitchen boys. Better to recruit some of those well-fed thanes we saw. Or their sons."

Shef crooked a finger and two halberdiers hustled a prisoner forward. A Norseman—bearded, pale-faced beneath windburn, a head taller than his two escorts. He held his left wrist awkwardly in his right hand, like a man whose collarbone is broken. The face was half-familiar: a man whom Brand had seen once at some forgotten campfire when the Viking army had still been as one.

"His three crews tried their luck raiding our lands near the Yare two weeks ago," Shef remarked. "Tell them how you got on."

The man stared at Brand with a kind of plea. "Cowards. Wouldn't fight us fair," he snarled. "They caught us coming out of our first village. A dozen of my men down with great darts through them before we could see where they were coming from. When we charged the machines they held us off with the big axes. Then more of them came round from behind. After they had dealt with us they took me along—my arm was broken so I could not lift shield—to see them attack the ships we had left offshore. They sank one with the stone-throwers. Two got away."

He grimaced. "My name is Snaekolf, from Raumariki. I did not know you men of the Way had taught the English so much, or I would not have raided here. Will you speak for me?"

Shef shook his head before Brand could reply. "His men behaved like beasts in that village," he said. "We will have no more of it. I kept him to say his piece and he has said it. Hang him when you can find a tree."

Hoofbeats came from behind them as the halberdiers hustled the silent Viking away. Shef turned without haste or alarm to meet the rider cantering down the muddy track. The man reached them, dismounted, bowed briefly and spoke. The men of the Wayland army, English and Norse together, stretched their ears to listen.

"News from your *burg*, lord jarl. A rider came in yesterday, from Winchester. King Ethelred of the West Saxons is dead, of the coughing-sickness. His brother, your friend Alfred the atheling, is expected to succeed him and take power."

"Good news," said Brand thoughtfully. "A friend in power is always good."

"You said 'expected'?" said Shef. "Who could oppose him? There is no other of that royal house left."

CHAPTER TWO

The young man stared out from a narrow window in the stone. Behind him, very faintly, he could hear the sound of the monks of the Old Minster singing yet another of the many masses he had paid for, masses for the soul of his last brother, King Ethelred. In front of him, all was activity. The wide street that ran east to west through Winchester was crowded with traders, stalls, customers. Through them pushed carts laden with timber. Three separate gangs of men were working on houses either side of the street, digging foundations, driving beams into the soil, fitting planks over timber frames. If he lifted his eyes he could see, round the edge of the town, many more men strengthening the rampart his brother had ordered, driving in the logs and fitting the fighting-platforms. From all directions came the sound of saws and hammers.

The young man, Alfred the atheling, felt a fierce satisfaction. This was his town: Winchester. The town of his family for centuries, for as long as the English had been on their island, and longer even than that, for he could number ancestors among the British and the Romans too. This Minster was his. His many greats-grandfather King Cenwalh had given the land on which it was to be built to the Church two hundred years before, as well as the land to support it and provide its revenues. Not only his brother Ethelred was buried here, but his father Ethelwulf as well, and his other brothers, and uncles and great-uncles in number more than a man could count. They had lived, they had died, they had gone back to the earth. But it was the same earth. Last of his line, the young atheling did not feel alone.

Strengthened, he turned to face the saw-edged voice that had been grating away behind him in competition with the sounds from outside. The voice of the bishop of Winchester, Bishop Daniel.

"What was that you said?" demanded the atheling. "*If* I come to be king? I *am* the king. I am the last of the house of Cerdic, whose line goes back to Woden. The *witenagemot,* the meeting of the councillors, elected me without debate. The warriors raised me on my shield. I am the king."

The bishop's face set mulishly. "What is this talk of Woden, the god of the pagans? That is no qualification for a Christian king. And what the *witan* do—what the warriors do—that has no meaning in the eyes of God.

"You cannot be king till you have been anointed with the holy oil, like Saul or David. Only I and the other bishops of the realm can do that. And I tell you—we will not. Not unless you satisfy us you are a true king for a Christian land. To prove this you must cease your alliance with the Church-despoilers. Remove your protection from the one they call the Sheaf. Make war on the pagans. The pagans of the Way!"

Alfred sighed. Slowly he walked across the room. He rubbed with his fingers at a dark stain on the wall, a mark of burning.

"Father," he said patiently. "You were here two years ago. It was the pagans then who sacked this town. Burned every house in it, stripped this minster itself of all the gifts my ancestors had put in it, drove off all the town-folk and priests they could catch to their slave-marts.

"Those were true pagans. And it was not even the Great Army that did it, the army of the sons of Ragnar, of Sigurth the Snakeeye and Ivar Boneless. It was just a troop of marauders.

"That is how weak we are. Or were. What I mean to do"—his voice rose suddenly and challengingly—"is see to it that bane never comes on Winchester again, so that my long fathers can rest in peace in their graves. To do that I must have strength. And support. The men of the Way will not challenge us, they will live in fellowship, pagans or no pagans. They are not our enemies. A true Christian king cares for his people. That is what I am doing. Why will you not consecrate me?"

"A true Christian king," said the bishop, slowly, carefully, "a true Christian king cares first and above all for the Church. The pagans may have burned the roof from this minster. But they did not take its land and revenues forever. No pagan, not the Boneless One himself, has taken all the Church land for his own, and given it to slaves and hirelings."

That was the reality, thought Alfred. Gangs of marauders, the Great

Army itself, might come down on minster or monastery and strip it of its goods, its treasures and relics. Bishop Daniel would resent it bitterly, torture to death every last stray Viking he caught. But it was not yet to him a matter of survival. The Church could re-roof its minsters, restock its lands, breed new parishioners and even ransom back its books and holy bones. Pillage was survivable.

Taking away the land that was the basis of permanent wealth, land the Church had booked to itself from death-bed donations over many centuries, that was more dangerous. That was what the new alderman, no, the jarl of the Way-folk had done. That had taught Bishop Daniel a new fear. Daniel feared for the Church. He himself, Alfred realized: he feared for Winchester. Rebuilding or no, ransoms or no, long view or short view—he would never see it ravaged and burned again. Church was less important than city.

"I do not need your holy oil," he said peremptorily. "I can rule without you. The aldermen and the reeves, the thanes and the councillors and the warriors. They will follow me as king whether I am consecrated or not."

The bishop stared unwinkingly at the set young face before him, shook his head with cold anger. "It will not be. The scribes, the priests, the men who write your royal writs and book your leases: they will not aid you. They will do as I tell them. In all your kingdom—if king you call yourself —there is not one man who can read and write who is not a member of the Church. What is more—you cannot read yourself! Much though your holy and pious mother wished you to learn the craft!"

The young atheling's cheeks flushed with rage and shame as he remembered the day he had deceived his mother. Had had the priest read one of her much-loved English poems over and over until he had learned it by heart. Then had stood in front of her reciting it and pretending to read from the book he had coveted. Where was the book now? Some priest had taken it. Probably had scraped the writing from it so he could inscribe on it some saintly text.

The bishop's voice rasped on. "So, young man, you do need me. And not only for the power of my subordinates, the power I lend you. For I have allies, too, yes, and superiors. You are not the only Christian king in England. The pious Burgred of Mercia, he knows his duty. The young man you dispossessed of Norfolk, Alfgar the alderman, and his worthy father Wulfgar, whom the pagans mutilated—they know their duty too. Tell me, are there none of your thanes and aldermen who might not follow one of them? As king?"

"The thanes of Wessex will only follow a man of Wessex."

"Even if they are told different? If the order comes—from Rome?"

The name hung in the air. Alfred paused, contemptuous reply checked on his lips. Once before in his lifetime Wessex had challenged Rome: when his brother Ethelbald had married his father's widow against all the rules of the Church. The word had come, the threats had been made. Ethelbald had died soon after—no one knew what of—the bride had been returned to her father, king of the Franks. They had not let Ethelbald's body lie in Winchester.

The bishop smiled, knowing his words struck home. "You see, lord king, you have no choice. And what you do does not matter in any case. It is only a test of your loyalty. The man you supported—Sheaf the son of the heathen jarl, the Englishman who was brought up as a Christian and then turned his back on it, the apostate, worse than any pagan, worse than the Boneless One himself—he has no more than weeks to live. His enemies ring him round. Believe me! I hear news that you do not.

"Sever your bond with him at once. Show your obedience to the Church your Mother."

The bishop leaned back in his new-carved chair, sure of his power, anxious to mark an ascendancy which would last as long as the young man in front of him might live.

"King though you may yet be," he said, "you are in our minster now. You have our leave to go. Go. And issue the orders I demand."

The poem he had learned for his mother years ago came back suddenly to the young atheling's mind. It had been a poem of wise advice for warriors, a poem from before Christian times.

"Answer lie with lie," it had said, *"and let your enemy, the man who mocks you, miss your thought. He will be unaware, when your wrath shall fall."* Good advice, thought Alfred. Maybe my mother sent it.

"I will obey your words," he said, rising humbly. "And I must beg you to forgive the errors of my youth, while I thank you for your prudent direction."

Weakling! thought the bishop.

He hears news that I do not? wondered the king.

To anyone who knew him—and to many who did not—the marks of defeat and shame and ignominious flight in the depths of winter, all were visible on Ivar Ragnarsson's face. The terrible eyes were still there, the eyes under frozen lashes that never blinked. But there was something in them that had not been there before: an absence, a withdrawal. Ivar walked like a man with something forever on his mind, slowly, absently, almost painfully, shorn of the lithe grace that had once marked him out.

It was still there when needed. The long flight from the fields of Norfolk across England to his brothers' base at York had not been an easy one. Men who had slipped out of sight when the Great Army passed that way before now emerged from every lane and byroad as a mere pair of exhausted men cantered back. Ivar and the faithful horse-swain Hamal, who had ridden to save him from the Way. At least six times the pair had been ambushed by angry peasants, local thanes, and the border-guards of king Burgred.

Ivar had dealt contemptuously with them all. Before the pair were out of Norfolk he had slashed the heads from two churls driving a farm-cart, taken their leather jackets and blanket coats, handed them to Hamal without a word. By the time they reached York his kills had been beyond count.

Three trained warriors at once could not stand against him, reported Hamal to a curious, fascinated audience. He means to prove he is still the Champion of the North.

Takes a lot of proving now, his audience muttered, the carls of the Army talking freely as was their right. Go with twenty long hundreds, come back with one man. He can be beaten.

That was what Ivar could not forget. His brothers, plying him with hot mead in front of the fire in their quarters by the minster, they had seen it. Seen too that their brother, never safe, now could not be trusted at all in any matter that required calculation. It had not broken their famous unity —nothing ever would—but now, whenever they talked among themselves, there were three and one, where once there had been four.

They had seen the change the first night. Silently, their eyes had met, silently they did what they had done before, telling none of their men, not admitting it even to each other. They had chosen a slave-girl from the Dales, wrapped her in a sail, gagged and bound her, thrust her into Ivar's quarters at dead of night while he lay, unsleeping and expectant.

In the morning they had come and taken away, in the wooden chest they had used before, what remained. Ivar would not run mad for a while, not fall into the berserk mood. Yet no sensible man felt anything but fear in his presence.

"He's coming," called a monk, poised at the entrance to the great workshop where the minster-men of York toiled for their allies-turned-masters. The slaves sweating at forge, vice or rope-walk redoubled their efforts. Ivar would kill the man he saw standing still.

The scarlet cloak and silver helmet stalked through the doorway, stood glaring round. Erkenbert the deacon, the only man whose behavior did not change, turned to meet him.

Ivar jerked a thumb at the workmen. "All ready? Ready now?" He spoke the jargon mixed of English and Norse that the Army and the churchmen had learned that winter.

"Enough of both to try."

"The dart-throwers? The stone-throwers?"

"See."

Erkenbert clapped his hands. Immediately the monks shouted orders, their slaves began to wheel and tug at a line of machines. Ivar watched them, his face blank. After his brothers had taken the chest away, he had lain without moving for a day and a night, his cloak over his face. Then, as every man in the army knew, he had stood up, walked to the door of his room, and screamed to the sky: "Sigvarthsson did not beat me! It was the machines!"

Since then, since he had called for Erkenbert and the learned ones of York to obey his wishes, the forge-din had not ceased.

Outside the workshop, the slaves set up the dart-thrower, identical to the one that had broken the first assault on York, inside the minster-precinct itself, training across a furlong of open space to the far wall. There a dozen churls hung a great straw target. Others wound feverishly on the new-forged cogs.

"Enough!" Erkenbert himself stepped across, checked the alignment of the barbed javelin, fixed Ivar with his eye, handed him the thong attached to its iron toggle.

Ivar jerked it. The toggle flew sideways, clanging unnoticed from his helmet, the line rising and falling in the air, a monstrous thump. Before the eye could follow it, the dart was buried deep—quivering in its straw bed.

Ivar dropped the string, turned. "The other."

This time the slaves tugged forward a strange machine. Like the twist-shooter, it had a wooden frame of stout beams. This time the cogwheels were not on top but at the side. They twisted a single rope, embedded in its strands, a wooden rod. At the end of the rod, a heavy sling, its pouch just clearing the ground. The rod quivered against its retaining-bolt as the slaves turned the levers.

"This is the stone-thrower," declared Erkenbert.

"Not like the one that broke my ram?"

The deacon smiled with satisfaction. "No. That was a great machine that threw a boulder. But many men were needed to move it, and it could shoot only once. This throws smaller stones. No man has made such a

machine since the days of the Romans. But I, Erkenbert, the humble servant of God, I have read the words in our Vegetius. And have built this
machine. The *onager* it is named: that is, in your tongue, 'the wild ass.' "

A slave placed a ten-pound rock in the sling, signed to Erkenbert.

Again the deacon passed a thong to Ivar. "Pull the bolt," he said.

Ivar jerked the string. Faster than sight the great rod leapt forward like a
great swinging arm.

Stopping with a crash against a padded beam, the entire weighted frame
jumped from the ground. The sling whirled round far faster than Shef's
self-designed stone-throwers. Like a streak the rock flashed across the
minster-yard, never rising—not lobbed but hurled. The straw target billowed into the air, slowly collapsed on its slings. The slaves cheered once
in triumph.

Slowly Ivar turned to Erkenbert. "That is not it," he said. "The machines
that rained death on my army, they threw high in the sky." He lobbed a
pebble upward. "Not like this." He hurled another at a pecking sparrow.

"You have made the wrong machine."

"Impossible," said Erkenbert. "There is the great machine for sieges. And
this one for men. None other is described in Vegetius."

"Then those bastards of the Way have made a new thing. One not
described in—in your book."

Erkenbert shrugged his shoulders, unconvinced. Who cared what this
pirate said? He could not even read, still less read Latin.

"And how fast does it shoot?" Ivar glared at the slaves twirling their levers. "I tell you, I saw the stone-throwers hurl another while the first was still in the air. This one is too slow."

"But it strikes hard. No man can resist it."

Ivar stared thoughtfully at the fallen target. Suddenly he whirled, yelled orders in Norse. Hamal and a handful of companions sprang forward, pushed the slaves out of the way, and heaved the cumbrous, tense-wound machine round.

"No," shouted Erkenbert, pushing forward. Ivar's arm clamped irresistibly round his throat, a wire-muscled hand forced his mouth shut.

Ivar's men pushed the machine round another foot, hauled it back a trifle as their leader ordered. One hand still effortlessly holding the limp deacon off the ground, Ivar jerked the string a third time.

The giant door of the minster—oak beams nailed across each other in double-ply, held fast over all with iron bands—exploded in all directions, splinters flying in slow arcs across the yard. From inside came a chorus of wails, monks leaping out, darting back, shrieking in terror.

They all stared in fascination at the great hole the boulder had smashed.

"You see," said Erkenbert. "This is the true stone-thrower. It strikes hard. No man can resist it."

Ivar turned, eyes fixed on the little monk in contempt. "It is not the true stone-thrower. There is another kind in the world of which you know nothing. But strike hard it does. You must make me many."

Across the narrow sea to the land of the Franks beyond, a thousand miles away in the land of the Romans, there within the gates of a minster greater than Winchester, greater even than York, deep silence lay. Popes had had many troubles, many failures, since the time of their great founder. Some had met martyrdom, some been forced to flee for their lives. Not thirty years before, Saracen pirates had made their way to the very gates of Rome, and had sacked the holy basilica of St. Peter himself which was then outside the wall.

It would not happen again. He who was now the equal of the Apostles, the successor of Peter, the holder of the keys of Heaven, he had set his face above all toward power. Virtue was great: humility, chastity, poverty. But without power none of those could survive. It was his duty to the humble, the chaste and the poor, to seek power. In pursuit of it he had put down many mighty ones from their high seats on their thrones—he, Nicholas I, Pope of Rome, Servant of the servants of God.

Slowly the hawk-faced old man stroked his cat, his secretaries and attendants sitting round him in silence. The foolish archbishop from the town in England, the town with the strange outlandish name—*Eboracum*, evidently, though hard to tell with his barbarous pronunciation—he had been dismissed with courtesy, and a cardinal deputed to show him all honor and provide him with amusement. What he had said had been nonsense: a new religion, a challenge to the authority of the Church, the barbarians of the North developing intellect. Panic and terror-stories.

Yet it corroborated his other information from England: Robbery of the Church. Alienation of land. Willing apostasy. There was a word for it. *Dispossession.* That was striking at the base of power itself. If that were to become known, there might be too many ready to imitate, yes, even in the lands of the Empire. Even here in Italy. Something would have to be done.

And yet the Pope and the Church had other problems, many more pressing ones, more immediate than this matter of English barbarians and Northern barbarians fighting over land and silver in a country he would never see. At their heart lay the partition of the Empire, the great Empire founded by Charlemagne, king of the Franks, crowned emperor in this very cathedral on Christmas Day 800, a lifetime before. For twenty years now, that Empire had been in pieces, and its enemies ever encouraged. First the grandsons of Charlemagne had fought against each other, till they had hacked out peace and partition. Germany to one, France to another, the great, long, ungovernable strip from Italy to the Rhine to a third. And now that third was dead and his third of the Empire divided once again among three, the emperor himself, eldest son of the eldest son, holding a bare ninth of what his grandfather had ruled. And what did that emperor, Louis II, care about it? Nothing. He could not even drive back the Saracens. What about his brother Lothar? Whose only interest in life was to divorce his barren wife and marry his fertile mistress—a thing he, Nicholas, would never permit.

Lothar, Louis, Charles. The Saracens and the Norsemen. Land, power, dispossession. The Pope stroked his cat and considered them all. Something told him that here, here in this trivial, far-off squabble brought by a foolish archbishop running from his duty, might be the solution to all his problems at once.

Or was the prickle he felt one of fear? An alert to the tiny black cloud that would grow and grow?

The Pope cleared his dry old throat with a noise like a cricket creaking. The first of his secretaries dipped his pen instantly.

" 'To our servants Charles the Bald, king of the Franks. To Louis, king of the Germans. Louis, emperor of the Holy Roman Empire. Lothar, king of

Lotharingia. Charles, king of Provence'—you know their titles, Theophanus. To all these Christian kings, then, we write in the same way . . .

" 'Know, beloved, that we, Pope Nicholas, have taken thought for the
greater security and the greater prosperity of all our Christian people. And
therefore we direct you, as you will have our love in the future, to work
together with your brothers and your kinsmen the Christian kings of this
Empire, to this effect . . .' "

Slowly the Pope outlined his plans. Plans for common action. For unity.
For a distraction from civil war and the tearing apart of the Empire. For
the salvation of the Church and the destruction of its enemies, even—if
what Archbishop Wulfhere had said were true—its rivals.

" '. . . and it is our wish,' " the dry, creaky voice concluded, " 'that in
recognition of their service to Mother Church, each man of your armies
who shall join this blessed and sanctified expedition shall wear the sign of
the Cross upon his clothing over his armor.

"Finish the letters in proper form, Theophanus. I'll sign and seal them
tomorrow. Pick appropriate messengers."

The old man rose, clutching his cat, and left the office without haste for
his private quarters.

"Nice touch about the cross," remarked one of the secretaries busily
drafting copies in the Pope's own purple ink.

"Yes. He got it from what the Englishman said, about the pagans wearing a hammer in mockery of the cross."

"The touch they'll really like," said the senior secretary, sanding vigorously, "is the bit about prosperity. He's telling them if they do what they're
told they can loot all Anglia. Or Britannia. Whatever it's called."

"Alfred wants *missionaries?*" said Shef incredulously.

"His very word. *Missionarii.*" In his excitement Thorvin betrayed what
Shef had come to suspect, that for all his scorn of Christian learning he
knew something of their sacred tongue, the Latin. "It is the word they have
long used for the men they send to us, to turn us to the worship of their
God. I have never before heard of a Christian king asking for men to be
sent to his country, to turn them to the worship of our gods."

"And that is what Alfred wants now?"

Shef was dubious. Thorvin, he could see, for all his belief in calm and
self-control, was carried away by the thoughts of the glory this would
bring him and his friends among the followers of the Way.

Yet it did mean something, he was sure, and not what it seemed. The
atheling Alfred whom he had met took no interest in pagan gods, and had,

as far as he could tell, a deep belief in the Christian one. If he was calling now for missionaries of the Way to be sent into Wessex it was for a deeper reason. A move against the Church, that was certain. You could believe in the Christian God and hate the Church that His followers had set up. But what did Alfred think he had to gain? And how would that Church react?

"My fellow priests and I must decide which of us, which of our friends are to go on this mission."

"No," said Shef.

"His favorite word again," observed Brand from his chair.

"Do not send any of your own college. Do not send Norsemen. There are Englishmen now who know well enough what you believe. Give them pendants. Instruct them in what must be said. Send them into Wessex. They will speak the language better and will be more easily believed."

As Shef spoke he stroked the carved faces on his scepter.

Brand had noted this before—that Shef did this now when he was lying. Shall I tell Thorvin? he thought. Or shall I tell Shef, so that he can lie better when need be?

Thorvin rose from his stool, too excited to sit. "There is a holy song," he said, "that the Christians sing. It is called the *nunc dimittis,* a song that says 'Lord, You may let Your servant die, for he has seen his purpose fulfilled.' I have a mind to sing it myself. For more hundreds of years than I can count this Church of theirs has spread, has spread, across first the Southern and then the Northern lands. They think they can conquer all of us. Never before have I heard of the Church giving up what once it won."

"They have not given up yet," said Shef. "The king asks you to send missionaries. He cannot say they will get a hearing, or make the folk believe."

"They have their Book, we have our visions!" cried Thorvin. "We shall see which is the stronger."

From his chair, Brand's bass joined in. "The jarl is right, Thorvin. Send freed slaves of the English to do this task."

"They do not know the legends," protested Thorvin. "What do they know of Thor or Njörth, of the legends of Frey and Loki? They do not know the sacred stories or the hidden meanings within them."

"They don't need to," said Brand. "We're sending them to talk about money."

CHAPTER THREE

That fine Sunday morning, as every Sunday morning, the villagers of Sutton in the county of Berkshire in the kingdom of the West Saxons drew together, as directed, before the hall of Hereswith their lord, thane of King Ethelred-that-was. Thane now, so they said, of King Alfred. Or was he still only atheling? They would be told. Their eyes roved as they counted each other, assessing who was present, whether any had dared to test the orders of Hereswith that all should be present, to attend the church three miles off and learn the law of God which stood behind the laws of men.

Slowly the eyes turned the same way. There were strangers in the little cleared space before the lord's timber house. Not foreigners, or not obvious foreigners. They looked exactly like the forty or fifty other men present, churls and slaves and churls' sons: short, ill-dressed in grubby wool tunics, unspeaking—six of them together. Yet these were men who had never been seen in or near Sutton before—something unprecedented in the heart of the untraveled English countryside. Each leaned on a long stout stave of wood guarded with strips of iron, like the handle of a war-axe, but twice the length.

Without seeming to, the villagers drew away from them. They did not know what this novelty meant, but long years had taught them that what was new was dangerous—till their lord had seen and approved, or disapproved.

The door of the timber house opened and Hereswith marched out, followed by his wife and their gaggle of sons and daughters. As he saw the lowered eyes, the cleared space, the strangers, Hereswith stopped short, left hand dropping automatically to the handle of his broadsword.

"Why are you going to the church?" called out one of the strangers suddenly, his voice sending the pigeons pecking in the dirt into flight. "It's a fine day. Wouldn't you rather sit in the sun? Or work in the fields if you need to? Why walk three miles to Drayton and three miles back? And listen to a man tell you you must pay your tithes in between?"

"Who the hell are you?" snarled Hereswith, striding forward.

The stranger stood his ground, called out loudly so all could hear. His accent was strange, the villagers noticed. English, sure enough. But not from here, not from Berkshire. Not from Wessex?

"We are Alfred's men. We have the king's word and leave to speak here. Whose men are you? The bishop's?"

"The hell you're Alfred's men," grunted Hereswith, freeing his sword. "You're foreigners. I can hear it."

The strangers remained braced on their staves, unmoving.

"Foreigners we are. But we have come with leave, to bring a gift. The gift we bring is freedom: from the Church, from slavery."

"You'll not free my slaves without my leave," said Hereswith, his mind made up. He swung his sword backhand in a horizontal cut at the nearer stranger's neck.

The stranger moved instantly, hurling his strange metal-ribbed staff straight up. The sword clanged on the metal, rebounded out of Hereswith's unpracticed hands. The thane crouched, groping for the hilt, eyes darting from one stranger to the other.

"Easy, lord," said the man. "We mean you no harm either. If you'll listen, we'll tell you why your king has asked us to come here, and how we can be his men and foreigners at once."

Nothing in Hereswith's makeup urged him to listen or to compromise. He straightened, the sword again in his hand, and lashed out forehand at the knee. Again the staff blocked it, blocked it easily. As the thane recovered his blade, the man he had attacked stepped forward and pushed him back with the staff across his chest.

"Help me, you men," bellowed Hereswith at the silent watchers, and charged forward, shoulder dropped and sword ready this time for a disemboweling thrust.

"Enough," said one of the other men he faced, thrusting a staff between his legs. The thane crashed down, started to scramble again to his feet. From his sleeve the first man jerked a short, limp canvas cylinder: the slave-taker's sandbag. He swung once, to the temple, crouched, ready to swing again. As Hereswith fell forward on his face, to lie unmoving, he nodded, straightened, tucked the sandbag away, beckoned to the thane's wife to come and treat him.

"Now," said the stranger, turning to his fascinated but still unmoving audience. "Let me tell you who we are, and who we were.

"We are men of the Way, from the North-folk. But this time last year we were slaves of the Church. Slaves to the great minster of Ely. Let me tell you how we became free."

The slaves in the crowd, maybe a dozen of the fifty men there and the same proportion of women, exchanged frightened glances.

"And to the freemen here," went on Sibba, once slave of the minster of Ely, then catapulteer in the Army of the Way, veteran of the victory over Ivar the Boneless himself, "to the freemen here we will say how we were given our own land. Twenty acres each," he added. "Free of toll to any lord, except the service we owe to Shef Jarl. And the service we give freely —freely, mark you—to the Way. Twenty acres. Unburdened. Is there any freeman here who can claim as much?"

This time the freemen in the crowd looked at each other, a low growl of interest rising. As Hereswith was dragged away, head lolling, his tenants edged closer to the new arrivals, ignoring the broadsword left forgotten in the dirt.

"How much does it cost you to follow Christ?" began Sibba. "Cost you in money? Listen and I will tell you . . ."

"They're everywhere," the bishop's bailiff reported. "Thick as fleas on an old dog."

Bishop Daniel's brows knitted at his servant's levity, but he held his tongue: he needed the information.

"Yes," the bailiff went on, "all men from Norfolk, it seems, and all claiming to be freed slaves. It makes sense. See, your grace, we have a thousand slaves just on our own estates here round Winchester and in the minsters and shires. The man you speak of, the new *jarl* as the heathens call him—he could have sent three thousand slaves in here to spread his word from Norfolk alone, if he sent them all."

"They must be caught," Daniel grated. "Rooted out like corn-cockle from amid the wheat."

"Not so easy. The slaves won't hand them over, nor the churls, from what I hear. The thanes can't catch 'em. If they do, they defend them-selves. They never travel in less than pairs. Sometimes they group together to be a dozen, or a score, no light matter for a small village to deal with. And besides . . ."

"Besides what?"

The bailiff picked his words with care. "What these incomers say—lies it may be, but what they say—is that they have been summoned in by the King Alfred . . ."

"The *atheling* Alfred! He has never been crowned."

"Your pardon, lord. By the atheling Alfred. But even some of the thanes would be loath to hand over men sent by the king to the Church. They say —they say this is a quarrel among the great ones and they will not interfere." And many would side with the atheling, last of the great line of Cerdic, against the Church anyway, thought the bailiff. But he knew better than to say it.

Liar and deceiver, thought the bishop. Not a month ago and the young prince had sat in that very room, eyes down like a maiden, apologizing and begging for direction. And he had left the room to call instantly for help from the unbelievers! And now he was gone, no one knew where, except that rumors came of his appearance in this part or that of Wessex, appealing to his thanes to deny the Church: to follow the example of the North-folk and the creed they called the Way. It did not help that he continued to protest that he remained a believer in Christ. How long would belief last without the land and the money to support it? And if things continued as they were, how long would it be before some messenger, or some army appeared at the very gates of the minster, ordering the bishop to surrender his rights and his leases?

"So," Daniel said at last, half to himself. "We cannot cope with this thing in Wessex. We must send outside. And indeed there is force coming from outside which will cure this evil so that it never raises its head again.

"Yet I cannot afford to wait. It is my Christian duty to act." And also, he added silently, my duty to myself. A bishop who sits quiet and does nothing—how will he seem to the Holy Father in Rome, when the moment comes to decide who shall bear rule for the Church in England?

"No," the bishop went on, "the heart of the trouble comes from the North-folk. Well, what the North-folk caused, the North-folk must cure. There are some who still know their Christian duty."

"In Norfolk, lord?" asked the bailiff doubtfully.

"No. In exile. Wulfgar the cripple, and his son. The one lost his limbs to the Vikings. The other lost his shire. And King Burgred too, of Mercia. It was nothing to me, I thought, who should rule East Anglia, Mercia or Wessex. But I see now. Better that the pious Burgred should have the kingdom of Edmund the Martyr than it should go to Alfred. Alfred the Ingrate, I name him.

"Send in my secretaries. I will write to them all, and to my brothers of Lichfield and Worcester. What the Church has lost, the Church will win back."

"Will they come, lord?" asked the bailiff. "Will they not fear to invade Wessex?"

"It is I who speaks for Wessex now. And there are greater forces than either Wessex or Mercia astir. All I offer Burgred and the others is the chance to join the winning side before it has won. And to punish insolence: the insolence of the heathens and the slaves. We must make an example of them."

The bishop's fist clenched convulsively. "I will not root out this rot, like a weed. I shall burn it out, like a canker."

"Sibba. I think we've got trouble." The whisper ran across the dark room where a dozen missionaries lay sleeping, wrapped in their blankets.

Silently Sibba joined his companion at the tiny, glassless window. Outside, the village of Stanford-in-the-Vale, ten miles and as many preachings from Sutton, lay silent, lit by a strong moon. Clouds scudding before the wind cast shadows round the low wattle-and-daub houses that clustered round the thane's timber one, in which the missionaries of the Way now slept.

"What did you see?"

"Something flashing."

"A fire not dowsed?"

"I don't think so."

Sibba moved without speaking towards the little room that opened off the main central hall. In there the thane Elfstan, their host, a man who protested his loyalty to King Alfred, should be sleeping with his wife and family. After a few moments he drifted back.

"They're still there. I can hear them breathing."

"So they're not in on it. Doesn't mean I didn't see anything. Look! There it is again."

Outside, a shadow slipped from one patch of darkness to another, coming closer. In the moonlight something flashed: something metal.

Sibba turned to the men still sleeping. "On your feet, boys. Get your stuff together."

"Run for it?" asked the watchman.

Sibba shook his head. "They must know how many of us there are. They wouldn't attack if they weren't confident they could deal with us. Easier to do that outside than dig us out of here. We must try to break their teeth first."

Men were scrambling to their feet behind him, groping for their breeches, buckling belts. One man undid a pack, began to haul from it strange, metallic shapes. The others queued in front of him, clutching the long pilgrim-staves all had carried openly.

"Force them down hard," grunted the packman, struggling to push the first halberd-head on its socket over the carefully designed shaft.

"Move fast," said Sibba. "Then, Berti, you take two men to face the door, one either side of it. Wilfi, you at the other door. The rest, stay with me, see where we're needed."

The movement and the clanking of metal had brought the thane, Elfstan, from his bed. He stared, wonderingly.

"Men outside," said Sibba. "Not friendly."

"Nothing to do with me."

"We know. Look, lord, they'll let you out. If you go now."

The thane hesitated. He called to his wife and children, dressing hastily, spoke to them in a low voice.

"Can I open the door?"

Sibba looked round. His men were ready, weapons prepared. "Yes."

The thane lifted the heavy bar that held closed the main double doors, and pushed them both open together. As he did so a groan came from outside, almost a sigh. There were many men out there, poised for a rush. But now they knew they had been seen.

"My wife and children—coming out!" shouted Elfstan. Quickly the children slipped through the door, his wife scurrying after them. A few feet beyond she turned, beckoned frantically to him. Her husband shook his head.

"They are my guests," he said. His voice rose to a shout, addressing the ambushers outside. "My guests and the guests of King Alfred. I do not know who are these thieves in the night, within the bounds of Wessex, but they will hang when the king's reeve catches them."

"There is no king in Wessex," shouted a voice from outside. "And we are men of King Burgred. Burgred and the Church. Your guests are vagabonds and heretics. Slaves from outside! We have come to collar and brand them."

Suddenly the moonlight shone on dark shapes, moving together out of the cover of houses and fences.

They did not hesitate. It would have been easier to catch their enemies

sleeping, but they had been told what their enemies were: released slaves, lowest of the low. Men who had never been taught swordplay, who had not been conditioned from birth to war. Who had not felt the bite of edges over the linden-shield. A dozen Mercian warriors swarmed together at the dark doors of the hall. Behind them, now that concealment was gone, horns blew for the assault.

The double doors of the hall were six feet across, a man's full arm-span. Room only for two armed men to enter at once. Two champions rushed in together, shields up, faces glaring.

Neither saw the blows that killed them. As they peered into the gloom for men to face them, faces to hack at, the halberds swept from both sides, at thigh level, below shield and mail-shirt. The halberd-heads, axe one side, spike the other, were twice the weight of a broadsword. One shore through a warrior's leg and deep into the facing thigh. The other sliced upward from the bone, deep into the pelvis. As one man lay in the flow of blood that would kill him in seconds, the other flapped and twisted, shrieking, trying to tear free the great blade lodged in bone.

More men pushed over them. This time spearpoints met them from in front, driving through wooden shields and metal rings, hurling men back into the confusion of the doorway, groaning from belly wounds. Now the long blades, sweeping in six-foot arcs, chopped down the mailed warriors like cattle before the poleaxe. For a few seconds it seemed as if the sheer weight and numbers of the first rush would break through the defenders.

But against the dim-seen menace, nerves failed. The Mercians scrambled back, those in front weaving desperately behind their shields, trying to drag their dead and wounded with them.

"So far so good," muttered one of the Waymen.

"They'll come again," said Sibba.

Four more times the Mercians came on, each time more warily, trying now, as they realized the tactics and the weapons against them, to draw the blow and evade it, to leap forward before the halberdiers could recover their cumbrous weapons. The Norfolk freedmen used their advantage of numbers, two men to face each door, a man striking from each side. Slowly the casualties on both sides grew.

"They're trying to cut through the walls," muttered Elfstan to Sibba, still on his feet as the sky began to pale.

"Makes no difference," replied Sibba. "They still have to climb in. As long as there's enough of us to block each gap."

* * *

Outside, a fair angry face stared at a bleeding exhausted one. Alfgar had come with the attackers to watch the destruction of the Waymen. He was not pleased.

"You can't break in?" he shouted. "Against a handful of slaves?"

"We've lost too many good men to this handful of slaves. Eight dead, a dozen hurt and all of them badly. I'm going to do what we should have done first."

Turning to his men, he waved a group forward to the undamaged gable end of the hall. With them they carried thorn fencing. They piled it against the wall, stamped it into a pile of thick brush. Steel struck flint, sparks dropping onto dried straw. The fire flared up.

"I want prisoners," Alfgar said.

"If we can get them," said the Mercian. "Anyway, now they have to come to us."

As the smoke began to pour into the drafty hall, Sibba and Elfstan exchanged glances. They could see each other now in the growing dawn.

"They might still take you prisoner, if you went out," said Sibba. "Hand you over to your own king. You being a thane, who knows?"

"I doubt that strongly."

"What are we going to do?"

"What is always done. We will wait in here for every breath we can draw, until the smoke is thickest. Then we will run out and hope one or two of us may get away in the confusion."

The smoke poured in more thickly, followed by the red gleams of fire eating at planking. Elfstan moved to draw a wounded man lying on the floor out of the smoke, but Sibba waved him back.

"Breathing smoke is the easy death," he said. "Better than feeling the fire in your flesh."

One by one, as their endurance waned, the halberdiers ran out in the smoke, trying to run downwind for a few yards of screen. Gleefully their enemies pounced, blocking their path, making them strike or lunge, leaping in behind with sword and dagger, and a long night of loss and frustration to avenge. Last and unluckiest ran Sibba. As he came out two Mercians, realizing by now which way their prey would go, stretched a rawhide rope across his path. Before he could rise or draw his short knife, there was a knee on his back, brawny arms on his wrists.

The last man left in the shell of his home, Elfstan stepped slowly forward, not running downwind like the others, but taking three long strides out of the smoke, shield raised, broadsword drawn. The Mercians running in hesitated. Here at last was a man like themselves. At a safe distance Elfstan's serfs and tenants watched, to see how their lord faced death.

Huskily Elfstan snarled a challenge, gesturing to the Mercians to come on. One detached himself, stepped forward, swinging backhand, forehand, clubbing upward with his iron shield-boss. Elfstan parried, edge to edge with the skill of a lifetime's practice, chopping with his own shield, circling one way then the other as he tried to detect a weakness in his enemy's wrist or balance or technique. For minutes the grave ballet of the sword-duel, the thing thanes were bred for, went on. Then the Mercian sensed the Wessex thane's exhaustion. As the shield-arm facing him drooped, he feinted a low cut, turned it into sudden short thrust. The blade drove in below the ear. As he fell, Elfstan struck one last failing blow. His enemy staggered, looked unbelievingly at the arterial blood spouting from his thigh, and fell also, struggling to cover the flow with his hands.

A groan rose from the men of Stanford-in-the-Vale. Elfstan had been a hard master, and many had felt the weight of his fist if slaves, or the power of his wealth if free. Yet he had been their neighbor. He had fought the invaders of the village.

"Good death," the Mercian captain said professionally. "He lost, but maybe he took his man with him."

Alfgar moaned with disgust. Behind him, men rolled the traveling cart of his father forward. Through the shattered palisade of the village, a further cortege advanced, black-robed priests in the van. In the midst of it the rising sun glittered on the bishop's gilded crozier.

"At least we have *some* prisoners," he said.

"Two?" asked Bishop Daniel disbelievingly. "You killed nine and caught two?"

No one bothered to answer him.

"We must make the best of it," said Wulfgar. "Now, how are you going to deal with them? 'Make an example,' you said."

The two freedmen stood in front of them, each held by two warriors. Daniel paced forward, stretched his hand out, pulled a thong from round one captive's neck, broke it with a jerk. He stared at what lay in his hand, did the same to the other prisoner. A silver hammer, for Thor, a silver sword, for Tyr. He tucked them into his pouch. For the archbishop, he thought. No, Ceolnoth is too much a weakling, feeble as the weathercock Wulfhere of York.

These are for Pope Nicholas. With this silver in his hand he may reflect that the Church in England cannot afford weakling archbishops any longer.

"I swore to burn the canker out," he said. "And so I will."

An hour later Wilfi of Ely stood tethered to the stake, legs tightly bound to prevent him kicking out. The brushwood burned brightly, caught at his woolen breeches. As the fire blistered his skin he began to twist in his bonds, gasps of agony forced from him despite his efforts. The Mercian warriors stared at him judgementally, interested to see how a slave-born bore pain. The villagers watched more fearfully. Many had seen executions. But even the wickedest, secret murderers and housebreakers, faced no more than the noose. To kill a man slowly was outside English law. Though not outside Church law.

"Breathe the smoke," yelled Sibba suddenly. "Breathe the smoke!"

Through the pain Wilfi heard him, ducked his head, breathed in great gasps. As his tormentors hesitated to approach, he began to fall forward in his bonds. As unconsciousness came on him, he rallied for an instant, looked upward.

"Tyr," he called, "Tyr aid me!" The smoke billowed up round him as if in reply. When it cleared he hung limp. A rumble of talk rose from the watchers.

"Not much of an example there," observed Wulfgar to the bishop. "Why don't you let me show you how to do it?"

As they dragged Sibba forward to the second stake, men went running at Wulfgar's word to the nearest house, came out moments later trundling the beer-barrel which even the meanest home could boast. At a gesture they stove in one end, tipped the barrel over, stove in the other to create a short stout cylinder. The barrel's owner watched unspeaking as his summer ale ran into the dirt.

"I've thought about this," said Wulfgar. "What else have I to do? What you need for this is draft. Like a clay chimney in a fireplace."

They tied Sibba, pale and glaring, next to the stake where his comrade had died. As they piled the brushwood deeply round him, Daniel stepped forward.

"Abjure your pagan gods," he said. "Return to Christ. I will shrive and absolve you myself, and you will be stabbed mercifully before you burn."

Sibba shook his head.

"Apostate," yelled the bishop. "What you feel now will only be the start of everlasting burning. Mark this!" He turned and shook a fist at the villagers. "His pain is what you will all suffer forever. What all men must suffer forever, if not for Christ. Christ and the Church that keeps the keys of heaven and hell!"

At Wulfgar's direction, they lowered the barrel over stake and condemned man together, struck sparks to the brush and fanned the blaze. The tongues of flame reached in, were sucked upward as the air burned out above them, leapt savagely at the body and face of the man inside. After a few moments the shrieking began. Continued, growing louder. A slow smile began to spread across the face of the limbless trunk that watched from its padded upright box.

"He's saying something," snapped Daniel suddenly. "He's saying something. He wants to recant. Put the fire out! Pull the brush away."

Slowly the burners raked back the blaze. Approaching cautiously, they wrapped cloths round their hands and lifted the smoldering barrel high over the stake.

Beneath it lay charred flesh, teeth showing white against blackened face and scorched lips. Flame had shriveled Sibba's eyeballs and was forced deep into his lungs as his body gasped for breath. He was still conscious.

His face lifted as the bishop approached, aware through its blindness that it was again in open air.

"Recant now," shouted Daniel for all to hear. "Make a sign, any sign, and I will cross you and send your soul without pain to Doomsday."

He bent forward under his miter to catch any word that burned lungs could pronounce.

Sibba coughed twice and spat the charred lining of his throat into the bishop's face.

Daniel stepped back, wiping the black mucus with disgust onto his embroidered robe, shaking involuntarily.

"Back," he gasped. "Put it back. Put it over him again. Restart the fire. And this time," he shouted, "he can call on his pagan gods till the devil has him."

But Sibba did not call out again. As Daniel raved and Wulfgar grinned at his confusion, as the warriors slowly moved in to pull the fire in on the bodies and spare the need for burial pit, two men slipped away from the back of the crowd, unseen by any except their silent neighbors. One was Elfstan's sister's son. The other had seen his home destroyed in a battle not of his concern. The rumor of the shire had told them where to take their news.

CHAPTER FOUR

S hef's face did not change as the messenger, staggering with fatigue after his long ride, poured out his news: a Mercian army in Wessex. King Alfred vanished, no one knew where. The emissaries of the Way mercilessly hunted down wherever they could be found. The Church proclaiming King Alfred and all allies of the Way anathema, stripped of all rights, to be neither helped nor harbored.

And everywhere, the burnings; or, by order of the bishop of Winchester, where the dreaded living corpse Wulfgar was not present, the crucifixions. Long lists of names of those caught: catapulteers, comrades, veterans of the battle against Ivar. Thorvin moaned, shocked, as the list ran on and on, moved even though those caught and killed were not of his race or blood and were only for a few short weeks of his faith. Shef remained seated on his camp-stool, thumb running again and again across the cruel faces of his whetstone.

He knew, thought Brand, watching, and remembering the sudden veto Shef had imposed on Thorvin's eager readiness to spread the word himself. He knew this would happen, or something like it. That means that he had sent his own folk, Englishmen, men he raised from the dirt himself, to what he must have known would be death by torture. He did the same for his own father. I must be very sure, very, very sure that he never looks at me in quite that same considering fashion. If I had not known before that he was a son of Othin I would know it now.

And yet if he had not done it I would be grieving for the death of Thorvin by now, not for a bunch of gangrel churls.

The messenger ran down, news and horror finally exhausted. With a word Shef dismissed him to food and rest, turned to his inner council sitting round him in the sunlit upper hall: Thorvin and Brand, Farman the visionary, Boniface the former priest with his ever-ready ink and paper.

"You heard the news," he said. "What must we do?"

"Is there any doubt?" asked Thorvin. "Our ally called us in. Now he is being robbed of his rights by the Church. We must march at once to his assistance."

"More than that," added Farman. "If there is a moment for lasting change, surely it is this. We have a kingdom divided within itself. A true king—Christian though he may be—to speak for us, for the Way. How often have the Christians spread their word through converting the king, and having him convert his people? Not only will the slaves be with us, but the freemen and half the thanes. Now is our chance to turn the Christian tide. Not only in Norfolk, but in a great kingdom."

Shef's lips set stubbornly. "What do you say, Brand?"

Brand shrugged massive shoulders. "We have comrades to avenge. None of us are Christians—your pardon, Father. But the rest of us are not Christians to forgive our enemies. I say march."

"But I am the jarl. It is my decision."

Slowly, heads nodded.

"What I think is this. When we sent the missionaries we stirred up the wasps' nest. And now we are stung. We should have foreseen it."

You did foresee it, thought Brand to himself.

"And I stirred up another when I took the Church's land. I have not been stung for that yet, but I expect it. I foresee it. I say let us see where our enemies are before we strike. Let them come to us."

"And let our comrades lie unavenged?" growled Brand.

"We will miss our chance of a kingdom, a kingdom for the Way," cried Farman.

"What of your ally Alfred?" demanded Thorvin.

Slowly Shef wore them down. Repeated his conviction. Countered their arguments. Persuaded them, in the end, to wait a week, for further news.

"I only hope," said Brand in the end, "that good living has not made you soft. Made us all soft. You should spend more time with the army, and less with the muttonheads in your doom-court."

That at least is good advice, thought Shef. In order to cool feelings, he turned to Father Boniface, who had taken no part, waiting only to record decisions or write down orders.

"Father, send out for wine, will you? Our throats are dry. At least we can drink the memorial for our dead comrades in something better than ale."

The priest, still stubbornly black-gowned, paused on his way to the door.

"There is no wine, lord jarl. The men said they were looking for a cargo from the Rhine, but it has not come. There have been no ships from the South for four weeks, not even into London. I will broach a barrel of the finest hydromel instead. Maybe the wind is wrong."

Quietly Brand rose from the table, stalked to the open window, stared at the clouds and the horizon. Why, he thought, I could sail from Rhinemouth to the Yare in my mother's old washtub in weather like this. And he says the wind is wrong! Something is wrong, but it is not the wind.

That dawn, the crews and captains of a hundred impounded trading vessels—half-decked single-masters, round-bellied cogs, English, Frankish and Frisian longships—all rolled unhappily from their blankets to stare at the sky above the port of Dunkerque, as they had done every day for a month and more. To see if the conditions were right. To wonder whether their masters would deign to make a move.

They saw the light that had come from the east, that had raced already across the tangled forests and huddled settlements of Europe, across river and toll-gate, *Schloss* and *chastel* and earthwork. Everywhere on the continent it had lit soldiers gathering, provision-carts mustering, horse-boys leading remounts.

As it swept towards the English Channel—though at this time men called it still the Frankish Sea—it touched the topmost banderole on the stone *donjon* within the wooden keep that guarded the port of Dunkerque. The guard-commander looked at it, nodded. The trumpeter wetted his lips, pursed them, sent a defiant bray down his metal tube. Immediately the quarter-guards answered from each wall, men began to roll from their blankets inside the keep. And outside, in the camp and the port, and along all the horse-lines that trailed off into the open fields, the soldiers stirred and checked their gear and began the day with the same thought as the sailors who were trapped in the port: this time, would their master stir? Would King Charles, with his levies, with the levies sent him by his pious and Pope-fearing brothers and nephews, give the sign for the short trip to England?

In the harbor, the skippers looked at their weathervanes, stared towards the eastern and western horizons. The master of the cog *Dieu Aide,* the cog which would carry not only the king but the archbishop of York and the Pope's legate himself, nudged his chief mate, jerked a thumb at the flag standing out stiffly from the mast. High tide in four hours, both knew. Current would be with them then and for a while. Wind in the right quarter and not dropping.

Could the landsmen get themselves down and embarked in time? Neither bothered to speculate. Things would be as they would be. But if the king of the Franks, Charles, nicknamed the Bald—if the king seriously wanted to obey the instructions of his spiritual lord the Pope, unite the old dominions of his grandfather Charlemagne, and plunder the wealth of England in the name of holiness, then he would never get a better chance.

As they watched the flag and the wind they heard, half a mile off in the *donjon* trumpets blaring again. Not for dawn, but for something else. And then, faintly, carried on the southwest wind, the noise of cheering. Soldiers acclaiming a decision. Without wasting words, the captain of the *Dieu Aide* jerked a thumb at the derricks and the canvas slings, tapped the hatches of the cog's one hold. Get the hatches off. Get the derricks over the side. We'll need them for the horses. The war-horses, the *destriers* of France.

The same wind, that dawn, blew across the bows of the forty dragon-boats cruising down the English coast from the Humber, almost in their teeth, making it impossible to rig sail. Ivar Ragnarsson, in the prow of the first boat, did not care. His oarsmen were rowing at their paddling-stroke, which they could keep up for eight hours a day if need be, grunting in unison as they heaved their oars through the water, feathering with the ease of long practice, continuing their conversations with a word or two as they swept them back, dipping and heaving again.

Only in the first six boats was there extra work for the men. In each, a ton and a half of dead weight squatted, carefully stowed before the mast: the onagers of Erkenbert, all the forges of York Minster had been able to turn out in the weeks Ivar had given them. Ivar had raged furiously about the weight, demanded that they be lightened. Impossible, the black archdeacon had replied. This is the way they are drawn in Vegetius. More convincingly, lighter models had knocked themselves to pieces in a dozen shots. The kick of the wild ass that gave these machines their name came when the throwing-arm struck the crossbeam. If there were no crossbeam the stone would not be hurled out with its astonishing force and velocity. A light crossbeam, however padded, would crack.

Ivar's meditations were interrupted by loud retching from behind him.

Each onager was served by a dozen slaves from the minster; in command of them all, torn deeply against his will from the studies and library of the minster, Erkenbert himself. Now one of the lubbers had succumbed to the long, North Sea swell and was vomiting his heart out over the side. The wrong side, naturally, so that the meager contents of his stomach blew back over the nearest rowers, provoking shouts and curses, disruption of the long, automatic rowing-stroke.

As Ivar stepped toward the disturbance, hand dropping to the gutting-knife at his belt, Hamal the horse-swain, the man who had saved Ivar from the lost battle at March, moved quickly. The slave grasped the man by the scruff of his neck. A violent blow across the side of the head, repeated as Hamal heaved the wretched man off his feet and flung him across the thwarts to the lee side, there to retch in peace.

"We'll have the hide off him tonight," said Hamal. Ivar stared unblinkingly for a moment, knowing well what Hamal was doing. Decided to leave it for the moment. Turned back to his thoughts in the prow.

Hamal caught the eye of one of the rowers, mimed wiping sweat from his brow. Ivar killed a man a day now on average, mostly from the valueless slaves of the minster. At that rate they would have no one left to wind a machine at all by the time they met the enemy. And no one could be sure who Ivar would turn on next. He could be diverted, sometimes, by sufficient cruelty.

Thor send that we meet the enemy soon, thought Hamal. The only thing that will cool Ivar's temper for good is the head and balls of the man who bested him—Skjef Sigvarthsson. Without that, he will destroy everyone around him. That is why his brothers have sent him out this time on his own. With me as his nursemaid, and the Snakeeye's foster father to report.

If we don't meet the enemy soon, thought Hamal, I am going to desert the first chance I get. Ivar owes me his life. But he is too mad to pay. And yet if he takes his rage out in the right quarter, something tells me there are fortunes yet to be gained, here in the rich kingdoms of the South. Rich and ripe to fall.

"It's a bugger," said Oswi, once slave to St. Aethelthryth's of Ely, now captain of a catapult-team in the Army of Norfolk and the Way. There were nods of agreement from his crew as they looked thoughtfully at their much-loved but not-quite-trusted artillery piece. It was one of the torsion-catapults, the wheeled twist-shooters. Every man in the crew was desperately proud of it. They had given it a name weeks before: "Dead Level."

They had polished every wooden part of it many times over. Yet they were afraid of it.

"You can count the turns you give to the cogwheels," said Oswi, "so it don't tighten too much."

"And I put my head right down on the ropes every time and listen to 'em," said one of his mates, "till I can hear they're in tune like a harper's harp-strings."

"But she'll still bloody well break one day when you don't expect it; they always do. Break one or two of us for breakfast."

A dozen heads nodded gloomily.

"What we need are stronger wooden arms," said Oswi. "They're what goes."

"Wrap 'em with rope?"

"No, that would work loose."

"I used to work in the forge at my village," the newest member of the team said hesitatingly. "Maybe if they had iron supports . . ."

"No, those wooden arms bend a bit," said Oswi firmly. "They have to. Anything iron would stop them doing that."

"Depends on the iron. If you heat and reheat and hammer it the right way the iron turns into what my old master called steel. But it's steel that bends a bit, not soft, like bad iron, but with spring in it. Now if we put a strip of that along the inside of each of the arms it would bend with the wood—and stop them flying apart if the wood broke."

Thoughtful silence.

"What about the jarl?" asked a questioning voice.

"Yes, what about the jarl?" came another voice from behind the half-circle. Shef, strolling round the camp in response to Brand's advice, had seen the cluster of intent faces and had walked silently up to overhear.

Consternation and alarm. Swiftly the group of catapulteers rearranged itself so that their newest member was left in the center, to face the unpredictable.

"Er, Udd here's got an idea," said Oswi, also shifting responsibility.

"Let's hear it."

As the new recruit, first hesitatingly, then fluently and with confidence, began to describe the procedure of making mild steel, Shef watched him. An insignificant little man, even smaller than the others, with weak eyes and a stoop. Any one of Brand's Vikings would have dismissed him immediately as useless to an army, not worth his rations even as a latrine-digger. Yet he knew something. Was it new knowledge? Or was it old knowledge, something many smiths had always known, given the right conditions, but had been unable to pass on except to an apprentice?

"This steel bends, you say," said Shef. "And springs back? Not like my sword"—he drew from its sheath the fine Baltic sword Brand had given him, made like his own self-forged and long-lost weapon of mixed strips of soft iron and hard steel—"but made in one piece? Springy all the way through?"

Udd, the little man, nodded firmly.

"All right." Shef thought a moment. "Oswi, tell the camp marshal you and your team are off all duties. Udd, tomorrow morning go to Thorvin's forge with as many men as you need to help, and start making strips the way you say. Fit the first pair to 'Dead Level' and see if they work. If they do, fit them to all the machines.

"And Udd: When it's done I want to see some of this new metal. Make some extra strips for me."

Shef walked away as the horns blew to dowse fires and to mount the night-guard. Something there, he thought. Something he could use. And he needed something to use. For in spite of the newfound confidence of Thorvin and his friends, he knew that if they just repeated what they had done before, they would be destroyed. Every stroke teaches its own counter. And he had enemies everywhere, in the South and in the North, in the Church and among the pagans. Bishop Daniel. Ivar. Wulfgar and Alfgar. King Burgred. They would not stand up to be shot at a second time.

He did not know what would come, but it would be unpredictable. It was vital to be unpredictable in reply.

The dream, or vision, came this time almost as a relief. Shef felt himself surrounded by difficulties. He knew he did not know the way through them. If some greater agency did, he would welcome the knowledge. He did not think it was Othin in his guise as Bölverk, Bale-Worker, who was guiding him, for all that Thorvin continued to urge him to accept the spear-pendant, the sign of Othin. But who else would help him? If he knew, Shef reflected, he would wear that one's sign.

In his sleep, he found himself suddenly looking down. Down from what seemed a great height, at what he realized, as his eyes cleared, was a great board. A chessboard, with the pieces on it. In the middle of a game. And the players of the game were the mighty figures he had seen before: the gods of

Asgarth, so Thorvin said, here playing at chess on their sacred board with squares of gold and silver.

But there were more than two playing. So gigantic were the shapes round the board that Shef could not bring them into focus all at once, any more than he could a mountain range, but he could see one of the players. Not the ruddy, Brand-shaped figure he had seen before, who was Thor, not the one with the axe for a face and a voice like a calving glacier, who was Othin. This one seemed somehow sharper, slighter, his eyes not level. An expression of intense glee crossed his face as he shifted a piece. Loki the Trickster perhaps. Loki, whose fire burned always in the holy circle, but whose followers went unknown.

No, Shef reflected. Tricky this god might be, but he did not have the Loki-look. The look of Ivar. As his vision cleared, Shef realized he had seen him before. It was the god who had looked at him as if he were a horse to be bought. And the expression on his face—surely this too was the owner of the ever-amused voice which twice had given him warnings. That is my protector, thought Shef. It is not a god I know. I wonder, what are his attributes, his purpose? What is his sign?

The board they were playing on, Shef saw suddenly, was not a board but a mappa. Not a mappamundi, but a map of England. He strained forward to see, sure now that the gods knew where his enemies were and what they planned. As he did so he realized that he was up on a mantelpiece, like a mouse in a king's hall. But like a mouse, though he could see, he could not understand. The faces were moving their pieces, laughing in voices like rumbles of thunder. None of it made any sense to him. And yet he was here, he had been brought here, he was sure, to see and understand.

The gleeful face had turned up toward him. Shef stood transfixed, unsure whether to duck back or to freeze. But the face knew he was there. It held a piece up to him, the other gods remaining intent on the game.

It was telling him, Shef realized, that this was the piece he had to take.

What was it? It was a queen, his eyes made out at last. A queen. With the face of . . .

The unknown god looked down, waved an arm dismissively. As if caught by a gale, Shef was toppling away, away back toward his camp, his bed, his blankets. As he fell he recognized in an instant whose the face was on the chess-queen.

Shef sat up suddenly with a gasp. Godive, he thought slowly, his heart thumping. It must be my own wish that sent me that vision. How could a girl affect the map of the contending enemies?

Outside Shef's sleeping-chamber, noise and upheaval, horses stamping, booted feet striding toward him past the cries of his bower-thanes. Pulling on a tunic, Shef opened the door before the boots reached him.

Facing him was a familiar figure: the young Alfred, still crowned with a golden circle, still as fresh-faced and full of nervous energy as before, but with a new grimness in his eyes.

"I gave you this shire," he said without preamble. "I think now I should have given it to the other one, your enemy. Alfgar. Alfgar and his cripple-father. For between the two of them, and my traitor-bishops and King Burgred my brother-in-law, they have hounded me out of my kingdom."

Alfred's expression changed, showed a sudden weariness and defeat. "I am here as a suppliant. Driven out of Wessex. No time to rally my loyal thanes. The army of Mercia marching on my heels. I saved you. Will you, now, save me?"

As Shef collected his thoughts to reply, he heard more running feet, coming from outside the circle of torches round Alfred. A messenger, too anxious and hasty to remember protocol. As soon as the man saw Shef standing in the doorway, he poured out his alarm.

"Beacons, lord jarl! Beacons for a fleet at sea. Forty ships at least. The men on watch, they say it can only be—it can only be Ivar."

As Shef watched the consternation on the face of King Alfred, something cold inside him drew a conclusion. Alfgar on one side. Ivar on the other. And what have they in common? I took a woman from one. The other took the same woman from me. At least I can be sure now that it was a true dream the god sent me, whoever he may be. Godive is the key to this. Someone is telling me to use her.

CHAPTER FIVE

Early in his experience of being jarl, Shef had discovered that news was never quite as good or quite as bad as it was made to seem on first hearing. So it proved again. Beacons were a good way of signaling danger, and direction, and even—with care—number. They said nothing about distance. The beacon-chain started far up the coast, in Lincolnshire. It could mean only that Ivar—if Ivar it was—had left the Humber with, as Brand had immediately pointed out, the wind dead in his teeth. He could be three days off, or even more.

As for King Burgred, with Alfgar and Wulfgar in his train, Alfred was sure that he was in pursuit and that he meant, on the urgings of his bishops, nothing less than the entire destruction of the land of the Way, and the submission of the whole of England south of the Humber to his rule. But Alfred was a young man who rode hard, and who had only his personal bodyguard with him. Burgred was famous for the splendor of his camp-furniture and the number of ox-wagons needed to carry it. Forty miles to him was four days' march.

Shef might expect a heavy stroke from each of his enemies. Not a sudden one.

It would have made no difference in any case. As Shef dealt with the immediate necessities of the situation, he thought only of what he knew he must do—and who he could trust in this situation to help him. There was only one answer to the latter. As soon as he could get rid of all his council-

members on one errand or another, he slipped through the gates of his
burg, sent back the troubled guards who had tried to accompany him, and
made his way as unobserved as possible through the crowded streets surrounding it.

Hund was, as he expected, busy in his booth, treating a woman whose
evident terror at the sight of the jarl suggested a guilty conscience: a drab
or a hedge-witch. Hund continued to treat her as if she were a thane's lady.
Only after she had gone did he sit down by his friend, unspeaking as
usual.

"We saved Godive once," said Shef. "Now I am going to do it again. I
need your help. I cannot tell anyone else what I am doing. Will you help?"

Hund nodded. Hesitated. "I'll help you any time, Shef. But I have to ask.
Why have you decided to do this now? You could have tried to get Godive
back any time the last few months, when there was far less on your mind."

Shef coldly wondered once more how much he could safely say. Already
he knew what he needed Godive for: as bait. Nothing could enrage Alfgar
more than knowing Shef had stolen her away. If he made it seem like an
insult from the Way, Alfgar's allies would be drawn in. He wanted them to
pursue Godive like a great fish striking. Onto the hook of Ivar. And Ivar
too could be baited. By a reminder of the woman he had lost, and the man
who had taken her.

But he dared say none of this to Hund, not even to his childhood friend.
Hund had been a friend of Godive too.

Shef allowed concern and confusion to show on his face. "I know," he
said. "I should have done it before. But now, suddenly, I am afraid for
her."

Hund looked his friend steadily in the eye. "All right," he said. "I dare
say you have good reason for what you do. Now, how are we going to
work it?"

"I'll get out at dusk. Meet me where we used to shoot the catapults.
During the day I want you to collect half a dozen men. But listen. They
must not be Norse. All English. All freedmen. And they must all look like
freedmen, understand. Like you." Undersized and underfed, Shef meant.
"With horses and rations for a week. But dressed shabby, not in the clothes
we've given them.

"And there's another thing, Hund, and this is why I need you. I am too
easy to recognize with this one eye"—the one eye you left me with, Shef
did not say. "When we went into the Ragnarsson camp that did not matter. Now, if I am to go into a camp with my half brother and stepfather in
it, I need a disguise. Now, what I thought was . . ."

Shef poured out his plan, Hund occasionally altering or improving on it. At the end the little leech slowly tucked his apple-pendant, for Ithun, out of sight, adjusting his tunic so nothing showed.

"We can do it," he remarked, "if the gods are with us. Have you thought what will happen here in the camp when they wake up and find you gone?"

They will think I have deserted them, Shef realized. I will leave a message, to let them think I have done it for a woman. And yet it will not be true.

He felt the old king's whetstone dragging at his belt, where he had tucked it. Strange, he thought, when I went into the camp of Ivar, the only thought I had in my head was to rescue Godive, to take her away with me and find happiness together. Now I mean to do the same again. But this time—this time I am not doing it for her. I am not even doing it for me. I am doing it because it must be done. It is the answer. And she and I: we are just parts of the answer.

We are like the little cogs that turn the ropes that wind the catapults. They cannot say they do not want to turn anymore, and neither can we.

He thought of the strange tale of Frothi's mill which Thorvin had told him, about the giant-maidens, and the king who would not let them rest. I would like to give them rest, he told himself, and the others who are caught up in this mill of war. But I do not know how to release them. Or myself.

When I was a thrall, then I was free, he thought.

Godive came through the women's door at the back of King Burgred's immense camp-pavilion and began to edge down the long rows of trestle-tables, at the moment unfilled. She had a task, in case anyone questioned her—a message for King Burgred's brewer to broach extra barrels, and instructions from Alfgar to stand over him while he did it. Actually, she had had to get out of the stifling atmosphere of the women's quarters before her heart burst with fear and grief.

She was no longer the beauty she had been. The other women, she knew, had noticed, were talking among themselves about what had happened to her, talking with malicious pleasure at the fall of a favorite. They did not know what the causes were. They must know that Alfgar beat her, beat her with increasing fury and frenzy as the weeks went by, beat her with the birch on her bare body till the blood ran and her shift stuck to her morning after morning. Such things could not be done quietly. Even in the timber hall of Tamworth, Burgred's capital, some noise carried through the

planks and panels. In the tents where kings spent the summer, the campaigning months . . .

But though they heard, and though they knew, there was no one who
would help her. Men would hide their smiles the day after a thrashing;
women, to begin with, spoke quietly and consolingly. They all thought
that it was the way of the world, however they speculated on how she had
failed to please her man.

None of them—except Wulfgar, and he no longer cared—knew the
weight of despair and dismay that came upon her whenever she thought of
the sin that she and Alfgar committed every time they lay together, the sin
of incest that must surely mark their souls and bodies forever. No one at
all knew that she was a murderess as well. Twice in the winter she had felt
the life swell within her, though—thank God—she had never felt it
quicken. If she had, she might not have had the strength to go into the
woods, find the dog's mercury, the birthwort, and drink the bitter drench
that she made from it to kill the child of shame in her own womb.

And even that was not what had made her face drawn and lined beyond
its years, her walk stooped and shuffling like that of an old woman. It was
the memory of pleasure that she hugged to herself. That hot morning in
the woods, the leaves above her head, the warm skin and thrusting flesh in
her arms: the sense of release and freedom.

An hour, it had lasted. The memory of it blotted out the rest of her
young life. How strange he had looked when she had seen him again. The
one eye, the fierce face, the air of pain mastered. The moment he handed
her back . . .

Godive's eyes dropped lower and she half ran across the space kept clear
outside the pavilion, crowded now with Burgred's personal guard, his
hearth-band, and with the hundred officers and errand-runners of the
Mercian army marching stolidly on Norfolk at their king's command. Her
skirts brushed past the group standing idly listening to a blind minstrel
and his attendant. Dimly, without thinking of it, she heard that they were
listening to a lay of Sigemund the Dragon-slayer: She had heard it before in
her father's hall.

Shef watched her go with a curious chill at his heart. Good, she was
there, with her husband, in the camp. Very good; she had failed completely to recognize him, though not six feet away. Bad that she looked so
ill and frail. Worse that when he saw her his heart had not turned over as
he expected, as it had done every time he had seen her since the day he
had known she was a woman. Something was missing in himself. Not his
eye. Something in his heart.

Shef dismissed the thought as he finished his song and Hund, his attendant, pushed forward quickly, bag outstretched in appeal. The listening warriors pushed the little man from one to the other as he moved round the ring, but in little more than good nature. His bag filled a little with bread, a lump of hard cheese, half an apple, whatever they had about them. This was no way to work, of course. What a sensible pair would have done was to wait till evening, approach the lord after dinner and ask permission to entertain the company. Then there would be a chance of proper food afterward, a bed for the night, maybe even a gift of money or a bag filled with breakfast.

But their own ineptitude fitted their cover. Shef knew he could never have passed for a professional minstrel. He meant instead to look like a part of the debris of war that covered all England: a younger son crippled in battle, cast out by his lord, turned away as useless by his family, and now trying to keep from starvation by singing memories of glory. Hund's skill had created a story on Shef's body that anyone could read by looking at him. First he had carefully and artistically painted a great scar on Shef's face, the slash-mark of an axe or a sword across the eyes. Then he had bandaged the fake scar with the filthy rags of an English army-leech, letting only the edges of it hint at what lay underneath. Then he had splinted and strapped Shef's legs beneath his wide breeches so that it was impossible for him to bend a knee; and finally, as a refinement of torment, strapped a metal bar to his back to prevent any free movement.

"You dropped your guard," he had said. "A Viking hit you across the face. As you fell forward you got the back of an axe, or a war-hammer, that crushed your spine. Now your legs can only trail behind you as you hobble on crutches. That's your story."

But no one had ever asked Shef his story. No experienced warrior needed to. Another reason that the Mercian companions did not bother to interrogate the cripple and his meager attendant was that they were afraid. Every warrior knew that such a fate one day might be his own. Kings and lords might keep a few cripples, pensioners, as signs of their own generosity or out of some family feeling. But gratitude or care for the useless were too expensive luxuries for a land at war.

The ring of listeners turned to other interests. Hund emptied the bag, passed half of the bits to Shef, squatted by him as they both devoured their gifts, heads down. Their hunger was not an act. For two days now they had worked closer and closer into the center of Burgred's camp, trailing behind it for ten miles each day, Shef slumped on a stolen donkey, living only on what they could pick up, sleeping each night in their clothes in the cold dew.

"You saw her," muttered Shef.

"When she comes back I will throw her the sign," replied Hund. Neither spoke again. They knew this was a moment of critical danger.

Eventually Godive could prolong her errand no further. Back in the women's quarters, she knew, the old woman Alfgar had set to watch over her would be growing suspicious, fearful: Alfgar had told her that if his whore of a wife found a lover, he would sell her to the slave-market in Bristol, where the Welsh chiefs bought cheap lives.

She began to make her way back across the still-crowded courtyard. There were the minstrel and his boy still. Poor folk. A blind cripple and a starveling. Even the Welsh would not buy such. How long would they live? Till the winter, maybe. They might outlive her at that.

The minstrel had raised his coarse brown hood against the slow drizzle that was turning the dust into mud. Or maybe it was against the cruel stares of the world, for his face was in his hands. As she came level with them, the attendant bent forward and dropped something onto the ground at her feet. Instinctively, she stooped for it.

It was gold. A gold harp, a tiny brooch for a child's dress. Small as it was, it would buy food for two men for a year. How could a wandering beggar have such a thing? Tied to it with a thread was—

It was a sheaf. Just a few cornstalks threaded together, but tied to make the shape unmistakable. But if the harp meant the minstrel, then the sheaf was—

She turned convulsively to the blind man. His hands came away from his face, bandage in them; she saw the one eye staring deep into her own. Gravely, slowly, the eye winked. As Shef dropped his face into his hands once more he said four words, low but clear. "The privy. At midnight."

"But it's guarded," said Godive. "And there's Alfgar . . ."

Hund stretched out his bag towards her, as if begging in desperation. As the bag touched her, he slipped a small flask from his hand to hers.

"Put it in the ale," he whispered. "Whoever drinks it will sleep."

Godive jerked back convulsively. As if rejected, Hund sank back, the minstrel dropped his face once more into his hands, as if too far gone in despair to look up. A few yards away, Godive saw old Polga hobbling towards her, reproaches already forming. She turned away, fighting an urge as she did so to leap, fighting an urge to run and embrace the old woman as if she was a young virgin with never a care or a fear. The lacerations on the backs of her thighs caught her woolen dress and slowed her to a cramped shuffle.

Shef had not expected to sleep on the edge of the abduction, but it had come upon him irresistibly. Too irresistibly to be natural, he feared. As he fell asleep, a voice was speaking. Not the now-recognized, amused voice of his unknown patron. The cold voice of Othin, fosterer of battle, betrayer of warriors, the god who took the sacrifices offered to Dead Man's Strand.

"Be very careful, mannikin," said the voice. *"You are free to act, you and your father, but never forget to pay me my due. I will show you what happens to those who do."*

In his dream, Shef found himself sitting at the very edge of a circle of light, in the dark but looking in. Within the light, a harper sang. He sang to a man, an old man with gray hair, but with a forbidding, cruel beaked face like the ones on his whetstone. The harper sang to this man. But he sang, Shef knew, for the woman who sat at her father's feet. He was singing a lay of love, a lay from the Southlands about a woman who heard the nightingale sing in an orchard and pined away helplessly for her lover. The old king's face relaxed in pleasure, his eyes closing, remembering his youth and the wooing of his dead wife. As he did so the harper, never missing a note, placed a runakefli—*a stick carved with runes—by the woman's skirt: the message from her lover. He himself was the lover, Shef knew, and his name was Heoden. The harper was Heorrenda the peerless singer, sent by his lord to woo the woman Hild away from her jealous father, Hagena the remorseless.*

Another time, another scene. This time two armies faced each other by a restless strand, the sea hurling in rollers over the kelp. One man stepped forward from the ranks, went toward the other. It was Heoden this time, Shef knew, come to offer bride-price for the stolen bride. He would not have done it if Hagena's men had not caught up with him. He showed the bags of gold, the precious jewels. But the other man, the old man was speaking. Shef knew he was rejecting the offer: for he had drawn the sword Dainslaf, which the dwarves had made, and which could never be sheathed till it had taken a life. The old man was saying he would be satisfied with nothing less than Heoden's life, for the insult put upon him.

Haste and pressure, pressure from somewhere. He must see this last scene. Dark, and a moon shining through scattered clouds. Many men lay dead on the field, their shields cloven, their hearts pierced. Heoden and Hagena lay close together in a death-grapple, each the other's bane. But one figure was still alive, still moving. It was Hild, the woman, who now had lost both husband-abductor and father. She moved among the corpses, singing a song, a galdorleoth *which her Finnish nurse had taught her. And the corpses began to move. Began to rise. Stared at each other in the moonlight. Lifted their weapons and began again to strike. As Hild shrieked in rage and frustration her lover and her father ignored her, faced each other, began again to hack, to chop at the splintered shields. So it would go till Doomsday, Shef knew, on the strand of Hoy in the far-off Orkney isles. For this was the Everlasting Battle.*

The pressure grew till he woke with a start. Hund was pressing a thumb under his left ear, to bring him awake silently. Around them the night was quiet, broken only by the stirring and coughing of hundreds of sleepers in their tents and shelters, the army of Burgred. The noise of revelry from the great pavilion had finally stopped. A glance at the moon told Shef it was midnight. Time to move.

Rising from their places, the six freed slaves Shef had brought with him, led by Cwicca the bagpipe-player of Crowland, went silently to a cart standing a few yards away. They clustered round it, seized the push-handles and set off. Immediately a great squeaking of ungreased wheels filled the night, provoking immediate complaints. The gang of freedmen took no notice, marched doggedly on. No longer strapped and bandaged, but still dragging himself on his crutches, Shef followed thirty paces behind. Hund stood watching them for a moment, then slipped away in the moonlight toward the edge of camp and the waiting horses.

As the cart shrieked its way toward the pavilion, a thane of Burgred's guard stepped across. Shef heard his snarl of challenge, heard his spear-shaft crack across some unfortunate's shoulder. Wails of complaint, expostulation. As the thane stepped closer to find out what the men were doing he caught the reek of the cart and stepped back again, gagging and waving a hand in front of his face. Dropping his crutches, Shef slid past behind his back and into the maze of the pavilion guy-ropes. From there he could see again the thane ordering Cwicca's gang back, Cwicca cringing but sticking to his litany of explanation: "Clean out them pots now, they said. Chamberlain said he don't want no shit-shoveling in daylight. Nor no shit-shovelers disturbing no ladies. We don't want to do it, lord, we'd sooner be in bed, but we got to do it, it's our hides if it ain't done by morning; chamberlain told me he'd have the skin off me for sure."

The whine of the slave was unmistakable. As he spoke he kept pushing the cart forward, making sure the aged reek of twenty years of human dung got well to the thane's nostrils. The thane gave up, walked away still waving a hand in front of his face.

It would be hard to make this a story for poets, Shef reflected. No poet had ever found a place for the likes of Cwicca. Yet the plan could never work without him. Slaves, freemen and warriors looked different from each other, walked and talked differently. No thane could ever doubt that Cwicca was a slave on an errand. How could an enemy warrior be so undersized?

The gang reached the door of the women's privy, at the rear of the great quarter-acre pavilion. In front of it stood the permanent sentry, one of Burgred's hearth-companions, six feet tall and fully armed from helmet to studded boots. From his place in the shadows Shef watched intently. It was a critical moment, he knew. Cwicca had blocked as much of the view as possible with his cart, but just the same a watchful eye might be there in the darkness.

The gang surrounded the companion-sentry, pressing round him, deferential but determined, pawing at his sleeve as they tried to explain. Catching his sleeve, catching his arm, pulling him down as a skinny arm shut off his throat. A momentary heave, a strangled half-cry. Then a spurt of blood black in the moonlight as Cwicca passed a razor-sharp knife across vein and artery and windpipe, cutting down to the neckbone with the force of one slash.

As the sentry fell forward, was seized by six pairs of hands and upended into the cart, Shef reached them, grabbing the helmet, spear and shield. In a moment he too was out in the moonlight, waving the dung-cart impatiently on. Now any watchful eye would see only what was normal: the armed six-footer waving forward a gang of dwarvish toilers. As Cwicca's gang got the door open, pressed round it with their shovels and buckets, Shef stood for a moment in full view. Then stepped back into the shadow as if to watch the slaves more closely.

A moment later and he was through the door. And Godive was in his arms, naked beneath her shift.

"I couldn't get my clothes," she whispered. "He locks them away every night. And Alfgar—Alfgar took the drink. But Wulfgar sleeps also within our booth, and he would drink no ale because it is a fast-day. He saw me leave. He may cry out if I do not return."

Good, thought Shef, his brain cold as ice in spite of the warmth in his arms. Now what I meant to do all along will seem natural to her. So much less to explain. Maybe she will never know that I did not come for her.

Behind him, Cwicca's men were pressing in, still giving the impression of men trying to work quietly but openly.

"I am going into the sleeping-chamber," Shef whispered to them. "The lady will show me. If you hear an alarm, flee at once."

As they stepped into the unlit passage between the little individual sleeping-places of Burgred's most trusted courtiers—Godive moving with the sureness of one who had walked it a hundred times—Shef heard Cwicca's voice behind him. "Well, since we're here we might as well do the job. What's a few buckets of shit in a day's work?"

Godive paused as they reached the lowered canvas flap, pointed, spoke almost soundlessly. "Wulfgar. To the left. He sleeps in our room many nights, so I can turn him. He is in his box."

I have no gag, thought Shef. I expected him to be asleep. Silently he caught the hem of Godive's shift, began to lift it up over her body. For a moment she caught at the material with automatic modesty, then gave way, let him strip her naked. The first time I have done that, thought Shef. I never imagined it would be no pleasure. But if she enters naked, Wulfgar will be confused. It may give me an extra moment.

He pushed her bare back forward, felt the wince and the familiar feel of dried blood. Rage filled him, rage at Alfgar, rage too at himself. Why had he not thought, not once these long months, what they must be doing to her?

Moonlight through the canvas showed Godive walking naked across the room to the bed where her husband lay in drugged sleep. A grunt of surprise, anger from the short, padded box to the left. In an instant Shef was standing over it, looking down into his stepfather's face. He saw the recognition, saw the mouth open in horror. Stuffed the bloody shift firmly between Wulfgar's teeth.

Instant resistance, a furious twisting like a giant trapped snake. Though Wulfgar had neither arms nor legs, he still struggled desperately with all the force of his back and belly muscles to get a stump over the edge of the box, maybe roll to the floor. Too much noise, Shef knew, and the privileged couples sleeping in the little canvas boxes around him would wake as well, perhaps decide to intervene.

Perhaps not. Even noble couples learned to turn a deaf ear to the sounds of love. The sounds of punishment too. Shef thought of Godive's scarred back, thought of his own, conquered the momentary repugnance. A knee in the belly. Hands forcing the shift deep down into the throat. Twisting the ends behind the head and knotting them, knotting them again. And then Godive was with him, still naked, thrusting forward the rawhide ropes Alfgar's men used to fasten their trunks of belongings onto the pack-mules. Quickly they ran the ropes round the sleeping-box, not tying Wulfgar down, but making sure he could not climb out, crawl across the floor. As they finished, Shef waved Godive to the other end of the box. Carefully they lifted it from its stand, placed it on the floor. Now he could not even tip the box over, make a noise.

The short struggle over, Shef took two paces across to the big bed, looked down at Alfgar, asleep in drugged slumber in the moonlight. His mouth hung open, a steady snore coming from his throat. Still a handsome man, Shef recognized. He had had Godive these twelve months and more. He felt no urge to cut his throat. He needed Alfgar still. For the plan. And yet a gesture. A gesture would make the plan work better.

Godive was coming forward, in gown and mantle now, recovered from the box where Alfgar had locked them. In her hand she held her little seamstress's scissors, a look of set determination on her face. Quietly Shef blocked her, forced the hand down. He touched her back, looked inquiringly.

She pointed to a corner. There it was, the bundle of birch-twigs, fresh ones, without blood. He must have been planning to use them later. Shef straightened Alfgar on his bed, folded his hands on his chest, placed the birch-bundle between them.

He moved over to where Wulfgar lay in the rays of the moon, eyes bulging, staring up with an unreadable expression: terror? disbelief? could it be remorse? A memory came to Shef from somewhere: the three of them, Shef and Godive and Alfgar, small children, playing excitedly at something —bulliers maybe, the game with the plantain-shoots, where each child took it in turn to cut at the other's shoot with their own, till the head of one or the other came off. And Wulfgar watching, laughing, taking a turn himself. It was not his fault he was a heimnar. He had kept Shef's mother, not repudiated her as he might.

He had watched his son flog his daughter half to death. Slowly, making certain Wulfgar saw every movement, Shef took the borrowed silver pendant from his pouch, breathed on it, polished it. Laid it on Wulfgar's chest.

The hammer of Thor.

Silently the two slipped from the room, headed through the darkness for the door to the privy, guided by the muffled sounds of scraping and clanking. A problem occurred to Shef suddenly. He had not thought of this in advance. A noble lady, gently bred and brought up. There was only one way out for her. Cwicca and his gang could walk out, protected by the obviously shameful nature of their task and their own size and gait, the unmistakable marks of the slave-born. He could seize the spear and shield again and walk with them, complaining loudly if need be about the shame of a noble thane escorting a shit-cart to see the slaves did not steal or loiter. But Godive. She must needs go in the cart. In her gown. With a dead body and twenty buckets of human dung.

As he got ready to explain to her, to speak of necessity, apologize, to promise a bright future, she stepped ahead of him.

"Get the lid off," she snapped to Cwicca. She put her hand on the fouled edge of the cart, vaulted into the dark, stomach-gagging reek inside. "Now move," came her voice from the depths. "This is fresh air compared with King Burgred's court."

Slowly the cart squeaked its way across the courtyard, Shef striding ahead, spear-shaft sloped.

CHAPTER SIX

S hef looked along the row of faces confronting him: all hostile, all
disapproving.

"You took your time," said Alfred.

"I hope she was worth it," said Brand, looking with incredulity at the drawn and shabby figure of Godive in her borrowed
churl-wife's gown, straddling the pony behind Shef's.

"This is not the behavior of a lord of warriors," said Thorvin. "To leave
the Army threatened on two sides, and ride off on some private errand. I
know you came to us first to save the girl, but to go now . . . Could she
not have waited?"

"She had waited too long already," said Shef briefly. He swung from his
horse, grimacing slightly from the pain in his thighs. It had been another
long night and day of a ride, though the consolation was that even coming
on hell-bent, with the fury of Wulfgar and the bishops to spur him, Burgred must still be two days behind.

Shef turned to Cwicca and his comrades. "Go back to your places in the
camp," he said. "And remember. This was a great deed that we did. You
will see in time that it meant even more than it seems. I will not forget to
reward you all for it."

As the men trotted off, Hund among them, he turned back to his councillors. "Now," he said. "We know where Burgred is. Two days behind and
coming toward us as fast as he can bring himself to march. We can expect
him to reach our boundary the second night from this.

"But where is Ivar?"

"Bad news there," said Brand briefly. "He came down on the mouth of the Ouse two days ago with forty ships. The Norfolk Ouse, of course, not the Yorkshire Ouse. Attacked Lynn at the river mouth straight away. The town tried to resist him. He battered the stockade down in a few minutes and stamped the place flat. No survivors to say how he did it, but there's no doubt it happened."

"The mouth of the Ouse," muttered Shef. "Twenty miles off. And Burgred about the same."

Without orders Father Boniface had produced the great map of Norfolk and its borders which Shef had had made for the wall of his main chamber. Shef stood over it, estimating, looking from place to place.

"What we have to do . . ." he began.

"Before we do anything," Brand interrupted, "we have to discuss the matter of whether you are still fit to be trusted as our jarl."

For a long moment Shef stared at him, one eye against two. In the end it was Brand's eyes that dropped.

"All right, all right," he muttered. "You're up to something, no doubt, and one day you may consent to tell us what."

"Meanwhile," Alfred put in, "since you went to such trouble to fetch the lady, it might only be polite to have some thought for what she is to do now. Not just leave her standing outside our tents."

Shef looked again from face to hostile face, focusing finally on Godive's eyes—once more brimming with tears.

There is no time for all this! Something inside him shrieked. Persuading people. Lulling people. Pretending they are important. They are all wheels in the machine, and so am I! But if they thought that they might refuse to turn.

"I am sorry," he said. "Godive, forgive me. I was so sure we were safe that my mind turned to other things. Let me present to you my friends . . ."

The dragon-boats cruised down the shallow, muddy stream of the Great Ouse river, the western frontier of the Wayland jarldom they had come to destroy, forty in line ahead. Some of the crews were keeping up a song as they wound through the green, summer countryside, the masts and furled sails marking their passage over the flat levels. Ivar's men did not bother. They knew the time without a song or a shantyman to mark it. Besides, wherever Ivar Ragnarsson stood there was now a cloud of strain and tension, even for veteran pirates who would boast and believe that they feared no man.

Not far ahead the helmsmen—the rower-reliefs and the cowed slaves who manned Ivar's machines, one to each of the front six vessels—could see a wooden bridge across the river: not much of a bridge, not part of a town, just the place where the road happened to cross the stream. Chance of ambush from it, none. Just the same, veteran pirates grew to be veterans by taking no unnecessary risks at all. Even Ivar, totally careless of his own safety as he was, did things the way his men expected. A furlong short of the bridge, the figure in the prow, resplendent in scarlet cloak and grass-green trousers, turned and gave one harsh call.

The rowers finished their stroke, recovered oars, and then dropped them in the water, blades reversed. Slowly the ship drifted to a stop, the rest of the fleet easing into close line behind. Ivar waved to the two clumps of riders on both banks, here easily visible in the flat meadowland round the city. They moved forward at a trot, to check the bridge. Behind them the crews began with the ease of long practice to unstep their masts.

No resistance. Not a man in view. Yet as the horsemen slid from their ponies and moved to meet each other on the wooden cart-bridge, they saw that men had been there. A box. Left clear in the middle of the track, where no one could fail to spot it.

Dolgfinn, captain of the mounted scouting party, eyed it without enthusiasm. He did not like the look of it. It had been left there for a purpose. It had been left there by someone who had a very good idea of how a Viking fleet approached. Such things invariably contained a message or a sign of defiance. Probably it was a head. And there was no doubt that it was meant to be delivered to Ivar. Just to confirm his opinion, there was a crude painting on the top, of a tall man in scarlet cloak, green breeches and silver helmet. Dolgfinn had no great fear for himself—he was Sigurth Ragnarsson's own foster father, sent by the Snakeeye himself to keep an eye on his insane relative, and if Ivar had any lingering concern for what any man thought, it was for his elder brother. Just the same, Dolgfinn had no particular relish for the scene that was likely to erupt. Someone would suffer for it, that was sure. Dolgfinn remembered the scene many months before, when Viga-Brand had dared and taunted the Ragnarssons together with the news of their father's death. Good material for a tale, he reflected. Yet things had not turned out so well afterward. Had Brand perhaps, plain man though he seemed to be, foreseen what would follow? And if so, what of this?

Dolgfinn put the thoughts from his mind. Trap it might be. If so, he had no choice but to test it. He picked up the box—not a head at least, too light—walked down to the edge of the water where the dragon-boat was edging in, leapt from shore to oar to thwart, and strolled toward Ivar standing on the half-decked prow, near the giant ton-and-a-half weight of his machine. Silently he put the box down, indicated the painting, whipped a knife from his belt and offered it to Ivar hilt-first, to pry up the nailed lid.

A king of the English would have waved forward a servant to do such a menial task. Chiefs of the pirates had no such dignity to stand on. In four brisk heaves Ivar had the nails out. His pale eyes looked up at Dolgfinn, while his face broke into an unexpected smile of pure pleasure and antici-pation. Ivar knew insult or provocation was coming. He liked the thought of something to repay.

"Let's see what the Waymen have sent us," he said.

Hurling the box-lid aside, he reached in.

"First insult. A capon." He lifted the dead bird out, stroked its feathers. "A neutered cockerel. Now, I wonder who that might signify."

Ivar held the silence till it was quite clear that neither Dolgfinn nor anyone else had anything to say, then reached down again.

"Second insult. Tied to the capon, some straw. Some stalks."

"Not stalks," said Dolgfinn. "That is a sheaf. Do I need to tell you who that is for? His name was often in your mouth a few weeks ago."

Ivar nodded. "Thank you for the reminder. Have you heard it said, Dolgfinn, the old saying: 'A slave takes vengeance at once, a coward never'?"

I did not think you were a coward, thought Dolgfinn, but he did not say it. It would have sounded too much like an apology. If Ivar meant to take offense, he would.

"Have you heard another old saying, Ivar Ragnarsson?" he countered. " 'Often from a bloody bag come bad tidings.' Let us riddle this bag to the bottom."

Ivar reached again, pulled out a third and last object. This time he stared at it with genuine puzzlement. It was an eel. The snake-like fish of the marshes.

"What is this?" Silence.

"Can anyone tell me?" Still only headshakes from the warriors crowding round. A slight stir from one of the slaves of the monks of York, crouching by his machine. Ivar's eyes missed nothing.

"I grant a boon to whoever can tell me the meaning of this."

The slave straightened up doubtfully, realizing all eyes were now on him.

"One boon, lord, given freely?"

Ivar nodded.

"It is what we call in English an *eel*, lord. I think it may mean a place. Ely, down the Ouse, Eel-island, only a few miles from here. Perhaps what it means is that he, the Sheaf, that is, will meet you there."

"Because I must be the capon?" inquired Ivar.

The slave gulped. "You granted a boon, lord, to whoever would speak. I choose mine. I choose freedom."

"You are free to go," said Ivar, stepping back from the ship's thwart. The slave gulped again, looking round at the bearded, impassive faces. He stepped forward slowly, gained confidence as no one moved to hinder him, leapt to the side of the ship, and then, in two moves, to a trailing oar and to the side of the river. He was off like a flash, heading for the nearest cover, running in awkward bounds like a frog.

"Eight, nine, ten," said Ivar to himself. The silver-mounted spear was in his hand; he poised, took two paces sideways. The leaf-blade took the running slave neatly between shoulders and neck, hurling him forward.

"Would anyone else care to call me a capon?" inquired Ivar generally.

Someone already has, thought Dolgfinn.

Later that night, after the ships had moored a cautious two miles north of the challenge-ground, some of Ivar's most senior skippers were talking quietly, very quietly, round their campfire well away from Ivar's tent.

"They call him the Boneless," said one, "because he cannot take a woman."

"He can," said another. "He has sons and daughters."

"Only if he does strange things first. Not many women survive them. They say—"

"No," cut in a third man, "do not speak. I will tell you why he is the Boneless. It is because he is like the wind, which comes from anywhere. He could be behind us now."

"You are all wrong," said Dolgfinn. "I am not a Wayman, but I have friends who are. I had friends who were. They say this, and I believe them. He is the *Beinnlauss*, right enough. But that does not mean 'boneless.'" Dolgfinn held up a beef-rib to point out which of the two meanings of the Norse word he meant. "It means 'legless.'" He patted his own thigh.

"But he has legs," queried one of his listeners.

"On this side, he does. Those who have seen him in the Otherworld, the Waymen, say that there he crawls on his belly in the shape of a great worm, a dragon. He is not a man of one skin. And that is why it will take more than steel to kill him."

Experimentally, Shef flexed the two-foot-long, two-inch-wide strip of metal that Udd, the little freedman, had brought him. The muscles on his arms stood out as he did so: muscles strong enough to bend a soft iron slave-collar by main force alone. The mild steel gave an inch, two inches. Sprang back.

"It works on the shooters all right," offered Oswi, watching with interest a ring of catapulteers.

"I'm wondering if it would work for anything else," said Shef. "A bow?" He flexed the strip again, this time putting it over one knee and trying to get the weight of his body behind it. The metal resisted him, giving only a couple of inches. Too strong for a bow. Or too strong for a man's arms? Yet there were many things that were too strong for a man's arms alone. Catapults. Heavy weights. The yard of a longship. Shef hefted the metal once more. Somewhere in here there was a solution to his puzzle: a mixture of the new knowledge the Way sought and the old knowledge he kept on finding. Now was not the time for him to work the puzzle out.

"How many of these have you made, Udd?"

"Maybe a score. After we refitted the shooters, that is."

"Stay in the forge tomorrow. Make more. Take as many men and as much iron as you need. I want fivescore—tenscore—as many as you can make."

"Does that mean we'll miss the battle?" cried Oswi. "Never get a chance to shoot old 'Dead Level' once?"

"All right. Udd chooses just one man from each crew to help him. The rest of you get your chance at the battle."

If there is a battle, Shef added silently to himself. But that is not my plan. Not a battle for us, at any rate. If England is the gods' chessboard, and we are all pieces in their game, then to win the game I must clear some of the pieces off the board. No matter how it looks to the others.

In the early morning mist King Burgred's army, the army of the Mark— three thousand swordsmen and as many slaves, drivers, muleteers and whores—prepared to continue its march in the true English fashion: slowly, grumpily and inefficiently, but for all that, with mounting expectation. Thanes wandered toward the latrines, or eased themselves onto any unoccupied spot. Slaves who had not done so the night before began to grind meal for the everlasting porridge. Fires began to burn, pots began to bubble, the voices of Burgred's guardsmen grew hoarse as they attempted to impose the king's will on his loyal but disorganized subjects: get the bastards fed, get their bowels emptied, and get them moving, as Cwichelm the marshal endlessly repeated. Because today we move into enemy territory. Cross the Ouse, advance on Ely. We can expect a battle any time.

Driven on by the fury of their king at the violation of his own pavilion, by the exhortations of their priests and the near-incoherent rage of Wulfgar the dreaded heimnar, the army of the Mark struck its tents and donned its armor.

In the dragon-boats, matters went differently. A shake from the ship-watch, a word from each skipper. The men were over the side in minutes, and every one dressed, booted, armed and ready to fight. Two riders trotted down from the advanced pickets half a mile away, reporting noise to the west and scouts sent out. Another word, this time from Ivar, and half the men in each crew stood down immediately, to prepare food for themselves and the others still formed up. Detachments swarmed round each of the ton-weight machines in the six lead ships, attaching ropes and rigging pulleys. When the word came they would sway them up from the strengthened yards, drop each one onto its waiting carriage. But not yet. "Wait till the last moment and then move fast" was the pirates' watchword.

The Wayman camp, four miles off in dense beechwood, made no sound and showed no lights. Shef, Brand, Thorvin and all their lieutenants had been round again and again the day before, impressing it on the most impatient Viking and dullest ex-slave. No noise. No straggling. Stay in your blankets till you're called. Get some rest. Breakfast by units. Then form up. Don't go outside the wood.

Obeying his own orders, Shef lay alert in his tent, listening to the muted bustle of the army waking. Today was a day of crisis, he thought. But not the last crisis. Maybe the last one he could plan. It was critically important, then, that this day should go well, to provide him with the start, the reserve of force that he would need before all was over.

On the pallet beside him lay Godive. They had been together four days now, and yet he had still not taken her, not so much as stripped off her shift. It would be easy to do. His flesh was hard, remembering the one time he had done it. She would not resist. Not only did she expect it, he knew she wondered why he had not. Was he another like the Boneless? Or was he less of a man than Alfgar? Shef imagined the cry she would make as he penetrated her.

Who could blame her for crying? She still winced every time she moved. Like his, her back must be scarred forever.

Yet she still had both eyes. She had never faced the mercy of Ivar, the *vapna takr*. As he thought of the mercy of Ivar, Shef's erected flesh began to shrink; the thoughts of warm skin and soft resistance dwindled like a catapult-stone going up into the sky.

Something else entered him instead, something cold and fierce and longsighted. It was not today that mattered, nor the fleeting good opinion of his men. Only the end. Stretched out, relaxed, perfectly aware of himself from crown to toe, Shef reflected on how the day might go.

Hund, he decided. Time for another call on Hund.

As the sun sucked up the morning mist, Ivar looked from his place with the ridge-line pickets to the familiar chaos of an English army advancing. Familiar chaos. An English army.

"It's not them," said Dolgfinn beside him. "Not the Way-folk. Not Skjef Sigvarthsson. Look at all the Christ-stuff, the crosses and the black robes. You can hear them singing their morning *massa,* or whatever they call it. So either Sigvarthsson's challenge was just a lie, or else . . ."

"Or else there's another army hiding round here somewhere, to finish off the winners," Ivar completed for him. The grin was back on his face, pinched and painful, like a fox nibbling meat from the wolf-trap.

"Back to the boats?"

"I think not," said Ivar. "The river's too narrow to turn forty boats in a hurry. And if we row on there's no certainty they won't mount and catch us. And if they do that they can take us out one boat at a time. Even the English might manage that.

"No. At our Bragi boast in the Braethraborg, my brothers and I swore to invade England and conquer all its kingdoms in revenge for our father. Two we have conquered, and today is the day for the third."

"And Sigvarthsson?" prompted Dolgfinn.

The grin spread wider, teeth showing like a rictus. "He will have his chance. We will have to see he doesn't take it. Now, get down to the boats, Dolgfinn, and tell them to unload the machines. But not this bank. The far bank, understand? A hundred paces back. And rig a sail over each one as if it was a tent. Have men ready to look as if they're taking them down when the English come in sight. But take them down English-style—you know, as if you were ten old gammers comparing grandchildren. Have the slaves do it."

Dolgfinn laughed. "You have trained the slaves to work better than that these months, Ivar."

The mirth had drained completely from Ivar's face, the eyes gone as colorless as his skin. "Then untrain them," he said. "The machines on that bank. The men on this." He turned back to his survey of the army coming forward, six-deep, banners waving, great crosses on standard-carts behind its center. "And send up Hamal. He will lead the mounted patrol today. I have special orders for him."

From his vantage point beneath a great flowering hawthorn, Shef looked out at the developing battle. The Army of the Way lay in its ranks behind and to either side of him, well spread-out and under cover of wood or hedgerow. The bulky pull-throwers were still not assembled, the twist-shooters with their horse-teams well to the rear. English bagpipers and Viking horn-blowers had all alike been threatened with disgrace, torment and forfeiture of a week's ale ration if they sounded a note. Shef was sure they had remained undiscovered. And now, as the battle seemed likely to be joined, both sides' wandering scouts would have been called into the center. So far so good.

And yet already there was a surprise. Ivar's machines. Shef had watched them being swayed from the boats, had noted the way the yards dipped and the boats heeled: heavy objects, whatever they were, far heavier than his own. Was that how Ivar had taken Lynn? And they had been put on the wrong bank. Safer from attack, maybe, but unable to move forward if the battle shifted the other way. Nor could even Shef's keen sight see how the machines were constructed. How would they affect his plan to fight the battle?

Even more, his plan not to fight the battle.

Cwichelm the marshal, veteran of many battles, would have halted the army if he could, as soon as his advance-guard reported the dragon-boats on the river in front of him. A Viking fleet was not what he had expected to fight. Anything unexpected should be scouted first—especially when dealing with the folk of the Way, whose many traps he remembered from the fight in the marsh when Sigvarth had died.

He was not left to make the decision. Vikings and Waymen were all the same to his king: enemies of decency. To Wulfgar and the bishops, all were heathens. Dragon-boats spread out in line? So much the better! Destroy them before they could mass together. "And if they are not Way-folk," the young Alfgar had added with pointed insolence, "so much less to worry about. At least they will not have the machines you fear so much."

Stung by the insult, aware that complex maneuvering would not work with the untrained country thanes who made up most of King Burgred's army, Cwichelm took his men over the slight ridge above the river at a brisk trot, he and his assistants well out in front, shouting their war-cries and waving their broadswords for the rest to come on.

The English army, seeing the hated dragon-boats in front of them, each crew clumped in a wedge before its boat, cheered and came on with enthusiasm. Just so long as they don't get disheartened, thought Cwichelm, dropping back till the ranks closed round him. Or get tired before the battle's even started. He settled his shield firmly on his shoulder, making no effort to lift it to guard-position. It weighed a stone— fourteen English pounds—the rest of his weapons and armor, three stone more. Not too much to carry. A lot to run with. Even more to wield. Through the sweat that ran into his eyes he noted dimly the men on the far bank struggling with canvas. Not often you catch Vikings napping, he thought. It's usually us that's up last.

The first volley from Erkenbert's onagers smashed six holes in the English battle-line, each stone driving clear through the six-deep ranks. The one aimed for the commanders in the center—conspicuous in gold and garnets and scarlet tunics—lifted a trifle high, at head height. Cwichelm never felt or saw the blow that drove his head straight back till the neckbone snapped, that reaped a file of men behind him and crashed on to bury itself in the earth just short of the cart from which Bishop Daniel was chanting an encouraging psalm. In an instant both he and the army were headless.

Most of the English warriors behind their visored helmets did not even see what had happened to their right or their left. They could see only the enemy in front of them, the enemy so tantalizingly gathered in isolated clumps and wedges, each one forty-strong in front of its ship, five or ten yards between them. In a yelling wave they ran forward to beat on the Viking wedges with spear and broadsword, hacking at the linden-shields, sweeping at head and leg. Braced and rested, Ivar Ragnarsson's outnumbered men strained every muscle to hold them for the five minutes their chief had demanded.

Through the carefully measured firing-lanes the catapults launched their irresistible missiles again and again.

*   *   *

"Something's happening already," grunted Brand.

Shef made no reply. For several minutes he had strained his one eye desperately to see what he could of the machines that were wreaking such havoc in Burgred's army. Then he fixed on one, counted his heartbeats carefully between one launch and the next. By now he had a good idea of what the weapons were. They must be torsion-machines—the slow rate of shot showed that, as did the smashing effect, the swirls of men bowled over as each missile struck. They were not on a bow principle. Little as he could see from a mile's distance, the square, high shape showed that. And the weight of them, the weight he could detect from the way they had to be slung on yards and pulleys—that showed they must be built stoutly to take some sort of impact. Yes. A little experiment, a closer look if he got the chance, and . . .

Time now to think more immediately. Shef turned his attention to the battle. Something happening, Brand said. And easy enough to guess what. After a few volleys, the men on the English side, nearest to where the stones were arriving, had started to edge sideways, realizing that safety lay in having wedges of their enemies between them and the machines. But as they edged sideways they hampered the efforts and the sword-arms of the champions trying to break through Ivar's crewmen. Many of those champions, half-blinded by their helmets, weighed down by their armor, had no idea what was going on, only that something strange was happening round them. Some of them were beginning to step back, to look for space to raise their visors, to shove off the men who should be backing them but were jostling them instead. If Ivar's men were concentrated they could use such a moment to break out. But they were not. They themselves were in small groups, each one liable to be swallowed instantly by superior numbers if they drove forward from their ships and the protecting riverbank. The battle hung in balance.

Brand grunted again, this time digging his fingers deep into Shef's arm. Someone by Ivar's machines had given an order to change targets, was enforcing it with kicks and blows. As the English swordsmen rushed forward, the clumsy standard-carts behind them were left exposed, each one with a waving banner on it—of king or alderman, or the giant cross of bishop or abbot. But now there was one fewer than there had been a moment ago. Splinters still flew in the air, turning end over end. A direct hit. And there again—a whole file of draft-oxen slumped onto their knees in a row and a wheel hurled itself sideways. From the Wayman army behind Shef and his group, all by now watching intently, there rose an exhalation, an exhalation that would have been a cheer without the instant kicks and curses of marshals and team-leaders. A cross held steady for a moment, then tipped inexorably over, crashed to the ground.

Something deep inside Shef clicked like a winding cogwheel. Thoughtfully, unnoticed in the rising excitement around him, he took a deep pull at the flask he had held all day in one hand: good ale. But in it was the contents of the little leather sack he had taken from Hund that morning. He drank deep, forcing himself to ignore the gagging reflex, the vile taste of long-rotten meat. How do you give a man a vomit, for a purge? he had asked. "That is one thing we *can* do," Hund had said with somber pride. Shef felt no doubt, as the drench went down, that that was exactly true. He drank the flask to its end, leaving not a drop as evidence, then rose to his feet. A minute, maybe two, he thought. I need all eyes.

"Why are they riding forward?" he asked. "Is it a charge?"

"A cavalry charge like the Franks do?" replied Brand uncertainly. "I've heard of that. Don't know that the English—"

"No, no, no," snapped Alfred, also on his feet, almost dancing with impatience. "It's Burgred's horse-thanes. Oh, look at the fools! They've decided that the battle is lost, so they're riding forward to rescue their lord. But as soon as he mounts . . . Almighty God, he's done it!"

Far away across the battlefield, a gold-ringed head rose into view from a ruck of bodies—the king mounting. For a moment he seemed to be resisting, waving his sword forward. But someone else had hold of his bridle. A clot of riders began to walk, then canter from the fighting. As they did so, instantly men began to shred away from the fighting-lines, following their leader, at first casually. Then briskly, hastily. Realizing the movement behind them, others turned to look, to follow. The army of the Mark, still undestroyed, still unbeaten, many of its men still unafraid, began to stream to the rear. As it did so, the stones lashed out again. Men began to run.

The Wayman army was all on its feet now, all eyes turning expectantly toward the center. The moment, Shef thought. Sweep forward when both sides are fully engaged, take the machines before they can change target, board the ships, take Ivar in flank and rear . . .

"Give me some horsemen," Alfred begged. "Burgred's a fool, but he's my sister's husband. I have to save him. We'll pension him off, send him to the Pope . . ."

Yes, thought Shef. And that will be one piece still on the board. And Ivar —even if we beat him Ivar will get away, by boat or horse, like he did last time. And that will be another. But we must have fewer pieces now. In the end, one piece alone. I want the mills to stop.

Blessedly, as he stepped forward, he felt some dreadful thing rising inside him, his mouth filling with the terrible cold saliva he had felt only once before, the time he had eaten carrion one hard winter. Grimly he clamped it down. All eyes, all eyes.

He turned, looked at the men rising from bracken and bush, eyes glaring, teeth showing with expectant rage. "Forward," he shouted, lifting his halberd from the ground and sweeping it toward the river. "Men of the Way . . ."

The vomit shot from his mouth so fiercely it caught Alfred high up on his enameled shield. The king gaped, uncomprehending. Shef doubled up, acting no more; his halberd dropped. Again the great retchings took him, again and again, lifting him off his feet.

As he rolled on the fouled earth the Wayman army hesitated, staring in horror. Alfred raised an arm to shout for his horse, for his companions, then dropped it, turned back to stare at the figure writhing on the ground. Thorvin was running forward from his place in the rear. A buzz of doubt ran along the ranks: What's the order? Are we going forward? Sigvarthsson is down? Who commands? Is it the Viking? Do we obey a pirate? An Englishman? The Wessex king?

As he sprawled in the grass, gasping for breath before the next upheaval, Shef heard the voice of Brand, looking down at him with stony disapproval.

"There is an old saying," it said. " 'When the army-leader weakens, then the whole army wavers.' What do you expect it to do when he spews his guts out?"

Stand fast, thought Shef, and wait till he's better. Please, Thor. Or God. Or whoever. Just do it.

Ivar, his eyes as pale as watered milk, stared out across the battlefield for the trap he knew must be there. At his feet—he had fought by choice at the tip of the wedge of his ship's crew—lay three champions of the Mark, each in turn eager for the fame that would ring through the whole of Christendom for the bane of Ivar, cruelest of the pirates of the North. Each discovering in turn that Ivar's slim height belied his extraordinary strength of arm and body, though not his snakelike speed. One of them, cut through mail and leather from collarbone to ribcage, moaned involuntarily as he waited for death. Quick as a snake's tongue Ivar's sword licked out, stabbing through Adam's apple and spine beneath. Ivar did not want sport, for the moment. He wanted quiet, for consideration.

Nothing in the woods. Nothing to either flank. Nothing behind him. If they did not spring the trap soon it would be too late. It was almost too late already. Round Ivar his army, without orders or briefing, was carrying out one of its many experienced battle-drills: securing a battlefield after victory. It was one of the many strengths of Viking armies that their leaders did not have to waste their energies in telling the rank and file how to do anything that could be turned into a routine. They could watch and plan instead. Now, some men went forward in pairs, one to stab, one to guard, making doubly and triply sure that no Englishman was lying still but conscious, ready to take a last enemy with him. Behind them came the loot-gatherers with their sacks, not stripping the dead of everything, as would be done later, but taking everything visible and valuable. In the ships, leeches were splinting and binding.

And at the same time every man kept a tense eye on their leader, for further orders. All knew that the moment of victory was a time to exploit advantage. They carried out their immediate tasks with savage haste.

No, reflected Ivar. The trap had been set, he was sure of that. But it had not been sprung. Probably the fools got up too late. Or were stuck in a marsh somewhere.

He stepped forward, placed his helmet on a spear, waved it in a circle. Immediately, from their concealment half a mile on the downstream flank of the English army, there broke a wave of riders, legs flapping as they kicked their horses into speed, steel glinting in the morning sun on point and edge and mail. The English swordsmen still shredding to the rear pointed, yelled, ran faster. Fools, thought Ivar. They still outnumber Hamal up there six to one. If they stood fast, formed line, they could finish him off before we got up to join in. And if we broke ranks to hurry they could win this battle yet. But there was something about armed riders that made scattered men run without even looking over their shoulders.

In any case Hamal and the mounted patrol—three hundred men, every horse that Ivar's army had been able to lay bridle on—had targets other than single fugitives. Now, after battle, was the time to destroy leaders, to ensure that kingdoms could never recover their strength again. Ivar noted with approval the swerve as fifty men on the fastest horses aimed to head off the gold-coroneted figure now being urged over the skyline by his horse-thanes. Others pounded down on the straggle of carts and standards making laboriously for the rear. The main body was galloping hard along the ridge-line, obviously intent on the camp and the camp-followers that must be there, out of sight but only a few hundred yards the other side of the ridge.

Time to join them. Time to get rich. Time for sport. Ivar felt the excitement rise in his throat. They had balked him with Ella. Not with Edmund.

They would not with Burgred. He enjoyed killing kings. And afterward—afterward there would be some one of the whores, maybe some one of the ladies, but anyway some soft, pale creature that no one would miss. And in the tumult of a sacked camp, with rape and death on every side, no one would notice. It would not be the girl that Sigvarthsson had taken from him. But there would be some other. Meanwhile.

Ivar turned, stepped carefully round the mess of entrails slowly spilling from the butchered man at his feet, replaced his helmet, waved his shield forward. The watching army, loot already stacked, men back in their ranks, gave a short, hoarse cheer and walked forward with him, up the hill, over the men they had killed themselves and the men the machines had slaughtered. As they tramped forward they shook out from their wedges to form a solid line four hundred yards across. Behind them the ship-guards already detailed watched them go.

So, from its concealment in the woods a mile upstream, did the Wayman army—confused, frustrated, already bickering over the limp shape of its leader.

CHAPTER SEVEN

We cannot afford to wait any longer," said Thorvin. "We must settle this matter for good. And now."

"The army is divided," objected Geirulf, the priest of Tyr. "If the men see you too ride away, they will lose heart even more."

Thorvin brushed the objection aside with an impatient gesture. Round him ran the cords with their holy rowan berries; the spear of Othin stood in the ground beside him next to the burning fire of Loki. Just as the time before, only priests of the Way sat in the sacred circle, with no laymen present. They meant to speak of things no layman should hear.

"That is what we have told ourselves for too long," replied Thorvin. "Always there is something more important to think of than this central one. We should have solved the riddle long ago, as soon as we began to think the boy Shef might indeed be what he said: the one who will come from the North. We asked the question, we asked his friend, we asked Sigvarth Jarl—who thought he was his father. When we could find no answer we passed to other things.

"But now we must be sure. When he would not wear the pendant, I said, 'there is still time.' When he left the army and rode to find his woman, we thought, 'he is a boy.' Now he pretends to lead the army and leaves it in disorder. Next time what will he do? We have to know. Is he a child of Othin? And if he is, what will he be to us? Othin Allfather, father of gods and men? Or Othin Bölverk, God of the Hanged, Betrayer of Warriors, who gathers the heroes to himself only for his own purposes?

"Not for nothing is there no priest of Othin with the army, and few within the Way. If that is his birth, we must know. And it may be that is not his birth. There are other gods than Allfather who walk in the world."

Thorvin looked meaningfully at the crackling fire to his left. "So: let me do what should have been done before. Ride to ask his mother. We know which village she comes from. It is not twenty miles off. If she is still there I will ask her—and if her answer is wrong, then I say we must cast him off before worse befalls us. Remember the warning of Vigleik!"

A long silence followed Thorvin's words. Finally Farman, the priest of Frey, broke it.

"I remember Vigleik's warning, Thorvin. And I too fear the treachery of Othin. Yet I ask you to think that Othin, and his followers, may be as they are for a reason. To keep off worse powers."

He too looked thoughtfully at the Loki-fire. "As you know, I have seen your former apprentice in the Otherworld, standing in the place of Völund the smith. But I have seen other things in that world. And I can tell you that not far from here there is far worse than your apprentice: one of the brood of Fenris himself, a grandchild of Loki. If you had seen them in the Otherworld, you would never again confuse the two, Othin and Loki, or think that the one might be the other."

"Very well," replied Thorvin. "But I ask you, Farman, to think this. If there is a war between two powers in this world, gods and giants, with Othin at the head of one and Loki at the other—how often do we see it even in this world, that as the war goes on, the one side begins to resemble the other?"

Slowly the heads nodded, even, in the end, Geirulf's, then Farman's.

"It is decided," said Farman. "Go to Emneth. Find the boy's mother and ask her whose son hers is."

Ingulf the healer, priest of Ithun, spoke for the first time. "A deed of kindness, Thorvin, that may come to good. When you go, take with you the English girl Godive. She has realized in her way what we have. She knows he did not rescue her for love. Only to use her as bait. That is no good thing for anyone to know."

Shef had been dimly aware, through first the racking cramps and then the paralyzing weakness that succeeded them, of the leaders of his army's factions arguing. At some point Alfred had threatened to draw sword on Brand, an action dismissed like some great dog brushing aside a puppy.

He could remember Thorvin pleading passionately for something, some rescue or expedition. But most of the day he had been aware of nothing except hands lifting him, attempts made to get him to drink, hands holding him through the retchings that followed: Ingulf's hands sometimes, then Godive's. Never Hund's. With just a fragment of mind Shef realized that Hund feared his leech-detachment might suffer if he saw too closely what he had done. Now, as the dark came on, he felt recovered, weary, ready to sleep: to wake to action.

But first the sleep must come. It had the nauseous taste about it of Hund's mold-and-carrion draft.

He was in a gully, a rocky defile, in the dark. Slowly he clambered forward, unable to see more than a few feet, lit only by a last pale light in the sky—the sky visible only many yards above his head, where the gully's jagged outline showed black against gray. He moved with agonized care. No stumble, no dislodgement of stone. Or something would be on him. Something no human could fight against.

He had a sword in his hand, gleaming very faintly in the starlight. There was something about the sword: it had a will of its own, a fierce urge. It had already killed its creator and master, and would gladly do so again, even though he was its master now. It tugged at his hand, and from time to time it rang faintly, as if he had knocked it on stone. It seemed to know about the need for stealth, though. The sound would be inaudible to anyone or anything except himself. It was covered, too, by the rushing of the water at the bottom of the gully. The sword was anxious to kill, and ready to keep silent till its chance came.

As he moved into the dream, Shef realized, as he often did, what sort of person he himself was. This time, a man impossibly broad of hip and shoulder, with wrists so thick they bulged round the gold bracelets he wore. Their weight would have dragged a lesser man's arms down. He did not notice them.

The man he was, was frightened. His breath came short, not from the climbing, but from fear. There was a sense in his stomach of emptiness and chill. It was especially frightening to this man, Shef realized, because he had never felt such a feeling before. He did not even understand it, and could not name it. It was bothering him, but not affecting him, because this man did not know it was possible to turn back from an enterprise once begun. He had never done it before; he would never do so till the day he died. Now he was climbing beside the stream, holding his drawn sword carefully, to reach the position he had decided on and to do the thing he had planned, though his heart turned over inside him at the thought of what he must face.

Or not face. Even this man, Sigurth Sigmundsson, whose name would live till the end of the world, knew he could not face what he had to kill.

He came to a place where the gully wall on one side was broken down, falling into a jumble of scree and broken stone, as if some great metal creature had smashed it and rolled it flat so that it could get down to the water. And as he reached it, a sudden overwhelming reek stopped the hero in his tracks, a reek like a solid wall. It stank of dead things, of a battlefield two weeks old in the summer sun—but also of soot, of burning, with some extra tang about it that attacked the nostrils, as if the smell itself would catch fire if someone struck a spark.

It was the smell of the worm. The dragon. Dawn-ravager, venom-blower, the naked spite-creature that crawled on its belly. The legless one.

As the hero found, in the jumble of stone, a crack large enough to take his body and crawled inside it, he realized he had not been too early. For the dragon was not legless, and seemed so only to those who saw it crawling forward from a distance. Through the stone the hero could hear a heavy stumping, as one foot after another groped forward; in between and all the time, the heavy slither of the belly dragging on the ground. The leather belly, if reports were true. They had better be.

The hero tried to lie on his back, then hesitated, changing position rapidly. Now he lay on one side, facing the direction from which the dragon must come, propped on his left elbow, right elbow down and sword across his body. His eyes and the top of his head projected above the track. It would look like another stone, he told himself. The truth was that even this hero could not lie still and wait for the thing to appear above him, or he—even he—would be unmanned. He had to see.

And there it was, the great head silhouetted against the gray like some stone outcrop. But moving; its armored crest and skull-bones like a metal war-machine rotating. The bloated swag body behind it. Some trick of the starlight caught one foot planted on the stone, and the hero stared at it, shocked almost into paralysis. Four toes, sticking out from each other like the arms of a starfish, but each one the size of a man's thigh, warty and gnarled like a toad's back, dripping slime. The very touch of one of those would kill from horror. The hero had just enough self-command not to shrink back with fear. The slightest movement now would be deadly dangerous. His only hope was to be a stone.

Would it see him? It must. It was coming toward him, directly toward him, padding forward with great, slow steps. One forefoot was only ten yards from him, then the other was planted on the stone almost on the lip of his crack. He must let it walk right over him, the hero thought with his last vestige of sense, let it walk right down to the river where it drank. And when he heard the first noise of drinking, of the water gushing up as it must into the belly above him, then he must strike.

As he told himself this, the head reared up only a few feet above him, and the hero caught sight of a thing of which no man had spoken. The dragon's eyes. They were white, as white as those of an old woman with the film-disease, but light shone through them, a pale light from within.

The hero realized what it was that he feared the most. Not that the legless one, the boneless longserpent, would kill him. That would almost be a relief in this terrible place. But that it would see him. And stop. And speak, before it began its long sport with him.

The dragon halted, one foot in mid-stride. And looked down.

Shef came from his sleep with a shriek and a bound, landing in one movement, just feet from the bed where they had stretched him. Three pairs of eyes stared at him, alarmed, relieved, surprised. One pair, Ingulf's, looked suddenly knowing.

"You saw something?" he said.

Shef passed a hand over his sweat-soaked hair. "Ivar. The Boneless One. As he is on the other side."

The warriors around Ivar watched him out of the corners of their eyes, too proud to show alarm or even anxiety, yet conscious that at any time now he might break out, turn on anyone at all, even his most trusted followers or the emissaries of his brothers. He sat in a carved chair looted from one of King Burgred's baggage-carts, a horn of ale in his right hand, dipped from the great keg in front of him. In his left hand he swung the gold coronet they had taken from Burgred's head. The head itself was on a spike in the stark ring surrounding the Vikings' camp. That was why Ivar's mood was grim. He had been balked yet again.

"Sorry," Hamal had reported. "We tried to take him alive, as you ordered, to pin him between our shields. He fought like a black bear, from his horse and then on foot. Even then we might have taken him, but he tripped, fell forward on a sword." "Whose sword?" Ivar had demanded, his voice quiet. "Mine," Hamal had said, lying. If he had indicated the young man who had really killed Burgred, Ivar would have taken out his spite and frustration on him. Hamal had a chance of surviving. Not an especially strong one, for all his past services. But Ivar had only studied his face for a moment, remarked dispassionately that he was a liar, and not a pretty one, and had left the matter there.

It would break out some other way, they were sure. As Dolgfinn went on with the tale of victory—prisoners taken, loot from the field, loot from the camp, gold and silver, women and provisions—he wished deeply that some of his own men would turn up. "Go round everywhere," he had told them, "look at everything. Never mind the women for the moment; there'll be plenty left for you before the night's over. But in the name of old Hairy Breeks himself, find something to keep the Ragnarsson amused. Or it could be us he pegs out for the birds tomorrow."

Ivar's eyes had shifted past Dolgfinn's shoulder. He dared to follow them. So—Greppi and the boys had found something after all. But what in the name of Hel, goddess of the dead, could it be?

It was a box, a wheeled box that could be tipped forward and trundled along like an upright coffin. Too short for a coffin. And yet there was a body inside. A dozen grinning Vikings pushed the box forward and tipped it to stand in front of Ivar. The body inside looked out at them, and licked its lips.

Ivar rose, putting down the golden coronet for the first time that evening, and stood in front of Wulfgar.

"Well," he remarked at last. "Not such a bad job. But not one of mine, I think. Or at least I don't remember the face. Who did this to you, heimnar?"

The pale face with its bright red, incongruous lips, stared back at him, made no reply. A Viking stepped forward, knife whipping clear, ready to slice or gouge on command, but Ivar's hand stopped him.

"Think a little, Kleggi," he urged. "It's not easy to frighten a man who's already lost so much. What's an eye or an ear now?

"So tell me, heimnar. You are a dead man already; you have been since they did this. Who did it to you? Maybe he was no friend of mine either."

Ivar spoke in Norse, but slowly, clearly, so an Englishman could pick out some of the words.

"It was Sigvarth Jarl," said Wulfgar. "Jarl of the Small Isles, they tell me. But I want you to know, what he did to me, I did to him. Only more. I caught him in the marsh by Ely—if you are the Ragnarsson, then you were not far away. I trimmed him finger by finger and toe by toe. He did not die till there was nothing left a knife could reach. Nothing you can do to me will equal what I did to him."

He spat suddenly, the spittle landing on Ivar's shoe. "And so may perish all you Godless heathen! And it is my comfort. As you die in torment, for you it is only the gateway to the eternal torment. I will look down from *Neorxna-wang*, from the plain of the blessed dead, and see you blister in

the heat. Then you will beg for the smallest drop from my ale-cup to cool
your agony. But God and I will refuse."

The blue eyes stared up, jaw set in determination. Ivar laughed suddenly, throwing his head back, raised the horn in his right hand and
drained it to the last drop.

"Well," he said. "Since you mean to be so niggard with me, I will do
what your Christian books say and return you good for evil.

"Throw him in the keg!"

As the men gaped, Ivar stepped forward, slashing at the straps which
held Wulfgar's trunk and stumps in place. Seizing him by belt and tunic he
lifted him bodily out of the container, took three heavy paces to the side,
and thrust the heimnar deep into the four-foot-high, hundred-gallon butt
of ale. Wulfgar bobbed, thrashing with the stumps of his arms, truncated
legs not quite reaching the bottom.

Ivar put one hand on Wulfgar's head, looked round like a teacher dem-
onstrating.

"See, Kleggi," he pointed out. "What is a man maimed like this afraid
of?"

"Of being helpless."

He pushed the head firmly down. "Now he can take a good drink," he
remarked. "If what he says is true, he won't need it on the other side, but
it's as well to be sure."

Many of the watching Vikings laughed, calling to their mates to come
and see. Dolgfinn allowed himself a smile. There was no credit in this, no
glory or *drengskapr*. But maybe it would keep Ivar happy.

"Let him up," he shouted. "Maybe he will offer us a drink from heaven
after all."

Ivar seized the hair, heaved Wulfgar's head up out of the frothing brew.
The mouth gaped wide, sucking in air by frantic reflex, the eyes bulged
with terror and humiliation. Wulfgar threw the stump of one arm over the
edge of the barrel, tried to lever himself up.

Carefully Ivar knocked it free, stared into the eyes of the drowning man
as if searching for something. He nodded, thrust the head back down
again.

"Now he is afraid," he said to Kleggi, standing by. "He would bargain for
his life if he could. I do not like them to die defying me. They must give
in."

"They all give in in the end," said Kleggi, laughing. "Like women."

Ivar thrust the head spasmodically deeper.

*   *   *

Shef hefted the object Udd had brought him. They stood in the center of an interested circle—all Englishmen, all freedmen, catapulteers and halberdiers together—near the front the gang Udd had collected to help him forge the strips of mild steel.

"See," Udd said, "we done what you told us. We made the strips, two-foot long. You said try and make bows out of them, so we filed notches in the ends and fitted strings. Had to use twisted gut. Nothing else strong enough."

Shef nodded. "But then you couldn't pull them."

"Right, lord. You couldn't, and we couldn't. But we thought about that for a bit, and then Saxa here"—Udd indicated another member of his gang —"said anyone who's ever carried loads for a living knows legs are stronger than arms.

"So: we took thick oak blocks. We cut slots for the metal near the front and slid the strips through, wedged 'em tight. We fitted triggers like we got already on the big shooters.

"And then we put these iron hoops, like, on the front of the wood. Try it, lord. Put your foot through the hoop."

Shef did so.

"Grip the string with both hands and pull back against your own leg. Pull till the string goes over the top of the trigger."

Shef heaved, felt the string coming back against strong resistance—but not impossibly strong. The puny Udd and his undersized colleagues had underestimated the force a big man trained in the forge could exert. The string clicked over the trigger. He was holding, Shef realized, a bow of sorts—but one that lay crosswise to the shooter, not up and down like a wooden handbow.

A grinning face from the crowd handed Shef a short arrow: short because the steel bow flexed only a few inches, not the half-arm's-length of a wooden bow. He fitted it in the rough gouge in the top of the wooden block. The circle parted in front of him, indicating a tree twenty yards off.

Shef leveled the bow, aimed automatically between the arrow-feathers, as he would have with a twist-shooter, squeezed the trigger. There was no violent thump of recoil as there would have been with the full-sized machine, no black streak rising and falling. Yet the bolt sped away, struck fair in the center of the oak-trunk.

Shef walked over, grasped the embedded arrow, worked it backward and forward. After a dozen tugs, it came free. He looked at it speculatively.

"Not bad," he said. "But not good, either. Although the bow is steel, I do not think in the end it strikes harder than the hunting bows we use already. And they are not strong enough for war."

Udd's face fell, he started automatically to make the excuses of the slave with a hard master. Shef held up a hand to stop him.

"Never mind, Udd. We are all learning something here. This is a new thing that the world has never seen before, but who made it? Saxa, for remembering that legs are stronger than arms? You, for remembering how your master made the steel? I, for telling you to make a bow? Or the Rome-folk of old, for showing me how to make the twist-shooters that started all this?

"None of us. What we have here is a new thing, but not new knowledge. Just old knowledge put together, old knowledge from many minds. Now, we need to make this stronger. Not the bow, for that is strong enough. The pull. How can we make it so that my pull up is double the strength of what I can do now?"

The silence was broken by Oswi, leader of the catapult-team.

"Well, if you put it like that, lord, answer's obvious. How do you double a pull?

"You use a pulley. Or a windlass. A little one, not a great big one like the Norse-folk use on their ships. Fix it to your belt, wind on one end of the rope, hook the other end of the rope over the bowstring, pull it up as far as you like."

Shef handed the primitive crossbow back to Udd. "There's the answer, Udd. Set the trigger further back, so the bow can flex as far as the steel will let it. Make a winding gear with a rope and a hook to go with every bow. And make a bow out of every strip of steel you have. Take all the men you need."

The Viking shouldering his way through the crowd looked suspiciously at the jarl surrounded by a throng of midgets. He had arrived only that summer, called from Denmark by incredible stories of success, wealth and profit, and of the Ragnarssons defeated. All he had seen so far was an army drawn up to fight that had then suddenly stopped in its tracks. And now here was the jarl himself, talking like a common man to a crowd of thralls. The Viking was six feet tall, weighed two hundred pounds, and could lift a Winchester bushel with either hand. What sort of a jarl is this? he wondered. Why does he talk to them and not to the warriors? *Skraelingjar* such as these will never win a battle.

Out loud he said, with a minimum of deference, "Lord. You are called to council."

His message delivered, he turned away, contempt in the set of his shoulders.

Greatly daring, Oswi asked what all had wondered: "Battle this time, lord? We got to stop that Ivar sometime. We wouldn't have minded if we'd done it sooner."

Shef felt the reproach, overrode it. "Battle always comes soon enough, Oswi. The thing is to be ready."

As soon as Shef stepped into the great meeting tent, he felt the hostility that faced him. The whole of the Wayman council was present, or seemed to be: Brand, Ingulf, Farman and the rest of the priests, Alfred, Guthmund, representatives from every group and unit of the joint army.

He sat down at his place, hand groping automatically for the whetstone-scepter left lying there for him. "Where is Thorvin?" he said, suddenly noting one absence.

Farman started to give a reply, but was immediately overridden by the angry voice of Alfred—the young king—speaking already in a fair approximation of the Anglo-Norse pidgin the Wayman army and council so often used with each other.

"One man here or there does not matter. What we have to decide on cannot wait. Already we have waited too long!"

"Yes," rumbled Brand in agreement. "We are like the farmer who sits up all night to watch the hen-roost. Then in the morning he finds the fox has taken all his geese."

"So who is the fox?" asked Shef.

"Rome," said Alfred, rising to his feet to look down at the council. "We forgot the Church in Rome. When you took the land from the Church in this county, when I threatened to take the revenues from it in my kingdom, the Church took fright. The Pope in Rome took fright."

"So?" asked Shef.

"So now there are ten thousand men ashore. Mailed horsemen of the Franks. Led by their king Charles. They wear crosses on their arms and their surcoats, and say that they have come to establish the Church in England against the pagans.

"The pagans! For a hundred years we have fought against the pagans, we Englishmen. Every year we sent Peter's pence to Rome as a token of our loyalty. I myself"—Alfred's youthful voice rose in pitch with indignation—"I myself was sent by my father to the last Pope, to good Pope Leo, when I was a child. The Pope made me a consul of Rome! Yet never have we had a ship or a man or a silver penny sent into England in exchange. But the day Church-land is threatened, Pope Nicholas can find an army."

"But it is an army against the pagans," said Shef. "Maybe us. Not you."

Alfred's face flushed. "You forget. Daniel, my own bishop, declared me excommunicate. The messengers say these Cross-wearers, these Franks, announce on all sides that there is no king in Wessex and they demand submission to King Charles. Till that is done they will ravage every shire. They come against the pagans. But they rob and kill only Christians."

"What do you want us to do?" asked Shef.

"We must march at once and defeat this Frankish army before it destroys my kingdom. Bishop Daniel is dead or fleeing, and his Mercian backers with him. No Englishman will challenge my king-right again. My thanes and aldermen are already gathering to me, and I can raise the entire levy of Wessex, from every shire. If, as some say, the messengers have overcounted the strength of the enemy, then I can fight them on even terms. I will fight them on any terms. But your assistance would be greatly welcome."

He sat down, looking round tensely for support.

In the long silence, Brand said one word. "Ivar."

All eyes turned to Shef, sitting on his camp-stool, whetstone across his knees. He still seemed pale and gaunt after his sickness, cheekbones standing out, the flesh round his ruined eye pulled in so that it seemed a dark pit.

I do not know what he is thinking, reflected Brand. But he has not been with us these last days. If what Thorvin says is true, about the spirit leaving the body in these visions, then I wonder if it can be that you leave a little of it behind each time.

"Yes, Ivar," repeated Shef. "Ivar and his machines. We cannot leave him behind us while we march to the South. He would grow stronger. For one thing, now Burgred is dead it will be only a matter of time till the Mercians elect a king to make peace with Ivar and save them from ravaging. Then Ivar will have their men and money to draw on, as he has already drawn on the money and the skills of York. He did not make those machines himself.

"So we must fight him. I must fight him. I think he and I are bound together now so that we cannot part till this is finished.

"But you, lord king." The whetstone-scepter was cradled in Shef's left arm while he stroked its stern, implacable faces. "You have your own people to consider. Maybe it is best for you to march to your own place and fight your own battle, while we fight ours. Each in our own way.

Christian against Christian and pagan against pagan. And then, if your God and our gods will, we shall meet again, and set this country on its feet."

"So be it," said Alfred, his face flushing again. "I will call my men and be on my way."

"Go with him, Lulla," said Shef to the leader of the halberdiers. "And you, Osmod," he added to the leader of the catapult-teams, "see the king has his pick of horses and remounts for his journey south."

As the only Englishmen on the council left, Shef looked round at those who remained, and broke into fluent, rapid Norse, tinged with the thick Halogaland accent he had learned from Brand.

"What are his chances? If he fights his way? Against these Franks? What do you know of them, Brand?"

"A good chance, if he fights our way. Hit them when they're not looking. Catch them when they're asleep. Didn't old Ragnar himself—bad luck to his spirit—did he not sack their great town back in our fathers' day, and make their king pay tribute?

"But if the king fights in the English way, with the sun high in the sky and everyone forewarned . . ."

Brand grunted doubtfully. "The Franks had a king in our grandfather's day: King Karl, Karl the Great—Charlemagne they call him. Even Guthfrith, king of the Danes, had to submit to him. The Franks can beat anybody, given time. You know why? It's the horses. They fight on horseback. About once in a blue moon they'll be there, with their saddles on, and their girthstraps tight, and their fetlocks plaited, or whatever it is they call them—I am a sailor, not a horseman, Thor be praised; at least ships never shit on your feet.

"But that day, that one day, you don't want to stand up to them. And if King Alfred's like all the other Englishmen, that's the day he'll choose."

"Horses on one side, devil-machines on the other," said Guthmund. "Enough to make anyone sick."

Eyes scrutinized Shef's face, to see how he would take the challenge.

"We will deal with Ivar and the machines first," he said.

CHAPTER EIGHT

Two figures dressed in the rags of incongruous finery cantered slowly down the green lanes of central England: Alfgar, thane's son, once favorite of a king; Daniel, a bishop without a retinue, still a king's deadly enemy. Both had escaped with difficulty from Ivar's riders by the Ouse, but had managed to end the day with a dozen guards between them, and money and rations enough to take them back in safety in Winchester. Then their troubles had begun.

First they woke one morning to find their guards had simply deserted in the night, perhaps blaming their masters for defeat, perhaps seeing no reason any longer to put up with Alfgar's caustic tongue, Daniel's outbursts of fury. They had taken the food, money and horses with them. Striding across the fields towards the nearest church-spire, Daniel had insisted that as soon as he reached a priest, his episcopal authority would provide them with mounts and supplies. They had never reached the spire. In the troubled countryside, the churls had abandoned their homes for the summer and had built themselves shelters in the greenwood. The village priest had indeed recognized Daniel's status, enough to persuade his parishioners not to kill the pair of wanderers, and even to leave Daniel his episcopal ring and cross, and the gold head of his crozier. They had taken everything else, including Alfgar's weapons and silver arm-rings. After that, for three nights in a row the fugitives had lain belly-pinched in the dew, cold and afraid.

Yet Alfgar, like his half brother and enemy Shef, was a child of the fen. He could make an eel-trap out of withies, could catch fish with a cloak-pin on twisted thread. Slowly the pair had ceased to hope for rescue, had learned to rely on themselves. The fifth day of their journey Alfgar had stolen two horses from an poorly guarded stud, and the herdboy's knife and his flea-infested blanket as well. After that they had made better time. It had not improved their humor.

At the ford of the Lea they had heard the news of the Frankish landing from a merchant disposed to be respectful to Daniel's cross and ring. It had altered their plan.

"The Church does not fail her servants," Daniel had declared, eyes red with rage and weariness. "I knew the stroke would fall. I did not know where or when. Now, to the glory of God, the pious King Charles has come to restore the faith. We will go to him and make our report—our report of those he must punish: the pagans, the heretics, the slack in faith. Then the evil Way-folk and the graceless adherents of Alfred will find that the quernstones of God grind slow, but they grind to the last grain."

"Where do we have to go?" asked Alfgar sullenly, reluctant to follow Daniel's lead but anxious to contact once again the side that might win, that might bring him vengeance on the ravisher, the bride-stealer, the one who had stolen first his woman, then his shire, and then his woman again. Every day he remembered a dozen times, with a shiver of shame, waking with the birch-twigs in his hand and the curious faces staring down: Didn't you hear? He took your woman? Trussed up your father, with no arms or legs, but just left you to lie there? And you never woke?

"The Frankish fleet crossed the Narrow Sea and landed in Kent," Daniel replied. "Not far from the see of St. Augustine in Canterbury. They are camped at a place called Hastings."

Surveying the walls of Canterbury, his base at Hastings left for a careful, six-day foray, Charles the Bald, king of the Franks, sat on his horse and waited for the procession trailing from the open gates to reach him. He was sure enough what it was. In the lead he could see holy banners, choirmonks singing, censers waving. Behind them, carried in a chair of state, came a gray-bearded figure in purple and white, tall miter nodding: surely the archbishop of Canterbury, the primate of England. Though back at camp in Hastings, Charles reflected, he had Wulfhere, archbishop of York, who would probably dispute this archbishop's claim. Perhaps he should have brought him and let the two old fools fight it out.

"What's this one called?" he asked his constable, Godefroi, sitting his charger next to him.

Godefroi—like his king, sitting easily in a deep saddle, high pommel in front, high saddle-bow behind, feet braced in steel stirrups—raised his eyes to heaven. "Ceolnoth. Archbishop of Cantwarabyrig. God, what a language."

Finally the procession reached its goal, finished its anthem. The bearers lowered the chair; the old man stumbled out of it and stepped across to face the menacing silent figure in front of him, metal man on armored horse. Behind him the smoke of burning villages smudged the sky. He began to speak.

After a while the king raised a gauntlet, turned to the papal legate on his left, Astolfo of Lombardy: a cleric without a see—as yet.

"What is he saying?"

The legate shrugged. "I have no idea. He seems to be speaking English."

"Try him in Latin."

The legate began to talk, easily and fluently in the Latin of Rome—a Latin, of course, pronounced in exactly the same way as the inhabitants of that ancient city spoke their own, modern tongue. Ceolnoth, who had learned his Latin from books, listened without comprehension.

"Don't tell me he can't speak Latin either."

The legate shrugged again, ignoring Ceolnoth's faltering attempts to reply. "The English Church. We had not known things were so bad. The priests and the bishops. Their dress is not canonical. Their liturgy is out-of-date. Their priests preach in English because they know no Latin. They have even had the temerity to translate God's word into their own barbarous speech. And their saints! How can one venerate names like Willibrord? Cynehelm? Frideswide, even! I think it likely that when I make my report to His Holiness he will remove authority from all of them."

"And then?"

"This will have to become a new province, ruled from Rome. With its revenues going to Rome. I speak only, of course, of the spiritual revenues, the proceeds of tithing, of fees for baptism and burial, of payments for entry into sacred offices. As regards the land itself—the property of secular lords—that must fall to its secular rulers. And their servants."

The king, the legate and the constable exchanged looks of deep and satisfied understanding.

"All right," said Charles. "Look, the graybeard seems to have found a younger priest with some grasp of Latin. Tell him what we want."

As the list ran on and on—of indemnities, supplies to be provided, toll to be paid to protect the city from sack, hostages to be delivered and laborers to start work immediately on a fort for the Frankish garrison to be installed—Ceolnoth's eyes widened with horror.

"But he is treating us as defeated enemies," he stammered to the priest who translated for him. "We are not enemies. The pagans are his enemies. It was my colleague of York and the worthy bishop of Winchester who called him in. Tell the king who I am. Tell him he is mistaken."

Charles, about to turn away toward the hundreds of mailed horsemen waiting behind him, caught the tone of Ceolnoth's voice, though he did not follow the words. He was not an uneducated man by the low standards of Frankish military aristocracy. He had learned a trifle of Latin in his youth, learned too some of Titus Livius's stories of the history of Rome.

Smiling, he drew his long, double-edged sword from his scabbard, held it like a merchant's balance.

"This will not need translating," he said to Godefroi. Then, bending from the saddle to Ceolnoth, he said slowly and clearly, two words.

"Vae victis."

Woe to the conquered.

Shef had considered all the possible plans he could use to attack Ivar's camp, weighed them like moves on a chessboard, rejected them one by one. These new ways of making war introduced complexities that could lead to confusion in battle, loss of lives, loss of everything.

It had been much easier when line had clashed with line, battled hand to hand until the stronger side won. He knew that his Vikings were becoming more and more displeased with these new things. Yearned for the certainty of the clash of arms. But the new ways had to be used if Ivar and his weapons were to be defeated. Old and new must blend.

Of course! He must weld the old and the new together like the soft iron and hard steel of a pattern-welded sword, like the sword he had forged and lost in the battle when Edmund was taken. A word formed in his mind.

"Flugstrith!" he cried, leaping to his feet.

"Flugstrith?" said Brand, turning from the fire. "I do not understand."

"That is how we will fight our battle. We will make it the *eldingflug-strith.*"

Brand looked disbelieving. "The lightning-battle? I know Thor is with us, but I doubt you can convince him to hurl his thunderbolts to clear our way to victory."

"It is not the thunderbolts I want. What I want is a battle fast as lightning. The thought is there, Brand; I feel I know what must be done. But I must make it clearer—as clear in my head as if it had already happened."

Now, waiting in the mist in the dark hour before dawn, Shef felt sure his battle-plan would work. The Vikings had approved it—so had his machine-tending Englishmen. And it had better work. Shef knew that after his rescue of Godive, and then his collapse as the army waited to attack, his credit with the council and the army too was almost exhausted. Things were being kept secret from him. He did not know where Thorvin had gone, nor why Godive had slipped away with him.

As he had before the walls of York, he reflected that in this new style of battle the fighting was the easiest part. Or at least it promised to be so for him. Yet somewhere inside himself his flesh still crawled with a kind of fear: not of death or disgrace. Fear of the dragon he sensed in Ivar's skin. He fought the fear and repulsion down, glanced at the sky for the first pale streaks of dawn, strained his eyes through the mist to see if he could see the outline of Ivar's battlements.

Ivar had made his fortified camp in exactly the same style as the one which King Edmund had stormed south of Bedricsward by the Stour: a low ditch and bank with stakes driven into it, forming three sides of a square with the river Ouse as the fourth side, his ships drawn up along the muddy bank. The sentry who paced the bank behind the stockade had been at that battle too, and lived. He needed no urging to keep alert. Yet to him the dark hours were the dangerous ones, short enough at this time of year. As he saw the sky beginning to pale, and felt the little wind that comes before the dawn, he relaxed and began to think of the day that might follow. He had no great desire to see Ivar Ragnarsson at his butcher's work again among his prisoners. Why, he wondered, did they not move on? If Ivar had been challenged to fight at Ely, he had met the challenge. It was Sigvarthsson and the Way-folk who must feel disgrace.

The sentry halted, braced himself chest-high against the wall of the stockade, fighting to keep alert. He brooded on the sounds he had heard so often in the last few days, coming from under the bloody hands of Ivar. Out there two hundred corpses lay in fresh graves, the product of a week's sacrifice and slaughter of Mercian prisoners taken after the battle. An owl called, and the sentry started, thinking for an instant it was the shriek of a spirit come for vengeance.

It was his last thought. Before he heard the thrum of the bowstring the quarrel drove through his throat. From the ditch, the figures who had crept up in the mist caught him, eased him to the ground, waited. Knowing the other sentries on the wall had been dispatched in the same instant, on the cry of the owl.

Even the softest of shoes makes a sound moving through the grass. The hundreds of running feet sounded like small waves rushing down a pebbled strand. Dark bulks loomed, moving swiftly toward the western palisade of the camp, their moment carefully chosen. They were black shapes against a black sky behind them. But the lightening sky in the east would silhouette the defenders when they awoke and rushed to battle.

Shef stood to the side, watching the attack, fists clenched: the success or failure of everything depended on the next few seconds. Taking the camp would be like taking York—only simpler and quicker. No clumsy, moving towers, no slow development of the attack in stages. This was being done in a way even the Ragnarssons would understand—in explosive attack, win or lose in the first minute.

His eager men had shaped the bridges, stout planks pegged together. Twelve yards long and three wide. Iron bands clamped the oars beneath the structure, their handles projecting to either side. Each handle grasped by a Viking, secure in the feel of the familiar wood, proud of the strength needed to lift the structure and run forward with it at the stockade of the camp.

The tallest warriors were in front. As they ran they grunted with the effort, not only from carrying the dead weight—but at the last moment they lifted it over their heads until the front was more than seven feet off the ground. Enough to clear the six-foot-high stakes of the camp.

And clear it they did with a final explosive heave as they leaped over the ditch, slammed wood down on wood, the men in the front springing clear at the last second and rolling down into the ditch.

But not those that ran behind. The instant the bridge was in place they thundered up it and leapt into the enclosure behind. Ten, twenty, a hundred, two hundred were over before the bridge-carriers could unsheathe their weapons and join in the attack.

Shef smiled into the darkness. Six had been built, six had attacked—and only one had not succeeded in topping the wall. It lay half in, half out of the ditch, while cursing Vikings crawled out from under it and joined the rush to the other bridges.

Screams of pain, roars of anger over there as the sleeping men realized that the enemy was in among them. First the thud of axes into flesh, then the clang of metal as men woke, seized arms, defended themselves. Shef took one last look in the growing light, saw that the warriors were following instructions and advancing in a steady line, slaughtering as they went.

But keeping position even after they had cut down the man they faced. Keeping pace with the murderous advance. Then Shef ran.

On the eastern side of the camp his English freedmen had waited in the darkness as they had been instructed, trotting forward to the attack only when they heard the first clash of battle. Shef hoped his timing had been correct. He had stationed them two hundred yards from the palisade. Estimated that if they ran forward when they heard the attack they would reach the camp when the armed struggle was joined and intense. All eyes should be on the Viking attack-force—all of Ivar's men rushing to the aid of their comrades. So he fervently hoped. He reached the corner of the camp just as the running men appeared.

Halberdiers led the way, each weighted with a great bundle of brushwood as well as his weapon. To be hurled into the ditch before the sharp blades were wielded against the stakes and the leather thongs that bound the palisade together.

The second wave of attackers approached, crossbowmen who pushed between the halberdiers, used knives to sever the last of the bindings, heaved stakes aside, climbed over and through them.

Shef followed them, pushing forward through the jostling ranks. No need to shout orders. The crossbowmen were following their long-rehearsed instructions, pacing forward ten carefully counted steps, then stopping and forming a line. Others halted behind them to make a double line that stretched from wall to river-line. Swift runners dashed forward to cut the tent-ropes, fled back to safety as the archers fitted bolts to cocked strings.

A few drabs and youths had seen them, had stood gape-mouthed and fled. But incredibly, none of Ivar's men seemed aware of their presence, totally taken up with the familiar clash of weapons coming from the other wall.

Shef stepped a pace beyond the double line, saw the faces turning toward him for the prearranged signal. He raised his arm, dropped it. The heads turned to their front, sighted for an instant. Then the sharp snap of a hundred strings released together.

The short, stout arrows shot across the camp, driving through leather and mail and flesh.

Already the front rank had hooked onto their tackle to reload, while the second rank stepped forward between them, looked to Shef, caught his signal, loosed their second volley.

Shouts of alarm and disbelief were now mingling with cries of pain as the warriors saw men falling, all to the rear of the battle. Heads turned,

faces pale in the dawn's light, to see the silent death that was striking them from the rear, while the Vikings of the Way still kept up their violent pressure from the front, expending energy furiously in an assault they had been promised would last only minutes.

The first row of bowmen was ready again. As each man finished loading, he stepped through the line in front to resume rank. Some faster than others. Shef waited impassively till the last had formed up—the lines must be kept separate if this maneuver was to work—before he dropped his arm again.

Four times the lines shot before the first of the defenders could turn, order themselves and race across the camp in a wavering line, hindered by collapsed tents and the embers of cooking fires. As they closed, the bowmen obeyed orders again. Shot if they had loaded, then turned and ran with the rest, through the ranks of halberdiers dressed behind them. The halberdiers shifted sideways to let their fellows pass, then closed ranks again in a solid line of points.

"Don't advance, just stand!" shouted Shef as he followed the last of the crossbows through. Few could hear him over the growing din of war-cries. Yet he knew this was the moment Brand had said would not work: the puny slave-born taking the full weight of a Viking charge.

The English obeyed their orders. Stood still, points leveled, second rank bracing the first. Even a man whose belly crawled with fear knew he had to do no more than he could. And the Viking charge did not come with full weight. Too many men shot down, and those the leaders; too many of the rest, uncertain, unprepared. The wave that came to hack at the wall of steel came piecemeal. Each man who ran in faced a point in front, blades chopping from either side. The blows they swung were caught by long shafts thrusting from the rear ranks. Slowly the Vikings drew back from the unshaken line, looking round for leadership.

As they did so a cry of triumph rang from behind them. Viga-Brand, seeing the battle-line in front of him thin and shred, had thrown his picked men through the center of what remained, to wheel instantly and to start to roll up the Ragnarsson line.

Beaten men began to throw their weapons down.

From the riverbank Ivar Ragnarsson stood and watched his men fall, then surrender. Sleeping in his ship, the *Lindormr*, he had rolled from his blankets too late to be more than an observer. Now he knew that he had lost this battle.

He knew why, too. The last few days of blood and slaughter had been a delight for him, a relief. The easing of some frenzy that had lain within him for many years, consoled only now and then and only for a time by the brief pleasures his brothers had arranged for him, or by the grand executions the Great Army had tolerated as appropriate. A delight for him; the army had slowly sickened of it. It had rotted their morale. Not much. Enough to make them put a little less than their best into the desperate defense they had needed.

He did not regret what he had done. What he regretted was that this attack could only come from one man, from the Sigvarthsson. The attack in the night, the instant breaching of his defenses. Then, when his warriors rallied for battle, the cowardly attack from the rear. The engagement was truly lost. He had fled a lost battle before—must he flee again? The victors were close on him, and on the other side of the river—moved across on clumsy punts and rafts five miles downstream—waited the ten torsion dart-throwers, lined up wheel to wheel, guided to their position by willing local churls. As the light strengthened, the twist-shooter teams lowered their sights on to the Ragnarsson ships.

On Ivar's ship, the *Lindormr;* the minster-slaves crouched round their machine. At the first noise of onset they had whipped the covers off it, wound and loaded. Now they hesitated, uncertain in which direction to shoot. Ivar stepped across and on to the gunwale.

"Boom off," he ordered. "Leave that. Push out from shore."

"Are you deserting your men already?" asked Dolgfinn, standing with a clutch of senior skippers a few feet away. "Without so much as a blow struck? That may sound bad when the story is told."

"Not deserting. Getting ready to fight. Come aboard if that's what you mean to do. If you mean to stand round like old whores waiting for trade, stay where you are."

Dolgfinn flushed at the insult, stepped forward with his hand on hilt. Feathers sprouted suddenly from his temple, and he fell. With the camp taken, the crossbowmen had fanned out again, shooting wherever they saw resistance. Ivar stepped behind the protecting bulk of the machine mounted on the prow of his ship. As the slaves clumsily poled the *Lindormr* out into the slow current, he pointed quickly to one man still on the bank.

"You. Jump. Over here."

Reluctantly Erkenbert the archdeacon gathered up his black robe, leapt the widening gap of water, landed staggering in Ivar's arms.

Ivar jerked a thumb at the crossbowmen growing ever more visible in the dawning light. "More machines you did not tell me of. I suppose you will tell me they cannot exist either. If I live past today I will cut your heart out and burn your minster to the ground."

To the slaves he shouted, "Stop pushing. Drop anchor. Drop the gangplank."

As the mystified slaves heaved the weighted, two-foot-wide plank from gunwale to shore, Ivar placed the stout protective beam of his machine behind him, took a firm grip on Erkenbert's right wrist, and leaned back to watch his army die. Unafraid, he had only one thought left: how to spoil his enemies' triumph, how to sour victory into failure.

Firmly escorted, Shef walked forward through the chaos of the camp. His helmet was strapped on, his halberd was over his shoulder. He had not yet struck a blow or dodged one. Ivar's army was no more. The Waymen were rounding up prisoners while a few survivors ran toward the river, running in twos and threes both ways along the bank to get away. There were not many of them, surely not enough to be a threat.

The battle was won, Shef told himself, and won easily, exactly according to plan. Yet something still chilled in his belly: too easy, he felt, too easy. The gods demand a price for favors. What was it to be? He began to run in earnest, heading for the helmet of Brand, now at the very tip of the Waymen's advance toward the river and the ships. As he did so, a flash of color came from the mast of one of the ships only a few yards ahead, gold catching the first direct rays of the rising sun. It was the Coiling Worm. Ivar had broken out his banner.

Brand slowed to a walk as he saw Ivar standing, one foot on the gunwale of the *Lindormr,* with six feet of water between the ship and the bank. Ivar was fully dressed, wearing his grass-green breeches and tunic, his mail-coat and silver helmet. He had thrown his scarlet cloak aside, but the polished boss of his shield caught the red light of morning. By his side stood a small man in the black robe of a Christian cleric, a look of horror on his face.

As men on both sides saw the confrontation, fighting finally stopped. The Vikings on both sides, Waymen and Ragnarssons, looked at each other, nodded, accepted that the battle was won and lost. As the English halberdiers, less businesslike in their attitudes, closed in, those Ragnarsson troops still resisting began hastily to throw their weapons down, put themselves under the protection of their former enemies. Then all, English and Norse, Waymen and pirates, faced inward, to see how their leaders would behave. At the rear of the watching ring, Shef struggled and cursed to get through.

Brand checked for a moment, breathing hard with the exertion of ten minutes' desperate struggle. Then he strolled forward toward the gang-plank. He raised his right hand, split between two fingers in King Edmund's battle the previous year. He moved the fingers to show how they had healed.

"We had words a while back, Ivar," he remarked. "I told you you should look after your women better. You did not take my advice. Maybe you don't know how to. But you said when your shoulder was whole you would remember what I said. And I said when my hand was whole I would remind you of it. Well, I have kept my word. Will you keep yours? You look as if you are thinking of sailing away."

Ivar grinned, showing his even teeth. Deliberately, he drew his sword and threw the decorated scabbard into the Ouse.

"Come and try me," he said.

"Why don't you come to fight on firm ground? No one will help me. If you win, you will have free passage back to where you stand now."

Ivar shook his head. "If you are so bold, fight on my ground. Here"—Ivar leapt forward onto the gangplank, took two steps forward—"I will take no advantage. We will both stand on the same plank. Then all can see who gives way first."

A buzz of interested comment rose as the watching men grasped the situation. At first sight the outcome of the fight looked evident. Brand outweighed Ivar by seventy pounds at least, out-topped him by a head and more, was as skillful and experienced with his weapons. Yet everyone could see the plank flex with one man's weight on it. With two, and one as heavy as Brand, how would the footing feel? Would both men be awkward and clumsy? Or just one? Ivar stood braced, feet as far apart as the plank would allow, sword-arm forward like a fencer, not crouched behind his shield like a warrior in a battle-line.

Slowly Brand walked forward to the end of the plank. He had his great axe in one hand, a small round shield buckled to his forearm. Meditatively he unstrapped it, threw it to the ground, took his axe in both hands. As Shef finally wormed his way gasping to the front, Brand leapt onto the plank, took two paces forward, and lashed suddenly backhand and upward at Ivar's face.

Ivar swayed easily away, moving only the six inches necessary to avoid the blow. Instantly he was beneath the stroke, chopping at a thigh. The blow was beaten down with the metal-shod haft of Brand's axe, counter-stroke slashing in the same movement at the wrist. For ten seconds the two men sent a rain of blows at each other, the cuts coming faster than the watchers could follow them: parrying, ducking, swaying their bodies to let thrust or slash go by. Neither man moved his feet.

Then Brand struck. Beating a blow from Ivar upward, he took half a pace forward, leapt high in the air, and came down with his full weight on the very center of the plank. It flexed, bounced upward, hurling both men off their feet. In the air, Brand swung the iron-shod butt of his axe at Ivar's head, connecting with a furious clang on his helmet's cheek-piece. In the same instant Ivar recovered blade and thrust with fierce dexterity through mail and leather, deep into Brand's belly.

Brand landed staggering, Ivar still in perfect balance. For a further instant both stood still, connected by the bar of iron between them. Then, just as Ivar tensed his grip for the savage twist that would rend gut and arteries forever, Brand hurled himself backward off the blade. He stood at the very end of the plank, groping with his left hand at the blood stream-ing through the torn steel.

With two hands Shef seized him by collar and waist and jerked him from the plank, thrust him staggering backward. The watchers roared disapproval, outrage, encouragement. Gripping his halberd in both hands, Shef stepped forward onto the plank. For the first time since the day he had been blinded, he looked full into Ivar's eyes. Tore his gaze away. If Ivar was a dragon, like the vision he had seen of Fafnir, then he might yet put on him the dragon-spell of terror and paralysis. A spell that could not be broken by steel.

Ivar's face split in a grin of triumph and contempt. "You come late to our meeting, boy," he remarked. "Do you think you can succeed where champions fail?"

Shef raised his eye again, stared deliberately into Ivar's face. As he did so he filled his mind with the thought of Godive—of what this man, this creature, had meant to do with her. What he had done with so many slaves and captives. If there was a protection against Ivar's spell, it lay in justice.

"I have succeeded where you failed," he said. "Most men can do what you cannot. That is why I sent you the capon."

Ivar's grin had turned into a rictus, like the bared teeth of a skull. He flicked the tip of his sword slightly. "Come on," he whispered. "Come on."

Shef had already decided what to do. He had no chance at all toe to toe with Ivar. He must use other weapons. Drag him down. Use Ivar's open contempt against him.

Shuffling gingerly forward along the gangplank, Shef aimed a clumsy two-hand thrust with the spear-point on the end of his shaft. Ivar batted it aside without moving eyes or body, waiting for his incompetent enemy to move closer or lay himself open.

Swinging the halberd way up over his head, Shef prepared for a mighty stroke, a stroke that would split an armored man from nape to crotch. Ivar grinned more broadly as he saw it, caught the moan of disbelief from the bank. This was no holmgang, where the parties were bound to stand still. Such a mighty stroke could be avoided by an old grandfather. Who would then step over and stab for the throat while the wielder was off balance. Only a thrall-bred fool would try it: and that was what this Sigvarthsson was.

Shef swung down with all his force, aiming not at Ivar but at the plank at his feet. The great blade, swung in a drawing cut, slashed clean through the wood. As Ivar, surprised and off balance, tried to leap back the two steps to his ship, Shef dropped the halberd, threw himself forward, grappled Ivar round the body. Fell instantly with him down into the cold, muddy current of the Ouse.

As the two men hit the water Shef gasped reflexively. Instantly his mouth and windpipe filled. Choking, he struck out for the surface. Was held and forced below. He had dropped the halberd, but his loose-fitting helmet had filled with water, was dragging his head down. A hand like a strangling snake was crushing his throat, but the other hand was free, was groping toward the belt and the gutting-knife in it. Shef grasped Ivar's right wrist in his left hand with the force of desperation.

For an instant both men broke the surface, and Shef managed to blow his lungs clear. Then Ivar had him again, was forcing him down.

Suddenly the cold inner revulsion that had held Shef half-paralyzed since the fight had started—the dragon-fear—was gone. No scales, no armor, no dreadful eyes to look into. Just a man. Not even a man, shrilled some triumphant fragment of Shef's mind.

Twisting fiercely in the water like an eel, Shef grappled his enemy close. Ducked his head, butted forward with the rim of his helmet. The rim which he had filed again and again to razor-sharpness. A crunch, something giving way, Ivar trying for the first time to wrench back. From the bank above there came a great roar as the craning watchers saw blood spreading in the water. Shef butted again and again, realized suddenly that Ivar had shifted his grip, had caught him in a stranglehold, rolled him under. Now Ivar was on top, face in the air, grimly concentrating on holding his enemy under. And he was too strong, growing stronger with every breath.

Shef's right hand, thrashing wildly, caught Ivar's knee. There is no *drengskapr* in this, thought Shef. Brand would be ashamed of me. But he would have taken Godive and cut her in pieces like a hare.

He drove his right hand firmly under Ivar's tunic, seized him by the crotch. His convulsive, drowning grip closed round the roots of Ivar's manhood, squeezed and twisted with every ounce of the strength years at the forge had given him. Somewhere, he heard dimly, there was a scream of mortal agony resounding. But the Ouse drowned it, the muddy stream poured choking in. As Shef's straining lungs also gave way and let in the cold, rushing, heart-stopping water, he thought only the one thing: Crush. Crush. Never let go . . .

CHAPTER NINE

Hund was sitting by his bed. Shef stared at him for a moment, then felt the sudden bite of fear deep within him, sat up with a jerk.

"Ivar?"

"Easy, easy," said Hund, pushing him back on the bed. "Ivar's dead. Dead and burned to ashes."

Shef's tongue felt too big for him to control. With an effort he managed to gasp, "How?"

"A difficult question," replied Hund judiciously. "It could be that he drowned. Or he might have bled to death. You cut his face and neck to pieces with the edge of your helmet. But personally, I think he died of pain. You would not loose him, you know. In the end we had to cut him free. If he had not been dead before, he would have died then.

"Funny," Hund added reflectively. "He was quite normal, you know, in body. Whatever was the matter with him and women—and Ingulf had heard many tales of it—it was in his head, nowhere else."

Slowly Shef's muddled brain disentangled the questions he needed to ask.

"Who got me out?"

"Ah. That was Cwicca and his mates. The Vikings just stood and watched, both sides. Apparently men trying to drown each other is a sport in their homeland, and no one wanted to interfere till they could see who had won. It would have been very bad manners. Fortunately Cwicca has no manners."

Shef thought back to the moments before he had faced Ivar on the swaying plank. Remembered the sudden shocking sight of Brand jerking himself backward off Ivar's sword.

"And Brand?"

Hund's face changed to an expression of professional concern. "He may live. He is a man of great strength. But the sword went right into his guts. It was impossible for them not to be pierced. I gave him the garlic porridge to eat myself, and then bent down and sniffed the wound. It stank, right enough. Most times that means death."

"This time?"

"Ingulf did what he has done before. Cut him open, stitched the gut, put it back. But even with the poppy and henbane drink we gave to Alfgar, it was hard, very hard. He did not lose consciousness. His belly muscles are thick as cables. If the poison starts to work inside him . . ."

Shef levered his legs over the side of the bed, tried to stand up, felt an instant rush of faintness. With the relics of his strength he fended off Hund's attempts to push him back.

"I have to see Brand. Especially if he is going to die. He has to tell me— tell me things. Things about the Franks."

Many miles to the south, a weary and dispirited figure crouched over the fire in the hearth of a wretched hut. Few would have recognized it as the one-time atheling of Wessex, the king that was to be. His golden circlet had gone—knocked from his helmet by the stab of a lance. His mail and shield decorated with animal-patterns had gone, too, stripped off and dropped in the intervals of desperate flight. Even his weapons were missing. He had cut his sword-scabbard free to run when, finally, after a long day's slaughter there had been no final alternative but flight or death—or surrender to the Franks. He had carried his sword drawn for miles, fighting again and again with his last few bodyguards to get free of the pursuing Frankish light cavalry. Then, as his horse died under him he had dropped it, rolled over. When the running fight had moved past his body and he had staggered to his feet again, there was nothing there. He had run off into the welcome dusk and the deep, thick forest of the Kentish Weald as empty-handed as a beggar. He had been lucky to see a glimmer of light before the night came. To beg shelter in the poor, starve-acre cottage where he now crouched, watching the oatcakes on the griddle while his reluctant hosts secured their goats outside. Discussed, perhaps, who they should betray him to.

Alfred did not think they would betray him. Even the poorest folk of Kent and Sussex knew now that it was deadly dangerous to so much as approach the Cross-wearers from across the sea. They spoke even less English than Vikings, cared no more for the harm they did than pagans. It was not personal fear that bowed his shoulders, brought the tears prickling unmanfully to his eyes.

It was fear for something strange at work in the world. Twice now he had met the young man Shef with the one eye. The first time he had had him in the hollow of his hand: he, Alfred, atheling and commander of an undefeated army; the other, Shef, at the very last end of his resources, about to be overwhelmed by the army of the Mark. That time the atheling had rescued the carl, raised him to alderman, or *jarl* as the Way-folk said. The second time Shef the jarl had been the one with the undefeated army; he, Alfred, had been the fugitive and the suppliant. Yet even then not a suppliant without hope or without resources.

And now how did things stand? The one-eye had sent him south, said each should fight their own battle. Alfred had fought his, fought it with all the men he could gather to his banner from the eastern shires of his kingdom, men who had come willingly to fight an invader. And they had been scattered like leaves in a gale, unable to hold the terrible charge of the mailed horsemen. Alfred was sure in his heart that matters had not gone so in the battle his ally and rival had meant to fight. Shef would have won.

Christianity had not entirely driven from Alfred and his countrymen the belief in something older and deeper than any gods—pagan or Christian ones: luck. The luck of a person. The luck of a family. Something that did not change with the years, something you either had or did not have. The great prestige of Alfred's royal house, the descendants of Cerdic, depended silently on a deep belief in the family's luck, which had kept them in power for four hundred years.

To the fugitive sitting by the hearth it seemed that his luck and that of his family had run out. No. It had been cancelled by the luck of a stronger figure—the one-eyed man who had started as a slave, a thrall in the heathen language, who had fought his way up past the execution-ground to be a carl in the Great Army of the North, and then up yet again to be a jarl. What greater proof of luck could there be? With so much of it in one man, how could there be any left for his allies? His competitors? Alfred felt the heart-chilling despair of someone who has given away the advantage in a contest, lightheartedly and without thought of consequences, only to see the advantage grow and grow, the initiative pass forever into the other's hands. In that bleak moment he felt it was over for him, for his family, for his kingdom. For England. He sniffed back a tear.

Smelled as he did so the reek of charring bread. Guiltily his hand darted to the griddle, to flip the oatcakes over to cook on the other side. Too late. Burned through. Burned inedible. Simultaneously Alfred's belly cramped inside him at the realization that after sixteen hours of desperate exertion there was nothing, nothing at all left to eat. And the door of the hovel opened to let in the churl and his wife, to fill the air with rage and blame. Nothing left to eat for them either. Their last food wasted. Burned by a good-for-nothing. A vagrant, too cowardly to die in battle, too lazy to do the simplest task. Too proud to pay anything for the meal and shelter they had offered him.

As they loaded curses on him, the worst of Alfred's punishment was the feeling that what they said was true. He could not imagine, ever, the slightest recovery. This was the bottom from which no one could climb. Any future there was would not be for him and his like, the Christians of England. It would be decided between the Franks and the Norse, the Cross-wearers and the Way-folk. Alfred walked into the shelterless night, heart breaking with despair.

This time it was Shef who sat by the bed. Brand turned his head very slightly to look at him, face gray under the beard. Shef could see that even the tiny movements needed for that caused agony, as the poison spread inside Brand's belly cavity to fight against the strength still locked in his massive frame.

"I need to know about the Franks," said Shef. "We have beaten everyone else. You were sure they would beat Alfred."

Brand's head nodded, very faintly.

"So what is dangerous about them? How can I fight them? I have to ask you, for no one else in the army has met them in the field and lived. Yet many say they have had years of good plunder from the Frankish kingdom. How can they let themselves be robbed and still be enemies even you would rather not face?"

Shef could see Brand trying to work out not the answer, but how to say the answer in fewest words. Finally he spoke, in a gravelly whisper.

"They fight among themselves. That is what has always let us in. They are no seamen. And they breed few warriors. With us—a spear, a shield, an axe—you are a warrior. With them, it takes a whole village to arm one man. Mail-shirt, sword and lance and helmet. But most of all, the horse.

Big horses. Stallions a man can hardly control. Have to learn to ride them with a shield on one arm and a lance in the other. Start when you're a baby. Only way.

"One Frankish lancer, no problem. Get behind him, hamstring horse. Fifty of 'em, problem. A thousand . . ."

"Ten thousand?" asked Shef.

"Never believed it. Aren't that many. Lot of light horsemen. Can be dangerous because they're quick, turn up when you don't think they're near."

Brand summoned his failing energies. "They'll ride over you if you let 'em. Or cut you up on the march. Stick to rivers is what we do. Or keep behind a stockade."

"To beat them in open field?"

Brand shook his head faintly. Shef could not tell whether he meant "Impossible," or "I don't know." After a moment Ingulf's hand fell on his shoulder, urged him out.

As he came blinking from the tent into daylight, Shef found himself once more besieged with problems. Guards to be detailed for the substantial plunder of Ivar's army, on its way to the treasury in Norwich. Prisoners' fate to be decided: some of them Ivar's torturers, some of them mere rank and file. Messages to be received and dispatched. At the back of Shef's mind there hung always the query: Godive. Why had she gone off with Thorvin? And what did Thorvin himself think was so important that it could not wait?

But now, immediately in front of him, Father Boniface, his own priest-turned-scribe, beside him another little man in clerical black with an expression of bitter, malignant spite on his face. Slowly Shef realized that he had seen him before, if only from a distance. In York.

"This is Deacon Erkenbert," said Boniface. "We took him from Ivar's own ship. He is the master of the machines. The slaves who wound the machines—slaves first to York Minster and then to Ivar—they say that he built the machines for Ivar. They say the whole Church in York now works night and day for the Ragnarssons." He looked down at Erkenbert with heartfelt contempt.

The master of the machines, thought Shef. There was a day when I would have given everything for a chance to talk with this man. Now, I wonder what he can tell me. I can guess how his machine works, and in any case I can go to see for myself. I know how slowly they shoot, how hard they hit. One thing I do not know: how much else is there in his head and in his books? But I do not think he will tell me that.

Yet I think I can use him. Dimly, Brand's words were working inside Shef's brain. Collecting into a plan.

"Keep close watch on him, Boniface," said Shef. "See the York slaves are well treated, and tell them they are free from this moment. Then send Guthmund to me. After him, Lulla and Osmod. And Cwicca, Udd and Oswi, too."

"We don't want to do that," said Guthmund flatly.

"But you could do it?" asked Shef.

Guthmund hesitated, not wanting to tell a lie, reluctant to concede a point.

"Could do it. Still don't think it's a good idea. Take all the Vikings out of the army, load them into Ivar's boats, press Ivar's men into service as galley-slaves, and head round the coast to some rendezvous near this Hastings place . . .

"Look, lord." Guthmund spoke pleadingly, as near to wheedling as his character would go. "I know, me and the boys, we haven't always been fair to the English you've hauled in. Called them midgets. Called them *skrael-ingiar*. Said they're no use and never will be. Well, they've proved us wrong.

"But there was a reason for what we said, and it goes double if you're going to fight these Franks and their horses. Your English can shoot machines. One of them with a halberd hits as good as one of our boys with a sword. But there's still a lot of things they can't do, no matter how hard they try. They aren't strong enough.

"Now these Franks. Why are they dangerous? Everyone knows it's because of the horses. How much does a horse weigh? A thousand pounds? That's what I'm telling you, lord. To even get a few shots in at these Franks, you'll have to hold them off for a while. Maybe our boys could do it, with the halberds and all. Maybe. They've never done it before. But it's dead sure they can't if you've sent them all off. What happens if you get caught with just a line of your little fellows between you and the Franks? They can't do it, lord. They haven't the strength." Nor the training, Guthmund thought silently. Not to watch armed men walk right up to you and start hacking away. Or ride up to you. They've always had us to help them.

"You are forgetting King Alfred and his men," said Shef. "He will have gathered his army by now. You know the English thanes are as strong and brave as your men—they just have no discipline. But I can supply that."

Guthmund nodded, grudgingly.

"So each group must do what it does best. Your men, sail. With the ships and the machines. My freedmen, wind their machines and shoot. Alfred and his Englishmen, stand still and do what they're told. Trust me, Guthmund. You did not believe me last time. Or the time before. Or when we raided the minster at Beverley."

Guthmund nodded again, slightly more willingly this time. As he turned to go he added one more remark.

"Lord jarl, you aren't a sailor. But don't forget another thing in all this. It's harvest now. When the night grows as long as the day, every sailor knows, the weather changes. Don't forget the weather."

The news of Alfred's total defeat reached Shef and his truncated army two days' march south. Shef listened to the exhausted, white-faced thane who brought the news in the center of an interested circle—he had abandoned the custom of council meetings in private as soon as the still-grumbling Guthmund and his Norse fellows had boarded their captured boats. The freedmen watched his face as he listened, marking that it changed expression only twice. The first time, when the thane cursed the Frankish archers —who had shot such a rain of arrows that twice Alfred's advancing army had been forced to stand and raise its shields, only to be caught motionless both times by the Frankish cavalry charge. The second time when the thane admitted that no one had seen or heard of Alfred the king since the day of the disaster.

In the silence that followed the story, Cwicca, presuming on his status as Shef's companion and rescuer, had asked what all thought. "What do we do now, lord? Turn back, or go on?"

Shef answered immediately. "Go on."

Opinion round the campfires that night was divided about the sense of that. Ever since the Viking Waymen had left with Guthmund, the army had seemed a different creature. The freed English slaves had always secretly feared their allies—so like their former masters in strength and violence, superior to any English master in warlike reputation. With the Vikings gone, the army marched as if on holiday: pipes playing, laughter in the ranks, calling out to the harvesters in the fields, who no longer fled at the sight of the first scouts and advance-guard.

Yet the fear the army had felt had also been a guarantee. Proud as they were of their machines, their halberds and their crossbows, the ex-slaves did not have the self-belief that comes from a lifetime of winning battles.

"All right saying 'Go on,'" said one anonymous voice that night. "What happens when we get there? No Alfred. No Norse-folk. No Wessexers to help out like we were promised. Just us. Eh? What then?"

"We'll shoot 'em down," said Oswi confidently. "Like we did with Ivar and them Ragnarssons. 'Cos we got the machines and they haven't. And the crossbows and all."

A mutter of agreement greeted his statement. Yet every morning the camp marshals came to Shef with a new and growing figure: the number of men who had slipped away in the night, taking with them freedom and the silver pennies already paid to each man from the spoils of Ivar, but forfeiting the promise of land and stock in the future. Already, Shef knew, he had not enough men in the ranks both to man his fifty machines—pull-throwers and twist-shooters—and to use the two hundred pulley-wound crossbows that Udd's forges had produced.

"What will you do?" asked Farman, Frey's priest, the fourth morning of the march. He, Ingulf and Geirulf the priest of Tyr were the only Norsemen who had insisted on staying with Shef and the freedmen.

Shef shrugged.

"That is no answer."

"I will tell you the answer when you tell me where Thorvin and Godive have gone. And why. And when they will come back."

This time it was Farman's turn to give no answer.

Daniel and Alfgar had spent many angry days of frustration, first finding the base of the Frankish Cross-wearers, and then getting through its guards and outposts to see its leader. Their appearance had been against them: two men in soiled and sodden cloaks after nights in the open, riding bareback on the sorry nags that Alfgar had stolen. The first sentry they had approached had been amazed to see any Englishmen come near the camp of their own will: the local churls had fled long since, taking their wives and daughters with them if they were lucky. Yet he had not troubled to call an interpreter for Alfgar's English or Daniel's Latin. After several minutes of shouting up at him above the gate of the camp stockade, he had meditatively fitted arrow to bow and shot it into the ground at Daniel's feet. Alfgar had pulled Daniel away at once.

After that they had tried several times to approach the daily cavalcade of warriors streaming out from the Hastings base, to rob and forage while King Charles waited unhurriedly for the further challenge he was sure must come. The first time had cost them their horses, the second, Daniel's episcopal ring, which he had waved too eagerly. Eventually, and in despair, Alfgar had taken a hand. As Daniel shouted angrily at a Frankish priest they had discovered picking over the ruins of a ransacked church, he pushed him aside.

"*Machina*," he said clearly, in the fragment of Latin he possessed. "*Ballista. Catapulta. Nos videre*"—he pointed to his eyes. "*Nos dicere. Rex.*" He waved at the camp with its flying banners, two miles off, made speaking gestures.

The priest looked at him, nodded, turned back to the barely coherent bishop and began to talk to him in strangely accented Latin, cutting Daniel's furious complaints short, demanding information. After a while he had called to his guard of mounted archers and set off back toward the camp, taking the two Englishmen with him. After that they had been passed from hand to hand, with cleric after cleric coming in to extract more and more of Daniel's story.

But now at last the clerics had gone. It was Alfgar, his cloak brushed and a substantial meal inside him, who stood in front of Daniel, facing a trestle-table, behind it a group of men with the look of warriors: one of them wearing the gold circle of royalty over a bald head. At his side stood an Englishman, listening carefully to what the king said. Eventually he turned to Alfgar, speaking the first English they had heard since they arrived in the camp.

"The priests have told the king," he said, "that you have more sense than the bishop behind you. But the bishop says that you two alone know the truth of what has happened up there in the North. And that for some reason"—the Englishman smiled—"you are anxious to help the king and the Christian religion with information. Now the king takes no interest in your bishop's complaints and proposals. He wants to know, first about the army of Mercia, second about the army of the heathen Ragnarssons, and thirdly about this army of heretics which his own bishops are especially anxious for him to meet and fight. Tell him all that, behave yourself sensibly, and it will do you good. The king will have to have some Englishmen he can trust once his kingdom is established."

Putting on his sincerest expression of loyalty, and looking the Frankish king firmly in the eye, Alfgar began his account of the death of Burgred and the defeat by the Ouse. As he spoke on, his English translated phrase by phrase into French, he began to act out the workings of the machines with which Ivar had demoralized Burgred's army. He laid stress on the machines which the Way-folk also had, and which he had seen again and again in the previous winter's battles. His courage rising, he drew the hammer-sign in wine on the king's table, told of the freeing of Church-slaves.

Eventually the king stirred, threw a question over his shoulder. A cleric appeared from the shadows, took stylus and wax, began to draw on his tablets the picture of an onager. Then a torsion-catapult. Then a counter-weight-machine.

"He says, are these what you have seen?" asked the translator.

Alfgar nodded.

"He says, interesting. His learned men know how to make them also, taking them from a book by one Vegetius. He says he did not know the English were learned enough to make such things. But among the Franks these are used only for sieges. To use them against an army of horsemen would be foolish. Horsemen move too fast for them to be effective. But the king thanks you for your goodwill, and wishes you to ride with him when he takes the field. He believes your knowledge of his enemies will be useful. Your companion will be sent to Canterbury, to await the inquiry of the legate of the Pope." The English interpreter smiled again. "I think your chances will be better than his."

Alfgar straightened, bowed, and walked backward from the table as he would never have done for Burgred, firmly resolving to find a teacher of French before nightfall.

King Charles the Bald watched him go, turned again to his wine. "The first of the rats," he remarked to his constable Godefroi.

"Rats with siege-engines they use in the field. Do you not fear what he says?"

The king laughed. "Crossing the Narrow Sea is like going back to the time of our forefathers, when the kings rode to battle in ox-chariots. In all this country there is nothing to fight but the Norse brigands, harmless away from their ships, and the brave, stupid swordsmen we beat the other day. Long mustaches and slow feet. No horses, no lances, no stirrups, no generals.

"We must take our precautions now we know their way of fighting." He scratched his beard thoughtfully. "But it will take more than a few machines to beat the strongest army in Christendom."

CHAPTER TEN

This time Shef was anxious for the vision he knew would come. His mind buzzed with doubts, with possibilities. Yet he had no certainty. Something must come, he knew, from outside to help him. It came usually when he was exhausted, or sleeping off a heavy meal. That day he had walked deliberately beside his pony, ignoring the chaff from the ranks. In the evening, had stuffed himself slowly with the porridge they had made from the last of the winter store, before the new grain came from the harvesters. He stretched out to sleep, fearful that his mysterious adviser would fail him.

"Yes," said the voice in the dream. Shef felt an instant surge of relief as he recognized it. The amused voice which had told him to seek the ground, which had sent him the dream of the wooden horse. The voice of the nameless god with the sly face who had shown him the chess-queen. This was the god who sent him answers. If he could recognize them.

"Yes," said the voice, "you will see what you need to know. But not what you think you need to know. Your questions are always 'What?' and 'How?' But I shall show you 'Why?' And 'Who?'"

Instantly he found himself on a cliff, so high up he could see the whole world stretched out before him, the dust-plumes rising, the armies marching, just as he had seen them the day they killed King Edmund. Again he felt that if he narrowed his eye exactly right, he would be able to pick out anything he needed to know: the words on the lips of the Frankish commander, the place where

Alfred lurked—live or dead. Shef gazed round anxiously, trying to orient himself so he could see what he needed to.

Something turned his head away from the panorama below, made him stare into the far, far distance, remote from the real world in space and time.

What he saw was a man walking along a mountain road, a man with a dark, lively, humorous face, one not entirely to be trusted, the face of the unknown god of his dreams. Now that man, Shef thought, drifting into the vision, that man has more than one skin.

The man, if man he was, came to a hut, a hovel in fact, a grubby shelter of poles and bark reinforced with turf and inept handfuls of clay on the chinks. That was the way men lived in the old time, Shef thought. They know better now. But who showed them better?

By the hut a man and a woman stopped their tasks and stared at the newcomer: a strange couple, both bent over from continuous work, short and squat in physique, brown haired and sallow, bow-legged, crooked-fingered. "Their names are Ai and Edda," the god's voice said.

They were welcoming the newcomer, showing him in. They offered him food, burnt porridge, full of husks, full too of stone particles from being hand-ground in a pestle and mortar, moistened only with goat's milk. The newcomer seemed undaunted by this welcome, talked cheerfully; when the time came, lay down on the heap of ill-cured skins between his host and his hostess.

In the middle of the night he turned to Edda, still dressed in her long black rags. Ai lay in a deep sleep, unmoving, stung perhaps by a sleep-thorn. The clever-looking man pulled up the rags, mounted upon her, thrust away without preliminaries.

The stranger in the vision rose next morning and went his way, leaving Edda behind him to swell, to moan, to bring forth children as squat and ugly as herself —but more active, more industrious. They carted dung, they carried brushwood, they tended swine, they broke clods with wooden spades. From them come, the Shef-mind said, the race of thralls. Once I too might have been a thrall. No longer.

The traveler went on his way, walking briskly, along through the mountains. The next night he came to a log cabin, well-built, its ends fitted into each other in deep, axe-cut grooves, a window on one side with solid, well-fitting shutters, a privy outside over a deep ravine. Again a couple paused from their work as the traveler came up to them: a stout and powerful pair, ruddy-faced, thick-necked —the man bald, with trimmed beard, the woman round-faced and long-armed, built for carrying burdens. She wore a long brown gown, but a woolen mantle lay close by to be put on in the cool evening. Bronze clasps lay ready to fix it on. He wore loose trousers like a warrior of the Viking fleets, but his leather shirt was cut into thongs at waist and sleeve, for show. This is how most folk live now, the Shef-mind thought. "Their names are Afi and Amma," said the voice.

Again they invited the newcomer in, offered him food, plates of bread with fried chops of pork, ready-salted, the grease from the frying running into the bread—food for heavy laborers and strong men. Then they retired for the night, all three lying down together on a straw mattress with woolen blankets to pull over them. In the night Afi snored, sleeping in his shirt. The traveler turned to Amma, wearing only a loose gown, whispered in her ear, took her soon with the same speed and zest as before.

Again the newcomer went on his way, left Amma to swell, to bring forth children with silent stoicism, as strong and well-built as herself, but maybe more intelligent, ready to try a new thing sooner. Her children tamed oxen, timbered barns, hammered out ploughs, made fishing nets, adventured on the sea. From them, Shef knew, came the race of carls. Once upon a time I was a carl too. But that time has gone as well.

On the newcomer went, his road tending now to the great plains. He came to a house set back from the road, a garth round it of hammered posts. The house itself had several rooms, one to sleep in, one to eat in, one for the animals, all with windows or broad doorways. A man and a woman sat outside it on a well-crafted bench, called to the wayfarer, offered him water from their deep well. They were a handsome couple, with long faces, broad foreheads, soft skin unmarked by toil. When the man stood to greet the stranger he overtopped him by half a head. His shoulders were broad and his back straight, his fingers strong from twisting bowstrings. "These two are Fathir and Mothir," said the voice of the god.

They led their visitor in, onto a floor strewn with sweet-smelling rushes, sat him at a table, brought him water in a bowl to wash his hands in, set before him roast fowl, griddle-cakes in a basin, butter and blood sausage. After they had eaten, the woman spun on her wheel, the man sat on a settle and talked with his visitor.

When night came the host and hostess seemed under some compulsion as they guided their guest to the broad feather bed with its down bolsters, placed him between them, lay while Fathir fell asleep. Again the visitor turned to his hostess, fondled her with fingers, served her like a bull or a stallion, as he had the two before.

The visitor went, the woman swelled, from her belly came the race of jarls, the earls, the fighting men. They swam fjords, tamed horses, beat out metal, reddened swords, and fed the ravens on the plains of slaughter. That is how men wish to live now, thought the Shef-mind. Unless it is how someone wishes them to live . . .

But this cannot be the end: Ai to Afi to Fathir, Edda to Amma to Mothir. What of Son and Daughter, what of Great-great-grandchild? And Thrall to Carl to Jarl. I am the jarl now. But what comes after Jarl? What are his sons called, and how far down the road will the wanderer go? The son of Jarl is King, the son of King is . . .

Shef found himself suddenly awake, perfectly conscious of what he had just seen, perfectly aware that in some way it related to himself. What he had seen, he realized, was a breeding program, designed to make better people as men bred better horses or hunting-dogs. But better in what way? Cleverer? Better at finding new knowledge? That was what the priests of the Way would say. Or quicker to change? Readier to use the knowledge they knew already?

One thing Shef was sure of. If the breeding was done by the tricky, amused face he had seen on the wanderer, the face that was also that of his god-protector, then even the better people would find there was a price to be paid. Yet the wanderer meant him to succeed. Knew there was a solution, if he could find it.

In the dark hour before dawn Shef pulled on his dew-soaked leather shoes, rose from the rustling straw pallet, wrapped his blanket-cloak round him and stepped out into the chill air of the late English summer. He walked through the still-sleeping camp like a ghost, with no weapon except the whetstone-scepter, cradled in the crook of his left arm. His freedmen did not ditch and stockade their camps like the ever-active Vikings, but at the edge sentries stood. Shef walked up to the shoulder of one of them, one of Lulla's halberdiers, leaning on his weapon. His eyes were open but he paid no heed as Shef walked quietly past him and out into the dark wood.

Birds began to chirp as the sky paled in the east. Shef picked his way carefully through the tangles of hawthorn and nettle, found himself on a narrow path. It reminded him of the path he had followed with Godive the year before, as they had fled from Ivar. Sure enough, it led to a clearing and a shelter.

The day was up as he reached the clearing, and he could see plainly. The shelter was a mere hut. As he watched it, the ill-hung door opened and a woman came out. An old woman? Her face was worn with care, and had the pale, pinched look of the chronically underfed. But she was not so old, Shef realized, standing silent and motionless under the trees. She looked round, not seeing him, and then sank down in the feeble sunlight by the side of her hut. Put her face in her hands and began to weep silently.

"What's the matter, Mother?"

She started convulsively as she heard Shef's question, looked up with terror in her eyes. As she realized there was only one man, unarmed, she calmed.

"The matter? An old story, most of it. My man was taken off to join the king's army . . ."

"Which king?" asked Shef.

She shrugged. "I do not know. It was months ago. He has never come back. All summer we were hungry. We are not slaves, but we have no land. With Edi not here to work for the rich, we had nothing. When the harvest started they let me glean grain from what the reapers missed—little enough. But it would have been enough, only it was too late. My child died, my daughter, two weeks ago.

"And now this is the new story. For when I took her to the church to be buried, there was no priest there. He had fled, driven out, they say, by the pagans. The 'Way-folk'? I do not know the right name. The men in the village were happy, they said now they would pay no more tithes, no more for Peter's pence. But what good was that to me? I was too poor to tithe, and the priest would give me a dole, sometimes, from what he had. And who was there to bury my child? How could she rest without the words said over her? Without the Christ-child himself to take her part in heaven?"

The woman began to weep again, rocking backwards and forwards. How would Thorvin answer this? Shef wondered. Maybe he would say that the Christians had not always been bad, till the Church went rotten. But at least the Church gave comfort, to some. The Way must do that as well, not think only of those who tread the path of the heroes to Valhalla with Othin, or to Thruthvangar with Thor. He fumbled at his belt for money, realized that he had none.

"You see now what you have done?" said a voice behind him.

Shef turned slowly, found himself confronting Alfred. The young king had dark rings under his eyes, his clothes were stained and muddy. He had neither sword nor cloak, but still wore mail, with a dagger at his belt.

"I have done? I think she is one of your subjects, this side of the Thames. The Way may have taken her priest away, but you took her man away."

"What we have done, then."

The two men stood looking down at the woman. This is what I have been sent to stop, thought Shef. But I cannot do it by following the Way alone. Or not the Way as Thorvin or Farman see it.

"I will make you an offer, king," he said. "You have a purse at your belt and I have none. Give it to this poor woman here, so that at least she may live to see if her man returns. And I will give you your jarldom back. Or rather we will share till we have defeated your enemies, the Cross-wearers, as I have already defeated mine."

"Share the jarldom?"

"Share all we have. Money. Men. Rule. Risk. Let our fates run together."

"We will share our luck, then?" said Alfred.

"Yes."

"There must be two conditions on that," said Alfred. "We cannot march under your Hammer alone, for I am a Christian. Nor will I march only under the Cross, for that has been defiled by the robbers of Frankland and Pope Nicholas. Let us remember this woman and her grief, and march under the sign of both. And if we conquer we will let our peoples find comfort and consolation wherever they can. In this world there can never be enough for everyone."

"What is the other condition?"

"That." Alfred pointed to the whetstone-scepter. "You must get rid of it. When you hold it, you lie. You send your friends to their deaths."

Shef looked at it, looked again at the cruel, bearded faces that ornamented each end: faces like that of the cold-voiced god in his dreams. He remembered the mound where he had got it, the slave-girls with their broken spines. Thought of Sigvarth sent to die by torture, of Sibba and Wilfi sent to the burning. Of Alfred himself, whom he had knowingly allowed to march to defeat. Of Godive, rescued only to be used as bait.

Turning, he hurled the scepter end over end into the deep undergrowth, there to lie once more among the mold.

"As you say," he said. "We will march under both signs now, win or lose." He held out his hand. Alfred drew his dagger, cut free his purse, threw it with a thump onto the wet ground by the woman's feet. Only then did he shake hands.

As they left the woman struggled with feeble fingers to pry at the lashings of the purse.

They heard the commotion before they had gone a hundred yards down the path: clash of weapons, shrieking, horses neighing. Both men began to run toward the Wayman camp, but the thorns and thickets held them. By the time they arrived, gasping, at the edge of the wood, it was over.

"What happened?" said Shef to the men who turned disbelievingly toward them.

Farman the priest appeared from behind a slashed tent. "Frankish light cavalry. Not many of them, maybe a hundred. They knew we were here, came all at once out of the wood. Where were you?"

But Shef was looking past him, at Thorvin pushing through the crowd of excited men, holding Godive firmly by one hand.

"We came just after dawn," said Thorvin. "Got here just before the Franks attacked."

Shef ignored him, looked only at Godive. She raised her chin, stared back at him. He patted her shoulder gently. "I am sorry if I have forgotten you. There are things—if . . . soon . . . I will try to make amends for what I did.

"But not now. Now I am still the jarl. First we must set guards on the camp, so we are not surprised again. Then we must march. But before that —Lulla, Farman, all priests and leaders to me as soon as the guards are set.

"And Osmod, one thing before that. Send twenty women to me now."

"Women, lord?"

"Women. There are plenty with us. Wives, friends, drabs, I don't care. As long as they can push a needle."

Two hours later, Thorvin, Farman and Geirulf—the only priests of the Way present among a half dozen English unit commanders—stared unhappily at the new device hastily stitched onto the army's main battle-banner. Instead of the white Hammer standing upright on a red field, there were now a Hammer and Cross, set diagonally, one across the other.

"It is dealing with the enemy," said Farman. "More than they would ever do for us."

"It is a condition made by the king for his support," said Shef.

Eyebrows raised as the priests looked at the shabby, solitary figure of the king.

"Not just my support," said Alfred. "The support of my kingdom. I may have lost one army. But there are still men who will fight against the invaders. It will be easier if they do not have to change religion at the same time."

"We need men, for sure," said Osmod the camp marshal and leader of the catapulteers. "What with this morning and the desertions we've had— seven, eight men to a team left, where we need a dozen. And Udd has more crossbows in store than men to use them. But we need 'em right now. And where are we to find them? In a hurry, like?"

Shef and Alfred stared uncertainly at each other, digesting the problem, groping for a solution.

An unexpected voice cut the silence from the back of the tent. Godive's.

"I can tell you the answer to that," she said. "But if I tell you, you must grant me two things. One, a seat on this council. I do not care to be disposed of in future like a lame horse or a sick hound. Two, I do not want to hear the jarl say again, 'Not now. Not now, because I am the jarl.'"

Eyes turned; first, in amazement, to her, then in doubt and alarm to Shef. Shef, hand fumbling automatically for reassurance to his whetstone, found himself looking into Godive's brilliant eyes as if for the first time. He remembered: the whetstone was no longer there, nor what it stood for. He looked down.

"I grant both conditions," he said hoarsely. "Now tell us your answer, councillor."

"The men you need are already in the camp," said Godive. "But they aren't men, they're women. Hundreds of them. You find more in every village. They may be only drabs to you, as the jarl said before. Needle-pushers. But they are as good as men for some things. Put six with every catapult-team. The men released can go to Udd, to carry a crossbow, or the strongest of them to Lulla, to use a halberd. But I would also advise this to Udd: pick as many of the youngest women as you can, those who are not afraid, and put them with your crossbows as well."

"We can't do that," said Cwicca incredulously.

"Why not?"

"Well—they aren't strong enough."

Shef laughed. "That's what the Vikings said about you, Cwicca, remember? How much strength does it take to pull a rope? Turn a lever? Wind a pulley? The machine gives the strength."

"They'll get frightened and run away," Cwicca protested.

Icily, Godive overrode him. "Look at me, Cwicca. You saw me climb into that dung-cart. Was I frightened then? And if I was, I still did it.

"Shef. Let me talk to the women. I will find the ones you can trust, and if need be I will lead them. Don't forget, everyone"—she looked round the circle challengingly—"it may be that women have more to lose than any of you. And so more to gain."

In the silence Thorvin said, still skeptically, "This is all very well. But how many men had King Alfred here when he marched against the Franks? Five thousand? Trained warriors. Even if we use every woman in the camp, how can a third of that number hope to win? People, men or women, who have never shot so much as a bird-bolt before? You cannot make a warrior in a day."

"You can teach someone to shoot a crossbow in a day," said Udd unexpectedly. "Just wind 'em and point 'em."

"Just the same," said Geirulf, Tyr's priest. "We learned this morning the Franks will not stand still to be shot down. So what are we to do?"

"Listen," said Shef, drawing a deep breath, "and I will tell you."

CHAPTER ELEVEN

Like a great steel reptile, the Frankish army moved out of its base at Hastings, a little after dawn. First, the light cavalry in their hundreds, armed only with steel caps, leather jackets and sabers: their duty, to search out the enemy, hold the flanks, exploit breakthrough. Then, file after file of archers, mounted like every man in the army, but expecting to dismount for battle, when they would close to within fifty yards of an enemy line and pour in the arrows from their breast-bows: their duty, to fix the enemy, make them raise shields to cover faces, crouch down to cover unarmored legs.

In the center, the heavy cavalry, the weapon which had brought the Franks victory after victory on the plains of central Europe. Each man with mail-shirt and thigh-guards, back and bowels protected by the high-reaching saddle, each man with helmet and longsword, and above all, shield, lance and stirrups. The kite-shaped shield to cover the body, the lance with which to strike overhand or underhand, the stirrups to brace the feet for the stroke. Few men, and no Englishman, could at once wield a lance in one hand, strap the other arm into an unmoving shield, and control a war-stallion with thigh-pressure and the fingertips of one hand alone. Those men who could, they believed, could ride down any infantry in the world, once they came out from their ships or their walls.

At the head of his main battle, nine hundred riders strong, King Charles the Bald turned in his saddle and looked back at the banners flying immediately behind him, at his guarded base beyond, at the ships clustered off the beach. His scouts had brought him good news. The last army south of the Humber, marching to meet him, careless and unprepared, but ready to give battle. That was what he wanted: one decisive shock, the leaders dead on the field, then surrender and the transfer of all the reins of government to his own hand. It should have come sooner, after the defeat of the gallant but foolish Alfred. Then the summer would not have been so far on.

At least the time was ripe. Maybe overripe. But today, or at worst, tomorrow, the decision would be made. Charles realized that his view was blurred by rain drifting in from the Channel. He turned, rode on, waved the English renegade up to ride by him with the translator.

"You live in this God-forsaken country," he said. "How long is this rain going to last?"

Alfgar glanced at the drooping banners, noted the slow wind from the southwest, thought to himself that it looked as if it was settled in for a week-long soak. Not what the king wants to hear, he realized.

"I think it will soon pass over," he said. The king grunted, urged on his horse. Slowly, as the army picked its way over the unharvested fields, the damp earth churned into mud—the advance-guards leaving a broad black swathe across the turf.

Five miles northwest, on a ridge a little south of Caldbeck Hill, Shef watched the Franks moving toward him. His banner flew from an ox-cart, the Hammer and Cross athwart each other. He knew the scouts would already have picked it up, told King Charles where he was. He had moved forward at dusk the day before, after the marauding Frankish light horse-men had pulled back to their base. His men—and women—had taken up their positions at night. Almost none of them were with him. This was a battle he could control no more. The real question, he knew, was whether his army could act according to plan—and keep on acting after they had lost touch with him and with each other.

One thing Shef was sure of: there were more people in his army than he knew about. All day the day before, he had overtaken little groups of men heading toward the battleground, churls with spears, woodsmen with their axes, even grimy charcoal-burners out of the Weald, called out by Alfred's summons of the *fierd,* the ancestral levy of Wessex and its dominions. All were told the same thing. Do not stand up to them. Do not form a line. Wait round the edges. Press in if you see your chance. It was a simple order, and they had taken it gladly, the more gladly from their king in person.

But the rain, thought Shef. Would it help or hinder? He would know soon enough.

The first shot came from the shelter of a half-burned hamlet. Fifty Frankish light horsemen, well forward and to the flank of the army's main advance, crossed the sights of "Dead Level." Oswi squeezed the trigger, felt the thump of release, saw the great dart flash half a mile. Driving clear into the solid target of horsemen. Instantly the team—seven men and four women—were rewinding, dropping the next bolt into its slot. Thirty slow heartbeats before it could shoot again.

The leader of the hobbelars saw his man on the ground, shaft driven below his ribs, and bit his lip with surprise. Siege-engines, in the open. Yet the answer was clear. Spread out, scatter the targets, ride round behind them. The shot must have come from the right, the open flank. He spurred his horse, shouting, sent his men pouring across the fields.

Thick hedgerows, designed to keep the cattle in and the wild pigs out, channeled his rush into a sunken lane. As the hobbelars swept by, faces looked out from the thorns. At ten-foot range, the crossbow bolts thumped into leather-jerkined backs. As soon as the bolts left the stocks, the shooters turned and ran, not even waiting to see if they had hit. In instants they too were astride ponies, spurring hard for cover.

"Ansiau's in trouble," remarked the leader of another conroy of horsemen, watching the growing turmoil. "An ambush. We'll hook round behind it and catch them between him and us. Teach 'em a lesson; they won't try it again."

As he began to lead his men round in a wide sweep, there came a thud in the air and a sudden terrible shrieking behind him: a great dart from nowhere, striking a man in the thigh, driving through, pinning the screaming man to his dead horse. Not from the ambush. From somewhere else. The leader stood up in his stirrups, searching round the featureless landscape for something to show him where to charge. Trees, fields of standing wheat. Hedges everywhere. As he hesitated, a crossbow-bolt, shot from a steady rest by a man under a hedge a hundred and fifty yards off, caught him full in the face. The marksman, a poacher from Ditton-in-the-Fen, made no attempt to leap to his feet and run. In ten heartbeats he was twenty yards away, crawling like an eel in a half-filled ditch. The waxed and twisted gut of his crossbow, he had already discovered, had took little harm from the wet. As the horsemen hesitated, spurred in the end toward the place where they thought the shot might have come from, the sights of another twist-shooter trained round.

Slowly, without horns or trumpets, like a cogwheel tightening a rope, twenty separate skirmishes began to grow into battle.

From his vantage point on the ridge, Shef saw the Frankish main force still riding forward: but slowly, at no more than a walk, with many checks. They did not like to advance without their flanks secured. And on the flanks, for long moments, there was scarcely anything to be seen. Then horsemen would appear, spurring round a copse, or charging a burned-out village in extended line. What they were charging or spurring after was usually invisible. Then, as Shef strained his one eye in the blurring rain, he caught a flash of movement far out to one side: a pair of horses side by side at full gallop, one of the twist-shooters bouncing behind, its team drumming their ponies with their heels in a long trail behind. Oswi and "Dead Level" pulling out at one end of a hamlet as the Franks poured in the other, the flanking movement that was meant to cut him off delayed and confused by shots from other directions. The catapult disappeared behind a dip in the ground. In seconds it would be unlimbered again, once more menacing a wide arc anywhere within its half-mile range.

Shef's strategy depended on three things. One was local knowledge: only those who lived, farmed and hunted over the landscape knew where there were passable tracks, safe lines of retreat. Every group he had sent out had attached to it a man or boy picked from those who had fled the area. Others were scattered in hiding places everywhere over twenty square miles, told not to fight but to guide and pass messages. The second thing was the shooting-power of the torsion-catapults with their great darts, and the new crossbows. Both were slow to load, but even the cross-bows would pierce mail at up to two hundred paces. And they were best shot by men lying down in cover.

The most important part of Shef's strategy was his realization that there are two ways to win a battle. Every battle he had ever seen—every battle fought in the Western world for centuries—had been won one way. By shock. By forming lines and clashing till one line broke. The line might be broken by axe and sword, as the Vikings preferred; by horse and lance, in the Frankish style; or by stone and dart, as Shef had introduced. Breaking the line meant winning the battle.

This might be a completely new way to win a battle. To have no line, to produce no shock, but to wear and shred the enemy away by missile attack. Only Shef's unprofessional and unwarlike troops would do it: it went against too many ingrained habits of lifetime warriors. Ground was not important. It was there to be yielded. Face-to-face courage was not important. It was a mark of failure. But there could be none of the usual battlefield boosts to morale—the horns, war-songs, leaders shouting, most of all the sense of comrades alongside you. In a battle like this one it would be easy to desert, or simply to hide, to come out when all was over. Shef hoped his teams would keep on covering each other: they had gone out in bands of about fifty—a catapult, twenty crossbows, a few halberdiers together. But it was in the nature of the battle that they would split up. Once that happened, would they come back again?

Remembering the dogged, snarling attacks that the Yorkshire peasants had put in against him in the snow outside York, he thought they might. The men and women out there could see the country over which they were fighting, see its unreaped crops, its burned barns and cut-down orchards. To the children of the poor, food and land were sacred. They had too many hungry winters to remember.

As he watched the battle develop, Shef felt an odd sense of—not of freedom, but freedom from care. He was only a cog now. Cogs had to turn when they were wound. But they did not have to think about the rest of the machine. That would wind, or it would break, and the cog could do nothing about it. It had only to perform its part.

He dropped a hand on Godive's shoulder, standing beside him. She looked sideways at his ravaged face, allowed his hand to lie there.

King Charles, still moving forward toward the ridge of Caldbeck Hill—where from time to time through the rain he could see the taunting banner of his enemies displayed—held up his hand for the twentieth time for his main battle to halt. The leader of his light horse cantered up to him, rain now soaking through his wool and leather.

"Well, Rogier?"

The hobbelar shook his head disgustedly. "It's like fifty dogfights out there all at once. No one stands up to us. We chase them out and chase them out. Then when we reform and fall back they come back after us, or they come in behind."

"What would happen if we just held together and rode forward? Up there." The king jerked his thumb at the banner on the skyline a mile away.

"They'd shoot the hell out of us all the way."

"But only as long as it takes us to ride a mile. All right, Rogier. Discourage these varlets and their bows as much as you can, but tell your men to ride forward in line with the main battle now. Once we have broken their center we can turn and deal with the flanks."

Turning, the king raised his lance and swept it forward. His riders cheered hoarsely, once, and began to push their horses into a trot.

"They're coming now," said Shef to Alfred, standing next to Godive. "But it's soft ground and they will save their speed for the last rush." Barely fifty people stood by the three leaders on the ridge, mostly runners and message-bearers, but he had kept one pull-thrower team by him, with its clumsy, immobile machine.

"Swan-stones," he ordered.

Glad to move after hours of inactivity, the team—men and women together—sprang to their places. They too had only one role to play today. Early in their practicing, Shef's English machinists had discovered that chipping grooves in the stones their engines lobbed produced a strange warbling note as they flew through the air, like the noise of a swan. For their own amusement they had competed to see who could carve out the loudest. Now Shef meant to send a signal to his scattered troops that all could recognize.

His team loaded, braced, loosed. Launched one eerily whistling stone to one flank, heaved the machine round, launched to another. The dart-thrower and crossbow teams still lurking in ambush in front of the Frankish advance heard the signal, hitched up, retreated and swung round to join their leaders for the first time that day. As they appeared one by one, Shef pushed aside the farm-carts which he had set on the skyline, set the machines in the gaps, posted crossbows inside the carts. For every man, woman and machine, a horse or a horse-team stood no more than five yards away, horse-holders ready.

Shef walked up and down the line, repeating the order. "Three shots from each catapult, no more. Start at extreme range. One shot from each crossbow, on the word."

As King Charles reached the foot of the ridge, his spirits rose in spite of the rain. His enemy had tried to harass and delay him, and now he was counting on the slope and the mud to take the force out of his charge. But the hobbelars had done their job in taking the casualties of skirmishing. And the English still did not appreciate the plan of the Frankish charge. Setting spurs to his horse, he drove up the hill at a canter rising to a gallop, overtaken in seconds by the counts of his bodyguard pulling ahead.

The catapults twanged, black lines streaking through the air, swirls in the massive body of metal plunging up the hill. Still they came on as the levers twirled behind the farm-carts. Again the musical notes, the streaks, the cries of pain from men and horses, the rear ranks hurdling over those who fell. Strange, Charles thought as the obstacle in front of him came into focus. A barricade, but no shields, no warriors. Did they think to stop him with wood alone?

"Shoot," said Shef as the front ranks of the charge reached the white sticks he had planted that morning. Then, instantly, in a Brand-like roar, drowning the simultaneous thump of the crossbows, "Now run! Hitch up and run!"

In moments the slope behind the ridge was a flood of ponies, crossbows well in the lead, catapults taking seconds to hitch up, one team-leader cursing a sticking toggle. Then they too were away. Last of the throng, Godive suddenly turned back, jerked the Hammer and Cross from its frame, swung astride her gelding, and pounded off, banner dragging behind her like a lady's train.

Eyes glaring, lances poised, the Frankish cavalry swept up to the ridge-line, furious to strike at their harassers. A few drove their horses straight at the gaps in the enemy line, whirled round, stallions rearing to strike with their steel hooves at the foot soldiers who must be lurking there.

No one. Carts. Hoofprints. One single siege-engine, the pull-thrower Shef had abandoned. More and more squeezed through the gaps between carts, some finally dismounting and hauling the obstacles away. The king gaped up at the stout wooden frame from which Godive had hauled the Hammer and Cross. As he did so, tauntingly, the same banner rose again, on another ridge-line above a tangle of wood and gully, a long half-mile away. Some of the hotheads in his ranks, fury undispersed by action, yelled and began to spur again toward it. Sharp orders brought them back.

"I have brought a knife to cut beef," the king muttered to his constable Godefroi. "But what is set before me is soup. Thin soup. We will go back to Hastings and think again."

His eye fell on Alfgar. "I thought you said this rain of yours would stop."

Alfgar said nothing, looked at the ground. Charles glanced again at the high frame from which the Hammer and Cross had been torn, still standing sturdily on its cart. He jerked a thumb at it. "Hang the English traitor," he ordered.

"I warned you about the machines," shrieked Alfgar as the hands seized him.

"What's he say?" asked one of the knights.

"I don't know. Some gabble in English."

*   *   *

On a knoll well to one side of the track of the Franks, Thorvin, Geirulf and Farman conferred.

"What do you think?" asked Thorvin.

Geirulf, priest of Tyr, chronicler of battles, shook his head. "It is something new. Completely new. I have never heard of such a thing before. I have to ask: who puts it in his mind? Who but the Father of Warriors? He is a son of Othin. And such men are dangerous."

"I do not think so," said Thorvin. "And I have talked to his mother."

"We know what you told us," said Farman. "What we do not know is what it means. Unless you have a better explanation, I must agree with Geirulf."

"This is not the time to give it," said Thorvin. "See, things are moving again. The Franks are retreating."

Shef watched the heavy lancers turn back from the ridge, with foreboding. He had hoped they would come on again, take more losses, weary their horses and exhaust themselves. If they pulled back now, there was too much chance that they would reach their base and come out another day of their choosing and renew the attack. Instinctively he knew that an irregular army cannot do one thing: defend territory. He had not tried to do so today, and the Frankish king had not tried to make him, sure that both sides desired the traditional, decisive clash. But there must be a way to make him attack. An undefended population all over southern England stood at the king's mercy.

He needed victory today. It meant taking greater risks for greater gains. Fortunately, retreating armies are vulnerable in a way that advancing ones are not. So far, hardly half of Shef's forces had been engaged. Time to commit the rest. Calling his errand-lads around him, Shef began to pass his orders.

Down on the sodden slopes rising from the sea to the downlands, the Frankish hobbelars were learning sense. No longer did they ride in bunched groups presenting easy targets. Instead they too lurked in cover, moving only when they had to and then in short gallops. By a path through a dripping copse, one group tensed as they heard running feet. As the barefoot lad rushed by, intent only on his message, one rider spurred out, slashed savagely with his saber.

"He had no weapon," said one of the Franks, looking down at the body draining blood into the rain-pocked puddles.

"His weapon was in his head," grunted the sergeant in charge. "Get ready to move again."

The boy's brother, running fifty paces behind, hid quiet as a vole behind a red-berried rowan tree, watched them go. Slipped off to find avengers.

The Frankish archers, so far, had done nothing but endure random shot, their bowstrings long since so wet as to be valueless. Their commanders, now, were using them to hold strategic spots as the army fell back. They, too, were starting to use woodcraft.

"Look." One pointed to a conroy of hobbelars falling back over a field, one of them suddenly clutching his side and tipping from his horse. The archers, behind a wrecked barn, saw a figure suddenly slip from a hedgerow, seize a pony, and ride off unseen by its victims. But straight toward their ambush. As it came round the edge of the barn at full gallop, two men drove their short swords into the pony's chest, seized the marksman as the pony collapsed.

"What devil's work is this?" asked one, snatching the crossbow. "See, a bow, arrows. What is this at the belt?"

"Never mind the belt, Guillaume," shouted one of his mates. "Look, it's a girl." The men stared at the slight, short-kilted figure.

"Women shooting men from cover," muttered Guillaume. "All right. We've time to teach her a lesson. Give her some memories to take to Hell with her."

As the soldiers crowded round the writhing, splayed-out figure, a dozen churls of the Kentish fierd crawled closer, wood-axes and billhooks ready. They could not stand up to mailed horsemen. Mere prowlers and robbers they could deal with.

Leaking men and horses, the great steel reptile oozed sullenly back toward its base.

King Charles, sunk in thought, did not notice the check in front of him till he was almost on his own archers. Then he paused, looked down. A sergeant caught his stirrup, pointed. "Sire, they are in front of us. Standing, for once."

The village reeve Shef had found was positive that a day's rain and the passage of thousands of horses would turn the brook between the Brede and Bulverhythe into a quagmire. Shef had decided to take the chance and believe him. His runners had got through—most of them. The pull-thrower teams with their heavy guards of halberdiers had closed in from the far flanks where they had waited immobile. Assembled their weapons, lined up five yards apart along a hundred and fifty yards of front. On a fine day, in the open, against cavalry, suicide.

Osmod the marshal, peering through the rain, judged the Frankish vanguard within range. As he called the order, twenty beams lashed the air together, slings whirled, stones shot into the sky.

Charles's horse reared as the brains of a dismounted archer flicked its face. Another stallion, leg broken, screamed and pawed at the air. Almost before one volley had landed another was in the air. For a moment the Frankish army, surprised again and again, came close to panic.

Charles rode forward bellowing, ignoring the stones now aimed deliberately at him. Imperiously he drove the archers forward, launching feeble arrows. Behind them, following his example, his heavy lancers broke into a slow trot. Into the quagmire where a brook had been.

Charles himself was pulled clear of his bogged horse by two counts of his stable, stood in the end to watch. His men floundered through, some on horses still, some on foot, to reach the machines that flung an unending rain of stones. They were met by a line of men in strange helmets, swinging and stabbing with huge axes like woodmen's tools. Robbed of the élan which was their birthright, the Frankish knights stood and fought them weapon to weapon. Slowly, the big men in mail forced their smaller, strangely armed adversaries back. Back. Almost to the line of the machines, which they must stand to defend.

Horn-blasts from both sides. Floundering through the mud, Charles tensed, expecting the counterattack, the desperate last charge. Instead his enemies turned suddenly, all together, and ran. Ran unashamedly, like hares or leverets. Leaving their machines to the conqueror.

Gasping with exertion, Charles realized there was no way to carry the things off. Nor to burn them. "Cut them up," he ordered. An archer looked doubtfully at the heavy timbers. "Cut the ropes! Do something to them."

"They lost a few," said one of his counts. "And they ran like cowards. Left their weapons behind."

"We lost many," said the king. "And how many swords and mail-shirts have we left behind us today? Give me my horse. If we reach base with half the strength we started, we'll be lucky."

Yes, he thought. But we're through. Through all the traps. And half, behind a safe stockade, may be enough another day.

As if to encourage him, the rain began to ease.

*   *   *

Guthmund the Greedy, sweeping down the Channel under oars alone, ignored the rain and welcomed the poor visibility it brought. If he was going to go ashore he would much prefer it to come as a surprise. Also, in rain or fog, there was a chance of snapping up information. In the prow of the leading ship, he pointed off to starboard, called an order to increase the stroke. In moments the longship was alongside the six-oar fishing-boat, its crew looking up in fear. Guthmund pulled the hammer-pendant from round his neck and showed it, noted the expressions fading from fear to wariness.

"We are here to fight the Franks," he called, using the half-English pidgin of the Wayman camp. The expressions relaxed another degree as the men realized they could understand him, took in what he said.

"You're too late," a fisherman called back. "They fight today."

"You'd better come aboard," replied Guthmund.

As he took in the sense of what the fishermen told him, his pulse began to beat stronger. If there was one principle of successful piracy, it was to land where the defenses were down. He checked again and again: the Frankish army had been seen marching out that morning. It had left camp-guards and ship-guards. The loot of the countryside, Canterbury included, was in the lightly guarded camp. The fishermen had no hope that the Franks would find anything but victory. Still, Guthmund told himself, if his friend and jarl was defeated, it could do no harm to rob the conqueror. And a stroke in the rear might be a vital distraction. He turned to the fishermen again with another string of questions: The fleet drawn up in a bay? The stockaded camp on a hill? The nearest inlet to it? Steep sides but a path?

In the drenching rain the Wayman fleet, rowed now by chained Ragnarsson survivors, pulled one by one into the narrow mouth of the stream below Hastings and its camp.

"Do you mean to climb the walls with ladders?" asked one of the fishermen doubtfully. "They are ten feet high."

"That's what those are for," said Guthmund, waving cheerfully at the six onagers being slung over the side by derricks.

"Too heavy for the path," said the fisherman, eyeing the way the boats heeled.

"I have plenty of carriers," replied Guthmund, watching keenly as his men, weapons poised, unshackled the dangerous Ragnarsson galley-slaves a few at a time and made them fast again to the onagers' frames and carry-bars.

As the narrow inlet filled with men, Guthmund decided to make a short speech of encouragement.

"Loot," he said, "lots of it. Stolen from the Christian Church, so we'll never have to give any back. Maybe we have to share it with the jarl, if he wins today. Maybe not. Let's go."

"What about us?" said one of the chained men.

Guthmund looked at him attentively. Ogvind the Swede: a very hard man. Threats no good. And he needed these men to use their full strength up the steep hillside.

"This is how it is," he said. "If we win, I'll let you go. If we lose, I'll leave you chained to the machines. Maybe the Christians will be merciful to you. Fair?"

Ogvind nodded. Struck by a sudden thought, Guthmund turned to the black deacon, the machine-master.

"What about you? Will you fight these for us?"

Erkenbert's face set. "Against Christians? The emissaries of the Pope, the Holy Father, whom I myself and my master called to this abode of savages? Rather will I embrace the crown of holy martrydom and go . . ."

A hand plucked at Guthmund's sleeve: one of the few slaves taken from York Minster who had survived both Ivar's furies and Erkenbert's discipline.

"We'll do it, master," he whispered. "Be a pleasure."

Guthmund waved the mixed party up the steep hillside, going first himself with the fishermen and minster-men to reconnoiter, the Ragnarssons struggling up next under their ton-and-a-half burdens. Slowly, still cloaked by the rain, six onagers and a thousand Vikings moved into position four hundred yards from the Frankish stockade. Guthmund shook his head disapprovingly as he realized that there were not even sentries posted on the seaward side—or if there had been, they had all drifted over to the other side to watch and listen to the far-off rumor of battle.

The first sighting shot from an onager bounced short, kicked up and flicked a ten-foot post stump-first out of the ground. The minster-men pulled out coigns, lifted the frames a trifle. The next volley of five twenty-pound boulders smashed down twenty feet of stockade in a moment. Guthmund saw no point in waiting for a second volley. His army headed straight for the gap at a run. The startled Franks, mostly archers, bow-strings useless, faced with a thousand veteran warriors ready to fight on foot at close quarters, broke and ran almost to a man.

*　*　*

Two hours after setting foot onshore, Guthmund looked out from the Frankish gate. All his training told him to parcel the loot, abandon the now-unnecessary machines, and get back to sea before vengeance fell on him. Yet what he saw looked uncommonly like a beaten army streaming back. If so, if so . . .

He turned, shouted orders. Skaldfinn the interpreter, priest of Heimdall, looked at him in surprise.

"You're taking a risk," he said.

"Can't help it. I remember what my grandpa told me. Always kick a man if he's down."

As his men saw the Hammer ensign break out over what they had thought was their secure camp, Charles the Bald felt the morale of his army break. Every man and horse was soaked, cold and weary. As they straggled out of the copses and hedgerows and formed once more into ranks, the hobbelars could see that at least half their number were still lying out in the sodden fields, dead or waiting for death from some peasant's knife. The archers had been mere passive targets all day. Even the core of his army, the heavy lancers, had left a third of their best on slope or in quagmire, with never a chance to show their skill. The stockade in front of him looked unharmed and heavily manned. No assault would go in willingly.

Cutting his losses, Charles stood in his saddle, raised his lance, pointed toward the ships drawn up on the beach or anchored in the road. Sullenly, his men changed their direction of march, angled down towards the beach on which they had landed weeks before.

As they reached it, one by one, the dragon-boats cruised round from the inlet where their crews had re-embarked. Rowed into position, halted all together on the calm sea, swung bows on with the skill of veterans. From a vantage point by the stockade, an onager tried a ranging shot. The missile plumped into the gray water a cable's length over the cog *Dieu Aide*. Gently, the onagers trained round.

Looking down on the crowded beach, Shef realized that where the Frankish army had shrunk, his had swollen. The dart-throwers and crossbows were in place as he expected, hardly fewer than when they had started. His stone-throwers were coming up at a rush, recaptured from where the Franks had left them, unharmed or hastily re-rigged and now carried along still assembled by hundreds of willing hands. Only the halberdiers had lost more than a handful. And in their place had come thousands, literally thousands of angry churls out of the woodlands, clutching axes and spears and scythes. If the Franks were to break out it would have to be uphill. On weary horses. Under withering fire.

Into Shef's mind, unbidden, came the memory of his duel with Flann the Gaddgedil. If you wanted to consign a man, or an army, to Naströnd, to Dead Man's Shore, you cast the spear over their heads as a sign that all were given to Othin. Then no prisoners could be taken. A voice spoke inside him, a cold voice, the voice he recognized as the Othin of his dreams.

"Go on," it said. "Pay me my due. You do not wear my sign yet, but do they not say you belong to me?"

As if sleepwalking, Shef drifted over to Oswi's catapult—"Dead Level," wound and loaded, trained on the center of the Frankish army, milling in confusion below them. He looked down at the crosses on the shields: remembered the orm-garth. The wretched slave Merla. His own torments at the hands of Wulfgar. Godive's back. Sibba and Wilfi, burned to ashes. The crucifixions. His hands were steady as they pulled out the coigns, trained the weapon up to launch its missile over the Frankish heads.

Inside him the voice spoke again, the voice like a calving glacier. "Go on," it said. "Give the Christians to me."

Suddenly Godive was beside him, hand on his sleeve. She said nothing. As he looked at her, he remembered Father Andreas, who had given him life. His friend Alfred. Father Boniface. The poor woman in the forest clearing. He looked round from his daze, realized that the priests of the Way, all of them, had appeared from somewhere, were gazing at him with grave and intent faces.

He stepped back from the catapult with a deep sigh.

"Skaldfinn," he said. "You are an interpreter. Go down and tell the Frankish king to surrender or be killed. I will give them their lives and passage home. No more."

Again he heard a voice: but this time, the amused one of the wanderer in the mountains, which he had first heard over the gods' chessboard.

"Well done," it said. "You defeated Othin's temptation. Maybe you are my son. But who knows his own father?"

CHAPTER TWELVE

"He was tempted," said Skaldfinn. "Whatever you may say, Thorvin, there is something of Othin in him."

"It would have been the greatest slaughter since men came to these islands," added Geirulf. "The Franks on the beach were worn out and helpless. And the English churls would have had no mercy."

The priests of the Way sat again in their holy circle, around the spear and the fire, within the rowan cords. Thorvin had picked great bunches of the freshest berries of autumn. Their bright scarlet answered the sunset.

"Such a thing would have brought us the worst of luck," said Farman. "For with such a sacrifice it is essential that no loot or profit be taken. But the English would not have regarded that. They would have robbed the dead. Then we would have had against us both the Christian God and the wrath of Allfather."

"Nevertheless he did not shoot the dart," said Thorvin. "He held his hand. That is why I say he is not a creature of Othin. I thought so once. Now I know better."

"You had better tell us what you learned from his mother," said Skaldfinn.

"It was like this," Thorvin began. "I found her easily enough, in the village of her husband the heimnar. She might not have talked to me, but she loves the girl—concubine's daughter though she is. In the end she told me the story.

"It was much as Sigvarth told it—though he said she enjoyed his attentions and she . . . Well, after what she suffered it is not surprising that she spoke of him only with hatred. But she bore him out up to the time when he lay with her on the sand, put her in the boat, and then left her and went back to his men and their women on the beach.

"Then, she said, this happened. There was a scratching on the boat's gunwale. When she looked over, in the night, there was a small boat alongside, just a skiff, with a man in it. I pressed her to know what sort of man, but she could remember nothing. Middle-aged, middle-sized, she said, neither well-dressed nor shabby. He beckoned to her. She thought he was a fisherman who had come out to rescue her, so she got in. He pulled out well clear of the beach, and rowed her down the coast, saying never a word. She got out, she went home to her husband."

"Maybe he was a fisherman," put in Farman. "Just as the walrus was a walrus and the skoffin was a foolish boy afraid of keeping watch on his own."

"I asked her—did he not want a reward? He could have taken her home. Her kin would have paid him, if not her husband. She said he just left her. I pressed her on this, I asked her to remember every detail. She said one more thing.

"When the stranger got her to shore, she said, he pulled the boat up on the beach and looked at her. Then she felt suddenly weary and lay down among the seaweed. When she woke, he had gone."

Thorvin looked round. "Now, what happened when she lay in this sleep we do not know. I would guess that a woman would know by some sign if she had been taken in her sleep, but who is to say? Sigvarth had been with her not long before. If she had any suspicion, she would have nothing to gain by mentioning it. Or remembering it. But that sleep makes me wonder.

"Tell me now." Thorvin turned to Farman. "You who are the wisest of us, tell me how many gods there are in Asgarth."

Farman stirred uneasily. "You know, Thorvin, that is not a wise question. Othin, Thor, Frey, Balder, Heimdall, Njörth, Ithun, Tyr, Loki—those are the ones we speak of most. But there are so many others in the stories: Vithar, Sigyn, Ull . . ."

"Rig?" asked Thorvin carefully. "What do we know of Rig?"

"That is a name of Heimdall," said Skaldfinn.

"A name," mused Thorvin. "Two names, one person. So we hear. Now, I would not say this outside the circle, but it comes to me sometimes that the Christians are right. There is only one god." He looked round at the shocked faces. "But he—no, it—has different moods. Or parts. Maybe the parts compete against each other, as a man may play chess, right hand against left, for sport. Othin against Loki, Njörth against Skathi, Aesir against Vaenir. Yet the real contest is between all the parts, all the gods, and the giants and monsters who would bring us to Ragnarok.

"Now, Othin has his way of making men strong to help the gods when they shall stand against the giants on that day. That is why he betrays the warriors, chooses the mightiest of them to die. So they will be in his hall the day the giants come.

"But it is in my mind that maybe Rig too has his way. You know the holy story? How Rig went through the mountains, met Ai and Edda and begot on Edda, Thrall. Met Afi and Amma and begot on Amma, Karl. Met Fathir and Mothir and begot on Mothir, Jarl. This jarl of ours has also been thrall and carl. And who is the son of Jarl?"

"Kon the Young," said Farman.

"Which is to say *Konr ungr* which is *konungr*."

"Which is King," said Farman.

"Who can deny our jarl that title now? He is acting out the story of Rig in his own life. Of Rig and his dealings with humanity."

"Why is the god Rig doing this?" asked Vestmund, priest of Njörth. "And what is Rig's power? For I confess, I know nothing of him but the story you tell."

"He is the god of climbers," replied Thorvin. "And his power is to make men better. Not through war, like Othin, but through skills. There is another old story you know, about Skjef the father of Skjold—which is to say, Sheaf the father of Shield. Now the kings of the Danes call themselves the sons of Skjold, the war-kings. Yet even they remember that before Skjold the war-king there was a peace-king, who taught men how to sow and reap, instead of living like animals by the chase. What I think has happened now is that a new Sheaf has come, however we pronounce the name, to free us from sowing and reaping and living only from one harvest to the next."

"And this is 'the one who comes from the North,'" said Farman doubtfully. "Not of our blood or tongue. One who has allied himself with Christians. It is not what we expected."

"What the gods do is never what we expected," replied Thorvin.

* * *

Shef watched the gloomy procession of disarmed Frankish warriors filing after their king aboard the ships that would take them home. With them Alfred had insisted on sending not only the papal legate and the Franks' own Churchmen, but also the archbishop of York, and his own Bishop Daniel of Winchester, Erkenbert the deacon and all the English clerics who had failed to oppose the invaders. Daniel had screamed threats of eternal damnation for the excommunicate at him, but Alfred had remained unmoved. "If you cast me out of your flock," he had remarked, "I shall begin my own. One with better shepherds. And dogs with sharper teeth."

"They will hate you forever for that," Shef had said to him.

"That is another thing we must share," Alfred had replied.

And so they had done their deal.

Both men single, without heirs. They would be co-kings, Alfred south of the Thames, Shef north of it, at least as far as the Humber, beyond which there still lurked the Snakeeye and his ambitions. Each named the other as his heir. Each agreed that within his dominion, belief in the gods should be free, for Christians, for Way-folk, and for any other that should appear. But no priest of any religion should be allowed to take payment, in goods or in land, except for a service agreed upon beforehand. And Church-land should revert to the crown. It would make them the richest kings in Europe, before long.

"We must use the money well," Shef had added.

"In charity?"

"In other ways too. It is often said that no new thing can come before its time, and I believe it. But I believe also that there can be a time for a new thing, and then men can stifle it. Or churches can stifle it. Look at our machines and our crossbows. Who could say they could not have been made a hundred years ago, or five hundred, in the time of the Rome-folk? Yet no one made them. I want us to get back all the old knowledge, even the numbercrafts of the *arithmetici*. And use it to make new knowledge. New things." His hand had clenched as if on the haft of a hammer.

Now, still watching the files of captives embarking, Alfred turned to his co-king and said, "I am surprised you still refuse to wear the hammer of our banner. After all, I still wear the cross."

"The Hammer is for the Way, united. And Thorvin says he has a new sign for me. I will have to see if I approve of it, for the choice is a difficult one. He is here."

Thorvin approached them, flanked by all the priests of the Way, behind them, Guthmund and a cluster of senior skippers.

"We have your sign," said Thorvin. He held out a pendant on a silver chain. Shef looked at it curiously: a shaft, with five rungs sticking out from it on alternate sides.

"What is it?"

"It is a *kraki*," replied Thorvin. "A pole-ladder. It is the sign of Rig."

"I have never heard the name of that god. What can you tell me about him that should make me wear his sign?"

"He is the god of climbers. Of wanderers. He is mighty not through himself but through his children. He is the father of Thrall, of Carl, of Jarl. And of others."

Shef looked round at the many watching faces: Alfred. Thorvin. Ingulf. Hund. There were some not there. Brand, of whose recovery he still had no news. His mother Thryth. He did not know if she would ever wish to see him again.

Most of all, Godive. After the battle a group of his catapulteers had brought him the body of his half brother—his mother's son, Godive's husband. Both he and she had looked for a long time at the purple face, the twisted neck, trying to find in it some memory of childhood, some clue to the hatred in the brain. Shef had thought of lines from one of Thorvin's old poems, said by a hero over the brother he had killed:

"I have been your bane, brother. Bad luck lay on us.
Ill is the Norns' doom, I will never forget."

But he had not said the words. He meant to forget. He hoped one day Godive would forget too. Forget that he had first saved her, then deserted her, then used her. Now that the constant stress of planning and action was over, he felt inside himself as though he loved her as much as he ever had before he rescued her from Ivar's camp. But what kind of love was it that had to wait for the right moment to be admitted?

So Godive had thought. She had taken her husband and half brother's body for burial, left Shef unsure when or whether she might return. This time he would have to decide for himself.

He looked past his friends at the prisoners still filing by—the sullen, hating faces—thought of the humiliated Charles, the enraged Pope Nicholas, the Snakeeye in the North with a brother now to avenge. He looked again at the silver sign in his hand.

"A pole-ladder," he said. "Difficult to balance on."

"You have to do it one rung at a time," replied Thorvin.

"Hard to climb, difficult to balance, to reach the top. But at the top there are two rungs to grasp on to. One opposite the other. It could almost be a cross."

Thorvin frowned. "Rig and his sign were known in the ages before there ever was a cross. It is not a sign of death. No. It is one of reaching higher, of living better."

Shef smiled, the first time he had done that for many days. "I like your sign, Thorvin," he said. "I will wear it." He slipped the Wayman's pendant round his neck, turned and looked at the misted sea.

Some knot, some pain within him was released, fled.

For the first time in his entire life he felt at peace.

ONE
KING'S
WAY

CHAPTER ONE

Frozen in the hard grip of the worst winter in memory, all of England lay under a frigid mantle of snow. The great river Thames was covered with ice from bank to bank. The road leading west to Winchester was a flint-hard, filthy track of frozen hoofprints and caked manure. The horses slipped on the ice, snorting out steaming vapors. Their riders, huddled and chilled, looked up at the dark walls of the great Minster and spurred their tired mounts with little result.

This was the 21st of March of the year of our Lord's Incarnation 867, and a day of greatest portent. A royal union was taking place today. Filling the pews were the military aristocracy of Wessex, every alderman, thane, and high-reeve who could possibly be squeezed within the stone walls, gaping and sweating, a low mutter of explanation and translation continually rising from them, watching intently as the whole elaborate ritual of coronation of a Christian king unrolled its stately dance.

In the right-hand pew at the very front of the nave of the great Minster at Winchester was Shef Sigvarthsson, co-king of the English—and king in his own right of all those parts of it north of the Thames which he could persuade into obedience. He sat uneasily, aware of the many eyes on him.

They saw a man whose age was hard to guess. His thick dark hair and smooth-shaven face made him seem young, too young for the gold circlet of royalty on his brow and the heavy bracelets on both arms. He had the height and the broad shoulders of a warrior in his prime—or of an ironsmith, which was what he had been. Yet for all his youth the dark hair was already streaked with white, and his face showed the betraying grooves of care and pain. His right eye-socket was an empty hollow, and the patch that covered it could not disguise the way the flesh had drawn and fallen in. The whole of England and half of Europe beyond knew how he had been half-blinded on the order of Sigurth Snake-eye, eldest of the sons of Ragnar. And how the smith's apprentice had taken his revenge by killing Sigurth's brother, Ivar the Boneless, Champion of the North, rising from near-thrall to carl of the Viking Great Army, to jarl under the orders of Alfred Atheling. Now to being king and co-ruler with Alfred himself, joint victors over the Frankish Crusade only the year before. Rumors ran everywhere about the meaning of the strange sign he wore round his neck as emblem of the Asgarth Way, an emblem none had worn before him: the *kraki*, the pole-ladder of the mysterious deity Rig.

Shef had no wish to see the coronation, still less the ceremony that would follow. The grooves of pain deepened in his face as he watched. Yet he understood why he had to be there, he and his men: to make a point, to support his co-king. It was Alfred's request, as close to a command as possible, that had brought him here.

"You don't have to take the Mass," Alfred had said firmly to Shef and his supporters. "You don't even have to sing the hymns. But I want you there at the coronation, wearing your pendants, wearing your crown, Shef. Making a show. Pick out your most impressive men, and look rich and powerful. I want everyone to see that I am supported fully by the men of the North, the conquerors of Ivar the Boneless and Charles the Bald. The pagans. Not the wild pagans, the slavers and sacrificers, like the sons of Ragnar: but the men of the Way, the Way of Asgarth, the pendant-folk."

They had at least managed to do that, Shef thought, looking about. Put on their mettle, the two dozen Way-folk selected to sit in the front ranks had responded nobly. Guthmund the Greedy was carrying more gold and silver on his person, in arm-rings, torque, and belt-buckle, than any five thanes of Wessex put together. Of course he had shared in three successive distributions of plunder under Shef, whose fame, though fabulous, was not all exaggeration. Thorvin priest of Thor and his colleague Skaldfinn priest of Njörth, though opposed to worldly display, had nevertheless dressed in shining white and brought with them their signs of office, the short hammer for Thorvin and the seaman's boat for Skaldfinn. Cwicca, Osmod and the other English freedmen now veterans of Shef's campaigns, though hopelessly unimpressive in person from youthful hunger, had managed to dress themselves in the unheard-of luxury of silken tunics.

They also carried carefully sloped the tools of their trade: halberds, cross-bows, and catapult-winders. Shef suspected that the mere sight of men so obviously English, so obviously low-born, and so obviously rich beyond the dreams of the average Wessex thane, let alone churl, was the most powerful silent argument for Alfred's success that could be found.

The ceremony had begun hours before with the forming of a great procession from the king's residence to the Minster itself—a walk of barely a hundred yards, but every yard of them seeming to demand some special observance. Then the high mass in the Minster, the nobles of the realm crowding up to take communion, not so much out of reverence as out of an earnest desire not to miss any luck or blessing that might be granted to others. Among them, Shef had noted, had been many seemingly incongru-ous figures, the undersized frames and rough clothes of slaves that Alfred had freed and churls he had promoted. They were now here to take the word back to their towns and villages: the word that there was no doubt, no doubt at all that Alfred Atheling was now Alfred King of the West Saxons and of the Mark, by all the laws of man and of the Christian God.

Also in the first row, towering over those around him, sat the Marshal of Wessex, the man chosen by custom as the most notable warrior of the kingdom hand-to-hand. The Marshal, Wigheard, was indeed an imposing sight, nearer seven foot than six and twenty English stone if an ounce in weight; he carried the king's state sword at arm's length as effortlessly as a twig, and had already shown uncanny ability to fence with a halberd as if it were a willow-wand.

There was one man in Shef's group, sitting immediately to his left, who had difficulty following the ceremony, who glanced again and again at the Champion. This was the giant Brand, himself champion of the men of Halogaland, still wasted and shrunken from the belly-wound he had taken in his duel on the gangplank with Ivar the Boneless, but slowly regaining strength. Brand, shrunken as he was, still seemed the bigger man of the two. His bones were almost too big for his skin, with knuckles like rocks, and ridges jutting out over his eyebrows like armor. Brand's fists, Shef had once noted by careful comparison, were bigger than a pint pot: not just huge, but disproportionate even to the rest of him. "Men grow big where I come from," was all that Brand would ever say.

The noise of the congregation died as Alfred, now thoroughly blessed and prayed over, turned to face them to take his oaths. For the first time Latin was abandoned and the service broke into English as Alfred's senior alderman asked the solemn question: "Do you grant us our rightful laws

and customs to be held, and do you swear after your power to grant
rightful dooms and defend the rights of your people against every enemy?"

"I do." Alfred looked round the packed Minster. "I have done so, and I
will do so again." A rumble of assent.

Now a trickier moment, Shef thought as the alderman stepped back and
the senior bishop stepped forward. For one thing the bishop was startlingly young—and for good reason. After Alfred's dispossession of the
Church, his excommunication by the Pope, the Crusade against him and
his final declaration of non-communion with Rome, every senior cleric in
his kingdom had left. From the Archbishops of York and Canterbury down
to the least bishop and abbot. Alfred's response was to promote ten of the
best remaining junior priests and tell them the Church in England was in
their hands. Now one of them, Eanfrith Bishop of Winchester, six months
before priest of a village no-one had heard of, came forward to ask his
question.

"Lord King, we ask you to grant to us protection for Holy Church and
due law and rightfulness for all those who are members of it."

Eanfrith and Alfred had been days working out the new formula, Shef
recalled. The traditional one had asked for confirmation of all rights and
privileges, tithes and taxes, ownerships and possessions—all of which Alfred had in fact taken away.

"I grant protection and due law," Alfred replied. Again he looked round,
again added words beyond tradition. "Protection to those within the
Church and without it. Due law to members of it and to others."

The highly trained choristers of Winchester, choirmonks and choirboys
together, burst into the anthem of Zadok the Priest, *Unxerunt Salomonem
Zadok sacerdos,* as the bishops prepared for the solemn moment of blessing
with the holy oil, after which Alfred would be literally the Lord's Anointed,
against whom rebellion was also sacrilege.

Shortly, thought Shef, would come the difficult moment for him. It had
been explained to him very carefully that Wessex, ever since Queen
Eadburh of wicked memory, never had a Queen, and that the King's wife
could have no separate coronation. Nevertheless, Alfred had said, he was
insistent that his new wife should be accepted by him in front of the
people, in honor of her courage in the defeat of the Franks. So, he had
said, after the donning of the regalia, sword, ring and scepter, he meant his
wife to come forward and be named before the congregation, not as
Queen, but as the Lady of Wessex. And who better to lead her to the altar
than her brother, Shef, also his co-king?

Who might have to yield his kingdom to the child of Alfred and the Lady, if he had no child himself.

This would be the second time he had given her away, Shef thought bitterly. Once again he must forget the love, the passion that had once bound them. The first had been to a man they both hated, and in punishment for that, it seemed, he must now hand her over to a man they both loved. As Thorvin nudged him with a mighty elbow, to tell him the time had come to step forward and lead the Lady Godive with her train of maidens to the altar, Shef met her eyes—her triumphant eyes—and felt his heart turn to ice.

Alfred might now be a king, he thought numbly. He himself was not. He did not have the right, or the strength.

As the choir broke into the *Benedicat* he decided that he would do it. Do the thing he wanted to, not just what he felt was his duty. He would take out the fleet, the new navy of the co-kings, to work out his inner anger on the enemies of the realm: the pirates of the North, the fleets of the Franks, the slavers of Ireland or Spain, anyone. Let Alfred and Godive find their own happiness at home. He would find peace in drowned men and shattered ships.

Earlier this same day, far to the north in the land of the Danes, a simpler and more terrifying ceremony had taken place.

It had begun before dawn. The bound man lifted from where he lay on the floor of the guard-hut had long since ceased to struggle, though he was neither a coward nor a weakling. Two days before, when the emissaries of the Snake-eye had marched into the slave-pen, he had known what would be in store for the man they chose. When they picked him from the others, he had known also that the least chance of escape was to be seized, and he had seized it: secretly gathered the slack in his wrist-chains as they marched him off, waited till the guards were hustling him over the wooden bridge that led to the inner heart of the Braethraborg, the stronghold of the three last sons of Ragnar. Then struck suddenly to his right with the chain, and hurled himself for the rail and the swift river beneath it—at the best to swim for freedom, at the worst to die his own man.

His guards had seen many such desperate attempts. One snatched at his ankle as he lunged for the rail, two others had him pinned before he could recover. They had beaten him systematically with their spear-shafts, not in malice, but to ensure he would be too stiff and battered to move swiftly again. Then taken off the chains and replaced them with rawhide thongs, twisting and wetting them with sea-water to dry even tighter. If the bound man could have seen his fingers in the dark, they would have been blue-black, swollen like a corpse's. Even if some god intervened to save his life, it would be too late now to save his hands.

But neither god nor man would intervene. The guards had ceased to acknowledge his existence when they talked among themselves. He was not dead, because for what he had to do a man was needed with the breath, and especially the blood, still in him. But that was all. There was no need for anything else.

Now, at the end of the long night, his guards carried him out of the longhouse where the great fresh-tarred flagship lay, and down the long row of rollers that led down the slipway to the sea.

"Here will do. This one here," grunted the burly middle-aged warrior in charge.

"How do we do it?" asked one of the others, a young man without the campaign-marks, the scars and silver arm-rings of the others. "I've never seen this done before."

"So watch and you'll learn. First, cut that rawhide round his wrists. No, don't worry," as the younger man hesitated, looked round automatically for any slightest glimpse of an escape, "he's a goner, look at him, couldn't even crawl if we let him go. Don't let him go, mind. Just cut his wrists free, right."

A few minutes of sawing, and the bound man staggered as the lashings freed, stared a moment in the pale but growing light at the hands in front of him.

"Now lay him out flat on that roller. Belly down. Feet together. Now see here, young Hrani, because this is the important bit. The thrall has to have his back upwards, for why you'll see very shortly. He can't have his hands behind him, same reason, and he mustn't be able to move. But he mustn't be able to stop himself moving either.

"So what I do is this." The middle-aged leader pressed his captive's face down on to the solid pine trunk he lay on, seized both arms and dragged them forward above his head, till the victim looked like a man diving. He pulled a hammer and two short iron spikes from his belt.

"We used to tie them, but I think you get a better roll like this. I saw something like it once in one of the Christers' churches. Course, they put the nail in the wrong place. Half-wits."

Grunting with effort, the veteran began to hammer a spike carefully through the junction of wrist and hand. Behind him, there came a rustle of many men moving. Against the dawn-light of the east, dark shapes began to show. Spears and helmets silhouetted against the sky where the sun would soon show its first glimmer on this, the first day of the warriors' new year, when day and night were the same length.

"He's taking it well," said the young man as his instructor started to hammer in the second spike. "More like a warrior than a thrall. Who was he, anyway?"

"Him? Just some fisherman we picked up on the way back last year. And he's not taking it well, he can't feel a thing, his hands have been dead for hours.

"Soon over now," he added to the man now firmly nailed to the log, patting his cheek. "Speak well of me in the next world. This could go a lot worse if I bungled it. But I haven't. Just lash his legs down, you two, no need for another spike. Feet together. He's got to turn when the moment comes."

The little group got to their feet, leaving their victim stretched out along the pine-trunk.

"Ready, Vestmar?" said a voice behind them.

"Ready, lord."

The space behind them had filled up while they worked. At the rear, away from the shore and the long sea inlet, lay hump after hump of dark shapes, slave-pens, workshops, boathouses, and in dimly-sensed ranks the rows of regular barracks that housed the trusted troops of the sea-kings, the sons of Ragnar—once four, now three. From the barracks the men had come streaming, all men, no women, no youths, to see the solemn spectacle: the launch of the first ship, the start of the annual campaigning season that once again was to bring terror and ruin to the Christians and their allies of the South.

Yet the warriors hung back, ranking themselves round the inlet's shore in a deep semi-circle. Pacing down to the very shore itself came only three men, all tall and powerful, men in their prime, the three remaining sons of Ragnar Hairy-Breeks: Ubbi the grizzled, despoiler of women, Halvdan the redbeard, the fanatical dueller and champion, dedicated to the warrior's life and code. Before even them, Sigurth the Snake-eye, so called for the whites that surrounded every part of his eye-pupils like the gaze of a snake: the man who meant to make himself King of all the lands of the North.

All faces were turning now to the east, to see if the first glimpse of the sun's disk could be seen on the horizon. Most years, here in Denmark in the month the Christians called March, only cloud. Today, good omen, clear sky, with just the light haze already turned pink by the still-invisible sun. A slight murmur came from the watchers as the readers of omens came forward, a stooped and aged band, clutching their holy bags, their knives and knucklebones and sheep's shoulder-blades, the instruments of divination. Sigurth watched them coldly. They were necessary, for the men. But he had no fear of a bad divination, a poor set of omens. Augurs who augured badly could find themselves on the sacrifice-stone as well as any other.

In the dead, intent silence, the man stretched out on the pine-log found his voice. Pinned and lashed as he was, he could not move his body. He strained his head back, and called out in a choked voice, aiming it at the midmost of the three men by the shore.

"Why can you do this, Sigurth? I was no enemy of yours. I am no Christian, nor man of the Way. I am a Dane and a freeman like yourself. What right have you to take my life?"

A roar from the crowd drowned his last words. A line of light showed in the east, the sun poking up over the near-flat horizon of Sjaelland, eastmost of the Danish islands. The Snake-eye turned, threw back his cape, waved to the men in the boathouse above him.

Instantly a creaking of ropes, a simultaneous grunt of effort, fifty men, the picked champions of the Ragnarsson army, throwing their mighty weight on the ropes attached to the spiked rowlocks. Out from the boat-house loomed the dragon-prow of the Snake-eye's own ship, the *Frani Ormr* itself, the *Shining Worm*. Grinding forward along the flat on the greased rollers prepared for it, ten tons of weight on a fifty-foot keel made of the stoutest oak-tree in Denmark.

It reached the top of the slipway. The pinned man craned his neck sideways to see his fate looming against the sky, and clamped his mouth shut to avoid the scream welling from inside him. One thing only he could avoid giving his tormentors, and that was the joy of a good omen, a year launched in fear and despair and shrieks of pain.

The men heaved at the ropes together, the prow tipped and began to slide down, thumping over each roller in turn. As it ground down towards him, as the projecting prow reached over him, the sacrifice called out again, meaning it in defiance: "Where is your right, Sigurth? What made you a king?"

The keel struck him accurately in the small of the back, rode over him and crushed down with its immense weight. Involuntarily, the breath pressed from his lungs in a weird cry, turning into a shriek as pain over-came any possible self-control. As the ship roared over him, its haulers running now to keep up, the roller to which he was nailed whirled round.

The blood of his crushed heart and lungs spurted up, driven out by the massive rounded keel.

It splashed upwards on to the flaring bow planks above him. The augurs watching intently, crouched low so as not to miss any detail, whooped and whirled their fringed sleeves in delight.

"Blood! Blood on the planks for the sea-king's launch!"

"And a cry! A death-cry for the lord of warriors!"

The ship surged on into the calm water of the Braethraborg fjord. As it did so the sun's disc rose fully above the line of the horizon, sending a long flat ray beneath the haze. Throwing aside his cape, the Snake-eye seized his spear by the butt and lifted it up above the shadow of the boathouse and the slipway. The sun caught it and turned its eighteen-inch triangular blade to fire.

"Red light and a red spear for the new year," roared the watching army, drowning out the augurs' shrilling.

"What made me a king?" shouted the Snake-eye to the passing spirit. "The blood I have shed, and the blood in my veins! For I am the god-born, the son of Ragnar, the son of Völsi, the seed of the immortals. And the sons of men are logs beneath my keel."

Behind him his army ran, crew by crew, towards their waiting ships, to take their turn by the stronghold's crowded slipways.

The same chill winter that held fast to England had fallen also on the other side of the channel. In the cold city of Cologne, on this same day, as Alfred was being crowned, eleven men met in a bare unheated room of a great church hundreds of miles to the south of the Braethraborg and its human sacrifice. Five of them wore the purple and white of archbishops' rank—none, as yet, the scarlet of a Cardinal. Slightly behind and to the right of each of the five sat a second man, each of these dressed in the plain black robe of a canon of the Order of Saint Hrodegang. Each was his archbishop's confessor, chaplain and counselor—of no rank, but of immense influence, with the best hope also of succeeding to the dignity of a Prince of the Church.

The eleventh man also wore the black robe, this time of a mere deacon. He looked covertly from side to side at the assembled gathering, recognizing and respecting power, but unsure of his own place at the table. He was Erkenbert, once deacon of the great Minster at York and servant of Archbishop Wulfhere. But the Minster was no more, sacked by the enraged heathen of the North the previous year. And Wulfhere, Archbishop though he remained, was a mere pensioner of his fellow-archbishops, an object of contemptuous charity like his co-Primate of Canterbury. The Church in England was no more: no lands, no rents, no power.

Erkenbert did not know why he had been called to this meeting. He did know that he was in deadly danger. The room was not bare because the great Prince-Archbishop of Cologne could not afford furniture. It was bare because he wished to have no cover for any possible eavesdropper or spy. Words had been said here that would mean death for all present if repeated.

The group had eventually, slowly, cautiously, come to a decision, feeling each other out. Now, the decision made, tension slackened.

"He has to go, then," repeated Archbishop Gunther, the host of the meeting in Cologne.

A circuit of silent nods around the table.

"His failure is too great to overlook," confirmed Theutgard of Trier. "Not only did the Crusade he sent against the province of the English meet defeat in battle . . ."

"Though that itself is a sign of the divine disfavor," agreed the notoriously pious Hincmar of Rheims.

". . . but he allowed a seed to be planted. A seed worse than defeat for one king or another king. A seed of apostasy."

The word created a momentary silence. All knew what had happened the year before. How under pressure from both the Vikings of the North and his own bishops at home the youthful King Alfred of the West Saxons had made common cause with some pagan sect—called, so they heard, the Way. Had then successively defeated the dreaded Ivar Ragnarsson of the Vikings, followed by Charles the Bald, Christian king of the Franks and deputy of the Pope himself. Now Alfred ruled unchallenged in England, though sharing his dominions with some heathen jarl whose name seemed almost a joke. But it was no joke that in retaliation for the Crusade sent against him by Pope Nicholas Alfred had declared the Church in England out of communion with the Catholic and Apostolic Church of Rome itself. Even less of one that he had stripped the Church in England of its lands and wealth, allowing Christ to be preached and served only by those who were prepared to earn their own livings by free offerings, or even—it was said—through supporting themselves by trade.

"For that defeat, and that apostasy, he must go," repeated Gunther. He looked round the table. "I say, Pope Nicholas must go to God. He is an old man, but not old enough. We must hasten his departure."

Now that the words had been spoken aloud a silence fell; it was not easy for princes of the Church to talk of killing the Pope. Meinhard, Archbishop of Mainz, a fierce, hard man, spoke in a loud voice. "Have we any way to do that?" he queried

The priest to Gunther's right stirred and spoke. "There will be no difficulty. There are men we can trust in the Pope's entourage at Rome. Men who have not forgotten that they are Germans like ourselves. I do not recommend poison. A pillow in the night. When he does not waken his office can be declared vacant without scandal."

"Good," said Gunther, "for though I wish his death, I take my oath before God that I wish Pope Nicholas no harm."

The group looked at him with faint signs of scepticism. All knew that only ten years before Pope Nicholas had deposed Gunther and deprived him of his see as a penalty for disobedience. As he had done also to Theutgard of Trier, while he had further rebuked and overruled even the pious Hincmar over a dispute with a mere bishop.

"He was a great man, who did his duty as he saw it. I do not blame him even for launching King Charles on his ill-fated Crusade. No, there is no harm in Crusades. But he made a mistake. Tell them, Arno," he added to his confessor. "Tell them our appreciation of the situation." He sank back, lifting the gold goblet of Rhenish wine on which so much of his archbishopric's revenue depended.

The younger man pulled his stool forward to the table, his sharp face gleaming with enthusiasm beneath close-cropped blond stubble. "Here in Cologne," he began, "we have made careful study of the arts of war. Not merely on the field of battle itself, but also in its wider context. We try to think not merely like a *tacticus*"—he used the Latin word, though up till then all had spoken the Low German of Saxony and the North—"but like a *strategos* of the old Greeks. And if we think *strategice*"—Hincmar at least winced at the strange medley of Greek and Latin—"we see that Pope Nicholas made a critical error.

"He failed to see what we here call the *punctum gravissimum*, that is, the heavy point, the point of main weight, of an enemy's attack. He did not see at once that the real danger, the real danger to the whole Church, lay not in the schisms of the East, or in the struggles of Pope against Emperor, or in the naval raids of the followers of Mahound, but in the little-known kingdoms of the poor province of Britannia. Because only in Britannia did the Church find more than an enemy: a rival, a supplanter."

"He is an Easterner," said Meinhard contemptuously.

"Just so. He thinks that what happens here in the West, here in the North-West of Europe, in Germany and Frankland and the Low Countries, is of minor importance. But we know that here lies destiny. The destiny of the Church. The destiny of the world. I dare to say it, if Pope Nicholas does not: the new chosen people, the only true bulwark against the barbarians."

He ceased, his fair face already flushing with pride.

"You will find no arguments on that score here, Arno," Gunther remarked. "So, once Nicholas is dead, he must be replaced. I know"—he raised a hand—"the Cardinals will not elect anyone to Pope who has any more sensible opinion, and we cannot expect to sway the Italians to sense. But we can sway them to nonsense. I think we are all agreed that we will use our revenues and our influence to ensure the election of someone we can count on to be popular with the Romans, well-born among the Italians, and a complete nonentity. I believe he has already chosen his papal name: Adrian II, they tell me.

"More serious is what must be done closer to home. Not only Nicholas must go. King Charles too. He also has been defeated, and by a rabble of peasants."

"Gone already," said Hincmar decisively. "His barons will not forgive humiliation. Those who did not share it with him cannot believe that Frankish lancers could be defeated by slingers and bowmen. Those who did are anxious not to share his disgrace. There will be a rope round his neck or a knife in his ribs without us stirring a hand. But who is to replace *him?*"

"Your pardon," said Erkenbert quietly. He had been listening with the greatest care, and slowly the conviction had come to him that these men, unlike the pompous and inefficient clerics of the English Church he had served all his life, actually respected intelligence more than rank. Juniors spoke without rebuke. They put forward their own ideas, and had them accepted. Or if they were rejected, it was with reason given, and after careful thought. Among these men, the only sin was to fail in logic, or in imagination. The excitement of abstract thought worked on Erkenbert more than the fumes of the wine in his goblet. He felt that at last he was among equals. Above all, he wished to have them accept him too as an equal.

"I understand Low German, for it is like my own English. But allow me to speak in Latin for the moment. I do not understand how King Charles the Bald of Francia can be replaced. Or what advantage any successor would be to this group. He has two sons, am I correct? Louis and Charles. He had three brothers, Ludwig and Pepin and Lothaire, of whom only Ludwig is still alive, and—is it seven living nephews, Louis and Charles and Lothaire . . ."

". . . and Pepin and Carloman and Ludwig and Charles," completed Gunther. He laughed briefly. "And what our English friend is too polite to say is that not one of them can be told from another. Charles the Bald. Charles the Fat. Ludwig the Saxon. Pepin the Younger. Which is which and what does it matter? So I will put it this way in his place.

"The seed of the Emperor, the great Charles, Charlemagne himself, has failed. The virtue is gone out of it. As we find a new Pope in Rome, so we must find a new king here. A new king's line."

The men round the table looked cautiously at each other, less cautiously as each realized that the unthinkable was being thought. Gunther smiled briefly at the effect of his words.

Greatly daring again, Erkenbert spoke. "It is possible. In my own country kings' lines have been deposed. And in yours—did not the great Charlemagne himself come to power through the deeds of his ancestors, who deposed the god-born to whom they had been servants? Deposed them and shore their hair in public, to show they were no longer holy? It could be done. What is it, after all, that makes a king?"

One man during the whole discussion had not spoken, though he had nodded in assent from time to time: the immensely-respected Archbishop of Hamburg and Bremen in the far North, the disciple and successor of Saint Ansgar, Archbishop Rimbert, famous for his personal courage in fanatical missions to and against the pagans of the North. As he stirred, all eyes turned to him.

"You are right, brothers. The line of Charles has failed. And you are wrong. Wrong in many ways. You speak of this and that, of strategy and the *punctum gravissimum* and the West and the East, and in the world of men what you say may have a meaning.

"But we do not live only in the world of men. I say to you that Pope Nicholas and King Charles had a worse failing than any you have seen. I pray only that we may not fall into it ourselves. I say to you, they did not believe! And without belief, all their weapons and their plans were straw and chaff, to be blown away on the wind of God's displeasure.

"So I will tell you that we do not need a new king, nor a new king's line. No. What we must have now is an Emperor! An *Imperator Romanorum*. For we, comrades—we Germans are the new Rome. We must have an *imperator* to mark it."

The others stared at him in silence, a new vision slowly forming in their minds. It was the blond-cropped Arno, Gunther's counselor, who broke it.

"And how is the new Emperor to be chosen?" he asked cautiously. "And where is such a one to be found?"

"Listen," said Rimbert, "and I will tell you. And I will tell you also the secret of Charlemagne, the last true Emperor of Rome in the West. I will tell you what it is that makes the true king."

CHAPTER TWO

The strong smell of sawdust and wood chips filled the air as Shef and his companions, rested now from the long ride from Winchester, strolled down to the keelyard. Although the sun had not long cleared the eastern horizon, hundreds of men were already working—leading up great carts loaded with wood and drawn by patient oxen, clustered round forges, bustling in and out of rope-walks. The noise of hammers and saws came from all directions, mixed with the furious voices of gang foremen: but no whip-cracks, no cries of pain, no iron slave-collars.

Brand whistled slowly and shook his head as he surveyed the scene. Only just released from his sick-bed, he was still carefully watched by his physician, the diminutive Hund. Until now he had seen none of what had been achieved over the long winter. And indeed, even Shef, who had driven the work on in person or by deputy every single day, found it hard to credit. It was as if he had released a torrent of energy rather than creating it. Again and again over the winter he had found his wishes anticipated.

After the fighting had ceased last year he had found himself with the resources and wealth of a kingdom to command. His first and most urgent task had been to ensure the defense of his precarious realm. He issued the orders and his commanders applied themselves eagerly—building war machines and training their users, recruiting troops, mixing his potentially refractory groups of freed slaves, Vikings of the Way, and English thanes performing military service in return for their leases of land. This accomplished he had set himself to his second task; to ensure the royal revenues. The job of recording all details of land and tolls, debts and taxes, till then carried on by custom and memory, he had passed on to the priest Boniface. With instructions to do in all the counties Shef now controlled what he had begun in Norfolk alone. It would take time and skill, but the results had already become visible.

The third task, though, was Shef's alone: and that was to build a navy. If there was one thing that was clear, it was that all the battles of the previous two years had been fought on English soil and paid for with English lives. The way to ensure defense, Shef had seen, was to stop the attackers, and especially the Vikings outside the Way, in the place where they reigned supreme: at sea. Supported by the accumulated wealth and taxes of East Anglia and East Mercia as well, Shef had started immediately to build a fleet.

He had had much help and experience to draw on. The Vikings of the Way contained many skilled shipwrights, quite ready to pass on their knowledge and skills if properly rewarded. Thorvin and his fellow-priests of the Way, immensely interested, had plunged into the work as if they had asked nothing better all their lives—as indeed was true. Conforming to their code of forever seeking for new knowledge and supporting themselves and their religion by their working skills alone. Smiths, carpenters, hauliers, poured from all over eastern England to the site Shef had chosen for his dock, on the north bank of the Thames. It lay within his own dominions but facing those of King Alfred, poised to guard—or to threaten —both the Channel and the North Sea, a short distance downriver from the commercial port of London, at the tiny hamlet of Creekmouth.

The problem had been direction. Holding all these skilled and experienced men to the plan Shef had formed, but which directly contradicted much of their life-times' collective experience. At first Shef had asked Thorvin to direct the site, but he had refused, saying he must be free to leave at any time if the demands of his faith required it. Then he had thought of Udd, the ex-slave who had, almost single-handed, invented the crossbow and made safe the torsion catapult. Thus—to some eyes—defeating both Ivar Ragnarsson, Champion of the North, and weeks later Charles the Bald, King of the Franks, at what men were coming to call the Battle of Hastings, 866.

Udd had been a disaster, soon replaced. Left to himself it transpired that the little man was only capable of taking an interest in things made of metal. He also could not direct so much as the boy who blew the bellows, from constitutional shyness. He had been removed and set to the much more congenial task of finding out everything that could be discovered about steel.

As confusion grew, Shef had had to think over his true needs: a man used to the sea and ships, used to organizing the work of others, but not so independent as to alter Shef's orders or so conservative as to fail to understand them. Shef knew few people. The only one of those who seemed even possible was the fisherman-reeve of Bridlington, Ordlaf, whose capture of Ragnar Hairy-Breeks two summers before had unleashed the fury on England. He it was, now, who turned to greet Shef's party.

Shef waited for him to kneel and rise. Early attempts to do away with the formal code of respect had foundered on the looks of hurt and uncertainty of Shef's thanes.

"I brought someone to see the work, Ordlaf. This is my friend and onetime captain, Viga-Brand. He comes from Halogaland, far, far in the North, and has sailed more miles than most men. I want his opinion of the new ships."

Ordlaf grinned. "He'll see much to stretch his eyes at, lord, however far he's sailed. Things no-one has seen before."

"Truth—right there is a thing that I have not seen before," said Brand. He waved at a pit a few yards off. Inside it was a man pulling one end of a six-foot saw. Another stood on the huge log above pulling on the other. Ready hands held the plank as they sawed it from the log.

"How does it work? I have only ever seen planks hewed out with adzes."

"Me too, till I came here," said Ordlaf. "The secret lies in two things. Better teeth on the saws—that is the work of Master Udd. And teaching these blockheads here"—the men looked up grinning—"not to push the saw, just *take turns pulling it*. Saves a lot of wood and a lot of work," he added in a normal voice. The plank eased to the ground, caught by helpers and the two sawyers changed places, the one beneath shaking dust and shavings from his hair. Shef noticed as they changed over that one wore round his neck the Hammer of Thor, as did most of the workmen on the site, the other an almost indistinguishable Christian cross.

"But that's nothing, sir," Ordlaf went on to Brand. "What the king really wants you to see are his pride and joy, the ten ships we're building to his design. And one of them, lord, now ready for your inspection, finished while you were in Winchester. Come and see."

He led them through the gate of a stout palisade to a ring of jetties projecting out into a still backwater of the river. There in front of them lay

ten ships, men working on all of them, but one, the nearest, evidently complete.

"Now, sir Brand. Did you ever see anything like that this side of Halogaland?"

Brand stared, considering. Slowly he shook his head. "It is a big one, right enough. They say the biggest ocean-going ship in the world is Sigurth Snake-eye's own *Frani Ormr,* the *Shining Worm,* that rows fifty oars. This is as big. All these ships are as big."

Doubt clouded his eyes. "What are the keels made of? Have you taken two trunks and joined them? If you have, well, maybe on a river or off the coast in fair weather, but for deep sea or long voyage—"

"All single trunks," said Ordlaf. "What you may be forgetting, sir, if you don't mind me saying so, is that up there in the North where you come from you have to work with the wood you can get. And while I can see men grow big enough up there, it isn't the same for trees. What we got here is English oak. And say what they like, I've never seen better wood or bigger wood."

Brand stared again, shook his head again. "Well and good. But what in Hel have you done to the mast? You've—you've put it in the wrong place.

And raked forward like a—like an eighteen-year-old's prick! How is that going to shift a ship that size?" Honest pain filled his voice.

Both Shef and Ordlaf grinned broadly. This time Shef took up the tale.

"The whole idea of these ships, Brand, is that they have only one purpose. Not crossing the ocean, not carrying men with spears and swords, not carrying cargo.

"These are ships for battle. Ships to battle other ships. Not by coming alongside and having their crews board each other. Not even by doing what Father Boniface tells me the ancient Rome-folk did, by ramming. No: by sinking the other ship and its crew along with it, and doing it from a distance. Now there's only one thing we know that can do that.

"You remember the pull-throwers I first made at Crowland that winter? What do you think of them?"

Brand shrugged. "Good against people. Wouldn't like to have one of those rocks fall into my ship. But as you know, you have to be the right distance to get a hit. Two ships, both moving . . ."

"Right, no chance. Now what of the twist-shooters we used against King Charles's lancers?"

"Might kill the crew, one man at a time. Couldn't sink a ship. The arrow they shoot would plug its own hole."

"That leaves us with the last weapon, the one that Erkenbert the deacon made for Ivar. Guthmund used them to knock down the palisade at the camp above Hastings. The thing the Rome-folk called the *onager*—the wild ass. We call it the mule."

At a signal deck-hands dragged tarred canvas away from a squat, square object mounted in the exact center of the nearest ship's undecked hull.

"What do you say to a hit from one of those?"

Brand shook his head slowly. He had seen the onagers shoot only once, and then from a distance, but he remembered seeing carts fly in pieces, whole files of oxen smashed to the ground. "No ship in the world could survive it. One hit, and the whole frame would go to pieces. But the reason you call it the mule is . . ."

"Because of the kick. Come and see what we've done."

The men walked up the gangplank to stare at the new weapon close up. "See," Shef explained. "These weigh a ton and a quarter. They have to. You see how it works? Stout rope down at the base, with two handles. You twist the rope both sides. It holds this bar"—he patted a five-foot beam standing upright, a heavy leather sling dangling from a peg at its top. "You force the bar down on to the deck, held by an iron clamp, and keep twisting. When it's at greatest strain you release the clamp. Bar shoots up with a rock in the sling, sling whirls round . . ."

"Bar hits the crosspiece." Ordlaf patted a thick beam on a massive frame, padded both sides with heavy sandbags.

"The bar stops, the sling releases, the rock keeps going. It throws flat and hard, anything up to half a mile. But you see the problem. We have to build it heavy, to take the kick. We have to have it dead over the center-line, so we can fix the frame down on to the keel. And because it weighs so much, we have to have it centered fore and aft as well."

"But that's where the mast should be," objected Brand.

"So we had to move the mast. That's where Ordlaf showed us some-thing."

"You see, sir Brand," Ordlaf explained, "where I come from we have boats like yours, double-ended and clinker-built and all. But because we're in it for fish, not for far voyaging, we rig them different. We step the mast forward of center, and we rake it forward too. And then, you can see, we cut the sail different. Not square, like yours, but on a slant."

Brand grunted. "I know. So if you take your hands off the steering oar she turns head into wind and rides the waves. Fisherman's trick. Safe enough. But slow. Especially with all this weight to shift. How fast is she?"

Shef and Ordlaf exchanged glances. "Not fast at all," Shef conceded. "Guthmund ran a trial against one of his boats before we put the mule in this one, and even without that weight, well—Guthmund sailed rings round her.

"But you see, Brand, we aren't trying to catch anyone! If we meet a fleet in the open sea, and they come to fight us, we'll sink them! If they sail away, the coastline has been defended. If they get past us, we'll follow and sink them wherever they go. This isn't a transport, Brand. It's a ship for battle."

"A battleship," added Ordlaf approvingly.

"Can you train it round?" asked Brand. "The mule, I mean. Can you point it different directions? You could with your dart-throwers."

"We're working on it," said Shef. "We tried putting the whole thing on a cartwheel, putting the cartwheel on an axle, and bedding the other end of the axle in a hole bored in the keel. But it was all too heavy to turn, and the kick kept breaking the axle. Udd has some idea of putting the whole thing on an iron ball, but . . . No. It will only shoot directly on the beam. But what we have done is fit two bars, two ropes, two sets of handles and so on, one either side. Only one crosspiece, naturally. But that means we can shoot to either beam."

Brand shook his head again. As they stood he had been feeling the ship heave gently beneath him, even in the Thames backwater, trying to estimate how she would feel in the open sea. A ton and a quarter of weight, much of it high up so that the machine stood higher than the gunwales. Sail pressure way off center-line. A wide yard so they could spread plenty of sail, he noticed. But tricky to handle. He had no doubt the fisherman knew his business. And there was no question what a hit from one of those rocks would do. Remembering the fragile frame of every boat he had ever sailed, their planks not even nailed to the ribs, but lashed with sinew, Brand could see the whole construction springing apart in a moment, leaving an entire crew struggling in the sea. And not even Sigurth Snake-eye's own fifty champions could fight against that.

"What are you going to call her," he asked suddenly. "For luck." His hand shot automatically to the hammer pendant on his chest. Ordlaf copied his gesture, fishing from under his tunic the silver boat of Njörth.

"We've got ten of the battleships," said Shef. "I wanted to call them after the gods of the Way, *Thor, Frey, Rig,* and so on, but Thorvin would not allow it. He said it would be bad luck if we had to say 'Heimdall is aground,' or 'Thor is stuck on the sandbank.' So we changed our minds. We decided to call each ship after one of the counties in my realm, and as far as we can we will crew her from that county. So this is the *Norfolk,* over there the *Suffolk,* the *Lincoln,* the *Isle of Ely,* the *Buckingham,* and all the others. What do you think?"

Brand hesitated. Like all sailors, he had deep respect for luck, and no wish to say the ill word that might bring down bad luck on the enterprise of his friend. "I think that once again you have brought a new thing to the world. It may be that your 'Counties' will sweep the seas. Certainly I would not care to encounter one, and men do not call me the timidest of the Norsemen. It may be that the kings of England will be the sea-kings in the future, and not the kings of the North.

"Tell me," he went on, "where do you mean to make your first cruise?"

"Across to the Dutch shore," said Shef. "Then up along the coast past the Frisian islands and into Danish waters. That is the main route the pirates come. We will sink every pirate ship we see. From then on any who wish to invade us must take the long sea-crossing from Denmark. But in the end we will destroy their bases, seek them out in their own home-ports."

"The Frisian islands," muttered Brand. "The mouths of the Rhine, the Ems, the Elbe, the Eider. Well, I will tell you one thing, young man. All that is pilot water. You understand what I mean? You will need a pilot who knows the channels and the landmarks, so he can find his way by smell and hearing if he needs to."

Ordlaf looked stubborn. "I've found my way all my life with no more than lead, lookout and log-line. Nor do I feel my luck has got any the worse since I left the monks who were my masters and found the gods of the Way."

Brand grunted. "I say nothing against the gods of the Way." Again, both he and Ordlaf touched their protecting pendants, and this time Shef, with a self-conscious gesture, reached also to pull out his strange ladder-like charm, the token of his patron Rig. "No, the gods may be well enough. But as for lead, lookout and log-line—you'll need more than that off Bremen! I say it, I, Brand, Champion of the men of Halogaland."

The listening workmen shifted and muttered. Some of those new to the yards nudged each other, pointing at the unfamiliar pendant of Rig.

Sun slanted through the high windows of the great library in the cathedral of Cologne, to fall on the open pages of several books spread across the massive lectern. Erkenbert the deacon, his short frame barely able to see its upper edges, stood lost in thought. He was alone. The *librarius,* knowing he had the archbishop's favor, and approving the intentness of his research, had left him to himself, even with the great and precious Bible, written on the skins of eighty calves.

Erkenbert was comparing texts. Could the fantastic tale that the archbishop Rimbert had told them days before possibly be true? It had convinced everyone else at the meeting, archbishops and counselors alike. But then it had flattered their pride, appealed to their sense of themselves as a nation, and as a nation continually rejected and undervalued by the power of Rome. Erkenbert did not share that feeling—or at least not yet. The English nation, remembering its conversion by the blessed Pope Gregory, had long boasted its loyalty to the Popes and to Rome. But what had Rome sent in return? If what Rimbert said was true, then maybe it was time to be loyal . . . elsewhere.

The texts, now. First among them was one that Erkenbert knew well, could have recited in his sleep. Nevertheless, important to look again. The four gospellers' accounts of the crucifixion of Christ all told slightly different tales—proof of their truth, of course, for who does not know that four men seeing the same thing will pick different parts of it to repeat? But John —John said more than the others. Turning the great, stiff pages, Erkenbert found the passage he wanted and read it, whispering the Latin words softly to himself and mentally translating them into his native English.

". . . *sed unus militum lancea latus eius aperuit*. But one of the soldiers pierced his side with a lance." With a lance, thought Erkenbert. With a Roman soldier's lance.

Erkenbert knew better than most men what Roman soldiers' weapons looked like. At what had once been his home at the great Minster of York, there had still remained standing much of what was formerly the headquarters building of the Sixth Legion of *Eboracum*. The legion had left York and Britain four hundred years before, called away to fight a civil war on mainland Europe, but much of its arsenal had remained behind, and much of what had not been stolen or used still lay in the vaults. The imperishable bronze fittings for the catapults Erkenbert had made for the heathen Ivar had been genuine old work, as good as the day they were made. Iron rusted, but for all that Erkenbert had seen on its stand, kept cleaned and polished as a trophy, the full panoply of a Roman legionary, helmet, cuirass, short-sword, greaves, shield and of course the iron-shafted Roman javelin, the *pilum*. Also called a *lancea*.

Yes, thought Erkenbert, that could have happened. And no question but that the lance, the Holy Lance, the lance that had pierced the side of the Son of God himself, could have survived physically. He had himself seen and handled weapons that might be as old.

But who might have thought to preserve such a thing? It would have had to be someone who recognized its importance at the very moment of its use. Otherwise the weapon would have gone back to the barracks, been mixed with a thousand others. Who could have set aside such a weapon? Not, thought Erkenbert, for all the archbishop had said, the pious Jew Joseph of Arimathea, whom John the gospeller mentioned four verses later. Such a man, if a disciple of Jesus, might well have been able to beg the body from Pilate, and to preserve the holy chalice in which Jesus had celebrated the Last Supper—though John said nothing of that. He would not have been able to gain possession of an infantry issue weapon from the Romans.

But the centurion, now. Erkenbert turned the pages of the Bible thoughtfully, moving from one Gospel account to the next. The centurion was mentioned in three out of four, and in all three he said almost the same words: Luke, "truly this was a righteous man," Mark, "truly this man was the Son of God," Matthew, "truly this was the Son of God." And in the fourth, in John, might the writer not have meant the centurion by "one of the soldiers"? If the centurion pierced the side of Jesus, as was his duty, and had seen or felt the miracle—what easier than for him to keep and treasure his own lance?

Now where did the centurion go after the Crucifixion? Erkenbert turned to another book, small, shabby, untitled, a book it seemed of letters, one after another, prattling of land and loans and debts, written by many authors, the kind of thing many efficient librarii would have sent to be scraped and re-used. Erkenbert fixed on the one of which Rimbert had told him. It seemed plain enough. A letter from Roman times, written in Latin—not good Latin, Erkenbert noted with interest, the Latin of a man who knew only the words of command, and to whom grammar was a mystery—and said at the top to be from one Gaius Cassius Longinus, centurion of Legio XXX Victrix. Describing in admiring terms the crucifixion at Jerusalem of a troublemaker, and now sent to the centurion's home at—Erkenbert could not read the name, but certainly something German, Bingen or Zobingen maybe.

Erkenbert pulled at his lower lip. A forgery? The letter had clearly been copied several times, but that was natural over the centuries. If the copier had been concerned to stress its importance, would he have made such a shabby copy, with such inferior penmanship? As for the tale itself, Erkenbert had no doubt that a centurion in Jerusalem in the Year of Our Lord 33 might well have been from the Rhineland. Or from England for that matter. Had the great Constantine, who had made Christianity the religion of the Empire, not himself been proclaimed Emperor on the very site of Erkenbert's own Minster at York?

The critical text was the third, a modern work, written no more than thirty years before, or so Erkenbert judged from its style. It was an account of the life and the death of the great Emperor Charlemagne, whose degenerate descendants, in Archbishop Gunther's view, now incompetently ruled the West. Much of it was familiar to Erkenbert already—the Emperor's campaigns, his fostering of learning. As Erkenbert never for a moment forgot, Charlemagne had called Alcuin, another man of York, another humble deacon like himself, from the English minster to control the destiny and the scholarship of the whole of Europe. Alcuin had been a man of great learning, true. But in literature, not in the practical arts. He was not an *arithmeticus,* as Erkenbert was. There was nothing to say an *arithmeticus* might not be as great a man as a poet.

But in this Charlemagne chronicle there was something Erkenbert had indeed never heard, till Rimbert had told them all of it. Not how the Emperor died, for that was known, but the portents that announced it. Erkenbert shifted the book into full sunlight and read intently.

The emperor, aged seventy, was returning, it said, from his forty-seventh victorious campaign, against the Saxons, in full majesty and power.

But then across the evening sky a comet had flashed. *Cometa,* thought Erkenbert. What we call the long-haired star. Long hair is the sign of the sacred king. That is why Charlemagne's ancestors had the kings they deposed shorn in public. The hairy star fell. And as it fell, the chronicle asserted, the emperor's horse shied and threw him. It threw him so violently that his sword-belt was torn off. And the lance he was carrying in his left hand flew from it and landed many yards away. At the same time, at the emperor's chapel in Aachen, the word "Princeps," or "Prince," had faded from an inscription the emperor had erected for himself, and never returned. The king had died weeks later, the chronicle said, insisting to the last that these portents did not mean that God had taken his authority from him. Yet of them all the greatest was the emperor's dropping of the lance, which previously he had carried everywhere with him—for that lance, the book insisted, was the *beata lancea* itself, the Lance of the German centurion Longinus, taken from its hiding-place in Cologne by Charlemagne in youth, and never leaving his side again in all his many campaigns and victories.

He who holds this Lance, the chronicle said, sways the destiny of the world. But no scholar knows where it is, for Charlemagne's counts diced for it after his death, and revealed only to each other who had been the winner.

And according to Rimbert no man knows now, thought Erkenbert, straightening up from his books. For by his account the Holy Lance was taken by Count Reginbald to Hamburg and treasured as a relic, inlaid with gold and precious stones. But since the heathens of the North sacked Hamburg twelve years ago, it has not been seen. Stolen away by some chieftain or kinglet. Destroyed maybe.

But no. For if it is the holy relic, God would guard it. And if it was made marvelous with gold and gems, even the heathen would respect it.

Does that mean that some petty chief among the church-despoilers shall be the overlord of Europe, the new Charlemagne? Remembering Ragnar Hairy-Breeks, whom he himself had put to the serpent-pit, and his sons, Ubbi, Halvdan, Ivar the Boneless and worst of all, the Snake-eye, Erkenbert felt his spine cringe in fear.

That could not be allowed. If the relic were in the hands of the heathen, it would have to be rescued, as Rimbert had urged so passionately. Rescued and transferred to the new emperor, whoever he might be, to unite Christendom once again. But what guarantee was there that this whole story, of lance and crucifixion and German centurion, was not just a fable? A forgery?

Leaving the books, Erkenbert strolled to the window and stared out at the peaceful spring scene. He had come to the library to check the documents, and check them he had. They seemed reliable. The story they told held together. Furthermore, he realized, it was a *good* story. He wanted to believe it. And he knew why he wanted to believe it.

All his life, Erkenbert reflected, he had been in the hands of bunglers. Incompetent archbishops like Wulfhere, incompetent kings like Ella and the fool Osbert before him, stupid thanes and illiterate priestlings, in their posts only because of some kinship with the great. England was a land where all his tools had been made of straw.

It was different here, in the land of the German Prince-Archbishops. Orders were carried out. Counselors were picked for their brains and their learning. Practical matters were attended to promptly, and those who understood them appreciated. Resources were far greater. Erkenbert knew that he had come to the great Gunther's attention simply because he had recognized the high quality of the Archbishop's silver currency, and asked how it was maintained. From the new mines, they had told him, in the Harz mountains. But a man who knows how to purify silver and separate out the lead is always welcome.

Yes, thought Erkenbert. He admired these people. He wanted them to accept him. But would they? He could sense their fierce pride in their own race and language, and knew that he was to that an outsider. He was short and dark as well, and knew how much they valued strength and the fair hair they thought a mark of their origin. Could his personal destiny ever be here? He needed a sign.

The rays of the sun had been moving all afternoon steadily westwards, across the lectern and the shelf of books beside it. As Erkenbert turned from the window it shone on an open page. Gold glittered from the massive illuminated capital on it, done with fantastic art in interlaced serpent-bodies, shining with silver and ruby patterns.

That is English art, thought Erkenbert. He looked again at the great Bible whose pages he had been turning, intent only on what they said, not on their art or origin. Certainly English work, and from Northumbria at that. Not York maybe, but Wearmouth or the *scriptorium* of the great Bede at Jarrow, from the time before the Vikings came. How did it get here?

How did Christianity get here? Hamburg and Bremen were pagan towns to Charlemagne. It was brought here by the English missionaries, by the men of my own blood, by the blessed Willibrord and Wynfrith and Willebald the breaker of idols. My ancestors brought them a great gift, Erkenbert told himself with a flush of pride. The Christian religion and the learning with which to understand it. If any check me with my foreignness, I will remind them of that.

Carefully, Erkenbert replaced the precious books on their shelves and let himself out. Arno, the archbishop's counselor, sat on a bench in the square outside. He rose as he saw the little deacon emerging.

"Well, brother? Are you satisfied?"

Erkenbert smiled with total confidence and enthusiasm. "Completely satisfied, brother Arno. You may be sure that the holy Rimbert has made his first convert of alien race. I bless the day he told me of this greatest of relics."

Arno grinned down, momentary tension relieved. He had come to respect the little Englishman for his learning and his foresight. And after all —were the English not only some other kind of Saxon?

"Well, then, brother. Shall we be about God's work? The finding of the Holy Lance."

"Yes," said Erkenbert fervently. "And after that, brother, the work it was sent for. The finding of the true king, the emperor of New Rome in the West."

Shef lay stretched on his back, drifting in and out of sleep. The fleet was due to sail next morning, and from all that Brand had said about the hardships of life at sea, it was important to sleep while one could. But it had been a trying evening. Shef had been obliged to host all his captains, the ten English skippers he had with difficulty found to command his "battleships," and the forty or more Way-Vikings who skippered his conventional craft. It had needed much drinking of toasts, with both groups anxious not to be outdone.

Then, when he had got rid of them and hoped for a confidential talk with Brand, his convalescent friend had been in sour mood. He had refused to accompany Shef in the *Norfolk*, saying he preferred his own ship and crew. He had insisted that it was bad luck to sail with so many men in the fleet who did not know the *haf*-words, the elaborate taboo-language by which sailors avoided mentioning directly such unlucky things as women, cats or priests. Finding that dismissed even by Thorvin, who did intend to sail in the *Norfolk*, he had fallen back on telling depressing tales from his homeland, tales mostly of the unknown creatures of the sea, the mermaids and marbendills, men who had angered the skerry-elves and been turned into whales, eventually one of a scoffer and scorner whose boat had last been seen being drawn under water by a long arm covered in gray hair. At that, Shef had broken off the conversation. Now he lay, afraid of what his dreams would show him.

When the dream came, Shef knew immediately—for once—exactly where he was. He was in Asgarth, home of the gods, and moreover he was standing exactly outside the greatest of the halls of Asgarth, Valhalla, Othin's home of the heroes. In the distance, though still inside Asgarth, he could see a vast plain, with what looked like a confused battle taking place on it: a battle with no battle-lines, where every man struck everyone else, falling and bleeding at random.

As the day wore on, men fell and did not rise. The battle resolved itself into a string of duels between single men. The losers fell, the winners fought again. In the end only one man was left, hideously wounded, leaning on a great bloody axe. Shef heard a dim and distant cheering: Hermoth, Hermoth.

The dead began to rise, their severed limbs reuniting, the gashes in their sides healing up. They helped each other up, the men who had killed each other laughing and showing how things had gone. Slowly they formed into ranks and began to march back to the great hall, twelve abreast, a column thousands long, the figure with the great axe at their head. They marched round the building a few feet from Shef's unnoticed person, wheeled left and tramped without breaking their ranks or their stride through the double doors of the hall, now flung wide. The doors slammed. Light even in Asgarth began to fade. Sounds of revelry rose from inside.

Now up to the door came limping a poor man, roughly dressed. As Shef looked at him he knew that only in Asgarth could such a creature remain alive. His back was broken in two, so that his upper half lurched along seemingly without connection to his legs. His ribs were splayed wide, his middle crushed flat as if by the stamp of some mighty animal. Burst entrails projected from his coat.

He reached the gate of Valhalla and stared at it. A voice came from inside, one of the mighty voices Shef had often heard before: not the amused and cynical voice of his own patron—or maybe his own father—the god Rig, fomenter of skills and trickery. No, a cold and gravelly voice. This is the owner of the hall, thought Shef. This is Othin the mighty himself.

"Who sent you, mannikin?" said the voice.

Shef could not hear the low reply, but the voice could.

"Ah," it said. "Well I know his mark. There will be a place for him here among my heroes. When the time comes."

The crushed man spoke again, still inaudible.

"You?" said the mighty voice. "There is no place here for the likes of you. Who

*are you to stand in line against the Fenris-brood, when I have need of men?
Away with you. Go round the back, to my kitchen-men. Maybe my chamberlain
Thjalfi has need of another trencher-licker."*

*The crushed man turned and hobbled away, round the building in the oppo-
site direction to that from which the marching host had come. On his face, Shef
saw as he passed, was an expression of such desolate despair as he hoped never
to see again.*

That is a man for whom even death has brought no peace, he thought.
Are even the gods allowed to do such harm? What need is it that drives
them to such evil?

CHAPTER THREE

From his vantage-point in the stern of the leading ship, Shef looked back at the long, trailing line. The *Bedfordshire,* fourth ship from the van, was sagging out of line again, as she had done ever since, by trial and error, they had picked on their present formation. All ten of the English "battleships," as Ordlaf insisted on calling them, were heading due east with the south-west wind behind them and on the beam, as easy a point of sailing as could be imagined, certainly far easier than their awkward sail up the first part of the Dutch coast from the Rhine mouth with the wind almost directly behind them. Just the same the *Bedfordshire* was wallowing slowly out to sea again.

No point in shouting to the ship behind, to pass on a message mouth to mouth till it reached the *Bedfordshire*'s skipper. He knew the importance of keeping in line, he had had it shouted at him time and time again by all the other skippers in turn every time they camped for the night. There was some error in his ship's construction. For some reason or other she made more of this "leeway" that Ordlaf was always complaining about. They would get it fixed when they returned to dock. Meanwhile the *Bedfordshire* would do what she always did: wallow out to sea till she was a hundred yards out of line, and then brace her sail round and awkwardly maneuver back into place. Where the others sailed along more or less straight, her progress was a string of shallow zig-zags, like the patterns on a welded sword.

It did no harm, at least for the moment, Shef concluded. He had realized one thing, though, and realized it some days before, almost as soon as
he and the rest of the landsmen had stopped retching over the side. That
was that the reason the Vikings ruled the seas, and could descend at any
spot in the Western world regardless of the precautions and the guards of
the Christian kings, was that they were very very good at something quite
unexpectedly complex and difficult: sailing boats.

The seamen and skippers Shef had recruited from the English coastal
ports were good enough sailors in their way, but it was not the Viking way.
Fishermen almost to a man, what they were good at was coming back
alive. Like Ordlaf, if the children's bellies had to be filled, they would put
to sea in almost any weather. They had no interest, though, in getting
anywhere unless it were to another likely bank or shoal, and certainly no
interest in going anywhere fast or unexpectedly. As for the crewmen from
the inland counties, aboard to man the mules and shoot the crossbows,
every detail of life at sea was a burden to them. At least six of them had
fallen overboard already while trying to attend to their natural functions,
though it was true that they had all been recovered from the calm and
shallow sea. The main reason Shef insisted on camping every night instead
of pressing on was that he dreaded the results of trying to cook afloat.

Shef turned from the problems of the *Bedfordshire* to the low, sullen,
sandy shore slipping by to the right—or to "steerboard" as the sailors
called it, the side of the ship which had the long steering-oar mounted.
Shef unrolled the long scroll of parchment on which he was attempting,
following his earlier experience, to draw a chart of these unfamiliar lands.
The natives on the coastal islands they had passed had told him a great
deal—they were, of course, Frisians, and the Frisians felt strong kinship
both with the English to whom they were related, and to the men of the
Way, whose religion and order had been founded by their own Duke
Radbod a hundred and fifty years before. But, more important, the Frisians
of the islands were the poorest of the poor. On the desolate sandbanks on
which they lived, sometimes twenty miles long but never more than a mile
across, no hut, no flock of sheep was ever more than ten minutes from a
Viking marauder. The islanders lived with little and stood ready to abandon that any moment.

That did not mean they were not happy to strike back. Once the news
had spread up along the islands that the strange fleet was an English one,
come to fight the Vikings, men had drifted in to every camp fire, eager to
speak for a mug of ale or a good silver penny of the new coinage.

The picture they gave was clear. As one rounded the Ijsselmeer the chain of islands began, running like the coast they sheltered slightly north of east. The islands' names seemed to become more familiar as one went further along. The Texel, Vlieland, Terschelling, which they had passed three days before—Shef did not know what those names meant. But then they had passed Schiermonnikoog, and further along a string of similar names, Langeoog, Spiekeroog, and Norderney. All these were easy to understand, for -oog was just the hoarse Frisian way of saying "ey," an island, an eyot, and -koog was the familiar Norfolk "key," a sandbank.

And all these islands were just sandbanks, drifts piled up over centuries by the rivers that flowed into the sea and that continually threatened to choke themselves with silt. The first slight break in the chain had been the Ems. Further up, the twin estuaries of the Jade and the Weser, with somewhere inside them the guarded bishop's town of Bremen. Just ahead, past Wangeroog, the last of the long Frisian island-chain now slipping past to starboard, lay the greater flow of the Elbe, with on it the port and stronghold of Hamburg under its powerful archbishop. Hamburg, famously sacked by the Vikings a dozen years before, so Brand said, who had taken part, but once again recovering, the very spear-point of the Empire of Christendom leveled at Denmark and Scandinavia beyond.

There would be a time to look into Hamburg and Bremen. But not now. Now the plan was to push ahead across the estuary of the Elbe, to the spot where the coastline turned north to the North Frisian islands, to Jutland, to the South Danes. And—so some of the seamen said—to the flatlands from which the English had come in their turn, centuries before, to the sack of Britannia and the overthrow of the Rome-folk. Shef felt a slight stirring of excitement. Who was to say that up there, there might not still be Englishmen left, who could be called to the defeat of what surely must be their Danish oppressors? But it would be enough if he could reach there —reach there and return, having tried his ships and given their crews confidence.

What he really needed, Shef reflected, still staring at the markings on his map, was a chart of what lay inside the island chain, between the islands and the main shore. If they could sail along there, his ships could defy wind and weather and water-shortage, cruise along as easily as on the Ouse or the Stour at home. Lurk inside shelter to pounce out on Viking fleets.

But Ordlaf had refused flatly to take the ships inshore, and Brand had backed him utterly. Pilot water, he had repeated. Don't try it without a man born and bred there and one you can trust. Shoals, banks, currents, tides. You can wreck a ship on sand or on chesil as easily as you can on

Flamborough Head. Easier, Ordlaf had added. At least you can see Flamborough Head.

Shef wondered obstinately how much of that was the Viking contempt for English seamanship. It had grown steadily during the days of their cruise, the Viking jokes getting continually more barbed till Shef had had to restrain the crew of the *Norfolk* from manning the mule and sending a few of the loudest laughers to the bottom. Since then they had evolved their current formation: the ten battleships cruising inshore and using all their efforts to keep up a decent speed, while the forty accompanying craft —all Viking-manned, all built on the shores of the Kattegat or the Norway fjords, but all bearing the Hammer and Cross of the Way kingdoms stitched to their sails—swept their contemptuous arcs far ahead and out to sea. Though never out of sight. Always one sail remained on the horizon, keeping a keen eye on the English lubbering along behind, itself watched keenly by the sharpest eyes in Brand's small fleet a further horizon away.

They can laugh, thought Shef. And they can sail too, I admit it. But this is like the sack of York, a new kind of battle. My men don't have to be the best sailors since Noah. They just have to be at sea. If the Ragnarssons want to get past us, or any other damned pirates out of the North, they must come in range. Then we sink them. The best sailors in the world can do nothing on shattered planks.

He rolled up his scroll, thrust it in its waxed leather bag, and walked forward to pat the comforting bulk of the mule. Cwicca, now senior catapult-captain of the fleet, grinned gap-toothed at the gesture. He had won forty well-stocked acres and a young bride for his part in last year's successes, wealth literally unimaginable for one who had been a slave of the monks of Crowland, owning nothing but a bone-and-bladder bagpipe. Yet he had left it all, his silk tunic apart, for this cruise. Hard to tell whether he hoped for more riches or more marvels.

"Sail turning this way," yelled the lookout suddenly from his uncomfortable stance on the single yard fifteen feet above Shef's head. "And more behind, I can see them! All coming straight for us."

The *Norfolk* heeled instantly as the more excitable crew-members rushed over to the left side, the backboard, to see for themselves. Moments of confusion as the boatswain and his mates kicked them back. Ordlaf shinning deftly up the knotted rope that led to the yard, following the lookout's pointing finger. Sliding back down again, face tense, to report.

"It's Brand, lord. All his ships tearing along together, fast as they can go, wind on the beam. They've seen something right enough. They'll tack and be alongside—" he pointed at the sky—"when the sun's gone so far."

"Couldn't be better," said Shef. "A still morning and a long afternoon to fight in. Nowhere for the pirates to hide. Serve the men their noon-meal early." He clutched his pendant, the silver pole-ladder. "May my father send us victory. And if Othin wants heroes for Valhalla," he added, remembering his dream, "let him take them from the other side."

"Well now, what do we make of that?" asked Sigurth the Snake-eye. He spoke to his two brothers, flanking him in the prow of the *Frani Ormr*. "A fleet in front, steering to meet us, and then suddenly they all spin round and take off as if they'd heard their wives were offering it free to all comers back home."

A voice behind him, the skipper of the *Ormr*, Vestmar. "Pardon, lord. Hrani here, the lookout, he wants to say something."

Sigurth turned, looked at the young man now being thrust forward. A young man, where almost everyone else on the ship, Sigurth's fifty picked champions, was in his prime. A poor man, too, without a gleam of gold on him, and a plain bone hilt to his sword. Picked out by Vestmar and added to the crew, Sigurth remembered, for his sharp sight. Sigurth did not bother to speak, merely raised an eyebrow.

Staring into the famous snakes' eyes with their white-bordered pupils, Hrani flushed and stammered. Then collected himself, swallowed, and began. "Lord. Before they turned I got a good look at the lead ship. There was a man standing in the prow, like you are, lord, looking at us." He hesitated. "I think it was Brand. Viga-Brand."

"You've seen him before?" asked Sigurth.

The young man nodded.

"Now, think carefully. Are you sure it was him?"

Hrani hesitated again. If he were wrong—Sigurth had a fearsome reputation for vengeances, and every man in the fleet knew of his and his brothers' consuming desire. To find and kill the men responsible for the death of their mad brother Ivar, Skjef the Englishman and Viga-Brand, Brand the Killer. If the brothers were disappointed . . . Yet on the other hand to lie to them, or to hide what one saw, both were equally dangerous. Hrani considered for a moment what he had actually seen, as the leading enemy ship rose on a wave. No, he had no real doubt. The figure he had seen was too big for any other man.

"Yes, lord. In the prow of the lead ship stood Viga-Brand."

Sigurth held his gaze for a moment, then slowly stripped a gold bracelet from his own arm, handed it over. "Good news, Hrani. Take this for your sharp eyes. Now tell me one more thing. Why do you think Brand turned away?"

Another gulp as the young man hefted the weight of the bracelet, hardly able to believe his luck. Turn away? Why would anyone turn away? "Lord, he must have recognized the *Frani Ormr,* and feared to meet us. Feared to meet you," he corrected hastily.

Sigurth waved a hand in dismissal, turned back to his brothers.

"Well," he remarked. "You heard what the idiot thinks. Now what do we think?"

Halvdan stared at the waves, felt the wind on his cheek, watched the faint dots of sail on the horizon. "Scouting ahead," he observed. "Fallen back on reinforcements. Trying to lead us on."

"Lead us on to what?" asked Ubbi. "There were forty of them. That's about what we expected, of our own folk known to be—" he spat over the side "—with the Waymen."

"More Wayfolk might have sailed south," suggested Halvdan. "Their priests have been stirring them up."

"We'd have heard, if there'd been any great number of them."

"So if the reinforcements are there," concluded the Snake-eye, "they must be from England. Englishmen in ships. A new thing. And where there is a new thing . . ."

"There you find the Sigvarthsson," completed Ubbi, his teeth showing in a snarl.

"Up to something," said Sigurth. "Up to something, or he wouldn't dare to challenge us, not at sea. Look, the Waymen are tacking, turning in to the land. Well, we'll take their dare. Let's see how good their surprise is. And maybe we can surprise them too."

He turned to Vestmar, standing a careful few paces to the rear. "Vestmar, pass the word. All ships ready for battle. Reef sail, rig the oars. But don't step the masts. Leave the yards up."

Vestmar goggled for a moment. He had been at a dozen sea battles round the coasts of Britain and Denmark, Norway and Sweden and Ireland too. Masts and yards were always stepped and stowed, to decrease the top-hamper, give the ships every yard of speed under oars that they could make. In close-quarter battle there were no men free to trim sails, and no wish for anything that would block a man's sight of arrow or javelin.

He caught himself, nodded, turned back, bellowing orders to his own crew and the ships nearest to him, orders to be passed on along and back to the hundred and twenty longships cruising behind and aside. Quickly, skillfully, the Ragnarsson fleet prepared for action.

*   *   *

Shef leaned over the backboard as Brand's ship, the *Walrus,* ranged easily alongside at the end of the long turn that had brought it and the rest of the Wayman fleet back into line with his own ten.

"The Snake-eye?" he shouted.

"Yes. It's the *Frani Ormr* in the lead right enough. They outnumber us three to one. Have to fight them now. If you tried to get away they'd sail you down before the sun started to sink."

"That's what we came for," called Shef. "You know the plan?"

Brand nodded, stepped back, pulled from round his neck a long red silken scarf. Stepping to the leeward side he let it stream in the breeze.

Instantly the ships behind him lowered the sails they had half-reefed and began to surge ahead, spreading into line abreast as they did so. A volley of orders from Ordlaf and the *Norfolk* began to check her already sluggish pace, while her consorts also began to range up on her, not moving abreast, but forming a close line, so close that the prow of each battleship almost overlapped the stern of the one ahead. Steersmen watched with anxious care as the clumsy craft edged up on each other.

At a wave from Cwicca, the catapult-crews lowered their throwing bars to the deck, fixed them with the well-greased sliding bolts, began to throw their weight on to the winding-handles to bring the stout ropes to maximum torsion. "Wind both sides," called Cwicca, looking at his master. "We might get a shot either way, God be good to us. I mean Thor be good to us." He pulled his hammer-pendant out to swing free.

Slowly the Wayman fleet edged into its agreed battle-formation, like an inverted T thrusting at the enemy. In front, lined up abreast, Brand's forty ships, sails now furled and masts stepped, moving forward at easy pace under oars alone—Shef could hear the men grunting as they put their weight into the easy swell of the waves. Behind their center, in line ahead and still under sail, the ten English battleships.

As the formation took shape, Shef felt the familiar sense of relief. All battles to him, he realized, had come to feel the same. Terrible, gnawing anxiety before they started, while he thought of the hundred and one things that could go wrong with a plan—skippers not understanding, crews not moving fast enough, the enemy coming up unexpectedly, before they were ready. Then the relief, followed instantly by a desperate curiosity. Would it work? Could there be something he had forgotten?

Brand was bellowing from the stern of his ship, breaking off to point forward urgently at the Ragnarsson fleet, now a bare half-mile off and closing quickly, oars threshing. What was he shouting? Shef heard the words and realized for himself at the same moment. The enemy were coming on to battle just as predicted. But their masts were still standing, though the sails were furled.

". . . he's smelled a rat!" came the tail-end of Brand's bellow.

Smell it or no, thought Shef. The rat is in range now. Now all it has to do is bite. From his neck he pulled a long blue scarf—Godive's gift, he remembered with a pang, given him the day she had told him she would marry Alfred. He streamed it to leeward, saw the faces turning as the lookouts saw it. Not a good luck memory, he thought. He loosed his grip on the silk, let the wind carry it into the yellow turbid sea.

Sigurth Ragnarsson, standing in the prow of his ship, noted the strangely-cut sails at the rear of Brand's thin line. Noted, too, the giant figure of Brand standing directly opposite him, waving an axe in ironic salute. Up to something, he thought again. Only one way to find out what it is. With elaborate care he stripped off his long scarlet cape, turned, threw it into the bottom of the boat. At the same instant a man stationed by the mast jerked a rope. From the top of the mast, above the yard, there flew free suddenly a great banner, with on it a black raven: the Raven Banner of the sons of Ragnar, woven it was said all in one night, with magic in its weft for victory. No man had seen it fly since the death of Ivar.

As the watching fleet saw it break out, each oarsman put his back into five mighty heaves, then simultaneously tossed oars upright and hurled them clattering into the longships' wells. Over the din, they gave one short cheer and seized up shields and weapons. Each steersman swung his suddenly accelerated boat so as to close on its next neighbor, boatswains swinging grapnels so as to lash them fast. As was always the custom, the fleet would gain momentum and then drift down on its enemies lashed together, to lock prows with the opposing fleet and there fight it out with spears and swords over the half-decked forecastles, till one side or other gave way and tried—usually unsuccessfully—to break free.

Brand saw the banner fly, saw the men bracing themselves for their last sudden spurt. Even as the oars bent under the first fierce stroke, he bellowed, in a voice fit to carry over an Atlantic gale: "Back oars and turn!"

The Wayman front line, carefully rehearsed, split instantly in the center. Brand's ship and all those to seaward of it swung hard to port, starboard oars pulling madly, port oars backing water. All those to shoreward swung hard the other way. Then, as the helmsmen struggled to keep from running foul of their fellows, the oars swung again, the fast maneuverable boats leapt away.

Shef, standing by the mast of the *Norfolk,* saw Brand's ships swerve away to left and right with the unanimity of two flocks of migrating birds. With a stab of fear—not fear for himself but for his plan—he realized the Ragnarsson fleet was closer than he expected and coming on fast. If those veteran warriors laid aboard him there could be only one ending. In the same moment he felt the *Norfolk* surge forward as Ordlaf spread sail to its fullest extent. Slowly the battleship swung round to port, presenting her starboard beam to the dragon prows not a hundred yards off. Behind her, her nine consorts swung round in close line ahead. Again the *Norfolk* picked up a yard or two of speed as the wind came more directly over her stern.

Shef heard Ordlaf shouting encouragingly: "The wind's rising! We'll get round in time."

Maybe, thought Shef. But just the same, they were too close. Time to check them. He nodded to Cwicca, crouched expectantly by the release.

Cwicca hesitated for only an instant. He knew the plan was to sink the lead center ship, the one with the great gilded snake's head on its prow. But his mule was still not bearing directly on it. Impossible to train it round. Waiting a split second for the heel of the waves, he jerked free the release bolt.

A flash of motion, a violent thud against the padded beam, a thud that shook the whole ship and seemed for an instant to check her way. The black streak that was a thirty-pound boulder lashing across the water. A streak that ended just behind the prow of the ship immediately to port of the *Frani Ormr.*

For a second or two the advancing line of ships seemed to roll on as if nothing had happened, sending Shef's heart leaping into his mouth. Then tiredly, irresistibly, the ship fell apart. The flying rock had smashed the stem-post to matchwood. The planks carefully fitted into it sprang from their notches. Below the waterline the sea rushed in, forced on by the ship's own motion. As it shot through the well the sinews holding planks to ribs and ribs to keel sprang apart. The mast, its keelson pulled from under it, swayed forward, held for an instant by its stays, then swung wearily to one side. Like a giant's club it scythed through the gaping crew of the ship next alongside.

To the watchers in the English line it seemed as if the ship had suddenly vanished, been pulled under by one of the water-hags of Brand's stories. For a moment or two they could see men apparently standing on the water, then fighting for their footing on loose planks, then down in the sea, or struggling for a hand-hold on the gunwales of the ships alongside.

And then the *Suffolk* too brought her mule to bear. Another streak flashed into the heart of the Ragnarsson fleet. And another as the third ship in line swung round.

Suddenly, as Shef gaped, noise seemed to be added to the battle. All at once he was aware of the snap of the crossbows, the song of the rope as Cwicca's handlers frantically wound their machine, the crash of rock on wood and waves of cheering as Brand's ships swung round to come in on the Ragnarsson flanks. At the same time Shef felt a sudden lash of rain and the ships opposite blurred for a moment. A rain shower passing over the sea. Would it soak the ropes and at this worst moment take his artillery out of action?

Out of the blur came three dragon prows, shockingly close. Not the snake's head of the enemy flagship, now a hundred yards behind them, but some other alert enemy skipper, who had cast his grapnels free and re-manned his oars, realizing his foe had no intention of closing to fight fair. If they managed to lay alongside . . .

Cwicca raised a thumb. Shef nodded. The bone-jarring thud again, the streak of movement that ended this time almost before it had begun, at the very base of the center ship's mast. Again, suddenly, no ship, just a flurry of planks and men gasping in the water.

The other two were still coming on, only yards away now, men in each prow with grapnels swinging, fierce bearded faces staring over their shields, a simultaneous deep grunt as the oarsmen took one last stroke to drive themselves over the gap.

A storm of cheering almost in Shef's ear and a great bulk like a whale shouldering past only feet in front of the *Norfolk's* bow. One of Brand's ships driving in under oars to intercept. Its prow swept along the starboard side of the Ragnarsson ship at a closing speed of twenty miles an hour, snapping the oars, hurling their butt-ends back to cave in the ribs and shatter the spines of the rowers. As the two ships ground past each other Shef saw the Wayman rowers rising from their benches to pour a storm of javelins over the side at point-blank range. The third Ragnarsson ship saw the carnage, swung away past the Norfolk's stern, picking up speed for the open sea.

Shef caught Ordlaf by the shoulder, pointed across a half-mile of sea filled with shattered ships, drowning men, and desperate combats of single ships and groups. Through the showers of rain and spray picked up by the rising wind he could see the Raven banner still flying. But already turned and moving east. The *Frani Ormr,* masterfully handled, had swerved its way unscathed through the English line, swung about and was already in full flight. As the two men watched her sail swept down from the yard, bellied out, and began to glide easily to safety.

"Follow," said Shef.

"She sails two yards to our one."

"Cut her off from the open sea while you have a chance. Drive her inshore."

"But that's the Elber Gat," protested Ordlaf.

Shef's fingers tightened commandingly on his shoulder.

CHAPTER FOUR

Sigurth Ragnarsson stared thoughtfully over his ship's port quarter. Significantly, he had not picked up his long scarlet cape, but had left his arms free for action. He braced himself against the *Ormr*'s heel on a long spear, iron-shafted, with a heavy triangular head. His brothers stood with their backs to him, also seeming relaxed but with weapons drawn. Discipline was savage in the Ragnarsson fleet. But the men in it were savage too, and these were picked veterans. They had no liking for turning from a battle, were already imagining what men might say about them later. Wondering if the Snake-eye had gone soft.

No point in trying to explain. Just keep them wondering a little while longer.

"What do you make of our friend behind?" said Sigurth to Vestmar, indicating the *Norfolk* laboring a long mile in their rear.

"It's a clumsy rig, but he can sail it," replied Vestmar briefly. "One thing, though. He doesn't know his way. See the lookout on the yard, and the skipper leaning over the prow looking for shoal water?"

"Plenty of that around," said Sigurth. He turned to look inland. A coast nearly featureless. The two small islands of Neuwark and the Scharhorn already passed. The silty current of the Elbe stirring beneath the keel, and then nothing till the base of Jutland and the fought-over lands between Denmark and the Empire of the Germans.

"All right. Strike sail. Get the men to the oars. And get someone in the bow with a lead-line."

Vestmar gaped, almost voicing a protest. A lead-line, he thought. But I know the Elber Gat like I know my wife's backside. And if we strike sail those bastards back there will be hurling their *iötunn*-rocks at us while we break our backs to get away. He swallowed the words and turned on his heel, calling hoarsely.

"We're gaining on them," called Shef. "Cwicca, stand by the mule!"

Ordlaf did not reply. He looked tensely at the sky, looked again at the ship they were pursuing, took the lead which his crewman in the bow had passed to him. Sniffed the mud sticking still to the wax at the end of the lead cylinder on the five-fathom rope. Stuck a tongue out, tasted it.

"What are you doing that for?"

"Don't know," muttered Ordlaf. "Sometimes you can tell if there's shell-fish, what kind of sand it is . . . If there's a shoal coming up."

"Look," snarled Shef. "He doesn't know where he is either, he's had a man in the bow swinging the lead this last two miles, just like you. Keep behind him, and if he doesn't run aground you won't."

Not as easy as that, young lord, thought Ordlaf, not as easy as that. There's other things, like the current—see him sliding through it like a snake while it grips our keel. And the wind, and these blasted squalls of rain coming down. And the tide. Is it still making? Now if I was at home in Yorkshire I'd feel it in my bones when we got to the full. But here in foreign parts who's to know when it turns? Can't be far off.

"Another quarter-mile and we're close enough for a shot," called Shef. "Get the oars out bow and stern. Just leave space clear round the mule."

As the grinning men heaved awkwardly in the short chop of the waves, the *Norfolk* picked up another trifle of speed, began visibly to close on the long dragon-shape ahead. Shef stared, estimating range and bearing.

"Right, that'll do. Take a good aim, Cwicca. Ordlaf, swing her to the right, no, to starboard, so we can shoot."

As the *Norfolk* swung to the steering-oar, the sail canted round. Yells of rage from Cwicca as its lower edge blocked his view. A scurry of sailors hastily heaving the ropes to brail up. Ordlaf cursing furiously as the oarsmen faltered in their stroke and the prow swung further, steadied, lurched back. As the sail finally jerked up out of their way Shef and Cwicca gaped for a moment, wondering where their quarry had gone.

"There!" In the instants of confusion the *Frani Ormr* had jinked like a hare, spun to port, and was now directly stern on to them, moving away at a frantic speed, oars flashing like the last moments of a race.

"Too far for a shot now," yelled Cwicca into Shef's ear, beside himself with excitement.

"They can't keep that up for long. Ordlaf, take us in after her."

Ordlaf hesitated, eying the long ripples of shoal water either side of the fleeing Viking. Shoal water half a mile wide between two long banks just showing. Beyond that, a waste of unknown banks and channels leading for miles to the featureless German shore.

The memory of the other skipper's lead-line reassured him. Dangerous water, but he doesn't know it either. If anyone strikes, he'll strike first. The *Norfolk* heeled round, bringing the wind on to her other beam, spread sail again and headed for the narrow channel in her enemy's wake.

That'll do, thought Sigurth, feeling the faintest grate of sand under his keel. We're through, at the very top of the tide. He caught a glint of relief in Vestmar's eyes as well, hastily dropped. One of the rowers blew out his cheeks and, greatly daring, raised an eyebrow at the helmsman. They had felt the pull of the sand under their blades these last minutes, had rowed shallow automatically like the seamen they were. Now they could feel the water deepening again. Maybe the Snake-eye had not lost all his luck. Maybe . . .

Behind them Sigurth could see the English ship still coming on, the hammer and cross half-visible on her sail. And behind her a squall blowing across the flat open estuary, a squall that would catch up with her . . . Now.

As the rain drummed down with sudden April fury Ordlaf peered tensely over the bow. The leadsman's voice in his ear rose to a shriek: "Two fathom now, skipper, two fathom and I can see the shoal!"

"In oars," bellowed Ordlaf in the same moment, "furl sail, stand by to back off."

Too late. As he shouted, one of the oarsmen, swinging stoutly but unskillfully, felt his oar turn under him, twist and throw him bodily off his bench, half over the side. Jammed in the sand, the stout ash wood held the weight of the driving ship for an instant, dragged her over, snapped into splinters. As the ship heeled, more oars caught, throwing the rowers this way and that. The last gust of the squall caught the sail, drove the keel on to the crest of a wave. Dropped her with a grinding thud on the sand. For seconds there was total confusion as Ordlaf and his mates, yelling fren-

ziedly, kicked men out of their way, heaved ropes, seized oars, tried first to
boom the ship off the bank on to which she had run, then to prop her at
least on an even keel. Slowly the noise died, the landsmen, their king
included, huddled nervously in the center of the boat. Shef found himself
facing a pair of reproachful eyes.

"We didn't ought to have done it. Run aground right on top of the tide.
Look—" Ordlaf pointed over the gunwale at the sandbanks already appearing to either side, as the sea started its long six-hour ebb.

"Are we in any danger?" asked Shef, remembering the way Ragnar's two
knorrs had run aground and gone to pieces before both of them two long
springs before.

"No, not danger of breaking up. It's soft sand, and we hit fairly slow. But
they took us in proper." Ordlaf shook his head with rueful admiration. "I
bet that skipper there knew where he was to the inch. Swinging away with
that old lead-line, and just drawing us on. And now a mile off and making
his way back to sea."

Shef looked round sharply, suddenly conscious of what might happen if
the Snake-eye and his picked crew came wading across the shallows. But
they were nowhere to be seen. He stepped to the prow and looked slowly
and carefully right round the flat gray horizon, looking for the mast, the
Raven banner that had been flying in front of them not ten minutes before.
Nothing to be seen. In some inlet or creek the *Frani Ormr* was lurking like
a poison snake, waiting for the tide and clear passage out. Shef sighed
deeply, tension released, and turned back to Ordlaf and the silent crew.

"Can we get off before nightfall?"

Ordlaf shrugged. "We can try and kedge her off. Keep everyone busy."

Hours later, the mood round the stranded ship had lightened, lifted by
hard work, sweat and a growing feeling that at least the battle had been
won, even if some of the enemy had got away.

The dropping tide—fifteen feet of drop in these parts—had revealed to
everyone what the *Norfolk* had done. She lay now half a mile from the
main Elbe channel, in a shallow valley between two long sandbanks, with
runnels and streamlets stretching in all directions through the rounded
hillocks of the shoals, broken here and there only by planks and ribs from
long-forgotten wrecks. At first Ordlaf had had the crew over the side,
digging round and under the keel with the intention of dragging the boat
bodily backward the way she had come. As the tide fell and the distance to
the main channel became clear, they had abandoned that idea. Not more
than sixty or seventy feet ahead there lay another deep-water channel, still
ten feet or more deep even with the tide almost out. Clearly the Ragnars-

son skipper had reached it, knowing well it was there, and then swung right or left while his enemy's attention was distracted. Inland towards Hamburg and the main channel, or out to sea by some unknown route, it made no difference now. Now the business of the *Norfolk*'s crew was to drag their ship the few feet needed to get her over the almost imperceptible crest of the shoal, and then down and into deep water. Already they had dug the sand away in front of her so that her bows now pointed definitely if gently down. But to shift her before the night-time tide, they needed a purchase.

Ordlaf had rigged one rope already, fixed at one end to the ship's anchor firmly planted in hard sand, passed round the base of the mast, and then handed to thirty men hauling together. The ship had stirred, groaned. Remained motionless.

"We need another rope," said Ordlaf. "With a straighter pull if we can get it, and room for the rest of the lads to heave. Best if we could fix it over there." He pointed to the sandbank the other side of the channel in front of them, maybe thirty yards wide.

"Have you got one long enough?" asked Shef.

"Yes. And we've fixed up another anchor out of halberd-heads. We just got to get it over there."

Shef heard a silent appeal. The *Norfolk,* big as she was in comparison with other vessels of her day, was far too small to carry even a dinghy in the cramped space that had to hold everything, crew and provisions. She had instead a tiny craft made of skin over a pole frame, more a coracle than a canoe, hard to steer and easy to capsize. Ordlaf or any of his Norfolk fishermen could handle it, but they were busy at skilled tasks. Any of the landsmen who made up the rowers and mule-team would certainly capsize it and drown.

Shef sighed. An hour before he had drawn out the last of the ship's scanty, daily-renewed store of firewood, and told Cwicca to light a fire on the sand, rig the ship's great iron kettle, and make what he could out of the hard rations: flour, salt fish and barley meal. To a hungry man the smell beginning to rise from the kettle was tempting. He looked at the sun already sinking down the sky, considered a night spent struggling in rising water, and gave in.

"All right. I suppose I was a fenman before they made me a jarl or a king. I'll do it."

"Can you handle it?"

"Watch me. If I didn't have the anchor to carry I could swim over in a dozen strokes anyway."

Ordlaf's boatswain loaded the anchor carefully in the bottom of the coracle, keeping sharp edges away from the hide, made certain the rope attached ran freely. Shef looked again at the kettle, calculated the distance and the chances of an upset, and removed the gold circle he wore as a sign of rank. He handed it to Hwithelm, a handsome youth of noble family and impenetrable stupidity who had been forced upon him as his ceremonial swordbearer, and who was already carrying his swordbelt.

"Hold that till I come back."

Hwithelm frowned at the casualness of the gesture, but slowly accepted its sense. "And your bracelets, lord?"

Shef thought for a moment, then slowly pushed the gold bracelet he wore on each bicep down and over his wrists, passed them to Hwithelm. They were unlikely to fall off, but if the coracle tipped over, as was likely enough, who knew what might happen?

He strolled to the edge of the channel, settled himself in the coracle, accepted the paddle, and shoved off. A difficult craft to steer with only one paddle and an awkward weight in it that brought the sea to within three inches of the gunwale. The trick lay in a twist of the paddle to straighten her up with every stroke. Cautiously Shef navigated across, tormented all the while by the smell of food, splashed ashore, dug the anchor in to cries of direction from Ordlaf. Then, with more haste as he heard the sounds of pottery bowls being served out, scrambled back in for the return crossing.

The rope was stretched across the channel. Easier than paddling was to sit with his back to the ship and haul himself along the rope, hand over hand.

Slowly Shef realized that the shouting from the ship had changed its tone, become urgent, frantic. He turned to the left, as he always did with his one eye, to see what was happening. Nothing visible, but Ordlaf with a look of horror on his face gesturing and pointing. Pointing to the right.

Shef swung hastily the other way, almost overturning the coracle with the jerk. For a moment all he could see was a black bulk throwing white water, almost on top of him. Then his mind took in what it saw.

The *Frani Ormr* bearing down on top of him, oars flashing, bow-wave curling to either side of the narrow channel. With mast stepped and snake-prow and dragon-tail removed she had lain concealed, no higher than a war-canoe, behind some nameless and invisible bank, watching her opportunity. Now she had seen it and was coming down as if to ram and trample her frail enemy under. In the same instant that he recognized the boat Shef saw a·scarlet-caped warrior leaning over the prow, a mighty spear balanced in his hand. His teeth showed in a grimace of hate and concentration. In that instant Shef knew that there was no chance such a man would miss his throw. The arm went back, the spear poised.

Shef hurled himself instantly over the side, down into the water, plunging desperately for depth. A great surge in the water pressed him further down till he felt the sand grate on his chest, for a moment he felt as if he would be caught between keel and sea-bottom, he scrabbled furiously up and away. Something struck him a glancing blow on the side of the head, an oar digging deep, and he dived again. Then his lungs would bear no more, he had to surface and breathe, but the surface was not there, he fought his way up with frantic strokes . . .

Shef shot gasping into the air a few yards behind the *Ormr*'s stern, stared wildly round him, struck out for the nearest shore. Found himself back on the sandbank where he had sunk the anchor. On the opposite bank someone had turned over the kettle, swords and halberds were being thrown to men clustered round their ship, a line of helmets showed over its gunwale as the dozen crossbowmen wound their weapons. Ordlaf was shouting directions, preparing to fight off an assault over the sand. No chance of bringing the mule to bear as the *Norfolk* lay, bows on to the channel and in any case tilted half over on one side.

The *Frani Ormr* was turning in her own length in the narrow channel, port oars pulling, starboard reversing. Turning not towards the *Norfolk*, but towards Shef, standing isolated on the wrong side of the deep water. Shef contemplated a plunge and a dozen strokes back to his friends, hesitated, imagining the harpoon plunging into his back as he swam. Too late. The prowless *Ormr* was stroking steadily towards him, a handful of men clustered by the side watching him intently.

Shef backed away, further up the sandbank, out of easy javelin range, wondering what came now. He was weaponless and alone. A cry and the oars stopped their beat, remained jutting out from the rowlocks. A man stepped over the side, on to one, walked down it in sailor's goat-skin shoes, jumped the last feet on to the hard sand. A young man, Shef saw watching warily a dozen yards away. But tall and strong, with a gold bracelet round one biceps.

A rush of air overhead, and another. Crossbow bolts from the *Norfolk*, trying to help. But a long carry from stranded ship to channel and then across the channel, and the bulk of the *Ormr* in the way. Shef backed further as the young man drew his sword. Three more men stepped on to oars and made their way towards him. Shef, sparing just one glance from his nearest enemy, recognized all three: Halvdan Ragnarsson, who had umpired his holmgang at York, Ubbi Ragnarsson the grizzled, and between

them Sigurth, who had taken Shef's eye at Bedricsward. As if remembering, Shef's empty eye-socket suddenly gushed salt water. The Ragnarssons
held axe, sword and spear. All three wore mail. The young man closest to
Shef did not.

Shef turned and began to run down the sandbank. It took him away
from the *Norfolk*, but that could not be helped. If he stayed where he was,
they would kill him, if he ran across the bank he would be floundering in
water again in a few strides. Mistake, he realized an instant later. He was
running the same way as the *Ormr* was facing, and she was keeping easy
pace with him on his right, shielding his pursuers from the crossbows and
with men ready for a shot with bow or javelin. He veered to the left,
hearing feet pounding on the sand behind him. The bank came to an end.
He hurled himself straight out into the water in a flat dive, took three,
four, powerful strokes, felt the sand under his belly again and scrambled to
his feet once more.

A dozen strides and he risked a look over his shoulder. The young man
had hesitated on the edge of the water, but was splashing through it, no
more than waist-deep. The Ragnarssons were behind, older men and
weighed down by their mail, but spreading out to cross the little channel
yards apart and cut off any break back. In front of him, and on both sides,
there lay nothing but a confusion of rounded banks, with pools and shallow runnels draining to the main channels. Every now and then one of the
runnels was a deep one. That was where they might catch him, still swimming as Sigurth aimed his spear or the young man caught his heel. But if
he got enough of a lead he could swim one of them and get away. Men in
mail would not be anxious to try a deep channel, and would lose sight of
him if they did.

Shef turned as the young man reached shore, and ran again. Ran just a
little slower than his best, swerving and glancing over his shoulder every
dozen yards, as if terrified. Fifty yards and splash through a shallow pool.
Fifty more and round a steeper bank. The *Ormr* a furlong away now and
powerless to intervene, the Ragnarssons spread out and calling to each
other to keep him in sight. The tall young man's panting easy to hear as he
closed the gap, raising his sword every few strides as if hoping to strike.

Vikings were poor runners, Shef remembered grimly. He swerved
through another knee-deep rivulet, leapt up the other side on to firm sand,
and swung round.

The young man paused in the water, then grinned exultantly and leapt
forward, sword up for a forehand cut. Shef sprang inside the blow, both
hands grabbing the right wrist, and backheeled his enemy's legs from

under him. Both went down with a thud on the sand, the sword bouncing away.

No time to grab it, and too risky to grapple. All the Viking had to do was hold him till the Ragnarssons got there. Shef stepped back, arms spread in the wrestler's stance. The young man faced him, still panting, still grinning.

"My name is Hrani," he said. "I am the best wrestler in Ebeltoft."

He closed, reaching out for a collar-and-elbow grip. Shef ducked and snatched for the knife at Hrani's belt. As Hrani dropped a hand to cover it, he straightened up, swinging his left arm backhand under Hrani's neck and thrusting a hip behind him. Off balance, the tall man fell backwards. On to a knee braced to catch his spine. In the same instant Shef heaved down with both arms and all the smithy-trained strength in his body.

A snap of spine, and Hrani looking upwards with terror in his eyes. Still holding him over one knee, Shef patted his cheek gently.

"You are still the best wrestler in Ebeltoft," he said. "It was a foul throw."

He pulled the knife from Hrani's belt and stabbed upwards, deep under the ribcage. Rolled the body aside and straightened, retrieving the sword with its plain bone handle.

A deeper channel just a few yards away. Shef trotted to it, hurled the sword thirty feet to the other side, plunged in and stroked swiftly across. Turned and stood on the shore to face the Ragnarssons, trotting up together, breathing hard. He ducked his head for a moment to let his empty eye drain, then looked across and met the Snake-eye's gaze.

"Come over," he called. "There are three of you, all great warriors. So was your brother Ivar. I killed him in the water too."

Halvdan strode into the water, sword raised. His brother Ubbi caught him by the shoulder.

"He would cut you down before you had your feet under you."

Shef grinned, deliberately exaggerating it, hoping to provoke a charge. If one man came across, he would try to kill him while the water still hampered his movements. If two or three crossed together, he would run again, confident that if nothing else he could outdistance them. He had the initiative now. This was a puzzle they had to solve. For they did not know he had made up his mind to run. If they all crossed together, the odds were that they would kill him, but he would get at least one blow in first. They might think, seeing the body of their henchman, that he was full of the fighting madness and would take their dare.

Without warning or backlift Sigurth's javelin came darting at his belly, launched without as much as a flicker of expression. Shef saw the flash, leapt with the reactions of youth into the air, kicking his legs wide. The shaft tapped him agonizingly in the groin as it flew through. Shef landed in a crouch on the sand, bit his lip to conceal the pain.

"At least your brother Ivar fought fair, standing on the same plank as I did," he called. "Did anyone tell you how he died?" His testicles crushed in my grasp, he thought, and his face cut to ribbons where I butted him with the edge of my helmet. I hope that was not the story they heard. For if he fought fair I certainly did not.

The Snake-eye turned away, not even bothering to draw his sword. He muttered something to his brothers and they turned too, stepping back towards the body of Hrani. Shef saw Sigurth stoop and retrieve the gold bracelet from Hrani's arm. Then the three began to make their way together back to their ship. They had not taken the dare.

Sigurth is a clever man, thought Shef. He turned and fled from the sea-battle rather than fight according to my plan. Now he has done the same again. I must remember, that does not mean that he has given up.

He looked round, assessing his own situation.

He was cut off from the *Norfolk*. It might or might not be attacked by Sigurth and his crew, might or might not win the duel. But in any case he did not dare to try to rejoin it. Impossible to say what ambushes Sigurth might lay in the sandbanks. He would have to go the other way, towards the unknown shore, across maybe a quarter-mile yet of sandbanks.

He had the clothes he stood up in, a flint and steel tied to his belt, and a poorly made iron sword with a bone handle. His stomach reminded him that he had not eaten since the noon-meal. He was already starting to shiver uncontrollably in his soaked woolen breeches and tunic. The salt water was irritating his empty eye, so that by some freak the other one wept continually. The sun was a bare hand's breadth above the flat horizon. And he could not stay where he was. The tide was rising. Soon he would be faced with a long swim rather than a walk.

He felt less of a king than ever. But then, he told himself, he had never felt truly a king at all. At least now that he was a man he had no master or stepfather to beat him.

Turning towards the German shore on the north bank of the Elbe, he thought to pick up the javelin Sigurth had hurled at him. A fine weapon, as was to be expected, iron-shafted for a foot below its long triangular head. The head itself of excellent steel, without marks of use. No silver inlay or decoration. The Snake-eye, sensible man, wasted no money on what he meant to throw at his enemies. Yet there were marks on the steel, runes. Tutored carefully by Thorvin, Shef managed to read them: "Gungnir," they said.

So, the Snake-eye thought it no desecration to imitate Othin himself. It was no heirloom or ancient weapon. Shef's smithcraft told him that this was new-forged. Thoughtfully, Shef sloped the spear over one shoulder, tucked Hrani's sword into his belt, and set out wearily and cautiously for the north bank of the Elbe across its guardian sands, just visible in the twilight.

Far to the north of the sandbanks of the Elbe, north even of the Ragnarssons' stronghold in Danish Sjaelland, the great college of the Way in far-off Kaupang lay still under deep snow on the Norwegian shore. Thick ice bridged the fjords from one bank to the other. Men out in the open moved hurriedly to the next place of shelter.

Yet between the rapid shapes of skiers one figure came to a halt, stood motionless in the snow: Vigleik of the many visions, most respected of the priests of the Way. Where he stood, birds began to flutter out of the sky, land around him, forming a circle. As the flock grew thicker, men pointed, called others to watch. Slowly a circle of men, priests and their apprentices and servants, formed outside the ring of birds, keeping a decorous fifty yards away.

One of the birds, a small redbreast, flew up from the throng, perched on Vigleik's shoulder, twittered loud and long. Vigleik stood unmoving in the snow, his head cocked as if paying attention. Finally he nodded courteously, and the bird flew off.

A second bird came, sat on his gloved hand where it clutched the pole of his skis. This time it was a tiny wren, its tail cocked up like a rider's spur. It too sang a long song, and waited. "Thank you, sister," the watching priests heard Vigleik say.

Then all the birds flew hastily up and off to safety in the branches. The newcomer was a great black crow, which did not sit by Vigleik but paced up and down in front of him, calling from time to time in harsh and challenging caws. It sounded as if it were jeering. Still Vigleik stood silent. In the end the bird lifted its tail, squirted a stream of droppings on to the grass, and in its turn flew off.

After a while Vigleik raised his eyes and stared into the far distance. When he dropped them, his face had changed back to its normal expression. Knowing the vision had passed from him, his colleagues ventured to approach. In the lead was Valgrim, admitted head of the College, and priest of Othin All-Father—there were few who cared to take such responsibility.

"What news, brother?" he said at last.

"News of the death of tyrants. And worse news. My brother the redbreast told me that Pope Nikulaus is dead in Rome-burg, smothered under a pillow by his own servants. He paid the price not for sending his men against us, but for losing."

Valgrim nodded his head, a smile of pleasure creasing his beard.

"My sister the wren told me that in Frankland King Karl the Bald is also dead. One of his counts told the story of how Karl's ancestors had the long-haired kings shaven to show that they were kings no more, and said that God had sent baldness to Karl to show he should never have been king. When Karl told men to lay hands on the count, the other counts rose and slew him instead."

Valgrim smiled again. "And the crow?" he prompted finally.

"That was the worse news. He told me there is a tyrant still living, though close to death today, Sigurth Ragnarsson."

"Tyrant he may be," said Valgrim. "Yet he is the favorite of Othin for all that. If the Way could win him to its side, it would gain a mighty champion."

"That may be too," said Vigleik. "Yet his creature the crow treats us as his enemies, the murderers of his brother. It threatened me, threatened all of us, with his vengeance. And yet the crow was not telling all the truth, I know. He was keeping something back."

"What?"

Vigleik shook his head slowly. "That is still hidden from me. Yet for all you say, Valgrim, I do not think the road to victory at Ragnarök lies through the likes of Sigurth Ragnarsson, with his sacrifices and his cruelty. It is not great champions alone that will overcome Loki and the Fenrisbrood. Nor is it blood that will bring Balder back from the dead. Not blood, but tears."

Valgrim's face flushed even in the cold at the challenge to his authority, and the mention of unlucky names and deeds. Controlling himself, he asked finally, "And at the end, when you seemed to look far away?"

"Then I saw eagles in the distance. First one mounted above the other, and then the lower one flew higher again. I could not see which would win in the end."

CHAPTER FIVE

Erkenbert the deacon sat in the sunlight behind a stout table, ink and parchment in front of him. It had been a long day's work, almost over now. But a deeply satisfying one. Erkenbert felt confidence, respect, almost awe creeping over him as he shuffled the thick pile of parchment sheets, filled with row after row of names: each one an application to join the ranks of the new Order which the archbishops of the West had proclaimed: the Order of the Lance, or in their tongue the *Lanzenorden*.

During their slow journey north from Cologne to Hamburg, Erkenbert had realized that there were special factors favoring the establishment of an order of warrior-monks here, in the German lands. In his native Northumbria, as indeed over the whole of family-conscious England, the thanes who formed the backbone of any army were good at one thing alone: establishing themselves comfortably on the estates granted them by the king. And then moving heaven and earth to see that not only did they hold on to them, however old, fat or unfitted for military service they became, but also that the estates were passed on in due form to their children. Sometimes they sent sons to perform service for them, sometimes they worked their way into royal or monastic favor by enforcing the king's dooms, or the abbot's, and witnessing any charter that needed a voice to swear one way or the other. However they did it, even if they had to send their daughters to tempt some magnate's lust, it was rare in England to find a parcel of land without some noble's son who thought he had a claim on it, or a noble's son who would prove in the end to be disappointed.

Not so in Germany. The warrior-class there had not been allowed to settle in and make itself comfortable. Service had to be performed. If it was not, a better replacement was found immediately. A middle-aged warrior had better have seen to his own security by the time his sword-arm stiffened, for his lord would feel no obligation to do it for him. As for the sons of warriors, there were many with little prospects, no assured future. In a sense, thought Erkenbert very quietly to himself, for all their concern with noble blood, they were more like peasants or churls than nobles, for they might be dispossessed at any moment. To such men, warlike though they were, to be allowed to enroll in an Order which would provide them a home and comradeship till the day they died, as if they were black monks, might well have unexpected appeal.

Yet he and his colleagues would not have had so much success in recruiting their serf-soldiers if it had not been for the oratory of Archbishop Rimbert. A dozen times as they made their way north from Cologne to Hamburg, Erkenbert had heard him call together the masses in whichever town they had chosen for their halt, and had heard him preach.

Always he took as his text the words of Saint Mark, "I will send you forth as sheep in the midst of wolves." He reminded his hearers how Jesus had forbidden Saint Peter to resist the soldiers when they came for him in the garden of Gethsemane, how he had urged his disciples to turn the other cheek, and if a man compelled them to go with him one mile, to go with him voluntarily for two. He would pursue the theme till he saw the looks of doubt, or disgust, on the faces of his warlike listeners.

And then he would say to them that what Jesus said was no doubt true. But what if a man compelled you to carry his pack for a mile, and you carried it from good will for two—and then instead of thanking you, he cursed you and told you to carry it another two, another ten, another twenty? What if you turned the other cheek and your enemy struck it again, and again, using his heaviest dogwhip? As his listeners stirred and muttered angrily, he would ask them why they felt anger. For were these things that he put to them not far less, not a hundred times less, than the insults and injuries they had had to endure from the pagans of the North? And then he talked to them of what he, Rimbert, had seen in his many years as the apostle to the North: daughters and wives ravished, men taken away and left to die in slavery, Christians on their knees in the snow, wailing as they waited to be sacrificed to the heathen gods at Odense or Kaupang or, worst of all, Swedish Uppsala. Wherever he could, he would tell each particular audience of what had happened to men or women from that town or that district—he seemed to have an inexhaustible stock of heart-rending stories, as who would not, Erkenbert reflected, if he had spent thirty years on the pointless and hopeless task of preaching to the heathen.

And when his audience's anger was at its height, when the serf-knights among them scowled and wrung their hands and swept off their leather caps in passion, then Rimbert would tell them his text: "I will send you forth as sheep in the midst of wolves. Yes," he would say, "the good priests of my missions, not one in ten of whom ever returns to his home, they have been sheep—and sheep they will remain. But from now on—and as he said this, his voice would rise to an iron clangor—when I send out my sheep, I will see that with each sheep there goes, not another sheep, not a wolf, no. But a great dog, a great mastiff of the German breed, with a good spiked collar round his neck, and twenty other wolfhounds running with him. Then we will see how the wolves of the North listen to the sheep's preaching! Maybe they will listen closely to his bleat in the future."

And Rimbert would condescend to joke and play with words, sometimes even imitating the noise of a sheep to set his audience laughing uproariously in the relief of its tension and anger. And then Rimbert would tell them, slowly and quietly, of his plan. To send mission after mission into the North, through the friendlier of the chiefs and kings of the heathen, each mission centered on a learned and pious priest, as had always been the custom, but each mission containing also a new and strong bodyguard for that priest: men of noble birth and knightly station, men without wives or children or ties, men expert with sword and lance and mace, men who could ride a war-stallion with shield on one arm and lance in the other, controlling it with knees and fingertips alone—men whom even the pirates of the North would walk carefully around, fearing to antagonize them.

And then, when he had their full attention, Rimbert would tell them of the Holy Lance, and of how, when it came back to the Empire, the spirit of Charlemagne would come again and lead Christendom once more to triumph over all its enemies. And he would invite suitable applicants to present themselves to his servants, to see if they were worthy of a place in the *Lanzenorden*.

Which was why Erkenbert now had the thick piles of parchment in his hand, covered with row after row of names: the applicants' names, their claims to noble birth—for no peasants or peasants' sons would be admitted under any circumstances—the lists of the worldly wealth they could bring to the order, and the details of their personal arms and equipment. In due course some names would be crossed out, some would be accepted. Most would be crossed out. And most of those not for failure in wealth or nobility, but because they could not pass the tests devised for them by the archbishop's *Waffenmeister,* his master-at-arms. Which, as Erkenbert ceased his writing, were going on in this place or that all over the wide exercise field outside the wooden stockade of much-sacked Hamburg. Men cutting at each other with blunted sword and shield. Men riding horses along a complex course of jumps and figures to strike down with a lance. Men grappling with each other, hand to hand, in the ring. And everywhere the grizzled *Waffenmeister* or the sergeants of his staff, noting, comparing, repeating names.

Erkenbert looked across at Arno, the counselor of Gunther, sent along with Erkenbert into Rimbert's archdiocese to watch, assist and report. They grinned at each other with the curious fellow-feeling that had grown between them, the small dark one and the tall fair one, each recognizing the other's delight in efficiency, in the exercise of pure intelligence.

"The Archbishop will get his first hundred easily," offered Erkenbert.

Before Arno could reply, another voice cut in. "He will only need ninety-nine now," it said.

Deacon and priest stared up from their stools at the newcomer.

He was not a tall man, Erkenbert noted, ever sensitive on this point. But his shoulders were extraordinarily broad, made to seem even more so by a pinched, narrow waist like a girl's. He was wearing a padded leather jacket such as horsemen wore under their mail. Erkenbert saw that extra strips had been sewn in to widen the upper body, neatly, but without any attempt to match colors. Beneath the jacket there seemed to be only a fustian tunic of the cheapest kind, and well-worn woolen breeches.

The eyes staring down were a bright, penetrating blue, the hair as fair as Arno's, but sticking up like the bristles of a brush. He had seen dangerous faces, and crazy faces, Erkenbert reflected, remembering Ivar the Boneless. He could not remember ever seeing a harder one. It seemed to have been chiseled out of rock, the skin stretched taut over prominent bones. Set on a neck as thick as a bulldog's, the head seemed almost small.

Erkenbert found his voice. "What do you mean?"

"Well, fellow, the archbishop wants one hundred, I make one, one less than one hundred—have you heard of the art of arithmetic?—that makes ninety-nine."

Erkenbert flushed at the jibe. "I have heard of arithmetic. But you have not yet been selected. First we need to know your name, and your parents'

names, and many other things. And you would have to go before the
Waffenmeister. In any case you are too late for today."

He felt a hand laid on his arm, Arno speaking softly and carefully.
"Colleague, you are correct, but I feel in this case we may make an exception. The young *herra* here is known to me, to us all. He is Bruno, son of
Reginbald, the Count of the Marches. There can of course be no doubt as
to his suitability on the score of ancestry."

Erkenbert reached irritably for the parchment. "Very well. If we are to
do this in proper form we must then proceed to the questions of wealth
and the contributions the applicant can bring to the order." He began to
write. "The name is Bruno, the son of a count must naturally be Bruno
of? . . ."

"Bruno von nowhere," said the soft voice. Erkenbert felt his writing
hand enclosed in a vast, irresistible grip, gentle but with metal cables
stirring beneath it. "I am the Count's third son, with no estate. I own
nothing but my arms and armor and my good horse. But let me ask a few
questions of you, little man with the paper. You speak *teutsch* well, but I
can tell you are not one of us. I have heard nothing also of your noble
family. I ask myself, who is this who has the right to say who shall and
who shall not be a *Ritter* of a noble order? No offense, I hope."

Arno cut in hastily. "The learned deacon is an Englishman, Bruno. He
fought in the Pope's army that was beaten and came to tell us the story. He
saw also the deaths of the famous Vikings, Ivar Boneless and Ragnar of the
Hairy Breeches. He has told us a great deal of value, and is heart and soul
for our cause."

The grip round Erkenbert's hand released, the blond man stepped back,
interest showing on his craggy face.

"Good," he said, "good. I am prepared to accept an Englishman as a
comrade. And there is one thing the little Englishman has said—take no
offense, friend, each of us has his strengths—one thing that is true. I must
certainly pass the *Waffenmeister*." His voice rose to a shout. "Dankwart!
Where are you, you old villain. Set me a test. No, do not trouble. I will set
them myself."

During the talk with Erkenbert, activity had ceased on the field. The
Waffenmeister, his sergeants, the so-far successful applicants had quit their
various tasks and come to cluster round the newcomer. They cleared a
lane for Bruno as he stepped away from the table.

In four bounds he had reached the great black horse standing unteth-
ered close by. He sprang into the saddle without touching stirrup or pommel, snatched a lance stuck in the ground, and was already in motion

towards the circuit of jumps and quintains. As his horse rose to the first hurdle Erkenbert realized the blond man had tucked his left arm theatrically behind his back, to make up for the fact that he carried no shield. His reins were dropped, he was controlling the stallion by knees and thighs alone. An overarm stab at the first quintain, an instant twist and leap. As dust rose from the field Erkenbert could make out only the crash of tumbling targets and a black centaur rising every few seconds over fence after fence. The more expert watchers had started to cheer every stroke. In what seemed moments the horse was back, the rider swinging again to the ground, breathing hard and grinning broadly.

"Did I pass that part, Dankwart? Tell the man with the paper, then, it doesn't count if he doesn't mark me down. But now, Dankwart, we have an expert watching, one who has seen real battles and seen great champions fight. I want to show him something and have his opinion. Who is the best man here today with sword and shield?"

The grizzled *Waffenmeister* pointed impassively to one of the applicants who had been sparring with his sergeants. A tall young man in a white surcoat over mail. "That one there, Bruno. He's good."

Bruno walked towards his proposed adversary, took one hand between his two, looked up at him with a curious tenderness, like a lady to her lover. "You agree?" he asked.

The tall man nodded. Sergeants handed each of them a shield, a heavy kite-shaped one of the horseman's pattern. Then a heavy sword, edges blunted, point carefully rounded. The two men stepped back, began to circle each other warily, each moving to the right, away from his opponent's sword.

Erkenbert, no expert, saw only a blur of motion, three repeated clashes as the tall man struck, low, high, backhand, whirling the sword as if it were weightless. Three solid determined parries from Bruno, twisting his wrist each time to take the blow at right angles on his own blade, ignoring the shield. Then as the fourth blow came he had stepped inside it, jerking the edge of his shield up to catch the descending sword just above its guard. As the tall man stepped back to recover his balance, Bruno's sword was in the air. It seemed for an instant as if three swords were striking at once, the tall man parrying desperately in all directions. Then his shield was down, his sword was up, he was in a half-crouch to parry a blow not struck. Bruno seemed even to pause for an instant, to weigh what was needed.

Then his sword swept through the gap too fast for sight. A thud, a gasp, and the tall man was sprawling on his back. Erkenbert realized a second after the blow that he had seen the count's son deliberately rolling his wrists at the moment of impact, to soften the blow. He had had no need to exercise his full force.

Bruno had already dropped sword and shield, was helping his opponent up with the same curious tenderness. He patted his cheek, looked closely into the other man's eyes, waving a hand in front of them to see if the other could focus. Relief crossed his face, he stepped back, grinning. "A good bout, young knight. I am glad we shall be comrades of the Order. Another time I will show you the trick of that feint, it is easy to learn." He looked round, acknowledging the applause of the circle of watchers, waving so that his opponent should be included in it.

Another thing about these Germans, thought Erkenbert, remembering the prickly, awkward insistence on rank and precedence of his homeland. They work together very easily. They like to form clubs and groups and companionships and all share their food and their beer. Yet they will still accept a leader who insists on being one of the men. Is that a strength or a weakness?

Bruno was approaching the table again, eyes shining with a kind of manic glee. "Now," he said, "will you write me down?"

As Arno reached for the pen and the parchment he laughed, bent over, collected Erkenbert's gaze and said with sudden gravity: "Now, comrade. They say you have seen the great champions, Ivar Boneless and maybe the warrior they call Killer-Brand. Tell me, how do you think one such as myself would compare with them? Tell me the truth, now, I take no offense."

Erkenbert hesitated. He had seen Ivar fight in battle against the champions of Mercia, though only from a fair distance behind. At closer quarters he had seen the duel on the gangplank between Ivar and Brand. He remembered Ivar's snake-like speed, the unexpected power in his relatively slender frame. Thought of what he had just seen, measuring the strength and leverage of the broad shoulders in front of him.

"Ivar was very quick," he said at last. "He could dodge a blow rather than block it, and still remain poised to strike back. I think if you had an open space to fight him in you might have worn him down, for you would be the stronger. But Ivar is dead."

Bruno nodded, face intent. "So what of Killer-Brand, the one who killed him?"

"It was not Brand who killed him. Ivar was too quick for Brand, mighty man though he is. No." The hatred in Erkenbert's heart welled up. "It was another who killed Ivar. The son of a churl, devil-possessed. He had only a dog's name to call himself, Shef, and he did not know his father. In fair fight you would defeat a hundred like him. And now they call him a king!"

The blue eyes were thoughtful. "Yet he killed a great champion, you say, fair fight or no. These things do not happen by accident. Such a man should never be despised. The greatest gift a king can have, some say, is luck."

By the time Shef reached solid ground he was chilled through, his teeth chattering uncontrollably. The rising tide had forced him to swim twice, no great distance but soaking him through each time. There was no sun to dry him. A fringe of seaweed marked the edge of tidal sand, with just beyond it a shallow dyke, obviously man-made. Shef scrambled to the top of it and turned to look out to sea, hoping against hope that he would see the *Norfolk* standing in to rescue him, and that in an hour or so he could count on dry clothes and a blanket, a hunk of bread and cheese, maybe a fire on the sand while someone else stood guard. At that moment he could imagine no greater reward for being a king.

There was nothing to be seen. The gray twilight made everything out on the flats seem the same, gray sea, gray sky, gray sandbanks slowly yielding to the water. He had not heard the clash of battle behind him as he made his way to the shore, but that did not mean anything. The *Norfolk* might have been carried by boarders. Or she might have been refloated and be continuing her single-ship duel with the *Frani Ormr*. Or both ships might long have sailed out once more to the open sea. There was no hope in that direction.

Shef turned the other way and contemplated the drab landscape in front of him. Plowed fields with shoots of green barley showing. Somewhere a few hundred yards off in the dimness black bulks that might well be grazing cows. All that showed a certain confidence here on the edge of the pirate sea. Were the men of this land great warriors? Or slaves of the Vikings? Or did they rely on the dangerous shoals to keep them safe? Whichever was true, their land was no great prize: flat as a man's hand, kept from the tide only by a six-foot dyke, muddy, sodden and featureless.

More to the point, there was no prospect of warmth in it anywhere. In a wooded country Shef might have thought to find a fallen tree to break the wind, boughs to pile under and over him to keep him out of the wet, maybe a drift of decaying leaves to rake over himself. Here there was nothing but mud and wet grass. Yet the cows and the plowed fields showed there was a village not too far away. Men never plowed more than a couple of miles from their homes and byres: the time it took an ox to travel that distance, morning and evening, was the most that any sensible man would add on to his day. So there must be a house, and with a house a fire, somewhere all but in sight.

Shef looked round for a gleam of light. Nothing. That was only to be expected. Anyone who had light and fire would have the sense to shut it in. Shef turned to his left, for no reason than that it was away from the land of the Christians and Hamburg further down the Elbe, and began to walk briskly along the dyke. If he had to, he decided, he would walk all night. His clothes were bound to dry on him in the end. He would be ravenously hungry by dawn, his body's resources used up by keeping out the cold, but that could be borne. He had fed well all the months he had been a king, and a jarl before that. Now was the time to use some of that up. But if he lay down in the fields, he would be dead by morning.

After only a few minutes of stumbling, Shef realized that he was crossing a track. He paused. Should he follow it? If the natives were hostile he could be dead well before morning. The patter of rain on his shoulders made his mind up for him. He moved cautiously down the track, his one eye probing the darkness.

The village was no more than a cluster of longhouses, their low walls showing just slightly darker than the sky. Shef reflected. No hall for a lord, no church for a priest. That was good. The longhouses were different sizes, some long, some short. One of the shortest ones was the closest to him. In the winter these folk, like the poor people of Norfolk, would bring their beasts in the house with them, for warmth. A small house meant few cows. Was it not true that charity was likeliest among the poor? He moved cautiously towards the door of the nearest house, the smallest. A chink of light through the wooden shutters.

He planted the Snake-eye's spear butt-down in the ground, pulled the sword from his belt and held it by the blade. With his right hand he pounded on the ill-fitting door. A scurrying inside, muttered words. It creaked open.

Shef stepped forwards into the ill-lit doorway, his sword balanced across both hands in token of submission. Without a pause he found himself lying on his back, staring up at the sky. He had felt no blow, had no idea what had happened. His arms and legs seemed to pay no attention to his insistent commands to them to move.

He felt a fist gripping the neck of his tunic, hauling him half upright, a voice in his ear muttering in a thick dialect, but comprehensibly, "All right, come along, get your feet under you, let's get you inside and have a look at you."

His legs sprawling, Shef staggered inside, his arm round someone's shoulder, and sank on to a stool by a meager fire.

For long moments he could pay no attention to anything but the warmth, holding his hands out to it, crouching over it. As the steam started to rise from his clothes he shook his head, rose unsteadily to his feet, and looked round. Facing him was a stocky man, hands on hips, with a mop of curly hair and an expression on his face of irrepressible good humor. From the thinness of his beard Shef realized that he was even younger than himself. In the background stood two older folk, a man and a woman, looking at him with alarm and distrust.

Shef tried to speak, realized his jaw was stiff and sore. An exploring hand found a growing lump on the right-hand side.

"What did you do?" he asked.

The stocky man grinned even more broadly than before, made swift darting movements with his hands and body. "Gave you a bit of a dunt," he replied. "You walked right into it."

Shef cast his mind back, amazed. In England, and among the Vikings, men hit each other with their fists often enough, but wrestling was the warrior's sport. By the time someone had raised his fist and swung it, even a grandfather should be able to duck out of the way. Even walking into a dark room, he would have expected to see a swing coming and at least react to it. Nor would you expect a swing to knock a man down. Fighting with fists was an affair of prolonged and clumsy bludgeoning, which was why the warriors despised it. Yet Shef had seen nothing and felt nothing till he was on the ground.

"Do not be surprised," said the old man in the background. "Our Karli does that to everyone. He is a champion. But you had better tell us who you are, or he will strike you again."

"I got separated from my ship," said Shef. "Had to walk and swim across the sandbanks."

"Are you one of the Vikings? You speak more like one of us."

"I am an Englishman. But I have been much among Norsemen, and can understand their speech. I have spoken with Frisians as well. You speak most like them. Are you Frisians? The free Frisians," Shef added, remembering how they liked to describe themselves.

Even the old woman laughed. "The free Frisians," said the stocky youth. "Living on sandbanks and running for their lives every time they see a sail. No, we are Germans."

"The archbishop's men?" inquired Shef cautiously. He could see his sword now, standing in a corner where they must have put it. If the answer were wrong, he would lunge for it and try to kill the stocky youth at once.

Again they laughed. "No. Some of us are Christians, some follow the old gods, some none. But none of us has any wish to pay tithes or kneel to a lord. We are the folk of the Ditmarsh," the youth ended proudly.

Shef had never heard the name from anyone before. He nodded. "I am cold and wet. And hungry," he added. "May I sleep inside your house tonight?"

"Sleep by the fire and welcome," said the older man, who Shef realized must be the father of the stocky one, the master of the house. "As for hunger, we have plenty of that ourselves. But you can dry yourself here rather than die out on the marsh. Tomorrow you must go before the village for a doom."

I have gone into a doom-ring before, thought Shef. But maybe the Ditmarshers' doom will be kinder than the Great Army's. Feeling his swollen jaw again, he moved to the side of the fire while the family of the house prepared itself for sleep.

CHAPTER SIX

Shef woke in the morning feeling strangely calm and rested. For a few moments he lay on the packed earth floor and wondered why. The fire was out, and he had kept from shivering in the night only by curling into a ball and gripping knees with arms. His clothes had dried from body heat, but dried stiff and harsh from salt water. His belly was pinched with hunger. And he was alone and without resources in a strange and probably hostile land. So why did he not seem more anxious?

Shef got to his feet, stretched luxuriously, and pushed open the wooden shutter, letting in the sunlight and the fresh air smelling of grass and blossom. He knew the answer. It was because his cares and responsibilities had fallen from him. For the first time for many months he did not have to think about other people's needs: how to feed them, how to persuade them, how to praise them to make them do his will. His childhood had made him used to cold and hunger. And to blows and the threat of slavery as well. But now he was no child, but a man in his prime. If anyone struck him he could strike back. Shef's one eye noted the weapons he had leant against the corner of the hut. Hrani's sword and Sigurth's spear. They were the only possessions he now had, apart from the pendant round his neck and the flint and eating-knife slung from his belt. They would have to do.

Out of the corner of his eye Shef saw that the older couple had emerged from their box-bed. The man went straight out of the door. That could be ominous. The woman pulled a quern from under their rough table, scooped grain from a barrel into it, and began to grind it with a hand-pestle. The sound brought Shef's childhood back even more strongly. As long as he could remember, every day had started the same way, with the sound of women grinding grain into flour. Only jarls and kings could live far enough away from daily necessity not to hear it. It was the task warriors hated most, though on campaign even they had to do it. Perhaps women hated it too, Shef reflected. At least it showed these people had food. His belly cramped in response to the thought, and Shef glanced again towards his weapons.

A touch on his arm. The young man with the curly hair stood there, grinning as always. He held out a hunk of black bread in a dirty fist, strong-smelling yellow cheese on top of it. As Shef took it, his mouth running instantly with saliva, he produced an onion, divided it in his palm with a crude knife, and passed Shef half.

The two squatted on the floor and began to eat. The bread was hard, old, full of bran and gritty with stone from the hand-quern. Shef tore it with his teeth, relishing every mouthful.

After a while, his stomach relaxing in its demands, he remembered the soreness in his jaw, the strange events of last night. As his hand went up to explore the swelling, he caught the young man—what had the woman called him? Our Karli?—grinning at the gesture.

"What did you hit me for?" he asked.

Karli seemed surprised at the question. "I didn't know who you were. Simplest way to deal with you. Simplest way to deal with everybody."

Shef felt a certain irritation rising. He swallowed the last lump of cheese, rose to his feet, spreading his arms and flexing the muscles in his back. He remembered the man he had killed yesterday, the young Viking from Ebeltoft. He had been a bigger man even than Shef, and Shef out-topped Karli by a head.

"You would not have done it if it had not been for the dark."

Karli was on his feet too, a look of glee on his face. He started to circle Shef in a strange shuffle, not like a wrestler's planted stance. His fists were doubled, his head sunk below his shoulders. Impatiently Shef stepped forward, hands grabbing for a wrist-hold. A fist jabbed at his face, he brushed it aside. Something struck him below the ribs on his right side. For an instant Shef ignored it, tried again to grapple. Then pain shot up from his liver, he felt his breath leave him, and his hands dropped automatically to guard the spot. Instantly his head snapped back and Shef found himself staggering back against the wall. As he straightened, blood ran down into his mouth, his teeth felt loosened.

A surge of anger drove Shef forward with lightning speed, aiming to body-check, trip and go for a bonebreaker hold. The body was not there, and as he whirled to reach the darting figure now behind him, he felt another blow in the back, a stab of agony from a kidney. Again he blocked a blow at the face, this time remembering instantly to swipe downwards to thwart the liver-punch that followed. Still no grip, and another blow high up on the cheekbone as he hesitated. But the circling had brought Shef into easy reach of the spear propped against the wall. How would that grin look? . . .

Shef stood up straight, spread his arms wide in token of defenselessness. "All right," he said, looking at Karli's grin. "All right. You would have knocked me down even if it had not been dark. I can see you know something I do not. Maybe many things."

Karli grinned even more broadly than before, and dropped his hands. "I expect you know some things too—a seafarer like you, with a spear and a sword as well. I have never been outside the Ditmarsh—hardly ever out-side this village. How about a trade? I will show you what I know, and you show me what you know. I could soon teach you how to strike and guard with your fists, like we do here in the Ditmarsh. You move very fast. Too fast for most of these ploughboys."

"A trade," Shef agreed. He spat on his palm and looked at Karli to see if he understood the gesture. The other grinned, and spat too. The pair slapped palms violently to seal the bargain.

As Shef wiped the blood from his nose with the back of his sleeve, they resumed their companionable squat.

"Now listen," said Karli. "You've more important things to learn right now than fist-fighting. My old man has gone out to tell the village you're here. They'll assemble outside, make the ring, and decide what to do with you."

"What are their choices?"

"First off, someone will say you're a slave. That'll be Nikko. He's the richest man in the village. Wants to be a lord. But silver is short in the Ditmarsh, and we never make slaves of each other. Having someone to sell in the market at Hedeby is what he thinks about all the time."

"Hedeby is a Danish town," said Shef.

Karli shrugged. "Danish, German, Frisian, we don't care. No-one tries any tricks on the Ditmarsh. They couldn't find the path through the fens. And anyway, they know there's no silver here. Lot to lose for a tax-collec-tor, nothing much to gain."

"If I don't want to be a slave, what's the other choice?"

"You could be a guest-friend." Karli looked at him sideways. "Like with me. That means exchanging gifts."

Shef felt his biceps, regretting the last-minute decision yesterday to strip the gold bracelets from them. One of those would have bought him hospitality for a year. Or a knife in the back. "What do I have, then? A spear. A sword. And this." He pulled the silver pole-ladder of Rig from under his tunic, and glanced across at Karli to see if he recognized the sign. No interest there. But Karli had glanced more than once at the weapons propped in the corner.

Shef stepped over to them, picked them up for a closer look. The spear with the 'Gungnir' runes: excellent steel, glinting new-forged, a beautiful balance in the hand. The sword: serviceable enough, but a little too heavy, the blade mere sharpened iron without a specially welded edge, beginning already to pock slightly with rust. Swords were more valuable than spears, the mark of the professional warrior besides. Still . . .

Shef held out the sword. "Take this, Karli." He noted the way the young man took it, the way he held the blade slightly off the square, disastrous for a parry. "And I will give you two more things. One, I will show you how to use the sword. Two, if ever we stay by a forge, I will forge it again for you to make it a better weapon."

The freckled face flushed with pleasure as the door opened. Karli's father came in, jerked a thumb over his shoulder.

"Come, stranger," he said. "The doom-ring is outside."

Some forty men stood outside in a rough circle, their wives and children forming a larger circle outside them. All the men were armed, but not well —spears and axes, but no mail or helmets. A few had shields on their shoulders, but not strapped on ready for use.

What the Ditmarshers saw emerging from the hut was a tall warrior, his calling unmistakable from his bearing: straight back, wide shoulders, no sign of the stoop or the cramped muscles of the peasant who had to follow a plow or bend every day over hoe or sickle. Yet he bore no gold or silver on him, carried only the long spear in his right hand. He was scarred as well, with one eyelid drooping over a sunken socket, and the whole side of his face seeming drawn in. Unnoticed blood smeared his face, and his plain tunic and breeches were dirtier than a peasant's. The circle stared at him, unsure how to read these signals. There was a low mutter of comment as Karli emerged behind him, gripping in inexpert hands the sword he had been given.

Shef looked round, trying to appraise the situation. The waking feeling of calm and confidence was still with him, unshaken by the brush with Karli. Thoughtfully he pulled the silver Rig-pendant up on its chain so that it hung outside his tunic. Another mutter of comment, men peering closer to try to identify the sign. Some of the men watching, maybe a quarter of those present, similarly hitched pendants into view: hammers, boats, phalluses. None like Shef's.

The man directly facing Shef stepped forward, a bulky man in middle-age with a red face.

"You came from the ships," he said. "You are a Viking, one of the robbers of the North. Even such as you should know better than to set foot on the Ditmarsh, where the free men live. We will enslave you and sell you to your kin at Hedeby. Or to the bishop's men at Hamburg. Unless there is someone who will pay to have you back—not likely, from the look of you."

Some instinct drove Shef forward across the ring, sauntering slowly till he came face to face with his accuser. He looked at him, tilting his head back to accentuate his greater height.

"If you know I came from the ships," he said, "you know there were two ships fighting. One was a Viking. It was the *Frani Ormr,* the great ship of Sigurth Ragnarsson. Did you not see the Raven Banner? The other one was mine, and Sigurth was running from it. Get me back to it and I'll give you a man's price in silver."

"What kind of ships chase Viking ships?" said the burly man.

"English ships."

The listening crowd made noises of surprise, disbelief. "It's true the first ship was a Viking," said a voice. "But he wasn't running. He was leading on. And he fooled the other skipper proper. If that second ship was English they must all be fools. Mast and sail all wrong, too."

"Take me back to it," repeated Shef.

Karli's voice came from behind him. "He couldn't do it if he wanted to, stranger. No boats. We Ditmarshers are bold enough in the marsh, but half a mile out to sea and that's pirate water."

The burly man flushed and glanced angrily round. "That's as may be. But if you've nothing else to say, one-eye, then what I said stands. You're my slave till I find a buyer. Hand over that spear."

Shef tossed the spear in the air, caught it at its point of balance, and feinted a lunge. He grinned broadly as the other man jumped clumsily away, then turned his back on him, ignoring the threatening axe. He began to stroll round the circle, looking into face after face, and addressing his words directly to the pendant-wearers in the circle. They were just like the

Norfolk farmers whose disputes he had so often judged as a jarl, he decided. Get their interest and exploit their village divisions.

"A strange thing," he remarked. "Man gets washed up on the shore, might be alive, might be dead, what do you do with him? Where I come from, the fishermen, if they have the cash, put a silver ring in their ears. You know what that's for. So if they drown and their bodies come to shore, the folk are paid for burying them. The folk would bury them anyway, in duty, but they don't like the idea of taking a last service for nothing.

"Now here I am, no ring in my ear, but not dead either. Why should I get worse treatment? Have I done any harm? I've made a gift to your Karli there, and in exchange he's knocked me down, bloodied my nose, loosened my teeth, and given me a sore jaw—so we're all good friends."

A rumble of amusement. As Shef had guessed, Karli was something between an object of admiration and a standing joke.

"Now what surprises me is our friend behind me." Shef jerked a thumb over his shoulder at the burly man. "He says I'm a slave. Well, maybe. Says I'm *his* slave. Did I go to his house? Did he capture me single-handed in peril of his life? Maybe you all decided that anything that fell off a ship belonged to him. Is that right?"

This time a definite rumble of rejection, and what sounded like a loud breaking of wind from Karli.

"So what I suggest is this." Shef had almost completed his circuit now, and was coming back face to face with the burly man. "If you want to make a slave of me, Nikko, then take me along to Hedeby and put me in the sale-ring. If you can make a sale, well and good. But then you must share the money with the village. Till you get to Hedeby, though, I stay free: no bonds, no collar. And I keep my spear. Sure, you can guard me as much as you like. Finally, till we get there I'll work for my keep." Shef tapped his pendant. "I have a skill. I'm a smith. Give me a forge and tools and I'll work at whatever you need."

"Sounds fair enough," called one voice. "I have a plowshare with its edge coming away, needs careful work."

"He don't talk like a Viking," called another. "More like a Frisian, only without the cold in his head."

"Did you hear the bit about sharing out?" called a third.

Shef spat on his palm and waited. Slowly, with hate in his eyes, the burly Nikko spat too. They slapped palms perfunctorily. As the tension slackened, Shef turned and walked back to Karli.

"I want you to come to Hedeby too," he said. "See the world. But we both have much to learn before we get there."

* * *

Forty miles out to sea, within sight of the Holy Island, the English fleet rocked on the waves, sails furled, like a flock of giant sea-birds. At the center four ships were lashed together for conference: the *Norfolk,* escaped from the muddy channels of the Elber Gat, the *Suffolk,* commanded by the senior English skipper Hardred, Brand's *Walrus* and the *Seamew* of Guthmund the Greedy, to represent the Viking Waymen. Feelings were running high, and strong voices carried over the water to the listening fleet.

"I can't believe you just left him on the Thor-forsaken sandbank," said Brand at a pitch just short of a bellow.

Ordlaf's face remained mulish. "Nothing else to do. He'd vanished out of sight, tide coming in, night coming on, no knowing if Sigurth and his picked champions weren't going to appear from the next sandbank. We had to get out of there."

"Do you think he lived?" asked Thorvin, flanked on either side by fellow-priests of the Way called from their ships.

"I saw four men go after him. Three came back. They didn't look pleased. That's all I can say."

"So the chances are he's stuck in the Ditmarsh somewhere," concluded Brand. "All those bastards have webbed feet."

"They tell me he's a fenman too," said Ordlaf. "If he's there, he's probably all right. Why don't we just go after him? It's daylight now, and we can pick our tide."

This time it was Brand's turn to look mulish. "Not a good idea. First off, no-one lands in the Ditmarsh, not even for water or an evening's *strandhögg.* Too many crews have vanished. Second, like I told you weeks ago, all this is pilot water. And you said you could find your way with lead and lookout! You got stranded, and you could again, maybe in a worse place next time.

"Third thing, though, is we still have the Ragnarssons around. They started off with a long hundred of ships, a hundred and twenty, the way you count. How many do you think we sank or captured?"

Hardred replied. "We captured six. The catapults sank at least a dozen more."

"Which leaves them a hundred, to our fifty. Less than fifty, since they boarded the *Buckinghamshire* and cut a hole in her bottom, and I have half a dozen ships too weakly manned now to be useful. And we won't take them by surprise again."

"So what do we do?" asked Ordlaf.

There was a long silence. Finally Hardred broke it, his careful Anglo-Saxon contrasting oddly with the camp-patois brewed from Norse and English of the others.

"If we are unable to rescue the king," he said, "as I am told we are, then I see it as my duty to return the rest of the fleet to English waters, to take instructions from King Alfred. He is my master, but the agreement between himself and King Shef"—he hesitated before coming out with the words—"was that one should succeed to all the rights of the other, if the other should pre-decease him. As may now be the case."

He waited for the storm of protests to die down, then went on, his voice gaining firmness. "After all, this fleet is now the main shield and protection of English shores. We know we can sink the pirates if they appear, and we will. That was the main aim and goal of King Shef, as of King Alfred: to have a peaceful coastline and a peaceful land behind it. If he were here he would tell us to do what I suggest."

"You can go," shouted Cwicca, the freed slave. "Go back to your master. Our master is the one who took the collars from our necks, and we won't leave him to have some webfoot half-breed put one on his."

"How are you going to get there?" said Hardred. "Swim? Brand won't take you. Ordlaf daren't, not on his own."

"We can't just sail away," pleaded Cwicca.

Thorvin's deep voice broke in. "No. But it is in my mind that we can sail on. Or some of us can. Something tells me that it is not Shef Sigvarthsson's fate to die silently, or to vanish. Someone may have him for ransom. Or for sale. If we go to a major port, where news is gathered, we will hear something of him. I suggest we go on to Kaupang, some of us."

"Kaupang," said Brand. "To the College of the Way."

"I have reasons of my own for going there, it's true," said Thorvin. "But the Way has many followers, and many resources, and the college is deeply concerned about Shef. If we go there we will get help."

"I won't," declared Hardred flatly. "Too far, too risky, hostile waters all the way, and we know now the 'Counties' aren't fit for a deep-sea crossing." Ordlaf nodded in glum agreement.

"Some go back, some go on," said Thorvin.

"Most go back, I think," said Brand. "Forty ships, even fifty ships, aren't enough to get through all the fleets of Norway and Denmark—the Ragnarssons, King Halvdan, the Hlathir jarls, King Gamli, King Hrorik, and all the others. They'd best turn back, to guard the Way in England. There are plenty who'd be glad to stamp it out.

"I'll take the *Walrus*. Go out deep sea, not hug the coast. I'll get through.

I'll take you, Thorvin, and your fellows, to Kaupang and to the college. Who else? How about you, Guthmund?"

"Take us!" Cwicca was on his feet, face red with rage. "We aren't turning back. Take me and my mates, and our catapult too, we can unship it from the *Norfolk* if that Yorkshire fart won't risk his skin. Cowpang, Ditfen, we'll take them all if we got to." A hubbub of agreement from the waist of the ship showed that the freed slaves of the catapult crews had been listening.

"Me too," said an almost inaudible voice from a small figure lurking behind the mast. Brand looked in several directions till he realized it came from Udd, the steelmaster, allowed on the cruise only in his former role of catapult crew spare hand.

"What do you want to go to Norway for?"

"For knowledge," said Udd. "I have heard men speak of Jarnberaland. Iron-bearing Land," he added, translating.

Another slight figure appeared to stand unspeaking by him. Hund, the leech, Shef's childhood friend, now with the silver apple of Ithun round his neck.

"Very well," said Brand decisively. "I'll take my own crew and the *Seamew* as consort. I'll have space for no more than ten volunteers. You Hund, you Udd, and you, Cwicca. Cast lots for the rest."

"And us as passengers," said Thorvin, nodding to his two fellow-priests. "Till we reach the college."

CHAPTER SEVEN

Shef stepped back a pace, his feet sinking into the soft mire. He twirled the peeled branch in his hand and eyed Karli carefully. The short man had lost his grin and gained a look of anxious determination. At least he had learnt to hold his sword right: edge and guard absolutely parallel with the line of his forearm, so that cut or parry would not be deflected. Shef moved in, swung forehand, backhand, thrust and sidestep, as Brand had taught him months before in the camps outside York. Karli parried easily, not quite managing to catch the light wood with his heavier blade, but well into line every time —the speed of his reactions was excellent. Still the same old problem, though.

Shef accelerated slightly, feinted low and rapped Karli briskly over the sword-arm. He stepped back and lowered his stick.

"You've got to remember, Karli," he said. "You aren't cutting brushwood. What you've got there is a two-edged sword, not a one-edged billhook. What do you think the second edge is for? It's not for your main stroke, because you always slash with the same edge, to get your full force into it."

"It's for the back-flick," said Karli, repeating his lesson. "I know, I know. I just can't make my muscles do it unless I think about it, and if I think about it, it's too late. So tell me, what would happen if I tried to face a real swordsman, a Viking from the ships?"

Shef stretched out a hand for the sword he had reforged, looked at its edges critically. It was not a bad weapon, not now. But with what he had

had by him at the forge in the Ditmarsh village, he had not dared to do too much. The weapon was still all of one metal, without the blends of soft and hard that gave a superior sword its flexibility and strength. Nor had he been able to weld on the hardened steel edges that were the sign of a master-weapon—no good metal, and a forge that would not get iron to more than red heat. So, now that they had left the village, every time he had fenced with Karli using his 'Gungnir' spear like a halberd, the iron edges of the cheap sword showed notches, to be taken out with hammer and file. Yet you could learn from the notches. If they were at right angles to the blade, Karli was fencing properly. A bungled parry showed cuts and shirrs of metal at odd angles. None this time.

Shef passed it back. "If you faced a real champion, like the man who taught me, you'd be dead," he said. "So would I. But there are plenty of farmers' sons in Viking armies. You might meet one of those. And don't forget," he added, "if you're facing a real champion, you don't have to fight fair."

"You've done that," guessed Karli.

Shef nodded.

"You've done a lot you don't tell me about, Shef."

"You wouldn't believe me if I told you."

Karli pushed his sword back into the wooden, wool-lined scabbard they had made for it, the only thing that would keep out the rust in the ever-lasting damp of the Ditmarsh. The two men turned and started back to the makeshift camp in the clearing thirty yards away, smoke trailing sullenly from the cooking fires into the misty air.

"And you don't tell me what you're going to do, either," Karli went on. "Are you just going to walk into the slave-ring and let Nikko sell you, like you say?"

"I'll walk into the slave-ring at Hedeby right enough," said Shef. "After that, things will go as they will. But I don't reckon to end up as a slave. Tell me, Karli, how am I coming along?"

He referred to the hours Karli had spent, in exchange for the fencing lessons, teaching him how to make a fist, how to strike straight forward instead of with the usual round-arm swing, how to step forward and put the weight of the body into a hooked punch, how to block with the hands and weave the head.

Karli's habitual grin spread across his face once more. "Just like me, I guess. If you met a real champion, a fist-fighter from the marsh, he'd be all over you. But you can knock a man down well enough, if he stands still."

Shef nodded thoughtfully. That at least was a skill worth knowing.

Strange that they should have so specialized in one fighting art, here in this unvisited corner of the world. Perhaps it was because they did so little trade and had so little metal that they fought by choice empty-handed.

Only Nikko bothered to look up as they rejoined the campsite, giving the pair of them an angry glare.

"We reach Hedeby tomorrow," he said. "Then your prancing will have to stop. I say, your prancing will have to stop," he repeated, voice rising to a shout as Shef ignored him. "The master you'll find in Hedeby won't let you fool around pretending to be a swordmaster. It'll be work all day and the leather across your back if you shirk! You've felt it before, I've seen you stripped! You're no warrior out of luck, just a runaway!"

Karli lobbed a handful of mud neatly into Nikko's campfire and the shouting died into exasperated mutters.

"It is our last night," said Karli in a low voice. "I've got an idea. See, we're coming out of the Ditmarsh. Be on the high road tomorrow, and the dry land, where the Danes live. You can talk to them then, but I'm not so good at it. But there's a village half a mile off, where the girls still speak good marsh-talk, like me—and you too, you still talk like a Frisian, but they'll understand you. So why don't we just slip off and see if there isn't anyone in the village who feels like a bit of a change from whichever mudfoot she's attached to?"

Shef looked at Karli with a mixture of irritation and affection. During the week he had stayed in the Ditmarsh village by the sea, he had realized that Karli, cheerful, open and thoughtless, was one of those men whom women invariably liked. They responded to his humor, his lack of care. He seemed to have tried his luck with every woman in his home village, and usually successfully. Some husbands and fathers knew, some turned a blind eye, all were careful about giving Karli an excuse to use his fists. But there had been general approval of Karli going off with Nikko and the others on their trading trip to Hedeby, whether they managed to include Shef as merchandise or not. Their last night in the hut Karli shared with his parents had been broken by continual scratching on the shutters and stealthy disappearances into the bushes outside.

They were not Shef's women, so he had no cause for complaint. Yet Karli made him anxious at some deeper level. In his youth, working at the forge at Emneth in the fen, and traveling round the neighboring villages on work-errands, Shef had several lusty encounters with girls—churls' daughters, even thralls' daughters, not young ladies whose virginity was prized and guarded, but ready enough to educate his ignorance. It was true they had never sought him out as they did Karli, perhaps put off by his unsmiling concern for the future, perhaps sensing his inner obsessions, but at least he had had no need to think he was lacking, or abnormal.

Then had come the sack of Emneth by the Vikings, the crippling of his foster-father, the capture and then the rescue of Godive. The moment in the little hut in the copse that summer morning, when he had become Godive's "first-man," and thought he had reached the summit of his ambition. And since then Shef had had no dealings with any woman, not even Godive after he had won her back, not even after they had put the gold circle of kingship on his head and half the trulls in England had been his for the taking. Shef wondered sometimes whether the threat of Ivar to castrate him had worked on his mind. He knew he was still a whole man —but then so had Ivar been, or so Hund had insisted, and he had been called "the Boneless," just the same. Could he have caught impotence from the man he had killed? Had his half-brother, Godive's husband, put a curse on him before he was hanged?

It was something in the mind, Shef knew, not in the body. Something to do with the way he had used the woman he loved as bait and as bribe, an inner agreement with her rejection of him and her marriage to Alfred, the most truthful man Shef had ever met. Whatever the case, he did not know the cure. Going with Karli might lead only to humiliation. Tomorrow he would be in the slave-ring, and the day after he could be facing the gelders.

"Do you think I stand a chance?" he asked, patting his ruined eye and face.

Karli's face creased with delight. "Of course! Great tall fellow like you, muscles like a blacksmith. Foreign accent, air of mystery. What you got to remember, these girls out here, they're *bored.* Nothing ever happens. They aren't allowed out near the road where anyone could grab them. No-one ever comes into the marsh. They see the same faces from the day they're born till the day they die. I tell you . . ." Karli expanded in fancies as to how the girls of the Ditmarsh had to amuse themselves for want of handsome strangers—or ugly strangers for that matter—while Shef stirred the stewpot and twisted strips of dough round twigs to toast in the fire. He did not think Karli's plan would work, or not for him at any rate. But he had gone on the naval expedition in the first place for one reason only: to shake off the black mood of Alfred and Godive's marriage. He would take any opportunity to break the spell upon him. But without any expectations. It would take more than a marshwife to remove his memories.

* * *

Hours later, walking back to camp through the marsh in the black night, Shef wondered again at his own lack of concern. Things had gone much as he had foreseen: the arrival in the village at the hour when folk left their doors and strolled round, the casual conversation with the menfolk to pass on news, Karli's meaningful looks and quick words with one listening girl and then another, while Shef held the attention of their male protectors. Then the ostentatious leaving at dusk, followed by the stealthy circuit back to a willow copse hanging over stagnant water. The arrival of the girls, panting, fearful and excited.

Shef's had been a pleasant plump girl with a pouting face. At first she had been flirtatious. Then scornful. Then, finally, as she realized that Shef himself had no hope or anxiety concerning his own failure, worried. She had stroked his ruined face, felt the scars on his back beneath the tunic. "You have had hard times?" she had said, half-questioning. "Harder than those scars show," he had replied. "Things are hard for us women too, you know," she had told him. Shef thought of what he had seen at the sack of York and in the ruin of Emneth, thought of his mother and her life story, of Godive and Alfgar and the bloody birch, of the stories of Ivar the Boneless and his dealings with women: remembered finally the slave-girls' bones, buried alive with their backs broken, which he had stumbled over in the old king's howe, and said nothing. Then for a while they had lain without speaking till the urgent noises coming from Karli and his mate had ceased once and then again. "I won't tell anyone," she had whispered as the other pair finally emerged damp and muddy from their hollow. He would never see her again.

It ought to worry him, Shef reflected, not to be a whole man. Somehow it did not. He paused, tested the footing of the stretch ahead with the butt-spike of his spear. In the darkness of the marsh something gurgled and plopped, and Karli drew his sword with a gasp.

"It was just an otter," Shef remarked.

"Maybe. Don't you know there are other things in the marsh?"

"Like what?"

Karli hesitated. "We call them thurses."

"Yes, so do we. Great big things that live in the mud and catch children who play too close. Giant women with green teeth. Arms covered in long gray hair that reach up and turn over a fowler's boat," Shef added, embroidering on one of the stories he had heard from Brand. "Merlings that sit and feast on the . . ."

Karli grabbed his arm. "Enough! Don't say it. They might hear themselves called and come."

"There are no such things," said Shef, confident again of his bearings and moving off on the slightly firmer ground between two sloughs. "People just make up the stories to explain why people don't come back. In marshes like this you don't need a thurs to make you vanish. Look, there's the camp through these alders."

Karli looked up at him as they reached the edge of the camp clearing, men already wrapped motionless in their blankets. "I don't understand you," he said. "You're always sure you know best. But you act like a sleepwalker. Are you sent by the gods?"

Shef noticed Nikko, awake and seated silently observing from the shadows. "If I am," he said, "I hope they have some help for me tomorrow."

In his dream that night he felt as if the nape of his neck were gripped in steely fingers, forcing him to look this way and then that.

The first sight he saw was somewhere on a desolate plain. A young warrior stood, holding himself upright with difficulty. Black blood covered his armor, and more ran down his legs from under the mail shirt. He clutched a broken sword in his hand and another warrior lay at his feet. From somewhere far off Shef heard a voice chanting:

> *Sixteen wounds I have, slit is my armor,*
> *Closed my eyes, I cannot see to walk.*
> *Angantyr's sword sliced me to the heart*
> *The sharp blood-pourer, poison-hardened.*

You can't harden swords in poison, thought Shef. Hardening is a matter of great heat and sudden cooling. Why is water not sudden enough? Maybe it is the steam that comes from it. What is steam anyway?

The fingers at his neck tweaked him suddenly, as if to make him pay attention. Across the plain Shef saw birds of prey flying, and the chanting voice said again:

> *The hungry raven roves from the South,*
> *The white-tailed carrion-fowl follows his brother.*
> *It is the last time I lay for them a table.*
> *It is my blood now the battle-beasts feast on.*

Behind the birds Shef thought for a moment he could see women, female shapes riding on the wind, and behind even them the dim sight of great doors opening: doors he had seen before, the doors of Valhalla.

So the heroes die, said another voice, not the chanting one. Even in the paralysis of his dream Shef felt a chill as he recognized the grim ironic tones of his protector, the god Rig, whose ladder-sign he wore round his neck. That is the death of Hjalmar the Magnanimous, the voice went on. Picked a fight with a Swedish berserk, provided two recruits for my father Othin.

The scene vanished, Shef felt his eyes twisted supernaturally elsewhere. A moment, and then another vision came into focus. Shef was looking down at a narrow pallet laid on an earth floor. It was somewhere aside from main rooms, maybe a blind passageway somewhere out of the way of passing feet, but cold and comfortless. On it an old woman was stretching herself out, carefully and painfully. Shef knew that she had just been told that she was bound to die, by a leech or a cunning man or a beast-doctor. Not from the lung-sickness that usually carried off the old folk in the winter, but from some growth or evil inside her. It hurt her terribly, but she dared not speak of it. She had no relatives left, if she had had a man or sons of her own, they were dead or gone, she lived now on the doubtful tolerance of those not her blood. If she gave trouble of any kind even her pallet and her bread would be withdrawn. She was a person of no importance.

She was the girl he had left in the marsh, come to the end of her life. Or she could be. There were others she could be: Shef thought of Godive's mother, the Irish slave whom Wulfgar his foster father had taken as a lemman and then sold away from her child when his wife grew jealous. But there were others, many many others. The world was full of desperate old women, and old men too, trying with the last of their strength to die quietly and not attract attention. Then they could creep into their graves and vanish from mind. They had been young once.

From the scene Shef felt such a wave of hopelessness as he had never imagined before. And yet there was something strange about it. This slow dying might be years in the future, as he had first thought when he seemed to recognize the woman. Or it might be years in the past. But for a moment Shef seemed to know one thing: the old woman praying for an unnoticed death on the pallet bed was him. Or had he been her?

Shef snapped awake with a jerk and a sense of relief. Round him the camp lay quiet in its blankets. He let his inhaled breath out slowly and relaxed his tensed muscles one at a time.

They came out of the marsh the next morning almost in a stride. One moment they were plodding forward through the black pools and across the shallow streams that seemed to flow in no direction, in a thin cold mist. Then the ground was rising beneath their feet, the mist cleared away, and barely a mile off across bare turf, Shef could see the Army Road marching along the skyline, with on it a continual to-and-fro of travelers. He looked back and saw that the Ditmarsh was invisible beneath a blanket of fog. It would clear in the sun and reform again at nightfall. No wonder that the Ditmarshers lived hand to mouth, and knew no invaders.

Shef was amused also to see how his companions changed as they came out on to the road. In the marsh they had been secure, confident, ready to sneer at the outside world and their neighbors. Here they seemed to put their heads down and hope to escape without attention. Shef found himself standing straight and looking round him, while the others stooped and closed up together.

Shortly a party on horseback caught up with them, ten or a dozen men riding together with pack animals, a salt-train heading north up the Jutland peninsula. As they rode past the Ditmarshers they called to each other in Norse.

"Here, see the mudfeet out of the fen. What have they come out for? Look, there's a tall one, must have been mother's little adventure. Hey, marshman, what are you looking for? Is it a cure for your spotted bellies?"

Shef grinned at the loudest laugher, and called back, in the fluent Norse he had learnt from Thorvin and then from Brand and his crew.

"What would you know about it, Jutlander?" He exaggerated the hoarse gutturals of the Ribe dialect they spoke. "Is that Norse you are speaking, or is it a disease of the throat? Try stirring honey in your beer and maybe you can cough it up."

The traders checked their horses and stared at him. "You are no Ditmarsher," said one of them. "You do not sound like a Dane either. Where are you from?"

"*Enzkr em,*" said Shef firmly. "I am an Englishman."

"You sound like a Norwegian, and one from the back end of nowhere at that. I have heard voices like yours trading furs."

"I am an Englishman," Shef repeated. "And it is not furs I am trading. These folk and I are going to the slave-ring at Hedeby, where they hope to sell me." He pulled his ladder pendant into view, turned his face full on to the Danes, and winked his one eye solemnly. "No need to keep it a secret. After all, I have to find a buyer."

The Danes looked at each other and rode on, leaving Shef well content. An Englishman, with one eye, and a silver pole-ladder round his neck. It only needed one friend of Brand, or of the Way, or even one of his skippers from last year's campaign gone home to retire to hear that, and Shef should at least have enough credit to get passage back to England: though he did not want to take ship from Hedeby on the Baltic shore.

Nikko scowled at him, feeling that the situation was slipping beyond his grasp. "I'll have that spear of yours before we reach the market."

Shef used it to point to the wooden stockade round Hedeby coming into view.

As he shuffled slowly forward in the line of merchandise for sale the next day, Shef felt his heart beating faster. He still had the inner calm—or was it indifference?—which had never left him since he woke up, king no more, in Karli's hut. Yet though he knew what he planned to do, he could not know how it would be taken. It depended on what a man's rights were. In the slave-market at Hedeby, what he and his friends could enforce, likely enough.

The market itself was no more than a cleared space on the shore, with a central knoll a few feet high to display the goods to the buyers. Behind it the tideless Baltic lapped gently on a thin strip of sand. To one side wooden piers ran out far into the shallow water, to enable the broad-hulled knorrs to come in and out with cargo. Around the whole ran a stout stockade of logs, flimsy enough in comparison with the Roman walls of York far away, but in good repair and heavily manned. Shef had heard little of the deeds of King Hrorik, who ruled in Hedeby and from it to the Dane-dyke thirty miles to the south. But his revenues depended entirely on the tolls he took from traders in the port, and he both guarded it and ruled it with a prompt and heavy hand. Shef glanced from time to time at the gallows erected in plain sight on the outermost jetty, a half-dozen bearded corpses dangling from it. Hrorik was anxious to show traders their rights would be protected. One of the many things Shef could not know was whether his plan might be taken as a discouragement to trade. But in any case, as the morning drew on and the line moved forward, his mood grew grimmer.

The lot being put up this time consisted only of women: six of them, pushed forward by a group of grinning Vikings. His man held each of them by the arm while their leader walked round the knoll shouting their merits out. All young girls, Shef could see. At a word, their mantles were pulled away and each stood in a short tunic, bare-legged to above the knee, the white skin drawing all eyes in the sunlight. Whoops filled the air, lewd suggestions shouted across the crowd.

"Where are they from?" Shef asked the armed guard standing near the slave-line. The man eyed Shef's build and bearing curiously, grunted a reply.

"Wends. See the white skin and the red hair. They catch them on the south shore of the Baltic."

"And who are the buyers?" Shef could see, now, a group of dark men in strange clothing pressing forward to inspect the women more closely. They wore head-cloths instead of standing helmeted or bare-headed, and the curved daggers in their belts glittered with precious metal. Some of them at all times faced outward, as if expecting surprise attack.

"Men from the Southlands. They worship some god who is a rival to the Christ-god. Great buyers of women, and they pay in gold. Have to pay high this year."

"Why is that?"

The guard looked at him curiously again. "You speak Norse, but don't you know anything? The woman-price went up as soon as the English market turned nasty. Used to get good girls from England."

The Cordovan Arabs were asking questions now, through an interpreter. A bystander relayed them to the crowd.

"He wants to know if they're all virgins."

Roars of laughter and a great bull voice crying, "I know the tall one isn't, Alfr, I saw you trying her out yesterday outside your booth."

The leader of the sellers looked round angrily, trying to scowl the barrackers into silence. The Arabs called to their interpreter, huddled together. Finally, a bid. Expostulation, rejection. But no counter-bids. A deal struck—Shef saw the flash of money as it was paid out, and drew in his breath at the sight, not of silver, but of gold dinars. A toll paid to the auctioneer, another to the jarl of King Hrorik, watching with careful eye, and the women were wrapped and hustled away.

Next to go forward was a strange figure, a middle-aged man in the remains of a black robe. He appeared to be bald, but a slight black fuzz grew on his scalp. A Christian priest, Shef realized, with a tonsure that had not been shaved recently. As he came out, another man pushed his way out of the crowd and seemed to go to embrace him: another priest, another black robe, but this time with fresh tonsure. A guard thrust him back, another called for bids.

Instant response, from a party of tall men, heavily-built and swathed in furs even in the spring sunlight. Swedes, Shef thought, remembering the accent of Guthmund the Greedy and some of the others he had met in the ranks of the Ragnarssons' Great Army. They were offering eight ounces of silver. One of them pulled a purse from his belt and threw it on the ground to back the offer up.

The priest who had been pushed away was back again, dodging the guards, spreading out his arms and shouting passionately.

"What's he say?" muttered the guard by Shef.

"He's trying to forbid the sale," Shef answered, catching some part of the gabble of Norse and Low German that the priest was using. "Says they have no right to sell a priest of the true God."

"They'll sell him too if he doesn't shut up," said the guard.

Indeed, the Swedes had thrown another purse on the ground, exchanged words with the auctioneer, were walking forward towards both men, satisfaction on their faces.

Another man stepped from the crowd and the satisfaction faded, replaced by looks of wary calculation. Shef, used to judging warriors, could see immediately why.

The newcomer was not a tall man, shorter than the shortest of the Swedes. But he was immensely broad across the shoulders. More, he moved with an easy confidence that set men back. He wore a padded leather jacket, worn and with different strips let into it here and there. His left hand rested on the pommel of a long horseman's sword. His hair stood up like a stiff, blond brush, over a face tight-drawn, clean-shaven, as hard as stone. But it was smiling.

The blond man put a toe under one of the purses, flicked it back to the Swedes, flicked back the other.

"You can't have him," he said in stilted Norse, his voice carrying in the sudden silence. "Neither of them. They are priests of Christ, and they are under my protection. The protection of the Lanzenorden." He called suddenly in a louder voice, and swept his arm around. Shef realized there were a dozen men mailed and armed close to the ring. They outnumbered the Swedes. But there were two hundred Norsemen watching, all armed as well. If they made common cause against the Christians . . . Or if King Hrorik's men decided to protect their trade and market . . .

"We'll pay for one of them," called the blond man conciliatingly. "Eight ounces. Christian money is as good as heathen."

"Ten ounces," said the leader of the Swedes.

The auctioneer looked questioningly at the blond man.

"Twelve ounces," he said in a slow, deliberate voice. "Twelve ounces and I will forget to ask how one of you comes to have a Christian priest—and what you others want Christian priests for. Twelve ounces and think you are lucky."

The Swede slipped his hand further down the handle of his axe, spat on the ground.

"Twelve ounces," he said. "And the money of Othin rings better than the money of any smoothface gelding of a Christian."

Shef felt the guard beside him start to move, saw Hrorik's jarl also begin to step forward. As he finished speaking the Swede threw his axe up to grip it in striking position. But before any of them had completed his movement there was a streak in the air, a thud, a gasp. The Swede was gaping down at a brass hilt protruding from the center of his body. Shef realized that the blond man had never attempted to draw sword, but had instead flicked a heavy knife from his belt and thrown it underhand. Before the thought had formed, the blond man had already taken three steps forward, drawn, and was standing with the point of his long sword resting exactly on the throat-ball of the seller.

"Do we have a sale?" he called, looking for an instant sideways at the hesitating jarl.

The seller, slowly and cautiously, nodded.

The blond man flicked the sword away. "Just a private disagreement," he remarked to the jarl. "Doesn't affect the market. Happy to settle with his friends anywhere outside the town."

The jarl hesitated, then nodded too, ignoring the shouts of the Swedes bent over the body of their leader.

"Pay the money and take your man away. And hold that noise, the rest of you. If you call men names you'd better learn to be quicker. If you have a grudge you're welcome to fight it out. But not here. Bad for business. Come on, somebody, get the next lot up here."

As the Christian priests embraced and the blond man rejoined his knot of mailed supporters, bristling with weapons, Shef found himself thrust forward on to the knoll. For a moment panic seized him, like an actor forgetting his lines on an unexpected cue. Then as Nikko bustled forward, and he saw the worried face of Karli just behind him, he remembered what he had to do.

Slowly he started to pull off his grubby woolen tunic.

"What's this?" said the auctioneer. "Strong young man, able to do simple smith-work, offered for sale by—some webfoot, who cares."

Shef threw the tunic to the ground, adjusted the silver pendant of Rig in the center of his chest, flexed his muscles in a parody of the behavior of farmhands at a hiring fair. The sunlight showed the old scars of flogging across his back, flogging he had received from the hands of his stepfather years before.

"Is he tractable?" shouted a voice. "He sure doesn't look it."

"You can make a slave tractable," shouted Nikko, standing next to the auctioneer.

Shef nodded thoughtfully, stepped over to the pair of them. As he did so he carefully spread the fingers of his left hand and then curled them into a tight fist, thumb outside the second joint, as Karli had shown him. He had to make this dramatic. Not a shove, not a scuffle.

Stepping forward on to the left foot according to Karli's demonstrations, he swung his left arm in a short arc, putting all the weight of his body behind it, and aiming as if to end with his fist behind his right shoulder. The left hook connected not with Nikko's jaw—Karli had advised against that for beginners—but with his right temple. The burly man, completely unprepared, dropped instantly to his knees.

Instantly Shef had him by the collar, jerked him to his feet, turned to face the crowd.

"One webfoot," he shouted in Norse. "Talks a lot. No good at anything. What am I bid?"

"I thought he was selling you," shouted a voice.

Shef shrugged. "I changed my mind." He stared round at the crowd, trying to overbear them with his one eye. What made a thrall? In the end, there must be consent. A thrall who simply disobeyed, simply fought back, could be killed, but was worth nothing. On the edge of the ring he realized there was a minor fracas going on, as Nikko's son and nephew came forward to his assistance, only to find Karli barring their path, fists raised.

"All right, all right," snarled the jarl almost in Shef's ear. "I can see the pair of you are unsaleable. But I'll tell you this—you still owe an auction fee, and if you can't pay it I'll take it out of both of you."

Shef looked round. A dangerous moment. He had hoped to see a friendly face before this, if the Danes met on the road had spread the word. Now he would have to settle with the toll-jarl on his own. He had only two possessions left. One hand closed round the silver pendant—that was his last resort. The other?

The 'Gungnir' spear thumped into the turf at his feet. Karli, beaming and rubbing his knuckles, waved cheerfully at him. Shef started to pull the spear out, to show the rune-marks on it to the contemptuous jarl, to try to strike a deal.

"If he's for sale, the one-eye," called a voice, "I'll buy him. I know someone who wants him bad."

With a feeling of doom at his heart, Shef turned to face the voice. He had hoped a friend would recognize him. He had not forgotten the chance that it would be an enemy, but had gambled that all the followers of the Ragnarssons, the survivors of the men he had known in the Great Army, would be with the Ragnarsson fleet at sea on the other side of Denmark. He had reckoned without the loose alliances, the continuous joinings and defections, of the Viking world.

It was Skuli the Bald, who had commanded a tower in Shef's scaling of the York walls the year before, but had then thrown in his lot with the Ragnarssons who had betrayed them. He was coming forward now, his ship's crew closed up behind him in a disciplined formation.

At the same moment some inner warning told Shef another face was staring at him fixedly. He turned, met a pair of black, implacable eyes. Recognized them instantly. Erkenbert the black deacon, whom he had seen first at the death of Ragnar in the snake-pit, and seen last being loaded aboard the transport-ships after the defeat of the Christian Crusade at Hastings. He was standing next to the rescued black-robe priest, talking rapidly to the blond German, and pointing.

"Skjef Sigvarthsson Ivarsbane," said Skuli, grinning, now only a few feet away. "I'm ready to pay more than market price for you. I reckon Ivar's brothers will pay me a man's weight in silver in return."

"If you can collect," snarled Shef, backing away and looking swiftly over his shoulder for a wall to set his back against. Karli was with him, he realized. He had drawn his sword, was shouting defiance in a growing hubbub. Shef saw instantly that he had forgotten everything he had been told, was holding the weapon like a thatcher cutting reeds. If the tension snapped, Karli would be dead within five heartbeats.

The blond German was within Shef's line of vision now as well, sword also drawn, his men trying to make a line between Shef and Skuli. He too was shouting something about a price. In the background traders and slaves were scattering, some trying to get well away, others drawing, seeming to align themselves with one faction or another. The guards of King Hrorik, taken off guard by this sudden outbreak among the customers, were trying to form a wedge to drive into the midst of the likely battle.

Shef drew a deep breath, hefted his spear. He would go straight for Skuli and take his chance with Erkenbert and the Christians. One act of charity first. He turned, meaning to club the unsuspecting Karli with the spear-shaft. If the little man was on the ground, maybe no-one would kill him, as they would if he tried to fight.

Something clung to the spear-point, weighing it down, hampering him. Something else over his face, blinding him. As he tore frantically at the blanket, trying to wrestle free, a soft concussion caught him on the side of the skull, and he found himself on one knee, struggling to rise, struggling to see. If he lost consciousness the next thing he might know was a Rag- narsson face intent on cutting the blood-eagle through his ribs.

Someone kicked Shef's feet from under him, and his head met the ground.

CHAPTER EIGHT

Sorry about that," said the fat face from the other side of the table. "If I'd heard about you just a little bit earlier I'd have bought you off your Ditmarsh friends myself, and no-one would have been any the wiser. But as a king yourself, you must know how it is. No king is cleverer than the information he gets."

Shef stared, trying to bring the face into focus, shook his head to clear it, and winced.

"There," said the face. "I don't think you've heard a word I've been saying. Where does it hurt?"

Shef rubbed his left temple, realized at the same time that the lump on his skull was on the right. A hand passed in front of his eyes, and he realized he was being tested for concussion.

"Lump on one side, pain on the other. Makes you think the brain is loose inside the skull, doesn't it?" the face went on conversationally. "That's why so many veteran warriors are—well—a little strange. We call it *vithrhögg*, the counter-blow. But I can see you're recovering now. Let me just run over some of what I said again.

"I'm King Hrorik of Hedeby and South Jutland. And you are?"

Shef grinned suddenly, realizing the gist of what was said to him. "I am your fellow-king, King Shef of the East and Middle Angles."

"Good. I'm glad it's all coming back. We have these riots in the marketplace pretty often, you know, and the lads have a drill for it. Throw sailcloth over all the weapons, and then clip everyone who looks dangerous while they're trying to get their blades free. We don't like losing customers permanently." A large hand poured wine into what Shef realized was a golden cup. "Take some water with that and you'll soon feel better."

"You lost a customer today," said Shef, remembering the knife standing from the Swedish buyer's heart.

"Yes, bad business that. But my jarl reports that the dead man gave provocation. Besides . . ."

A plump finger jerked Shef's pendant from under the tunic which, he realized, someone had found and put back on for him.

"You're a man of the Way, right? So you don't have much time for Christians. None at all, from what I hear of your victory over the Franks, and I dare say they have even less for you. But down here I have to keep a very close eye on them. There's only the Dane-dyke between me and Othin knows how many German lancers. It's true they fight among themselves all the time, and it's truer that they're even more frightened of us than I am of them. But I really don't like to go stirring up trouble, especially in matters of religion.

"So I've always let the Christians send their priests up here and appeal for converts, and never said a word when they started baptizing the slaves and the women. Of course, if the poor souls wander off into the countryside and end up sold, or thrown into the bog for good luck, I can't do anything about that. I keep order in Hedeby and along the trade-road, and I judge disputes at the Thing. Telling my subjects what to believe or who to leave alone . . ." The fat man laughed. "*You* know how risky that would be.

"But this is something new. This spring, when the priests came north from Hamburg, three or four of them, each one had an escort with him. Not big enough to call an army, not even big enough to be a serious menace, and plenty of cash to pay their way. So I let them in. But I tell you something," the face leaned forward, "as one king to another. Very dangerous men. Very valuable men. I wish I could hire half-a-dozen of them. That one you saw, the blond one with the hair like stiff wire, my guard captain says he's the fastest man he's ever seen. Very tricky too."

"Faster than Ivar Ragnarsson?" asked Shef.

"The Boneless One? I was forgetting that you had bested him." Shef's vision seemed to clear as the wine did its work, and he looked more sharply at the big man leaning back in his wooden chair till the stout back of it creaked. Gold circlet on his head, heavy gold chain round his neck and thick bracelets on his arms. An air of simple good-nature, like the host of a peaceful town tavern. But sharp eyes under heavy brows, and a network of scars along the muscled right forearm, the places where a dueller picked up cuts. A successful dueller, for failed ones did not live long enough for the scars to heal.

"Well. I certainly owe you one for that. He used to worry me badly, and his brothers still do." A heavy sigh. "It's a hard life for a king down here, with the Empire and the Christians growling the other side of the Dane-dyke, and fifty sea-kings to the north forever disputing which shall be king over all. The Christians say they need an emperor now. Sometimes I think we do too. But there. If we thought that we'd have to decide who it was. Maybe me. Maybe you. Maybe Sigurth Ragnarsson. If it was him neither you nor I would live to see the day, nor want to.

"But I'm forgetting myself. You've had a hard time, I can see that, and you look as if you could use a good dinner too. Why don't you sit in the sun somewhere this afternoon, till it's time for the night-meal? I'll see it's all safe."

"I owe some money," said Shef. "That man I hit in the slave-ring—he did bring me here, and feed me for a week. I ought to pay him. And then I need money to buy passage home. If there are English traders in the port, I can borrow from them, on my own credit and that of my co-king Alfred."

Hrorik held up a ringed hand. "All dealt with, all paid for. I sent the Ditmarshers off very happy, I always try to keep in with them too, they can be a nuisance when they're angry. The one young one insisted on staying behind, though. Don't thank me, you can always pay me back.

"But as for the passage home. Well, not just yet."

Shef looked at the shrewd, jolly face. In the corner behind it he could see 'Gungnir' propped against the wall. He had no illusions about being able to reach it.

"Stay here with you?"

"I've sold you on, as a matter of fact," said Hrorik, winking.

"Sold? Who to?"

"Don't worry, not Skuli. He offered me five pounds of silver. The Christians went to ten, and a pardon for all sins from the Pope written in purple ink."

"Who then?"

Hrorik winked again. "Your friends from Kaupang. The priest-college of the Way. Made me an offer much too good to refuse. Said something about a trial. Better than being tried by Sigurth Snake-eye, though? Wouldn't you say?"

*   *   *

With a length of stout blood-sausage in his belt, a long black loaf under his arm, and a twist of salt in one hand, Shef strolled out into the strong afternoon sunshine, bidden by King Hrorik to go out and rest till dinner. Half-a-dozen guards surrounded him, there to ensure at once that no-one molested him and that he did not escape from the town. Karli, for once rather subdued, accompanied them, sword still slung from his belt, and carrying Shef's spear over one shoulder.

For a few minutes the little group walked through the crowded streets of Hedeby, full of booths selling amber, honey, wine from the south, fine weapons, bone combs, shoes, pig-iron and everything else that might be traded into or out of the Scandinavian lands. Then, as Shef grew tired of the constant edging and jostling, he caught sight of a low green mound, within the town-stockade but without buildings or people on it. He pointed to it wordlessly and headed over. The pain in his head had gone, but he still walked slowly and carefully, afraid to set if off again by some movement. He felt also as if information from the outside was filtering through to him slowly, as if he were under a foot of clear water. He had a great deal to take in and think about.

He reached the mound and sat down on the top of it, looking out over the bay of the Schlei and the green fields to the north of it. Karli hesitated, then drove the butt-spike of the spear into the soft turf and sat down also. The guards exchanged glances. "You have no fear of the howe-bride?" asked one of them.

"I have been in a howe before," said Shef. His belt-knife had gone, he noticed: Hrorik was taking no chances at all. He passed the sausage to Karli to cut up, and began to break up the bread. The guards gingerly sat or squatted in a ring around them.

After a while, belly full, back pleasantly warmed by the sun, Shef pointed out to the fertile landscape facing them outside the town's perimeter. The river Schlei ran to the north of the town, and on the opposite shore he could see hedged fields, plowmen driving their ox-teams, brown furrows growing along the green, and rising out of the trees here and there, the curls of smoke from chimneys. To an Englishman, the Viking lands appeared as the home of fire and slaughter, its inhabitants seamen and raiders, not plowmen and charcoal-burners. Yet here, at the center of the Viking storm, the land looked more peaceful than Suffolk on a summer day.

"I have heard that this is where the English came from once upon a time," Shef said to the nearest guard. "Are there any Englishmen still living over there?"

"No," said the guard. "Just Danes. Some of them call themselves Jutes, if they don't want to admit connection with the sea-kings from the islands. But they all speak the Danish tongue, just like yourself. That bit of land is still called Angel, though. It's the angle between the Schlei here and Flensborg Fjord on the other side of it. I dare say the English came from there right enough."

Shef reflected further. So much for his hope, once upon a time, of rescuing oppressed Englishmen from Danish rule here in Denmark. Still, it was strange that the Ditmarshers did not speak Danish, living next to them as they did. Strange too what they did speak: not English, nor Danish, nor yet exactly that strange language the priest had spoken this morning, a kind of German. Something with bits of all of them, and yet perhaps most similar to the Frisian Shef had got used to hearing from the men of the islands off the Dutch coast. Once upon a time this borderland had been a melting-pot of tribes. Now lines were being drawn more carefully: Christians this side, heathens that, German spoken here, Norse there. Yet the process was a long way from finished. The guard called his language Danish, *dönsk tunga,* others called the same language Norse, *norsk mal.* The same people called themselves Danes one day and Jutes the next. Shef was king of the East Angles and Alfred of the West Saxons, but both sides would agree that they were at bottom Englishmen. The German tribes were ruled by the same Pope and the same royal family as the Frankish tribes, but did not think of themselves as connected. Swedes and Gauts, Norwegians and Gaddgedlar. One day all of this would have to be sorted out and made clear. There was an urge to do it already. But who would succeed in drawing the lines, in imposing law on some level higher than Hrorik's "good for business" ethic?

Without much surprise Shef observed the blond German walking towards them out of the town, the man who had killed the Swede and rescued the priest-slave that same morning. Hrorik's guards saw him too, reacted without even a pretense of warriorly calm. Two instantly barred his path with swords drawn and shields raised, the other four poising javelins at ten feet range. The blond man smiled, unbuckled his sword belt with exaggerated care, let it drop to the ground. As the guard commander snapped orders at him, he stripped off also his leather jacket, set it down, peeled a heavy throwing-knife from under his sleeve, a short needlepoint from inside his boot. One man closed, searched him roughly and thoroughly. Finally, grudgingly, they stood back and let him pass, the javelins still poised. As he stepped the last few feet towards Shef Karli, too, drew his sword and stood in a posture of suspicious truculence.

The blond man looked at the way Karli held the sword, sighed, and sat down cross-legged facing Shef. His smile this time indicated a secret complicity.

"My name is Bruno," he remarked. "I am here with the mission of the Archbishop of Hamburg-Bremen to the Danes. Ransoming some of our people back, you know. And they tell me you are the famous Shef Sigvarthsson, the bane of the even more famous Ivar." He spoke Norse with a marked accent that made the name "Sigvarth" almost into "Siegfried."

"Who told you that?"

The smile of complicity and understanding again. "Well. As you guessed, it was your little countryman, the deacon Erkenbert. He is a passionate little fellow, and will hear no good of you at all. Yet he cannot deny that you beat the Ragnarsson sword to sword."

"Sword to halberd," corrected Shef. He added no further details.

"So. That is not often a winning game. But you use odd weapons. May I glance at your spear?" Bruno rose and studied the spear planted in the grass at Shef's side, carefully not touching it, hands behind his back.

"An excellent weapon. Newly-forged, I see. I take an interest in spears. And in other things too. May I see what you have round your neck?"

Ignoring the growl of doubt from Karli, Shef pulled out his silver pendant with the Rig-sign on it, and let Bruno, seated once more, stare intently at it.

"And what would you call that, now?"

"It is a *kraki*," said Shef. "A pole-ladder. A center pole, with rungs either side. It is the emblem of my god."

"Yet I believe you were baptized a Christian? Such a shame, that one who belonged to the true God should go over to a pagan idol. Do you feel no urge to change back? Might you not, if certain—difficulties—were cleared from your path?"

Shef smiled for the first time in their exchange, remembering the horrors inflicted on him and on others by the black monks, by Wulfgar and Bishop Daniel. He shook his head.

"I would not expect you to change your mind the first time anyone suggested it. But let me give you two things to think about," the blond man went on.

"One is this. I have no doubt all this fighting and struggling looks as if it is about land and money. And it is! Hrorik would not let me have you because he thought he had a better deal elsewhere, and he does not want to strengthen us in any way. I know you won over the English kingdoms to your heresy of freedom for all gods by abolishing the tithes men have to pay to the Church. But beneath that struggle, I am sure you know well that there is something deeper. A struggle not just of men, but of other powers."

Remembering the strange sights he had seen, the compelling voices of his protectors and the other gods in the strange Asgarth-world of his dreams, Shef slowly nodded.

"There are powers which it does no man good to be associated with. Our Church calls them devils and demons, and you may think that is just the Church's prejudice, protecting its—what is the word?—its single-trade in salvation for the soul. Well, I know priests too, and I too despise their concern for money, for buying and selling the things of God.

"But I tell you, Shef Siegfriedsson, as one warrior to another: a great change is coming, and there is One coming who shall bring it. On that day the kingdoms will be overthrown and cast into a new mold, and the priests —yes, and the archbishops and the Popes who think to control it, they will be controlled. On that day you do not want to be on the wrong side."

"And how will anyone know which is the right side?" said Shef, observing the gleam of passion on the hard, stony face. Hearing the ring in Bruno's voice the guards edged closer, as if expecting some outbreak of sudden violence.

Bruno's face split in another of his unexpected and strangely winning smiles. "Oh, there will be a sign. Something pretty unmistakable, I expect. A miracle, a relic, something sent from God to work in the world, a chosen leader to use it." He rose to his feet, prepared to go.

"You said you had two things to tell me," prompted Shef. "Be on the right side when the kingdoms are shaken, that was one. The other?"

"Oh yes. Of course. I have to tell you you are in part mistaken about your own sign. I hope you recognize others better. What you have round your neck, you may call it a *kraki* in Norse, or a 'ladder' in your language and mine. In Latin, though—you have heard Latin from the priests? Well, they would call it a *graduale*. From *gradus,* a step, you know."

Shef waited, not sure of the point.

"There are those who believe in the Holy Graduale. The Franks call it the Holy Graal. Dreadful the way the Franks talk Latin—can you imagine a language in which *aqua* turns into *eau?* Yes, the Holy Graduale, or Grail, that is what you have round your neck. It's supposed to go with the Holy Lance, some say."

Bruno stepped over to his pile of clothes and weapons, and slowly resumed them, covered all the time by javelins. Finally he looked at Shef, nodded a farewell, and strolled peacefully back towards the town and the markets.

"What was all that about?" Karli asked suspiciously. Shef did not answer. The feeling of being underwater was growing on him, as if he were now fathoms deep, but in clear water which hid nothing from his view. Still looking out over the peaceful fields of the Angle, he felt the pinch on his neck that told him his sight was being directed. On top of the green fields and the furrows and the curling smoke-plumes of cottages, other pictures began to impose themselves.

He was still looking at exactly the same place, but the buildings of Hedeby were no longer there, there were more trees, less plowland. This is the Angle as it was when the English left it, something told him. Ten long warboats were cruising into the Schlei, much the same as those of Sigurth Ragnarsson, but different, more primitive in design: no mast or sail, only oars, and a stiffer, crankier air, without the living suppleness of the full-fledged Viking ship. War canoes with rowlocks. Shef's sight followed them as they pulled up river, found an inlet, paddled along it into a small, shallow lake. The crews streamed out, never more than thigh-deep in the water, dispersed into the countryside, began to come back late in the day, laden with metal, with sacks and barrels, cattle and women. They settled down by their ships, lit fires as night came on, began to slaughter the beeves and rape the women. Shef watched unmoved: he had seen worse in reality, without the distancing of his vision.

The men of the land had not gone, had fled only to find their weapons and gather their strength. Now they had a leader. Where the canoes had paddled into the lake he felled trees, threw them in to block the exit. Then the land-folk began to close in on the scene of rape and riot. Arrows flew from the trees. The raiding party abandoned their entertainments, ran to their weapons, gathered to beat off the attack. Some women slipped away, crawled into the darkness or into the black water of the lake. Others were struck by flying arrows, cut down by angry raiders.

The people of the land made a line and pressed forward, shields raised. The raiders met them, the two sides hacked at each other over yellow linden shields for a few minutes, then the land-folk fell back. Once more arrows flew from the trees. A voice called out from the dark forest, promising to give all the raiders to the war-god, hang them on trees for the birds. The raiders gathered their ships, tried at dawn to break out the way they had come, met the tangled tree-trunks of the barricade. During a long morning's fighting, Shef saw—speeded up as if all was done by two armies of ants—the raiders defeated, split up, blankets thrown over their weapons so that the survivors were borne down or pinned between shields. In the end ten war-boats, their gunwales hacked and splintered, lay on the edge of black mud, a hundred and twenty grim-faced prisoners standing or lying by them.

The victors cleared the site of bodies and weapons, brought them all to the captured ships, urged on by the orders of their leader. Shef expected to see the prisoners stripped of armor and valuables, the loot divided. Instead the men began to smash holes in the boats' planks. They drove the captured spears into tree-trunks and bent them so that the iron shafts were useless. They snapped the bows and arrows, punched holes in the bronze helmets, took the swords, heated the blades in fire to destroy their temper, and then rolled the blades up with tongs into twisted spirals. Finally they turned to their prisoners, marched each one to a cauldron, bent him over it, cut his throat and bled him into it like a Michaelmas pig. The bodies were stacked in the boats, pushed out into the lake to sink, the broken weapons left on the boggy shore.

Everyone went away. For years everything lay as it had been left, the place avoided by all except the occasional awed or daring child. The boats and bodies and weapons sank slowly, maggot-ridden, into the black mud. Even more slowly, the lake dried out. Now cows pastured on it, all memory of what had happened there long gone, both among the victor-Angles whose descendants now lived far across the sea, and among the men of the islands to whom no word of their defeated expedition had ever come back.

And why do they do that? Shef found himself asking. The scale of what he was watching changed, he was no longer looking at real earth, at real history, instead he seemed to be viewing a drawing, a drawing that moved. Across a bare plain, the sun rose. Only it was not the sun, it was a ball of fire in a chariot, drawn by horses. The horses ran in terror, foam-flecked. Across the sky behind them ran giant wolves, tongues lolling, determined to pull down the horses and eat the sun. When the sun is hidden, or the moon, something told him, it is a wolf's shadow falling across it. One day the wolves will catch up and blood rain from the sky before sun and moon go out.

From the plain a great tree rose, giving air and shade and life to all the worlds beneath its branches. Looking closely, Shef saw that it twisted continually in pain. Beneath the earth, at its heart-root, he could see a giant serpent gnawing on it, venom dripping from its jaws. In the sea swam an even more monstrous serpent, rising from time to time to draw down a ship under full sail with one snap of its jaws. Deep beneath both the tree-serpent and the ocean-serpent Shef's new sight could see the dim outlines of some even more monstrous shape, chained to the foundations of the world, but writhing in pain so that the earth shook. It too was tormented, continually it struck back, one day it would break free to urge on the wolves of the sky and the serpent of the sea.

That is the world the pagans know of, Shef thought. No wonder they hate and fear their gods and seek only to propitiate them with cruelty. Their gods are afraid too, even Othin Allfather fears Ragnarök but does not know how to avert it. If there were a better way for the pagans to follow, they would take it. He thought of Thorvin's preachings of the Asgarth Way. Thought too of the White Christ, the suffering face under a crown of thorns which he had once seen on a wooden statue at Ely Cathedral, of the martyred King Edmund who had died under Ivar's chisel.

But that is not the whole story, something told him. Only a part. One day you may see the world as the Christians see it. Till then, remember this. Remember the wolves in the sky and the serpent in the sea.

The pleasant warmth on Shef's back had faded. As his normal sight slowly returned to him he realized that he was still looking out across the Schlei, his eyes wide open and unblinking. The green fields were still there, but the afternoon sun had faded, clouded over. His guards had drawn back, were muttering anxiously to each other as they stared at him.

Closer, a man knelt on one knee, looking deeply into his face. Shef recognized the white clothes and rowan-berry necklace of a priest of the Way, noted the silver boat which said that this was a priest of Njörth, the sea-god.

"I am Hagbarth," said the priest. "I am here to take you to Kaupang. My colleagues have been very anxious to meet you, to test you on their own ground. Fortunate for us that you came here from England."

He hesitated. "Will you tell me what you have just seen."

"Nothing but the world as it is," said Shef.

"To see things the way they are, that is a rare skill," answered Hagbarth. "And even rarer in broad daylight. Maybe you are the true prophet that Thorvin says, and not the false emissary of Loki that others declare. I will bear witness for you. We must go now."

"To Hrorik's hall?"

"And on to Kaupang."

Shef rose from the ground, stiffer and more cramped than he should have been. As he plodded down from the knoll towards Hedeby, he reflected on what he had seen. Was it his own mind telling him to accept the Christian Bruno's offer? Was it a warning, telling him of the true nature of the world he was entering, the world of the sea-kings, shaped by blood and horror over a hundred generations?

As they came to the edge of the town, they saw a coffle of slaves marched by. Shef looked at them, surprised to see such wretched folk find a market: old men, old women hobbling along, all with faces marked by a lifetime of toil, mere bags of bones like old oxen fit only for slaughter and the broth-pot.

"Are they worth bringing to market?" he asked.

"The Swedes buy them for the sacrifice at Uppsala," said one of the guards. "Summer and winter, a hundred oxen, a hundred horses, a hundred men and women they sacrifice and hang in the great oak groves at Uppsala. They say that without it the kingdom of the Swedes would fall, and the sky come down on their heads. If you can get no more work out of your thrall, you can always get one last payment that way."

One of the other guards laughed. "Keeps all the thralls working as hard as ever they know how, too. Maybe it's us should pay the Swedes."

CHAPTER NINE

Against the startling blue sky the great mountain line stood out in brilliant white. In fold after fold the range tumbled down to the black water at its foot—black only where the outflowing river kept a channel clear. Elsewhere thick ice still covered the shallow water of the bay, joining the mainland to the islands scattered along the shore. A thin powder of fresh snow covered the trees on the islands, and the ice between them. Where wind had swept the snow away, the ice lay old and transparent, still feet in thickness, but taking its color from the black depths beneath.

In the prow of the longboat, Shef and Karli watched, awestruck. In the land they had left, spring was far advanced, the buds out and the birds singing and nesting. Here there was no fresh green, only the dark gloom of the conifers, and the bright sun seemed only to be thrown back by the hard snow. The longboat was moving slowly now, under oars alone and they at no more than the paddling stroke. Hagbarth had furled sail in the night, as soon as he felt the loom of the land on either side, as soon as he knew they were within the deep bay that ran up in the end to the town of Oslo. Now, from time to time, the crew heard the sharp rap-rap of ice chunks striking the boat's fragile planks. Standing above them on the very gunwale itself, holding on with one hand as he leaned outboard, a crewman called sharp directions to the helmsman at the steering-oar, directing him away from the greater ice-lumps, the small islands that came drifting down the current from the land.

"Not much risk from ice this late in the spring," Hagbarth had said, the

first time his southern passengers had jumped to their feet in alarm at the knocking beneath their feet. "But we won't risk it just the same."

Shef had been profoundly glad, and Karli even gladder, of the reduction in speed, and not just out of fear of what awaited them at journey's end. Neither man, not even Shef, had made a fast passage in a Viking longboat before. It was an experience very different—Shef now realized—from the stately waddle of the *Norfolk* up the Dutch coast, the sickening roll and lurch of sailing in a Yorkshire fishing-coble. The Viking boat, Hagbarth's own *Aurvendill*, had seemed to slide over the water like a great, supple snake. Each wave as it came towards them rose far above the gunwales, looked down on the undecked hull, seemed certain to crash down on it in a swamping torrent. Then the prow rose, swarmed up, seemed like an intelligent creature to look over the other side and begin its downward curve while the stern-post was still rising. After a while Shef, his nerve starting to return, found Karli sitting staring in horror at the lower planks below the waterline. They shifted continually, moving away from the boat's ribs and then moving back again, held only by lashings of twisted root or sinew. Often the gaps were large enough for a man to put foot, hand, or even head through. At such moments there seemed to be nothing except habit holding the side-planks together at all. For a while after that both Karli and Shef sat together, convinced deep in their bellies that if they slackened the tension of their watch, the charm would break and the sea come rushing through.

As for anything striking the egg-shell's sides, the thought was unbearable. Shef had once asked Hagbarth if Norsemen ever carried horses or oxen from place to place, and if so, how they prevented the beasts from rushing to and fro in panic. Hagbarth had laughed. "If you put a horse in my *Aurvendill*," he said, "I have always found that any of them, even the fiercest stallion, takes one good look round him and then stands very, very still." Shef could see why.

And yet they had had to hurry, ice or no ice, running under full sail all the time during daylight, moving at a speed only a little under a horse's full gallop or a man's all-out sprint, as fast as a young man would go if he had nothing to carry and no more than a quarter of a mile to cover. For hour after hour. In the twelve hours of daylight on their first day Shef thought they might have traveled more than a hundred and fifty miles, though it was true they had tacked continually, making it less than that in a straight line. In the two nights and two days of their voyage, maybe four hundred all told—four hundred miles to bring them from the spring of flatland Denmark to the settled chill of Norway and the mountains.

All the way Hagbarth, explaining their haste, had commented on the immediate dangers on one or either side. Ships of King Hrorik had convoyed them up the South Jutland coast by night and through the Great Belt, the gap of water between the Danish mainland and Othin's own island of Fyn. Not too much risk there, Hagbarth had said. Hrorik has an arrangement with King Gamli of Fyn. But then they had swerved sharply out to sea with dawn and the turn-back of Hrorik's escorts. King Arnodd of Aalborg, Hagbarth had explained. Not hostile, does business like anyone else. But part of his business is robbing ships. Anyone without his leave, not related to him or his jarls, or just too weak to resist. Anyway, he feels threatened now: has to keep up a reputation.

Who's threatening him, Shef had asked, wondering already if the sea-legs he had acquired weeks before would keep off sea-sickness in the strange swoopings of the *Aurvendill*. Hagbarth had spat carefully past Karli's vomiting form and jerked a thumb to starboard, to the dim shapes of Fyn and Sjaelland beyond.

"The real bastards," he had said briefly. "Your friends. The Ragnarssons.

Their base is over there, the Braethraborg, and the Emperor of the Greeks himself wouldn't want to meet them at sea. Don't worry," he had added. "As far as we know the Snake-eye took the whole lot south to meet you, and they haven't come back yet. If they have, they'll be coming round the point over there on the backboard right about now. Unless they've strung out to make a nice long line from coast to coast just ahead."

Even after they had cleared the menace of the Skaggerak and were sailing, wind abeam, ten miles off the long coast of the South Swedes, Hagbarth's conversation was a long list of human hazards: King Teit of the East Gauts, King Vifil of the West Gauts, reports of independent pirates off the Weder islands, rumors of a fleet of broken men out of the Small Lands trying their luck up towards Norway, King Hjalti of the Farmsteads, and always—or so Hagbarth had said, though by this time Shef was suspecting him of deliberate terrorization—the possibility of the fearsome kings of the West-fjords taking a change from their usual raiding-grounds in the Atlantic islands and against the Irish, and coming over to vex the Swedes, whom they hated.

"In your country," Karli had asked once, pale with sickness and terror, "can anyone call himself a king?"

"Not *anyone*," Hagbarth had said with all seriousness. "It helps if you can call yourself one of the god-born, and there are plenty of people to check that. Us for a start, we priests of the Way. And there are some who are too proud to lie about their ancestry, like the Hlathir jarls—if they are descended from anyone it must be the trolls.

"But as a rule, if you can raise a fleet, say sixty ships or so, and you can find yourself a base on land, even if it is only a few square miles like the Braethraborg—the Ragnarssons took that from old King Kolfinn of Sjaelland, and defied him to take it back—then you can call yourself a king. Sea-king is what they usually say."

"And how do you get to be a king of somewhere? Like the Farmsteads or the Small Lands or the Midden-heaps or the Further Cow-byre," asked Shef, temper strained by fear.

"Get a Thing to accept you," said Hagbarth briefly. "Easiest way to do that is to stand in the clearing and say you're king and you're going to tax everybody. If you get out of the clearing, you're probably a king. God-born or no."

The tension had only slackened at dawn that day when Hagbarth, looking carefully round him at the first blink of dawn, had pronounced them within the waters of the Norwegian kings, Olaf and Halvdan.

"Kings of Norway?" Shef had asked.

"Kings of the Westfold and the Eastfold," Hagbarth replied. "One each, but co-kings of both. And don't look like that, what about you and Alfred? You're not even brothers. Half-brothers, that is."

Further argument had been cut out by the appearance from either side of heavily-manned warships, each half the size again of the *Aurvendill*, long pennants flying. Shef knew enough of the sea to recognize them as coast-defense craft only, unfit for a deep-sea passage or a hard gale because of their riveted keels, but capable of jamming in a hundred warriors each for a short while, untroubled by the need to carry rations and water. As the ice narrowed in from either side they closed up, eventually falling into line astern, each ship paddling gently into the whirlpools made by the one ahead, as the oars dipped and pulled in the dark water.

Ahead Shef could see what looked like a substantial township, many log houses with plumes of smoke rising from all of them. At its center rose a large hall, horns jutting from ridge and gables. Further away, outside the town but below the mountains, he could see with his one sharp eye a collection of larger buildings, some of them strangely shaped, but all half-hidden by the firs. Where the town ran down to the shore, dozens of boats of all sizes lay at jetties. And, at the largest and longest of the jetties, he could pick out what seemed to be a welcoming committee. Or a group of jailers. Shef looked longingly at the islands scattered thickly to the left. The ice was barely fifty yards away now. Then a few hundred yards more to the land, and on every island plumes of smoke to show shelter and habitation.

All ruled by the co-kings, of whichever Fold it was. If your heart did not stop beating as soon as you touched the freezing water. If you did not freeze solid as soon as you climbed out of it.

Shef belatedly realized that he cut hardly a kingly figure himself. He had started the trip in exactly the same tunic, breeches and leather shoes that he had worn continually since he had struggled ashore on the Ditmarsh two weeks before: bemired, salt-stained, blood-stained from his own blood and the Viking he had killed on the sandbanks, with a fortnight's accumulation of tar-patches, spilt broth, and sweat on top. It was no worse than what he had worn most of his boyhood in the Norfolk marsh, but Vikings, he had noticed, were cleanlier than Englishmen, or at least than English churls. Only Karli sat next to him when they came to eat. As they sailed further north and the sea-wind came keener, Hagbarth had tossed each of them a thick blanket, which they now hugged round them.

By contrast to their squalor, Shef could pick out on the jetty scarlet capes, gleaming armor, polished shields reflecting the sun, and in a solid body at the water's edge, the shining white clothes of the priests of the Way, competing with the snow behind. Shef ran a hand ineffectually through his hair, dislodging a louse, and turned for advice to Hagbarth. Then turned back again, with sudden incredulous joy.

One figure over there by the shore stood out even among the tall shapes around him. Surely—yes, that must be Brand. Scanning quickly along the jetty, Shef realized that there were other men there in a little knot, smaller than the rest as Brand was bigger. And one of them showed up in a bright flash of scarlet—it was the silk tunic the ex-slave Cwicca wore for great occasions. Now that he knew what he was looking for, Shef could pick them out readily. Brand there well to the fore, Guthmund the Greedy standing beside him, and in a self-effacing clump to the rear Cwicca and Osmod and a gang of their mates. Shef looked again at the white tunics and cloaks of the priests of the Way, standing at the very edge of the jetty. Yes, Thorvin was there among them, and Skaldfinn too, and Hund: outnumbered, though, by a cluster of other priests, one formidable figure near the front almost rivaling Brand even in size. And there was another group there as well, standing separate both from the priests and from Brand and his friends. A puff of wind from the mountains caught the pennants held by standard-bearers, and for a moment Shef saw the Hammer of the Way, white on black, and from the group he could not identify a blue streamer with a strange design he did not recognize. He looked a mute question at Hagbarth.

"It is the Gripping Beast," said Hagbarth, dropping his voice, the jetty now only fifty yards away.

"Of King Halvdan? Or King Olaf?"

"Neither," said Hagbarth with a touch of grimness. "Of Queen Ragnhild."

The crewmen tossed oars, dropped them clattering into the bottom of the boat. Ropes flew out from prow and stern, were caught and snubbed to tree-trunk bollards. The *Aurvendill* settled gently alongside the jetty. The gangplank was thrown across.

Shef hesitated, conscious of his own appearance. Facing him, the big unknown priest looked down, what seemed to be scorn and mistrust on his face. Shef remembered the last time he had stood face to face with an enemy on a gangplank: when he had killed Ivar, Champion of the North. No-one else could ever say that. Shedding his blanket, and snatching the 'Gungnir' spear from Karli's ready hand, he stepped on to the gangplank, strode across it, meaning to force the priest to stand back.

As he reached the other end an arm like the base of a mast quietly thrust

the priest aside, and Brand shoved forward, holding out an immense fur cape, made from the skin of a white bear, its brooch and chain of gold. In an instant he had wrapped it round Shef's shoulders, fastened the links. Then he fell to one knee, his face still only just below Shef's own level.

"Hail, King of the East and Middle Angles," he called. On the signal, Cwicca and his mates, and the crews of the *Walrus* and the *Seamew* further behind, cheered and clashed their weapons.

Brand, who had never knelt in his life before, winked one staring eye, and jerked his head infinitesimally at the others on the jetty. Shef caught the hint, turned to Hagbarth, who had followed him up the gangplank.

"You may present your colleagues," he said imperiously.

"Why, this is—ah—King Shef, may I present to you Valgrim the Wise, Head of the College of the Way and priest of Othin? Valgrim, this is . . ."

Valgrim was paying no attention. With a scowl for Brand, he reached out one hand, seized the spear in Shef's grip, and turned it so that he could read the runes on it. After a moment he released the spear, turned and walked wordlessly off.

"He didn't like that," muttered Brand. "What do the runes say?"

"Gungnir. It's not my spear anyway, I took it from Sigurth Ragnarsson."

Most of the other priests of the Way had moved off after their leader, leaving Thorvin and Hund behind. As they departed, Shef saw the other group coming towards them under the blue and silver banner. He gaped up at it: a strange design, of a beast with snarling face, seemingly throttling itself with one paw while clutching its own ankle with another. He dropped his eyes, found himself face to face with the most striking woman he had ever seen.

He would not have thought her beautiful if some one had described her. Since his childhood Shef had framed his ideas of beauty on Godive: tall but slight of figure, with brown hair, gray eyes, and the perfect complexion she had inherited from her Irish slave-concubine mother. This woman was tiger to Godive's sleek leopard: as tall as Shef, with broad cheekbones and great green eyes set wide apart. Her breasts swelled out the dark green gown she was wearing, and heavy hip-bones showed through as she walked. Two long plaits hung round her face and over her shoulders, held in place by a heavy gold band low over her forehead. She was not a young woman either, Shef realized belatedly, but double his age or Godive's. At her side walked a young boy, maybe ten years old.

Confused, and unwilling to face the woman's stare, Shef dropped on one knee to the boy's level.

"And who are you?"

"I am Harald, son to King Halvdan and Queen Ragnhild. What happened to your eye?"

"Someone put it out with a hot needle."

"Did it hurt?"

"I fainted before it was finished."

The boy looked scornful. "That was not *drengiligr*. Warriors do not faint. Did you kill the man who did it?"

"I killed the man who caused it. The one who did it is standing over there, and the one who held me. They are friends."

The boy looked nonplused. "How can they be friends if they blinded you?"

"Sometimes you will take from your friends what you will not from your enemies."

Belatedly Shef realized the boy's mother's thigh was only inches from his blind side. He rose to his feet, conscious as he did so of the strong female warmth. There, on the jetty, with dozens of men all around, he could feel his manhood stirring as it had not for all the Ditmarsh girl's efforts. In another moment he would feel the urge to throw her down on the wooden deck—if he were strong enough, which he doubted.

The queen looked scrutinizingly at him, seemingly aware of what he felt. "You will come when I call you, then," she said, and turned away.

"Most men do," muttered Brand again in Shef's ear.

Over his voice, as he watched the green gown retreating magnificently towards the snow, Shef heard a sound he would once have picked out through any distractions: the clink-clink, beat-beat of light and heavy hammers working at a forge. And other sounds too which he could not place.

"We've a lot to show you," said Thorvin, finally making his way up to his former apprentice.

"Right," said Brand. "But first, the bath-house. I can see the lice in his hair, and it puts me off even if Queen Ragnhild likes it."

"He came stalking ashore with one eye and a spear in his hand with the 'Gungnir' runes on it," growled Valgrim. "What else has he to do to declare himself Othin? Ride an eight-legged horse? He is a blasphemer!"

"Many men have one eye," replied Thorvin. "And as for the 'Gungnir' runes, he did not have them cut. The only reason he has the spear is that Sigurth Snake-eye threw it at him. If there is a blasphemer, it is Sigurth."

"You have told us that when he first appeared to you out of nowhere two winters ago he said he came from the North."

"Yes, but all that he meant was that he came from the north of his kingdom."

"And yet you have presented this to us as if this accident were proof that he is the One we await. That he is the One who will come from the North to overthrow the Christians and put the world on its better path. If this aping of Othin is an accident, then what he said to you was an accident. But if what he said to you was a sign from the gods, then this too is a sign. He is setting himself up as Othin. And I, the priest of Othin in this college, I say that such as he cannot have Othin's favor. Did he not refuse the Othin-sacrifice when he had the Christian army at his mercy?"

Thorvin fell silent, unable to see a way round Valgrim's logic.

"I can tell you that he is one who sees visions," put in Hagbarth. "And not only in his sleep."

The listening priests, a score of them together, looked at him with interest. They had not formed their holy circle nor set up the holy cordon of rowan-berries round the spear and the bale-fire: what they said was still unprivileged, not done under the guidance of the gods. Still, they were not forbidden to speak of holy things.

"How do you know?" grunted Valgrim.

"I saw him in Hedeby. He sat on a mound outside the town, a grave-

mound, an old king's howe. They told me he made his way there un-
prompted."

"Means nothing," said Valgrim. He quoted derisively lines from one of
the traditional poems of the past:

"Then the bastard sat on the barrow,
When the princes parted the spoil."

"Bastard or not," Hagbarth went on. "I saw him with his eyes wide open,
seeing nothing and replying to no-one. When the fit passed I asked him
what he had seen and he replied, he saw things as they were."

"What did he look like when the fit was on him?" asked a priest with
the sign of Ull the hunter-god round his neck.

"Like him." Hagbarth jerked a thumb at the most respected of the
priests in the conclave, Vigleik of the visions, seated unspeaking at the end
of the table.

Slowly Vigleik stirred. "One other thing we must remember," he offered.
"The evidence of Farman priest of Frey, our brother still in England. He
says that two winters ago he was in the camp of the Ragnarssons, searching
for new knowledge, trying to see whether even among the Loki-brood
there might be the One we await. He had seen Thorvin's apprentice whom
they now call King Shef, but he knew nothing of him, thought him only an
English runaway. Yet the day after the great battle with King Jatmund he
too saw a vision, in daylight. A vision of the smithy of the gods. In it he
saw Thorvin's apprentice in the shape and place of Völund, the lame
smith. And he saw Othin speak to him. Farman told me, though, that
Othin did not take him under his protection. So maybe Valgrim, as priest
of Othin, is right to fear him. There may be other plans than Othin's."

Valgrim's chest swelled with rage, both at the challenge to Othin's plans
and at the thought that he might be a prey to fear. He did not venture to
defy Vigleik. Among the priests who had gathered to the College from the
whole of Norway, and the other Scandinavian lands, there were more who
knew of Vigleik the Seer than of Valgrim the Wise—wise in the ways of
kings and the arts of government. One of the arts of government was to
keep silent till the moment came.

"Guidance may come to us," he said pacifically.

"Who from?" asked a priest from Ranrike to the north.

"From our holy circle, when the time comes to form it."

"Also," said Vigleik, "if we are fortunate, from King Olaf. He is the wisest
of kings on the earth, though not the most lucky. I suggest we invite him
to attend our conclave, to sit outside the circle. He is not the One, though

once we thought he might be. Yet if anyone may recognize a true king, it is he."

"I thought Olaf Elf-of-Geirstath was dead," muttered the Ranrike priest to one of his back-country fellows.

Washed from head to foot in a great tub of heated water, his hair cut short and scrubbed again and again with lye, Shef stepped cautiously across the old, hard-packed snow of the College's precinct. His clothes had been taken away and replaced with a hemp shirt and tight-fitting woolen drawers, a thick wool tunic and trousers over them. Brand had repossessed the bearskin cape, muttering that if he found lice in that he would send Shef out to hunt down another one, but he had replaced it with a mantle of homespun. His gold bracelets again shone on Shef's biceps, though he had refused to replace the gold circlet of kingship on his cropped head. He walked clumsily in a pair of thick winter boots borrowed from Guthmund, padded out with wound rags. In spite of the cold and the snow, he felt warm for the first time in days.

Udd the undersized steelmaster kept pace with him. After the rough administrations of Brand, Shef had greeted Cwicca and the rest of his faithful gang, handed Karli over to them, scowling distrustfully, and told them to consider him a new and valued recruit, and then become aware that Udd was standing to one side, tongue-tied as ever. One only became aware of Udd when he had something to say or to show. It was certainly something to do with metal. Remembering the forge-noises he had heard from the jetty, Shef clapped Udd on the shoulder, added a final warning about good behavior to Karli, and followed Udd out into the open. Cwicca and the other English ex-slaves who had come to this unknown land in the north had promptly slammed the door, wedged every chink they could find, and returned to their normal habit of clustering round the fire in as much animal warmth as they could manage.

Udd was not heading towards the place from which familiar forge-noises came, but to a small building separate from the main frequented halls and dormitories. As they walked a figure shot suddenly past them at a speed no man could match. Shef jumped to one side, fumbling for the sword at his belt, saw the figure sweep away down the slope to the township well below.

"What was that?" he gasped. "Skates? On snow? Downhill?"

"They call 'em skis," said Udd. "Or ski-runners or something. Wooden boards you tie to your feet. They all use 'em up here. Strange folk. But now look at this." He pushed the door open and led Shef into an empty shed.

For a few moments Shef could see nothing in its dark interior. Then, as Udd fumbled open a shutter he saw a great stone wheel lying in the middle of the shed. As his eyes grew used to the dimness, Shef realized that there were actually two wheels, one over the other. A machine of some kind.

"What do they do?" he asked.

Udd lifted a trapdoor, pointed under the shed to a channel below. "When the snow melts there's a stream under here. See the wheel down there? With the paddles on it? Water flows, turns the paddles. Axle on that wheel turns these two above. The surfaces touching each other have channels cut in 'em. Pour grain in. Grinds the grain."

Shef nodded, remembering the monotonous noise of the old woman grinding corn in the Ditmarsh hut, the job that never ceased, the job that warriors hated.

"Does it much faster than women with the old pestle and mortar," Udd added. "Mind you, it's been frozen solid since we got here. They say when it's working it grinds as much corn as forty women working all day. The folk come up from the town and pay the priests to use it."

Shef nodded again, reflecting on how the monks of Saint John or Saint Peter would have appreciated such an addition to their income. He saw the potential of the device. But he could not understand Udd's interest: it was notorious that the little man cared for nothing but metal. Best not to rush him.

Silently Udd led his king out and down the slope to a second shed. "This is like rung two," he said, with a glance at Shef's ladder-emblem. "And this is down to us. See, ever since last year the priests here have been fascinated by what they heard of our catapults. Cwicca and his mates have already built a couple, to show 'em how we do it. But they'd already got the idea of the little wheels: the cog-wheels, you know. And the priest who was working with the mill, he got the idea of using real big cog-wheels not to wind a catapult but to make a different mill."

The pair approached the second building. On one wall of it, another big wooden wheel with paddles, exactly like the first one: but set vertically in the snow-choked ravine, not horizontally. Clearly the water would turn this even better, with a better purchase. But what use would an axle be turning two vertical millstones? The corn would run straight through them and never be ground at all. It was the weight of the stone that did the grinding.

Still silently Udd led Shef in and pointed to the gearing. At the end of the millwheel-axle an immense iron cog-wheel stood vertical. Its teeth meshed into a matching horizontal cog, fitted over a stout oak axle. Below it, on the same axle, the two familiar stone wheels. Above them, a hopper showed where men could stand to pour in sacks of kernels.

"Yes, lord, it's well-done. But what I wanted to say was there's something to do with this that these folk haven't thought of yet. See, lord," Udd dropped his voice, though there was no-one near, no-one within a furlong of them. "What's our problem with iron? With making it, like?"

"Beating it out," said Shef.

"How many days does it take a man to get fifty pound of iron out of, say, five times that amount of ore?"

Shef whistled, remembering the hours he had spent pounding out the slag for his first home-made sword. "Ten," he guessed. "Depends how strong the smith is."

"That's why smiths have to be strong," agreed Udd, looking down at his own puny frame. "I couldn't ever be one. But then I thought, if this mill does the work of forty grinding-slaves, women that is, could it not do the work of, say, twenty smiths?"

Shef began to feel a familiar warning itch in his brain. Many minds were working here, as they had worked to make the catapults, the pulley-wound crossbow. Some priest of the Way had thought of the water-mill. Some long-dead Roman had left behind the cog-wheels. Shef and his crewmen had rebuilt the catapults. And from hearing about that alone, some other priest had worked out how to transfer the force in the flow of a river to the task he needed in a different dimension. Now Udd had returned that thought to his own obsession. It was as if people too were cog-wheels, the one fitting into the other, one brain turning the next.

"How could stone wheels grind iron?" he asked cautiously.

"Well, lord, what came to me was this." Udd dropped his voice even further. "What everyone's always thought in this line is, a wheel drives a wheel. But I thought, what if it doesn't? What if it drives something a different shape? And much, much bigger? See, axle turns here. Turns a shape like this. The shape turns, and all the time it's turning, it's lifting a heavy weight, as heavy as a millwheel. Only not a millwheel, a hammer. But when it gets to this point here—it stops lifting. The hammer drops instead. A really heavy hammer, a hammer six smiths couldn't lift, not even if they were as strong as Brand! And hammering as fast as the axle on this mill-wheel turns. How long would it take to beat out fifty pounds of iron then? Five hundred pounds?"

The little man's pale face shone with excitement, the thrill of the inventor. Shef caught the feeling, felt his palms itch to start the work.

"Listen, Udd," he said, trying to keep a cool head. "I don't see what you mean about the shape to lift and to drop."

Udd nodded energetically. "That's what I've been thinking about every night in my bunk. What we need, I reckon, is something like this . . ."

On the floor of the hut, planks overlaid with a thin layer of drifted snow from under the warped door, Udd began to draw a cross-section of a reciprocating cam. After a few moments Shef seized his own straw and began to draw as well. "If it turns like this," he said, "you'd have to have a groove on the handle of the hammer, to stop it flying off. But does it have to have a hammer-shape?"

An hour later Thorvin the smith-priest, coming from his doubtful meeting, saw the tall king and the puny freedman walking down the snowy path, their arms waving wildly as they designed imaginary machines. For an instant he understood Valgrim's doubts. Farman and Vigleik might see the One King in their visions. No vision or prophecy had ever included a word, he was sure, about scrawny foreign thrallborn assistants.

CHAPTER TEN

In the Scandinavian lands, in the year of Our Lord 867, the peoples were much the same, but the lands themselves greatly different. In spite of centuries of bickering, jealousy and war, the Danes, Swedes and Norwegians were all much more like each other than anyone else. There is every difference, though, between the fertile pastures of the Danish islands and the Jutland peninsula, or the long coastline of Sweden in the sheltered tideless Baltic, and the fjord-splintered Atlantic-facing stretch of Norway, with its immense and almost pathless spine of mountains, the Keel. The Norwegians said even then of the Danes that only Danes could have an eighteen-hundred foot hillock as the highest spot in all their kingdoms, and call it Himinbjerg, Sky Mountain. The Danes said of the Norwegians that if you put ten Norwegians together, eleven would call themselves kings and lead fifteen armies to war against each other. The jokes had a basis in fact, in geography and history. Travel for the Norwegians was not impossibly difficult, for there were passages all the way up the coast with its thousands of islands, and in the long winter ski-runners could travel over the snow faster than any horse could gallop. Yet it might take two days to go round by sea rather than cross a ten-thousand-foot sheer-rising mountain mass. It was easier in Norway to divide than to unite. Easy too, in a land where there was a boatyard on every one of a thousand fjords, to raise a fleet and crew it with the younger sons who counted their fathers' farmlands in fractions of an acre.

In this land of little kingdoms and brief alliances, forty years before, there had been a king called Guthroth. He was king of the Westfold, the land to the west of the great fjord that runs up to Oslo and divides the main Norwegian mass from the borders with Sweden. He was a king not much better, or much worse, than his neighbors and rivals the kings of the Eastfold, of Ranrike, Raumrike, Hedemark, Hedeland, Toten, Akershus and all the others. His subjects, a few score thousand, maybe enough to make the population of a decent English shire, called him the Huntsman because of his hobby, which was hunting women—a dangerous and difficult hobby, even for a king, in a land where every cot-carl had spear, axe and half-a-dozen Viking expeditions behind him.

But Guthroth persevered. In the end his first wife Thurith, daughter of the king of Rogaland, died, worn out with vexation at her husband's infidelities and the trouble and expense they caused, and Guthroth thought at once of replacing her. His eye fell on the daughter of the king of the tiny kingdom of Agdir, no more than a town and a handful of villages: Asa, daughter of Hunthjof the Strong, a virgin of unmatched beauty. To Guthroth it seemed that her charms might stir again in him the youth that seemed to be passing. But Hunthjof the Strong refused Guthroth's offers, saying that his daughter would not need to go sniffing other women's beds to see who had been in them. Stung by the insult and the rejection, Guthroth did his only great deed beyond the normal expected from kings of a warlike people: he gathered his men and came down on Agdir on skis on a dark winter's night, just after Yule, when men were still sleeping off the Yule-ale. He killed Hunthjof the Strong in fair fight at the door of his bedchamber, though it is true that Guthroth was fully awake and fully armored, while Hunthjof was half-drunk and wholly naked; then seized Asa, bundled her into a sleigh and dragged her back to the Westfold roped to the sleigh-posts. There Guthroth's own priests declared the wedding, and Asa was dragged off willy-nilly to the bedchamber.

Her beauty fulfilled Guthroth's expectations, and nine months later she gave birth to her son Halvdan, later called the Black from his hair and his rages. Guthroth slowly let out the breath he had been holding, and forbore to tie Asa's wrists to the bedposts every night when he slept, knowing that women with a child to defend would become more sensible and less grudge-bearing than before. He still made sure even the knife she used to pare an apple with was pointless and no sharper than would serve to cut soft cheese.

Yet he had forgotten that a woman can work through other men as easily as in her own right. One dark evening, just after Yule the year after

Asa's father's death, Guthroth emptied the great aurochs-horn of beer which he kept on his table without a stand, so that it had to be drained in one draught, and shortly staggered out to piss on the snow. As he did so, while his hands were occupied with his breeches, and before he had begun to empty his bladder, a young lad stepped round the corner of the royal hall and thrust a broad-bladed spear through his belly, fleeing instantly on skis. Guthroth lived long enough to say that the killer had said only, "Those who kill drunken men should always stay sober," and then died, trying still to complete his piss.

Guthroth had an acknowledged and legitimate son by his first wife Thurith, a strong lad of eighteen winters called Olaf. Men expected that he would appease his father's ghost by sending Queen Asa into the howe with him, and make a clean sweep by leaving the child Halvdan, his half-brother, out in the forest for the wolves. He did not do so. And when asked why not—it was a sign that men did not fear him as much as a king should be feared that they were able to ask—he said that he had dreamed a dream. In it he saw a great tree spring from his step-mother's womb, a tree with blood-red roots, a white trunk, and green leaves that spread all over Norway and even further across the world. So he knew that a great destiny waited for Asa's children, and would not thwart the gods and bring down bad luck by trying to avert it.

Olaf, then, spared his stepmother and protected his half-brother, but from that time he himself had little good fortune, and men said that he had thrown away his own luck. In the years to come he was overshadowed in battle by his half-brother, Asa's son, who won himself a kingdom across the fjord in the Eastfold. And Olaf's own only son, Rognvald, whom men called the Magnificent for his courage and his gifts to poets, died when a trifling scratch in a mere skirmish swelled and went bad and defied the leeches even of the Way.

By contrast Halvdan won himself not only the new kingdom of the Eastfold, which he loyally shared with his one-time protector, and his grandfather's kingdom of Agdir, but also a wife whom even the imperious Queen Asa could not despise, as she did all other women. This was Ragnhild, daughter of King Sigurth the Hart of Ringerike. Like Asa, she too had been carried off from her father, but not by Halvdan. While her father was traveling through the mountains, he was ambushed by a mountain-chieftain, a wild man and a berserk called Haki. For all his berserkergang, Sigurth wounded Haki three times before he was killed, and cut off his left arm, so that Haki lay abed for a long winter, unable to enjoy his virgin bride. Just about the time he might be calculated to have recovered enough to do the deed, Halvdan struck first like his father. He took fifty picked men into the mountains and fired Haki's hall in the night. As Ragnhild ran out to greet her rescuers, they snatched her up and drove away across a frozen lake. When the pursuers got to the lake and saw the reindeer-sleighs disappearing, Haki knew that he would never catch them up nor live down the shame of losing both his arm and his bride. He threw himself on his own sword's point to rise again unmaimed in Valhalla. And so Halvdan won the most beautiful bride in the North and the only woman fit to match the mother-in-law for temper, and did so in time to enjoy her virginity despite the appearances: or so he always believed. Before long she too gave birth to a son, Harald, whom men called the Fairhaired in contrast to his father.

These, then, were the rulers of the Westfold in the time that the priests of the Way settled there and made the trading town of Kaupang their center and headquarters: first King Guthroth, then King Olaf, then King Olaf and King Halvdan together, with Harald Fairhair the only son of either of them able to succeed. And as important at least as any of the men, Queen Asa mother of Halvdan, and Queen Ragnhild mother of Harald.

Seated on a bench before an open window in Hedeby, Erkenbert the deacon considered the names both of King Halvdan (the Black), and King Olaf (Elf-of-Geirstath, whatever that might mean), and attached carefully the name of their kingdom or kingdoms: the Eastfold and the Westfold, both parts of that larger grouping that men called *Northr Vegr,* the Northway. He did not think that either of them was the man he had been told to look for. Olaf the Elf, certainly not. Erkenbert's notes said this man was over fifty, and notorious for his bad luck, though he did seem nevertheless to have retained his kingdom. But he also did not occur on any of the lists Erkenbert had made—doubtful and based on shaky memories though they were—of who had and had not been present at the great raid on Hamburg after which the Holy Lance of Longinus had disappeared.

The other one might be a bit better as a possibility. He was widely feared and respected, something of a conqueror on the tiny depressing scale of the Northern lands, said to be the main obstacle in Norway to the Ragnarssons' goal of spreading their power. His ships challenged quickly and kept all interlopers at a distance. Yet Erkenbert did not think this Halvdan fitted the bill either. When Bruno had given him the task of collecting all available information on the kings and chieftains and jarls of Scandinavia, to try to determine who might hold the Holy Lance, he had told him to look for three things. One, success. Two, connection with the raid on Hamburg. Three, sudden change: a failure who suddenly became a success would betray the mighty influence of the great relic more surely than anything else. There was no sign of that with Halvdan. He seemed to have ground his way to power in an unremitting way from birth, or at least from his youth.

Against his will—for he had not wanted to come on this mission to the north, and would rather have stayed in Cologne or Trier or even Hamburg or Bremen, finding out more of the mysteries of power—Erkenbert was beginning to feel the intellectual challenge of the problem Bruno the count's son had set him. "Someone must know the answer," Bruno had said. "They just don't know they know. Ask everyone we meet about everything. Write all the answers down. Look to see what kind of pattern emerges." And this Erkenbert had done, interrogating first the few Christian converts they had made in Hedeby—low-value informants these, mostly women and thralls who knew nothing of the reputations and records of the great ones—then the Christian priests they had rescued, then those guards of King Hrorik who would speak to them out of politeness, and finally, paying heavily in wine from the South, the skippers and helmsmen of the boats that put in, often famous warriors themselves and sensitive as harlots to shifts in reputation.

A shadow darkened the door and the senior knight of the Order of the Lance, Bruno himself, edged his freakishly broad shoulders through the opening.

He smiled, as he did so readily. "What is the betting today?" he asked. "Any new runners in our little horse-race?"

Erkenbert shook his head. "If we have heard the answer already, as you say, I cannot recognize it," he said. "The one most like the picture you want is still the young man who killed Ivar and bested Charles. He has come from nowhere. Everyone talks of his deeds and his luck. He is a close associate of Viga-Brand, Brand the Killer, who was certainly present at the sack of Hamburg."

Bruno shook his head regretfully. "I thought so too," he said. "Right up till the time I spoke to him. He is a strange one, and I think maybe he has something to do with all this. Yet he had only one weapon, and though it was a spear it was most certainly not *the* spear. Too new, wrong shape, marked with heathen runes, though I could not read them. I think you have got him on your brain, and will not drop him. Maybe that is preventing you from recognizing the true holder. Tell me some more about some of these heathen kings."

Erkenbert shrugged, picked up once more his mounting pile of vellum.

"I have told over to you the kings of Denmark and Norway," he said. "Now in Sweden and Gautland between them there may be as many as twenty more. From the north, King Vikar of Roslagen, aged fifty, elected at the Ros-Thing twenty years ago, said to be rich but peaceful, takes tribute from the Finns and never comes south."

Bruno shook his head.

"How about King Orm of Uppland, controls the great Kingdom Oak and the temple-sacrifices at Uppsala, said to be powerful but disinclined to personal combat, took the kingdom by force twenty years ago?"

"He sounds a bit more likely, but not much. We'll keep an eye on him. You know," Bruno reflected, "for all their recent defeats, I wonder if Sigurth Ragnarsson or one of his brothers couldn't be our man. After all, even Charles the Great had some setbacks, against the Saxons."

Erkenbert was unable to repress an involuntary shudder.

"I think we may have to get a little closer to the action to find out for sure . . ." Bruno went on.

In the hut to which they had been assigned in the college precinct at Kaupang, the English ex-slaves and Karli the Ditmarsher were exchanging stories of the Hidden Folk. There was a companionable mood in the warm tight-closed room. Hama, one of the catapulteers, had a split lip. Cwicca had an eye swollen shut. Karli was nursing a bitten ear, and had a lump on the side of his head where Osmod, seeing man after man knocked down by Karli's fists, had hit him over the head with a billet of firewood. The group had ceased to mock each other's accents, and were trying to find common ground in explaining the strange world around them.

"We believe in things called thurses," said Karli.

"Us too," agreed Cwicca the fen-man. "They live in holes in the marsh. If you're out in a punt after wild duck, you don't want to go putting your pole into any old thurs-nest. Fowler who does that, he don't come back."

"Where do these creatures come from?" asked one of the men.

"They don't come from anywhere, they've always been here."

"What I heard," said Cwicca, "is this. You know we're supposed to be descended from Adam and Eve. Well, one day the Lord God came down and asked Eve to show him her children. Well, she showed him some of them, but some of them weren't washed, 'cause she was an idle slut, so she told them to hide. And at the end the Lord God said 'Those children you hid from me, let them remain hidden.' And since then those of us who come from Eve's children who were seen, we're human, but those who come from the others, they're the Hidden Folk, who live in the marshes and on the moors."

The story was considered, but not much liked. Every man there but Karli had been a slave of the Church, first recruited and then freed by Shef and the army of the Way. Christian doctrine was familiar to them, but they associated it with slavery.

"I can't see that has anything to do with what they've got up here," said another voice. "No thurses up here, 'cause there's no marshes. What they've got up here is nixes. In the water. Only there's no water 'cause it's all frozen."

"And trolls," put in another.

"I never heard that word," said Osmod, "what's a troll?"

"Great gray things what live in the rocks. And they call 'em trolls because they trundle down the hill at you."

"One of the locals told me this," said the split-lipped Hama. "There was a man lived up in the mountains, called Lafi. And one day when he was hunting, two troll-wives caught him and dragged him off to their lair in the mountains, and used him as a stud. They wore nothing but raw horse-hides, and they lived on nothing but meat and fish. Sometimes the meat was horse or sheep, but sometimes they wouldn't show him where it had come from, but he had to eat it just the same. After a while he pretended to fall ill, and while the young troll-wife was out hunting, the other one asked him what would cure him. And he said, nothing but rotten meat that had been buried for five years. So she said she knew where there was some of that, and off she went. But because she thought he was too sick to get out of bed, she didn't roll the stone quite shut in front of the cave. And he got out and ran for it. They picked up his scent and came after him, but he smelt wood-smoke and ran till he got to a camp of charcoal-burners, and they got their weapons and faced out and kept the troll-wives off. And then they all went down the mountain and got to safety.

"But nine months later, when he came out of his house, there was a baby on the doorstep all covered in gray hair. After that he was afraid ever to go out at night. I don't know what happened to the baby."

"So they aren't animals, then. They can breed with us, like," reflected Osmod. "Maybe there's some truth in Cwicca's story."

"Maybe we better leave Karli out for the troll-women," came a suggestion.

"Yes, and then if there's any trouble from any old troll-daddy, he can just knock him down."

* * *

Outside, ignoring the laughter coming from the dark hut, Brand was trying to talk seriously to Shef.

"I tell you," he said, "she's dangerous. Deadly dangerous. The most dangerous thing you've met since you stepped on the gangplank to face Ivar. Worse than him, even, because when you faced him he already knew he was bound to lose in the end. She doesn't think that. She has more to play for."

"I don't know why you're worried," said Shef. "I've never so much as spoken to her."

"I saw the way you looked at her. And her at you. What you need to realize is that she's only interested in one thing, and that's her son Harald. There are prophecies about him. First people thought the prophecies meant his father. Then they switched to thinking it meant him. Ragnhild certainly thinks it means him.

"But now you come along and people start saying maybe you're the one, the big king that everyone's been waiting for, the one who'll rule all Norway."

"I wouldn't even have got to Norway if they hadn't bought me off Hrorik and brought me here."

"Well, you're here now. And people like Thorvin—he means no harm, but he's responsible just the same—people like Thorvin telling everyone you're the son of the gods and the one who comes from the north and I don't know what else. You have visions, you're *in* visions, Hagbarth says one thing and Vigleik says another. You have to expect people to listen. Because behind it there are things no-one can just laugh off as old wives' tales: you're a thrall who got to be a king, I saw it myself. You put Alfred to one side, and he was one of the god-born, descended from Othin, even the English admit that. You took the surrender of the king of the Franks. What are a few hedge-wife prophecies to that? Of course Ragnhild thinks you're dangerous. That's why she is."

"What happens tomorrow?" asked Shef.

"The priests of the Way meet in holy circle. They have to decide about you. You won't be there. Nor I."

"What if they decide Thorvin is wrong? Surely then they can just agree I'm nothing to do with them and let me go. After all I have supported the Way, I wear its pendant, I have helped them establish themselves on Christian soil. Any of its priests are welcome to come to my kingdom any time and pursue new knowledge. More than welcome," Shef added, thinking of what he and Udd had discussed.

"And if they decide the other way, that you are the one they seek?"

Shef shrugged. "If there's going to be any change in the world, I'm more likely to start it in England than stuck up here where no-one ever comes."

Brand frowned, displeased to hear Norway disregarded. "And what if they decide you are not the one they seek, but you have been masquerading as him? Or even more likely, that you are not the one they seek, but a rival and an enemy. That is what Valgrim the Wise thinks, and he has a point. He is sure that the great change in the world which shall destroy the Christians' power must come from Othin. And everyone agrees you are not from Othin."

He tapped Shef on the chest with a mighty forefinger. "Though you go round looking as if you ought to be, with your one eye and that damned spear. Valgrim thinks you are a threat to Othin's plan. He will try to have you condemned for that."

"So Valgrim thinks I'm a threat to Othin's plan. And Ragnhild thinks I'm a threat to her son's future. And all because I learnt to build the catapults and the crossbows, to twist rope and forge wheels and bend steel. They ought to realize the real danger is Udd."

"Udd's only five feet tall," snarled Brand. "People don't think he's a danger because they don't even know he's there."

"That's a real danger for you, then," answered Shef. Musingly he added words he had learnt from Thorvin:

"All gates, ere you go through,
Look round you, peer round you.
Not evident to any, where un-friends sit
  In every hall."

Far up the mountain-side, a man sat amid the dark, who had forfeited the family luck, had felt it go out of his possession. Some men said they could see the luck, the *hamingja*, of a family or a land or a kingdom: usually a giant woman, fully-armed. Olaf had not seen that. But he had felt the luck flow out of him all the same. It was the loss of luck that had been the death of his son, Rognvald the Magnificent. His father had killed him.

Now the same father had to decide whether the sacrifice he had made had been pointless. It was the new one, the one-eye. Olaf had watched him come ashore, to be greeted by the Way and his dangerous bitch of a sister-in-law. Even from a distance, Olaf had felt the luck flowing from him. So great it was that it had overpowered the luck of the Othin-born kings of Wessex. It could easily now overpower even the destiny that Olaf had foreseen for his half-brother's family. For the future, as Olaf well knew, was not fixed. It was a matter of potentials. Sometimes the potentials could be changed.

Should he intervene? Olaf had brought the Way to Westfold many years before, respecting both its material power through new knowledge and the spiritual power of its visionaries and dreamers. With material power he had had little to do. With the mystical power, much. If he had not been a king, he could have rivaled Vigleik in visions. Except that Vigleik saw what had happened, what was happening. Olaf saw what would happen. If he could blot out the desire to do so.

Olaf reflected wordlessly on what part he would play in the morning, when the Way formed its circle, and called on him, as it would, to sit outside it, to listen and advise. If he chose to put down the one-eye, he knew, he would gain a majority and reestablish the plan to which he had sacrificed his own life and his son's. But if he did that, he would be sacrificing another future. From very far away, Olaf felt the faint tingle of a thought searching for his own, searching for what he knew and trying to pick a path out of the same tangled indications as his own. There were Christian priests as sensitive in their inquiries as himself. Yet they were too late: he already knew what they were looking for, he was closer to the balance point.

As the sun left the sky entirely, the man in the grove found his skis, walked to where the snow began out of the protecting trees, and began to snake his way down the hill. Behind him, wolf-howls rose. As his skis hissed past the outlying farms, the bonders caught sight of him and muttered to their wives. "There is the elf-king. He has been again to the stone ring, to Geir-stath, to take counsel from the gods."

CHAPTER ELEVEN

Inside the great boat-shaped hall, the priests of the Way had formed their holy circle. White cords marked it off from the outside world, with the sacred rowan-berries hanging from them—berries faded now, with the spring coming on, from their autumn scarlet. Inside the circle, more than forty priests sat together, the largest conclave any of them had ever known, drawn for the most part from Norway, where the Way was strong, but also from Denmark, from Sweden, with a few scattered converts or missionaries even from the isles of the Atlantic, from Ireland, or from Frisia where the Way had been born almost two centuries before. One even, Hund the leech, from England, accepted formally at the sponsorship of his master Ingulf the week before.

At one end of the circle stood the silver spear of Othin, at the other the burning bale-fire of Loki. By tradition, this fire, once the conclave had begun, could not be refueled: nor could conclave continue once the fire was so far dimmed that no spark could be seen in the ash.

Valgrim the Wise stood by the spear of Othin, not touching it, for no man had the right to claim it for himself, but reminding them that he was the only priest among them who dared take to himself the dangerous service of Othin. He served the God of the Hanged, Betrayer of Warriors, rather than the homelier or friendlier gods like Thor, the farmers' help, or Frey, bringer of fertility to men and animals. Ten paces behind him, almost hidden in the shadows of the shuttered hall, there stood a great chair of carved wood, with built-up sides and a canopy covered in a design of interlacing dragons. A pale face looked out from the deep shadow, the gold circle on its brow catching ruddy gleams from the Loki-fire: King Olaf, host and protector of the Way, there by invitation to observe and if need be advise, but not to vote, or speak without express request.

The shuffling of stools and muttered conversation slowly died. Valgrim let it die away, waiting for his moment: he had opposition, he knew, and needed every advantage to overbear it. The only man standing, he looked round, waited till all eyes were on him.

"The Way has come to a turning-point," he said suddenly. He waited again. "We have our first false prophet."

That is what we are here to determine, thought Thorvin. But he let Valgrim continue. Better to have the issue out in the open.

"For a hundred and fifty years the Way has spread. At first slowly, and only here in the North where the words of Duke Radbod took root. Now we begin to have followers in many places. Even followers of alien blood and language. Even followers baptized in infancy to the Christ-god. And who can doubt that this is good?

"For we must remember our aim and our purpose. Aye, and our vision. Duke Radbod saw that we who worship the true gods would be brushed aside by the Christ-god, if we did not do as his followers do: preach a word, say a message, bring news of where our spirits go to, and where they come from. And do one thing they do not do: allow all words and all messages to be spoken, not say like the Christ-priests that those who do not obey them in every respect must be tormented for ever for no sin other than disobedience.

"That was our first aim. To preserve ourselves and our peoples and our teaching against men who would destroy them all utterly. But after the aim there came the vision. I have not seen it, but there are others in this hall who have. Different men"—Valgrim looked round the circle, nodding at this face and that, showing the others that he knew exactly who he meant and that they were present to deny him if they did not agree—"different men who yet saw the same vision.

"And that vision is of another world than this one. A world where every land we know, ours among them, obeys the Christian god. But where men live like beasts on a slave's holding, so crowded that they cannot breathe, ruled by rulers they never see, sent to war like pigs to the slaughter-place. And worse things than that. Our wise men and seers call this the Skuld-world: the world that shall be—unless we stop it.

"Yet stop it we can! There is another world wise ones have seen. Aye, and this one I have seen myself"—Valgrim's gray bush of a beard nodded as he stared round. "A world so strange we see it only in fragments, and cannot understand all of those. I have seen men floating in the black of an airless sea, somewhere between the worlds, and thought at first they were the most wretched of all sinners, cast out from all the worlds because even Nithhögg could not bear to gnaw their bones. But then I saw their faces and saw that they were like men on some great adventure: and some of them men of our own blood and language, world-farers so great that any skipper alive today would be no more than a child to them. I do not know how this came about, or will come about, but I know that is the true path for true men: not the path of the Christ-fearers. So all my days I have sought new knowledge.

"One more thing I know, and that is why we must take this path besides the desire for knowledge and power and glory. That is because we are not alone."

Valgrim looked round again, trying to impress these last words, his own conviction, on men who might have agreed with everything he said so far.

"All men know that around us there are the Hidden Folk. Not danger-ous to us here down in the settlements, dangerous only, it may be, to the hunters in the mountains and the children playing by the water-side. But they are not the only Hidden Folk. Somewhere out there, we know, are creatures with power to match the gods, not trolls or nixes, but the *iötnar* themselves, foes of god and man. And the Loki-brood as well, those who are not of one skin, those who walk in different shapes, half-human, half-dragon, or half-whale.

"In the end, we believe, the great day will come when gods and men on one side will battle the giants and the Hidden Folk on the other—and on that other side too there will be many men, the Christ-worshipers, the deserters. Those who have been misled. That is why Othin takes the war-riors to him, to form the host that will march out from Valhalla on that day of Ragnarök. Other hosts there will be too, from Thruthvangar for Thor and Himinbiorg for Heimdall, and from all the others, sailors and ski-runners and leeches and bowmen. But Othin's host will be the greatest and the hardiest, and most hope of victory lies in it.

"We dare not divide our hosts. The battle is not yet certain. If the Way takes the wrong path now, we will be divided and lost. I say that the one-eyed Englishman who carries the Othin-spear and yet does no homage to Othin, I say that he is the false prophet leading us on the false path. We must reject him now to fulfill our true destiny: which is to hail the One King, the One King whom our prophecies say will come to us from the

North. The One King who will change the world and bring victory instead of defeat on the day of Ragnarök."

Valgrim ceased, and settled the spear-pendant firmly on his broad chest. He waited for the denial he knew would come.

It came from a quarter he had hoped would support him. Vigleik of the many visions stirred on his stool, looked down at the unusual emblem he bore, the bowl of Suttung the mead-guardian, bringer of inspiration, and spoke.

"What you say of visions may be true, Valgrim, but while what we see is one thing, what we understand of it is another. Now I have said this to you before, and if you cannot deny it you must tell me what it means. We know our brother Farman saw the one-eyed Englishman—saw him when he had two eyes. Saw him in vision in Asgarth, home of the gods, and set in the place of Völund, lame smith of the gods. And Farman saw All-Father speak to him. None of us has seen this of any other mortal man. So why should I not think that this man has a divine destiny?"

Valgrim nodded. "I know your visions are true, Vigleik, and Farman's also. You saw the death of the tyrants last month, and news has come through on the trade-ships since, that you saw the truth. So the one-eye may have been seen as Völund. But just as you say, seeing is one thing and understanding is another. Now what does the story of Völund tell us?"

He looked round again, sure his audience was with him, all keenly interested in the story of their sacred myths. "We all know that Völund's wife was a swan-maiden, but that after she left him he was taken by Nithhad, king of the Njar-folk. Nithhad desired his craft as a smith, but feared his escape, so he cut his hamstrings with a knife and set him to work in the smithy at Saevarstath. And there what did Völund do?"

Valgrim's voice fell into the deep chant of the Way-priests:

"He sat, he did not sleep, he struck with the hammer.

Always he crafted the cunning thing for Nithhad.

"He made him fine bracelets and necklaces of gold and gems. He made him bowls for his ale and cunning runners for his sledges. He made him swords that would cut linen by sharpness and anvils by strength. But when Nithhad's two young boys came to see the marvels, what did he do? He lured them into his smithy, promised to show them fine things, showed them a chest."

Again Valgrim's voice turned to the chant:

"They came to the chest, they craved the key.

It was malice they opened when they peeped in.

"He killed them, he buried their bodies under the forge, of their teeth he made necklaces, goblets of their skulls, brooches of their shining eyeballs. Gave them all to Nithhad. And when Nithhad's daughter came to him to mend a ring, what did he do? Stupefied her with beer, raped her, thrust her out.

"She told her father, weeping. He came to Völund to take his head. And Völund, his hamstrings severed—he put on the wings he had made in the smithy, and flew away. What was the cunning thing he had made for Nithhad? It was his revenge. For that is his name, Völund. From the cunning thing, vel."

The conclave sat silent, pondering the story they all knew. "Now I ask you," said Valgrim, "who is the hero of this story? Völund for his cunning, as we are told? Or Nithhad for his attempt to restrain it? I tell you, Vigleik, where this Englishman is concerned, he is Völund, right enough. And we are Nithhad! He will kill our sons and rape our daughters. That is to say, he will deny us our own issue and turn us into creatures to breed his getting for him. Nithhad made only one mistake, which was to try to use Völund's skill and think he was safe when he was only lamed. He should have killed him and made sure work! For men like Völund or the English-man are not safe when they are crippled. For they are like Völund's wife, the swan-maiden: they are not men of one skin. But it is not a swan that the Englishman turns into, on the other side. Rather, a dragon, or a mound-dweller, a mold-man. Hagbarth, I ask you: did you not report that he said *he had been in a mound before?*"

The hall stirred with excitement and appreciation at Valgrim's unex-pected explanation. They saw Hagbarth nod slowly, reluctantly confirming what Valgrim had said.

Thorvin broke out in reply, as Valgrim had known he would. "This is all well enough, Valgrim, but you are only twisting words. Of course the lad had been in a mound before—he took the old king's treasure from it. He dug his way in with a mattock and fought his way out, like a hero. He did not *live* in one. If Viga-Brand were here he would mock you for saying he should have left the money in the ground. I ask all here, look beyond words. Look at actions. Shef Sigvarthsson, give him his proper name, he turned a whole country to the Way. He drove out the Christ-church. If he let Christ-priests stay, it was only as if they were any of us, made to pay their own way and work for their own believers. He killed Ivar Ragnars-son. And is there any doubt that he is a seeker for knowledge, who will give up anything for that knowledge?"

Thorvin raised his hand for silence. "If you do not believe me, listen."

Outside, not far away, the priests could hear a familiar sound, but not one they had expected to hear with all of them in conclave. Across the precincts of the college, across the old, much-trodden snow, there came the clink-clink of the heavy hammer, dimly over it the roaring of forced draught from a bellows. Men working at the forge.

At the forge, Shef had just completed the careful reforging and re-tempering of the sword he had given Karli. Now it was set aside to cool, before reassembly of blade, guard, hilt and pommel. Now Udd had taken over. The little man was conducting a demonstration. He stood to one side of the fire, directing, while Shef, stripped to his breeches and a protective leather overall, handled the pieces of iron and steel with tongs. Cwicca crouched on one knee, pumping the leather bellows that fed the draught to the charcoal-glowing forge. The rest of the English catapulteers, seven of them, Hama, Osmod and the others, with Karli making an eighth, squatted on their heels along the wall, enjoying the warmth and adding their comments.

"Right," said Udd. "They're all red-hot. Take the first spike and lay it down to one side."

Shef took a red-hot iron spike, the raw material for a dagger or spearhead, and laid it carefully across the mouth of a pottery bowl, not letting it touch the still-frozen earth of the floor.

"Take the next one and put it straight away into the snow-water."

Shef lifted it with the tongs and plunged the red-hot metal into a leather bucket full of barely-melted snow, gathered a few minutes before from outside. A cloud of steam rose with violent hissings.

"When the metal's cold, take it out and bend it between your hands."

Shef waited a minute or two, plucked the spike out, felt it gingerly to make sure there was no residual heat. Bent it between his hands. He had a good idea of what would happen, but was content to let Udd make his demonstration his own way. As the muscles stood out on Shef's forearm, the metal spike suddenly snapped in two.

"Now try the other one."

Shef handled this one, still warm even in the chilly air, with rags. This time he needed no force. The metal bent in his hands like wire, remained bent without any sign of springing even after he let it go.

"Same metal," lectured Udd. "If you quench it, it gets hard and brittle— takes a good edge, but no strength. But if you just cool it, it bends. Neither hard nor strong."

"As much use as an old man's dick," said a catapulteer companionably.

"More use than yours," retorted Karli.

"Shut up," said Udd, bold only in the making of steel. "Now, Shef, my lord that is to say. Take the bent one. Bend it straight again. Put it back in the fire and heat it red-hot once more.

"Now, quench it." Again the hissing and the cloud of steam. "Return it to the fire. But this time, don't let it get red-hot. Heat it gently—slow down on the bellows there, Cwicca. Let it get to the color of straw."

Udd peered over with near-sighted anxiety. "Now, that's enough. Take that out and let it cool slowly."

Shef followed instructions, this time more unsure of what would happen. As a working smith, he knew well the virtues of quenching and the dangers of annealing. His way of combining the qualities of strength, hardness and suppleness, however, had always been to work different grades of metal together in strips. The thought of going back to a strip once annealed had never occurred to him. Nor did he see the significance of the third gentle heating. As the metal cooled he looked with satisfaction at the returning blisters on his hands. They had got too soft while he had played at being a king.

"All right," said Udd. "Now try it."

Shef picked up the iron spike and bent it in his hands. It flexed powerfully, giving but then striving to regain its shape.

"This is how you made the crossbow strips," he remarked.

"In a way, lord, yes. But this is different." Udd's voice dropped with a kind of reverence. "This iron is the best I have ever seen. The ore it comes from takes half—a quarter—of the working we are used to. How long does it take a forge to make ten pounds of iron in England?"

"Two days," suggested Shef.

"Here you would get forty in the same time for the same labor. That is one reason the Vikings are so well-armed, I think. Their iron is better. It costs far less time and charcoal to make. So every man can have iron tools and weapons, not just the rich. The iron comes from Jarnberaland, far to the east across the mountains. The Way-folk say they have a mine there and men to run it.

"But there is still more we have discovered, lord."

In the heart of the forge there lay a pile of what appeared to be ash. Using long tongs, Udd hauled it out, dragged it onto the earthen floor, briskly swept away the covering cinders to reveal a metal plate.

"This has been in the fire for hours, since last night. I have kept the fire going all that time, while the rest of you were snoring."

"Karli wasn't snoring, he was out after women."

"Shut up, Fritha. It is a plate made like the spike, by cooling, and then quenching, and reheating, so it was strong and springy. Then I heated it again and kept it in the fire. And all the time it was in the fire, I kept piling the charcoal round it. Now lord, when it has cooled, I want you to thrust it with your spear, with the great spear you took from the Snake-eye."

Shef raised an eyebrow. The 'Gungnir' spear's massive head was made of the best steel he had ever seen. The plate Udd had been working on was perhaps an eighth of an inch thick, the thickness of the metal guard that protected a warrior's hand in the center of a shield. Much thicker and the shield would be too heavy to move easily. But Shef had no doubt the steel spear-head would punch straight through.

As the plate cooled, Udd set it up directly against the wooden logs of the forge wall. "Strike now, master."

Shef stepped back, balanced the shaft, imagined he had in front of him a deadly enemy. He stepped forward onto the left foot, swung body, arm and shoulder, trying to strike through plate and wall to a space a foot behind both, as Brand had often taught him.

The shaft jarred in his hands, sprang back. Incredulously, Shef looked at the thin plate. Unmarked. Undented. He looked again at the needle-point of 'Gungnir.' For half an inch the triangular point had been punched flat.

"That's hardened steel," said Udd flatly. "I thought it would be good stuff for mail. But I found you can't work it. It's unbendable. But if you made the mail, and then hardened it . . ."

"Or if you made thin plates like this and then just sewed them on . . ."

In the considering silence one of the catapulteers remarked, "What I don't see is how it all comes from the same stuff. Some's hard and brittle, some's soft and bendy, some's springy, some's so hard you can't scratch it. What makes the difference? Is it something in the water?"

"Some of the Vikings think that," said Udd. "They believe it's best to use a slave's blood for the final temper."

The ex-slaves looked at each other, reflecting on fates they had missed.

"Or some try oil. There may be some sense in that. All this steam. You've seen sweat jump off a hot blade? Well, water tries to get away from hot metal, and when you're quenching you don't want it to get away. So oil might be better.

"But I don't think it's that. It's the heating and cooling that do it. And I think it's something to do with the charcoal as well. If you can keep the metal touching the coal, something passes between them. That's my belief."

Shef walked to the door, stared out across the snow to the fjord and the islands lying in it, still trapped in thick ice. Out there on one of the furthest islands, he knew, was the queen he had seen on his first arrival, Queen Ragnhild, with her son, her husband away seeing to his taxes in the Eastfold. Out there on the island they called Drottningsholm, Queen Island. He watched his breath condensing in the frosty air, and wondered about sweat on iron, iron sizzling in the water-bucket, men blowing on their hands to warm them, steam rising from hot bodies in cold air. What was steam, he wondered?

Two men were carrying a bucket towards him across the snow, slung between them on a pole. There was something strange about that. You would expect slaves to be given a task of that kind, but those men were not slaves: too tall, too well-dressed, swords at their belts. Behind him Shef could hear Cwicca ordering Karli to the bellows and taking a turn at following Udd's instructions. Through the inexpert beating of the hammer he could hear the faint squeak of leather shoes on snow.

The men reached the forge door, set their bucket down carefully. Shef found himself, as so often with these Norwegians, looking up to meet their eyes.

"I am Stein, of the guard of Queen Ragnhild," said one of them.

"I did not know guards carried buckets," observed Shef.

Stein scowled. The noise at the forge had ceased as the men inside heard conversation, and Shef knew they were crowding into the doorway, ready to support their leader if needed.

"This is a special bucket," said Stein, mastering his temper. "A gift from the queen to you, the Ivarsbane. It is winter-ale. Do you know what that is, southerner? We brew our strongest ale, and then in the hardest of the frost we set our vats outside. The water in the ale freezes, we break the ice off the top and throw it away. The longer you do it, the more water the ale loses, and the stronger is what remains. It is a drink for heroes—like you, if you are the slayer of Ivar."

Stein's expression showed doubt, increasing as Cwicca and the others jostled their way out to peer into the tawny liquid. Not one of the Englishmen was less than head and shoulders shorter than the two Norsemen, and even the stocky Karli was dwarfed.

Stein fumbled at his belt. "The queen told me also to say this. The drink is for you and your men, as you choose. But the queen said you came ashore with nothing, so she sent you a cup. The cup is for you alone. For you alone."

He freed what he had been carrying and passed it over. Shef turned it over in his hands, surprised. From the way Stein talked he had expected a goblet of gold or silver, something precious. Instead it was a plain mug of hollowed beechwood, such as any churl might drink from. As he turned it over he saw marks on the bottom. Runes. A message.

His errand done, Stein turned away with his companion, not waiting for thanks. Shef recovered himself, called to his own companions. "All right, let's get that inside where it's warm. Fritha, run down to the hut and get your mugs and a ladle if you can find one. Let's at least have a drink. And Udd, heat up a couple of spikes, we can mull this ale and see what it's like hot. Just the thing for this country. Hama, get on the bellows for him, Osmod, get some more fuel for the fire."

As the ex-slaves bustled round, Shef stepped into the cool bright sunlight to read the scratched runes. They were in the Norse style he had learned from Thorvin, but unfamiliar in some ways. Slowly he puzzled out their sense.

"*Bru er varthat, en iss er thykkr,*" they read. "The bridge is guarded, but the ice is thick."

What bridge? Shef looked out again over the fjord. Out there the islands lay in the dense ice. Now he looked for them, he could see thin strips running from one island to the next: long lines of logs, set in the water each autumn and allowed to freeze there. The furthest island out was Drottningsholm. She had said he would come to her when she called him. And now she had. Shef realized Karli was watching him with a raised eyebrow. For him alone, she had said. But if he were to go prowling like a tomcat, it might be best to take an experienced companion.

In the hall of conclave, tempers were running high. The higher because everyone there knew they would soon have to make a final decision. The bale-fire had long since fallen from a blaze to a glow, and now in the darkening hall only a few embers shone out. The fire might not be refueled, nor the conclave continue once no spark could be seen.

"So what is it you propose?" said Valgrim to Thorvin. As the debate had gone on, the two men had emerged as leaders of factions, increasingly speaking against each other. With Thorvin were the majority of the priests of Thor, of Njörth and of Ithun, practical men with clear skills to which they were devoted, smithcraft, seamanship and shipbuilding, medicine and surgery. These men appreciated the advances and the experiments that Shef's Way-kingdom had made, and were eager to continue on that path. Thorvin's followers also included the alien priests, the Frisians, those whose native language was not Norse. Against him were Valgrim, the one priest of Othin, and the majority of the priests of Frey, along with those of Ull, Heimdall, Tyr and the lesser gods. Devotion to them was strongest in

Norway itself, and among the least-traveled or most-isolated of the followers of the Way.

"Let the lad return to England," said Thorvin promptly. "Take as many
of us as we can with him. Make his kingdom there the strongest in the
North, a place where we can recruit wealth and followers. From it, set up
our challenge to the Christ-god. Never before have we taken followers
from him, always his priests have crept into our lands to steal followers
from us. Let us support this, the first true success we have had.

"And what is your proposal, Valgrim?"

The big man replied as promptly. "Hang him on a tree as a sacrifice to
Othin. Fit out the greatest fleet we can, with the assistance of King
Halvdan and King Olaf, and go down to take over his kingdom before the
English know what has become of him. Then do as you say, Thorvin. Only
with the priests of the Way in charge, not some unknown foundling."

"If you hang him on a tree you reject the messenger of the gods!"

"He cannot be the messenger of the gods. He is not a Norseman, not
even a Dane. Most of all, Thorvin, even you have admitted it. He may wear
a pendant, he may see visions, but he has no belief. He is not a true
believer!"

"You talk like a Christian!"

Valgrim's face purpled, and he started to stride towards Thorvin, who
slipped his hand down the haft of his ceremonial hammer. As the other
priests started to rise from their stools, to come between the two men,
another voice cut through the chill air, one that had not spoken during the
angry debate: that of Vigleik of the visions.

"You spoke of fitting out a fleet, Valgrim, and you of setting up a kingdom, Thorvin. Maybe it is time, before the bale-fire goes out, to call on the
advice of a king and a commander. You have heard our words, King Olaf
Elf-of-Geirstath. What wisdom do you have for us?"

The figure in the carved chair rose to his feet and walked forward to the
very perimeter of the corded circle. His face was grave, lined with care. In
it there was something of the air of majesty: none, though, of the air of
instant decision seen in every Viking jarl or skipper, let alone king. His
eyes seemed to look through what was in front of them, to some event or
chance beyond.

"Have I leave to speak?" asked Olaf. He waited for the growled assent of
the conclave. "Then I have this to say, having heard all that has been said
here on both sides.

"All of you know, I think, though you may not wish to say it to my face,
that I am a man who has lost his luck. The luck of his family. I can tell you

that I did not lose it, nor give it away. I only knew that it would go, and then that it had gone. I am different from other men only that I knew it, instead of finding out much later, or never. I know a great deal about luck.

"Some men will tell you that the luck of a family, the *hamingja* as we say, is like a giant-woman fully-armed, that the lucky can see as they see the spirits of the land. There are stories of men who saw their guardian-spirit leave them and go to another. They may be true. But that is not what I saw. Truly I saw nothing—except the dream of the great tree of which you have doubtless heard.

"What I felt was like the feeling in the air before the lightning-flash. I knew the flash would come, I knew it would go from me to another. I knew that that other was of the line of my brother. When I was young I thought it was my brother Halvdan. Now I know it was not. Till a few days ago I thought it was my brother's son Harald, whom they call Fairhair.

"Now I am not sure again. For again I have the feeling, the feeling before the flash. It comes to me that luck is going to shift again, to pass out of my line altogether—and maybe to the young man Shef."

The listeners stirred, and Valgrim's faction eyed each other doubtfully.

"Yet I was wrong before, over Halvdan. Maybe I am wrong again. But not, I think, wholly. As I grow old it seems to me more and more that luck is not a thing that one has or has not, like youth or strength. It is more like light, where a lesser light remains what it was, but cannot be seen any longer when a greater light outshines it. Like a candle still burning in a sunlit room. Except that maybe the greater light steals light from the lesser even, even puts it out.

"I have heard the history of the young man Shef. He brought bad luck to his own king Jatmund. He did not quail before the luck of Ivar. He was rescued, they tell me, by one of the god-born, the king Alfred, descended from Othin. Soon after the rescue that king was a beggar, to be rescued in his turn. I think this young man draws the luck from others. Where he comes, luck goes. He may take it even from my own blood, where I thought the luck of Norway rested—where it did rest, till you brought him here to challenge it."

"All this is mere talk," rumbled Valgrim. "We must have proof."

"Proof comes from a test. Let us test his luck against the luck of Harald and Halvdan, against the queens Asa and Ragnhild."

"How do we do that?"

"Agree to the test and I will tell you. But agree quickly, before the bale-fire goes out."

The forty priests looked at the tiny glowing spark that was all that was left, muttered together. Then, slowly, both Thorvin and Valgrim nodded their agreement. As a Tyr-priest knelt down and blew gently on the last remaining ember, King Olaf began to speak. Before he had finished, Valgrim was already shaking his head in dissatisfaction.

"Too unsure," he growled. "I need a clearer sign."

"You may get a clearer sign than you wish, Valgrim. I spoke of light and luck. There is another way to see it. Some of you believe that all our lives are spun by the three spinners, Urth, Verthandi and Skuld. But they spin not single threads, rather a great web, the threads crossing over each other. Where the threads cross each other, they fray! Beware the man with a strong life-thread, Valgrim. Especially if that thread crosses yours."

Vigleik stirred himself to speak. "I have seen the Spinners," he said. "Their loom-weights are skulls, their shuttles are swords and spears, their web is human gut."

"That is in the Skuld-world," said Thorvin flatly. "That is what we mean to change."

CHAPTER TWELVE

The two men crept cautiously through the dark woods to the edge of the ice. The snow had hampered them badly, lying in uneven drifts in the hollows and forcing them to push through the tangled fir-branches. Yet they had not dared to use the paths through the woods—anyone who saw them might have challenged them, and while they were not forbidden to move around at night, they had no wish to cause stir or comment. Karli had grumbled steadily at first as snow fell from the trees and crawled down his neck, repeating that he knew plenty of places where they could find friendly women without all this trouble. But as Shef pushed on Karli had fallen silent, accepting the expedition as one of the strange preferences for a particular woman that even the sanest of men might have. It would be an exploit, after all, he told himself, to seduce a queen. Maybe there would even be a princess for himself.

Where the wood ran down to the ice, the snow stopped, brushed away by the wind, or melted by the sunlight that got through the fringes of the fir-trees during the lengthening days. Shef and Karli walked forward more easily and stood for a few moments looking out at the scene, considering their course.

They had made a circle away from the college and the town behind it, and were now on the end of a long point jutting out on the western side of the bay. On the far side of the bay, maybe a quarter-mile off, were the chain of islands that led to Drottningsholm. There was no moon, and the

sky was covered by thick cloud driven on by a strong wind from the
south-west, but even so they could see the tree-covered island nearest the
shore standing out black against the mirk of the sea and sky. Just visible as
a black streak was the long line of logs which led from mainland to island.
They could not see the guard-posts at either end, but there was no doubt
they were there. The question was, could the guards see two men silhouetted against the ice?

"The wind has swept the snow off," Shef whispered to Karli. "We won't
stand out against the white."

"But why isn't the ice white too?" Karli replied.

Both men knelt and looked closely at the ice-cover in front of them. It
seemed black and forbidding, yet still thick as cathedral walls. There was
no give in it, clearly frozen still all the way down to the mud at the bottom.
Shef stepped out cautiously, jumped up and down in his leather-soled
boots. Both men had tied rawhide round their footwear for better grip and
less noise.

"It's solid. We can do it. And if the ice is black, better for us."

Cautiously, both stepped out and began to walk gingerly across the ice
to the center of the island before them. Both crouched, as if that would
make them harder to see. At each step they planted their feet carefully and
delicately, as if the ice might shatter beneath them at a sudden shock.
Every now and then one or the other would tense, thinking he felt the first
shiver that would mean thin ice. Then they plodded on again. Shef had his
spear in one hand, the point carefully beaten and filed out once again to
needle-sharpness. Karli had taken the wooden sword-scabbard from his
belt, frightened to trip over it, and now held sword and scabbard together
in both hands, as if it were a balance-pole.

As the island drew nearer both men began to breathe more freely. At the
same time the sense of exposure grew on them. The trees ahead were a
dark menace, they themselves out on the flat without a vestige of cover.
Sense told them that the black night and low clouds covered them, that
there was no light in the sky to pick them out. Nevertheless, if they could
see the island, surely the island could see them. As they came up to the
shore, they both accelerated their pace, darted instantly into the shadow of
the trees.

They sat for a while, hearts thumping, waiting for noise of movement or
challenge. Nothing came. Only the steady hiss of the wind in the trees.

Shef turned to Karli, muttered, "We'll go round the edge of this island,
keeping to the ice by the shore. When we see the next bridge ahead of us
we'll decide what to do about it."

For some minutes they shuffled warily round the edge of the island. Once they caught a whiff of wood-smoke and stood stock-still. But the trees remained unbroken, not even a cottager's landing-stage jutting out into the water. They shuffled on.

The bridge to the next island almost caught them by surprise. They shuffled round a small spit of land, and saw it in front of them, not twenty yards off, and plain to see, two tall men leaning on their javelins. Could even hear their muttered conversation. Quickly the two intruders pulled back into shelter.

"What we ought to do," whispered Shef, "is make a detour out to sea, to keep well away from them."

"Don't fancy that," muttered Karli. "I want to keep where the ice is thick."

"If the ice wasn't thick enough, she wouldn't have told us to take it."

"Women are funny. And she could be wrong. Anyway she's not out here with fifty feet of cold water under her."

Shef reflected for a moment. "Let's try this, then. We'll start from here, and go parallel with the bridge, where the water's shallowest and the ice thickest. But we won't walk, we'll crawl. Keep right down, there's not so much for them to see. Anyway, they're watching the path, not the ice."

As they set out, crawling awkwardly in their heavy clothing, beards skimming the ice, Karli began to wonder. If the ice is so thick, why are these Norwegians only guarding the bridges? Why are they guarded at all? Are these people just stupid? Or does the queen . . . ?

His friend was yards in front of him and moving like an angry adder. No time for debate. And the ice seemed thick as ever. Karli crawled quickly behind, trying not to eye the seeming safety of the log-bridge twenty yards off.

As soon as they reached the second island both men crawled to the side away from the bridge, slithered round behind another of the many tiny spurs jutting out from the shore, stood up and bolted once more into the cover of the trees, breathing hard. The cold of the ice had bitten through their layers of wool and leather. They put their weapons down carefully, pulled off the sheepskin mittens Brand had given them, blew on frozen hands. Carefully Shef eased a leather bottle from its belt-sling, pulled out its stopper.

"Winter ale," he muttered. "The last of it."

Each took a long pull. "Tastes like ale," muttered Karli, "but it doesn't feel like it. You can feel your gullet glowing as it goes down, no matter how cold it is. Shame we can't make this stuff where we come from."

Shef nodded, thinking again for a moment of water freezing on ale, of steam leaping from a hot blade. No time to pursue that thought.

"Drottningsholm's the next island," he said. "We know the king isn't there, and that no men are allowed to sleep overnight on it. One more crossing . . ."

"And we're like two cocks in the hen-roost," completed Karli.

"At least we can see what the queen wants from us."

I know what she wants from you, thought Karli, but kept silent. Slowly, they worked their way round the shore of the second island.

The bridge this time was easy to spot, but well away from the point where they caught their first sight of Drottningsholm. They stood in the trees, looking across and calculating the odds. They were on the western point of another small bay, Drottningsholm perhaps a furlong off. The eastern point was another furlong away, and the bridge ran from its tip to the further island.

"Just as easy to start from here as go over near the bridge," said Shef. "And we won't need to crawl. We're far enough away so no-one will see us from the guard-post, and we'll be getting further away all the time."

"All right," said Karli. "I guess if the ice was going to break, it would have broken by now. We've seen no holes in it. It hasn't creaked or anything."

Shef gripped his shoulder, took his spear in both hands, and set out across the flat, black, windswept expanse.

"All right, where is he?" Brand stood in the doorway of the fetid communal hut, glowering down at the eight Englishmen facing him. He had been drinking worriedly in a tavern in the port of Kaupang with Guthmund and their crews, when he had been called away by news that the Way-priests' conclave had ended. After a brief interview with Thorvin he had headed straight for the quarters Shef shared with Karli, now treated as his bodyservant. Found both missing, and headed on to the catapulteers' hut.

Faced with an angry man nearer seven feet high than six, the ex-slaves reverted to servile custom. With imperceptible shuffles they moved into a tight group with at its front Osmod and Cwicca, the burliest and most self-confident of them. Their faces took on a look of stony ignorance.

"Where's who?" said Osmod, playing for time.

Brand's enormous fists opened and closed. "Where—is—your—master —Shef?"

"Don't know," said Cwicca. "Ain't he in his quarters?"

Brand took a step forward, murder in his eye, paused as he saw Osmod, once captain of the halberdiers, cast a quick glance towards a rack of weapons. He turned, marched out, slamming the door.

Outside Hund, Shef's childhood friend, now a faithful priest of Ithun, stood patiently in the crusty snow. "They won't talk to me," Brand snarled. "You're English. They know you're his friend. See if you can find out what's up."

Hund stepped into the hut. A murmur of voices, all talking English in the thick Norfolk dialect common to them all. Finally Hund appeared, beckoned Brand once more into the hut.

"They say they don't know for sure," he translated. "But putting one thing and another together, they're fairly sure he got a message of some sort. They suspect that he has gone to visit the queen Ragnhild at Drottningsholm. He has taken Karli with him."

Brand goggled. "Gone to Drottningsholm? But no man's allowed on the island overnight. And the bridges are all guarded."

Cwicca grinned, his gap teeth showing. "That's all right, skipper," he said in the Anglo-Norse pidgin of the Wayman army in England. "We're not so dumb. We know that. If he's gone, he'll have slipped across on the ice, see? We went down and had a little look this afternoon. It's still plenty thick enough, no sign of cracking."

Brand stared at Cwicca and the others, horror evident on his face. He tried to speak, failed, tried again.

"Don't you English fools know anything?" he said in a hoarse whisper. "In the fjords this time of year, the ice doesn't crack. It rots from the bottom up. Fills with water. Then one morning it isn't there any more. It doesn't crack. It just sinks!"

The wind struck them with redoubled force as soon as Shef and Karli were well out on their last stretch of ice, as if they had come out from under the lee of some unseen headland. With it came a whirl of horizontal, driving rain. Shef flinched as the first drops struck his face, expecting stinging hail or ice-storm. Then he put his hand up to the drops that trickled down his face, and wondered. Rain. So the frost had broken. Would they be able to get back, once across? No time to worry about that now. And in the rain they had no need to fear being seen by the bridge-guards.

"Listen," he said to Karli. "I don't like this rain. The ice may crack. We can both swim. The thing to do, if it cracks under us, is keep your head up. Don't get caught under the ice and not know which way to turn. If we're in a hole in the ice, swim to the edge of it and put your weight on the ice. If it cracks, go forward and try again. When we get to somewhere thick enough to bear us, crawl out and keep crawling. And Karli, tuck your sword in your belt again. You may need two hands."

As Karli fumbled to obey, moved by some impulse, Shef looked up at the dark shore still a hundred yards in front, hefted the 'Gungnir' spear in his hand, trotted two paces forward, turned and hurled the spear ahead of him. He saw it streak forward, land, and skid on along the ice, its clatter drowned by the hiss of the rain.

As his foot came down he felt the ice give. Both men stood motionless for a moment, listening for the crack. Nothing. Still ice under their feet.

"Maybe it just came loose from the shore," muttered Karli.

They stepped on, cautiously, planting their feet with utter delicacy. One step. Two.

Cold bit into Shef's boot as he put it down. Water. A puddle on the ice? Water in the other boot. Suddenly the cold was at his knees, his thighs, he felt his vitals retract convulsively. Shef stared round for the break in the ice, but there was nothing there, his feet were still planted solidly but the ice was dropping beneath . . .

The black water closed over Shef's head and he found himself struggling desperately to stay afloat. There were hands round his neck, clutching from behind, hands like Ivar's, as if Ivar were back from the dead.

Shef turned furiously inside Karli's panic clutch till they were face to face, brought his hands up together inside Karli's embrace, joined them and swung them down edge first on the bridge of Karli's nose. Reared up out of the water and swung again, felt gristle give beneath the blow. Reared up to swing again, felt the strangling clutch release.

"Sorry, all right, I'm all right." Karli let go and began to tread water. Shef realized at once the furious bite of the water. He had swum in cold water often enough, in the fens, for sport or to cross where there was no bridge. This was different. The cold had bitten through every garment he wore, filled them all, was draining the strength from his body with every instant that passed, the cold and the waterlogged wool and leather both combining to drag him down into the mud.

And he had lost any sense of direction. Shef thrust his body out of the water as high as he could manage, twisting his one eye round to see if he could see the island, or the other shore, or ice still solid to swim towards. Nothing. Nothing.

Or there? Was that a deeper black in the night? He caught the shape of Drottningsholm against the sky, seized Karli's shoulder, dragged him in the right direction. Both men began to strike out with the strength of panic, first with a clumsy overarm stroke, then as their sodden clothes pulled them down with a gasping short-armed breast-stroke. Their legs trailed under them. Kick your boots off, thought Shef. They always say, kick your boots off. But mine are laced with rawhide, and anyway. Anyway it's too cold. I have to get out or die.

The first touch of mud under his feet made him try to stand immediately, and his head sank instantly beneath the surface. He pulled himself up, flailed again overarm till he felt mud beneath his belly. Staggered up, felt his feet slide from under him, seized a tree-root on the shore and dragged himself forward and out. From behind came a gasp, feeble splashing. Shef marked the helpful root, turned, plunged back into the water, seized Karli and dragged him by main force the last few yards to shore. With one hand he grabbed the root again, twined the other in Karli's curly hair and shot him forward onto the freezing beach. Both men rose gasping and choking to their knees.

As they did so Shef knew for certain that if they did nothing they would die there of cold, in less time than it would take a careless priest to say a Mass. The water had burned like fire. Now they were out in the air the cold was even worse. Already he had little sensation across his body, the feeling of bitter pain was going, he felt a pleasant relaxation pulling him down.

"Strip," he snarled to Karli. "Get your clothes off. Wring them out."

His own hands fumbled at the toggles of his coat, seemed unable to find them. Karli had somehow got his sword out of his belt and out of his scabbard, was sawing at his own fastenings. He passed it to Shef, who dropped it from numb hands. For moments, a desperate silent struggle in the dark as they peeled off layer after layer. Naked at last, they were flayed by the wind, doubled over. But the rain flurry had gone, the harsh wind dried them in seconds. Shef groped for his tunic, wrung it out, doubled it and wrung it out again, driving out the half-frozen salt slush. As he struggled into it again, for an instant he felt an illusion of comparative warmth.

Pure illusion. They would still die here on the shore before daybreak. But at least a moment to think.

As Shef groped for his breeches, he saw movement in the trees. Not men. Too low down for the queen's guards. Wolf-shapes creeping closer, belly-down, lips already drawn back over snarling teeth. But not wolves. The queen's wolfhounds, bought at fabulous prices from the market in Dublin, and turned loose each night for her safety.

Only the water's edge saved the two men in their first rush, for the men backed into it by some primeval instinct, and the dogs could not come at them from all sides. As the big leader ran silently in, Karli, sword snatched up, swung a violent blow at its head. The edge turned as it connected, still gripped in inexpert hands, and the dog seized Karli's wrist in its jaws.

It had seized a fighter of instant reflex, poor swordsman though he was. In a moment Karli had thrust his left thumb deep into its eye, shaken it off, mad with pain, and thrust the sword into Shef's hands, snarling incoherently. Shef met his first attacker with a barefooted kick in the throat. As it came back for a leap at his groin he snatched the sword, dropped the point, and spitted its heart as it sprang.

The pain-crazed leader had seized another dog in its jaws and the two were rolling over and over in a snarling tangle. Padding round them a fourth animal the size of a calf gathered itself and made a leap for Karli's throat. He met it as he would a rough-and-tumble fighter in the brawls of the Ditmarsh, dropping his head instantly to butt it in the teeth, hooking with both hands at its body, trying to break ribs, rupture liver. The dog fell back, off balance, caught itself and poised for a second spring.

As it did so Shef leaned across and swept off one foreleg at the knee-joint, flashed the point in the muzzle of the dog that was threatening him, cut forehand at the dogfight still going on a yard away and instantly backhand at the last dog springing forward. Don't go for the kill, he thought. Take the easy maim instead. Dogs are safer than men for you only have their jaws to worry about.

One wolfhound was down dead, another hobbling off on three legs. The half-blind leader, further disabled by a slash on the side, had had its throat torn out by the dog it had attacked. That animal was backing off, disconcerted, a low rumble in its throat as warning, but not ready to continue the fight. Only one hound still faced them, teeth showing, lunging a few inches forward and then backing off again as it eyed the menace of the sword-point. Karli, bleeding now from both head and wrist, scrabbled in the water for a rock, dragged one out and hurled it furiously at three feet range. Struck on the shoulder, the dog whuffed indignantly, turned and streaked into the shadows.

The two half-naked men staggered again towards their clothes, groped in the freezing pile of wool and leather, struggled again to wring them out and get them on. As the adrenalin of the fight faded, Shef realized that he had no movement left in his fingers at all. He could use them as hooks, but tying a lace or fastening a belt was beyond him.

Slowly he wrapped his fingers round the sword-hilt again, knelt by the body of the dog he had spitted. Drove the point deep into its belly and sawed feebly downwards. A rank smell of punctured gut and coils of pale intestine pushing their way out. Shef dropped the sword, pushed his frozen hands into the body cavity and groped for the creature's heart.

A dog's body temperature is higher than a human's. The still-hot blood poured over Shef's fingers like liquid fire, seemed to run up his body. He thrust his arms deeper into the body cavity, up to the elbows, wishing he could crawl entirely inside. Karli, seeing what he had done and why, hobbled painfully over and fumblingly followed his example.

As sensation came back, Shef withdrew, pulled on his wet but no longer dripping breeches, fastened the belt, clambered into his water-sodden leather coat. His woolen hat was somewhere in the waters of the fjord, the sheepskin mittens lost in the darkness. Against his warmed hands, his feet felt like blocks of ice. Slice open another dog? Short of absolute necessity, he could not make himself do it. Clumsily he tipped water from his boots, thrust his feet inside, feeling as if the toes might break off at any moment. He made no effort to refasten the cut thongs on boots or coat.

"What do we do now?" asked Karli. He passed Shef the sword, holding on to the wooden scabbard as a makeshift club.

"We came to see the queen," said Shef.

Karli opened his mouth to reply, then closed it. The woman had trapped them, that was obvious. Unless maybe it was her husband all along. He had known deceits like that before. But the queen's hall and its outbuildings were the only shelter on this island. If they did not have shelter and fire they would be dead before dawn. Karli plodded after Shef through the fir-thickets, hoping to stumble on a path. He had hoped for a princess. He would settle now for a friendly drab, any draggletail housemaid with a fire and a blanket in a corner.

In the endmost room of the queen's hall at Drottningsholm, two women sat facing each other from either side of a glowing fire. Each sat straight-backed in a hard wooden chair, each glittered with ornaments, each had the air of a woman rarely refused, and never safely. Other than that they were dissimilar. They had hated each other from the moment of first meeting.

Queen Asa, widow and murderess of King Guthroth, mother of King Halvdan, had centered all her hopes on her boy. But as soon as he grew beyond infancy he had feared and distrusted her. Had she not killed his father? In youth he had pursued women as had his father and in contempt of his mother, in manhood he had turned Viking and spent every summer on campaign, every winter planning the next or consolidating the last. Disappointment had withered Asa, turned her brown, shriveled and cruel.

Queen Ragnhild, wife of King Halvdan, had no liking for her mother-in-law or the son whose bed she occasionally shared. Often she wondered whom she would have chosen for herself, if her father had been spared to arrange marriage for her. Sometimes she wondered if even Haki the one-armed berserk might not have made a better match, mountain-troll though he was. As she came to her full strength and influence she consoled herself when necessary with one or other of the stalwarts of her guard. Her husband insisted that no man might stay overnight on her island, for the sake of his own good name and the legitimacy of their one child. But much could be done in the daytime. Ragnhild was like Asa in only one further respect: she too centered her life on her only son, the boy Harald. If Ragnhild had allowed it, the boy's grandmother might have turned a fraction of her disappointed love from son to grandson. It was one theme where their interests ran together.

"Midnight already," said Ragnhild in the warm silence. "He will not come."

"Maybe he never bothered to try."

"Men do not turn their back on invitations from me. I felt his mind as he stood on the dock. He could no more refuse me than my hounds a bitch in heat."

"You describe yourself well. But you could have done as much without the play-acting. Bitch that you are, you could have sent your hound Stein to cut him down."

"His friends of the Way would have protected him. That would have drawn in Olaf."

"Olaf!" The old queen spat out the word. She owed her life to her stepson's forbearance, and the life of her child. She hated him the more, and the more still because her child did not feel as she did, consistently respected and deferred to his elder half-brother, for all Olaf's name for bad luck and Halvdan's history of conquest.

"And your son, my husband, would have supported his brother," added Ragnhild, twisting the knife she knew was there. "It was better done as I did it. His body will be found in a week's time, when it swells, and men will say what fools the *Enzkir* are, to walk out on rotten ice."

"You could have left him," suggested Asa, determined to give her daughter-in-law nothing. "He was no risk. A one-eyed stripling from a country far away, from the slavelands. Who would think such a man a risk to a true king like Halvdan? Or even to your puny Harald? You would do better to fear that half-troll Viga-Brand."

"It is not size that makes the king," said Ragnhild. "Or the man."

"You would know," hissed Asa.

Ragnhild smiled contemptuously. "The one-eye had luck," she said. "That was what made him dangerous. But luck lasts only till it meets a stronger luck. The luck that is in my blood, the luck of the Hartings. It is we who will make the One King in the North."

The door behind them creaked open, letting in a blast of freezing air. Both women sprang to their feet, Ragnhild seizing the iron stake she used to summon her thralls. Through the door stumbled two men, one tall, one short. The short one pushed the door closed, dropped its latch, this time pushed home the peg that prevented it being opened from the other side.

Shef pulled himself straight, walked wearily across the room, sword still in hand, forced himself not to drop groveling in front of the blessed glowing embers. His features were barely recognizable, caked with mud and the filth of shore and forest. Blood and slime covered his hands and matted the hair on his forearms. Where his skin showed it was blue with cold, a touch of deadly white on his nose and forehead.

"You sent me a message, lady," he said. "You warned me of the bridge-guards, but you lied about the ice. I met your dogs, too, here and there on the shore. Look, this is their hearts' blood."

Ragnhild raised the iron spike she had snatched up, beat with it on an iron triangle hanging above the fire. As Shef moved forward, sword raised, she stood motionless.

The slave-girls had been asleep, though not yet dismissed, on pallets out of sight. Four of them tumbled through the door that led to the main hall and the other apartments, rubbing their eyes and pulling dresses straight. It was not wise at any time of night to be slow in answering the summons of either queen. As Asa often said, she would be entering her grave-mound soon now, and she still had not chosen who should keep her company in death. The women, young or middle-aged but all with weary careworn faces, lined up hastily, daring only to cast side-glances at the two strange men. Men? Or marbendills from the deep? Queen Ragnhild might press even a marbendill into her service.

"Hot stones into the steam-room," snapped Ragnhild. "More fuel for this fire. Heat water in basins and bring towels. Bring two blankets—no, one blanket for that one and my fine robe of ermine for the English king. And girls—" The women halted in their first obedient scurry. "If I hear that anyone hears of this, I will not ask which one of you told them. There is always a Swedish ship in port, and space on the temple trees at Uppsala."

The women ran out. Ragnhild looked from her full height down at Shef, still standing irresolute in front of her, and then across at Asa.

"There is no arguing with the stronger luck," she said. "Best to join with it."

CHAPTER THIRTEEN

Shef sat on a broad wooden bench which almost filled the tiny dark room, lit only by a single wick burning in a dish of whale-oil. Beneath it a covered trough of hot stones radiated heat, scorching heat that shriveled the mouth-lining and stung the nose with the stink of pine-resin from the wooden walls. He luxuriated in it, feeling the deep chill thaw from his bones. Feeling also the need for instant decisions recede. He was in others' hands now. Even Karli was no longer his responsibility. He did not know where they had taken him.

At the queen's instructions, the slave-women had pulled him away, taken off his filthy, clammy clothes. One of them had rubbed his face furiously with handfuls of snow taken from the fast-shrinking drifts out-side, to prevent the frostbite that had already attacked it. Others had poured warm water over him, rubbed him with lye, scrubbed off the dirt and blood and animal fat from his hands. Dimly he had realized that they had also taken his sword, that something or other of the same kind was happening to Karli, but the sudden entry into warmth had half-stupefied him. Then they had led him into the steam-room and left him.

For a while he sat, not even sweating in the fierce heat, just letting the warmth soak through to his half-frozen marrow. Then as weariness came over him he lay back, propping his head against a wooden billet, and fell into a light, uneasy sleep.

* * *

Somewhere in the dark above him, his fate was being discussed. He heard the now-familiar rumble of mighty voices. One spoke for him, he realized, one against.

"He should have died on the ice," said the hostile voice: cold, authoritative, unused to contradiction, the voice not only of the Father but the Ruler of gods and men.

"No-one should blame a man for saving himself," argued the second voice: Shef knew he had heard it many times, recognized it as the voice of his patron, perhaps his father, Rig the cunning.

"He threw away the spear, the spear with my own runes on it. He denied me sacrifice. He does not follow the heroes' road."

"The less reason, then, for taking him to you. He would not find a place in Valhalla, would not be an obedient recruit for your Einheriar."

The first voice seemed to hesitate. "And yet . . . There is a cunning there. Too few of my champions have that. Maybe it is a quality I will need on the day of Ragnarök."

"You do not need it yet. Leave him where he is, let us see where his luck takes him. He may do you service in his own fashion." The second voice was lying, Shef knew, he could tell it by the sweet reason that dripped from its tongue. It was buying him time.

"Luck!" said the first voice, suddenly amused. "Let us see that, then. If he has a luck, it will be his own, for mine he has thrown away. And he will need powerful luck to survive the dangers of Drottningsholm. We will watch."

The two voices drifted away in a rumble of agreement.

Shef came to himself with a start. How long had he slept? Not long, he thought. It was too hot for anyone to lie comfortably. He was sweating now, and the bench under him was damp. Time to get up and look about him. He remembered the lines of poetry he had heard from Thorvin:

Not evident to any, where un-friends sit
In every hall.

As he rose to his feet, the door of the tiny room creaked open. There was a fire lit in the room outside, and from the glow behind her, he realized that the figure standing in the doorway was the queen, Ragnhild. He could not see what she was wearing. As she came forward, closing the door, she pressed close to him.

"You have shed your jewelry, queen," he said with a roughness in his throat. He could feel himself stirring at the woman-smell that came from her, stronger even than the pines.

"No-one can wear gold in the room of hot stones," she replied. "It would burn. So I have shed my rings and armlets. See, even my brooch has gone."

She caught his hands, held them to her gown, ran them down its lapels. The gown fell open. Shef's hands cupped the heavy swell of her breasts, realized she wore nothing but the one open garment. His arms went round her, his hands stroked down the long muscular slope of her back, gripped her buttocks fiercely. She pressed forward, thrusting her pelvis into him, pushing him back. The bench caught him behind the knees and he sat back with a thud.

As the sweat poured suddenly from his body, the queen straddled over him, thrust herself down on his rigid erection. For the first time since he had entered Godive two years before in the Suffolk wood, Shef felt the inner warmth of a woman's body. It was as if a spell had been released. Half-amazed at his own ability, he tore the gown aside, seized the queen by her hips, began to thrust upwards violently, still sitting.

Ragnhild laughed, steadying herself on his shoulders. "I have never known a man so active in this room," she said. "Usually the heat makes them as slow as a gelded steer. I see that this time I shall not need the birch-twigs."

Unknown time later, Shef walked to the outer door of the hall, opened it, peeped cautiously out. In front of him, to the east, he could see a thin line of light over the Eastfold hills far on the other side of the fjord. Ragnhild looked over his shoulder.

"Dawn," she said. "Soon Stein and the guards will be here. You will have to hide away."

Shef pushed the door open, let the air in on his naked body. In the last few hours he had been first frozen, then all but roasted. Now the air felt only pleasantly cool and fresh. He took deep breaths of the clear air, thought he could scent in it the green smell of grass thrusting up through the vanishing snow. Spring came late to Norway, but then plants and animals and people all made up for lost time. He felt more alive and alert than he had since his boyhood. The danger threatened in his dream was forgotten.

He turned, seized Ragnhild once again, began to push her to the floor. She resisted, laughing. "The men will be here. You are very vigorous. Have you never had your fill before? Well, I promise you—you will have it again tonight. But now we must hide you away. The girls will not talk, and the men will not look. They know better. But we must not give Halvdan any excuse for trouble later."

She pulled Shef, still naked, away from the door.

Karli wondered where they had hidden his friend—he supposed he now had to call him, his master. He himself was lying on a straw mattress in a garret reached by a ladder through the slave-women's quarters. A small unshuttered window gave light, but he had been warned not to look out. His gashed wrist and head had been bandaged, and he was wrapped in a warm blanket.

The ladder creaked, and he reached for the sword which he had picked up when they separated him from Shef. But it was only two of the slave-women coming up together. He did not know their names: plain, brown-haired women, one his own age, one ten years older with a deep-lined face. They carried his clothes, washed clean and dried by a fire, a loaf of hard bread, a crock of ale and another of curds.

Karli sat up, grinned, reached appreciatively for the ale. "I would stand up and thank you properly, ladies," he said. "But all I have on is this blanket, and what I have behind it might shock you."

The young one smiled faintly, the older one shook her head. "There is not much that shocks those who live on this island," she said.

"How is that?"

"We have other things to worry about. The queens play their games, with men and the king and the boy Harald. In the end one of them will lose, and pay the forfeit, and be carried to the grave-mound. Queen Asa has already started to put aside the things that will go in it with her, the sledge and the cart and the jewels and the fine clothes. But neither she nor Ragnhild will go alone, when they go. They will take attendants—maybe one, maybe two. I am the least valuable of those here. Maybe Asa will take me, or Ragnhild send me. Edith here is the youngest. Maybe Ragnhild will be jealous and send her."

"Edith," said Karli, "that is no Norse name."

"I am English," said the younger girl. "Martha here is a Frisian. They took her from her island in a mist. I was caught by the slavers and sold in the market at Hedeby."

Karli stared at them. Up till then all three had spoken in Norse, the women quite fluently, Karli still uncertain. Now he changed his speech to the Ditmarsh language, related to Frisian and English, which he knew Shef could easily understand.

"Did you know that my friend and I are not Norsemen either? He is a
king in England. But they say he was once a thrall, like you. And they tried
to sell him in Hedeby only weeks ago."

"Tried?"

"He knocked the man who said he was his master down, and threatened
to sell him instead. A good joke, and not a bad punch. But listen—I know
my friend, and I know he has no love for slavers. When we get back to our
friends, shall I ask him to buy you from the queens here? He would do it if
he knew you were English, Edith, and he would take Martha too."

"You aren't going to get back to your friends," said Martha flatly. "We
hear a lot. Queen Ragnhild fears your friend. She thinks he may take the
place she means for her son. She meant to kill you both last night. Now
she means to drain your friend's manhood, get a child from him, in case
his blood is the one destined for rule. Once she has that child in her belly,
your friend will find the henbane in his porridge. And you too."

Karli looked uncertainly at the loaf he had been gnawing.

"No," the woman went on, "you are safe yet. As safe as we are. Till she
has got what she wants."

"And how long will that take?"

Martha laughed for the first time, a short and mirthless bark. "Putting a
child in a woman's belly? You are a man, you should know. As long as it
takes to walk a mile? Less, with most of you."

"More with me," muttered Karli. His hand had strayed automatically
and unresisted to Edith's knee.

Valgrim the Wise looked carefully at the dripping spear, its steel head
already showing rust. He spelled out the runes on its iron shaft.

"Where did you find this?" he asked.

"On the shore of Drottningsholm," said Stein, the guardsman. "When
we went back on to the island this morning, as usual, I sent men to round
up the dogs as we always do. They couldn't find them, and the queen
Ragnhild told me she had been disturbed by their howling and sent her
maids out to bring them in. When I asked more, she flew into a rage and
told me to get out before she had my ears cut off. I guessed something was
wrong and sent out a guard-boat to row along the shore, now the ice has
gone. They found this."

"Floating?"

"No, the head's too heavy. They said it was close to the shore, in about
three feet of water. The head was lodged on the bottom, but the shaft was
still bobbing about."

"What do you think it means?"

"They could have drowned on the rotten ice," suggested Stein. "It all went quite suddenly early last night, when the rain came on."

"But you don't think so?"

"It's the dogs," said Stein. "There's something fishy there, and Ragnhild is hiding something."

"Maybe a man?"

"Probably a man."

Both heads turned to the third man in the room, the remote unbending figure of King Olaf.

"This seems to affect the good name of your family," said Valgrim, a trifle uncertainly.

The king smiled. "What you are thinking is that it is also a good test of luck. If King Shef was on the rotten ice last night, and survived, that was one test passed. If he got past the wolfhounds, that was another. You want me to set him a third?"

"Third time pays for all," said Stein.

"I agree. A third test it is, and then no more, from me or from you. Agreed."

Valgrim nodded, reluctantly, eyes full of calculation.

"Then I will send word to my brother that there is reason to think things amiss on Drottningsholm. I have never done that before, and he knows I would not do it lightly. So he will believe me and give permission for a thorough search of the island and every building in it, from end to end. You must think how you would make it, Stein. And if intruders are found there, hiding, then they must go to the king's justice. It will be heavy, when he thinks the good name of his son Harald is concerned.

"Till then, Stein, you had better double the guards on the bridges, both from Drottningsholm to the second island, and from that to the third and to the mainland. A bold man could swim between the islands too, so have your guard-boats out between them. I need not tell you to make sure there is no boat a man could steal.

"If this is to be a test, it is in your hands to make sure it is a strict one. Do not come to me afterwards and say, this was no fair test, any man might have escaped. You must make sure that the only escape is by Völund's path, through the air! Then if King Shef escapes, we will know that Völund he is, in whatever shape."

Stein and Valgrim nodded again.

"And no word to his friends," added Valgrim. Out of the window of the high room where they sat, he could see Thorvin walking across the college precinct, Brand at his side. Both men looked deeply anxious.

"No word to his friends," Olaf agreed. "I will play fair on this one, Valgrim. See you do too. Otherwise it is no test of king's luck."

As he turned and went out, Valgrim and Stein looked at each other.

"He said make it a strict test," said Stein. "I could make it a little stricter than he plans."

"Do that," said Valgrim, looking again at the 'Gungnir' runes on the spear he still held. "No strictness is too harsh for the man who pretends to come from All-father."

"And if his luck does prove stronger?"

Valgrim hefted the spear, shook it like a man about to strike. "I think it has left him already. I hated him for aping my master Othin. I hate him more now he has thrown away my master's token."

From the shadows of the great hall, Karli watched his friend-and-master musingly. All the signs, he thought. I should have realized earlier.

Almost from the moment of their first meeting—certainly from the first time they had talked together—Karli had unconsciously assumed that Shef was the elder of the two, the wiser, the more widely-traveled, the more weapon-skilled. It had given Karli no sense of inferiority. His own animal spirits were too strong for that, and he remained unshakably confident in his own ability to knock any man down with his fists, and bed, if not any woman, at least any woman reasonably good-humored. He did not feel inferior to Shef. But he had assumed that Shef knew as much as he did.

A mistake. He should have realized that where women were concerned, this tall warrior with the scars and the mighty friends was no more than a boy. He was behaving like a boy now. A boy who has met his first woman. What he had been doing with Queen Ragnhild all day, Karli did not know, but now night had fallen and the guards had been withdrawn he still could not take eye or hand off her. As he spooned the strong salt stew into his mouth, his left hand lay on the queen's bare arm, lightly stroking it. Every time she spoke he leaned close to her mouth, laughed, took every chance to touch her again. Karli had heard stories of witches who sucked away a man's manhood. In his experience there was no need of witchcraft. Sexual skill, consciously exercised, worked on any man—the first time anyway. Once you realized there were more fish in the sea than ever came out of it, you might be protected. But Shef did not know that yet. And there was no way of telling him. When Karli had approached him after being freed from the garret, Shef had been pleased to see him, but vague, reluctant to talk or plan or even think about what had happened. He was slit-struck.

It was up to him, then. Karli had no doubt that for all the warmth and the food and the careful attention, he and Shef were in greater danger than they had been on the ice. What Edith and Martha and their two friends had told him had chilled him deeply. Shef was against slavery because he had been threatened with being a slave. Karli was against it because he had no experience of it. In the uncivilized and poverty-stricken Ditmarsh there was neither room nor work for slaves. They might sell shipwrecked strangers to other strangers, but they kept no thralls themselves. The constant fear under which a thrall like Edith or Martha lived was a new thought to him.

And fear made people good listeners. Their lives depended on knowing what might happen and taking the few pitiful precautions open to them. So Martha not only bore with the contempt and bullying she received from the Norwegian female housekeeper who came in with the guards each morning and left with them each night. She encouraged it, making mistakes to provoke a beating and a flood of words. What the massive Vigdis had said after Martha dropped the pan was that a time was coming for idle sluts. Aye, and maybe not them alone. Why else the doubled guards? And don't think to swim off like the spineless eel your father. The men have brought up boats to the channel between each island. When the king comes we'll see who's useful enough to let live and who is fit only for howe-bridal.

Vigdis obviously did not know what the guards were for, and thought it some royal intrigue: maybe King Halvdan tired of his mother waiting to die, or of his wife and her independence. But the slave-women knew better. The dogs, they said. Men coming round to look in their pens, ask where the others were, why they had not all come home, why they could not be heard baying if they were still loose somewhere on the island. We cleared up the bodies before first light, Edith had said, and the rain washed away the blood, but in the soft ground it would not take a tracker to see that people had been doing something.

A night or two's grace, thought Karli, still watching Ragnhild and Shef, the sour queen Asa sitting glaring at both across the table. I know. The slave-women know. Shef will not listen. And Vigdis has not told the queens. Well, one thing is for sure. They will not notice if I am not there. Quietly he went through the door to the little cramped room where the slave-attendants waited.

"Have you thought what to do?" whispered Edith.

Karli squeezed her hip. "I am a Ditmarsher," he said. "I know something about water. I need to build a"—he hesitated for the right word—"a boat?"

"There are no boats on the island. No planks, no tools. It would take weeks to fell trees. And anyway, they would hear you!"

"I don't mean a boat like that," said Karli. "I mean"—he turned to the Frisian woman Martha—"we call it a *punt.*"

"For the duck-hunters," said Martha, nodding. "But what do you need to make that?"

Hours later Karli bent sweating over the contraption he had put together on the island's seaward shore, furthest removed from the guard-posts. Its flat bottom was simply a door. There had only been one whose absence would not be immediately noticed the next day—the one that led to the slave-women's stinking latrine. Probably neither the guards nor the queens knew such a place existed, let alone whether it had a door or not. Karli had lifted it bodily off its hinges and carried it out. He could have stood on that alone and poled himself along if he had been able to keep to shallow water. But he knew he would have to do better than that, make a seaward circle before he ran in to the shore. He needed a place to stand if he was not to be tipped off by every wave. And something like a bow to cut the water. Done with no tools and no noise.

Slowly and clumsily he had cut away one edge of the door with his sword, sharp but not serrated. Iron skewers from the kitchen had nailed down billets of firewood toward the stern, hammered in with a flat stone muffled by layers of cloth. On top of that he had fixed a flat wooden tray with four nails worked loose with his fingers and pulled stealthily out of the ornate wooden planking at the rear of the hall. Finally, growing impatient and trusting to luck that the damage would not be seen next morning, he had pulled away one strake of planking low down to the ground, snapped it over his knee. He was trying now to drive three more nails through the planking into the cut-away edge of the door, to make a bluff, square bow. Once it was done he would have a makeshift imitation of the craft the Ditmarsh fowlers steered through their everlasting bogs. He would neither row nor pole it, but scull it over the stern with a single oar —snapped planking again, wedged into a split fir-branch. It would do, if the water stayed calm. If no-one picked him out from a guard-boat close in, or one of the king's giant coastal patrol warships further out. If he met no creature of the deep.

At the last thought Karli's hair bristled. Deep within himself, he knew he was afraid. Not of water, not of men. He and the English catapult-men had idled away too many hours telling each other monster-stories, and passing on those they had heard from the Vikings. In his own land Karli feared the fen-thurses. The English feared boggarts, hags, and groundles. The Vikings told stories of all of them, and stranger creatures still, skoffins and nixes and marbendills and skerry-trolls. Who knew what might not be met, out at sea, in the dark? All it would take would be a gray-haired hand reaching up and seizing an ankle as he sculled six inches above the water. Then the things would feast at the sea-bottom.

Karli shook himself, drove home the last nail with a flat stone, straightened up.

The voice in his ear murmured, "Going fishing?"

Frightened already, Karli leapt straight over his punt, turned in the air, came down braced for flight, gaping to see what threat had crept up on him. Almost, he relaxed when he saw the amused, contemptuous face of Stein the guard-captain, standing there fully-armed but thumbs still hooked in his belt.

"Surprised to see me?" suggested Stein. "Thought I wouldn't be back till morning? Well, I thought a little extra care wouldn't hurt. After all, if men aren't allowed on Drottningsholm after dark, nor are you. Eh?

"Now tell me, short-legs, where's your taller friend? Stallioning away up at the hall? He'll lose more than an eye when we hand him over to King Halvdan. Do you want to go along with him?"

The sword Shef had retempered for Karli still lay on the ground where he had been using it. Karli lunged forward, seized its hilt, straightened up. The shock had worn off. No hag from the deep. Just a man. On his own, seemingly. With helmet and mail, but no shield.

Stein dropped a hand to his own sword-hilt, drew and stepped round the boat. Karli was no dwarf, but Stein out-topped him by head and shoulders, outweighed him by fifty pounds. How fast was he? Plenty of farmers' sons in Viking armies, Shef had said.

Karli cocked his elbow and threw his weight into a forehand slash, not at the head, too easy to duck, but at the point where neck met shoulder, as Shef had taught him.

Stein saw the beginnings of the movement, knew before the sword was drawn back where the blow was aimed, where it would fall. He had time to tap his foot once before his riposte. In one movement he turned his own sword in his hand, drove the base of his blade in a short chord to intersect the longer arc of Karli's blow. The blades clanged once. Karli's shot into the air, knocked from his grasp. A twist of the wrist, Stein's point rested in the hollow of Karli's throat.

Not one of the farmers' sons, then, Karli thought sickly. Stein's face creased with disgust. He dropped the point to the ground.

"It's not the skin that makes the bear," he remarked. "Nor the sword the warrior. All right, you little freckle-faced bastard, talk or I'll cut you up for bait."

He bent forward, thrusting his chin out and up. Karli's feet shuffled from the fencing position he had taken to the one that came naturally to him. He shrugged a left hand feint out of habit and swung instantly with the right hook to the side of the jaw.

This time Stein's decades-drilled reflexes failed him completely. The blow caught him standing flat and still. As he straightened his sword for the killing counter-stroke, another blow snapped his head back and a third from six inches' range crashed into his temple. As he slumped forward Karli side-stepped and swung a hand-edge chop at the back of his neck: illegal in the Ditmarsh ring, but not against husbands or rivals met at night. The veteran sprawled his six foot four full-length at Karli's feet.

Out of the shadows came Martha, the middle-aged slave-woman. Terror stood in her eyes as she saw the lying man.

"I came to see if you were gone. That is Stein the captain. It is the first time he has ever come spying at night. They must know you are here! Is he dead?"

Karli shook his head. "Help me to tie him before he comes round."

"Tie him? Are you mad? We cannot guard him for ever, or keep him silent."

"Well . . . What are we going to do with him?"

"Cut his throat, of course. Do it now, quickly. Put his body on your boat and roll it off in the water. It will be days before he is found."

Karli retrieved his sword, stared at the unconscious man. "But I've never killed anyone. He's . . . He's done me no harm."

Martha's face set, she stepped forward, bent over the man now starting to push himself up from the ground. She snatched the short knife from the sheath he carried on his belt, felt its edge for a moment, hurled the helmet aside and pulled his head back by the hair. Reached forward and round, drove the point in deep under the left ear. Dragged it round in a deep, slicing semi-circle. Blood spouted from the severed arteries, Stein cried out, his voice coming as an expiring whistle from the great hole in his windpipe.

Martha released his head, let the body fall forward, wiped the knife automatically on her filthy apron. "You men," she said. "It's just like killing a pig. Only pigs don't steal other pigs from their homes. Don't bury them alive. He'd done you no harm! How much have he and his like done me? Me and my kind?

"Don't just stand there, man! Be off with you. And take this carcass with you. If you are not back within two days we'll all go to join him. Wherever he's gone."

She turned and fled into the darkness once more. Karli, his throat dry, queasily began to drag his clumsy craft into the shallow water and then to load the dead weight on it.

CHAPTER FOURTEEN

An hour later, Karli tucked his single oar cautiously between his thighs, straightened up on his precariously rocking craft, and stretched his overworked shoulder muscles. As soon as he started he had realized how different the sea was, even the sea of a landlocked fjord, from the shallow muddy waterways of the marsh. The gentlest of waves made the door pitch and toss. To keep his balance at all he had to straddle as near as he could to the center, which meant that his sculling-platform was behind him, not where he needed it. By trial and error he had found a way to stand, one foot far forward, one braced against the edge of the wooden tray. Fortunately he had made the oar long enough to reach the water even so.

There were two ways for a Ditmarsh fowler to scull, an easy way and a hard way. The balance problem ruled out the easy way—standing upright on one leg with the oar in the crook of the other knee, swinging it with both hands. He had had to switch immediately to the hard way, oar under one arm, other arm swinging the oar up and down, left to right in a continuous figure-of-eight. Karli had unusual balance, unusual strength in the arms and shoulders for a man of his weight. He could manage. Only just, and only slowly.

Still, no-one had picked him out. At the beginning he had poled his way out into water deeper than the length of his oar, then with relief pushed the dead body off the front edge and felt his wooden plank rise. The mail took the body down. It would rise again soon, but by then Shef would be rescued or Karli gone to join Stein in the next world.

Then he had sculled away from the island in a straight line towards the black shape of the Eastfold hills across the fjord. Five hundred weary strokes, fighting to keep his balance all the way. Then he had turned, looked cautiously behind him to Drottningsholm and the islands. He could make them out, but with no detail. He did not think that in the clouded, moonless night anyone from the guard-posts could see a crouching man on an invisible raft against the black sea.

He had turned and started to make his way towards Kaupang harbor to the north. Wind and tide were behind him. He kept changing arms as the weariness grew. It was discouraging to be able to see nothing, no lights, no sign of progress. He could have been on a shoreless sea, paddling from nowhere to nowhere.

As long as there was nothing out here with him. Over the hiss of the wind and the surge of the sea, Karli realized he could pick out something else. A steady creaking, something rhythmic, something chopping the water. He looked behind him, full instantly of terror at some strange water-hag swimming behind him for its prey.

Worse than that. Against the black sea and the sky Karli made out a shape, a fierce head lifted high, like a monster questing for swimmers. The dragon prow of one of King Halvdan's giant warships, out rowing his endless summer blockade. Karli could see the white splash of the oar-thresh, hear the rhythmic creak of the rowlocks, the grunting of the rowers as they put their weight on the oars. They were rowing very slowly, not going anywhere special, conserving their strength. Lookouts stood at prow and stern, alert for skippers trying to evade King Halvdan's taxes, for pirates sneaking by to raid Eastfold or Westfold. Karli lay down immediately on the plank, careless of the water soaking him. He dropped his face, pulled his hands back into their sleeves, trapped the oar beneath his body. On a dark night, he knew from much avoidance of husbands and fathers, nothing showed up more than white skin. He tried to look like a piece of floating wreckage, skin crawling as he imagined the bowmen taking aim.

The oars thundered in his ear, the door pitched and heaved as the bow-wave of the great warship went by. No challenge, no shot. As the stern-tail crawled past the corner of his eye he heard the lookout call something, an indistinct reply. Still no challenge. Nothing to do with him.

Carefully and shakily he climbed back on to his feet, retrieved the oar, began to scull slowly after the warship's receding stern. As he began to count off his strokes once more he felt the door begin to rise again beneath his feet. Another bow-wave? No, something greater, something closer, the whole clumsy contraption tipping over almost on to its side. Karli dropped on to his knees, clutched the edge, as he did so heard a great snort in the water not six feet away.

A fin his own size cruised gently past, standing straight up almost at right angles to the water. Beneath it a huge body rolled black and gleaming. Ahead of him the fin turned, cruised back to intercept. A head came out of the water, broad enough to engulf the door in one snap. Karli caught the flash of brilliant white barring beneath the black upper body, saw an intelligent eye observing him.

The killer whale, a bull orca out foraging for seals ahead of the rest of its school, considered tipping the man-thing off its floe and snapping it to pieces in the water, but decided against. Men-things were hardly fair prey, a gentle, irresistible voice told it. There was no excitement in chasing them. Sometimes porpoises followed their ships, and porpoises were a good catch. Not tonight. It ceased to follow the warship, ignored the thing on the floe, swam inexorably off to find its companions.

Karli straightened again, realized the warmth inside his breeches was his own piss. Shakily he took up the scull, began to count off his strokes. This country was not safe. Both the men and the animals were just too big.

In their hut, the English catapulteers were preparing their breakfast and at the same time checking their weapons. Light was just showing in the sky, but ex-slaves rose early, out of habit. Besides, in spite of the pendants they all wore, in spite of being at the heart of their adopted religion, they felt uneasy, isolated, unsafe. Their leader had vanished, no-one knew where. They were surrounded by men of alien speech and unpredictable temper. In their hearts they knew that most of the Norsemen they met thought all foreigners were just slave-material waiting to be seized. They had come to Kaupang as men of a conquering army. Slowly their status seemed to be slipping away. If they were disarmed they would be back to tilling fields and herding goats, working under the lash once more. Without saying it, every one of them had determined that that was not to happen. If need be, they would have to break out. But how?

In the army of the Way in England there had been three main divisions: crossbowmen, halberdiers, catapulteers. No-one had made any effort to train them as swordsmen, though each carried a broad, single-edged sax-knife in his belt, as useful for firewood as for enemies. But Udd had made sure that each man there, whatever his original trade, carried and knew how to use one of the latest model crossbows, no longer wound by belt-pulleys, the spring-steel bow cocked instead by a long, pronged lever. It fitted under the bowstring and latched onto inset bolts. With a single, heaving effort the bow was cocked as the pull was exerted against a foot stirrup on the front of the bow's wooden frame. Osmod and three of the others also carried their unwieldy halberds, the combination axe and spear that Shef had invented for himself to make up for his lack of weight and training.

But the group's main weapon stood outside the hut: the mule, the stone-hurling catapult they had unshipped from the Norfolk and loaded into Brand's *Walrus*. The Thor-priests had been busy ever since they arrived, observing it, watching them shoot it, getting them to build further models of the two other styles of catapult they knew, the twisted-rope dart-shooter and the simpler stone-lobbing pull-thrower that the Way had already deployed on three battlefields. It was said that King Halvdan had ordered experiments on fitting mules to bow and stern platforms on his coastal patrol craft, large enough to take them if maybe too weak in the keel to stand the repeated shock of recoil. But till then the mule outside was the only one in the North.

There was one further innovation that no-one as yet had tried. Udd's invention of case-hardened steel as yet seemed all but useless. The material, once hardened, was too hard to work with any tools they had. Udd had suggested hardened crossbow-bolts, but as the others pointed out, the ones they had would go through any known armor anyway, so why bother? In the end Udd had made one thin round plate of the new steel, two feet in diameter, and pegged it on to a standard round shield of linden wood. Few warriors if any carried iron shields. The weight was so great that the shield could not be wielded for more than a few moments. Soft linden wood was used instead, to catch and trap the enemy's point or edge, usually with an iron boss as hand-guard. The plate Udd had made was so thin that if it had been normal iron it would have added no protection. But the case-hardened steel would turn any ordinary sword, spear or arrow, and weighed no more than a second layer of wood. Udd and the others had not yet worked out what the utility of the new shield was—none at all to men who fought as they did. It was a case where a new technique had not yet found a use.

At first, in the early-morning hubbub, no-one heard the scratching at the door. Then, as it was repeated, Cwicca paused. The rest fell silent. Fritha and Hama snatched up crossbows, cocked them. Osmod stepped to one side of the door, poised his halberd. Cwicca jerked out a peg, lifted the latch, swung the door open.

Karli fell in on hands and knees, barely able to support himself. The
seven men inside gaped at him, then slammed the door shut and sprang to
help.

"Get him on the stool," snapped Osmod. "He's soaked. Hah, not all
water either! Get his clothes off, one of you bring him a blanket. Rub his
hands, Cwicca, he's half-frozen."

Karli, supported on the stool, was pointing towards a mug. Osmod
passed him the strong warmed beer, watched it go down in a dozen gulps.
Karli finished, breathed out, sat up straighter.

"All right. I'll be all right in no time. Just cold and wet and dead-tired.
But I've got news.

"First, Shef is alive, on Drottningsholm. The message he got was a trap
but we got there just the same. So he's on the island, he's alive but he
won't be much longer if he stays there. Trouble is, that queen of theirs is
screwing him senseless and he won't leave. We're going to have to go and
get him. But he won't come of his own free will and they've reinforced the
guards over the bridges. And he's not the only one there who needs rescuing . . ."

Karli poured out his story to a ring of faces that grew grimmer as he
went on. At the end Osmod silently passed him a refilled mug, looked at
Cwicca, who as catapult-captain shared the leadership with him in Shef's
absence.

"We've got to get him off. We could do it ourselves, but we'd never get
away afterwards. That's what we've got to think about. Now, who in this
place can we trust?"

"How about Hund the leech?" asked Cwicca.

Osmod considered a moment. "Yes, I'd like to have him with us. He's
English, and he's the lord's oldest friend, and he's a Way-priest besides."

"Thorvin the priest, then?" suggested one of the hammer-wearers. Faces
round him twisted dubiously. Cwicca shook his head.

"He's more loyal to the Way than he is to King Shef. This is Way
business, somehow. You can't tell which road he'd turn."

"Can we trust any of these Norskers?" asked one of the others.

"Maybe Brand."

A pause while they thought it over. Finally, Osmod nodded. "Maybe
Brand."

"Well, if we got him on our side, it's easy. He's nigh seven foot tall and
built like a stone wall. He's the Champion of wherever-it-is, isn't he? He's
just going to walk through them guards like piss through snow."

"I'm not so sure about that," muttered Osmod. "He got a sword right through his belly last year. They've patched him up, right. But they didn't patch his head up, did they? I don't know that he'd be champion of anywhere any more."

"Are you saying he's gone yellow?" asked Fritha, incredulous.

"No. But I'm saying he's got a bit careful, like he never was before. In this country full of berserks, or whatever they call 'em, that's almost the same thing."

"But you still think he'll help?"

"As long as we don't ask too much." Osmod looked round, frowning. "Seven of us here, and Karli. Where's Udd?"

"Where do you think? Now the water's running he's up at the mills, seeing how they work. Took a hunk of bread up as soon as light showed."

"Well, go and get him back, someone. The rest of you, listen. Because here's what we'll do . . ."

". . . So that's our plan," concluded Osmod, looking grimly across the table at Brand. "And that's what we're going to do. The only question we've got for you is, are you in or are you out?"

Brand stared down consideringly. Though both men were sitting, Brand's face was still a foot above the Englishman's. It was a real surprise, he reflected, how these men of Shef's had changed. Everything in Brand's make-up, culture and experience had told him all his life that a slave was a slave and a warrior was a warrior, and there was no way of making the one into the other. A warrior could not be enslaved—or only with massive precautions, like those King Nithhad had taken for Völund, and look where that had got him. And slaves could not be made into warriors. Not only did they not have the skills, they didn't have the heart either. During the battles in England the year before Brand had revised his opinion, a little. Ex-slaves were useful, he concluded, for war-with-machines, because they could be made into machines themselves: doing what they were told, heaving on ropes and pulling toggles to order. That was all.

But now here was one not just making up a plan of his own, not just telling him, Brand, that he was going to do it, but defying Brand to stop him. The giant Halogalander felt a mixture of irritation, amusement, and something like—anxiety? Fear was not something he would ever readily admit to.

"Yes, I'm in," he said. "But I don't want my crew mixed up with it. And I don't want to lose my ship."

"We want to use your ship to get away in," said Osmod. "Sail back to England and get out of here."

Brand shook his head. "Not a chance," he said. "King Halvdan's got this coast sewed up as tight as a frog's ass. And the *Walrus* can't fight off one of his patrol ships, they're twice our size."

"Use the mule."

"You know how long that would take to ship, not just to carry, but to mount it so it can shoot. Anyway, any ship not specially designed will just fall to pieces if you shoot that thing off in it."

"So how do we get away after we've got King Shef back off this queen? Are you saying it can't be done?"

Brand chewed his lip. "We can do it. Maybe. Not by sea. I think the best thing is this. I'm going to invent an errand and get off now—say I'm going out in the hills for some sport, they'll believe that after a winter cramped up indoors. I'll buy horses for the lot of you. When you've done your bit, meet me at a place I'll tell you. Then we all have to ride like smoke till we're out of Halvdan and Olaf's territory—they won't know right off which way we've gone. Then we all cut across country to the Gula Fjord. My helmsman Steinulf will take over here for me. I dare say with the Way behind him, or anyway with Thorvin and Skaldfinn and their friends, he'll be able to get the *Walrus* free and take it round the coast to meet us. Even if there's trouble, Guthmund should be able to get away with the *Seamew*. All meet up at the Gula and head back to England, like you said."

"You don't want to be in on the attack?"

Brand shook his head silently. Osmod in his turn stared across the table. He too had always believed that a slave and a warrior were two different breeds, as different as sheep and wolves. Then he had found that given a reason and a fighting chance, he had wolf in him. Now he wondered about the giant figure facing him. This was a man famous even among the fierce, quarrelsome, everlastingly competitive heroes of the North. Why was he now standing out? Leaving the dangerous work to others? Was it right that a man who recovered from a wound that took him to the gates of death was never the same man again? He had stood by the door and felt the cold wind come through . . .

"You can leave that to us, then," said Osmod. "Us Englishmen," he added, rubbing the point in. "Do you think we can do it?"

"I think you can do it the way you said," replied Brand. "You Englishmen. What worries me is getting you all across the mountains to the Gula Fjord. You've only met the civilized Norwegians so far. The ones who live up in the back hills, where we're going—they're different."

"If we can handle King Halvdan's guards, we can handle them. And

what about you? You're the champion of the men of Halogaland, aren't
you?"

"I think taking you midgets across Norway will need a champion. I shall
feel like a dog taking a troop of mice through Catland. They're going to
think you people are just so many free dinners."

Osmod's lips compressed. "Show me where we are to meet you with the
horses then, Lord Dog. I and the other mice will be there. Maybe with a
few catskins."

The little convoy moving down to the bridge and the islands beyond it
looked as ragged and unthreatening as it could be made. In the lead an old
farm-horse pulling a battered cart, with one man walking by its side chir-
ruping encouragingly to it. The cart's load was invisible, but a dirty tarpaulin held it all down, one end flapping loose. On the other side of the horse
walked Udd, the smallest of the men, gaping near-sightedly at the horse-
collar: a Norwegian invention which few Englishmen outside the catapult-
teams had ever seen. It enabled a horse to pull twice the weight of the ox-
style straight pole, and Udd, characteristically, had forgotten about the
point of their journey in fascination at the new artifact.

Round and behind the cart straggled eight more men, the six remaining
English catapulteers, Hund the leech, his white priest-clothes hidden under a gray mantle, and Karli. None carried a weapon in sight other than
their belt-knives. Halberds were stowed inconspicuously on nails along the
sides of the cart. The crossbows, already cocked, lurked under the loose
tarpaulin.

As the cart dipped down to the shore, two guards by the side of the
bridge straightened up, retrieved their javelins from the ground.

"Bridge is closed," one of them shouted. "Everyone's off the island. Can't
you see the sun, nearly down?"

Osmod pushed forward, shouting indistinctly in poor Norse. There
were six men on this post, he knew. He wanted them all outside. The man
leading the horse joined in, continuing to walk forward.

One of the guards had had enough. He jumped back, javelin poised,
shouted at the top of his voice. Other men came suddenly out of the hut to
one side, handling axes, picking up shields. Four more of them, Osmod
silently counted. That was right. He turned and raised a thumb to the
others clustered round the cart.

In an instant the crossbows were out and leveled, six of them, with Udd
slipping back to seize his and join in.

"Show 'em," said Osmod briefly.

Fritha, the marksman of the group, sighted and released. A sharp twang and an instantaneous thud. One of the men with shields gasped, his face suddenly white, stared down at the iron quarrel which had driven through his shield and deep into his upper arm. Fritha dropped the bow forward, thrust his foot into the stirrup, jerked over the goat's foot lever, dropped a second quarrel into place.

"You're all marked," called Osmod. "These bows will go through any shield or armor. You can't fight us. Only die. Drop what you're holding and go into the hut."

The guards looked at each other, brave men, but unnerved by the lack of face-to-face challenge, the threat of being shot down from a distance.

"You can keep your swords," offered Osmod. "Just drop those javelins. Go in the hut."

Slowly they dropped spears, shuffled backwards, watching their enemies, trooped into the guard-hut. Two Englishmen ran forward with bars, hammers, nails, quickly and roughly nailed bars across the door and the one shuttered window.

"We learnt something from King Shef," remarked Cwicca. "Always work out what you're going to do before you do it."

"They'll soon bust out," said Karli.

"Then they'll reckon they've got us trapped. That'll give us a bit more time."

The cart rolled on to the bridge, in winter logs embedded in ice, in summer with planks laid over the logs now floating. The men were carrying crossbows and halberds openly now, easy to see in the long Northern twilight. But there should be no-one to see or challenge till the other side of the first island and the next bridge.

Hearing the cart roll towards them, and knowing there should be no-one there, the pair of guards manning the second bridge had more warning and more time to decide what to do. Facing a line of crossbows, one of them immediately and sensibly turned and ran, hoping to get away and call for help. Aiming carefully, Fritha put a bolt through his thigh that brought him instantly down. The second man carefully grounded his weapon, eyes glaring vengefully.

Hund walked from his place at the rear to glance at the wound the crossbow-bolt had made, clicking his tongue at the spreading blood, the bolt buried firmly in bone.

Osmod joined him. "Nasty job getting that out," he remarked. "Still, better alive than dead, and the best leeches in the world over at the college at Kaupang."

Hund nodded. "You, fellow, when you take him to master Ingulf to have his leg mended, give him the regards of Hund the priest and say the Englishmen spared this man's life, at my urging. Till then, pad the wound, check the blood-flow." He showed his silver apple-pendant, sign of Ithun goddess of healing, and turned away.

The cart rolled over the second bridge, over the second island, and on to the final span to Drottningsholm. Occasionally looking behind them for signs of pursuit, the freedmen closed up. This time, they knew, they would have to fight.

The third guard post was the main one, a dozen men. They had already spent the day in serious anxiety, following the disappearance of their captain Stein. They had searched every part of the island for him except the queens' quarters, found nothing. They waited now only for word from King Halvdan before they searched the queens' hall too, but even so they did not expect to find him. They knew enemies were nearby, whether human killers or monsters from the deep. Some had seen a school of orcas cruise by, their great fins showing, and wondered if Stein had been fool enough to enter the water. The faint shouts they had heard from the brief clashes to the north had alarmed them further. As the cart and its escort came into view they moved on to the bridge to block it, four men abreast, three deep.

From the rear rank an arrow flew, aimed at the horse's head. Whatever the cart and its cargo, they meant to block it. Wilfi, leading the horse still, now carried the new case-hardened shield. He lifted it, caught the shaft square on. It leapt back, point blunted.

Cwicca, Osmod, Hama and Lulla walked forward, halberds ready, dropped on one knee to make a hedge of points facing the Norsemen forty feet away. Four crossbowmen stood behind them.

"Drop your weapons," shouted Osmod. He had no hope that his order would be obeyed. A dozen veteran warriors surrender to less than their own number of strangers? Their mothers would disown them. Yet Osmod felt at least a flicker of compunction about shooting men down who were all but helpless, helpless against weapons they did not understand. He waited for the bows to be bent, the javelins to poise before he shouted again.

"Shoot!"

Four crossbows twanged together. At forty feet, against standing targets, no-one could miss. The Viking front line collapsed, one man lifted off his feet by the impact of the bolt, many foot-pounds of energy stored in sprung steel and delivered in a moment. A man in the second line gasped and flinched as a bolt passed through the man in front and plowed up his rib-cage.

Another man broke from the pile of fallen round his feet and hurled himself forward, sword circling back for one mighty slash. Foam splattered his moustache as he ran, desperate for glory and for one blow. He called hoarsely on Othin as he came. A crossbow bolt from the near-sighted Udd hissed past one ear, another from the inexpert Karli flew over his head.

As he came within three strides Osmod straightened from his kneeling position, gripped his long halberd close to the base, thrust forward in a long point from low down. The charging warrior ran straight on to it, splitting his own heart on the leaf-blade, running forward with the last strength in his body till the cross-fixed axe-blade and spike stopped him short. His last breath left him with a grunt, his eyes stared forward in shock.

The sword fell from his hand, the life left him. Osmod twisted the shaft once, cleared his blade, withdrew, dropped back to kneel. A series of clicks behind him as the crossbows cocked again.

The six men in front of him broke and ran, four sideways along the shore, two away along the bridge to Drottningsholm. Osmod gestured briefly. "Put those two down," he said. "Let the others go."

Bodies were dragged aside, and the cart rolled forward for the last time, the old horse now encouraged into a trot, some of the Englishmen behind it walking backwards, alert for pursuit. Osmod and Cwicca jogged in front of the others, eyes probing in the dim light for what they had been told to expect.

"There," said Cwicca, pointing. "Tell Udd and Hund to secure the boat, they're easily spared. They only have to push it off and row it round the point."

Osmod called directions, and the two men broke away. "The rest of you, put your shoulders to the cart and get it up this slope. The hall's on the other side, and we have to hurry now."

Heaved on by the horse and eight men, the cart rocked up a brief slope, came through a copse of firs, and broke out into a clearing. In the center of it stood the Hall of the Two Queens, steep-roofed, ornately gabled, stags' antlers nailed up above the doorways. No sign of life except a frightened face peeping from behind a low shutter, but smoke seeped into the air from its one chimney.

The men swung the cart round so that its rear pointed at the hall, whipped away the tarpaulin, dropped the tilt, clustered round the squat bulk of the mule in the wagon-bed.

"Not there," called Karli. "That's the slaves' room you're pointing at. They'll have him there, in the private chamber. Train round right, right another six feet."

The ton-and-a-quarter mule could not be lifted from its bed without immense effort. Instead the horse-holder slowly shuffled the horse round, inching the cart sideways on its solid axles.

"On!" grunted Cwicca hoarsely, raising his arm in the team's well-practiced drill. Fritha the loader lifted a twenty-pound water-smoothed rock from the bed of the cart, fitted it into the sling. The crew, all but Cwicca and Hama the launch-man, vaulted over the sides of the cart. They had not shot their weapon, with its monstrous kick, from inside a confined space before, and were not sure what effect it would have.

Cwicca checked his target again, dropped his arm in the signal to shoot.

Shef lay back in the great feather bed, in complete relaxation. In all his life he had never spent so much time lying down before, except when he was bedridden with the marsh-fever. A man who was awake should be working, or eating, or at rare intervals merry-making. That was what everyone he knew believed. The idea of rest did not enter their minds.

They were wrong. A day and a night now, he had hardly stirred from the great bed, except to eat his meals. Even those had been brought to him by the slave-women during the day. He had never felt better.

But then maybe that was the queen. She too had come to him at frequent intervals during the day, more frequent than he had ever imagined possible. In Shef's stern and gloomy home, dominated by the pious, angry Wulfgar his stepfather, all forms of sexuality were forbidden to all on Sundays, on the eve of Sunday, during Lent, in the Advent season, during the fasts of the Church. The servants had evaded his rules, of course, and even more the village folk, but sexuality had taken on an air of furtiveness, something to be snatched, got over in between bouts of work, or between sleep and wake. Someone like Queen Ragnhild had been the stuff of dreams, beyond the imagination or experience of any village-youth.

And what he had done had been beyond his imagination too. In amazement, considering what he had already performed, Shef felt his flesh beginning to rise again at the thought of what he had seen and felt. Yet the queen would not return for a while, gone out, she said, to walk along the shore. Better to save his strength. Better to sleep again, warm and well-fed. As he closed his eyes and lay back against the duck-down bolster, Shef thought vaguely of Karli. Better see what he was doing. One of the slave-

women would know. He had never asked their names. Strange. Perhaps he
was beginning to behave like a king at long last.

*In his dream, Shef was standing by a forge, as he had before. It was not the great
forge of the gods of Asgarth, which he had once visited, yet it was like that forge
in that the whole working space was littered with boxes, logs, rough tables. There
were hand-holds nailed here and there to the wall.*

*They were there, Shef remembered, because this smith was lame. In the body
he now inhabited, he remembered the keen pain as they slit his sinews with the
knife, the laughing face of his enemy Nithhad, the promise Nithhad had made
him.*

*"You will not run far now, Völund, with your hamstrings cut, neither on feet
nor on skis, hunter of the forest. And cut sinew never grows back. Yet your hands
are unharmed, and you still have your eyes. So work, Völund, mighty smith!
Work for me, Nithhad, make me precious things by day and by night. For there
is no escape for you by land or by water. And I promise you, husband of the
Valkyrie though you are: if you do not earn your bread every day, you will feel
the lash like the lowest dog of a Finn among my thralls!"*

*And Nithhad had had him trussed up then and there and given him a taste of
the leather for proof. Still Völund remembered the pain in his back, the shame of
being beaten without reply, the glittering eyes of Nithhad's queen as she
watched. His wife's ring had glinted on her finger as she did so, for they had
robbed him as well as mutilated him.*

*Shef-who-was-now-Völund beat furiously on the red iron as he remembered,
not trusting himself in this mood with copper or silver or the red gold that
Nithhad demanded most.*

*As he limped and heaved himself from side to side he saw bright eyes watch-
ing him. Four of them. The two young sons of Nithhad, come to see the fire and
the clangor and the sparkling jewels. Völund paused, looked at them. Nithhad
let them come freely, sure that his slave could never escape, sure too that no
matter how crazy he was for revenge, Völund would never take a revenge for
which he could not escape retaliation. In the belief of the North, that would be
exchanging one for two, neither sensible nor honorable. A revenge was no
revenge unless it was complete.*

*High above, in the rafters to which his great smith's arms could swing him,
lay the wings Völund had made: the magic wings to take him away. But first the
revenge. The complete revenge.*

*"Come and see," called Völund to the watching faces. "See what I have in my
chest here."*

He reached inside it, pulled out a chain of gold links with a jewel between each one, red, blue and green in complex pattern. "Or see this." He showed for an instant a box of walrus ivory with carved scenes upon it, inlaid with silver. "See, in the chest, there is much besides. Come, look in the chest, just peep over the side if you dare."

Slowly the two boys came out into the light of the fire, holding each other's hands. One was six, the other four, the children of Nithhad and his second wife, the enchantress, far younger than their half-sister, the maiden Böthvild who also came to eye him sometimes from the shadows. They were fine boys, shy but friendly, not yet spoilt by their father's greed, their mother's cunning. One of them had given him an apple the day before, saved from his own meal.

Völund waved them over, opened the chest, held its massive lid open with one hand. He was careful to hold it by the handle. Many an hour had he spent, in time stolen from sleep, welding on the edge to it, the sharpest edge he had ever made in his life. They were good children, and he did not wish them to feel pain.

"Come, see!" he said again. They peered over, squeaking like mice with excitement. Their necks were over the iron lip of the chest. Völund, cruel man that he was, averted his eyes as he prepared to slam down the lid . . .

I do not want to be in this body, thought Shef, fighting against the god's fingers that held him firmly, forced him to watch. Whatever lesson I am being taught, I do not want to learn it.

As he began in some unknown way to squirm free he saw another sight, far below the forge, somewhere in the deep rocky bowels, not of Middle-earth, but of the walls that surround the Nine Worlds of men and gods and giants together. A great figure, with the savage unpredictable face of a god, chained with monstrous fetters to the foundations of the universe. A great serpent hissing and spitting venom in its face, the face contorted with pain and yet still aware, still thinking, still looking beyond the pain.

The figure was the chained god Loki, Shef realized, whom the Way-priests believed had been bound and tormented by his father Othin for the murder of his brother Balder. Yet who would break free and return to revenge himself on gods and men, with his monster-children on the Last Day itself. The enormous staple on one wrist-fetter had been pulled almost free from the wall, Shef saw. When it came loose Loki would have one hand free to throttle the tormenting serpent sent by his father Othin. Already he seemed free enough to beckon, to be signaling to his allies, the monster-broods in the forests and in the depths of the sea. For an instant his furious eyes seemed to look from his prison up towards Shef.

As he tore himself away again Shef felt one more trickle of the thoughts of Völund.

Do the deed, they ran. Do it now. And then, then to scoop out the skulls and

carve them like walrus ivory, then to polish the teeth till they shine like pearls,
then to take the glistening eyeballs from their orbits . . .

Back in his own body again, Shef felt a monstrous slam, saw for an instant a
sharpened lid swinging down.

The slam was real. He could feel the tremors of it still shaking the bed.
Shef kicked his feet free of the linen sheet and woolen blanket, leapt from
the bed, lunged for tunic, breeches and shoes. Was this the queen's husband come for him?

The door swung open and the boy Harald rushed in. "Mother! Mother!"
He stopped as he saw only Shef sitting on his mother's bed. Without a
pause he pulled his little eating-knife from his belt and lunged at Shef's
throat.

Shef parried the blow, caught the thin wrist, twisted away the knife,
ignored the furious kicks and punches from the free hand. "Easy, easy," he
said. "I was just waiting here. What is happening outside?"

"I don't know. Men with a—with something that throws rocks. The wall
is all smashed in."

Shef let the boy go, darted through the door from the bedchamber to
the queens' parlor. As he did so a concerted charge smashed down the
door from the main hall, and a wave of men poured in, knives drawn and
crossbows pointed. Shef recognized Cwicca at the same moment that they
recognized him, began to step forward waving his arms frantically for
them to stop.

Karli sprang out of the ruck and came forward, shouting something
inaudible in the din of voices.

"There's no need for it!" Shef bellowed back. "I'm all right. Tell them all
to stop."

Karli laid a hand on his arm, trying to drag him towards the door.
Furiously, Shef threw it off, realized at once that Karli meant to knock him
unconscious once more. He dodged the left lead, got a hand up in time to
block the right swing, ducked his head into Karli's already-broken nose
and grappled his arms, trying to prevent him getting in a clear blow. As
they struggled, Shef felt other hands on him, arms and legs, men trying to
pick him up bodily and carry him off like a sack. He heard a voice gasp in
his ear, "Hit him with the sandbag, Cwicca, he won't stop fighting."

Shef dropped Karli, swung the men holding his arms into each other,
trampled his way free of the man clutching his leg, filled his lungs for
another and more commanding bellow.

Behind him, the old queen Asa had also entered the room. One of the

English raiders stood goggling at the struggle in front of him, unable to bring himself to join in and lay hands on his master. Seizing the iron stake by which she summoned her slaves, the old queen struck him smartly over the head, snatched the seax-knife from his belt as he slumped. Took three quick hobbling paces towards Shef, the cuckolder of her son and danger to her grandson, still standing unawares with his back to her.

At the same moment the little boy Harald, also standing staring at the struggle, felt the prompting of generations of warrior-ancestors. With a shrill cry he too raised his knife again and ran forward to attack the invaders of his hall. As he ran past Shef at a line of grown men, Shef scooped him up and hugged him to his own body, wrapping both arms round him to prevent his struggles. He tried to shout again, "Everybody just stand still!"

The faces confronting him turned to alarm, men started to spring forward. Shef turned with the speed he had learned in the wrestling ring, Harald still clutched to his body.

Queen Asa thrust savagely upwards with the broad-bladed knife. Shef felt a thud, a prick of pain over his ribs. Looked down at the boy in his arms. Saw him turn up his face, start to ask some disbelieving question. Saw the knife driven clean through the boy's heart and body. The knife in the hands of his grandmother.

Somewhere, again, Shef heard a lid slam. Slam again and again.

The room had gone completely still and silent. Shef released his grip, slowly straightened the small body out, laid it on the ground.

As he looked down, his eyes seemed for a moment to blur. He seemed to be looking not at the slight shape of a ten-year old, but at a grown man, tall and burly, with a mane of hair and beard.

This was Harald Fairhair, said a cold, amused, familiar voice. *Harald Fairhair as he would have been. You are his inheritor now. You inherited his treasure from King Edmund, and paid with your youth. You inherited his luck from King Alfred, and paid with your love. Now you inherit destiny from King Harald. What will you pay with this time? And do not try to shirk my visions again.*

The moment passed. Shef was once more in the parlor, staring down at a bloodstained shape. Harald was dead now. Shef had felt the life go. Arms were at his shoulders again, hustling him away, and this time he did not resist. Behind him Queen Asa took slow step after slow step towards the body of her grandson, reaching out a tentative, shaking hand. Shef lost sight of her as they ran him through the door into the hall, out through the main door shattered by the catapult-stone, into the open.

Outside the hubbub broke out again, someone shouting, "But she's still got my knife," other voices snarling at him, Osmod counting, "Seven, eight, nine, all right, that's the lot, get moving." Cwicca appeared from somewhere with a firebrand and the barrel of dry kindling the slaves used, hurled first one and then the other into the cart, watched the flame spread as he slashed the horse free of its traces.

"They won't get our mule," he shouted.

"What are you doing with those women?" Osmod shouted as Karli came into the light, a woman in each hand and two more running anxiously behind him.

"They've got to come with us."

"It's only a six-oar boat, there's no room."

"They have to come. Especially now the boy's dead. Their throats will be cut at his burial."

Osmod, ex-slave himself, argued no more. "All right, move it."

In an untidy stream nine men and four women ran down the path leading to the little beach where Martha had killed Stein only the evening before, Cwicca and Osmod bringing up the rear, crossbows raised. Half way down it, Shef heard a great shriek split the air behind him. Ragnhild returned from her walk along the shore. Behind it, men's voices shouting. The guardsmen they had left behind, rallied and anxious to avenge their defeats.

The run turned into a headlong dash, each person making for the beach and the boat they could see waiting, Udd and Hund with oars poised ready to shove off. Men and women poured over the thwarts, seized oars or were pushed out of the way. The overloaded boat jammed on the shingle, Shef and Karli leaped out again and heaved it bodily out six feet, ten, till the beach shelved away and they were dragged in over the sides, only inches above the water. Six men found their places, braced their feet, took one pull, another, as Osmod hoarsely called the time.

Framed by the light from the now fiercely-burning cart, Shef saw the figure of Queen Ragnhild walking down the beach, her arms stretched out. Arrows from the men behind her skipped over the water, but Shef ignored them, waved down the crossbows poised to answer.

"Luckstealer!" she cried. "Bane of my son. May you be the bane of all those around you. May you never know woman again. May no son succeed you."

"It wasn't his fault," muttered Wilfi from the bow, rubbing his head where the iron stake had split it. "It was that daft old woman who took my knife."

"Shut up about your knife," growled Fritha, "you should have held on to it."

As the bickering continued, the boat pulled steadily away into the black dark, waiting for concealment before bending round away from Halvdan's cruisers to the mainland no more than a short mile off.

Shef stared over the stern till he could see no longer, at the woman still raving and weeping by the shore.

CHAPTER FIFTEEN

Alfred, King of the West-Saxons, co-ruler with the absent King Shef of all the English counties south of the Trent, watched his young bride with slight nervousness as she walked the last few steps to the top of the hill overlooking Winchester. There was some chance—the leeches could not yet be sure—that she might be carrying his child already, and he feared she might overtax her strength. He knew though that she hated protection, held his tongue.

She reached the top, turned and looked out over the valley. It was already a mass of white blossom, where the Hampshire churls had planted the apple trees for their beloved cider. On the broad fields the other side of the stockaded town teams could be seen plowing, men following the slow oxen up and down the furrows; very long furrows because it took the eight-beast teams so long to make a turn. Alfred followed her gaze, pointed to a spot in the middle distance.

"Look," he said, "there is a team plowing with four horses, not eight oxen. It is on your own estate. Wonred the reeve saw the horse-collars the men of the Way used for their catapult-teams, and said he would try it for plowing. He says horses eat more than oxen, but if they are hitched properly they are stronger and faster and do much more work. He says he is going to start breeding horses for size and strength as well. And there is an advantage no-one thought of. It takes a good part of a churl's day to get out to the further fields and back if he is leading a yoke of oxen. With the horses they ride out and back, so they have more time in the fields."

"Or more time to rest, I hope," said Godive. "One reason poor churls live so little time is that they have no rest but Sunday, and the Church takes that."

"Used to take that," corrected Alfred. "Now it is up to the churl."

He hesitated a moment, patted her shoulder gently. "It is working, you know," he said. "I don't think any of us ever realized how rich a country can be if it is left at peace, with no masters. Or only a master who cares for the country. But the good news comes in every day. What King Shef, your brother, told me is perfectly correct. There is always someone who knows an answer, but nearly always it is someone whom no-one has ever asked before. I had a group of miners visit me yesterday, men from the lead mines in the hills. They used to be owned by the monks at Winchcombe. Now the monks have gone, they work the mines themselves, for my reeve and the alderman of Gloucester. They told me that the old Rome-folk used to mine silver in the same hills, and that they think they could do the same.

"Silver," he mused. "If the black monks had known that, they would have whipped their slaves till they died in search of it. So the slaves did not tell them. They tell me because they know I will give them a share. And with new silver—it is not long ago that every time we minted the money was worse, and soon Canterbury money would have been as bad as York. Now, with the silver I put back from the Church hoards, a Wessex penny is as good as any in Frankland or the German lands beyond. And the traders come in from everywhere, from Dorestad and Compostella, and the Franklands too if they can evade their own king's ban. They all pay harbor-dues, and I use it to pay my miners. The traders are happy, and the miners are happy, and I am happy too.

"So, Godive, you see that things are not as bad as they were, even for the churls. It may not seem much, but a horse to ride and a full belly even in Lent is happiness to many."

A bell began to chime from the Old Minster in the town below, its strokes ringing out over the steep valley. Ringing for a bridal, probably: the priests who remained in Wessex had found that if they were to keep any worshipers for the White Christ they had to use their assets of music and ritual, more impressive still than the strange tales of the Way-missionaries from the North.

"It still rests on war, though," she replied.

Alfred nodded. "It always did. I saw this valley a desolation of burnt fields when I was a boy. The Vikings took the town and burnt every house in it except the stone Minster. They would have pulled that down if they had had time. We fought them then and we fight them still. The difference is that now we fight them at sea, so the land is spared. And the more it is spared the stronger we are, and the weaker they grow."

He hesitated again. "Are you missing your—your brother? I know well that all this goes back to him. If it had not been for him I would have been dead, or a penniless exile, or at best a puppet-king with Bishop Daniel holding my strings. Or some Viking jarl, maybe. I owe him everything." He patted her hand. "Even you."

Godive dropped her eyes. Her husband always referred to Shef, now, as her brother, though she knew that he knew that there was no blood relationship between them, that they were stepbrother and stepsister only. Sometimes she thought that Alfred had realized the truth of their relationship, maybe the truth too that her first husband had really been her half-brother. But if he suspected, he was careful to ask no further. He did not know that she had miscarried twice, deliberately, while she had been first married, taking the dangerous birthwort. If she had believed in any god, the Christian one or the strange pantheon of the Way, she would have prayed to him or them for a safe delivery for what might now be in her womb.

"I hope he is alive."

"At least no-one has seen him dead. All our traders know there is a reward for any news, and a greater one for the man who brings him back."

"Not many kings would pay to have a rival return," said Godive.

"He is no rival to me. My rivals are across the Channel there, or up in the North working mischief. It looks safe as we sit on this hill and look over the fields. I tell you, I would feel twenty times safer if Shef were back in England. He is our best hope. The churls call him *sigesaelig,* you know, the Victorious."

Godive squeezed her husband's arm. "They call you Alfred *esteadig.* The Gracious. That is a better name."

In the great tent of striped canvas many days' march and sail to the north, the conference was less happy. The tent had been pitched with its rear into the wind, and the front wall brailed up so the men inside it could also look out. They looked out over a drear landscape of moor and heather, marked here and there by columns of smoke rising, the marks of the harrying parties coming down on one clump of wretched bothies or another. The three Ragnarssons left alive sat on their camp stools, ale-horns in hand.

Each had a weapon stuck into the ground beside him, spear or spiked axe, as well as their swords belted on. Twice already that spring, since the battle off the Elbe, one jarl or another had tried to challenge their authority. Sensitive as cats to the constant ebb and flow of reputation on which power rested, all three knew they had to offer their followers a scheme. A bribe. A proposition. Or there would be tents struck in the night, ships missing at the next rendezvous, men gone to try their fortune in the service of some sea-king better favored by luck.

"This is keeping the lads busy," said the grizzled Ubbi, nodding at the smoke-columns. "Good beef, good mutton, women to run down. No casualties to speak of."

"No money," completed Halvdan. "No glory either."

Sigurth the Snake-eye knew his brothers were just setting the problem up for him to deal with, not offering a criticism. The brothers never fought, hardly ever disagreed. Their relationship had survived even the psychotic Ivar. The other two waited for him to respond.

"If we go south again," he said, "we run into those rock-throwers again. We can sail rings round them, we know that. But they have the advantage now. They know we're up here in Scotland, because they kept us out of the Channel. All they have to do is harbor somewhere on the coast near their northern border, wherever they choose to draw it. If we sail downcoast, they hit us. If we go round them—and we don't know where they are—they get to hear about it, come down after us, and hit us in harbor, wherever we are. The risk is either meeting them at sea, or getting our ships battered to bits while we're on land. We might end up having to cut our way from coast to coast. And I don't think any of the lads, however big they talk, fancies meeting the rock-throwers at sea again. You can't fight standing on a bundle of planks."

"So we're beat," nudged Ubbi. All three men laughed.

"Maybe what we need is some rock-throwers of our own," suggested Halvdan. "That's what Ivar thought. He made that little black-robed bastard, what was his name? Erkinbjart? He made him make some. Pity the little bastard got away."

"That's for next year," said Sigurth. "Can't change horses in mid-stream, and for this year we have to go with what we have. This year we'll pass the word in the slave-markets that we pay high prices for men who can shoot these throwers. Someone will bring one in. And if they can shoot them they can build them. Put someone like that together with a real ship-builder, and we'll have something that can outsail those clumsy English tubs and outfight them too.

"But right now we need something to put heart into our lot and silver into their pouches. Or the hope of silver in their heads, anyway."

"Ireland," suggested Halvdan.

"We'd have to go north about round the tip of Scotland now, the place will be aswarm with Norwegians before we get there."

"Frisia?" offered Ubbi doubtfully.

"Poor as Scotland, only flatter."

"That's the islands. How about the mainland? Or we could try Hamburg again. Or Bremen."

"That hasn't been lucky water for us this year," said Sigurth. His brothers nodded, both of them showing their teeth in involuntary snarl. They remembered the humiliation on the sandbank, coming back from a fruitless hunt with no quarry and a man missing. The humiliation of being outmaneuvered, so that they had to stand back from a challenge from a single man.

"But I think that's the right idea," said Sigurth. "Or nearly the right idea. We'll keep the lads busy over here for a few weeks yet, give this whole country a complete shaking. Let them know they just have to enjoy themselves, there's something bigger coming. Then we'll go back across the North Sea, direct crossing, head for the granite isles."

His brothers nodded, knowing he meant the islands of the North Frisians, facing the Ditmarsh, Fohr and Amrum and Sylt, three islands of rock amid a waste of shifting sands.

"Then we go down the Eider and hit Hedeby."

Halvdan and Ubbi stared at each other, considered. "They're our own people," said Halvdan. "Sort of. Anyway, they're Danes."

"So what? Have they done us any favors? That fat trader-king Hrorik wouldn't even sell the man we want to Skuli. He let the Way-priests take him off to their bolt-hole."

"Maybe we ought to hit them instead."

"Right. What I'm thinking," said Sigurth, "is if England is ruled out for us right now, we'll find better returns in our own countries than foraging round these poor places. Riskier, I know. But if we take Hedeby and Hrorik's gold, then there'll be all the more to support us if we go for Halvdan and his idiot brother Olaf. Sure, there'll always be some who'll drop out, got a brother in Kaupang or a father in Hedeby. Plenty left. And the ones we beat in one place will join us for the next place."

"Roll up the North first," said Halvdan. "Set you in place as the One King of all the Northlands. Then come back to the South."

"With a thousand keels, and rock-throwers in the front of them," amplified Ubbi.

"To finish the Christians once and for all . . ."

"To fulfill our Bragi-boast long ago . . ."

"To get revenge for Ivar."

Halvdan got up, drained his horn, pulled his spiked beard-axe out of the ground. "I'll go round the tents," he said. "Drop a few hints. Say we've got a plan, and everyone will get a shock when they know it. Keep them quiet just a few weeks longer."

Erkenbert the deacon stood inside a great ring of ancient stones. It was the doom-ring of the Smaaland peoples, the Little Countries between Danish Skaane and the giant confederacy of the Swedes extending hundreds of miles to the north, a country with many kings striving always to establish one *Sveariki,* one empire of the Swedes. It was the Smaalanders' spring assembly, when men came out of their snowed-in cabins and began to prepare for the short but welcome summer.

Erkenbert had carefully dyed his worn black robe so that it shone even blacker, a violent contrast with the furs and homespuns that surrounded him. His attendant had also once more shaved every inch of his tonsure, so that the bald ring on his head stood out even more strongly. "We don't want to hide away," Bruno had said. "That's the old style. Trying to get by on sufferance. We want them to see us. Get Christianity in their faces." Erkenbert had meditated a sharp reply on the virtue of humility, but had withdrawn. For one thing few men any longer cared to answer back to the Master of the *Lanzenorden,* as men were already calling him. For another Erkenbert could see the sense in the policy.

The Smaalanders were selling off slaves, as usual. Mere bags of bones, most of them, ill-fed during the winter and now a doubtful speculation for the summer and the work-period. The emissaries of the Uppsala king Orm were buying the cheapest, as usual. Don't bother with most of them, Bruno had said. Funds are low. But this one he had to have.

A burly farmer pushed forward into the ring as his turn came, towing with him in one fist an emaciated figure. The slave was dressed in no more than tatters, and shook uncontrollably with cold. Through the rags his ribs showed. A cough racked his body every few seconds, and he stank of the midden where he had slept for warmth.

A chorus of jeers greeted the arrival, from the seller's neighbors. "What do you want for him, Arni? If he was a chicken you'd have to use him for soup. Even the Swedes won't take him. He won't live till the next sacrifice."

Arni glared round indignantly. His eye fell on Erkenbert advancing deliberately across the sale-ground. Erkenbert walked composedly up to the thin man, put his arms round him, held him closely.

"Don't worry, sirra, we have heard of you, we are here to rescue you."

The stink attacked Erkenbert's nostrils, but he bore it, remembering the Book of Job. The thin man began to weep, causing a fresh barrage of jeers and hooting from the crowd.

"How can you rescue me, they will take you too, they are animals, they care nothing for the rights of God . . ."

Gently Erkenbert disengaged himself, pointed behind him to the group from which he had come. Ten *Ritter* of the *Lanzenorden* stood in a double line, every man mailed, helmeted, with metal gauntlets shining. In each man's right hand was a short pike, butt on the ground, point forward at exactly the same angle. "These people are good warriors," Bruno had said. "But they have no discipline. We will show them some. It keeps them uncertain."

"What do you want for this man?" said Erkenbert, speaking loudly so the watchers could hear.

Arni, a devout disciple of Frey, spat on the ground. "To you, Christling, twenty ounces of silver."

Derision from the crowd. Eight ounces was a good price for a man in full vigor, twelve for a pretty girl.

"I will give you four," shouted Erkenbert, still playing to the crowd. "You have saved the other sixteen on food and clothes over the winter."

Arni did not see the joke. Face purpling, he strode forward towards the much smaller man.

"Shaveling! Four ounces! You have no rights here. By the law of the Smaalanders any man who catches a Christ-priest has the right to enslave him. What is to hinder me from taking you and your four ounces."

"You have the right to enslave a Christ-priest," replied Erkenbert unmoved. "Do you have the strength?"

At the psychological moment the uncanny shape of Bruno made its way out of the crowd, from the point opposite the watching ranks of the *Ritters*. He pushed gently through the watching men, edging them aside with his ape-like shoulders. He carried no pike, but wore the same armor as his men. His left hand rested on the pommel of his trailing, over-length sword.

Arni glared round him, observing the sudden silence, realizing that in an instant he had become the one under test. He tried to rally the crowd round him.

"Are we going to take this? Are we going to let these men come in here and steal our slaves away?"

"They're paying cash," observed a voice from the crowd.

"And what will they do with the men they take? Such as these—" Beside himself with fury, Arni turned and cuffed his slave violently across the side of the head, sending him sprawling and weeping to the ground. "Such as these should go to the groves of Uppsala, as a sacrifice to the true gods, not go back to preach more lies about sons of virgins and the dead risi—"

Arni's voice cut off in mid-syllable. Moving like the tufted lynx of the forests, Bruno had covered the four paces between them. His hand shot out faster than anyone could see. But they could all see now that his gauntleted fingers had closed on the throat-ball, the Adam's apple of the Smaalander, held it in steel pincers. He lifted slightly, and the farmer rose on struggling tiptoe.

"Filth," said Bruno. "You have laid hands on the servant of the living God. You have spoken blasphemy against our faith. I will not kill you in the doom-ring, where blood must not be shed, but do you care to meet me in the dueling-ground, with sword and buckler, or axe and spear, or any weapon you care to choose?"

Unable to move or speak, the farmer goggled helplessly.

"I thought not." Bruno released him, turned on his heel, barked a command. In one drilled movement the front rank of his *Ritters* stamped forward, paces one-two-three, stood at attention once more. "Continue with the sale."

"Four ounces," Erkenbert repeated. We mustn't rob them, Bruno had said, or they *will* fight. But we don't have to pay over the odds either. Still, we must rescue Sirra Eilif the priest. Only he knows anything of the kings in the back country behind Birka. We need him to help us with our search. I am anxious to hear more of this King Kjallak they speak of, from up on the borders of Iron-bearing Land.

Massaging his throat, the farmer wondered whether he dared hold out for more, met Erkenbert's black hostile eyes, decided he did not. He nodded.

Erkenbert threw a small purse at his feet, took Eilif the priest gently by one arm, withdrew with him to the ranks of the *Ritter*, now joined once more by Bruno. The priest and the deacon moved to the security of the central file, Bruno snapped commands, the armored men sloped their pikes and marched away, feet slamming down together like a single man.

The Swedes and Smaalanders watched them go, turned again to their business.

"What did you think of that?" said one tall Swede to another.

"Think of that? That's the bastard who killed King Orm's man at Hedeby. He must make a habit of this. I don't know what he wants, but I'll tell you this. We're seeing some new kind of Christian."

The other nodded thoughtfully, looked round to see if any might over-hear. "If there's a new kind of Christian around, maybe we all need a new kind of king to deal with them."

CHAPTER SIXTEEN

Brand had protested briefly and furiously at the unexpected appearance of four women from the boat. Not enough horses. We'll have to leave them. When they told him what had happened on Drottningsholm his protests ceased. "We'd better get out of here," was all he said. "Now his son is dead Halvdan won't rest till everyone involved is dead as well. Or he is. I don't think he'll touch my crew, or not till he finds out that I left with you. But we have to be out of the Westfold faster than anyone has ever left before. You drop behind—you're left behind."

Shef said nothing to all this. Stumbled as he walked with his dark thoughts still on the island. And the dead boy. Some part of him was still trapped back there, sealed between the warm thighs, engulfed by large breasts.

They had set off along a path that led directly up into the mountains, twisting and winding through the everlasting dark pine- and fir-forest. Ten Englishmen, four women, Karli and Brand, with a dozen horses between them. And deadly pursuit sure to follow them in the morning.

Yet almost from the start it seemed that Brand's fears had less ground than he thought. One of the ex-slaves, Wilfi, had said immediately that in his life in England he had been a forerunner, the slave sent on ahead of his master when his master travelled, to see to his lodging and food at every halt. Running forty miles a day, Wilfi said, was as easy to him as walking twenty to another man. He needed no horse. The women rode double, or else one would ride while the men took turns trotting at their side with a hand on the saddle.

It was a long night's riding, dawn was slow in coming. At first light Brand called a halt to cook, water the horses at a stream, and give the mountain ponies a chance to forage in the new swift-growing grass. The slaves quickly built a fire, crushed grain and made their everlasting porridge. Then they were ready to start again while Brand was still groaning and massaging his stiff thigh-muscles. When he looked round in surprise at the column already forming up, Osmod told him with a certain relish: "You forget, master. A slave has to go on whether he wants to or not. It is free men who have to be persuaded, or think a blister, or hunger or thirst are good enough excuses to stop."

And Vikings, fast movers though they might be by the leisurely standards of the armies of the Christian West, were seamen or ski-runners rather than horsemen. For all his urgency it was Brand who held the party up. No horse the party had could carry his giant frame for long. During the long day that followed the long night, Osmod finally took charge, reorganized the mounts so that each man or woman in the party took a turn on foot as well as riding, and told Brand to take two horses, riding one and leading the other in turn, or else, on the flatter and broader stretches, running between the two with a great arm hooked over each saddle-pommel.

"Will we make it?" Cwicca asked finally when they stopped for a second time, to hobble the horses in a patch of thick new growth. The rest of the party listened anxiously for the answer. Brand looked round, tried to estimate where they were and how far they had come.

"I think so," he said. "We have come faster than I thought possible. And we must have had a start anyway, since Halvdan did not know which way we went."

"He'll find out, though?" queried Cwicca.

"There'll be riders out now to tell him who is moving through his territory. But they have to reach him, get his orders, come back and try to carry them out. All that time we're heading the other way. Three more stages like the two we've done and we're out of the Westfold. Won't stop Halvdan sending killers after us, but he can't order anyone to block the road."

"But we're not taking any risks," said Osmod. "As soon as the horses have eaten their fill, we move on."

"We have to sleep sometime," protested Brand.

"Not for days yet. When people start falling off their horses, then we can sleep. Or else tie them on."

The party pushed on again, wearily, with aching feet and grumbling bellies. But never a word of complaint. The women led the way, looked back sharply at the slightest sign of flagging.

Slowly, though, they began to realize that the real threat lay not behind them but in front. In mountainous and little-traveled Norway, all roads and paths went naturally through every farmstead on the route. A chance for the isolated farm-folk to hear news or to give it, a chance for the traveling pedlars to sell their clothes or wine or salt. To begin with, at every farmstead they came to, Brand had bargained for extra horses, buying one here and two there till the party were fully mounted with animals to spare. Yet though he paid immediately in good silver pennies, the farmers seemed loath to sell. "I'm being too quick," he explained. "They want me to hang around and bargain for half a day. Nothing much happens up here. They like to spin things out. Paying the price asked and moving on —it doesn't seem honest to them. Anyway, it's natural they're going to wonder who we are. Ten midgets who can't speak the language properly, four women in slave-gear, one man in a dream"—he pointed at the unspeaking Shef—"and me. They're bound to be uneasy. I told you, I'm taking a bunch of mice through Catland."

Trouble stirred first the day after Brand declared them free of the Westfold. They had crossed a watershed and were winding their way down through a steep valley, water rushing down on both sides of it, and animals newly-released from their indoor winter pens grazing gratefully wherever the new grass showed. The party came down, as they had a dozen times before, on a farmstead, a cluster of buildings arranged in a rough square. Work had stopped immediately as the men of the farm moved over to inspect the new arrivals, to exchange words with Brand, to call out the women and children. Slowly Shef, his mind still turning continually over the little boy who had died in his arms, realized that the mood at this farmstead was somehow different. The menfolk were not just uneasy or suspicious, they were amused. They had come to some kind of conclusion. Shef looked round more alertly. How many of them were there? Were there still as many as there had been at the start? How many in his own party?

A shriek came suddenly from behind the cow-byre. A voice calling out in English. Edith's voice, the youngest and prettiest of the women. Without words Cwicca, Osmod and the rest seized their crossbows and streamed towards it, Brand, Shef and the farm-folk following at a run.

As they came round the corner of the barn they saw two Norsemen holding Edith. One held her from behind, trying to clamp a hand over her mouth. The other had hold of one leg, was trying to grasp the other. As he heard feet behind him, the second man let go, turned.

"She's used to it," he said. "Look at her. Just a whore of a slave. Does it all the time. Why shouldn't we get a turn too?"

"She's no slave," snapped Osmod. "And she never was your slave."

"Who are you to say?" The other farm men, half a dozen of them, had come round now, were siding with him and the other man still clutching Edith. "She has no rights here. Nor have you. If I say you're a slave you'll soon be one."

Shef pushed his way forward, made the Norseman meet his eye. They were not in danger here, he knew, or at least no immediate danger. He had heard the crossbows click, and though the Norsemen had axes and knives to hand, they would be riddled before they had a chance to use them. But if they did that, even if they killed every man, even if they killed every woman and child as well, as Viking raiders would have done in England, still the news would go out and a hue and cry raised. These men had to be made to back down. But they had decided, in their unthinking way, that they were dealing with lesser beings.

"Just leave us this one," suggested the Norseman, "and the rest of you can ride on."

Edith screamed from behind the covering hand, thrashed violently. She thinks we might just do it, thought Shef.

Brand stepped from behind him, the axe he had taken from his saddle sliding through his massive palm. It was a mighty weapon, the haft a three-foot shaft of ash, the curved convex edge a foot long from horn to horn. The iron head was inlaid with serpent-patterns in silver, the welded steel blade flashing bright against the darker iron. A long spike jutted from the back of the head, for balance, and for the back-stroke. It was the weapon of a champion.

"Let her go," he said. "Unless you want to fight me. All of you, or one at a time. I don't care."

The Norseman who had spoken first looked up at him. He was not as big as Brand—no-one Shef had ever seen was—but once again Shef realized what giants the Norwegians were. The Norseman was a good four inches taller than Shef himself, far broader and heavier. He was considering the challenge, Shef realized. Was it worth it? What was the risk?

Brand flicked his axe into the air, let it twirl over and over, caught it without glancing up.

The Norwegian nodded slowly. "All right. Thorgeir, let her go. I don't think she's worth it. This time. But someone will catch you before you get out of the mountains, big man. Then we'll see why you're running slaves through the Buskerud. Slave-blood in you too, maybe."

Shef saw Brand's knuckles whiten on the axe-handle at the insult, but he made no move. Edith, released, ran instantly to the center of the group that faced her, crossbows cocked and leveled. Slowly, facing outwards, the women, the Englishmen and Brand retreated to their horses, silently gathered up their possessions. Two of the horses were missing, stolen during the brief confrontation.

"Don't fuss about it," muttered Brand. "Just get going and keep going." The column wound through the farm-buildings and middens. A child threw a clod of earth after them as they left, and then the rest joined in, mingling earth and stones with taunts and jeers that followed them half a mile on their way.

The party camped that night in more comfort than ever before, spreading out their meager supply of blankets and taking time to cook the salt meat and dried onions they had bought a day before. But they ate silently and anxiously. A sentry remained on his feet all the time, watching the trail before and behind them.

As the others rolled themselves up to sleep, Osmod and Cwicca came over to sit next to Shef and the still-silent Brand.

"We're not going to get very far like this," said Osmod. "The news will go ahead of us, along paths we don't know. We could have trouble at every farmstead. If there's a village or a town it could be worse."

"I told you," Brand replied. "Like taking a nest of mice through Catland."

"We were relying on our dog," said Cwicca.

Shef looked at Brand with instant alarm. He had seen Brand challenged or provoked several times during the campaigning winter, in the camps round York or East Anglia. Provoked a good deal more gently or carefully than this, and by men many times more formidable than Cwicca. The response every time had been the instant blow or grapple: a broken arm, a man knocked senseless. This time Brand sat motionless, seemingly deep within himself.

"Yes," said Brand finally. "You were relying on me. You still can rely on me. I gave my word to see you through to the Gula Fjord, and I will do my best to keep that word. But there's something you ought to know. I know it now, if I didn't before.

"I have been a warrior for twenty-five winters. If I were to count up the men I have killed or the battles I have seen—well, it would sound like a saga of one of King Hrolf's champions, or of old Ragnar Hairy-Breeks himself. In all that time no-one can say I ever turned tail, or held back when the spears crossed."

He looked round fiercely. "You have seen that! I should not need to boast here.

"But the fight with Ivar took something out of me. I have been wounded many times, and left for dead more than once. I never felt in my own heart that I was dead. When Ivar dodged my blow and got his sword through me I felt the blade in my guts, and I knew, I knew that even if I could get myself off it and live that day, then I would die within two more. I knew. It took less time than a heartbeat, but I could never forget it. Not even after Hund over there sewed up my torn guts and my belly and nursed me through the fever and the draining pus. I am as strong as ever I was now. But I cannot forget what I once knew."

He looked round again at the others. "And the trouble is, you see, up here in the mountains, where every district has its champion, and *mannjafnathr* is what they do all the time, comparing men to see which they think is the deadliest, they can feel it. That man back there knew he wasn't my match—knew I had killed a dozen farmhands like him before my beard was fully grown. But he could tell as well that my heart wasn't in it. Just a little more time to think about it, and he might have taken the risk."

"You are as strong as ever," said Osmod. "You would have killed him. Better for all of us if you had."

"I expect I'd have killed him," Brand agreed. "He was only the cock of his own midden. But funny things happen when a man loses heart. I have known great warriors stand still with the piss running down their breeches till they were cut down. They freeze, and the Valkyries, Othin's daughters, the Choosers of the Slain, throw their fear-fetters over them."

The Englishmen sat in silence. Finally Osmod spoke again. "That's it, then. We'd better go through every place we come to all closed up and ready from now on. Halberds showing, crossbows cocked. I wish these silly bastards up here had seen crossbows work. Then they'd be more frightened. But we can't shoot somebody just to show them.

"One other thing," he added. "Edith didn't go off behind that barn just because she's dumb, you know. She was called over. By a woman. Woman speaking English, not Norse. She must have heard us talking among ourselves. A slave-woman. Been here twenty years."

Brand nodded heavily. "They have been running slaves out of England for fifty years now. I dare say every farmstead in the whole of the North has its English grinding-slave, or half-a-dozen of them, and men-thralls for the heavy work out in the fields as well. What did she want?"

"Wanted us to take her with us, of course. Spoke to Edith because she thought she'd be sympathetic. Then the men came round the corner, must have been watching."

"Did you speak to the slave-woman?" asked Shef, finally breaking out of his own internal struggles. "What did you tell her?"

"Told her she couldn't come. Too much trouble for us. I should have said the same to Edith and the others, even if they were down to have their throats cut over some dead prince-brat's tomb. The woman back there was from Norfolk," Osmod added. "They stole her out of Norwich twenty years ago, when she was a girl. Now she'll grow old and die up here."

He and Cwicca got to their feet, walked away, began to spread out their blankets.

Shef looked at Brand, did not venture to speak. What the big man had said must have cost him as much grief and inner shame as breaking down in public tears might have done to someone lesser. Shef wondered what sort of man he would be in the future. Could they ever nurse him back to health in his mind, as Hund had done with his body? Long after the rest of the camp was asleep, except for the patrolling sentry, Brand sat restless, moodily breaking sticks and feeding them into the fire.

The next day, as they jogged along through the mountain pinewoods, moving now without the frantic haste of the rush from Halvdan's kingdom, Shef found Udd riding by his side. He looked down with some surprise. Udd normally had little or nothing to say except when there was forge-work to be done.

"I've been thinking about those millstones," said Udd. "They're not very much use up here, because the water only flows half the year. And when it does it's like that." He pointed to the mountain-stream ahead of them, pouring down in a thin deep channel over a succession of six-foot drops in the hillside.

"What they need here is something more the same all the time."

"Like what?"

Udd licked a finger, held it up in the air. "No shortage of wind up here, is there?"

Shef laughed. The thought of wind, a thing no-one could see or measure or weigh or even catch, driving the most massive thing that men ever used, the great weight of the millstone, was impossible.

"Wind can drive a ship, though, can't it?" said Udd, reading his leader's thought. "If it can drive a ship that weighs ten tons, why not a stone that only weighs one?"

"Wind's not like water," said Shef. "It comes from different directions."

"That doesn't stop the sailors, does it? No, what I was thinking was this . . ." As they rode on, Udd began to outline his idea of a sail-powered wind-mill, mounted on a rotating frame that could be turned to face the wind by a post like a ship's rudder. As he made objections, received answers, added his own notions, Shef found himself slowly drawn more and more into the deep incommunicable excitement of the inventor. Riding behind them, Cwicca nudged Karli.

"He's got him talking then. About time too. I was getting worried riding through this place with two leaders, both of them in some other world. I wish we could do the same for the other." He indicated the giant figure of Brand, slouching along at the head of the column with one arm over his over-burdened horse's saddle.

"He may be more of a problem," cut in Hund from behind them. "I wish we could just get him to his ship."

The challenge came not at any of the farmsteads they passed through that day, nor the next, though they rode through all of them greeted only by lowering faces and men standing silently by their barns and byres. Forewarned, Shef looked round keenly at every place they came to for signs of the others there, besides the men. Twice he caught sight of thin faces peeping from behind shutters: women hoping for a miracle, or maybe only for a friendly word in their own tongue. In his sleep he thought to hear the grinding noise of the querns, on and on for twenty years, thirty years, marking out a life of hopeless toil.

But at least the farmsteads spread only over a few yards, had in them never more than ten or a dozen men and boys, of all ages, not likely to test their strength against a well-armed body of their own number, even if the strangers came of slave-race and were headed by a doubtful champion. Where the road over the mountain passes finally dipped down into a dale, and the dale ran down to meet two more, the little cavalcade saw before them a cluster of houses spreading out where the streams intersected, and rising above them all a taller building, more than one story, its gables and side-posts fantastically carved into dragon shapes.

Brand reined in, turned to face the others. "That's Flaa," he said. "It's the main town of the Hallingdal district. They have a temple there. Just try to ride on through as if it was another farm-garth."

As they rode through the small square at the center of the settlement, the bulk of the timber church to their left, men emerged from between the houses, blocking the path forward and on all sides. They were fully armed, spears and shields ready, bows in the hands of the youths and boys behind the warriors. Shef heard the click of the crossbows being cocked yet again. They might kill or cripple their own number, he was sure. After that they stood little chance against the thirty or forty men that would be left. Pick one direction and break out?

A man was coming forward to greet them, no weapon drawn, right hand up for parley. He and Brand stared at each other.

"Well, Vigdjarf," said Brand. "We haven't met since Hamburg. Or was it the raid on the Orkneys?"

"The Orkneys it was," said the other man. He was shorter than Brand by some way, but heavily-built, thick-necked and balding. Squat arms bulged with muscle over gold bracelets: a bad sign in both ways. This man had made heavy profits out of something, and here in the poor mountain lands it would not be from rearing cattle.

Vigdjarf looked pointedly at the hammer pendant on Brand's chest, then past him at the clump of horses, men and women behind him. "You are in strange company," he remarked. "Or maybe not so strange. Once people start wearing things round their necks I always think it's the next thing to turning Christian. And then what? They start talking to the other slaves, start helping them to run off. Start being one yourself. Are you that bad yet, Viga-Brand? Or is there a bit of your old self yet?"

Brand slid off the pony he had been riding, walked forward, axe in hand. "You can cut the talk, Vigdjarf," he said. "When we last met I never heard a peep out of you. Now you think you're something. Well, what's it to be? Are you and your cousins just going to try to jump us? Because if you do we'll kill a lot of you, that's for sure."

Behind him Osmod raised a crossbow, sighted on the thick oak of the temple door, squeezed the trigger with its carefully-ground sear. A flash too fast for sight, a thump echoing round the silent square. Osmod reloaded without haste, four easy movements, a click, another square iron bolt dropped home.

"Try digging that out," Brand went on. "Or have you got some other deal? Just you and me, maybe, man to man."

"Just you and me," Vigdjarf confirmed.

"And if I win?"

"Free passage through, for all of you."

"And if you win, Vigdjarf?"

"We take the lot. Horses, slaves, men, women. We can find a place for the women. Not the men. Thralls who've been allowed to run around thinking they're people get funny ideas. They'll go to the sacred tree, to hang for Othin's ravens. Maybe we'll keep some of them, if we think they're safe. But you know how we deal with runaways up here. If we don't kill them we geld and brand them. Only safe thing to do.

"But you've got another way out, Brand. You personal, I mean. Just walk away from them. They're not your folk. Join us, hand them over, no trouble for you or me, we'll even cut you in on the profits."

"No deal," said Brand. He flipped his axe up, to grip it in both hands. "Here and now?"

Vigdjarf shook his head. "Too many people want to watch. I told them you'd say that. Now they're coming down from all the garths in three dales. We've marked out a duelling-ground down by the river. Tomorrow morning. Me against you."

As Shef stood listening to the talk, the talk that might condemn him to the gelding-iron, the brand, and the iron collar, he felt the familiar pinch at the back of his neck which meant his vision was being directed. This time he did not struggle against the sight he was being shown. As had happened when he sat on the howe by Hedeby, his eye remained open, he still saw the small muddy square, the wooden temple, the armed men tensely waiting. But at the same time another picture swam across his vision, filling his brain, as if the eyeball they had taken from him were somewhere else, reporting on what it saw as well as the one still in his head.

He saw a great mill, like the one Udd had first shown him at the college in Kaupang, two horizontal stones, the one turning over the other, fed by a hopper from above. But no cog-wheels, no water running. Instead the mill-room was dry, like the middle of summer in a hot year, and the dust rose chokingly from the ground with never a drop of water to lay it.

Through the dust a man moved, a single figure thrusting slowly and steadily at a bar. The bar, thick as the steering-oar of a warship, was set into the upper millstone, and as the man pushed so the millstone moved round and round. And the man moved round and round, in the same weary circle, never resting, never coming to an end, never seeing anything but the same dusty room.

Yet in fact he could see nothing, Shef realized, for the man was blind, his eye-sockets empty. The man slacked his pace for a moment, trying to get better grip for his footing. Instantly a lash from somewhere, a red stripe springing up across the naked, filthy back. Though he was blind the man looked back, as if bothered by some fly he could not quite get to grips with. His hands were fettered to the bar he pushed with great gyves of iron. As he put his weight on the bar again, Shef saw the monstrous muscles stand out on arms and back and sides. There seemed to be nothing between them and the skin. The man was as strong as Brand, as tight-drawn muscularly as Shef himself. Long black hair curled down over his shoulders.

That is a way of milling Udd has not thought of, Shef reflected as the vision began to blur, he came to himself again. Use a man instead of an ox, or a horse, or a dozen grinding-slaves with hand-querns. But I do not think my protector in Asgarth has sent me this to tell me about milling, any more than he sent me the Völund-vision to warn me of open chests. Then he meant to tell me the boy had to die. And the slam of the chest closing was the crash of the catapult-stone, the mule-stone. Now the mill-stone . . . It means something more immediate than cog-wheels or gearing.

"Tomorrow morning," said Brand, repeating Vigdjarf's words. "Me against you."

Shef pushed his horse forward till it drew level with Brand's side. "Tomorrow morning," he said, looking down from horseback at the burly Vigdjarf. "But not you against him. Our champion against yours."

As the warrior eyed the crossbows and opened his mouth to protest, Shef cut in quickly. "Your champion may have choice of weapons." Vigdjarf looked thoughtful, suspicious, eyed the group behind Brand, then nodded agreement.

From somewhere, not too far away—or was it in his own head?—Shef could hear the dreary, slow creak of a millwheel turning.

CHAPTER SEVENTEEN

hef realized a man was coming towards his little group bivouacked in a fenced yard on the edge of the village's common grazing land. He seemed uncertain rather than hostile or aggressive. Indeed, as he reached the group he paused, sketched what might have been a clumsy bow—performed by someone who had heard of the custom but never seen it done. His eyes were on the white priest-clothes of Hund, now badly soiled, and the Ithun-apple that hung round his neck.

"You are a leech," he said.

Hund nodded, remained seated.

"There are many in this village who are sick, or with wounds that have not healed. My son broke his leg, we bound it up but it is crooked, he can put no weight on it. My mother has the eye-sickness. There are others—women whose childbirth tore them, men who have had the jaw-ache for years, no matter what teeth we pull . . . Leeches never come up here. Will you look at them?"

"Why should I?" said Hund. The priests of the Way did not believe in humility, had never heard of Hippocrates. "If our champion loses tomorrow you are going to hang us, or maim us and enslave us. If you brand me tomorrow, why should I heal your sick today?"

The man looked uneasily at the others in the group. "Vigdjarf did not see that you were a leech. I'm sure . . . Whatever happens . . . He did not mean you."

Hund shrugged. "He meant my companions."

Shef got to his feet, looked down at Hund, winked his one eye barely perceptibly. Hund, who had known Shef since they were boys, caught the hint, looked away, his face unreadable.

"He will come," said Shef. "When he has unpacked his leech-tools. Wait for him over there."

As the man walked away Shef said to Hund, in an urgent undertone, "Treat the ones he shows you. Then demand to see the others. Even the thralls. Ask anyone you think you can trust about the mill. The mill we can hear creaking. Whatever happens, be back here at dusk."

The disk of the sun was already poised on the jagged mountain-tops as Hund walked back to the others, looking weary. The brown stains of dried blood showed on the sleeves of his tunic. From time to time during the afternoon, the listeners had heard faint cries of pain: a leech at work in a place where even poppy and henbane were unknown.

"Much to do up here," said Hund, sitting down and accepting the bowl of food Shef passed him. "I had to break that child's leg again to set it properly. So much pain in the world. And so much of it easy to cure. Warm water and lye for the midwives' hands would save half the women who die in childbirth."

"What about the mill?" demanded Shef.

"Late on they brought a thrall-woman to me. They did not want to, told me it was useless, and so was she. They were right. It was useless. She has a growth inside her and even in Kaupang with assistants and my best potions I doubt I could save her. But I tried to ease her pain. Her pain in the body, that is. There is no cure for what is in her mind. She was an Irish woman, stolen from her home when she was fifteen, forty years ago. They sold her to some man up here. She has never heard a word of her own tongue since, had five children by different masters, all taken away from her. Now her sons are Vikings, stealing women on their own. Never ask yourself why there are so many Vikings, so many Viking armies. Every man breeds as many sons from slave-women as he can. They do to fill the ranks."

"The mill," said Shef firmly.

"She told me there is a mill, as you said. It was set up only last year by a Way-priest who came up here, one of Valgrim's friends. Last year, too, they brought up a man to turn it. How can a man turn a mill?"

"I know," said Shef, remembering the god-vision he had seen. "Go on."

"She says the man is an Englishman. He is kept locked up there all the time. Twice he has broken free and run into the hills. Both times they ran him down. The first time they beat him with rawhide outside the temple. She said she saw that. She said he is a man of great strength. They lashed him for as long as it would take to plow an acre, and he never cried out except to curse them. The second time he ran, they . . . did another thing."

"What was that?" asked Brand, listening keenly.

"When they say slaves are gelded, it usually means they cut off their stones, like a bullock or a cut stallion. To make them tame and docile. They did not do that with him. Instead they cut off the other thing that makes you a man. They left him his stones. He is still as strong as a bull, and as fierce. He has the desires of a man. But he can never act like one again."

The men listening stared at each other, each one wondering what his fate might be in the morning.

"I'll tell you one thing," said Cwicca definitely. "I don't care what promises anyone makes. If Brand loses tomorrow—and Thor send he won't—the man who beats him gets my first bolt right through him. And then we're all going to start shooting. We may not be able to get out, but I'm not going to be a thrall here. These mountain-trolls are as bad as the black monks."

A rumble of assent came from the others, men and women together.

"She said one more thing," Hund went on. "She said he's mad."

Shef nodded, reflectively. "A mad Englishman," he said. "As strong as a bull and as fierce. We will loose him tonight. I know there are sentries watching us. But they will expect us to try to sneak off with the horses. All of us will go to the latrine separately once the sun is down, but three of us will hide the other side of it till full dark. Me. You, Karli. You, Udd. Put your smith-tools inside your tunic, Udd. And a flask of grease from the meat-pot. Now, Hund, show us as much as you can about how the village is laid out . . ."

Hours later, in deep darkness lit only by the stars, the three men clustered in shadow outside a rough hut on the outskirts of the village: the place of the mill.

Shef glanced round at the lightless houses not far away, waved Udd forward. A heavy door, barred, the bar clamped down and secured with a heavy iron bolt. No lock on the bolt. There only to prevent someone getting out. No need for Udd's skill yet. The little man slipped the bolt, raised the bar, stood ready to open the door.

Shef fumbled with lamp and strike-light, catching the sparks, blowing on the tinder, finally lighting the wick that floated in the whale-oil container, and sliding down the thin-shaved, transparent horn screen that let light out but shielded the wick from wind. A risk to show a light out here, however carefully shielded by tunic and body. But if what Hund said was right, a greater risk to plunge into the beast-den blind.

The light working at last, Shef signaled to Udd, who jerked the door open. Shef slid inside like a snake, Udd and Karli just behind him. He heard the door pulled softly shut as he looked inside at the great mill. At the huddled shape lying under sacking a few feet away, by the wall. He stepped forward one pace, two, his eye drawn to the massive bar jutting out from the center of the upper wheel, the thick chain leading from it to . . .

A flash of movement and something was lashing at his ankle. Shef leapt in the air, still holding the lamp incongruously upright, came down three feet back.

The hand missed his ankle by an inch. A bone-wrenching thud. Shef found himself staring down in the uncertain light of the lamp at a pair of glaring wide-set eyes. The thud had been a chain jerked to the very last fraction of its run by a collar round a thick neck. The eyes glaring up showed not a flicker of pain, only bitter rage at having failed.

Shef's eye went to the chain. Yes, from the bar to the collar. Another chain from the collar to a shackle set deep into the wall. The hands gyved together and chained also to the collar, so that they could not move further than from waist to mouth. Why had all this been done? Slowly Shef realized it was so that the chained man could be dragged from the wall to the bar, and from the bar back to the wall again, without anyone having to go within his reach. The room stank. A latrine bucket. It was doubtful if the man used it. A pot for water. He must use that. No food, no light, only sacking to cover himself with in the cold air of the mountain spring. How had he lived through the winter? The man wore only a single ragged tunic, torn till one could see the matted hair of his chest and body.

The chained man was still waiting, still watching, without so much as a blink. Waiting for the blow. Hoping the striker of it would come within range. Slowly he shuffled back, attempting with an imbecile cunning to look afraid. Trying to tempt Shef forward, within the reach of the chain.

Something stirred within Shef's memory. Disfigured as he was, hair and beard trimmed only where they fell to the length of the circling mill-bar, the man looked familiar. And, amazingly, something like recognition was dawning in his eyes as well.

Shef sat down, carefully out of reach. "We are Englishmen here," he said. "And I have seen you before."

"And I you," said the man. His voice creaked as if he had not used it for many days. "I saw you in York. I tried to kill you, one-eye. You were near the front of the men who broke in. Standing next to one of the Viking whoresons, a giant. I struck at him and you parried the blow. I would have killed him with the back-stroke and you a moment later. But the others got between us. And now you are in the Viking lands to make sport of me, traitor."

His face twisted. "But God will be good to me, as he was to my king Ella. At the end I can die. God send me a free hand before that!"

"I am no traitor," said Shef. "Not to your king Ella. I did him a favor before he died. I can do you one too. A favor for a favor. But tell me who you are, and where I have seen you."

The crazy twist of the face again, like a weeping man determined never to shed a tear. "Once I was Cuthred, captain of Ella's hearth-band, his picked champions. I was the best warrior from Humber to the Tyne. The Ragnarssons' men pinned me between shields after I had killed half a score of them. Gyved me and sold me for my strength."

The man laughed silently, throwing his head back like a wolf. "Yet there was something they never knew, that they would have paid gold to know."

"I know," said Shef. "You put their father in the worm-pit, to die of adder-bite. I was there. I saw it and that is where I saw you. I know something else too. It was not your doing, but that of Erkenbert the deacon. Ella would have set him free."

He leaned forward, not quite close enough. "I saw you throw Ragnar's thumb-nail on the table. I stood behind the chair of Wulfgar my stepfather, whom the Vikings made a *heimnar*. The man who brought Ragnar to York."

The mad eyes were wide with surprise and disbelief now. "I believe you are the devil," Cuthred muttered. "Sent as a last temptation."

"No. I am your good angel, if you still believe in the White Christ. We are going to set you free. If you promise to do one thing for us."

"What is that?"

"Fight Vigdjarf the champion tomorrow."

The head turned back like a wolf's again, on it a look of savage glee. "Ah, Vigdjarf," Cuthred husked. "He cut me while they held me. He has never come within my reach again. Yet he thinks he is a bold man. Maybe he will stand up to me. Once. Once is all I need."

"You must let us come close to get your shackle out. Get your collar off."

Shef waved Udd forward. The little man, a bundle of tools in his hand, stepped forward like a mouse towards a cat, one pace, two. Within range. And Cuthred had him, one great paw round his face, one gripping his neck, ready for the snap.

"A poor exchange for Vigdjarf," reminded Shef.

Slowly Cuthred released Udd, looking at his own hands as if he did not believe them. Karli lowered the point of his sword. Udd, shaking, stepped forward again, peered near-sightedly at the iron, began to try to work it loose. After a few moments he turned back to Cuthred, stared at the collar.

"Best to file the collar off, lord. It might make a noise. Can't help hurting him, too."

"Keep greasing the file. Do you hear, Cuthred? He may hurt you. Don't lash out. Save it for Vigdjarf."

The Yorkshireman's face twisted, he sat immobile while Udd slowly filed and greased and filed again. The lamp burned its oil, began to gutter. Finally Udd stood back. "It's through, lord. Needs pulling back."

Shef stepped forward, with caution, Karli standing just out of reach, sword poised again. Cuthred waved him away, grinned, put his hands up, seized the two ends of the thick collar still twisted round his neck. Pulled. Fascinated, Shef saw the muscles standing out like cables on his arms and chest. The stout, cold iron bent into a bow as if it were peeled greenwood. Cuthred stepped free, dropping collar and chains with a crash. He knelt, seized Shef's hands in both his own, pressed them to his head, pressed his head to Shef's knees.

"I am your man," he said.

The lamp went out finally. In the darkness the four men cautiously eased the door open, went out into the starlit night. Like shadows they crept back through the village, snaked back to their camp-site, keeping the hobbled horses between them and the Norwegians' sentry. The fire was still burning, tended by the watchful Edith.

As he saw the woman, Cuthred made a choking noise in his throat, seemed ready once again to pounce.

"She is English too," whispered Shef. "Edith, feed him with all we have. Talk to him quietly. Talk to him in English." As the others started to stir in their blankets, he crept over to Cwicca. "And you talk to him too, Cwicca. Give him a pint of ale, if there's any left. But first, quietly, cock your crossbow. If he lunges for anyone, shoot him. Now I'm going to sleep till dawn."

* * *

Shef stirred, not at first light, but as the sun first started to show over the mountain tops that hemmed in the valley on both sides. It was cold, and dew lay thick on the single blanket. For a few moments Shef was reluctant to stir, to break the little cocoon of warmth his body had created. Then he remembered the mad eyes of Cuthred, and sprang up.

Cuthred was still asleep, his mouth open. He lay with a blanket pulled over him and his head pillowed on the breast of Edtheow, oldest and most motherly of the slave-women. She lay awake but unmoving, one arm crooked round Cuthred's head.

And then he was awake. His eyes flicked open without a transition, took in Shef staring at him, took in the men beginning to light fires, roll blankets, head for the latrine. Fell on Brand, also on his feet, also studying Cuthred.

Shef never saw Cuthred move. He saw the blanket fly one way, behind it Cuthred must have sprung to his feet in one movement from a lying position, before his eyes could focus he heard the crash and grunt of knocked-out breath as Cuthred drove into Brand with his shoulder. Then they were both on the ground, rolling over and over. Shef saw Cuthred's thumbs drive at Brand's eyes, saw Brand's great quart-sized hands grip the Englishman's wrists, try to bend them back. Then the two were locked for an instant, Cuthred on top, neither able to force the other back. Cuthred twisted his hands free, jerked the knife from Brand's belt and leapt to his feet with the same uncanny speed. Brand too was struggling up, but Cuthred had the knife swinging forward for the killer stroke under the chin.

Osmod grabbed his forearm as he struck, pulled the knife aside. Then Osmod was rolling on the ground, knocked sideways by a backhand blow from the pommel. Cwicca had both hands on the knife-wrist. Shef ran in, seized Cuthred's left arm, twisted for a bone-breaker hold. It was like seizing the fetlock of a horse, too thick to manage. As Cwicca on one side and Shef on the other grappled with an arm each, Karli stepped forward, face alive with excitement.

"I'll quieten him," he yelled. His feet shuffled, his shoulder dropped, he swung with both hands, left-right-left, hooking into Cuthred's unguarded belly, driving upwards to go under the ribs and reach the liver.

Cuthred lifted Shef bodily off the ground one-handed, smashed an elbow into the side of his head, jerked an arm free. A fist like a bludgeon came down on Karli's head, he stamped violently on Cwicca's feet, failed to dislodge the desperate grip on his knife-wrist, reached across to seize the knife left-handed.

Staggering to his feet again, Shef saw Udd sighting deliberately with a crossbow, started to shout "Stop!", realized that in one instant either Cwicca would be disemboweled or Cuthred shot dead.

Brand stepped forward, between Cuthred and the crossbow. He said nothing, made no attempt to grip the other man. Instead he held out his axe, balanced across both palms.

Cuthred stared at it, ceased to reach for the knife, reached instead for the axe-helve. Paused. Cwicca, gasping, slowly let go, retreated out of range. Half-a-dozen crossbows were leveled now. Cuthred ignored them, staring only at the axe. Slowly he reached out and took it, felt the balance, swung it backwards and forwards.

"I remember now," he muttered hoarsely in his Northumbrian English. "You want me to kill Vigdjarf. Ha!" He hurled the axe upwards, twirling it so that it span in the air, the light flashing off its brilliant edge, caught it at its balance point as it came down. "Kill Vigdjarf!" He looked round as if expecting to find his enemy in sight already, began to move towards the village like a landslide.

Brand jumped in his way, arms spread, calling out in his primitive English. "Yes, yes, kill Vigdjarf. Not now. Today. Everyone watch. Now eat. Get ready. Choose weapon."

Cuthred grinned, showing a set of gums with a few sparse front teeth remaining. "Eat," he agreed. "Tried to kill you before, big man, in York. Try again later. Now, kill Vigdjarf. Eat first." He buried the axe-head with a chunk deep in a tree-stump stool, looked round, saw Edtheow coming towards him with a hunk of bread, took it from her and began to gnaw at it. She gentled him like an anxious horse, rubbing his arm through the filthy tunic.

"Oh yes," said Brand, looking at Shef still rubbing a buzzing ear. "Oh yes. I like this one. We've got a berserk here. Very useful people. But you do have to get them pointed the right way."

Under Brand's direction the entire camp got to work on Cuthred, scurrying round him like men with a champion race-horse. First, food. As he gnawed his way through the crust Edtheow brought him, the ex-slaves heated their staple oat porridge, passed him a bowl of it, began to warm over the stew they had made the night before from unwary chickens pecking too near the camp-site, diced onions and garlic into it. Cuthred ate continuously, supervised by Brand and Hund together. They gave him only small amounts at a time, seeing him scrape each bowl down to the wood before passing him the next one. "He needs the food for strength," muttered Brand. "But his belly's shrunk. Can't handle much at a time. Give him a pint of ale to slow him down. Now, get that tunic off him. I'm going to wash and oil him."

The catapult-crew prized hot stones out of the bed of the camp-fire, dropped them into a leather water-bucket, watched the steam rise. But when Shef stepped forward, making gestures to take off the tunic, Cuthred scowled, shook his head violently. Looked at the women.

Realizing he did not wish to show the shame of his mutilation, Shef waved the women away, stripped off his own tunic. Turned deliberately so that Cuthred could see the flogging-scars on his own back, scars his stepfather had put there, pulled the tunic back on. Fritha and Cwicca stretched out a blanket on the ground, made signs that Cuthred should lie on it facedown, then cut the tunic from his body with their sax-knives.

When they saw his back the ex-slaves looked at each other again. In places the flesh had been flogged off clear through to the spine, only thin scar-skin covering the vertebrae. With lye and warm water Fritha began to sponge off a winter's accumulation of filth and dead skin. When he had finished, Brand came forward with his own spare pair of breeches, signed to Cuthred to put them on. The men stared elaborately into the far distance while Cuthred donned them. Then they sat him on a tree-stump while Fritha worked on his arms, face and chest.

Shef observed him carefully as they did so. Cuthred was, indeed, a big man, far bigger than any of the ex-slaves, bigger by a long way than Shef himself. Not the size of Brand—the breeches were rolled up twice at the ankles, and hung so loose at the waist that Brand's belt would have gone round him twice. But he was different from almost any man Shef had ever seen, any of the warriors he had known from Brand's crew or from the Great Army. Someone like Brand had no paunch or beer-belly, but he was thick-set, he ate well every day, his muscles were covered with a thick coat of padding to keep out the cold. If you seized him over the ribs you could pull out a handful of flesh.

By comparison with Cuthred, Brand was shapeless. On the mill-slave, turning a great weight with arms and legs and back and belly hour after hour, day after day, week after week, fed on little more than bread and water, the muscles stood out as if they had been drawn on paper. Like those of the blind man Shef had seen in his fleeting vision. It was the combination of strength and thinness that made Cuthred so blindingly fast, Shef realized. That and his madness.

"Start work on his hands and feet," ordered Brand. "See, he's got toenails like a bear's claws. Trim them, or we'll never get shoes on him, and he needs them for grip. Let me see his hands."

Brand turned them over and over, testing to see if they flexed. "Hands like horn," he muttered. "Good for a sailor, bad for a swordsman. Give me some oil, I'll rub it in."

Cuthred sat as they worked on him, oblivious to the cold, seemingly taking the attention as his due. Perhaps he was used to it from his former life, Shef thought. He had been captain of the companions of the King of Northumbria, a rank you could reach only by fighting your way up. Cuthred must have fought more duels than he could remember. Besides the marks of torture, old scars of point and blade were showing up beneath the shaggy mat of hair. Like a horse, he must have grown his own pelt in the heatless hut through a mountain winter. They began to trim his hair and beard with the group's one pair of precious scissors. "Don't want anything blowing in his face," Brand explained.

He passed over his spare tunic to go with the breeches, a splendid one of dyed green wool. Cuthred shrugged into it, unfastened the breeches, tucked it in and tied the rope belt round himself once more. Washed, trimmed and dressed, did he look different from the wretched creature they had rescued, Shef asked himself.

No, he looked just the same. Any sane person, meeting Cuthred on a path or road, would have jumped off it and climbed a tree, as if he had met a bear or a wolf-pack. He was as crazy and as dangerous as—as Ivar the Boneless, or his father Ragnar Hairy-Breeks. He even looked like Ragnar, Shef remembered. Something in the stance, in the careless eyes.

Brand began to show Cuthred the weapons they had available. A poor selection. Cuthred looked at Karli's treasured sword, sniffed, bent it without words over his knee. Looked up at Karli's grunt of shock and protest, waited to see if it would come again, grinned as the stocky Ditmarsher fell silent. He tossed the seax-knives aside contemptuously. Osmod's halberd interested him, and he fenced for a few seconds with it, whipping its great weight round one-handed as if it had been a willow-wand. But the balance was wrong for a one-handed weapon. He put it aside, scrutinized Brand's precious silver-inlaid axe.

"What is its name?" he asked.

"*Rimmugygr*," said Brand. "That is, 'Battle-troll.' "

"Ah," said Cuthred, turning the weapon over and over. "Trolls. They come down from the mountains in the winter, peer through the shutters at chained men alone. This is not the weapon for me. You, chieftain," he said to Shef. "You wear gold on your arms. You must own a famous sword to lend me."

Shef shook his head. After the battle at Hastings his thanes had insisted that a king must have a great weapon, had picked out for him a sword of the finest Swedish steel, with a gold hilt and its name engraved on the blade: *Atlaneat,* it had been. He had left it behind in the treasury, carried only a plain sailor's cutlass. He had left the cutlass behind on the trip to Drottningsholm, taking only the 'Gungnir'-spear. But Cwicca had brought the cutlass with him when they rescued him, he had pushed it back in his belt. He unsheathed it, handed it over. Cuthred looked at it with much the same expression he had shown for Karli's. It was a single-edged sword with a heavy back, slightly curved, made of plain iron though with a good steel blade welded on by Shef himself. Not a weapon to fence with, just a slashing sword.

"No back-swing with this," muttered Cuthred. "But force in the first blow. I'll take it."

On impulse, Shef passed him also the shield that Udd had made, case-hardened steel pegged over plain wood. Cuthred looked at the thin metal with interest, scrutinized its odd color, tried to strap it on. Strap would not meet buckle over his forearm till they had punched an extra hole in it. He stood up, bare sword in hand, shield strapped on. His face grinned like the mask of a hungry wolf.

"Now," he said. "Vigdjarf."

CHAPTER EIGHTEEN

A man stood at the perimeter of the camp, fully armed, a short staff in his hand: a marshal, come to call them to the dueling ground. Shef rose to mask Cuthred from him, jerked a head to Brand to do the talking.

"Are you ready?" called the marshal.

"Ready. Let us repeat the terms of the duel."

As the others listened, Brand and the marshal went over the terms of the agreement: only hewing weapons, champion against champion, free passage staked against return of all those alleged to be thralls, at the disposal of the winner. As they heard that condition laid down, Shef felt the tension rising among the English, men and women.

"Win or lose, we aren't having none of that," Osmod muttered. "All of you, keep your bows and bills right handy. You women, hold all the horses' bridles. If our man goes down—which he won't, of course," Osmod added, glancing hastily at Cuthred, "we're going to try to bust our way out."

Shef saw Brand's shoulders tense with disapproval as he heard Osmod's unsporting orders, but he continued talking. The marshal, unable to speak any English, paid no attention. Cuthred grinned even more widely than before. He was behaving with a strange restraint for the moment, back on his stool, making no effort to show himself. Either the familiar ritual of a duel-morning had gripped him, or else he was relishing the surprise they had planned for Vigdjarf.

The marshal turned away and Brand walked back to the group, already prepared to move, horses loaded, packs strapped. At the last moment Cuthred's eye fell on the small hatchet they used for firewood. He twitched it from its strapping, passed it to Udd. "Put an edge on that with your file," he ordered.

The party led on through the short village street, already deserted. In the small square outside the temple clustered not only the entire population of the little town, but also scores more, men, women and children from the length of the dales, eager to see the clash of champions. They had left the one street clear for Brand's party to enter by, but as they passed through men with spears and shields moved to block further exit from it. Osmod looked round with calculating eye, trying to spot the weakest place in the circle surrounding them. Saw none.

Immediately facing them, outside the temple door itself, scarlet cloaks marked Vigdjarf and his two seconds. Brand looked round, eyed Cuthred carefully, nodded to Osmod and Cwicca either side of him. "Wait," he said, holding up a finger. "Wait for the call."

Cuthred took no notice. He had taken the sharpened hatchet and was holding it in his left hand, along with the shield-strap. With his other hand he had begun to flip Shef's cutlass into the air, letting it turn over and over in its unbalanced way, seizing it by its guardless hilt every time it came down. Murmurs were beginning to run round the crowd as some of them recognized him, realized it was the mill-thrall, speculated what it might mean.

With Shef at his side, Brand began to walk out to meet the others. "Should we have tried to get some armor on him," muttered Shef. "Your mail? A helmet? A leather jacket, even? Vigdjarf has everything."

"No point with a berserk," said Brand briefly. "You'll see."

He halted seven paces from the others, raised his voice for the watching crowd as well as the challengers.

"Ready to try your luck, Vigdjarf? You could have tried me years ago, you know. But you didn't feel like it then."

"And you don't feel like it now," replied Vigdjarf, grinning. "Have you decided who's going to try me? You? Or your one-eyed friend bare-handed here?"

Brand jerked a thumb over his shoulder. "We thought we'd try the one in the green tunic behind us there. He's very keen to fight you. He *really* feels like it."

Vigdjarf's grin faded as he peered across the square to where Cuthred stood, now clear of the others, standing out in plain sight, still tossing the sword up and down. He had started now to throw the hatchet from hand to hand as well, tossing it left to right and back again while the sword was still in the air.

"You can't send him out to fight me," said Vigdjarf. "He's a thrall. He's my own thrall. You must have stolen him in the night. I can't fight my own thrall. I appeal to the marshals." He looked across to the two armed and armored men waiting either side of the square.

"You're very quick to call people thralls," said Shef. "First you say some travelers are thralls, and they have to fight you to prove they're not. Then when someone wants to fight you, you say he's a thrall too. Maybe it would be simpler if you just said everyone was a thrall. Then all you'd have to do would be make them act like thralls. Because if they don't—they aren't."

"I won't fight him," said Vigdjarf positively. "He is my own property, stolen in the night, and you are all night-thieves." He turned to the marshals, began to protest again.

Brand looked over his shoulder. "If you won't fight him, that's up to you," he remarked. "But I can tell you one thing for sure. He's going to fight you. And anybody else who gets in his way."

With a hoarse bellow, Cuthred had stepped away from his handlers, was walking forward across the square. His eyes were set and unblinking, and as he came he began to sing. From his brief career as a minstrel, Shef recognized the song. It was the old Northumbrian lay of the Battle of Nechtans-mere, where the army of the Northern English had been wiped out by the Picts. Cuthred was singing the part where the valiant retainers refused to fly or surrender, but formed the shield-wall to fight to the last man. Hastily Brand and Shef moved out of his path, saw him go by, still walking slowly but braced for a pounce at every step.

Vigdjarf, facing him, grabbed at his second's cloak, waved again to the marshals, saw them all back away, leaving him face to face with the enraged man he had gelded.

At five paces range, Cuthred charged. No feinting, no feeling-out. No defense. The attack of an enraged churl, a swineherd or a plowboy, rather than a king's champion. The first blow started with the tip of the curved cutlass touching Cuthred's spine and came down in a sweeping arc at Vigdjarf's helmet. Reflex alone would have served to block it, for any but a joint-locked grandfather. Vigdjarf, still yelling protests to the marshals, had his shield up without thought, took the blow full on the shield-boss.

Dropped almost to his knees, driven down by the sheer weight of the blow. And the second one was already in the air, and the third after it.

Making no attempt to guard, Cuthred danced round his enemy, slashing from every angle. Splinters flew from the iron-rimmed and bossed linden-shield at every blow, in instants Vigdjarf seemed to be holding only a hacked remnant. A furious clang echoed round the square as for the first time Vigdjarf managed to get his sword up for a parry.

"I don't think this is going to last very long," said Brand. "And it's going to be nasty when it finishes. Mount up, everyone. Shef, get some rope."

Cuthred's attack had not slowed at any moment, but Vigdjarf, a veteran, now seemed to have pulled himself together. He was using both sword and the fragment of battered half-moon of shield left to him to block strokes. He had also realized that Cuthred never parried, never got into a position to do so. The shield in his hand might as well have been there only for balance. Twice in quick succession he lunged out of a parry, stabbing for the face. Both times Cuthred had sprung sideways already, angling for another cut.

"He's going to get one home," muttered Brand, "and then . . ."

As if remembering his wits, Cuthred suddenly changed tactic, instead of hacking at the head and body, stooped, slashed backhand at the knee. Vigdjarf had seen that many times, far more often than the crazed attack he had just survived. He leapt over the stroke, came down crouching and swung in his turn.

With a groan of dismay the English watching saw the slash come down full across Cuthred's thigh. They waited for the spurt of arterial blood, the last agonized stroke, easily blocked, the sideways topple and the killing slash or stab. This was how it always ended. Vigdjarf's teeth showed across the square as he waited for Cuthred to crumple.

But not this time. Cuthred sprang, whirling the sword at his enemy's head and in the same clumsy movement lashing out with the hatchet in his shield-hand. There was a single meaty thud, and the hatchet was buried through helmet and skull.

Cuthred had let go of the hatchet and grasped Vigdjarf's sword-wrist with his shield-hand. As Vigdjarf clubbed desperately and unavailingly at him with his broken shield, he stepped in, drove the cutlass home under the mail, started sawing deliberately back and forward. Vigdjarf began to scream, dropped his sword, began to try to claw the cutlass away. Cuthred was talking to him, holding him up now, shouting words into the dying face.

Horror-stricken, not at death but at loss of dignity, the marshals and Vigdjarf's second rushed forward. In the circle Shef realized that prudent men were starting to hustle their wives and children away, back through the narrow streets or into doorways. Still bare-handed, he stepped forward, shouting to the marshals to stand back.

Cuthred dropped his still-bleeding enemy on the ground and without warning charged again. One of the marshals, still holding his staff out and trying to shout some warning, dropped, cut from neck to breastbone. As the sword jammed on bone, Cuthred swung his shield for the first time at the other, knocked him staggering backwards, seized the sword from the dying marshal's hand, and slashed the second's leg off at the knee. Then he was in motion again, charging without pause or hesitation at the crowd of Vigdjarf's supporters grouped outside the temple.

A spear flew to meet him, a heavy iron-shod battle-spear thrown with full force at ten feet range. Straight for the center of the body. Cuthred dropped the case-hardened shield across his heart. The spear met it full on, did not sink in, dragging down his shield-arm, bounced back as Gungnir had when Shef had first tried the metal.

A yell of surprise and alarm and suddenly all that could be seen were turned backs, Cuthred slashing at them, men falling or fleeing, the shout going up: "Berserker! Berserker!"

"Well, now," said Brand, looking round at the suddenly-deserted square, "I think if we just ride away very very quietly . . . Perhaps pick up some of these useful bits and pieces scattered around, like that sword there— you don't need it any more, do you, Vigdjarf? You were always a bit too hard on the thrall-women for a proper *drengr*, that was my opinion. And now it's been the death of you."

"Aren't we going to bring poor Cuthred along?" said Edtheow indignantly. "I mean, he's saved us all."

Brand shook a disgusted head. "I think we would all be better just having nothing to do with him."

Cuthred was lying motionless in the mud fifty yards down the street on their way out of the town, two heads lying by him, their long hair twisted in his grip. Shef was suddenly pushed aside by Hund who stared in fascination at the left thigh where Vigdjarf's full-blooded slash had gone home.

A deep, deep cut, six inches long, white bone glinting at the bottom of it. But like a cut in dead meat, only the barest trace of blood.

"How has that happened?" asked Hund. "How could a man not bleed from that? Keep walking with the muscles severed?"

"I don't know," said Brand, "but I've seen it before. That's what makes a berserk. People say that no steel bites on them. It bites all right. But they don't feel it. Not till later. What are you doing?"

Hund had produced needle and gut thread, was beginning to stitch the edges of the great gash together, stitching large at first, then turning and going back over with small precise movements like a tailor. Blood began to seep and then to well from the wound as he did so. He finished, wrapped lengths of bandage round and round, rolled his patient over, turned back his eyelids. Shook his head wonderingly.

"Put him over a horse," he ordered. "He ought to be dead. But I think he's just fast asleep."

He had to use his knife to saw through the hair of the severed heads to get them out of Cuthred's clench.

"Yes," said Brand judiciously. "There're lots of theories about berserks. I don't take much notice of most of them, myself."

They were riding along the crest of a ridge, as they had been for some days now, first winding up, then seemingly more or less on a level, now perhaps with the down-stretches lasting longer than the ups. To their right lay a long sweep of valleys with water glinting in them and here and there the bright green of fresh grass. To their left the land fell more sharply, into a waste of fir and pine, and they could see little ahead but the ridge rising and falling, with chain after chain of blue mountains lifting into the far distance. The air was cold and keen, but filled the lungs with life and the sharp smell of the pine-woods.

Behind Brand and Shef, and the interested Hund riding close beside them, a string of ponies stretched out for a hundred yards, with people walking here and there among the riders. More people than there had been when they left Flaa the week before. As the English had made their way through a now-deserted countryside, a countryside that emptied before them, figures had crept out to join them, emerging from the woods by the road, stalking softly into the firelight when they camped: runaway slaves with the collars still round their necks, most of them English-speaking. Drawn by the rumor of the free folk moving through the land, headed by a giant and a one-eyed king, and guarded by a mad berserk of their own race. Most of the ones who had come in were men, and not all of them thralls or churls by birth. It took determination and courage to break free from one's masters in an alien country: and when they could get them, the Vikings were very ready to enslave former thanes or warriors, valuing them for their strength. After brief debate, Shef had agreed to accept all those who could find their way to them, though he would not search farms or pursue their owners to liberate the countryside. Men who could break free, and women too, might be an increase in force. There was no hope any more of passing unnoticed.

"Some people say the word really means 'bare-sarks,' " Brand went on. " 'Bare-shirts,' that is, because they'll fight in their shirts alone, with no armor. I mean, you saw our mad friend back there—" he jerked a thumb at Cuthred, who now, amazingly, was well enough recovered to sit on a pony. He was riding near the back of the cortege, well-surrounded and escorted by those he seemed able to tolerate. "No defense at all, and no interest in it. If we'd put armor on him it's my belief he'd have torn it off. So 'bare-shirt' makes a kind of sense.

"But there's others say it's really 'bear-sarks,' like 'bear-shirts.' Because they act like bears, that just come at you and can't be frightened off. What they mean is that they're really, you know—" Brand looked round cautiously and dropped his voice, "like Ivar, *not men of one skin*. They change into another shape, sort of, when the fit takes them."

"You mean they're werewolves," suggested Shef.

"Were-bears, yes," Brand agreed. "But that doesn't make sense, really. The were-shape runs in families, for one thing. But a berserk can be anybody."

"Can this condition be created by drugs?" asked Hund. "It seems to me that there are several things that can take a man out of himself, can make him think he is a bear, for one thing. In small quantities, the juice of the nightshade berry, though that is also a deadly poison. Some say you can make an ointment of it mixed with hog-lard, and smear it on. It makes people think they are flying out of their bodies. And there are other growths with similar effect."

"Maybe," Brand said. "But you know that wasn't the case with our madman. He'd had nothing but what we ate, and he was as mad as ever before we even fed him.

"No, I don't think it's really very hard to understand at all. Some men like fighting. I do myself—not as much as I used to, maybe. But when you like it, and you're used to it, and you're good at it, the noise and the excitement lifts you, you can feel it swelling inside you, and at its peak you feel you are twice as strong and twice as quick as you usually are, and you do things before you know you've done them. Being a berserk is like that, only much, much more. And I think you can only get to that if you have some special reason inside you. Because most men, even when they're caught up with the excitement, remember somewhere deep down what it feels like when you get hit, and how you don't want to go home with just a stump, or what your friends look like when you shovel them into a hole. So they keep using their shields and their armor. But a berserk's forgotten all that. To be a berserk, deep down, you have to not want to live. You have to hate yourself. I've known some men like that, born like that or made like that. We all know why Cuthred there hates himself and doesn't want to live. He can't bear the shame of what they did to him. He's only happy when he's wiping it out on someone else."

"So you think the other berserks you knew had something wrong with them too," said Shef thoughtfully. "But maybe not in their bodies."

"That was the case with Ivar Ragnarsson," Hund confirmed. "They called him the Boneless, from his impotence, and he hated women. But he was normal in body, I saw that for myself. He hated women for what he could not do, and he hated men for what they could do that he could not. Maybe the same is true with our Cuthred, only with him he was made like that, he did not make himself. I am amazed at the way he healed. That cut was all the way through the thigh and into the bone. But it did not bleed till I began to dress it, and it has healed like a surface scratch. I should have tried tasting his blood, to see if there was something strange in it," he added thoughtfully.

Brand and Shef looked at one another for a moment in alarm. Then their attention was distracted. The ridge-path made a sharp turn to the left, by a cairn of stones, and as they followed it round the land seemed to part before them.

There, down far below, was a deep valley with at the end of it a new and silver gleam. Too big for the mountain streams they could see everywhere, a gleam that led widening out to the horizon. On it, for those with the far-sight of seamen, little flecks of color.

"The sea," muttered Brand, reaching out and gripping Shef's shoulder. "The sea. And look, there are ships riding at anchor. That is the Gula-fjord, and where the ships are is the harbor for the great Gula-Thing. If we can reach there—maybe my *Walrus* will be there. If King Halvdan did not take her. I think—it's too far away—but I could almost think that one moored far out was her."

"You can't tell one ship from another ten miles away," said Hund.

"A skipper can tell his ship ten miles away in a fog," retorted Brand. He kicked heels into his weary pony's barrel sides and began to plunge forward down the slope. Shef followed more slowly, waving to the rest to close up.

They caught up with Brand as his overburdened pony flagged, and managed to persuade him to halt as night came on, still several miles from the site of the Gula-Thing and its harbor. When they finally rode or walked next morning into the half-mile wide cluster of tents, turf booths, and temporary shelters, all of them leaking smoke into the Atlantic breeze, a small knot of men stood to greet them: not warriors in their prime wearing armor, Shef was concerned to note, but older men, even greybeards. Spokesmen for the community, the counties served by the Thing, and the kinglets or jarls who guaranteed its peace.

"We hear that you are robbers and night-thieves," said one of them without preamble. "If you are such you may be hunted down and killed without penalty by all the free men who come to this Thing, and you have no share in its peace."

"We have stolen nothing," said Shef. It was not true—he knew his men stole chickens from every farmyard and butchered sheep for their stewpot without compunction—but he did not think that these petty thefts were the problem. As Osmod said, they would have paid for food if anyone had offered to sell it to them.

"You have stolen men."

"The men were stolen in the first place. They came to us of their own free will—we did not seek them out. If they have freed themselves, who can blame them?"

The Gula-men looked uncertain. Brand followed up in a more conciliating tone. "We will steal nothing within the circuit of the Thing, and will observe its peace in every respect. See, we have silver. Plenty of it, and gold as well." He slapped a clinking saddle-bag, pointed to the precious metal shining on Shef's accouterments and his own.

"You will promise to steal no thralls?"

"We will steal no thralls and harbor no thralls," said Brand firmly, waving Shef to silence. "But if any man following us or here already wishes to claim that any of our company is or ever was his thrall, then we will make counter-suit against him for enslaving a free man without right or justice, and claim against him for every injury, blow, insult or mutilation suffered in the course of that slavery. As also for each year spent in slavery, and for loss of rightful earnings during that time. Furthermore . . ."

Knowing the intense glee with which the Vikings pursued legalities of even the most trivial kind, Shef cut him off. "Adjudication to be settled by stated champions on the dueling ground," he added.

The Norwegian spokesmen looked at each other with some uncertainty.

"Furthermore we'll be out of here as soon as ever we can," offered Brand.

"All right. But don't forget. If any of you gets out of hand—" the old man looked over Shef's shoulder at the lowering figure of Cuthred, slouched on his pony with Martha and Edtheow gently patting an arm each "—then you will all be responsible. There are five hundred men here. We can take you all if we have to."

"All right," said Shef in his turn. "Show us where to camp, show us the water place and let us buy food. And I need to hire a forge for the day."

The spokesmen parted, let the little cavalcade pass through.

King Alfred's good silver pennies met with immediate approval inside the Thing-ground, and within hours Shef, stripped again to the waist and wearing a charred leather apron, was beating out metal at a hired forge with borrowed tools. Brand had headed straight off to the harbor a mile away, the rest had been told to establish a perimeter with stakes and rope and not stray outside it; Cuthred had been settled down with a carefully-organized team of minders. His likes and dislikes were well-known to everyone by now. He responded well to Udd, for some reason, probably because of the little man's total lack of any threat, and would listen for hours to Udd's boring monologues on the subject of metalworking. He liked the motherly comfort of the older and plainer women. Any sign of sexual display or intimacy from one of the younger women, even an accidental turn of hip or glimpse of calf, was likely to set his face in murderous lines. He tolerated the weakest of the thralls and freedmen, obeyed Shef, sneered at Brand, bristled at any sign of strength or competition from other men. If Karli, young, strong and popular with the women, so much as came into sight, Cuthred's eyes would follow him. Shef, noticing it, had told Karli to keep well away from him at all times. He had also told Cwicca and Osmod to set up a rota: two men with crossbows to watch Cuthred at all times, without being seen to do so. A tame berserk was valuable, especially for crossing hostile country. Unfortunately there were no tame berserks.

As some form of protection for their straggle of runaways, Shef had begun by beating out a dozen Wayman pendants. Only of iron, for the silver Waymen preferred had other uses at the moment. But at least they would be distinctive. To make them more so, Shef had made all of them his own emblem, the pole-ladder of Rig. None of the people they had rescued knew what it meant, but they would wear it as a talisman.

His next task was to see every man had at least some form of weapon: not for use, or at least he hoped not, but as a mark of status in a world where every free man carried at the very least spear and knife. Shef had bought a bundle of ten-inch spikes used to fix timber where doweling pegs would not do, and was beating each into a spearhead, to be sunk into ash-shafts and lashed tight with wetted rawhide. They would outfit their newest recruits. The catapulteers still had their halberds, knives and cross-bows. Shef had taken back his cutlass from Cuthred, and straightened once more Karli's cheap and ineffective sword. The fight at Flaa had yielded a handful of other weapons, including Vigdjarf's sword, picked up and handed over to Cuthred.

The last of the spearheads done, Shef turned to his final job: converting the case-hardened shield into an offensive weapon for Cuthred. Although he seemed to have forgotten all his training in scientific fencing with shield and broadsword he kept the shield by him at all times. He was parted from it only with great difficulty and stood close and watched as Shef, remembering Muirtach and Ivar's Gaddgedill followers, decided to remove the double leather grips for hand and forearm and put a straight handhold across the shield's center on the inside. Cuthred grunted what might have been approval, then, with great reluctance, let Shef take the shield to the smithy where he fixed one of the ten-inch spikes to its middle on the outside. There was no way of driving a hole through the metal without ruining a dozen punches, so he would weld it on to the case-hardened surface. A tricky job, involving desperate efforts by relays of bellows-men to keep the metal glowing as near white-hot as they could manage.

Straightening, finally, Shef picked the shield up, rotated it from side to side in his left hand, and reflected that what was hard even for his smithy-trained muscle would be light work for Cuthred. He turned and walked out of the borrowed booth. Found himself face to face with a newcomer. He rubbed the smoke from his eyes, blinking in the sunlight, and recognized a grinning Thorvin, Brand just behind him.

"I see you are yourself again," said Thorvin, gripping his hand. "I told Brand that if you were well we need only head for the sound of the hammer."

CHAPTER NINETEEN

When King Halvdan knew that his son was dead," Thorvin explained an hour later, seated comfortably on a camp-stool with a mug of bought ale in his hand, "he went into a giant-rage. He told his mother that she had lived too long, put a rope round her neck, and told her to stab and hang herself at the same time as a sacrifice to Othin, so that little Harald might join the warriors in Valhalla. She did it willingly, or so I heard.

"Then he found that Brand was missing, and Shef's men as well, and decided to take it out on Brand's ship and crew. But they barricaded themselves in a hall in the college of the Way, and called on some of the rest of us to protect them. Valgrim sided with Halvdan, and many of his followers too, and for a while it seemed there might be civil war even within the college of the Way.

"But Halvdan did another thing. It could not be hidden from him that Shef had been on the island of Drottningsholm, and one of Stein's guardsmen confessed that he had been invited there. So Halvdan had Ragnhild to blame as well, and swore that she should follow his mother into the mound for her disloyalty and carelessness over his son."

"Well." Thorvin took another pull at his ale. "He was dead the next day. Dead in his bed. Died a straw-death, like a worn-out thrall."

"What symptoms did he show?" asked Hund, sitting close by on the ground.

"Ingulf said, henbane poisoning." Karli, also allowed to listen to the informal council, rolled his eyes, opened his mouth to say something, shut it again as he caught Thorvin's eye.

"So then there were men gathering everywhere, and oaths of vengeance on all sides. It was said that King Halvdan's conquests would seize the chance to break free of the Westfold rule, Queen Ragnhild was supposed to be going back to her people to raise an army to send after the killers of her son, the skippers of the coast guardships all came into port to protect their own interests, Brand's crew got back to the *Walrus* and asked me to take to flight along with them."

"But you didn't?" Shef guessed.

Thorvin shook his head. "There was Way business to settle first. Besides, everything quieted down suddenly. King Olaf then showed what was in his hand. Did you ever wonder," Thorvin inquired, "why they call King Olaf *Geirstatha-alfr*, Elf-of-Geirstath?"

The listeners shook their heads mutely. After a moment Cwicca volunteered, *"Alfr* is what we call *alf*. Like in Alfred or Alfwyn. One of the Hidden Folk, but not ugly or vicious like a fen-thurs or a mountain-troll. Elf-women mate with men sometimes, and the other way round, or so they say. They are wise, but they have no souls."

"What happens to them when they die, then?" asked Thorvin. He looked round, observing the uncertain shrugs and headshakes of his listeners. "None of us knows, though some say they go to a world of their own, one of the nine worlds of which this is the midmost. But others say that they die. Die and then return again. And some say that the same may happen with men born of women. Now that is what King Olaf believed of himself. He said that he had been on this earth before, and that he would yet return in the person of one of his blood. Or if not—for now he has none of his blood or his brother's living—then his life would pass into some other keeping.

"He said, Shef, that he had set a test for you with Valgrim, and that you had passed it. He said that you had taken the luck of his lineage with you, and that from now on his luck and his spirit would flow through yours. And he told me to tell you that you had passed his test and Valgrim's, and he would now hold both Eastfold and Westfold for you. As your underking."

Thorvin rose, walked over to where Shef sat, and carefully closed Shef's hands round his own. "King Olaf told me that I was to place my hands in yours on his behalf. He accepts you as the true king, the One who is to come from the North, and asks you to return to take your proper place in his kingdom and in the college of the Way."

Shef stared round at a ring of equally surprised faces. The very idea of an under-king did not come easily to the Norse or the English alike. A king was someone who acknowledged no superior, by definition. How could an under-king, who accepted an over-king, be a king, rather than a mere jarl or *hersir?*

"How did his men take this?" asked Shef tentatively. "Olaf has been supported by his brother for many years, has he not? Since they say he lost his luck to him. If the districts were thinking of revolt, Olaf would be able to do little against them. Especially if he declared himself under-king to a stranger."

Thorvin smiled. "No-one had any time to say anything. After all these years Olaf moved like—like a Ragnarsson. He burned Ragnhild's brother in his hall, before he could get his boots on. He had all the prominent men of the Eastfold who had spoken of revolt and independence brought to him in their shirts with ropes round their necks, and made them beg for their lives. He called a full meeting of all the priests of the Way, in conclave with the fire burning, and made Valgrim say in conclave how he had tested you, and made him admit that you had passed. There was no standing up to him. And now he is out, going from Thing to Thing in his own territory, making the men of each district accept his authority—and yours."

"And what about Ragnhild?" asked Shef. "How has Olaf dealt with her?"

Thorvin sighed. "She got away. Went back to her father's territory somewhere. I believe Valgrim went with her. His followers were convinced by Olaf, mostly, but his spite against you was too strong. He felt you had bested him."

"Still. The way is clear for us to go back. Back to Kaupang, and then back to England. How soon would you be ready to start, Brand?"

Brand scratched his head. "We have the two ships here, *Walrus* and Guthmund's *Seamew.* But you have picked up a lot of people coming across the country, the ships will need to be provisioned for so many passengers. Two days after next dawn."

"So be it," said Shef. "We return south two days after next dawn."

"When we first met," said Thorvin, "you said you came from the north. Now you are very quick to want to return to the south. Are you sure that you have come as far as you need to along the *northr vegr,* the North Way?"

"You mean there's places north of *here,*" muttered an unidentifiable English voice from the circle of listeners. "I thought only trolls lived north of *here.*"

Many hundreds of miles to the south, in the great palace of the Archbishop of Cologne, the plotters who had removed Pope Nicholas met again. Not all of those present at the first meeting had returned: Hincmar of Rheims was missing, delayed by his own affairs. But his absence was more than compensated by a throng of lesser prelates, bishops and abbots from the length of the German-speaking lands, all now ready and eager to be associated with the founders and rulers of the famous *Lanzenorden*. Archbishop Gunther looked round at them with both satisfaction and contempt. It was good to find so many supporters, a good sign too of the weakening of the power of the new Pope that so many were ready to attend a gathering that old Pope Nicholas, at least, would have denounced as treasonable. Yet as numbers increased, so strength of purpose was diluted. These men here were followers of success. Success would have to be provided for them. Fortunate that there was so much.

Gunther's chaplain and assistant Arno was coming to the end of the report he had been invited to deliver. "So," he concluded, "recruitment to the *Lanzenorden* continually increases. Teams of priests and guardians have entered all the northern lands. Many captives have been rescued or ransomed and sent home, among them many of our brothers in Christ enslaved over many years by the heathen. And while we move freely into the heathen lands, their assaults on us and on our Frankish brothers have ceased, or slackened."

Because they are afraid to come down the Channel, Gunther thought grimly. They fear the English apostates, not us. He let none of his doubts show on his face as he led the applause. As it died down another voice cut across Arno's smiling satisfaction. The voice of Rimbert, the ascetic, Archbishop of Hamburg-Bremen and the major force in the spread of the new Order.

"Yet for all this," he said. "For all the recruits and the money and the slaves rescued, we are no nearer the Order's true purpose. We have not found the Lance, the holy relic of Charlemagne. And without that all our success is as a tinkling cymbal. As vain as the ribbons on a strumpet's sleeve."

Gunther shut his eyes for a moment as the grim voice rasped on, opened them to note the alarm spreading across many faces. For if the saintly Rimbert did not believe in his own creation, who else should?

"Yes," replied Arno, shuffling his papers. "That is true. Yet I have reports here from the most daring of our teams sent into the heathen lands, a report sent by the English deacon Erkenbert, strong in the strength of the Lord, at the instructions of his commander Bruno son of Reginbald."

The very mention of Bruno's name, Gunther noted, created a wave of relief. Even Rimbert nodded acceptingly, not continuing with his denunciation.

"The learned Erkenbert reports that he and Bruno and their men penetrate ever deeper into heathendom, fearing no persecution. They test every king and kingdom for signs of the Lance at work, and have found nothing yet. Nevertheless, the learned Erkenbert says we must remember that it is a gain in knowledge every time one learns nothing."

Arno looked up, saw that this thought had proved too hard for all his audience, and tried again. He was speaking to an audience at least theoretically literate, and could afford an appeal to writing. "He means that if one has a list of names—like the list of witnesses to a charter, each one written below the other." Puzzled nods from most of the bishops and abbots, following so far. "Then every time one crosses such a name *off,* there are fewer names left to consider. If one crosses every name off but one, then that one must be the one you seek. So, you see, even a negative result— even finding a nothing—tells you something."

Silence greeted this exposition. Faces looked by no means convinced. Archbishop Rimbert finally broke it.

"The efforts of our brothers in heathendom are beyond praise," he said. "We must support them with every man and every mark we can raise." He looked round challengingly. "I say, every man and every mark! Yet for all that, I do not think the Lance of Longinus, the Lance of Charlemagne, the Lance of the Emperor-to-be: I do not think this will be brought to light by the hand of man alone."

While Brand and Guthmund sought out provisions for their sail south, Shef spent much of his time wandering round the great meeting, half way between a shire-court and a summer fair, watching how the Norse-folk did their business. Those of his band who could be allowed to wander freely did the same, but there were few of them—Cuthred remained under guard at all times, and the runaway slaves never left the perimeter that Shef had marked out except to visit communal latrines, in groups with Brand or Guthmund supervising.

The Thing was a strange custom, Shef concluded. Rightly speaking, it had not happened yet. Round about Midsummer's Day was the traditional time for the Gula-Thing, still some weeks off. At that time many law-cases would be decided by the thirty-six chosen wise men of the Thing-lands, the three *fylkir* of Sogn, Hord and the Fjords. These were the areas that provided so many of the horde of summer pirates that sailed south every year. It was therefore no easy business to summon a man for murder, for land-disputes or for a paternity case at midsummer, when they might be, or pretend to be, away. So a kind of reduced court met much of the time, trying usually to get some agreement without the matter going to the final decision of the wise. At the same time trade and business of many kinds never ceased, with ships continually coming and going.

Shef was amazed at the wealth on display. England was a rich country in land and in food, he had realized during the short period that he had ruled some of it. But the Viking lands had had coined silver and even gold flowing in to them for two generations or more. The well-off among them would pay high prices for luxuries, making it worth while for strongly-manned ships to come up from the south, past the pirates of Rogaland. And the flow of materials from the north included luxuries that Shef had never seen. He was, now, rich himself from the taxes of East Anglia, some portion of them held by Brand in the *Walrus* for his use. At Brand's urging Shef bought for himself a hooded coat of the best waterproof sealskin, the hood fringed with wolf hair on which a man's breath would never freeze, even in the coldest weather. A two-edged sword of the finest Swedish steel, its hilt cut from the twisted horn of some fabulous beast of the northern seas that Brand called a narwhal. A bag for sleeping in, sealskin again on the outside, wool on the inside, with between them a thick layer of down from the northern birds. Shef, reluctant to spend money which he never felt was his, had nevertheless spent enough nights shivering in thin clothes and blanket to be ready never to feel cold again. He had marveled at the patience with which these goods were assembled, wondering how long it would take to trap and pluck the rare eider-birds that gave the best and warmest down in the world. But Brand had laughed when he mentioned this.

"We don't catch them," he said. "We make the Finns do that."

"Finns?" Shef had never heard the word before.

"Up north," Brand pointed, "where Sweden and Norway run close together, beyond Halogaland where I live, the world turns into a place where no man can grow anything fit to eat, not rye, not barley, not even oats. Pigs die of cold, and cows have to be stall-fed all winter. There the Finns live, without houses, in skin tents, wandering from place to place with their herds of reindeer. We put tribute on them, the *Finn-skatt*, the Finn-tax. Every man of them has to pay so much a year, in skins, in furs, in down. They spend their time hunting and fishing, so it goes easily for them. What they catch beyond their tax, we buy off them and sell all together to the traders here or further south. The kings of the world dress in furs caught by my Finns, and they pay kings' prices too! But I buy the stuff in the first place for butter and cheese. No Finn can milk a cow, and no Finn can walk past a bowl of milk. It is a good trade."

Good for you, thought Shef. It must be a difficult tax to collect.

Trading done, he had walked over to the area where legal cases were settled. Most of the time, just men standing in groups, fully armed, leaning on their spears, but listening for the most part to what their friends or their adversaries had to say, and to the advice of the wise men of their district. The Gula-Thing had strict laws, but few men knew what they were, since they had never been written down. It was the task of the wise to learn as much law as they could, or all of it if they wished ever to be law-speakers, and to announce it to disputants. They might then wriggle or quibble, try to find other laws more suitable for their case, or simply intimidate their opponents into accepting a cheap settlement, but they would not simply deny the law existed.

Yet there were some matters, often involving seduction, rape, adultery or woman-theft, where the law might be clear but where passions ran high. Several times during the two days Shef heard voices suddenly raised and the clang of weapons. Twice Hund was called away to patch and bandage, and once men rode away with set faces and a corpse of their own slung over a horse.

"Someone will get burnt out over that one," Brand remarked. "Hard men round here, they can get away with things for a fair while. Then the neighbors get together, come down and torch the place. Kill everyone who tries to get out. Works even on berserks, eventually. As the poem says:

Every wise man shall count himself warlike
  With moderation.
Or find, when he comes among the fierce ones,
  No man has no match."

On the second afternoon, as Shef lounged in the sunshine watching Guthmund bargain furiously for two barrels of salt pork—his bargaining tactics were much admired, even by the victims, who swore that they could never believe a famous abbey-robber could express such passion over a mere clipped penny. Then Shef noticed men's attention start to waver, heads turn, and then a general drift begin up to the stones of the doom-ring. Guthmund broke off, releasing the pork-merchant's collar, slapped his money down, and began to follow the drift, Shef hastening after him.

"What's up?" he asked.

Guthmund had picked the story out of the crowd. "Two men agreed to settle their business Rogaland-style."

"Rogaland-style? What's that?"

"The Rogalanders are poor, couldn't afford proper swords till recently, just carried cutlasses like the one you had, or timber-axes. But they really mean business just the same. So if they decide to fight a duel, they don't square off inside an enclosure marked with hazel twigs, or fight a formal holmgang like you did once. No, they stretch out a bull's hide, and both men stand on it. Not allowed off. Then they fight with knives."

"That doesn't sound too dangerous," Shef ventured.

"First they tie their left wrists together."

The place for duels of this kind was in a hollow, so men could line the sides and watch. Shef and Guthmund found places high up. They saw the bull's hide carefully laid out, the contestants brought forward. A priest of the Way spoke words which they could not hear, and the two men slowly stripped off their shirts and stepped out in their breeches alone. Each held in his right hand a long, broad knife, like the seax-knife Shef's catapult-men carried, but with a straight blade and sharp point—a stabbing weapon as well as a chopping one. A leather rope was tied first to one wrist, then the other. Shef noted that there was maybe three feet of slack left. Each man took half the slack and held it in his bound left hand, so that the fight began with the backs of the left fists touching. One man was young, tall, with long fair hair braided down his back. The other twenty years older, burly and bald, an expression of grim anger on his face.

"What's it about?" Shef muttered.

"Young one got the other one's daughter pregnant. He says she consented, the father says he raped her in the field."

"What does she say?" Shef asked, remembering similar cases from his own time as a judge.

"I don't think anyone asked her."

Shef opened his mouth to ask further, realized it was too late. More words spoken, a ritual request to accept mediation, now impossible to take without shame. Two headshakes. The law-speaker stepped carefully off the bull's hide, made a signal.

Instantly the two men were in motion, springing round each other. The father had stabbed at the first flicker of the judge's hand, stabbed low under the linked hands. But at the same moment the young man had dropped his slack and sprung back to the full extent of the rope.

The father dropped his slack too, snatched forward at the rope trailing from his enemy's wrist. If he got it he could hold the younger man to him, keep him no more than one arm's length, perhaps pull him close and stab him in the body. But to commit yourself to a mortal stroke left you open to a mortal counter. In this kind of duel it was easy to kill your enemy. If you cared to give him the chance to kill you.

The older man's snatch missed, the younger one was leaping away, keeping near the edge of the hide. Suddenly he stretched forward, slashed his enemy across the back of the arm. A shout as the blood showed, a sneer in answer from the wounded man.

"Easy in this game to give a scratch," Guthmund remarked. "But a scratch won't settle it. Loss of blood, if it goes on a long time—but it never does."

The fight had reached a kind of pattern, one man trying to close, stabbing always underneath the two arms, jerking and grabbing at the rope that joined them. The other ignoring the rope, keeping away, flicking quick slashes at arm or leg, but taking care not to let his knife catch, to trap him for an instant.

He did it once too often. The bald father, bleeding from a dozen minor wounds, took yet another slash high up on the left biceps. Caught the retreating hand, the knife-hand, with his own tied left. Started to twist it savagely, shouting something Shef could not catch over the crowd noise. The seducer lashed out with his own left hand, desperately trying to catch the other's knife-hand in his turn. But the older man had twisted, holding the knife away behind his body out of reach, feinting to thrust low, then high, twisting the caught wrist all the time.

With no other hope left the trapped man kicked both feet off the ground, tried to catch the other's thighs in a scissors grip, sent him staggering. As the two fell locked to the ground Shef saw blood spurt, heard the groan of released breath from the spectators close up. The judge stepped forward, pulled the two men apart. Shef saw one knife jutting from deep in the chest of the young man. As they rolled the other over he saw a second hilt standing up from the older man's eye.

Women were shrieking, rushing forward. Shef turned to Guthmund, ready to rebuke a system that lost a woman husband and father in the same heartbeat, and a child father and grandfather. But the words died in his throat.

Cuthred was striding down the hollow, spiked shield in one hand, sword in the other. Behind him trailed Fritha and Osmod, Udd a pace or two after them, all carrying crossbows but looking helpless. As Shef started to shove his way forward, he heard Cuthred's crazy voice lifted in pidgin Norse.

"Bunglers! Nithings! Have to be tied together not to run away. Hold a man to be cut. Fight an Englishman, why don't you, one with hands free. One hand tied, give you choice. Hornungs, sons of drabs! You, you there."

White spittle was flying from his mouth, and a circle was steadily widening round him, leaving him isolated with the two dead men at his feet. Staring down, Cuthred slashed suddenly at one of them, opening a great gash across the young man's dead face. He began to stamp his feet and breathe in great gasps, ready to charge the entire crowd.

Shef stepped in front of him, waited for recognition to show in the mad eyes. Reluctant recognition.

"They won't fight," said Shef slowly. "We'll have to find a better time. And striking a corpse is foul play, Cuthred. Foul play for an *ordwiga*, a *herecempa*, a *frumgar* like yourself, a king's champion. Wait for the Ragnarssons, for the killers of your King Ella."

Cuthred's face worked at the string of honorifics, all of which he had earned in former life as captain of the King of Northumbria's guard. He looked at his bloody sword, at the corpse he had struck, threw his weapon down and burst into racking sobs. Udd and Osmod closed on either side, took his arm, started to lead him away.

Mopping sweat, Shef turned to meet the disapproving look of the duel-judge, the law-speaker.

"Mutilating a dead body," the Norseman said, "is punishable by a fine of . . ."

"We'll pay," said Shef. "We'll pay. But someone ought to pay for what has been done to that live one."

The next morning, Shef stood by the narrow gangplank leading to Brand's prized and cherished ship, the *Walrus*. Guthmund's *Seamew*, already loaded, rocked easily in the water twenty yards out, a row of faces looking over the low gunwale. Loading the ships had not been an easy business. Each rowed eighteen oars a side and carried a normal crew of forty. To this had had to be added Shef, Hund, Karli and Thorvin, the eight men of the catapult crew, the four women they had rescued from Drottningsholm, Cuthred, and the train of runaways they had attracted in their ride across Upland and Sogn—nearly thirty all told, a large number to add to the cramped quarters of two narrow ships.

But now they were not all there: Lulla, Fritha and Edwi of the catapult crew, all missing. Had they been cut off somehow? Were they being hidden somewhere in the Thing area, destined for slavery or revenge, or even sacrifice? At the thought of his men being strung up on the temple trees of some backwoods town, Shef's patience snapped.

"Get all the men off," he shouted to Brand. "You too Guthmund. We can muster a hundred men between us. We'll go through this place and turn every tent over till they hand our men over. Anyone doesn't like it, he'll get a bolt in his belly."

Shef became aware that Cwicca and the others were not reacting with the enthusiasm he would have expected. They had donned their glassy expressions, always a sign they knew something they did not dare to reveal.

"All right," Shef said. "What's up with those three?"

Osmod, usually the spokesman on difficult occasions, spoke up. "It's like this," he volunteered. "We've been walking round, some of us, looking at things. And all they're talking about here is catapults and crossbows and that. They've heard a lot about them, don't know how they work. So we said, naturally, that we knew all about catapults, and as for crossbows, well Udd here practically invented them. So they say—by this time they'd stood us all a drink or two—they say, 'very interesting, do you men know what's happening down south?' 'No,' says we, naturally enough, since we don't. So then they say . . ."

"Get on with it!" Shef bellowed.

"They're paying big money for experienced catapult men, men who know how to build and shoot them. Big money. We think Lulla and Edwi and Fritha have decided to go in for that."

Shef stared for a moment, uncertain how to react. He had freed those men. They were landholders back in England already. How could they go off and take service with anyone, leaving their lord? But then they were free men, because he had freed them . . .

"All right," he said. "Forget it, Brand. Osmod, the rest of you, thank you anyway for staying. I hope you won't lose by it. Let's get on board and get going. Back in England in two weeks, if Thor sends us a wind."

He did not, or not immediately. All the way down the long fjord from where the Gula met the Sogn to the open sea, the two boats pulled steadily into the teeth of a fresh breeze, low in the water from their weight of passengers and stores. Brand spelled the rowers, rotating the male passengers with his own men.

"Get round the ness," he remarked. "Wind'll be on our beam then, we can stop rowing and sail south. What's that ahead?"

Round the point of the promontory that guarded the Gula-fjord, little more than half a mile away, came a ship. A strange ship, not like the traders and fishing-boats they had passed half a dozen times already. Her blue and white striped sail bellied in the breeze behind her, a pennant flew from her mast, blowing towards them so they could see it only fitfully as a gust took it wide. Something wrong with her sail. Something wrong with her size.

"Thor aid us," said Brand at the steering-oar. "It's one of Halfdan's coastguard ships. But she's got two sails. She's even got two masts. I never saw such a thing in all my born days. What have they done all that for?"

Shef's one sharp eye caught sight of the banner, the Gripping Beast design on it.

"Turn," he said. "Get us out of here. It's Queen Ragnhild. And she means us no good."

"It's a big ship, but we're two to one, we can fight her . . ."

"Turn," shouted Shef, recognizing something about the motions of the men on deck.

Brand caught on in the same moment and sent the *Walrus* heeling round in a turn so violent that the rowers were sent skidding along their benches.

"Back starboard," he shouted. "Pull backboard. Now pull together. Pull hard, get the stroke up. And drop the sail and sheet home, you in the waist there, help him, Narr, Ansgeir. Guthmund . . ." His voice carried over the water to their companion lagging a furlong behind. The *Walrus*, wind now behind her, began to scud back the way she had come.

Watching the pursuing ship, Shef, as he had expected, saw her yaw to bring her beam round. "On the word, swing her hard to starboard," he said quietly. "Now."

The *Walrus* swung briskly round. At the same moment Brand shouted to his crew to lift their oars, let the boat run freely under sail. The oars heaved smartly together out of the water. A hum in the air, three oarsmen together span out of their seats, landed in the belly of the ship, cursing or moaning. Shattered pieces of oar flew up in the air, splashed slowly into the sea. The mule-stone that had smashed through them just above head-height flew on, hit the water, bounced from wave to wave to wave before sinking.

"They were talking about fitting one of those," said Brand. "But they said she'd never take the recoil. Must have rerigged her internally along with the two masts."

"But who's crewing the mule?" asked Shef, still watching the ship behind them trying to make up lost distance, alert for any second swerve that would bring the mule round to bear. It was fortunate this was a stern chase and Ragnhild's men could not shoot over the bow. "Renegades of mine? But where would they have got them from?"

"The Way has been very interested in all that you did," put in Thorvin, standing close to Brand. "They built copies of all the machines you made. Valgrim could have built the mule and found a crew. Some of his friends are priests of Njörth, would know how to rebuild a ship. What are we going to do? Run back into the Gula-fjord and hope to fight them on land?"

Shef was once more staring intently at the activity in the bow of the pursuing ship. She had lost way by turning beam-on to shoot, and now both were under sail the *Walrus* and her consort were making ground with every wave. The ships had begun half a mile apart. Now they were certainly more than that. Even at that distance, though, Shef was certain that he could make out a tall figure, a tall female figure, standing in the very prow of the ship, long hair streaming disheveled. Ragnhild coming after him. Chasing him, however fast they sailed, into a long fjord with no other exit. And they were certainly doing something strange in the prow there.

Could they have built a mule that did not need to be bedded low down and centrally in a ship?

Light showed behind Ragnhild, fire, a strong fire blazing brightly. At the same moment Shef's brain recognized the motions of the men round it. He had never seen a catapult being wound from in front of it before, but that was what they were doing—had been doing, for they had just jumped back to clear the view for the shooter, just like Cwicca's crew. Not a mule, one of the great dart-shooters he had used himself to release Ella and to break Ivar Ragnarsson's army.

As Shef turned to shout at Brand to swerve again, he saw the light suddenly coming straight at him with inconceivable speed, rising and falling slightly a bare six feet over the waves. Involuntarily, Shef cringed. Bent forward, arms over belly, sure the machine would send the great javelin-size bolt straight through body and spine.

A thump just below his feet, sending him staggering. Instant reek of burning tar, burning wood. Brand yelling hoarsely and a lurch as he abandoned the steering oar to look over the side. Then Shef was shoved aside by men running up from the waist of the ship with bailing buckets, trying furiously to lean over far enough to reach the water, scoop it up, throw it on to the great fire-arrow that had slammed into the *Walrus,* come clean through her rear planking three feet from Shef's leg, was now setting fire to planks and thwarts at once.

"Use the drinking water!" shouted Brand. The driblets of sea-water his crew were bailing up from the waves barely within reach were making no impact on the mass of pitch and tar on the bolt's head, jammed through the planks. And the fire was spreading. If it caught the sail . . . A man ran from the water-barrel by the base of the mast, lost his footing and fell, bucket going wide into the bilge. Others hesitated, torn between the sea just out of reach and the water-barrel too far away.

Cuthred slouched from his place near the bow. No-one had ventured to ask him to row. He had an axe in his hand. Standing over the fire-arrow, he smashed three strokes down through the *Walrus*'s frail planking, bent over the side, thrust the bolt further through till the blazing head stood well out from the ship's inner side. Swung the axe again, shearing through the thick wood with one blow. Picked up the severed head, ignoring the flames that ran up his arm, tossed it over the side. As Cuthred turned sneering to Brand, Shef realized that the ship behind them had yawed again.

Machine-war, he thought sickly. It comes too fast. Even a brave man wants to stop, to shout "Wait till I'm ready!" Helplessly, he saw the mule-stone come blurring towards him, again seeming to come directly at him, not the ship, him personally, aiming for his rib-cage, to shatter the thin bones and crush out the heart.

The stone hit the water thirty yards short, bounced like a child's skimming-stone, bounced again, and hit the *Walrus* like a hammer just forward of the steering-oar. Planks stove, a rowing-bench hurled from its socket, green water poured through. But only a hole, not the complete shattering and disintegration of a ship struck on keel or stem-post.

You were a king before, Shef told himself. Now they say you are an over-king. And what are you doing? Cringing. Waiting for help from a madman. This is not the way for a leader. You have destroyed men from a distance before. You never thought how you would behave when the other side had all the machines.

Shef stepped up to the stern again, leaving the others to deal with the leak. Ragnhild's ship was still coming on behind them, while men worked to wind their machines, prepare for their next shots. One or other would sink them, once they had learnt to hold their hand till they were in proper range. Meanwhile they had come back under full sail almost to their starting-place. Shef could see a crowd down by the Thing-harbor, watching them. And just in front lay the island, the Gula-ey, on which the Thing itself had been held in years gone by. Shef eyed the narrow channel between it and the shore, considered the size of Halvdan's warship, remembered the trick Sigurth Snake-eye had played on him. He did not think an experienced Viking skipper would fall for that one.

He caught Brand by the shoulder, pointed. "Take us through there."

Brand opened his mouth to argue, closed it as he caught the tone of utter certainty in Shef's voice. Silently he leant on the oar, steered between rocks, waved peremptorily to Guthmund to follow. After a few moments he ventured to say, "We'll lose the wind in a moment."

"All right." Shef was watching the ship behind. As he expected, she had shifted course. Not going to follow. Going to go round the island to the left as they had to the right. Take the wind on the beam, keep up speed, overhaul the two ships she was pursuing, destroy them at close range. Probably their skipper thought his enemies intended to beach and escape on foot. Ragnhild would have a plan for that too.

But for a few moments the island would be between them.

"On the word," said Shef quietly, "furl sail, turn, and row back as fast as ever you can. Once we're past it'll be a rowing match. With a ship that size and with that much extra weight, we're bound to win."

"Unless she just sits and waits for us. Then we're rowing back to face catapults at fifty yards."

Shef nodded. "Turn now."

The *Walrus* and *Seamew* turned together, began to row back, the men at the oars heaving in an intent silence. The only noise they could hear Shef realized, was the hum of voices on the shore a hundred yards away. He hoped pointing fingers would not give his plan away. What Brand said was right. This was like two children chasing each other round a kitchen table. If the chaser just stopped, the one who doubled back would run right into him. Shef did not think the chaser would stop. That ship there, however experienced the skipper, was commanded by Ragnhild, he knew. She would not stop to think. She wanted to run him down. Besides that, he had seen the men lining the bulwarks, waving weapons and shouting. They had acquired machines, but they did not think like machine-warriors yet. Their instinct and training was to close and overwhelm, to break the line by force and weight. Not to sit back and shoot from a distance, use their weapons' range.

As the *Walrus* scudded out from the channel and back the way they had come, Shef looked over the starboard quarter. Relief filled him. Halvdan's ship had raced round the island, realized too late what had happened, was only turning now in a flurry of flapping sails. Badly handled, too. The crew and skipper had evidently still not worked out the problems of their two-mast rig. Nearer a mile off than half a mile, and no chance of catching up. Brand's oarsmen were throwing their weight on the oars now, one of them singing and the rest giving the refrain each time they swayed their oar-handles forward. Three men were bending planks back into place, plugging gaps with sealskin and sailcloth. The way was clear to run out into the open sea and south again.

Karli caught Shef's arm and pointed ahead. A small skiff, rowed by one man, paddling out from the harbor to intercept them.

"It's Fritha," he said. "Must have changed his mind."

Shef frowned, stepped forward to the bow again, seizing a rope. As the *Walrus* came up on the small skiff he heaved the rope across, saw Fritha grasp it. He made no attempt to haul his boat alongside but abandoned it, dropping the oars and swinging himself waist-deep through the water till he could clutch the *Walrus*'s side. Shef seized his collar, heaved him over, stood looking down forbiddingly.

"What happened? Silver not paid on time?"

Fritha gasped, struggled dripping to his feet. "No, lord. I had to tell you. The Thing is full of the news. A ship came in ahead of that one there. We knew the queen Ragnhild was coming before you did. But the ship said another thing. As she sailed up the coast, she—the queen—told every harbor along the coast that if you escaped her she would pay a bounty for your head. A great bounty, all her inheritance. Every pirate in Rogaland is looking for you now. All along the coast. Two hundred miles of it."

And Rogalanders are poor, Shef reflected, but they really mean business. He looked at Thorvin.

"It seems the way south is blocked. I will have to be the one who comes from the North after all."

"We say the words," said Thorvin. "But the gods put them there."

CHAPTER TWENTY

Sure they'll come after us," said Brand. He held a seal's flipper in one hand, gnawed carefully along one of its long bones, sucked the blubber noisily from the skin, hurled the remains into the sea. As an afterthought he wiped both greasy hands carefully on his beard, rose to his feet, slouched off towards the boathouses of Hrafnsey, his island home. Over his shoulder he shouted, "But they won't find us. And if they do, we'll see them first."

Shef looked after his retreating figure. Brand worried him more and more. Shef had known him for almost two years now, and at no time could Brand ever have been taken as a model of courtly etiquette. Nevertheless, by the admittedly low standards of Viking armies his behavior had been normal enough: rough, violent and noisy, but capable of finer feeling and even of an element of show. Brand had cut a fine figure at the wedding of Alfred and Godive. When Shef had arrived at Kaupang, Brand had put up a very creditable impersonation of a courtier welcoming an honored king. He had always been clean and careful about the hygiene of the camp.

As the ships had run further and further north, racing up the seemingly endless coastline of Norway with the wind behind them, always the long jagged coast to starboard and a turmoil of reefs and islands and tidal skerries between them and the Atlantic on the backboard, Brand's behavior had steadily changed. So had his accent and that of his Halogaland crew. They had always spoken oddly compared to the other Norwegians. As they neared the everlasting ice their accents had thickened, their voices grown gruffer, they had begun to revel, it seemed, in oil and grease. They ate their bread ration soaked in seal-fat, scattering pinches of salt on it. They ate the fish they caught raw, and sometimes alive: Shef had seen a man pluck a herring from the sea on his line and sink his teeth into it immediately, the fish still flapping in his hands. One day Brand had reduced sail as if looking carefully for landmarks, and finally steered into a beach. His crew had piled out whooping before the boat had even come to the shore, run up the beach to a cairn, and started instantly to demolish it and dig into the sand beneath. The stench that came up sent Shef and his English crewmen reeling backward to a safe distance, where they were joined by Guthmund and his Swedes from the *Seamew,* for once in complete agreement with the English as against the Norwegians.

"What out of Hel have you got there?" Shef had shouted from the safe side of a wood fire, the smoke in his nostrils.

"Rotten shark liver," Brand had shouted back. "We buried it on the way down to age a bit. Like to try a bite?"

As one man the Swedes and English had moved another fifty yards down the beach, pursued by guffaws and shouts of "It's good for you! Keeps out the cold! Bite a shark and he can't bite you!"

Once they got to Hrafnsey things had got worse. The island itself was about five miles long and two wide, and relatively flat. Much of it could be grazed, some even plowed. It lay opposite the most desolate coastline Shef had ever seen in his life, far bleaker and more jagged than even the mountains of Norway running down to the Oslo fjord. Even past midsummer, snow could be seen everywhere. The mountains seemed to run straight and undeviating down into icy water, with only here and there the barest glimpses of green growth on little shelves and ledges, for all one could see inaccessible from the water or from the mountain-tops above them. For many days Shef continued to find it impossible that anyone could live and find food there. Yet Brand's crew had dispersed for the most part into the rocky wilderness like water into sand, pulling away in two- and four-oared rowboats, or in small sail cobles. In every fjord there seemed to be a farm, or at least a hut or cluster of stone-walled turf-roofed cabins.

The truth was, Shef had realized, that these people, though they grew some oats and barley in favored places, were essentially carnivores. The freezing water teemed with fish, easy to pickle in brine for the winter. Seals were everywhere also, competing with men for the fish and so doubly valuable to kill. There was enough grass to graze cows and sheep in the summer, and to make hay to feed them through the winter. Goats could be turned out to forage for themselves on the mountains. These Norsemen of the furthest North put an immense value on milk and butter, whey and curds and cheese, milking all their animals, sheep and goats as well, twice daily through the summer, and preserving all of it which they did not consume immediately. It was indeed a rich land that they lived in, though it seemed no more than rock. But it needed special qualities to survive in it. Some of Brand's men had taken Karli, the flatlander from the Ditmarsh, and a few of Guthmund's crew bird's nesting after eggs, to be found in vast quantities on every cliff and skerry during the breeding season. They had returned helpless with laughter after half a day, depositing the white-faced outlanders on the shore with exaggerated care. Only someone with no nerves at all and no slightest sense of vertigo could swing down the iron-bound cliffs on fingertips and toeholds alone. A man could not marry on Hrafnsey, Brand had told Shef, till he had gone to a certain stone two hundred feet above the jagged rocks of the shore, balanced on it—for it was a stone that moved in the wind—bent over the edge, touched his toes and then pissed into the surf below. It was his grandfather's time since any man had slipped: the fear of falling had been bred out of Brand's line and that of all his fellows.

None of this made the Halogalanders easier to live with. From the start Shef had worried about how they were to get away. Then he had worried about how, if they did not get away—and Brand seemed content to wait for pursuit rather than try to counter-attack or avoid it—they were to live through the winter with their great trail of useless mouths, Englishmen and Swedes who could not harpoon seals, climb cliffs or digest the buried livers of the enormous basking sharks. "Catch more fish," was all Brand would say. He seemed unworried about everything, content only to be back in his alien home, making plans only for the collection of the Finn-tax.

Shef had many things to worry about besides Brand. They crowded on him as he lay sleepless in the short twilights of the northern summer. For one thing, on the long voyage up the coast he had had time to talk to all his crew members, Cwicca, Hama, Udd, Osmod and the others, who had all occupied their time at the Gula Thing by collecting as much gossip as possible. The Norwegian Thing-goers were startlingly well informed—though it was not so startling when you reckoned the volume of trade and warfare that passed through their hands. Piecing together what they had said, Shef realized that his own actions had caused far more repercussions in the Scandinavian lands than he had ever imagined. The whole of the Norse-speaking world was alive with interest in the new weapons that had defeated the Franks and the Ragnarssons. That was why high prices were on offer to genuine experts. The sea-battle off the Elbe had also been reported on in detail, and plans for fitting catapults to ships were far advanced. There was no point in raiding to the south any more, some said, till the Norse were on even terms once more, or better, against their English prey.

Expectation was mounting, too, about the Ragnarssons' counter-stroke. According to Osmod, the most accurate informer, there was very definite feeling that the Ragnarssons would have to do something. They had failed in Northumbria, failed to avenge their father properly. Lost one of their number, failed to avenge him too. Failed at the start of their great counter-raid in the spring, failed even to buy the man they saw as the origin of their misfortunes when he stood for sale on the slave-block. That story was well-known, Osmod said, and men were laughing openly as they heard about it. Wiser men felt that the Ragnarssons must do something. Only the year before it had been common knowledge that Sigurth the Snake-eye meant to establish his brothers on the thrones of England and Ireland, and then return with their aid to unify all Denmark under his own rule, as had never been done since the days of the mythical Skjöldungs. And now what did they say of him? That he could not catch a man on a sandbank with the tide coming in. Many laughed, Osmod repeated, but others said that you could be sure of one thing: the Ragnarssons would return from their forays in Scotland ready for some desperate stroke. Sensible kings in Denmark had forbidden their subjects to raid abroad, and were calling up their fleets and armies for home defense.

And then there were the Christians stirring. Here it was Thorvin who had told Shef most, Thorvin who had been so exultant the year before at the thought of Christian kings calling in Wayman missionaries. Now, he said, it began to look as if the boot were on the other foot. Report after report had come in to him of strange behavior in the markets and at the Things of the south Scandinavian lands: Christian priests not just coming in to try to make converts, as they had for decades, among the slaves and the poor folk and the women of the country, usually finding themselves mocked and enslaved in their turn. No, coming in with a swagger and a guard, returning insult with insult and violence with violence, buying back their own. And asking questions. Questions about the raid on Hamburg sixteen years before. Questions about kings. Writing down the answers. Not trying to save souls, no, looking for something. Thorvin had heard especially, and in tones of deepest admiration, about the man they called Bruno.

But there Shef had been able to tell Thorvin of what he had seen in the market at Hedeby, and of the conversation he had had afterwards. What had surprised him was not that the Vikings were impressed by Bruno—anyone as fast and skillful as he was would naturally be a success in the Viking world—but that Bruno had continued on from Hedeby, into the country of the Swedes, the Smaaland counties and the two Gautaland provinces south of the great Swedish lakes.

Thorvin had told him one thing especially that he did not know before. "Do you know why so many of us are called Eirik?" Thorvin had asked. "It is because of the Eiriksgata, or better one should say the *Ein-riks-gata*. The road of the one ruler. No man can become king of all the Swedes, it is said, unless he has traveled that road. It goes round all the Things of all the provinces. The true king must go to each Thing, and declare himself king in each assembly, and overcome any and all challenge. Only once a king has done that is he king over all the Swedes."

"And who was the last king who ever did that?" Shef had asked, remembering what Hagbarth had told him months before about the way you became a king, though it might be no more than king of the Eastfold, or the Fjord-countries, or as Shef had said mockingly, of the Next Midden or the Further Cow-byre.

Thorvin had pursed his lips and shaken his head slowly, remembering history so old it was myth. "Maybe King Ali," he had said. "Ali the Mad, uncle of King Athils. The Swedes say he was king over all Sweden, including the Gautlands and Skaane. But he cannot have held those lands for long—his nephew was put to scorn by King Hrolf on Fyrisvellir Plain. You know. You saw that yourself," he added, reminding Shef of one of his own visions.

It seemed to Shef sometimes that the wide-shouldered Bruno was touring the Scandinavian lands as if he meant to follow the Einriksgata himself, to make them Christian by force from above rather than by conversion from below. If so, the Wayman victory in England with East Anglia and Alfred's kingdom would be canceled out, and more, by Christian victory in the North. He could not imagine it would be so. Still, it fretted him that he had no news, no further news once every last bit of nourishment had been chewed from what his men reported. It fretted him even more that he was up here at the very last edge of the inhabited world, while great matters were stirring in the center. Driven away to a land of birds' eggs and shark liver, while the armies marched in the south.

And indeed the armies marched and the fleets maneuvered. While Shef and his men twisted rope and shaped wood, setting up catapults, mules and dart-shooters to cover every seaward entrance to Hrafnsey for the attack of Ragnhild, the Ragnarssons came down like a cloud on the Ditmarsh and the islands of North Frisia, sending King Hrorik into a frenzy of recruiting and appealing and gathering stores for siege in Hedeby. The Archbishop of Hamburg-Bremen, the ascetic Rimbert, hearing stronger and stronger reports from his agents in the North, doubled the forces of the Knights of the Holy Lance and sent them in their own ships across the Baltic, with the enthusiastic support of his brothers in Cologne and Mainz and Trier and even beyond. The Frankish descendants of Charlemagne bickered and sparred for the succession to Charles the Bald, with the new Pope—the Popelet, men called him—lending his support now to one, now to the other. And in a season of unexpected peace Godive's child grew in her womb, while her husband received the deputations of many kingless English counties, anxious to join in what they saw as the new Golden Age without either Church or pagans.

But Shef waited on events, his whereabouts known to none, relieving his feelings only by constant work at the forge and among his fellow craftsmen.

Cwicca's gang were attempting to make winter wine in summer. They had been vastly impressed by the strong drink they had been given in Kaupang, and had managed to buy a small barrel between them at the Gula-Thing. It was gone now, but they had time on their hands, and Udd had explained his theory to them.

"What they do with winter wine," he lectured, "is freeze the water out of it, so that what remains is stronger."

Nods and general agreement.

"Now steam is water." There was more discussion about this point, but everyone had seen steam rising from damp ground, or sweat turning into steam when it hit a hot iron. "So if we heat beer up till the steam comes off it, we'll get the water out of it just as if it had been frozen. It won't be winter wine. It'll be kind of summer beer."

"But it'll be stronger," said Cwicca, wanting to get the main point straight.

"Right."

The men had got a tub of beer—most of the scanty barley production of Hrafnsey went into brewing rather than bread—put half of it into the largest copper pot they could borrow, and heated it over a gentle fire, careful not to burn the bottom of the pot out. Slowly the thick brew began to bubble, the steam rose off it in the thick-walled, low-roofed brewhouse. A score of men and half a dozen women were jammed in together, the catapult-team and with them the kraki wearers, as they were called, the rescues of the trek across the Upland.

Udd, presiding, watched carefully, superintending the fire-tenders, beating away attempts at preliminary tasting with his largest beechwood ladle. Finally, watching the level in the pot, he judged that almost half of the beer had been steamed away. Two men lifted it carefully away from the fire, waited for it to cool.

Udd had learnt some very elementary man-management over the months, enough for him to give the honor of first taste to someone else, and to someone who would value it. He passed over Cwicca and Osmod, the gang's natural leaders, called forward one of the recent rescues, a big silent man whom the freed but still class-conscious English suspected of having been a thane of King Burgred before the Vikings captured and enslaved him.

"Ceolwulf," he called out. "I expect you've been used to good stuff. Come and try this."

The former thane stepped forward, took the wooden mug held out to him, sniffed the liquid, drank deeply, rolling it round his mouth before swallowing.

"What does it taste like?" asked Karli anxiously. "Is it as good as the last barrel?"

Ceolwulf paused to give weight to his words. "What it tastes like," he said, "is water that's been used for washing old musty grain. Or maybe it's very very thin old porridge."

Cwicca seized the mug from him, drank deep in his turn, lowered the mug with an expression of complete disbelief. "You're wrong there, Ceolwulf," he said. "What this tastes like is gnat's piss."

As the other men dipped their mugs into the pot to confirm the judgment, Udd stared open-mouthed at the brew, the fire, the condensing steam on the membrane that covered the glassless window.

"The strength was there," he muttered. "It's not there now. It must have gone off in the steam. But it doesn't go off when you freeze drink. The ice and the steam are different. The ice is water. So the steam must be— something else." Experimentally he put out a finger, ran it along the steam-wet membrane, licked it.

"So don't keep the brew that's left," he concluded. "Keep the steam. But how to collect it?" He looked consideringly at the copper pot.

Weary and anxious, Shef decided to spend an afternoon in the steam-bath. It was a small wooden hut built out on the end of a pier, with a platform beside it overhanging the deep water of the fjord that led down to the Hrafnsey harbor. Every day men lifted hot stones out of the pit where they had been heating overnight and trundled them along to the hut, where they lay glowing for hour after hour. It was a common thing for those who had nothing to do, or who were weary from some task or other, to stroll along and sit in the heat for an hour or so, dropping water on to the stones, and from time to time going out on to the platform for a plunge into the freezing water.

When Shef stepped in to the dark hut, he realized there was someone already there, sitting on one of the benches. Peering into the gloom, he saw from the light of the opened door that it was Cuthred, sitting not naked, like every other man who went there, but in a pair of ragged woolen drawers. Shef hesitated, went in. He did not know of anyone else who would willingly sit in the dark with Cuthred, but something told him he had nothing to fear. Cuthred did not forget, even in his berserkergang, who had released him from the mill. He had said, also, once he found out how Shef had recognized him, and that Shef had been there at the start of the whole story, the capture of Ragnar, that he knew their fates were twisted.

After they had sat together in the dark for a while, Shef realized that Cuthred had started to talk, very quietly, and almost to himself. He was talking, it appeared, about Brand.

"Big fellow, he is," Cuthred muttered. "But there's nothing special about size. I've known some almost as big, and one or two who were taller. That Scotty I killed, he was seven feet tall, I measured him. Brittle-boned, though. No, it's not the size that gets me about that son of a bitch, he's just not normal. His bones are wrong. Look at his hands, they're twice the size of mine. And his eyes. Over his eyes."

A hand reached out, rubbed firmly across Shef's eyebrows, the voice muttered on. "See. Normal people, they have nothing under their eyebrows, just a socket. I haven't felt his eyebrows, can't get close enough, but I've looked carefully. He has a bone ridge there, makes his eyebrows stick out.

"And his teeth, now." Again the hand, peeling Shef's lower lip down. "See, most people, nearly everyone, the top set of teeth goes over the lower set. When you bite with your front teeth, it's like scissors, the one sliding over the other. Now his teeth aren't like that. I've watched for a long time, and I reckon his teeth fit edge to edge, they don't slide over each other at all. When he bites, it's like an axe on a block. And his back teeth, they must be real grinders. Something very strange about him. And not just him, quite a lot of them round here. His cousins have it too. But he's the worst.

"And there's another thing. He's hiding something round here. You know, lord—" for the first time Cuthred acknowledged that he knew who he was talking to. "You know that these days I spend a lot of time rowing round by myself."

Shef nodded in the darkness. Cuthred had indeed taken to rowing round in a little two-man dory he had borrowed, or commandeered. There was a general feeling of relief that he was out of the way for as long as he was.

"Well, I went right round the island first time, and then I went down the coast a bit to the south, and then I went up to the north, not very far, because I started late in the day. But when I got back from that one they were waiting for me at the dock. Brand, and about four of his cousins, all with spears and axes and their armor on, as if they were ready for trouble.

"Now, that got me mad right off. But I'm not as mad as they think I am. I reckon they'd have liked me to be, that day. But I got out of the boat, and got right up close to Brand where I could get my hands on him if anything started—he knew what I was doing.

" 'Now listen,' he said, talking very carefully. 'I mean you no harm, but I want to give you a warning. Go round in your boat. That's all right. Go anywhere you like—round the island, out to the seal-skerries, anywhere to the south. Not north.'

" 'I've just been north,' I said. 'No harm in that that I could see.'

" 'You can't have gone very far,' he said. 'You just went up to Naestifjorth, that's what they call the next big fjord north of here. That's all right. Most of the time. The next one is Midfjorth. You don't want to go in there.'

" 'And the one after that?' I asked him, pushing him a bit.

"Well, he shut his jaw like a wolf-trap. In the end he just said, 'You don't want to know about that at all. Stay away from it.' "

"That's strange," said Shef. "After all they go north often enough, all of them, to meet the Finns and collect the Finn-tax. They say no-one really lives north of here, not Norsemen anyway, just the Finns. But they seem to know their way north all right."

"But when the ships go north," Cuthred answered, "they go outside the line of the skerries. I've been asking round, as much as I can, and Martha, she asks the women-folk for me. North of here, on the real coast, inside the skerries—that's no-go country. I wonder why. They're hiding something. When I walked off, after they'd warned me, I heard one of Brand's cousins say something to him, trying to calm him down. 'Let him go,' he said, 'he's no loss.' So he really was trying to warn me, of something they think really is dangerous. But they don't want it talked about just the same."

Cuthred's low voice slowly drifted off to a list of other insults and spites that had been put upon him, while he toiled at the mill. Men and women who had mocked him, the bitter cold of the mountain winter, the way he had tried to block the shutter with dirt, the way the shutter kept opening again, faces that had appeared at the window, the way they had rattled the door trying to reach him in the night . . .

Relaxing in the heat, Shef's mind slowly lost its incessant turning over of the problems of Bruno and Alfred and Sigurth and Olaf, of the dead Harald and Ragnhild, yes, and Godive too. His head sank back into the corner, against the pine-scented wooden walls, he dropped into an uneasy sleep.

He was still in the dark, but a different dark—not the warm, comfortably-scented, mildly companionable one he had left, but a place cold and still and smelling of earth and mold. Yet it was not an enclosed place. It was a road, and there was a mount beneath him, carrying him along at an unearthly pace, with a strong swarming movement, as if it had more legs than a horse should.

The horse was Sleipnir, Shef realized, the eight-legged steed of the father of the gods. But he, the rider whom Shef was accompanying in his dream, was not All-father. He could feel what sort of a person it was, and it was not a god, but a man. A madman, like Cuthred, but without Cuthred's reasons. The main emotion he felt—he felt it all the time—was a furious glee at meeting and overcoming obstacles. His memories were a blur of slashing and slicing and trampling, broken only by the oblivion of drink. Of Othin's mead. The rider of Sleipnir, something told Shef, was Hermoth. It was a name he had met before. The name the champions had shouted in celebration and praise at the end of the long day's fighting at Valhalla. The champion for the day, before the host of Othin, the Einheriar, returned to the hall, their death-wounds magically healed, for an evening of carouse before the next day's contests. Hermoth had won more often than any other hero, more often than Sigurth Fafnisbani, more often than Böthvar Bjarki. So they had chosen him for this exploit, the most vital Othin had ever dispatched a hero on.

To bring back Balder from the dead. The Shef-mind that observed all this knew a little of the dead god, Balder, had heard a story from Thorvin. Now it came to him not as a story but as a series of flashes of sight. Balder, Othin's son, most beautiful of all the gods. Though he was a male god, he was too beautiful to be called handsome. Shef could see no picture of him, just a blur through Hermoth's mind of brilliant light, that seemed to blaze from the flesh of the god.

So beautiful was Balder that the gods, fearing ever to lose him, had made all created things take an oath not to harm him. Iron had sworn, and fire, and disease, and terrible old age, and the giant-brood even, unable to resist his beauty, and every fish and snake and animal in the world, and every tree in the wood. One thing had not sworn: the little, weak, sappy mistletoe plant that climbs up the oak-tree. It could do no harm if it wanted to—or so the gods reasoned.

And once the oath had been taken, Balder was invulnerable, and so the gods, amusing themselves in much the same way as their earthly followers, made sport out of setting up Balder the beautiful as a target and throwing at him every kind of edged and pointed weapon that came to hand. One god could not join in —Hoth, Balder's brother, who was blind. But one day a voice came to him in his blindness and said, would he not like to join in. Yes, he replied, but I am blind. And the voice said, I will set you in the right place and direct your arm. Throw this. And the voice put in his hand a spear made of the mistletoe plant, but hardened with magic arts.

The voice was Loki's, the trickster of the gods, enemy of gods and men, father of the monster-brood. Hoth took the spear and threw.

Hermoth's ears were still ringing with the great cry of lamentation that went up when the gods, and then all other created things, realized that Balder was dead, realized because of the way the light went instantly out of the universe, so that all things became mundane and dreary and dull, as they have stayed forever since. In his mind's eye he could still see the great pyre on which Othin had laid his son, in the funeral ship that would take him down to the Hel-world. Saw how even the giants had been bidden to the funeral and had come. Saw the giant-woman Hyrrokkin push the boat out, weeping—Hermoth had been one of the four champions chosen to hold her wolf-steed with viper-reins. Saw, just as the boat was pushed out along the slipway, Othin bend and whisper something in the ear of his dead son.

What had that word been? He did not know. It was his task, now, to ride to Hel and fetch Balder back.

The horse was out from its constricting walls now, clattering out on to a great bridge that sprang through the air—what air this could be in the world below, Hermoth did not know. He was passing ghosts now, shades that looked anxiously at him, aware of the clatter of the hooves, unlike their own silent passage. They were insignificant ghosts, pale men and women, children, not ghosts chosen for Valhalla or the groves of Frey. And at the bottom of the bridge there, there were gates.

As Sleipnir tore towards them they swung slowly shut. Hermoth stooped, whispered encouragement in the ear of his steed.

A clenching of muscles, a leap so high it seemed they would strike the lower surface of Hel itself. The gates were behind them, the baffled guardians gaping in their track.

This time it was a wall, a wall that ran up, or so it seemed, to the sky that was not there. Yet there was a crack, a tiny crack, at the top. Too small for Sleipnir, too small for Hermoth. Hermoth did not need to be told that this was magic. He drew rein, cantered up, stopped, dismounted. Beat with his massive knuckles on the stone wall, beat till his knuckles were bloody, ignoring the pain, as he always did.

A voice from the other side. "Who is that, that does not beat like a pale ghost from Hel?"

"Hermoth I am, Othin's boy, Othin's errand-rider. I come to speak to Balder."

Another voice, and this one Balder's, slow and dragging and weary, as if the mouth were filled with mold. "Go home, Hermoth, and tell them: I may not leave unless the whole world weeps for me. And I know. Just as there was one thing that would harm me, so there is one thing that will not weep. Tell them." And the voice trailed away as if being dragged down some long and dusty corridor.

Hermoth did not hesitate or falter, for such was not his nature. He knew certainty when he heard it. And he had no fear of returning with such a discouraging message. He mounted and turned again to ride back. Thought for a moment. Reached inside his tunic, where he had stowed a black cock from Asgarth, one of Othin's own breed.

He whipped the knife from his belt, slashed the head from the cockerel, threw first the head, and then the body, with the accuracy of the great ones through the crack between wall and sky.

A moment later he heard a sound through the stone wall, a sound so strong it seemed to make the wall reverberate. A cock crowing. Crowing for dawn, for new life, for resurrection.

Wondering, Hermoth turned to ride back through Helgate and over the Giallar-bridge that divides the Hel-world from the other eight. He did not know what this meant, but he did not think it would be a surprise to Othin.

What was it that Othin had whispered to his dead son on the pyre?

Shef's head jerked upright, conscious that something was going on outside. His body ran with sweat, he had slept too long. For an instant he thought the shouting must mean that at long last, Ragnhild had come. As she had done once before when he slept in the steam-room. Then his ears caught the sound of exultation, delight, not dismay. They were shouting something. What was it? "The wind, the wind?"

Cuthred was at the door, gripping the handle. The door had stuck, as they often did in the heat, and Shef's heart thumped for an instant—few worse fates than dying baked in the heat of a steam-bath, but it had been known to happen. Then the door snapped open, and the light and cold air streamed in.

Cuthred took two paces out and leapt over the railing into the water below. Shef followed him, gasping as the bitter-cold water closed over his head. After his experience on the ice Shef had thought he would never willingly enter cold water again, but steam-baths changed your mind. The two men swam together to the ladder that led out to the platform where they had hung their clothes, climbed out, gaping at the horde of running men who seemed to have appeared from nowhere.

They were running down to the boats, all of them. Not the sea-going boats, the *Walrus* and *Seamew,* but the dories, the rowboats. Hauling out boats Shef had never seen. And there were other boats, pulling into the harbor like demons, with the men of the fjords shouting. All shouting the same word. This time Shef caught it. Not the wind. "The grind! The grind!"

Shef and Cuthred stared at each other. Down below, at the harbor, Brand saw them slowly rubbing themselves dry. He made a trumpet of his hands, bellowed up to them.

"We are leaving your men behind. No room in the boats for idiots when the grind comes! You two follow if you want to see something."

Then he was off, in a boat, balancing on the thwart with a great lance in his hand.

Cuthred pointed to the little two-oar boat he had commandeered, tied up ten feet away on the shore. Shef nodded, looked round for his narwhal-hilted sword, remembered that as usual he had left it by his bunk. No time to go for it now, he had the eating-knife strapped to his belt. Cuthred stowed sword and spiked shield as ever in the bottom boards, grabbed the oars, began to pull out into the long fjord that led to the open sea. As they rowed out Shef saw the English catapulteers standing by the machines that now guarded entrance to the harbor. They were shouting "What? What is it?"

Shef could only shrug helplessly as Cuthred rowed on.

CHAPTER TWENTY-ONE

A s Cuthred rowed the two-oared boat down the fjord, Shef saw a young man bounding down the rocky slope from one of the outlying farmsteads, waving desperately to be picked up. Shef signed to Cuthred to pull over.

"Maybe he can tell us what's going on."

The young man stepped out from one sharp-pointed rock to another, gauged the rise and fall of the boat on the waves, and dropped into the prow like a seal sliding on to a rock. He was smiling broadly.

"Thanks, mates," he said. "The grind comes every five years maybe. I don't want to miss it this time."

"What is the grind?" said Shef, waving down Cuthred's furious scowl.

"The grind?" The young man sounded as if he was unable to believe his ears. "The grind? Why—it's when the whales come, in a flock, a school. Come inside the skerries. Then, if we can get outside them, we drive them inshore, beach them. Kill them. Blubber. Oil. Whale-meat for the whole winter." His teeth showed in an ecstatic grin.

"Kill a school of whales?" Shef repeated. "How many will there be?"

"Maybe fifty, maybe sixty."

"Kill sixty whales," snarled Cuthred. "If you could do it, you lying Norse walrus-get, you could never eat them if you sat and ate till Doomsday."

"They're only the pilot whales," said the young man, sounding hurt. "Not the sperm whales or the big baleen whales. They're only ten, twelve ells long."

Fifteen to eighteen feet, thought Shef. Maybe it could be true.

"What do you kill them with?" he asked.

The young man grinned again. "Long lances," he said. "Or else this." He pulled a knife from his belt, long, broad, single-edged. Instead of a plain point it had a long sharpened hook, sharpened, Shef could see, on both its outside and inside edges.

"A grind-knife," the young man said. In his thick accent, the "f" became a "v", the long "i" an "oi." "*Grindar-knoivur*. Jump out of the boat in shallow water, straddle the whale, feel for its backbone, stab in to the side of it. Pull back. Cut the spine. Ha! Ha! Much meat, fat for the winter."

As the boat emerged from the mouth of the fjord, the young man looked round, saw the trail of dories all pulling rapidly away from them to the north, and without further words sat down on the thwart next to Cuthred, took an oar and began to row alongside him. Shef was surprised to see a sour grin on Cuthred's face, perhaps at the young Norseman's obvious assumption that Cuthred the mighty berserk needed assistance.

Ahead of them Shef saw the boats eventually ease to a halt, form a loose circle on the waves. And then, perhaps a half-mile beyond, Shef saw for the first time the school of whales they were pursuing: first a slow white spout against the gray sea, then another, then more of them all together. And beneath them, just a glimpse of black backs rolling easily in turn.

The men in the boats saw the rise as well, Shef could see them standing up, shaking their long-headed lances, and hear faint cries of excitement. Even from a distance, though, he could hear Brand's bull roar shouting them down, giving what sounded like a long string of explicit orders, boat by boat.

"You have to have a grind-captain," the young man explained between strokes. "If the boats do not work together, the whales will slip out. Everybody works together, and then we all share equally. One share for each man, one share for each boat, captain gets a double share."

Shef's boat came up with the main cluster just as they began to separate and move off. At the last moment the young man stood up, hailed a relative, and stepped from boat to boat with the same ease that he had joined them, pausing only to wave a cheerful farewell. Then all the Norse whaleboats, mostly four- or six-oared, moved off in a long unraveling string. Brand, positioned at the center of the line, turned to Shef as his boat moved off and shouted across the waves: "You two! Stay at the back, and don't do anything. Keep out of it!"

For a long time, Cuthred swung determinedly at the oars, maintaining station on the last boat in the long line. He seemed, Shef thought looking at his sweating frame, to have grown even stronger in the last few weeks, as solid food put a layer of fat over his tight-drawn mill-slave muscles. Yet it was hard work for one man to keep up even with the four-oared boats, all manned by skilled seamen. Cuthred stuck to it grimly. But in any case the whaleboats were not rowing at their maximum speed all the time. As the chase progressed, Shef realized there was a skill in it, a form of tactics.

Brand's first aim had been to get a line of boats outside the whale-pod, to the west, between them and the skerries that marked off the coastal channel from the open Atlantic. Once he had done that, he tried to move them inshore. Boats would swerve in close to the pod, and then stop, the crew leaning over and slapping the water with their oars. What this sounded like to whale-ears, who could tell? But the whales plainly did not like it, swerving away, trying to escape. Sometimes they tried to accelerate, to get round the far end of the line of boats. Then the lead dories would swing across, beat the water, force them to slow or turn back. Once it seemed as if the whale-leader had decided to turn round and swim back to the south, towards Shef and Cuthred bringing up the rear. For minutes the water was churned by black backs swarming close together, some swimming forward, some already turning back. Then all the boats moved in together, shouting and splashing, herding the whales towards the rocky shoals they feared.

Brand was relying also on panic, Shef realized as he got them moving again. And he had a particular place in mind. It was not enough to drive the whales on to the rock-bound coast. If it came to that they might turn and break through the line by sheer force. They had to be driven on to a killing-ground: a beach, for choice, but anyway an inlet or cove that they would be prepared to swim into but whose mouth could be firmly blocked. Best, too, if it could be done at high tide so that the ebb would leave the beasts stranded.

Slowly Brand jockeyed boats and whales till he had them where he wanted. The whales in a frothing mass just outside the entrance to the bay he had marked, the boats in a semi-circle from point to point of the bay. Then Brand waved his lance in one wide sweep and the boats moved in.

Brand himself made the first kill, his boat coming up alongside a slow-swimming cow-whale, while he leaned out, one foot on the gunwale, and drove home the long lance with its barbed head just forward of the low dorsal fin. From their position fifty yards behind Shef and Cuthred could see the instant flow of dark blood into the water—water whipped up instantly into a frenzy by lashing flukes.

The dying whale must have emitted some underwater bellow of agony, for the rest of the pod seemed to panic immediately, leaping forward away from the terror in their rear. Instantly they found themselves in the shallows, bellies grinding on gravel, tails rising out of the water as they fought for room. The other boats came in as one for the kill, a headsman in each prow looking for a place to plant his barb, the men shouting each other on.

As he watched Shef saw the first man leave his boat. It might have been the young man they had ferried, clutching his grind-knife, but he was followed by a dozen others, plunging recklessly into the turmoil of heaving bodies, seizing fins and trying to straddle their prey. Knives raised, plunged, plunged again as the men tried to find the vulnerable spot between vertebrae, where the hooked knife, hauled upwards, could sever the spinal cord and cause instant death. The whales twisted and thrashed, unable to fight back, unable to swim out, trying only to keep their tormentors from the kill.

"Looks risky," muttered Shef.

"But it isn't." Cuthred's voice had a note of disgust in it. "No more than killing sheep. Those things don't fight back, I don't think they have any teeth even. You could get squashed between two of them, but they're not even trying to hurt each other."

A group of men had hold of one whale and were running it up the beach as far as they could, seizing it by its fins and by the spears and blades protruding from it. They left it squirming weakly and ran down into the water for another. Already the whole surface of the bay had turned red from the streams of arterial blood pumping into it from the whales' punctured hearts. From the melee Shef saw a calf whale struggling free, having abandoned its dying mother. Barely six feet long, it floundered out of the shallows and made towards them for the open sea. A boat steered in front of it, a man leapt on to its back, grind-knife flailing. The spurt of blood that rose leapt into the boat, splashing his oar-mates. Shef heard them roar with laughter, saw another group on the shore already starting to flense the blubber from a dying whale, cramming handfuls into their mouths, and shouting with manic glee.

"I think we've seen enough of this," said Cuthred. "Nobody ever called me squeamish, but if I hurt people it's because I don't like them. I've got nothing against whales. I don't even like whalemeat."

He began to pull away from the cove of butchery, with Shef's silent agreement. The Norsemen, intent on their work, ignored them. By the time Brand thought to look up, they had gone.

* * *

Outside the cove, Shef was surprised to see how far the sun had gone down. At this time of year in a latitude as high as theirs, there could hardly be said to be a night-time. The sky remained pale continuously. Yet the sun did drop below the horizon for a short while every day. It was now close to it, the low red disc beneath the clouds sending long shadows across a placid sea. Cuthred bent to the oars and urged the boat along what would be a long trip back to a bed and fire. Shef became aware that it was hours since he had eaten or drunk; and he had begun the long boat-ride dehydrated from the steam-bath.

"Have you anything to eat in the boat?" he asked.

Cuthred grunted, "I always keep something in the cuddy there in the stern. Butter and cheese, a crock of milk, fresh water. Let me get us going and we can take turns to row and eat."

Shef found Cuthred's provision box in its compartment and hauled it out. It was well stocked, but for the moment Shef was content to drink water, chew on a wrinkled apple stored from the autumn before.

"You know," he remarked between bites. "This is the place Brand warned you away from. Inside the skerries, north of the island. I guess none of them come here much, from what he said. But with the grind out they wouldn't take any notice of where they were. And if there was anything dangerous it probably wouldn't want to mess with the grind boats. Not all of them together, all worked up."

"But it might just fancy two men on their own with the sun dropping," concluded Cuthred. His teeth showed in a snarl. "Well, just let it try."

Shef threw his apple-core overboard, squinted into the long shadows, reached forward and put a hand on Cuthred's brawny arm. He pointed silently.

Perhaps a quarter of a mile away, a giant fin showed above the water. It seemed almost man high, stuck straight up at right angles to the water. A black back showed beneath it, and then more of them, fins coming up out of the water, backs swirling and then dipping down like the top of enormous wheels.

"Killers," said Cuthred positively. They had seen several schools of them on the journey north in the *Walrus*, and each time Brand had gone to the side and regarded them speculatively. "Never heard of them attacking a ship," he had said. "Never heard of them attacking a boat either. But then, you wouldn't. If one of them decided to attack a boat there wouldn't be anyone left to tell about it. Seals are their meat. People must look pretty much like seals to them. I never go in the water if there's any of them about."

The lead fin suddenly changed course, angling sharply towards them. Without hesitation Cuthred swung the boat and headed for the rocky shore a hundred yards off. There was no chance of landing on it, it ran straight down into the water, but any kind of shoal or rock projection would keep the great beast off. It had certainly seen them, or sensed them. The fin was coming straight at them, a white wave cresting in front of it as it tore through the water.

The orcas had sensed the blood spilled in massive quantities into the water. They might have been following the pod of pilot whales themselves, intending to close in and make a kill. Could such a creature feel frustration at being forestalled? Resentment at the snatching of so many potential prey all at once? Anger against the land-apes, for so easily and ruthlessly destroying the whale-kind? It might just have been excitement from the blood, and a sportive urge to even the score against men moving so confidently out of their native element. The bull orca raced down on the small boat with menace in his very line. Shef felt instantly that he meant to toss the boat in the air, catch the men as they came down, and chop them to bits in the water with snaps of his great cone-toothed mouth.

"Head in," he called to Cuthred. "Right against the rock."

The boat glided along a sheer rock face, the two men reaching out for handholds to pull it closer in, uncomfortably aware of the deep water still only feet away. The fin lowered, rose up again till its tip was higher than Shef's head, sitting on the thwarts, and the whale surged alongside, almost rasping the boat's seaward gunwale. Shef saw the white markings under the black top, heard the sharp exhalation from the blowhole, saw its cold and careful eye on him. The tail slapped the water, the whale sounded, turning for another pass.

Shef seized an oar, thrust it against the rock, drove the boat a few yards along. Only feet away was the dark opening of a cove, a rocky inlet too small to call a fjord. Inside that the whale would be cramped, might turn away. The rest of the school were here now, sweeping past less closely than the bull-leader, filling the air with the spray from their blowholes.

Cuthred pushed too hard and the boat swerved away from shore. The bull was there instantly, boring in head first. Shef swung an oar, jerked the boat's bow back towards the inlet shore. As one man they thumped the oars into the rowlocks, heaved furiously, two strokes, three, rocketing into the quiet water of the inlet.

Something beneath them, lifting them irresistibly, the boat almost out of the water, starting to tip. If he fell in the water, Shef knew, the next thing he would feel would be great jaws about his middle. He hurled himself sideways, kicking with all his strength, and landed with one leg in the water and the other foot on a tiny rock ledge. A thrust, a heave and he was scrambling on to a tiny flat place, a hearthrug-sized patch of shingle on the rocky shore.

The boat turned over completely as the whale shook its body. Cuthred was launched out like a diver, turned in the air, a shower of objects coming down with him as the boat spilled its contents. His spiked shield, the one made of case-hardened steel, landed a foot from Shef's hand. He watched numbly as Cuthred splashed into the water and the whale turned.

Cuthred trod water for an instant, then seemed to find footing under him. He stepped backwards towards the land, only six feet from where Shef crouched, still thigh deep. Somehow, his sword was in his hand, he leveled it at the great black-and-white jaws boring in. The whale swerved and as it did so Cuthred thrust forward in a classic "long point," arm and body rigid.

A thump of contact, a sudden flurry, a slap of water from the tail. Then the whale was gone, leaving a thin trail of blood in the sea, and shattered planks where the boat had been.

Cuthred slowly straightened, wiping his sword on his wet sleeve. The provision box floated a few feet from him. He stepped forward again, up to his middle, and without haste gathered it in, turned and waded over to the ledge where Shef still crouched motionless.

"How do we get off here, then?" he asked. "I don't fancy swimming."

They crouched for a few minutes on the steep rock, looking across the little inlet. The whales were still there, cruising in and out. Once one of them rose to the stern of the boat, floating half-intact ten yards out from shore, took it without haste in its jaws, crunched down.

The two men turned awkwardly to look behind them at the rocky shore. The best that could be said was that it was not completely vertical, rather a stiff slope, steeper than the roof of a house, but made of a jumble of stone. There were handholds and footholds in plenty for a scramble. But the mountain-side seemed to go on and on, up to the pale sky with never a break. It could take hours to reach the top, hours with never a place to rest. Yet there was no choice. Slowly and carefully, aware of the deadly water a few feet away, the men gathered their meager possessions together. Cuthred had his sword and spiked targe. Impossible to carry them while scrambling up the mountain. After a moment Shef took the sword, cut a length from one leather shoelace, tied sword and shield together and showed Cuthred how to sling both on his back. The rope handles on the provision box could be extended, retied so as to make carrying straps. Shef fixed that on to his own back, made certain his short eating-knife was still in its sheath, the fire-flint he always carried next to it. He carried nothing else except the gold bracelets on his arms, was unarmed save for the belt-knife.

They began, carefully and slowly, to make their way up the mountain-side. For what seemed an age they crept from rock to rock, on all fours all the way, trying to angle round vertical precipices, never quite coming on the impassable, never finding a place to stop, to sit or even stand in safety. Shef's thigh muscles began to ache, then to jump spasmodically. At any moment, he felt, the cramp might strike. Then he would lose his grip and fall, or roll, all the way to the water. Looking down, he saw nothing but unforgiving stone all the way down to the metal-gray sea, still patrolled by the orca fins. He forced himself to thrust himself up another few feet. Brace a foot, push again, haul with all the failing strength of his arms.

A voice was talking to him. Cuthred's, just a few feet above. "Lord," it said. "Three more steps, two more steps. A place here to rest."

As if in reaction to what Cuthred said, Shef felt the searing pain of cramp in his right thigh. He knew he had to override it, but there was no strength left. He felt the leg give way, tightened his fingers despairingly on their last hold.

Fingers seized his hair, yanked mercilessly with terrible strength. Shef felt himself lifted off his feet like a puppy, hauled up and over a ledge. He lay belly down, gasping. Cuthred seized him by his breeches and hauled him the last few feet, rolled him over and began to knead his thigh.

After a score of deep indrawn breaths, Shef felt the pain ease. He knuck-led involuntary tears from his eyes and sat up.

They were on what seemed for all the world like a narrow path, no more than a foot and a half wide, but luxury after the mountain-side. It ran along the side of the inlet, visible either way for only a few yards. Just on the seaward side of the place where they sat, it seemed to fork, one part continuing to run along horizontally, the other turning uphill.

Cuthred pointed to the second fork. "I reckon that might go up to the highest point of the ness," he said. "Good lookout point. I'll go along there, see what there is. Maybe we can find some wood, light a beacon. The whalers are bound to come back past here sometime."

Not for a while, Shef thought. And even then they may decide to keep outside the line of the skerries, as they do when they're not hot on the trail of the grind. But Cuthred had already slipped away, sword and shield now ready in his hands. What made this path anyway, Shef reflected. Goats?

What else could live up here but mountain goats? Strange that they had worn such a clear track.

Suddenly aware again of his own hunger and thirst, he unslung the provision box, pulled out the milk crock, took a long slow draught of it. As he set it down again, he felt depression and despair settle round his shoulders like a heavy blanket.

The view in front of him was unutterably bleak: gray sea far below, tossing restlessly on gray stone. Above it, just rock and jumbled scree rising all the way to a ridge far above the level where Shef sat. And above that, another higher ridge, and another, rising up to the snow that never melted. White snow and gray stone merged into a sky from which every hint of color had been washed. No hint of green grass, no hint of blue sky, only the everlasting paleness of the high latitudes. Shef felt as if he were at the end of the world, and about to fall off it. The sweat of toil and pain was drying on him, turning him cold and clammy in the little bitter wind that whispered along the mountain-side.

If he died here, who would know? The gulls and the carnivorous skuas would eat his flesh, and then his bones would bleach for ever in the wind. Brand would wonder what had happened for a while. He might never bother to pass word to the south, to Godive and Alfred. They would forget him in a few seasons. His whole life seemed to Shef, in those moments, to be a remorseless pursuit from one disaster to another. The death of Ragnar and the beating he had got from his stepfather. The rescue of Godive, and his blinding. The battles he had fought, and the price he had paid for them. Then the stranding on the sandbank, the march to Hedeby, the way Hrorik had sold him to the Way in Kaupang, the disaster on the ice, his betrayal by Ragnhild, and the killing of little Harald. It all seemed of a piece: momentary success, bought by pain and loss. And now here, stranded beyond hope of rescue, in a place where no human foot had trod since the beginning of time. Maybe it would be better to let go now, fall down the hillside, and vanish from sight for ever.

Shef slumped back, shoulders against the stone, the provision box still open by his side. He felt the sight coming on him, taking over his mind and body in his exhausted, waking swoon.

I told you before, something told him. Remember the wolves in the sky and the serpents in the sea. That is what the pagans see when they look at the world. Now see another picture.

Shef found himself in the body of another man, like himself, exhausted, in pain, close to despair and even closer to death. The man was stumbling along a rocky slope, not as steep as the one Shef had just climbed. But the man was in worse shape. There was something heavy on his shoulder, grinding into it, but he could not put it down or move it to the other. It was rubbing grimly into his back too, and the back was afire—Shef's own back twinged with remembered sympathy, from the pain of a fresh flogging, the sort that tore open the skin and slashed deep into the flesh and bone beneath.

Yet in some way the man welcomed the pain and the exhaustion. Why? He knew, Shef felt, that the more exhausted he became, the shorter his sufferings would soon become.

They were there. Wherever there was. The man dropped the burden he had been carrying, a great wooden beam. Others took it, men in a strange kind of armor, not mail but metal strips. They fitted it to a still larger beam. Why, Shef realized, this is a cross. I am seeing the crucifixion. Of the White Christ? Why would my patron-god show that to me? We are not Christians. We are their enemies.

They had stretched him out and were driving home the nails, one through each wrist, not the palms where flesh would tear through as soon as full weight came on them, but between the bones of the forearm. Another through the feet, a tricky job to line them both up. Mercifully, by this stage the pain was not coming through to the Shef-mind observing. Instead, it looked hard at the men doing the grim task.

They were working quickly as if they had done this many times before, talking to each other in a language Shef did not understand. Yet as the moments went by he found he could catch a word or two: hamar, they said, nagal. But for "cross" they said, not rood as he expected, but something that sounded like crouchem. Roman soldiers, so Shef had always been told, but talking some kind of German dialect, with a garbled kitchen-Latin thrown in.

The man on the cross fainted as they hauled him up. Then his eyes opened again, and he was looking out, as Shef was doing now, as Shef had done years before after his blinding. Then he had seen the vision of Edmund, the martyred Christian king, coming to him with his backbone in his hand, and then passing on—elsewhere. So there was a place for Christians to go, as well as the Valhalla of the pagans.

The sun was already beginning to sink over Calvary. For a few brief seconds, Shef saw it as the dying man, or man-god, saw it. Not the chariot drawn by terrified horses and pursued by ravening wolves of pagan belief, just as the earth and sea below were not the haunt of giant serpents seeking only to destroy mankind. Instead the man looking up saw, not chariot nor disk of gold, but a glowing bearded face looking down, full of both sternness and compassion. It

*looked down on a world of creatures that threw up their arms to him and begged
for help, for forgiveness, for mercy.*

*Eloi, eloi, cried the dying man, lama sabachthani. My God, my God, why
hast thou forsaken me.*

*The glowing face shook in denial. Not a forsaking, a cure. A bitter potion for
the sins of the world, an answer to the beseeching arms. And now a final mercy.*

*A man stepped forward from the ranks drawn up at the foot of the cross, red
cloak above his armor, red hackle cresting his iron helmet. Inoh, he said in the
same half-German gabble that his soldiers had used. Giba me thin lancea.*
"Enough, give me your lance."

*The dying man found a sponge at his lips, sucked at it feverishly, tasting the
thin sour wine that the soldiers had as a daily ration to mix into their water. As
the blessed relief flowed down his parched throat, tasting better than anything he
had drunk in the world before, the centurion below freed the lance from the
sponge he had held up, dropped it two feet, poised it carefully, and then thrust
home under the ribs to split the convict's heart.*

*Blood and water ran over his hand, and he gazed at the mixture with sur-
prise. At the same moment he felt the world shift around him, as if something
had forever altered. He looked up, and instead of the grim burning sun of this
parched and desert land, he saw what seemed to be his own dead father's face
smiling down at him. Around him a thrill of exultation seemed to rise from the
sand, and beneath his feet a cry of relief came from the rocks, from under the
rocks, from Hell itself where the prisoners saw their promised salvation.*

*The centurion swayed, caught himself, looked down again at the ordinary
issue lance dripping blood and water down his hand and arm.*

*Now that is what the Christians see, said the voice of his guardian to Shef.
They see a rescue from outside where the pagans see only a fight they cannot
win and dare not lose. All well and good—if there is a rescuer.*

The vision faded, left Shef sitting on the barren rock. He blinked, thinking
about what he had seen. The trouble is, he saw in a moment of contrast,
that the Christians put their trust in rescue, and so do not struggle for
themselves, just put their faith in their Church. The pagans struggle for
victory, but they have no hope. So they bury girls alive and roll men under
their longships, for they feel there is no good in the world. The Way must
be between these two. Something that offers hope, which the pagans do
not have: even Othin could not bring back his son Balder from the dead.
Something that depends on your own efforts, which the Christian Church
rejects: to them salvation is a gift, a grace, not something mere humanity
can earn.

He sat up, bothered by a sudden feeling of being watched, looked round for Cuthred, realized he had still not returned. He groped once more for the open provision box, hoping food and drink would put better heart into him. More milk, thick cheese and biscuit.

Seemingly sprung from out of the stone, a figure appeared before him. Shef found his mouth hanging open in mid-bite.

CHAPTER TWENTY-TWO

It took Shef a moment to realize that the figure was a little boy, a young child. Yet he was hardly little. He stood about five feet high, no shorter than Udd the metalworker, and a good deal broader. He could have been a small man. Yet something in the earnest innocence of his stance suggested youth.

And he did not look like any man at all. His arms hung low, his head slanted forward on an impossibly thick neck. Small eyes peered out under heavy eyebrows. He was dressed in—nothing. No, he had on a rough kilt made of some kind of skin. But it almost vanished against his own pelt. The child was covered from head to foot in long gray hair.

His eyes were fixed unmoving on the piece of cheese Shef was in the act of lifting to his mouth. His nostrils flared suddenly as he smelt it, and thin drool began to run from the side of his mouth. Slowly Shef took the cheese from the biscuit he had laid it on and passed it wordlessly to the strange boy.

Who hesitated, not wanting to come closer. Finally he came forward two paces, in a kind of awkward shamble, stretched out a long gray arm, and snatched the cheese from Shef's hand. He sniffed it, the nostrils flaring again, and then took it into his mouth with one sudden snap. He chewed, eyes closing in a kind of rapture, thin lips pulled back over what seemed to be massive canine teeth. His feet shuffled in an incongruous, involuntary dance of glee.

Finns can't turn down cheese or milk or butter, so Brand had said. He did not think this creature was a Finn. But maybe it felt the same way about food. Still moving gently, Shef handed over the crock with the remains of Cuthred's milk in it. Again the careful exploration with the nostrils, the sudden decision and the instant draft. As he—or it—drank, it bent its knees oddly so as to tilt its body back. It could not throw its head back to drink like a proper person, Shef realized.

Finished, it dropped the crock. The noise as it shattered on the stone seemed to startle it, it looked down, looked across at Shef. Then, there was no doubt, it said something, and the something had all the tone of "I'm sorry." But Shef could understand not a syllable of what it said.

And then it was gone, whisking away down the path for a couple of paces, and then just gone, vanished, gray pelt merging with the gray stone. Shef scrambled to his feet and ran stiffly to the point where it had disappeared, but there was nothing to be seen. It had vanished like his own dream.

One of the Huldu-folk, Shef thought. You have seen one of the Hidden People, the people who live in the mountain. He remembered Brand's tales of the things that pulled people underwater, the long gray arms stretching out to seize boats. And the tales Cwicca and his gang told, of men caught in the mountains by female trolls and forced to serve them. They had been telling one only the other night: of a great wizard, a wise man, who had made it his task to free some island in the Northlands from the trolls and the Hidden People. He had gone all over the island, saying the words of power and driving the creatures out so they could harm men and women no more. In the end he had had himself lowered down the last cliff on the island to finish the job. But as they let out the rope from above, a voice had come from the cliff itself. "Manling," it had said, "you must leave some place for even the hidden folk to be." And with that a gray arm had come from the cliff and plucked the man from his hold and hurled him on to the rocks below. It didn't make sense, Shef had told them. Who could have heard the words but the man on the rope, the man hurled to his death a moment later? Suddenly the story seemed to make much better sense.

Cuthred was still nowhere to be seen. Shef opened his mouth to shout, closed it. Who could tell what might hear? He picked up a stone flake from the ground, scratched an arrow on the lichen-covered stone, pointing in the direction he was taking, inland. He left the provision box lying and began to sidle along the rocky narrow path as fast as he could.

It twisted on along the side of the inlet, but far above it, for perhaps half a mile, often narrowing to a bare foothold, never quite vanishing entirely. One of Brand's bird's-nesters would have followed it without hesitation.

Karli the flatlander would have frozen with terror. Shef, a flatlander too, hobbled on carefully, sweating with fear and exertion, trying not to look down.

And then there was a clearing in front of him. In the dim half-light Shef looked round cautiously. A clearing? At least a flat place with a thin poor covering of grass and weeds in the everlasting stone. Why had they not seen the green from the sea? Because the whole place was hidden, in a dip in the ground between sea and mountain. On the other side of it, a chink of light. A fire? A cabin?

Stepping very cautiously forward, Shef realized it was indeed a cabin. Stone walled, turf roofed, set against the further hillside as if it had grown there. Even at fifty yards Shef could hardly be sure he was seeing it, though a dim glow came from some chink or other in its wall.

As he thought that, Shef realized that his left hand was actually resting on another wall, right by him. He had walked up to another building and still not seen it. Yet a building it was, and a big one, a lean-to of stone slabs running forty feet from the point where the path came out to what might be a door at the other end. He could smell something too. Smoke, and a faint flavor of food.

Hand on knife, and moving as gently as a fowler creeping up on a nest, Shef ghosted up to the door. Not a door, a leather curtain pegged across. He slipped the thongs off the pegs and eased inside.

For twenty heartbeats he was unable to see. Then his eye adjusted. Dim light was coming in from cracks in the wall, and from an opening in the roof, under which a low fire glowed. A carcass hung over it. It was a smokehouse, Shef saw. All along the far side stood rack after rack of split, smoked and dried fish. All along the near side, tubs of more fish, salted, fish and meat. In front of him, hanging from a peg, a seal carcass, with more in rows down the length of the building. He stretched a hand up to feel. The peg was of stone, the hook that supported the split seal of wood, not carved but bent and allowed to grow into the correct shape. Nothing he could see was of metal. Only wood, and stone.

The carcasses grew bigger as he walked fascinated down the row. Seal. A walrus, so large it stretched from roof to floor. And then a bear. Not the brown bear of the forests in the south, common in Norway, still to be found in the deep woods of England. No, a creature as much bigger than that as an orca was bigger than a porpoise, far bigger than Shef as it hung there flitched and jointed. White fur still showed on it here and there. It was a great white bear like the one that had furnished Brand's best robe, an animal that had cost three lives to bring down, or so Brand said.

He was almost at the smoke now, where the fire glowed and the light came in from the roof. What was this creature that the mighty hunter of the mountains had brought down? Not a seal, not a walrus, not a porpoise nor a bear. Shef realized that there, turning gently in the smoke, hanging from a peg, was a man. Halved, stripped, gutted and chined, like a pig, but still certainly a man. Others too, racked behind him, men and women as well, hanging like so many flitches of bacon, some by the throat, some by the feet. The women's breasts drooped on their naked flanks.

Shef saw that there were other things piled carelessly in a corner. Clothes, mostly, thrown there in disorder. Glint of metal here and there, silver and enamel work and iron too. Whatever had caught and killed these people cared nothing for booty. It had all been tossed aside like horns or hooves or anything inedible. Was there a weapon there?

Two pegs on the wall supported between them a dozen long-shafted spears. Shef picked one up, realized immediately it was worm-eaten and bent from lying for years in the heat. He rummaged through them as silently as he could.

Junk, all of them. Split shafts, bent heads, metal thick with rust. He had to find something. He had only his tiny beltknife against a creature that could kill walruses and polar bears.

There. There was one. At the bottom of the pile Shef glimpsed a shaft that seemed to be sound. He picked it up, hefted it, felt relief sweep over him at the thought he was now not completely defenseless.

Somehow, as he hefted it, the idea of using it to strike and kill repelled him. It was as if a voice was telling him: "No. This is not the tool for such a purpose. It would be like trying to pick hot metal from the forge with a hammer, or beating out iron with the haft of your tongs."

Puzzled, Shef looked for a moment at what he held, his eye continually glancing in fear towards the entrance. A strange weapon. Not the sort anyone made nowadays. A leaf-shaped blade unlike the massive triangular head of Sigurth's 'Gungnir,' a long iron spike below it set into an ash shaft. Traces of ornamentation on it. Someone had even cut into the iron and then set gold into the tracery. Once there had been two gold crosses at the base of the blade. The gold was gone now, betrayed only by a fleck of color, but the chiseled crosses remained. A war weapon, from the iron spike, and a javelin from its weight. But who would put gold on a javelin which you hurled at your enemy?

Someone had valued it, at any rate. Some one of the carcasses now hanging in the smoke. Shef hefted the weapon uncertainly once more. It was madness not to take any weapon that would give him a chance of survival in this deadly place. Why had he already put it back, laying it gently once more across its pegs?

Alarmed suddenly by some faint stir of air behind him, Shef span round. Someone, or something, coming. He crouched, looking along the floor beneath the rows of human and animal bodies.

Someone was walking towards him. With a flush of relief Shef recognized the cross-tied breeches of Cuthred. He stepped out into plain sight, beckoned his companion over, pointed wordlessly to the hanging corpses.

Cuthred nodded. His sword was bare in one hand, his shield ready in the other.

"I told you," he whispered hoarsely. "Trolls. In the mountains. Peered at me through the windows of the hut. Rattled the door in the night to try to get in. They smelt meat. Thick bars they have on the doors in those mountain villages. Not that all of them need them."

"What do we do?"

"Get them before they get us. The cabin opposite, you saw it? Let's go. Have you no weapon?"

Shef shook his head mutely.

Cuthred stepped behind him, picked the spear he had just laid down from its pegs, held it out to him. "Here," he said, "take this. Go on," he urged, seeing Shef's reluctance, "it doesn't belong to anyone any more."

Shef stretched out a hand, hesitated, gripped the weapon firmly. In the warm, smoky dark there came a faint ringing sound, as if the metal head had struck stone. Shef felt a kind of relief again. Not relief from defenselessness, rather relief that the weapon had been handed to him. It had passed from its owner to the master of the smokehouse, and then to Cuthred, the man who was not a man. It was right for him to hold it now. Maybe not to keep it, maybe not to strike with it. But hold it, yes. For now.

The two men made their way out into the suddenly sweet-smelling air.

They moved across the small open space like two ghosts, treading carefully round the weeds to prevent the faintest brush or rattle. One mistake here, Shef thought, and they too would be hanging in the smoke. Had the little boy run ahead to warn his people? His father? He had seemed grateful rather than fearful or hostile. Shef did not want to have to kill him.

The door of the cabin, like that of the smokehouse, was covered with a pegged leather curtain, seemingly of horsehide. Should they try to lift it gently, or slash it down and charge through? Cuthred had no doubts. He waved Shef silently to hold the top of the curtain, then took his sword and applied its razor-sharp edge to each of the retaining loops in turn. The curtain hung loose, held only by Shef's hand. Cuthred nodded.

As Shef dropped the curtain, Cuthred whisked inside, sword poised. Then stood motionless. Shef moved in after him. The cabin was empty of life, but not bare. To their left stood what must be the main room, a rough table in the center with stools round it made of driftwood. The stools were of immense size. Shef would have had to climb up to sit on one. In the far corner a black entrance seemed to lead into the rock. The whole scene was lit by a wick burning in a stone bowl of oil.

Perhaps the inhabitants were all asleep. It was midnight, certainly, even though the sky remained light. But Shef had noted that in midsummer the Norse-folk lost most sense of time, sleeping when they needed to, and sleeping very little, as if they saved that up for the appalling winters. The Huldu-folk could be the same.

To their right, though, that must be the sleeping-chamber, reached through another narrow opening. Shef braced himself for what might have to be a killing thrust, and slid through the doorway, javelin poised. Two beds, yes, like shelves in the rock, to conserve warmth, heaped with skins and furs. Shef moved closer to check that the furs were all animal furs, not the gray pelt of a troll. No, nothing there.

As he turned to sign to Cuthred a great crash sent his heart into his mouth. He sprang forward to see what had happened. In the middle of the other room, by the overturned table, Cuthred was grappling savagely with a troll.

A female troll. She too wore a kind of kilt round her waist, but breasts swelled beneath her gray pelt, long hair hung down her back like a horse's mane. She had hidden inside the larder in the rock, leapt out as Cuthred closed on it. With one hand she grasped the spike on his round targe, with the other the wrist of his sword-hand. The two swayed backwards and forwards, Cuthred trying to free a weapon, she trying to wrest them away. Her teeth flashed in a sudden snap at Cuthred's face.

Shef gaped, amazed for a moment at the woman's strength. Cuthred was putting out every ounce of effort that he had, grunting furiously as he heaved at her, the immense muscles straining in his arms. Twice he had her off the ground, lifting her two hundred pounds easily, but she clung on.

Then suddenly she was moving forward, Cuthred pushed back, and as she gained momentum she thrust a heel behind his ankle and tripped him. The two went over together, the troll on top, and Cuthred's sword and shield went sprawling. An instant later and she had whipped a stone knife from her belt, was driving it at Cuthred's throat. Cuthred caught her wrist with one hand, and again they were frozen in a desperate test of strength.

The javelin was a hindrance in the narrow doorway. As Shef stepped sideways to try to angle through the door of the sleeping chamber, the dim light from outside was blocked. The master of the house, the hunter of the mountains, had returned. He stepped soundlessly through the outer door like a moving slab of rock, turned towards the struggle.

Even stooping, his skull brushed the ceiling. His arms hung almost to the floor. His shoulders were round and sloping, not square like a man's, but even so the space between his shoulder-blades was wide enough to fit a sword-blade lengthwise. His back was turned to Shef, whom he had not noticed, his attention fixed on Cuthred and the female.

Shef poised the spear. He had one chance for a completely unprotected strike, at spine or kidneys or angling up under the ribs for the heart. Not even a giant could survive that. In front of him, he knew, was the man-eater.

As he poised for the strike, a sense filled Shef suddenly of the utter dreariness of the place. He had felt it before, sitting on the ledge of the mountain path, a sense of colorlessness, harshness, hostility. Then in the passing vision he had seen and felt the world begging for a rescue, for a release, and the sun-face granting it; granting what had not been granted to Hermoth, or to Balder. The iron lance-shaft by his cheek seemed to exude both warmth, and a kind of weariness, an urge to desist from slaughter. The world had seen too much of it. Time for a pause, a change.

The female troll squatting on Cuthred's chest suddenly shot head-first across the room and crashed into the legs of the male, sending him staggering backwards almost on to Shef's spear-point. Cuthred had forced her back so that all her strength was pushing forwards, then dropped his hands, seized her ankles and hurled her clean over his head. He twisted and came to his feet, sword once again in hand, confronting the male troll with a grin of reckless fury. A snarl like a bear's came from the male troll as he thrust the female out of the way.

Shef slammed his spear-butt on to the stone floor and shouted at the top of his voice, "Stop!"

Both trolls jumped round to face him, eyes swiveling between the threat in front and the threat to their rear. Shef shouted again, this time to Cuthred gliding forward, "Stop!"

At the same moment the small male troll he had seen on the path ran through the outer door, clutched the large male round the legs and pattered out a long stream of syllables. Shef stepped through the narrow doorway of the sleeping-chamber, spread his arms wide and carefully propped his spear in a corner. He waved imperiously at Cuthred, who hesitated, doubtfully lowered his sword.

What of the trolls? Shef looked at them in the light of the lamp, looked again, looked a third time at the great male, standing staring down at him with a puzzled expression. A familiar puzzled expression. Gray pelt, round skull, strange undershot jaw and massive teeth. But something—something in the eyebrows, the cheekbones, the square set of head on pillared neck. Gently, Shef walked forward, took the male's enormous hand, turned it over in his own. Yes. Huge fingers, a fist that if doubled would be the size of a quart-pot.

"You look like someone I know," said Shef, almost to himself.

To his surprise the troll grinned broadly, showing huge canines, and replied in halting but recognizable Norse.

"I think you meet my good cousin Brand."

According to Echegorgun—much of the substance of what he had to say was passed on in the end to Shef by Cuthred over many days and many campfires—the Hidden People had once lived much further to the south, in Norway and in other countries below what Echegorgun called the Shallow Sea, the Baltic. But as time went by and the climate changed they had

followed the ice north, harried all the way and all the time by the Chinned
Ones, the Thin People, the Beaters of Iron—Echegorgun had many names
for them. Humans were not, of course, formidable—Echegorgun laughed
at the very thought that they might be, making a strange harsh noise deep
in his throat. But there were a lot of them. They breed as fast as the seals,
he said, or as fast as the salmon spawn. And in groups they were dangerous, more so as they acquired metal. It seemed that the memories of the
Hidden People went back to the days before humans had metal, when all
the Walking Creatures, humans and Hidden Ones, had only stone. But
once the humans had metal, first bronze—Echegorgun called it the brown
iron—and then true iron, gray iron itself, the old equality between the
species, if species they were, began to break down. Echegorgun would not
admit or concede it, but Shef thought sometimes that the fast-breeding
which Echegorgun so much despised and thought less than fully sapient,
had something to do with the metal. Beating iron out of ore does not come
naturally, is the result of learning based on trial and error based on initial
lucky accident. Short-lived creatures with little to lose and strong reasons
for wanting to distinguish themselves among their too-many competitors,
they would be much more likely to waste time on mere experimentation
than the longer-lived, slow-maturing, slow-breeding True Folk (as they
called themselves).

Whether that were true or not, over the centuries the True Folk had
become the Hidden People, keeping to the inaccessible mountains, developing the skills of hiding themselves away. It was not so difficult,
Echegorgun said. There were more True Folk around than most of the
Thin Ones realized. They did not inhabit the same ranges, or even the
same times. The Norse in Halogaland, Echegorgun said, being specific,
were almost entirely coastal. They went up and down the sea road, the
North Way from which the country got its name, they built their huts in
the fjords, they pastured their animals in the bits of summer grazing they
could reach. Rarely did one find any of them more than a few miles inland.
Especially as those who did penetrate inland, exploring or hunting, were
not at all likely to return.

The Finns were more of a nuisance, for they roamed widely with their
reindeer herds, their sledges and bows and traps. Yet their roaming was
mostly in the summer and in the day. In the winter they kept to their tents
and their cabins and their regular trap rounds, all easy to avoid. The snow
and the ice, the dark and the high places, Echegorgun said, they belong to
us. We are the People of the Dark.

And what about the dead men you hang in your smokehouse, Shef asked him on the afternoon of their first meeting. Echegorgun took the question seriously. It was the seal-skerries that caused the trouble, he said. The Thin Ones had to be kept off them, or at least off those of them he regarded as his own. Shef slowly realized that Echegorgun, like the rest of his people, was as near amphibious as a polar bear, which are often found swimming contentedly well out of sight of land. His pelt kept the cold out, and was as waterproof as a seal's. Any of the adults would think little of swimming a couple of miles in the freezing water to a skerry, there to club seals or harpoon walruses. Sea-mammals were a great part of their diet. They did not like the Thin Ones to go there, and discouraged them by ambush. The stories about gray arms turning boats over were true. As for smoking and eating their prey—Echegorgun shrugged. He could see no harm in eating your kill. The Thin Ones might not eat the Hidden People, but they would kill them for any reason or for none, not because the Hidden People ate their food. So which was worse?

In any case, there was no real need for ambushes and killings, if everyone kept to their side of known lines. Trouble might arise in times of famine. If the grain crop failed—Echegorgun thought it was bound to fail three years in ten—then the Thin Ones started to come out and hunt the skerries in desperation. Don't eat grain, that was the answer, don't breed so fast you have to rely on chancy foods. But real northerners, the real northerners among the humans, Echegorgun said, emphasizing this distinction, they did not let things get so far. They knew their place, and they knew his. The humans he killed, they were always visitors who did not respect the slowly-evolved boundaries.

"Like the man who left this?" said Shef, holding up the spear he had taken.

Echegorgun took it, felt it, snuffed at the metal in a considering way with his great flaring nostrils. "Yes," he said. "I remember him. A jarl of the Tronds, from Trondhjem. Foolish people. Always want to take over the Finn-tax and the Finn-trade, take it from Brand and his family. He came up here in a longship. I followed it till they camped on an island, he and two others went to hunt birds' eggs. After he had gone—he and some more—the rest lost heart and went home."

"How did you know he was a jarl?" asked Shef.

"The Huldu-folk know a lot. They are told some things. They see many more, in the dark, in the quiet."

Echegorgun would say no more at that point, but Shef was confident that he and Brand's family had ways of getting in touch with each other—sign left on a skerry maybe, rocks left a certain way till there was need of communication, and then altered to bring out an envoy. The Hidden Folk might have been an advantage to the Halogalanders, in getting rid of unwanted rivals from the south. Brand and his family in return kept pressure off certain fixed areas.

And besides, there was family feeling. Echegorgun smiled salaciously when Shef hinted at it. Years before, he said, the father of Brand's father Barn, a man named Bjarni, had been stranded on a skerry by a shipwreck. He had had food with him, good food, milk and whey, and had set it out as bait for the Hidden People. A girl of that race had seen it, taken the bait. He had not caught her, no, how could a Thin One catch even a girl of the True Folk? But he had shown her what he had got for her, and she had been enticed. You Thin Ones are thick in one place, Echegorgun said, his eyes rolling to Cuthred sitting close to the female he had wrestled.

Echegorgun went on to say that the girl, his own aunt, had kept the baby men called Barn till it was evident that it would be smooth-skinned, or too smooth-skinned to live like the True Folk. Then she had left it by its father's door. But first Bjarni, and then Barn, and then Brand, had remained conscious of their kinship at need.

Shef heard little of what was said then, for he had begun to worry about Cuthred. Thin Ones might be thick in one place, but Cuthred had no place at all. He had been behaving well up in the north, yet one thing Shef was sure of: any reminder of his mutilation, any sexual display by a male or provocation by a female, and Cuthred would revert to the berserker. And yet it was strange. He was sitting talking to the female Miltastaray, daughter of Echegorgun and sister of the little boy Ekwetargun, as if she were Martha or one of the least-challenging of the slave-women. Perhaps it was because he had overpowered her. Perhaps it was because she was female, but so different that there was no need or expectation of flirtatiousness between them. Either way, Cuthred seemed secure and safe, for the moment.

Shef turned his attention back to Echegorgun's story. By this time the five creatures—men and a woman? people? humans and not-humans?—had left the hut and were sitting out under a risen sun in the flat patch between hut and smokehouse. From where they were they could see a calm gray metallic sea, with islands rising from it, but were sheltered from closer observation. The Hidden Folk had a keen sense of "dead ground," Shef was to note. They kept always out of direct lines of sight, whatever else they seemed to be doing.

"So you see much, and are told more?" he said. "What do you know about me? About us?"

"About him," Echegorgun pointed with his underslung chin to Cuthred, "much. He was a thrall in the mountains south of here. Some of our people tried to get him out. Maybe they would have eaten him, maybe not. You people are hard on your own kind. I know what they did to him. It would not mean so much to us. We think of other things than mating.

"About you." Shef found deep brown eyes fixed on him. "There is no news of you. But people are following you."

Shef laughed. "That is no news to me."

"Other things are following you too. The killer whales that attacked you —sometimes they do that, I know, if they feel like sport or if something annoys them. But I have seen that school of them going up and down, and they are not from near here. They have come up from the south, like you. Maybe after you.

"Still, if you know people are following you, I need not tell you the rest."

Echegorgun stretched his enormous arms, over nine feet from finger-tip to finger-tip, with an air of complete indifference.

"What rest? Are other people following me now?"

"There is a ship hidden in the Vitazgjafi fjord half a day's swim south of Brand's farmsteads on Hrafnsey. I would have warned him but he is away with the grind—the grind, you understand, is within his rights. He was careful not to drive them ashore here or near here. But anyway, he is away, and the ship is down there waiting. A big ship. It has two . . . two sticks. Those things you put cloths on. A big fair-haired woman shouts orders at the menfolk." Echegorgun laughed. "She needs a winter with me to calm her."

Shef considered furiously. The woman was Ragnhild, the ship the one that had tried to sink them in the Gula-fjord. "What do you think they mean to do?"

Echegorgun looked at the sun. "If they did not attack last sunset, they will attack this one. The two ships Brand has will not be ready to fight. He will have taken them up to the grind-beach and loaded them up with oil and meat. The strangers will catch everyone else asleep or tired. The grind makes much work."

"Will you not warn them?"

Echegorgun looked surprised, as far as his flat hair-covered face would show it. "I would warn my cousin Brand. For the rest—the more Thin Ones kill each other, the better. I know you spared me when you could have struck me with the spear, so now I spare you, for True Folk keep their bargains, even if they have not been said. You fed my boy, my

Ekwetargun as well. But I would be wiser to twist your head off your shoulders and hang you with the others."

Shef ignored the threat. "I can tell you one thing you do not know," he said. "I am a man who has authority. I am a king in my own land. Some say I am a sort of a king even here. And I speak for many people. Here is one sign of my authority." He showed the Rig-token, the kraki, round his neck, and pointed to the one he had made for Cuthred. "It may be I could do something for you. For you and your kind. Make the men stop hunting you. Let you live in a place less stony. But you would have to do something for me. Help me defeat those men from the south, and the woman with them, and their ship."

"Well, I could do that," said Echegorgun carefully. He rose to a strange squatting position, gripping his bare feet in his enormous hands.

"How? Would you warn Brand? Would you—fight on our side? You would be a mighty warrior if we gave you iron to use."

Echegorgun shook his massive head. "I will do neither of those. But I could speak to the whales for you. They are worked up already. If they thought I had killed you, they might feel like listening to me. And these are stranger whales, of course. If they were my own folk I would not deceive them."

CHAPTER TWENTY-THREE

Bruno, *Hauptritter* of the *Lanzenorden,* stood in front of a double rank of his armored knights, pikes sloped, standing immobile at attention as he had made their custom. All were looking at the ceremony taking place a hundred yards in front of them. They could have got a better view by marching closer, but one could not be sure how the natives would take interference in their sacred custom. Bruno had no objection to interfering with the barbaric customs of the natives, but this was not the time.

A roar came from the thousand throats of the men clustered at the center of the doom-ring of the Gautish peoples, a roar and a clashing of weapons on shields.

"What's that mean?" muttered a voice from the rear rank. "They've made a decision?"

"Silence in the ranks," said Bruno, though without heat. The *Lanzenorden* believed strongly in the theoretical equality of all its members, without the savage discipline that had to be imposed on armies of peasants. "Yes, look, they have a king. *Habeunt regem,*" he added, parodying the formula for the election of a Pope.

A figure rose, swaying wildly, from the throng in front of them. A man lifted on a shield by a dozen eager supporters. Once he caught his balance, he looked round, drew his sword, shouted out his name and the traditional formula of proclamation. "I am the king of the Gauts. Who denies it?"

A moment's silence, then the clashing of weapons again. A week before, and a dozen chieftains would have denied it. Fighting it out hand to hand would have deprived the Gautish peoples of most of their ruling class, the rich and the god-born together. So for days the meeting, the *Gautalagathing,* the Thing of those bound by the Law of the Gauts, had been abuzz with messengers, rumors, offers of support and retractions, deals and promises. Now it was all settled. Till the next shift of power.

The crowd began to disperse towards the smell of roasted oxen and the great vats of beer which the new king would provide as part of the price of his election. The German *Ritters* watched them with a certain envy, a certain scorn. Bruno decided to hold them in their ranks a little longer, to make certain no-one went down to the party, got into a fight.

Another figure was coming towards them, the scrawny black-clad Englishman, Erkenbert. As he came closer Bruno saw a slight flush of excitement on his pale face, and felt his own heart thud in anticipation. The Englishman was holding one of his everlasting lists.

"Do you think you've found it?" said Bruno as soon as the other was in earshot.

"Yes. Down at the tents I found an old man. Too old to attend the election, but not so old that he had lost his memory. He was at the raid on Hamburg. More than that, he was among the men who sacked the cathedral. He remembers closely who was there—especially closely, for he feels still that he was cheated of some share of the loot. He gave me a complete list of the chieftains present, seven of them who led more than a dozen ships' crews, he says. Now, and this is the important thing. Six of those chieftains we have news of already, and we know they do not fit."

"So it must be the seventh?"

"So it would seem. His name is Bolli. He is jarl of the Tronds."

"And who in Hell are the Tronds? I've been in this God-forsaken country half a year, I've heard of more tribelets and kinglets than my father has pigs in sties, and I never heard of the Tronds."

"They live far in the north," said Erkenbert. "Far up the North Way, where they seek to control the fur-trade."

"Far in the north they may be," muttered Bruno, "but if there were a new king there, an emperor-in-being, we would still have heard about it. I begin to wonder if our method is wrong. Or could even the holy Rimbert have made some mistake? Perhaps there is no Holy Lance."

"Or perhaps it is lying in a treasury, unnoticed."

Bruno's face took on an expression quite unfamiliar to Erkenbert, one of depression and defeat. "I can't help thinking," he said, "you tell me the

Lance is in Norway. We hear also that the great struggle for power in the North is going to take place where we left in the spring, at Hedeby in Denmark, everyone is full of it. And here we are, running round provincial gatherings in Sweden."

"Gautland," corrected Erkenbert.

"Same place. I have gone in the wrong direction."

Erkenbert reached up and patted the disconsolate knight on his enormous shoulder. "Whom God loves, he chastises," he said. "Think of King David in the wilderness. Think of Samson at the mill, and how in the end he brought down the great temple of the Philistines. God can bring forth a miracle at any time. Did He not deliver Joseph from Potiphar, and Daniel from the lions' den? I will tell you the holy text you must remember: *Qui perseravabit usque ad finem, ille salvabitur.* He who shall persevere to the end, he shall be saved. To the end, though. Not to near the end."

Bruno's face slowly cleared. He wrung Erkenbert's hand in a careful grip. "Thank you," he said. "Thank you. Wise words. We shall find out more about these Tronds. And meanwhile, I shall hope that God has some errand for me in sending me to these parts."

Hrorik, King in Hedeby, gnawed his beard as he listened to the reports of his scouts.

"Definitely the Ragnarssons?" he queried.

"Definitely. We got close enough to see the Raven Banner."

"Flown only when all the bastards are together. Well, at least there's one bastard fewer of them now. And him the worst bastard of them all. A hundred and twenty ships, you say, and harbored on the mainland opposite Sylt?" Hrorik calculated thoughtfully. "Well, the Ragnarssons are always bad news, but that could be worse. They have to get through the marsh first, and then they have to get over our good wooden walls. I know all about their rams and the tricks they learned from their father. I think we ought to be able to see them off."

One of the scouts cleared his throat. "More bad news, lord, I'm afraid. Catapults. We saw them unloading them. Big jobs, weighing a ton, I would say. Three or four of them."

Hrorik's face regained its concerned expression. "Catapults! What sort were they? Were they the stone-throwers we've heard about, or the dart-throwers, or what?"

"We don't know. Never seen one work. We've just heard these stories, same as you. They all come from men who've been defeated by them."

"Thor help us. This is where we need some men who know about these things."

Hrorik's port-warden, sitting in on the conference, broke in. "I can help you there, lord. I got a report from a skipper yesterday. He was up at the Gula Thing. He said there had been a lot of excitement up there—I'll tell you another time. But at the end of it he said that one of our ships had recruited two Englishmen and was bringing them south. Englishmen," he added with emphasis. "Those are the real experts. These are guys who were there when Ivar got his, and the Frankish king too. Ship should be in in a couple of days."

"So. While Sigurth Snake-arse crawls through the marsh, we can have these men building machines to fight his machines. That's good. But let's do the obvious things too. If the Ragnarssons are there on the west coast, the east coast's clear. So let's get ships out to King Arnodd, and King Gamli, and ask them to send every ship and man they can spare. Clean out the Ragnarssons, and we'll all sleep easier."

"Clean out the Ragnarssons," said the port-warden, "and maybe it'll be time to have just one king in Denmark."

"Just don't say that anywhere else," agreed Hrorik.

Many days' sail to the north, far from the gathering war-storms that would determine the fate of many kingdoms, Shef and Cuthred crouched immobile in the shadow of a rock. Twice they had got into what they thought was good cover. Both times Echegorgun had moved them out, muttering in his own strange language. "You Thin Ones," he said finally. "You don't know how to hide. Or how to look. I could walk through one of your towns in broad daylight and you would never see me." Shef did not believe him, but he had to acknowledge the uncanny skill of the Hidden People in vanishing, in the day, at night, or in the pale twilight that had come again after another long day of sleep and waiting.

In front of them, Echegorgun stood knee deep in the water at the edge of the inlet. He had led them down to it by barely manageable paths, the men slipping and scrambling on the rock, propped up by Echegorgun or Miltastaray, sometimes lowered from one place to the next. Finally, once they were concealed to his satisfaction, Echegorgun had told them to sit motionless, and watch. Watch what a True Person could do. They would see something no Hairless One had seen for many a lifetime. How the True Folk called their kinfolk, the whales.

Now Echegorgun stood facing out to the open sea. High above, Miltastaray kept watch for any boats that might appear, ferrying men or meat between the place of the grind and Brand's threatened home on Hrafnsey.

In one hand Echegorgun held a long paddle, its blade curiously rounded, cut laboriously with stone tools from the trunk of a mountain-aspen. Strange curlicues ran around its inside face. Echegorgun held it up, high above his head, the grotesque length of his arm suddenly clear. Then he brought it down with all his strength on the calm water. The sound of the slap seemed to run from horizon to horizon, as the ripples ran out into the Atlantic swell. Again Echegorgun brought it down. And again. The two men crouched, wondering how far the sound would run above water. And how far below it.

After a dozen blows, Echegorgun turned and put the paddle carefully on a rock on the steep shore. He took another implement, a long tapering tube, made out of layers of coiled and glued birch-bark, and took another cautious step further out, waist-deep now, standing on some unseen projection. He put the thinner end of the tube in his mouth, the trumpet end deep in the water.

From where they crouched, and even in the dim light, Shef could see the prodigious back widening as Echegorgun took a deep breath, a deep breath like the indraft of a bellows. Then he blew.

No sound reached the men on the shore, but after a few moments the air seemed to buzz, to vibrate noiselessly. Was the surface of the sea shivering in sympathy? Shef could not tell, though he strained his one eye to see. He had no doubt that beneath the water some immense disturbance was taking place.

The blowing went on and on, Echegorgun breathing in continually and somehow blasting out at the same time. Shef was not sure, but he felt dimly that the "notes" Echegorgun was playing altered now and then, according to some unknown code. He remained motionless, feeling the chill of the high latitudes creeping up on him, feeling his muscles stiffen, the cold stone strike through his breeches. He did not dare to move. Echegorgun had said that at any disturbance he would break off. "Just one pebble rolling," he had warned. "If the whale-folk were to think I was playing with them, even foreign whale-folk . . . I could never swim safely again."

Beside him Cuthred too sat like a rock image. But then, barely perceptibly even from two feet, his eyes moved, his chin rose a trifle, pointing. Between the shore and the skerries, a fin rose. The straight-up, right-angle fin of the killer-whale, the orca. It was coming towards them, not quickly, deliberately. From time to time the head too rose, and a spout went up, white against the gray islands. The orca was taking a good look. Behind it, well behind it, the rest of the school followed.

Slowly the fin came closer. As it closed, Echegorgun's breathing seemed to slacken, as if he were cutting down the underwater noise. He seemed to be blowing with a shorter, more varied rhythm. Finally the fin closed right up, the orca swimming along parallel with the shore, turning, cruising slowly back. Every time it turned it kept its eye on the strange gray creature standing waist-deep in the water. Shef felt his skin contracting at the thought of what might happen. A lunge of the jaws, a sweep of the tail, and Echegorgun would be off his feet and off the rock. Even his mighty frame would be no more than a bull-seal to the killer. Nothing was safe with them in the water, not the tusked walrus, nor the polar bear, not even the great whales which they tore to pieces while they were still alive.

Echegorgun put his tube carefully down on the rock behind him. Then, slowly, he sank down, submerging shoulders and head in the water, and began to swim out. The killer watched, giving him room. The men on shore could see little, only what showed above water. Yet it began to seem, after a while, as if Echegorgun was acting out some kind of pantomime. Sometimes he seemed to mimic a whale's motion, sometimes a man swimming. Once it seemed to Shef as if he kicked his heels above the water, and rolled over violently: a boat turned upside down? The killer's movements began to synchronize with his own, they swam up and down together, both moving at a fantastic speed for a human, a bare stroll for a whale.

And then the fin swung away, a great tail slapped the water twice, as if in farewell. The other fins cruising up and down offshore swung too, in unison. All together the school began to race down the sound at top speed, the whales arcing in and out of the water in a complex ballet, as if in exultation. They raced away to the south, towards Hrafnsey.

Echegorgun remained in the water till they were out of sight, cruising up and down with an easy overarm stroke, only skull and arms showing, with a faint flurry where his heels touched the surface. At a distance, just another seal. Finally he turned, swam into shore, heaved himself out, shook himself easily like a dog.

"Well," he said in Norse. "Come out now, Thin Ones. I told them the one who wounded their leader was dead. They asked, and the one they followed? Dead too, I said. They were disappointed. It was easy to tell them there were more whale-foes in the ship. The great ship going into Hrafnsey now. They said they would find sport with it."

"Going into Hrafnsey now?" said Shef. "How are we to get there?"

"There is a way," said Echegorgun. "No Thin One would find it, but I can show you. One thing I had better tell you, though. The whale-folk are not good at telling Thin Ones apart. Nor do they care much. Anyone on the water is at risk tonight."

"Show us how to get across," said Shef. "I swear to repay you for all this. Even if I have to become king of this land to do it."

The men of the two-masted ship moving under light sail towards Hrafnsey harbor had had a long voyage up the Norwegian coast in which to get used to their unfamiliar weapons and sail-rig. For the most part they were men of Agdir, Queen Ragnhild's homeland. In the turmoil following the sudden death of Halvdan and the seizure of power by Olaf, one of the skippers of King Halvdan's fleet had decided his best interests lay with Ragnhild, and had placed his ship at her service. Most of his crew had not stayed with him, but had deserted, their places taken by Ragnhild's own men. With them had come Valgrim the Wise, defeated in his plan to control the College of the Way, and eager to take revenge on the one who had thwarted him. Not only him—but also to set the Way and his misguided colleagues back on the true path of Othin, the path that would lead to victory, not defeat, at Ragnarök. He and his backers had built the catapults and trained their users. They were eager, too, to redeem their failure in the Gula Fjord.

Yet the driving force behind them all, skipper, crew and Valgrim as well, was the hatred of Queen Ragnhild for the man who had killed her son, or caused him to be killed. The man who had stolen the luck to which she had pledged her life. Ragnhild had seen her mother-in-law Queen Asa go to the gallows without blinking, had poisoned her husband King Halvdan without a tremor. One day, maybe, she would breed a new race of kings from her own loins. But before that the beggar-Englishman she had seduced, hidden, and thought to use to clear the path for her son: he must go to Hel to serve her son and her for all eternity.

As the great warship closed on Hrafnsey, its goal, its crew had ceased to follow the coastline and had moved offshore, into the Atlantic rollers but out of sight of land, coming in again only a few miles from where they reckoned their quarry to be. There they had lain upon a deserted inlet, one of the thousands on that jagged coast, seen by no-one. Or at least, no human.

Yet they had not lacked for close information. After the butchery was over at the grind, the real work had started for the men of Halogaland. Vital to cut the carcasses up and salt as much meat as possible. Even more vital to rig the cauldrons on the beach itself, strip off the blubber, start the long job of rendering down the whale-oil, immensely valuable for lamps, for fuel and even for food through the long winter nights. Firing the cauldrons was not a problem. Once the oil had been cooked out of the blubber, the strips that were left became fuel for the next rendering. But every barrel the Halogaland coast possessed would hardly be enough for the sudden windfall of wealth that the grind brought. Boats were passing up and down in all directions, loading up barrels, towing strings of them, sending messages for urgent assistance. One whale-boat with two men in it passed by the fjord where Ragnhild's warship lay, to be snapped up immediately by its pinnace.

The Norsemen, mostly and with exceptions like Ivar the Boneless and his father Ragnar, were not torturers of each other, whatever they might do to slaves. Ragnhild had taken them on board and told them plainly that they had two choices: to be beheaded at once over the side of the ship, or to tell her the situation at Hrafnsey. The fishermen had decided to talk. Ragnhild knew the outline of the harbor, including its catapult defenses and its two longships. She knew, too, that half the men of the area were still boiling blubber at the grind-beach, and the rest were exhausted from hours of loading and unloading, making trip after trip between beach and harbor. What she did not know was that Shef and Cuthred were missing. Her prisoners had simply not noticed, preoccupied with other things.

What they had noticed and told her was that Brand, desperate for men, had taken the English catapulteers from their posts, and Guthmund's Swedes as well, and set them to work on the jetty, since they were all manifestly useless at anything to do with whales. Listening with half an ear to Cwicca and Osmod's protests, and their demands that something should be done to search for their master Shef, Brand had sent a sentry up to the harbor-point, with instructions to sound a horn for help if he saw any strange craft approaching. The sentry had sat down on the soft turf with his back against a stone and immediately fallen asleep.

Ragnhild's ship, the *Crane*, moved into Hrafnsey harbor a few moments before sunrise lit the pallid sky, meeting no challenge, its oversized crew of a hundred and twenty men ready for action. They nudged each other as they saw the bulks of the catapults against the sky, unmanned and untended.

Brand, down at the jetty supervising the unloading of another cargo of barrels from his own *Walrus*, saw nothing till the first catapult-stone whirred across the water.

It was aimed with deadly skill. The men of the *Crane* had had time to practice, and no shortage of good round rocks to practice with. Coming from a bare two hundred yards, the distance between jetty and harbor-point, it struck the *Walrus* full on the prow. The prow kicked back, the planks that fitted into it all sprang loose. If the ship had been running under sail she would have gone to the bottom like a stone. As it was, she merely sprang apart and settled gently on to the rock ten feet beneath her keel, mast still jutting upwards.

Brand stared, gaping, unable to realize what had happened. The second stone shattered the jetty a few feet from him, sending half a dozen men into the water. At the same moment, light flared on the dark decks of the *Crane*. The dart-shooter's crew, anxious to try their fire-arrows once more. As they sighted, Ragnhild stepped behind them.

"There," she snapped. "There. Aim for that big barrel. Surely you can hit that this time."

The crew trained their weapon round a trifle, sighted again, released the retaining toggle. The fire-dart shot across the water, its flight indicated by a line of fire. Slammed into the barrel of whale-oil just unloaded from the ruined *Walrus*. Instantly a tongue of flame shot into the sky, burning with a pure and brilliant light. The men on the shore stood out immediately as dark shadows, shrieking and running in confusion, some to put the fire out, some to fetch their weapons, the English catapulteers beginning the long run round the harbor and the point behind it to reach their aban-doned weapons.

Ragnhild's skipper, observing, grinned with satisfaction. His name was Kormak, son of an Irishwoman, with long experience in the never-ending Irish wars. He knew when his enemy had lost the initiative.

"Close up to the jetty," he ordered. "You with the stone-thrower, sink that other big ship there, the Swedish one. Dart-thrower, set light to the barrels and then the houses. Boatswain, pick twenty men, furl sail, and take the ship back out a hundred yards under oars once the rest of us are ashore. I don't want anyone trying to take the *Crane* while we're busy. The rest of you, we'll land on the jetty and go straight through the village."

"And remember," shouted Ragnhild over him, "the one-eyed man. Six gold arm-rings for the one-eyed man."

Beside her, Valgrim hefted the 'Gungnir' spear he had taken from Stein, and Stein from the shore where Shef had thrown it. A good weapon, he thought. To drink the blood of a heretic.

Not far away, but too far, Shef saw the flame suddenly light up the sky. He stood on the shore of the mainland a bare quarter of a mile from the edge of Hrafnsey island. But he had no boat. He would not have believed that they could even get so close so quickly. But Echegorgun, Miltastaray and Ekwetargun with him, had led them inland over paths not even a goat could find, and then over a surprisingly easy ridge-route to the coast close by where they stood. Though they had rowed for hours two days before, they must have walked only five miles, cutting across the base of a peninsula.

"How do we get across?" he asked.

"Swim?" suggested Echegorgun.

Shef hesitated. A quarter of a mile was not so far. But this water, he knew, was always bitter cold. And besides—he could not forget the threat of the whales.

Cuthred nudged him and pointed. Lit up now by the red glow in the sky, they could see the black dot of a whale-boat, with more behind it, pulling frantically down from the grind-beach. Men carrying a load down, or coming back for water.

"More Thin Ones," said Echegorgun. "We go now. Do not speak of us except to my cousin Brand. If you go on the water in a boat, you will speak to no-one again."

"Wait!" said Shef sharply. "Can you tell where the whales are?"

Echegorgun nodded. "Hear them in the water. I know already. They are outside the harbor, watch the strange ship. Unhappy. They want small boats to tip over, not big ship to ram. Don't go in boats."

"Can you tell us if they go into the harbor? If it's safe for a few minutes just to row across?"

Echegorgun sniffed doubtfully. "You hear a noise like a walrus sounding, you row across. Make it quick." An instant later he had vanished, his great bulk disappearing seemingly into a rock.

"Noise like a walrus sounding?" muttered Cuthred. "Might as well be an angel belching for all the good . . ."

Shef ignored him. He had stepped on to the highest point he could reach, waving the lance he had recovered in wide sweeps over his head. Moments later the leading whale-boat saw him, hesitated, pulled over.

"Stop the other boats," said Shef. "No, do as I say. I know the place is under attack. We have to go in together, not a few at a time."

Slowly the dories gathered, nine or ten of them, maybe forty or fifty men, fierce and skilled seamen, but unarmored and unarmed except for the long whale-lances some of them carried, their flensing-axes and grind-knives.

"You're going to have to listen very carefully to what I say," said Shef. "First, there is a school of killer whales out by the harbor, and we don't want to row into them. Second, we will know when they have gone into the harbor . . ."

As a buzz of incredulity greeted his words, he thumped his lance-butt on the rock and raised his voice commandingly over it.

Kormak was doing to the men of Hrafnsey much as they had done to the whales. Deliberately, he kept up the pressure to make them panic, though he knew their form of panic would be a headlong assault. As the *Crane* moved up to the jetty, stones whirred from her mule, each one smashing a house. Fire-arrows thumped into wood and oil, turning the whole settlement into a conflagration. Few were killed, few were hurt, the fighting strength of the defenders was hardly diminished. But they had no time to think. Besides, as Brand saw his beloved *Walrus* a wreck, saw his winter store and his warehouses going up in flames, his heart swelled till it seemed to burst his jerkin. No time to fetch his mail, no time to array the men. Between the flames he stood, his face working, clutching his axe 'Battle-troll' and waiting for the despoilers to set foot on land.

As the side of the *Crane* touched the jetty, the men Kormak had detailed off sprang ashore, forming an immediate armored front six wide. At the same time Kormak bent, said a quiet word to his boatswain. Two men slipped ashore, walking along the jetty's side struts, one each side. At the right place they heaved a rope across, made fast.

Kormak pushed forward to the center of the front rank, stepped on two more paces, arranged the men in the Viking wedge. Then they began to move forward, shouting in unison. Kormak waited for the furious charge he expected.

It came. Seeing the confident figure striding towards him, Brand, the doubts and fears that had afflicted him since the duel with Ivar entirely wiped out by fury and loss, ran forward, axe raised. Behind him, in a ragged wave, came the men of Hrafnsey with what weapons they could snatch up.

"A big fellow," remarked Kormak to his nearest shield-companions. He raised his shield to guard and shouted a taunt, unheard in the roar of flame.

As Brand charged forward, the boatswain, crouched in shadow, raised the rope. Brand's feet went from under him and he hurtled sprawling forward, full-length, his weight shaking the jetty. 'Battle-troll' skidded out of his hand. With a roar, Brand started to scramble to his feet, but at the same moment Kormak slammed him mercilessly, with every ounce of force he could summon, on the side of the head. Brand shook his head, continued to struggle upwards. Disbelievingly, Kormak swung his lead-shot loaded sandbag again. This time the giant went down on all fours.

The charging men behind him hesitated, some also brought down by the rope. Two ran on, were met by a concentrated volley of javelins, fell bristling. The rest wavered, then ran in ones and twos back into the blazing village.

"Tie him up," said Kormak briefly. He waved his troop forward, aiming to drive out the stragglers, establish a perimeter, and take control of boats, food and weapons. Hunting down the fugitives would be the job after that. He wished the one-eyed man had charged with Brand. It would have kept Ragnhild off his back.

The English catapulteers being employed as unskilled labor down at the jetty had run at the first stone. They had no weapons, and no impulse to fight in defense of the settlement. In the dark beyond the firelight, they rallied, gasping, round Cwicca.

"Shouldn't never have taken us away from the mule," said a voice in the darkness. "We knew they were coming, we told him, but no, he would have . . ."

"Shut up," said Cwicca. "Thing is, if we get up there now we can train round and shoot up that ship of theirs, no bother. That'll get them back aboard her in a hurry."

"No good," said Osmod. "Look."

He pointed to the *Crane*'s pinnace, loaded with armed men, now pulling across the harbor in the direction of the two untended catapults. Kormak had thought of that too.

Kormak had not thought of the whales. The orcas had been shadowing the *Crane* all the way in, eager to attack. Yet the bull leader had held off. He had an accurate sense of the *Crane*'s bulk, knew she was the biggest man-thing he had ever come across. Maybe if he rammed her head on, she would fill and sink. Maybe not. The scratch he had received from Cuthred irritated him, but at the same time gave him caution. The sport he wanted was to tip a boat like an ice-floe, to snap up the men inside like unwary seals. So he hesitated, and his school with him, cruising up and down at the harbor-mouth, half an eye on the *Crane* and the commotion, half an eye on the interesting but shore-sheltered whale-boats he had sensed lying under cover of the mainland a quarter of a mile away.

Then he heard the regular thumping oars of the pinnace, and hesitated no longer. Filled with the cruel urge, more than hunger, of the fox in the hen-roost, he swept down the harbor channel, with his school behind him.

"No good," said Osmod again. "Great holy suffering Christ." Driven back to childhood, he made instinctively the sign of the Cross to ward him from evil, over the hammer still slung round his neck. No-one corrected him. Staring at the pinnace, they saw all together the great fin that rose man-height behind the boat, the black-and-white body that reared beneath it.

Boat and men went over with hardly a cry. For an instant, bobbing heads. Then fin after fin cutting through the water as the killers went into their established ritual for striking at a great whale, a blue or a sperm or a finner, swinging in in turn, snapping with the great jaws and swinging out of the way of the next. But where a bite from a full-grown orca would merely wound a sixty-foot blue, it snapped a man in half. The flurry was over in seconds, the whales sounding again to hide their presence.

"I met one of those things out on the water," muttered Karli, his face white. "I told you it could have turned me over as easy as winking. The fin's as tall as I am. What are its teeth like?"

Cwicca roused the others from their paralysis. "Well, Thor help them, but look. The road's clear to the mules. Let's get up there."

Still gaping at the threatening fire-lit water, the catapulteers started to run round the harbor to their machines.

On board the *Crane,* all attention was concentrated on the charge and fall of Brand. No-one saw the pinnace go under except the two fishermen, still prisoner and lashed to the outer gunwale. They looked down at the water under them, trying to estimate its depth. Slowly, looking over their shoulders, they started with new determination to work their hands free.

On the mainland coast, Shef saw the flames leaping again. The men in the boats were grumbling, reluctant to believe in a threat from orcas, desperate to see what was happening at their homes. Behind him came a strange sound, a kind of long violent blowing snuffle, followed by a slap like a tail striking water.

"What was that?" he asked.

"Sounded like a walrus going down," said one of the men in the boats. "But it can't be, not . . ."

"All right," snapped Shef. He raised his lance high and called out to all the boats. "It's safe now, maybe just for a few moments. Row right across as fast as you can go, beach on the shore right opposite and get out. Don't go into the harbor. Do you hear, don't go into the harbor. Now row."

He sat down in the prow of the lead boat, Cuthred in the stern. The whale-men bent to their oars, sent the boat skimming over the calm sea. Shef twisted from side to side, fearing at any moment to see the fins racing again towards him. The boats reached the mid-point of their passage, raced on. As they closed on the island shore, outside the harbor entrance, maybe half a mile still from the main settlement and hidden from it by a hill, Shef felt the speed slacken.

"Why don't we just push on in?" called one of the oarsmen.

"Believe me," said Shef. "You wouldn't like it."

His boat grounded her prow on shingle, followed by most of the others. The men scrambled out, heaving their boats higher, snatching out their makeshift weapons. One boat ignored Shef's shouts, skimmed on towards the harbor entrance, disappeared from sight round the point. Shef shook his head in disgust.

"I still don't see why . . ." began another dissident. Cuthred, patience exhausted, clubbed him on the side of the head with a sword-pommel, seized him by the throat, dragged him again on to his feet.

"Do what he says and obey your orders," he snarled. "Got it?"

Shef waved the fifty men he had into a double extended line and led them off in a broad arrow formation. He kept them at a swift walk, curbing any impulse to run. They would need their breath if they had to fight armored men. His plan was to swing wide round the hill at the harbor mouth, and come out of its cover down the stream on which the main settlement stood, to drive the invaders back into the water. Maybe by then they would have dispersed to rape and loot. He hoped so. Surprise was his only chance now.

The catapulteers reached the first mule and paused for a moment. Man one, or man them both? Even with Karli added, they had less than two full teams.

"Just the first one for now," Cwicca decided briefly. "Get winding."

They had slacked the twisted ropes off before leaving. It was never good to keep them under torsion for too long. The winding levers were still stacked in their place, though, and the men sprang to it. At the same time Cwicca called Karli to assist him. One improvement they had made in the weeks of waiting. They had never before been able to train their machine round more than a few inches. On a ship, one had to aim the ship rather than the mule. However, by trial and error Udd had solved the problem. They had put the heavy machine on small iron-rimmed wheels of its own, not so that it could be drawn overland like the lighter dart-throwers, but so that those small wheels could rest on a larger one, placed flat on the ground and flanged to keep the smaller ones in place. Two strong men could tip the whole ton-and-a-quarter forward on its unmoving axle and train it round by a balancing trail.

Straining, Karli and Cwicca lifted the trail, walked the machine round from its first position covering the harbor entrance to bear on the *Crane* now slowly sweeping away from the jetty.

"Round half a pace more," grunted Cwicca. "Back a hand's breadth. Right. Tip her forward, hammer in two wedges, no, three."

They tipped the machine forward so it pointed, now, down at the water. The ropes were wound, the throwing bar straining at its retaining bolt. Cwicca fitted a thirty-pound rock into the sling, drooping from the bar, checked the very precise angle of the hook from which the sling's catch had, at the right moment, to fly free.

"Ready. Stand clear. Shoot."

The bolt was pulled back, the bar shot up with inconceivable force, the sling whirred round, adding its own vector to the force of the twisted ropes. The boulder shot across the water in a flat hard line.

And missed. The crew had wedged the machine down as far as it would go. But it was a hard business altering for range downwards. The rock skimmed narrowly over the decks of the *Crane* and splashed into the water in the center of the widening gap between ship and jetty. The plume it threw up hurled spray into Kormak's face, as he turned back from the won skirmish on the jetty.

"Thor aid me," he said. "What happened to the pinnace? They were supposed to secure that machine." Then he began to bark orders. A threat to his ship was the most serious thing, everything else trivial, winning the battle, securing prisoners, even appeasing Ragnhild.

As the queen realised Kormak meant to turn back from sacking the settlement, the settlement she was sure contained her son's bane, skulking somewhere away from the fighting, she flew at him with teeth and nails. He shook her off as she clung to his arm, shrieking her demands.

The important thing to do, he saw straight away, was to get the *Crane* over on the other side of the harbor, where the catapults could not train down far enough to shoot. The ship needed more men, and in a hurry. There were still a dozen skiffs and dories lying round the jetty and the shingle by it. Quickly Kormak detached fifty men to hold the foot of the jetty, ordered the rest into the boats, jamming in as many as they could carry. At the last moment he stopped, ordered two men out of the nearest, replaced them with the still groggy Brand, hands lashed firmly behind his back.

"Let's get him safely stowed," he remarked, stepping into the same boat. He thrust a furious Ragnhild away from him again. "Lady, we'll come back for you. If the man you want is anywhere, he's on the shore. I suggest you go look for him yourself. Give way," he added to the oarsmen.

As a second stone thumped into the sea, aimed this time at the first boats creeping out, and missing once more, fifty men set out to cross the intervening hundred yards of water.

Shef brought his group hurdling over the stream and into the blazing village by the landward end of its one muddy street. As they moved down it, jogging now, men moved out of the flames and shadows to join him, adding themselves to the line, eager to support the first sign of concerted resistance. Shef felt the wolfish force of their anger sweeping him along. There was no way to halt them now. They were going to hurl themselves on the invaders whatever he said or did.

Yet the Halogalanders had no armor, and the only shield in the party was Cuthred's. The enemy were fully equipped, Shef could see them standing in a solid rank across the base of the jetty, unshaken and unafraid. In seconds he would have to lead the charge. What chance had he of surviving it? Standing in the center of the front rank, a target for every spear? This was the way of the world. Shef poised his lance. There was no way he could see of altering it. He tried to call up within himself the fighting urge he had felt when he killed Hrani the Viking on the sandbank. There was no response. The lance in his hand seemed to drink it, to send out an urge instead to delay. To pity, not to strike. The men on his right and left were looking sideways at him, expecting the word to charge. Something made Shef sweep the lance out sideways, holding them back.

Behind the shield-wall on the jetty, the rising sun cleared the surrounding hills and shone for the first time that day full on the water. It caught the fins and bodies of the killers as they swept in for the second time from the deep water, confident of what they had to do, emboldened by their first success. A great cry went up from the water as the men in the dories realized what was coming towards them.

Brave men, some of them struck out with spears and swords as the black-and-white bodies rushed in. Valgrim the Wise, standing disbelieving in the prow of his boat, swung back the 'Gungnir' lance to use as a harpoon. Too weak, too slow. The boats were taken from underneath. A blow from a snout, propelled at thirty miles an hour by a body tons in weight, and each boat disintegrated. The heavily-armed men splashed or sank in the water, and as they did so the jaws tore at them, into them, the killers sweeping backwards and forwards in the pattern they used for hunting seals or porpoise. In seconds the bay ran as red as the cove of the grind. But this time with man-blood, not with whale's, crewmen's mixed with that of their skipper, and that of Valgrim the Wise, priest of Othin, now sacrificed to Othin's own creatures. Unnoticed by any, the spear with the 'Gungnir' runes drifted gently to the bottom: it had brought its last owner no luck.

Shef's charging line faltered as the men took in what was happening, a thing no-one had ever seen before. Seeing their enemies stare and hesitate, Kormak's detachment turned as well. Both sides stood, struck with horror. There was no way for anyone to intervene.

After a time, Shef stepped forward, spoke to what seemed to be the leader of the men on the jetty. "Put your weapons down," he said. "We will give you life and limb, and passage home when we can. There is no way for you to escape now. And there has been bloodshed enough."

Lips pale, the leader looked at his men, saw their shaken and horrified expressions, the fight drained out of them. He nodded, slowly laid down sword and shield. Cuthred moved forward, shouldered a path through the others for Shef, walked with him to the end of the jetty to see the end of the story.

As he did so, a figure rose from the planking, shrieking recognition. Ragnhild, knife in hand, unmoved by the slaughter, desperate for revenge. She came at Shef like a fury, knife low for the thrust. Shef saw her come, recognized the green eyes he had kissed, the hair he had clenched in climax. The lance drooped disregarded in his hand, he groped for words of apology. She was shrieking something as she ran in, he caught only the words ". . . killed my son!" He stood, arms wide, paralyzed, hoping for a word of explanation, another miracle.

Cuthred stepped between them, the knife-thrust screeching off the hard surface of his shield. Automatically he lifted it to thrust her off. Ragnhild's eyes widened with sudden shock. Then she fell backwards, dragging Cuthred's targe with her. The targe with the foot-long spike Shef had welded on himself. It had driven through her heart below her breasts.

"As God's my judge," said Cuthred, "that was an accident. I never killed a woman in my life."

"Too many killings," said Shef. He stooped, searching for signs of life. Her lips were still moving, still cursing him. Then they ceased, and he saw her eyes roll upwards. As he stepped away, Cuthred walked forward, put a foot on Ragnhild's outstretched arm, and jerked his shield free. He shook his head in self-reproach, looked to see if his leader had noticed what he had done.

But Shef's eyes had turned from the corpse on the jetty to the blood-stained, fin-slashed water. Then, disbelievingly, he looked again across the bay. There, in the shallows opposite, two figures were sitting, visible in the growing daylight. Behind him a murmur of amazement arose as more and more men saw the astonishing sight. The second thing they had seen that morning that no living man had ever seen before. One of the Hidden People.

Echegorgun, gauging the whales' mood exactly, had swum easily and confidently across the narrow strait after the whale-boats. He had seen Shef take the men on shore, had seen the one over-confident boat sweep on into the harbor, to be met and butchered by the whales. He had kept well back, but had followed the whales on into the harbor, sure that he would hear if they turned towards him. He had cruised along the shore, only the tip of his skull showing, and that looking like yet another gray rock. He had watched the doings of the men with interest, but without concern— till he had seen two men load an unmistakable figure into a boat. Brand son of Barn son of Bjarni. His own aunt's grandson.

Echegorgun knew exactly what would happen next. He had a couple of minutes only in which to avert it, alter it. Like a seal he had launched himself across the water, clung for a moment to the stern of the *Crane,* gauged the distance between himself and the lead boat with Kormak in it, felt the swarm and flurry of whale-flukes only yards away. He submerged, striking out like an otter.

Brand, bound helpless in the bottom of the boat, Kormak's foot resting firmly on his chest, saw only a great gray hand seize the gunwale. Then the boat tipped. Tipped towards Echegorgun, tipped a fraction before the first whale struck. As the men shouted and raised their weapons, an irresistible clutch seized his tunic, dragged him over the side and down deep, deep, away from the splintering planks and thrashing limbs on the surface.

For a second Brand felt all the superstitious horror of his race. Seized by the marbendill, dragged down to the monster's dinner at the bottom of the sea. And yet, in that flash, he had half-recognized the hand. He lay motionless, not resisting, holding his one deep-drawn breath.

Slowly the grip dragged him through the water, powered by the great muscles of the not-man. Under the *Crane's* keel. Across the bay. Into the shallows. As they both came up, releasing their breath in a final gasp, Brand stared into the face next his own. The face staring back. As Echegorgun produced a flint knife and began to cut free the ropes that held Brand's arms, they explored each other silently, for similarity, for family resemblance.

Finally Brand spoke, sitting in the shallow water. "I have left messages for you and your folk in our secret place," he said, "and I have always kept to our compact. Yet I never expected to see you here in the daylight. You are of the race that grandfather Bjarni met."

Echegorgun smiled, showing his massive teeth. "And you must be my good cousin Brand."

CHAPTER TWENTY-FOUR

It is an expensive business finding you shelter," said Brand wearily.

Shef said nothing. He might have replied that it had sometimes been profitable too, but allowances had to be made for Brand's state of mind. He was not sure how many days had gone by since the battle—in the high latitudes it was hard to tell. Everyone seemed to have been furiously at work for longer than they could bear, stopping only when they fell asleep. And yet—it was an ominous sign—dark was returning to the sky. Summer was past, winter coming on. It came on very fast in Halogaland.

However many days it had been, the settlement still looked barely survivable. All three of the ships in the harbor were sunk or unserviceable. By sheer bad luck Cwicca and his crew had found the range and managed to depress their machine just as the battle was won, and put a rock neatly through the base of the *Crane's* mast. Driven by terror of the whales her crew had managed to pole her over and beach her, but she would never sail again. The *Walrus* still sat at the bottom of the harbor, her mast poking forlornly above the surface. The *Seamew* had caught fire and burnt. Though there were small craft of all kinds available, there was no ship big enough to sail south for Trondhjem, the nearest port, and return with provisions. In time, one would be made from the salvaged planks and timbers—for of course there was little large wood readily available on the barren coast or the wind-swept islands. For the same reason rebuilding the burnt huts would be hard, for all the local skill in using stone and turf. Much of the precious windfall of the grind had gone up in flame, and with it the storehouses and warehouses where Brand kept not only the furs and feathers and skins of the Finn-tax, which he traded, but also the meat and cheese and butter on which he lived.

And besides Shef's train, and Guthmund's crew, there were maybe seventy survivors off the *Crane*. They had been promised their lives, and no-one had suggested breaking the promise. But they all ate. There was no way everyone on the island could live through the coming winter, however hard they fished and sealed. Many of the Halogalanders had quietly slipped back to their homesteads, making it clear they wanted no part of Brand's problem. They would live. It would be the strangers, and their hosts, if they were fool enough to share, who would die.

"At least we have gold and silver," Brand went on. "That doesn't burn. The best thing we can do is put a boat together, a makeshift, load it with every man we can squeeze in, and send it off south. If it hugs the shore it might get to somewhere with food to spare. Then turn Ragnhild's Westfolders out, buy as much as we can, and head north again."

Again Shef forbore to say anything. If Brand were not so tired he would have seen the faults in the scheme. The Westfolders would be many enough to overpower their guards, take the money, and leave the settlement as foodless as ever. As it was, guarding them was taking far too much of everyone's resources. They would have to be sent off on their own. If they could be brought ever to venture out to sea again, with their new terror of the whales.

"I am sorry," said Brand, shaking his massive head. "I have experienced too much to make any sensible plan. A marbendill for a cousin! I knew, but now everyone does. What will folk say?"

"They will say you are fortunate," broke in Thorvin. "There is a priest of the Way in Sweden, whose special devotion is to the goddess Freyja. His craft is the breeding of animals, the way you must cross-breed or in-breed to get the best-yielding cows or the woolliest sheep. He has spoken to me often of mules, and the breeding of dog and wolf, and such things. As soon as he knows, he will come here. For it seems to me that we and the seamen are more like dog and wolf than we are horse and donkey. For your grandfather Bjarni bred with one of their females, and she had a child, your father Barn. But Barn too had a child, and that was you, and your ancestry is plain if we see you together. If Barn had been a mule, a human mule, that could not have happened. So we and the marbendills are not so far apart. Maybe there is more marbendill blood in the race than we knew before."

Shef nodded. The thought had come to him before as he looked at the northerners, with their massive frames, their eyebrow-ridges, their hairy skins and bushy beards. But he had not aired the thought. He noticed that the word "troll" was being used more sparingly around the settlement, replaced by "sea-folk" or "marbendill," as if others were also reckoning their ancestry.

"Well, be that as it may," said Brand, looking slightly more cheerful. "I do not know what we are to do. I wish, I don't mind saying it, I wish I had the good advice of my cousin."

But Echegorgun had slipped away very soon after dragging Brand to the shore. He had seemed for a short time pleased with the attention he received, and certainly pleased by Brand's gratitude. Then the noise seemed to irk him, and he had vanished as only the Hidden Folk could. He had also taken Cuthred with him, both of them apparently swimming the firth back to the mainland. Echegorgun was impressed by Cuthred.

"Not quite a Thin One," he had said. "Stronger than Miltastaray, anyway. And look at the hair on his back! Grease him well, he could swim with the seals too. Miltastaray likes him. He could be a good mate for her."

Shef had gaped at the last thought, and then said cautiously, unsure how to put it. "I thought you said, Echegorgun, that you knew what had happened to him. Well, what happened was that some of the other Thin Ones, they cut off, well, not what makes him a man, but what . . ."

Echegorgun cut him off. "I know. It means less to us than to you. You know why you live such short lives? Because you mate all the time, not just in season. Every time you do it, more of your life gone. A thousand times for every child, I have listened at many windows! Hah. Miltastaray would look for something else in a man."

And with that they had gone. Shef had had time only to speak to Cuthred and ask him to ask Echegorgun to bury his human kills, like a civilized person, instead of smoking them like a—like a marbendill. "Tell him we'll pay him in pigs," he had said.

"You haven't got any pigs," Cuthred had replied. "Anyway, I prefer pigs to people."

Perhaps they would all have larders like Echegorgun's before the winter was out, Shef thought. As the circular discussion between Thorvin, Brand, Guthmund and the others continued, he got up, brooding, and walked away. He carried with him the lance he had taken from the smokehouse: it felt more comfortable than the 'Gungnir' spear, or the expensive swords he had acquired and lost. The best thing to do when you were faced with an insoluble problem, he had found, was to ask everyone about it till you met the one who knew the answer.

He found Cwicca and the gang sharing a scanty meal in a break from their work of trying to recover planking from the wrecked ships. As he approached, they stood up respectfully. Shef wondered for a moment. They did that sometimes. Sometimes, misled by his accent when he was speaking English, they forgot and treated him as one of themselves. They seemed to be doing that less often.

"Sit," he said, but remained standing himself, leaning on the lance. "Not much to eat, I see."

"And there's going to be less," agreed Cwicca.

"There's talk of sending the prisoners away in a ship, when we've built it. If we could build two we could trust someone to go south for food."

"If we could build two," demurred Wilfi.

"If we can get anyone to sail it," added Osmod. "Right now everyone's so scared of whales they'd run aground if they saw a spout."

"Dead right too," put in Karli fervently. "I mean to say one thing, lord. You know I saw one of those things when I poled across from Drottningsholm? Right out on the water, close up? Well, one of those here was the same one. I saw a bite-mark on his fin. Same thing here. It looks as if— well, as if they followed us up."

Or followed you up, he thought but did not say. The English ex-slaves had told him many strange stories of their master, whom they both venerated and felt at home with. He had believed few of them. Now, he was beginning to wonder. Was there a penalty, he thought, for a man who had greeted the son of a god by knocking him down. There had not seemed to be one so far.

"Well, if we don't do something we'll all starve to death," said Shef.

The ex-slaves considered the prospect. Not an unfamiliar one. Many slaves, and as many poor folk, died in the winter, from cold or hunger or both. They had all known it to happen.

"I had an idea," said Udd, and then stopped, with his usual shyness in front of a group.

"Was it about iron?" asked Shef.

Udd nodded vigorously, recovering his nerve. "Yes, lord. You know that ore we saw down at the College at Kaupang? The sort that took so little working, because there's so much metal in the stone? It comes from Jarnberaland. Iron-bearing Land."

Shef nodded encouragingly, with no idea where this thought was leading. They couldn't eat iron, but sarcasm would cut Udd off completely.

"There's a place called Kopparberg too. Copper Mountain. Well, the thing is, they're both over there." Udd pointed across the harbor to the mountainous shore opposite. "On the other side of the mountains, I mean. I thought, if we can't sail, we could walk. It's not as if there's nowhere the other side."

Shef looked at the jagged forbidding shore, thought of the terrible cramping struggle up the side of Echegorgun's inlet. The path they had come upon. The easy ridge route Echegorgun had taken to bring them out opposite the island.

"Thank you, Udd," he said. "I'll think about that."

He walked on till he found Guthmund the Swede. Guthmund was in unexpectedly good spirits. He had lost his ship, and there was every chance of dying of starvation. On the other hand, the loot from the *Crane* had been surprisingly good. Ragnhild had taken half her ancestral treasure with her, to buy men and revenge, and it had been recovered from the wreck. Deaths in the attack had meant fewer people to share it with, too. Guthmund greeted his young leader with a smile. They called him Guthmund the Greedy. His ambition was to become Gull-Guthmund, or Gold-Guthmund in English.

The smile vanished as Shef asked him about what Udd had said. "Oh, it's up there somewhere all right," he agreed. "But I wouldn't know where exactly. You folk don't realize. Sweden is a thousand miles long from end to end, all the way from Skaane to the Lapp-mark. If Skaane is Swedish," he added. "I am from Sodermanland myself, I am a true Swede. But I guess, I guess this is about as far north as Jarnberaland."

"How can you tell?"

"By the way the shadows fall. If you measure a shadow at noon, and you know how far it is from midsummer, you can tell how far north you are. It is one of the crafts of the Way, Skaldfinn Njörth's priest once showed me."

"So if we went up there and walked due east we would come to Jarnberaland in the country of the Swedes."

"You might not have to walk all the way," said Guthmund. "I have heard it said that there are lakes up there in the Keel, the central range, and they run east and west. Brand told me that when the Finns on this side raid the Finns on the other—Kvens they call them—they take bark boats and paddle along them."

"Thank you, Guthmund," said Shef, and walked on again.

* * *

Brand looked incredulous when Shef reported the results of his conversations to him and Thorvin, still sitting together. "Can't be done," he said flatly.

"Why not?"

"It's too late in the year."

"A month after midsummer?"

Brand sighed. "You don't realize. Up here summer doesn't last long. On the coast, all right, the sea seems to keep the snow and ice off for a while. But just think. Remember what it was like in Hedeby, like spring, you said. Get to Kaupang and it's still ice-bound. And how far is that? Three hundred miles north? Here you're another six hundred. A few miles in from the coast—and that's as far as I've ever been, even chasing Finns—and there's snow on the ground more than half the year. The higher you go, the worse it gets. The high mountains never melt at all."

"So cold is the problem. But Udd's right, is he, it is Jarnberaland on the other side, maybe two hundred miles off? Ten days' travel."

"Twenty days' travel. If you're very very lucky. In some of the country I've seen three miles is a hard day. If you don't get turned round and die walking in a circle."

"Still," Thorvin put in, pulling at his beard, "there is something few people know. And that is that the Way is strong in Jarnberaland. Naturally, for we are craftsmen and smiths. And smiths go to iron. There are priests of the Way there, working with the folk who mine the iron. Some say it is as good as a second College. Valgrim was against it. He said there could only be one College."

And he the head of it, Shef thought. Valgrim's errors had finally caught up with him. He had been in the boats that rowed back to the *Crane,* and only two of the men in them had survived, Brand and a young man who had remained hunched into a ball ever since they pulled him on shore, making small noises of fear. Ragnhild could have died that way too, Shef told himself. Just an accident. Another of the ones that surrounded him. Part of his luck, Olaf Elf-of-Geirstath would say, and King Alfred with him.

"So if we crossed the mountains," Shef went on, "we might even find help the other side."

"But you can't cross the mountains," Brand repeated, exasperated. "The mountains are full of Finns and—"

"And the Hidden Folk," Shef completed for him. "Thank you, Brand." He rose to his feet and walked off yet again, the lance marking his paces.

* * *

The final word came from a man whose name he did not know, one of the *Crane's* crew, sweating in the pale sunlight as he and his mates heaved rocks on to a sled, to drag to the settlement to make a few more winter shelters. Halogalanders watched them from a distance, carrying bundles of seal-harpoons. Shef, still unsure of his proper course, paused to watch them for a moment.

One of them looked up. A relative of Kormak, he spoke bitterly. "Today we sweat, you watch. We were defeated—but not by men, by whales! That cannot happen twice. Next time you will find no protectors. The Roga-landers are still looking out for you, and Ragnhild's kin will pay her bounty. And behind them, the Ragnarssons. Sigurth Snake-eye will pay as much for you as Ragnhild would have. If you go south, you will meet someone. You will never see England again, one-eye. The only man who could get through what waits for you would need an iron skin. Like Sigurth Fafnirsbane. And even he left a weak spot!"

Shef looked down reflectively. He knew the story of Sigurth who killed the dragon Fafnir—he had seen a part of it himself, in vision, seen the dragon-mask. He knew too that Sigurth had been betrayed by his lover, and killed by her husband and his kin, once they found out that the dragon's blood that had made his skin impenetrable had been checked at one spot by a leaf that stuck to it, and left him vulnerable only in the back. He, Shef, had had an angry lover as well, though she was dead, and her husband too. And he had killed a dragon, if Ivar Boneless might be considered as such.

The parallels were too close for comfort. And it was true enough that the North Way down the coast was also the one way south, and all too easily blocked.

"I hear what you say," he answered. "And I thank you for your warning. But you meant it in malice. If you have nothing better to say, do not speak next time." He reached out, carefully, and tapped the angry Viking on the very throat-ball with the point of his lance.

The human mind is strange. Nose-bleeds start from fear. A stammer is cured by a shock, feeble old women start from their beds in a crisis and lift great timbers from their sons' bodies. Kormak's relative knew he had spoken too freely. Knew that if the one-eyed man ran him through with the lance, there would be no complaint against him. As the point touched his throat, his gullet froze with fear. And remained frozen.

As Shef walked away one of his mates said to him in an undertone, "You chanced it there, Svipdag."

Svipdag turned to him, eyes wide. Tried to speak. Tried again, and again. Nothing came out but a low gargling. Men saw the terror in Svipdag's eyes as he realized that he meant to speak, but had been robbed of the ability as if a cord had been tied round his windpipe.

The other prisoners looked after Shef's retreating back. They had heard stories of him, of the death of Ivar, of Halvdan, of how King Olaf had handed over all his luck and his family's into this man's keeping. They knew he bore the sign of some unknown god round his neck, his father, some had heard.

"He said, 'do not speak,' " one of the Vikings muttered. "And now he can't!"

"I'm telling you, he called the whales in too," said another.

"And the Hidden Folk come to his help."

"If I'd known all that, Ragnhild could have whistled herself hoarse before I came on this gods-forsaken trip."

"You don't have to do this, you know," said Brand when Shef told him of his decision. "We'll think of something. Get those greedy louts from the *Crane* out of the way, things'll look better. We can send some lads south in the dories, maybe buy a boatload of food in Trondhjem, and a boat to put it in. *You* don't have to walk off into the snow, even if someone else does."

"That's what I'm going to do anyway," said Shef.

Brand hesitated, embarrassed. He felt he had spoken too gloomily earlier, provoked this insane decision. He remembered when he had first taken Shef under his protection, after they had put his eye out. He had taught him Norse, taught him how to use a sword properly, taught him the way of the *drengr,* the professional marching warrior. And Shef had taught him much too. Raised him to glory, and to riches—for the crisis now was one of food and fuel and ships, not of money.

"Look, no-one I know of has ever been deep into those mountains and come back, let alone come out the other side. Maybe the Finns do, but they're different. It's wolves and bears and cold. And where are you if you get through? Sweden! Or Swedish Finnmark, or somewhere. I can't see why you're doing this."

Shef thought for a few moments before replying. "I think I have two reasons," he said. "One is this. Ever since I went to the cathedral this spring, saw Alfred and—and Godive marry, I've felt that things were getting out of my hand. People pushed me, and I went along. I did what I had to. From the sandbank to the slave-market to Kaupang to the queen. Across the Upland and up to here. Chased by the Ragnarssons and Ragnhild and even by the whales. Now I think I've retreated as far as I

mean to. From now on I'm going to go back. I have been deep into the
darkness, into the smokehouse of the Hidden Folk, even. Now I have to
get into the light. And I don't mean to go back the way I came."

Brand waited. Like most of the men of the North, he believed deeply in
luck. What Shef was saying was that he meant to change his luck. Or
maybe that his luck had turned. Some people would say that the young
man had luck and to spare. But no man could judge of another's luck, that
was clear.

"The other reason?" he prompted.

Shef pulled his pole-ladder pendant forward from his chest. "I don't
know if you think this means anything," he said. "Do you think I have a
god for a father?"

Brand did not reply. "Well," Shef went on, "I keep seeing things, as you
know. Sometimes asleep, sometimes awake. I know someone is trying to
tell me things. Sometimes it's very easy. When we found Cuthred, I had
been shown to look for a man turning a great mill. Or had I heard the mill-
wheel creaking already? I don't know. But then, and the time when Cwicca
broke down the wall of the queen's house to get me out, I had a warning.
A warning about something that was happening right then.

"All that's easy enough. But I have seen other things that are not so easy.
I saw a hero dying, and an old woman. I saw the sun turn into a chariot
pursued by wolves, and into a father-god's face. I saw a hero ride to rescue
Balder from Hel, and I saw the White Christ killed by soldiers of the
Rome-folk who spoke our own tongue. I saw the heroes in Valhalla, and I
saw how those who are not heroes are received there.

"Now all those sights were trying to tell me something. Not something
easy. Not only from one side, from the pagans or the Christians. What I
think they were trying to tell me—or maybe I am telling myself—is that
there is something wrong. Something wrong with the way we all live. We
are sliding into the Skuld-world, Thorvin would say. Virtue has gone out
of us, out of us all, Christians and pagans. If this pendant means anything,
it means that I must try to put it back. One step at a time, as you mount a
ladder."

Brand sighed. "I see your mind is made up. Who will go with you?"

"You?"

Brand shook his head. "I have too much to do here. I cannot leave my
own kin unfed and unsheltered."

"Cwicca and his gang will come, I think, and Karli. He came with me for
adventures. If he gets back to the Ditmarsh he will be the greatest story-

teller they ever had. Udd for sure, maybe Hund, maybe Thorvin. I have to speak again to Cuthred, and to your cousin."

"There is a skerry where I can leave a message," Brand conceded reluctantly. "Your chances would go up a great deal if he would accompany you. But maybe he thinks he has done enough."

"What about provisions? What can you spare us?"

"Not much. But you will have the best of what we still own." Brand pointed. "One thing. Why are you still carrying that old weapon? All right, you picked it up in the smokehouse when you had nothing else, but look at it. It's old, the gold inlay is worn off, the blade is thin, it has no crosspiece. Not half the weapon Sigurth's 'Gungnir' was. Give it to me, I'll find you a better one."

Shef hefted the weapon thoughtfully. "I call it a good spear that conquers," he said. "I'll keep it."

CHAPTER TWENTY-FIVE

I n the end the group that Shef led to the foot of the mountains numbered twenty-three, all but three of them English speakers by birth. Cwicca, Osmod, Udd and their three remaining mates Fritha, Hama and Wilfi had joined him without question, as had Karli. So had Hund, saying that he had a feeling they would have need of a leech. More to Shef's surprise, Thorvin had agreed to make the trip, giving as his excuse that as a smith he wanted to see Jarnberaland and the College's outpost there. Once the news of the attempt spread, Shef had been much more surprised to find a deputation come to him, headed by Martha, the woman from Frisia, once a slave of Queen Ragnhild, and by Ceolwulf, the rescued slave whom the others suspected of having been a thane.

"We don't want to þe left here," they said. "We have been too much among the Norse-folk, and want to find our way home. Our best chance is with you."

"Not a good chance," Shef told them.

"Better than the one we had a while ago," said Ceolwulf grimly.

So the party was expanded by four women and eight men. Shef had wondered whether to argue that the women would not have the strength to make the journey, but the words died as he thought them. He had traveled from Kaupang to the Gula with them, and they kept up as well as the men, certainly better than the puny Udd or the short-legged Osmod. As for the male ex-slaves, all of them wearing still their Rig pendants, Shef had not the heart to leave them. They might be an asset. Certainly some of them, like the formidable Ceolwulf, had talents of their own. They had fought well if briefly in the skirmishes against the crew of the *Crane*: some had died, over-anxious to get in a blow against the race that had enslaved and tormented them.

The last member of the party was Cuthred. Brand had gone off one evening in the growing dark, making it clear that he was not to be watched or followed. As had been the custom of his family, he had left a message in a secret spot that his Hidden Folk relations knew. In some private code he had passed the news that he needed a meeting. But Echegorgun had not replied, or appeared. Instead Cuthred had walked in two mornings later. His clothes were dry and he was carrying his sword and shield, so he had not swum the narrow firth from the mainland. Echegorgun must have had some kind of boat or water-craft, but Cuthred was as close-mouthed about that as if he had already become a Hidden One himself.

Told what was intended, he listened, nodded, sat silent during the day, and disappeared again in the dark. When he returned a second time he brought discouraging word.

"Echegorgun won't accompany you," he said. "He says he has been seen too often already. He says I am to come with you instead."

Shef raised an eyebrow. Cuthred spoke as if he had a better alternative —maybe to join the Hidden Folk for good, as a kind of exchange for the child Barn many years ago.

"He says he will keep an eye on you, or on us," Cuthred went on. "And he will pass the word to his relatives not to interfere with us. That is a great threat removed. You know why most hunters from here have never come back. They ended up smoked like stock-fish. But that still leaves the bears and the wolves. And cold and hunger. And the Finns. We will have to take our chances with them."

Shef had agreed, having no choice, and turned to his preparations. In the end Brand had paraded every single member of the party in front of him, and gone through their equipment minutely. All had stout and well-greased boots that reached up to the calf. Thick leggings and thick wool trousers over them, for women as well as men. Wool tunics, skin mantles, hemp shirts. "Sweat is a danger," Brand told them. "Freezes on you. Hemp soaks up the sweat better than wool. Better not to sweat. Just do everything at an even pace, but never stop unless you have a fire. That is the way to keep warm, but not too warm." He had made sure that everyone had a bag to sleep in. Not, alas, the magnificent model Shef had bought at the Gula, which had burnt with so much else. But a store of feathers had survived the fire, and everyone had a two-layer bag of some material, wool or skin, padded with the down of the seabirds. Mittens and hats, scrims to go round the neck and pull across the face in a blizzard. For each person, in a back-pack, ten day's food, mostly dried fish and seal-meat, or the strong cheese made from sheep or goat's milk. Not enough, but a person walking all day in the cold needs four pounds' weight of food a day. Carry more, travel less. "If you see anything living, eat it," Brand said. "Spin out what you carry as long as you can. You will be hungry before you reach the other side."

The party's weapons had been carefully selected as well, and not for war. The catapulteers carried their crossbows and their knives. Even Osmod had been made to abandon his halberd, too heavy and cumbersome. Thorvin had his smith's hammer, Hund was empty-handed. The others carried either wood-axes or spears, stout-shafted ones with cross-pieces, not javelins or harpoons. "For bear," Brand explained. "You don't want one of them walking up the shaft at you." Four short hunting bows were spread among the group as well, given to those who considered themselves good shots. Cuthred carried the sword they had taken from Vigdjarf, and his spiked shield. Shef had his lance as well as a broad sharp-pointed Rogaland knife taken from the *Crane*.

Finally, Brand had insisted on pressing upon them six pairs of the strange sticks the Norwegians slid on, the skis. "None of us can use them," Shef protested.

"Thorvin can," Brand replied.

"I learned too," added Ceolwulf. "Learned the first winter."

"You might need to send scouts out," Brand urged. What he thought was that some might survive, even if all did not.

At dawn, some fourteen days after the battle and the burning, the party set out. They were carried over the first stretch in the first ship Brand's folk had managed to make from salvaged parts: planks from both the wrecked ships, keel made from one half of the *Crane*'s originally riveted main timber. The ship was short, wide, and lacking in proportion, named by Brand in disgust the *Duckling*. Nevertheless she moved reasonably enough under sail, the party packed into her roomy waist with the six-man crew working round them. There had been some argument about where they should all be set down, Brand opting for a fjord which ran furthest into the tangled mass of mountains, and so cut down their marching distance as much as possible. But Cuthred vetoed the choice with total confidence. "Echegorgun said not," he reported. "He said, go to the fjord that leads to the triple-horned mountain. Then head due east. That way we will strike a line that may lead us down to the great lake that runs across Kjolen, the Keel."

"A line, or a path," queried Shef.

"A line. There are no paths. Not even Hidden Folk paths. In the deep mountains, they need no paths."

He had almost said "we," Shef noted.

So, in a chill wind, twenty-three laden figures stood at the very end of a deep fjord. The sun had climbed high up the sky. Even so, it was only just high enough to clear the mountain-tops, and half the fjord still lay in deep shadow. On the other side the snow-capped peaks lay reflected in deep still water, stirred only by the faint ripples of the *Duckling* being poled out from shore. The humans seemed a mere scattering of forked twigs under the impassive gray bulks, their path a mere slash in the rock down which bright water bounded.

Brand called out across the water, "Thor aid you."

Thorvin made the sign of the Hammer in reply.

"Lead on," said Shef to Cuthred.

Twelve days later, Shef knew he had calculated wrong. He was cutting a twelfth notch in a stick he had carried tucked in his belt since the first few days, and the rest were watching him. They were watching him because he had a dry stick.

That was part of the miscalculation. The first day had been as bad as Shef had thought it would be, remembering the agony of the climb up the shore, where he had met Ekwetargun. The mountain-side had never been a vertical wall, to be scaled. Yet it had never flattened out enough to become a place where a person could walk, either. First the thigh muscles ached. Then the arms began to join in, as the weary climbers pulled themselves up more and more, pushed with their legs less and less. The breaks for rest became longer, more frequent, the pain worse at each restart.

All that Shef had predicted. After all, it was only a matter of climbing, say, five thousand feet. Five thousand steps would do it. We must have done three already, he told the others. Two thousand steps! We can count them. And though he had been wrong about the number, he had been right that there would be an end.

So, then, for a few days, high spirits. Cooped up in slave-quarters or on ship-board for so long, the English had revelled in the air, the sunlight, the immense distances they could see, the exhilarating bareness. The bareness. That was the trouble. Even Thorvin had confided to Shef that he had expected to meet what the Norwegians called *barrskog*, thickets of scrub. But they were far above the tree-line here. Each night, each fireless night— for they had carried no wood—the cold seemed to clamp down more fiercely. Food was rationed strictly. It never seemed enough. Maybe if they had had a fire to boil their meat in, they began to mutter to each other, the dried seal-meat might have felt as if it filled a belly. As it was, it seemed to be like chewing leather. An age to choke down, and only cramp in the guts once it was there. Night after night, Shef woke from his cold sleep, even in the down-lined bag, dreaming of bread. Bread with thick yellow butter on it. And honey! With beer, thick brown beer. His body cried out for it. None of them had had much fat on their bones to begin with, and their bodies were beginning to break down muscle for want of anything else to use.

So they stared at his stick, wanting him to shave it down, use it for tinder, light a fire and burn—burn the sere brown grass and moss that covered the rolling upland plateau. It was impossible. But they thought it.

At least they had made some distance, Shef reflected. Neither hills nor woods had detained them, though swamp and bog had. Yet they had not come upon the lake he had hoped for, and all Cuthred would say was that it must be further on. A lake, he said, with trees round it, with bark that would make light boats. So Echegorgun had assured him. Pity Echegorgun won't come and show us, Shef had felt like saying again and again, keeping silent in view of Cuthred's doubtful loyalties.

A few days ago he would have told himself that at least the party was staying united. The ability of the ex-slaves to endure hardship had been a great asset. Where proud warriors would have argued and fought and blamed each other, making something out of every blister or bellyache, Shef's party had behaved to each other like—well, like women, Shef had to say. When Martha got the gripes one morning and might have delayed their start, it was Wilfi who acted the fool and distracted attention. When Udd, the weakest of the party, began to limp and go whiter and whiter in the face trying to disguise it, afraid that he would be abandoned, it was Ceolwulf who halted the march, dressed Udd's sore heel with his own ration of sealfat, and walked by his side to encourage him.

Yet the strain was starting to tell, showing in bickerings. Cuthred, especially, was getting worse again. The day before Karli, still irrepressible when it came to women, had caught up with Edith as she walked ahead, and fondled her buttock for a moment. He and Edith had been bed-partners since Drottningsholm, when the chance came, and she had not protested. But Cuthred, walking behind, had said nothing, merely caught

Karli a great sweeping blow on the ear. For a second Karli had squared off to him. Then he saw Cuthred's ostentatious openness to the punch, knew that the counter would be lethal, dropped his shoulders and turned away. Now Karli was humiliated. Not as much as Cuthred had been, but there was enmity there now, and spreading as people took sides.

Shef tucked the stick back in his belt, looked up at the stars coming out in the frosty air. "Sleep now," he said. "March at dawn. We've nothing better to do. We'll find wood tomorrow, and Cuthred's lake."

When the leader weakens, then the army is hindered, so goes the proverb. When the leader has to joke, then the army is weak already.

Somewhere above, a mind was watching. Looking down at the little comfortless party, nipped by the cold and by the belly-pinch, one of them at least sobbing silently with an internal pain. It watched with satisfaction, tempered only by caution.

He survived my whales, it thought. He survived my disciple's test. He carried my spear and he still bears my mark, but he does me no honor. Has never done me honor. But what is honor? The important thing is, he weakens me and mine for the day of Ragnarök.

Yes, thought the Othin-mind, I have slept little since the death of my son. Since they took Balder from me, and the best of my men, my Einheriar, failed to bring him back from Hel. Since then the world has been gray and dull, and so it will stay till the day of Ragnarök. And if we do not conquer on that day, what hope is there? But this creature, this manling born in a bed, wants to make the world better as it is, to give men happy lives before Ragnarök comes. If that belief spreads, where will my Einheriar come from?

He must die here and his thoughts die with him. And his followers too. And yet there is a loss there, a loss there as well. For the creature with my one-eye has a kind of wisdom—I wonder who put it there? Sometimes he reminds me of one of my other sons. In any case, he sent me a great champion for the day of Ragnarök, Ivar Slayer-of-Kings, who now fights daily in Valhalla with his fellows. And the one he takes with him, he is a great champion too, the mutilated one. There are no women in Valhalla to irk him, he would be welcome. Baptized to the White Christ he may have been, but there is no belief there now, he could be mine, come to me for my collection. But to do that he must die with weapon in hand.

It would be a pity to lose him. Even the one-eye, he has a kind of cunning, and that is scarce enough in the fields round Valhalla. What shall I send them? Shall I send my wolves?

No. If the wolves ate them, that might be well enough. But just now they would eat the wolves and find them tasty. No, the whales failed and Valgrim failed, and the old iötunn was never mine but rather the brood of Loki. The wolves would fail too. So I will send them snow. And in the snow, my Finns.

The flakes began to whisper down out of the sky shortly after dusk, at first just one or two, seeming to crystallize rather than fall. Then bigger flakes, and bigger, and a wind rising out of the north to drive them on. Around midnight the two sentries, seeing the snow starting to drift around and over the humped sleeping bags on the bare ground, decided to wake people up and make them shake themselves clear. The camp turned into a slow shuffle of exhausted men and women struggling out into the cold air, shaking their bags down, moving to a new spot, lying down, feeling the hard ground beneath them turn to slush under their own escaped body heat. They began to shuffle unconsciously to get into the lee of each other, the camp moving slowly piece by piece downwind.

Some time before dawn Shef, realizing what was happening, made a line of backpacks and raked snow over them to create a makeshift wall, putting the party behind that in ranks, the weakest in the middle and the strongest on the edges. Few people slept much for all that. Dawn broke on people tired, hungry, and still fireless.

There was no moving till the snow stopped, as it did after a few hours. They looked out then on a featureless white plain, the sun hidden behind clouds. Shef felt a momentary stab of doubt. During the night he had lost all sense of direction. With the sun hidden . . . He had heard that there was a kind of clear rock that so concentrated the rays that you could see the sun even through cloud, but there was none of it in this group.

He controlled his fear. Which way they went was no longer material. They had to find wood and shelter, and any way that led to that was good. Salvaging the skis from under the snow, he told Thorvin and Ceolwulf, their only skilled users, to go in different directions as far as was visible, to look for a break in the plateau.

Only after they had left did he think to count heads. They were one short. The missing woman was Godsibb, a fair, silent, sad girl, who had trudged along without complaint ever since they had taken her from Drottningsholm. Even Karli had not bothered to try his luck with her. She had never responded even to his good cheer. They found her body, a hump in the snow surprisingly far away, showing how much they had moved in the night.

"What did she die of?" asked Shef after they had swept the snow off the body with their hands.

"Cold. Exhaustion. Hunger," said Hund. "People have different levels of resistance. She was a thin girl. Maybe her bag got damp. Nobody noticed her in the night and she fell into the snow-sleep. It is a peaceful way to go —better than the fate Queen Asa would have given her," he added, trying to deflect Shef's self-criticism.

Shef looked at the worn face, too tired for a young girl's. "She came a long way to die here," he said.

And in dying she had caused him a problem, too. Impossible to bury her in the frozen ground. Could they leave her in the snow, under the snow? It would look all right as they marched away, but no-one could avoid thinking of what would happen when the snow melted and left her exposed.

Hund touched Shef's arm and pointed silently. On a knoll a hundred yards away, a four-legged shape looked at them, then sat down to wait, tongue lolling. Others drifted up behind it, took in the situation, and sat or lay down.

There were different views about wolves. Some of the English were quite used to them, said they were hardly dangerous at all. Brand had contradicted that with his usual finality. "They'll pull you down," he said. "Not frightened of people at all. Of course they won't attack a score of you, armed and together. Two men off in the forest, that's another story."

The wolves meant they could not possibly leave Godsibb, not till they could find earth to lay her in, fire to soften it, and stones to pile on her grave. Carrying her would just weaken the carriers further. If they ended up with another corpse to carry, and another . . .

Shef called two men over, told them to tie her in her bag, attach ropes to it and drag her through the snow when they moved on. He waved aside Fritha's eager offer to shoot a wolf with his crossbow. Waste of a bolt. There would come a time when their need would be greater. Meanwhile the hunting bows had been lost in the night, put down on the ground and buried in the snow. Shef organized the party into a line and made them move back over the whole area they had covered in the night, back to where he thought was their original campsite, probing with feet and gloved hands. They found two of the four bows but only one quiver of arrows, also a set of skis and someone's discarded backpack. By then it might have been noon, and not a step advanced on their journey. A poor start for the first day of bad weather. Shef scowled at the man who had lost his pack, and rubbed the lesson home with harsh words.

"Keep everything by you. Or on you. Don't leave anything ever till the

morning. Or there won't be a morning. And remember, your mother isn't
with us!"

Thorvin and Ceolwulf were back, looking annoyingly warm and cheerful from hours of positive action.

"Head that way," said Ceolwulf, pointing. "There's a dip, a valley going
down, and what looks like trees a few miles off."

Shef reflected. "All right," he said. "Look. Just two of you might not be
safe, with our new escorts. Pick four of the youngest and show them how
to use these skis. Then take them forward, ahead of us. Even your beginners will be faster than people floundering in snow. When you get to the
trees, break wood and bring back as much as you can carry. A fire will put
heart into people, and make it easier for them to walk on. I will bring
everyone on as fast as I can. Take care not to lose sight of us, and come
back at once if the snow begins again."

The skiers went ahead of them, Thorvin and Ceolwulf calling advice and
helping fallers to their feet. Shef and the rest, sixteen of them towing one
body, kept on trudging forward, occasionally stumbling into drifts. The
snow crept down boots and inside mittens.

Piruusi the Finn reveled in the snow, the first fall of the year, early and
welcome. He had left his snug skin tent at dawn, watered the bone runners
of his sleigh and left them to ice, wiped his face and his skis with yellow
reindeer-fat, and skimmed away, bow in hand. He hoped for ptarmigan or
Arctic hare, but anything would be welcome, even nothing. Winter was
the time of release for the Finns, and if it came early, then their ancestral
spirits looked kindly on them.

As he swept up to and past the tent of old Pehto, the shaman, Pehto
came out and hailed him. Piruusi stopped, frowning. Pehto was too powerful with the spirits to vex, but he called always for attention, respect,
food and fermented milk.

Not this time. Capering professionally and shaking his rattle, Pehto
nevertheless for once spoke sense. "To the west, Piruusi great hunter, lord
of the reindeer. To the west, something comes. Something with power,
Piruusi, and a god's disfavor. Aiiee!" And he began a manic stamping
dance, which Piruusi ignored.

Nevertheless he swung out of the low birch wood, its leaves already
turning brown from the first frost, and pushed up the gentle slope to the
west. His skis hissed smoothly across the snow, Piruusi moving without
thought and without effort. Ski-poles were slung across his back, but on
anything less than a full slope he had no need of them. More important to

hold the bow and arrow, ready for a shot at any moment. One lived in the winter wild by preying on every opportunity. Never turning down a chance.

There was something there, sure enough. Had the old fraud really seen them with his mystic vision? Perhaps he had risen early to look, for they were plain enough, a straggle across the snow. First, men on skis. Men! They fell over every hundred paces, worse than boys, as if they were babies. And behind those, clear enough to Piruusi's long-sighted eyes, a herd of them, moving like oxen, floundering along, kicking up snow with every step. They dragged a makeshift sled or travois with them.

Piruusi had never paid a Finn-tax, but those of his cousins who lived nearer the shore did so. It was worth it not to have their summer fisheries and fowling-trips cut short by the murderous seamen. Time, Piruusi thought, for someone to pay a Norse-tax in return. He skimmed back to the cluster of tents, men and women inside the flaps cooking over their hot fires of dried reindeer dung, called the menfolk to their skis and bows.

Shef's party regained their strength as they reached the first clump of trees, mere dwarf birch, but desperately welcome. Shef called the skiers back to join the marchers, anxious that no-one should be lost sight of.

"We'll get into the trees, find shelter," he called. "Then we can have a fire and cook. At least we'll be off the moor."

As if in answer, an arrow from behind a tree struck Wiferth, struggling with his skis, in the base of the skull. He fell instantly, dead as a herring before he struck ground. Moments later the air was full of the zip of arrows, the trees full of figures flitting from one trunk to another, never showing for more than an instant, calling encouragement to each other in some unknown language.

Many of Shef's party were veterans. They crouched immediately, shook out into a rough circle, moved behind what cover there was. But the arrows came from all sides. Not shot with much force—Shef saw Ceolwulf grimace and pull an arrow from the brawn of his thigh, seemingly with little effort—but deadly to throat or eye. The shooters were quite close in.

"Fritha," Shef called, "use your crossbow. The rest of you with bows, shoot if you're sure, not otherwise. If you don't have a bow, lie down."

The crossbow clicked as Fritha cocked it. Cuthred, using his initiative, stepped over to behind Fritha, batted an arrow away with his shield, stood over him to guard his back. Fritha sighted on a tree-trunk with a Finn behind it, waited for the man to bob out for his shot. As the Finn emerged, Fritha squeezed the trigger.

Hit in the center of the chest at thirty yards, the Finn flew backwards, the bolt buried up to its feathers. Piruusi, ten yards away, looked over in surprise. The Norse were not bowmen! Nor had he seen a bow. He had no martial tradition, no urge for glory. He fought like a wolf, like a predator. If the prey offered resistance, withdraw, wait. The Finns drew back, still shouting and releasing arrows.

"Well, that seemed easy enough," muttered Shef, rising to his feet.

"Wait till we try and move," answered Cuthred.

A few hours later, with still time left before the dark came down, the position was clear enough. Shef's party had lost two dead—they now had three corpses to drag—and half a dozen with minor arrow wounds. Crossbows or the threat of them kept the Finns at a distance, but Shef believed only a couple of the dozen bolts shot had taken effect. They had not too many left, and the Finns were growing adept at creeping up, shooting, and skimming away in the trees. They were deep in the wood now, and the shelter they had looked forward to so eagerly was proving a menace. On the open moor they had left, their longer-range weapons would have been decisive. It was a bad prospect for the night. Time to fell trees, make a barricade. At least they could have their promised fire.

As the first axeman struck at a birch tree, Shef noticed a bundle wedged in its branches. He stared up. A long bundle. An ominous long bundle.

He pointed it out to Thorvin, both men crouching for fear of the flying arrow. "What is that?"

Thorvin pulled his beard. "I have heard that up here, where the ground is often frozen too hard to bury their dead, they place them in trees instead."

"We are in the Finns' churchyard?"

"Hardly a church. But a burial place, yes."

Shef waved the axeman on, looked round for other tree-bundles. "Get a fire lit," he called. "A big one. Maybe they will pay a ransom for their dead."

Piruusi, watching, scowled again. The fire the Norse-folk had lit silhouetted them, would make them good targets in the night. But that was his own grandmother they had cut from her rest! What might they do? Not burn her? A burnt ghost lost its body in the other world, would come back to haunt its careless relatives. His grandmother had been trouble enough while she was alive.

Time, Piruusi thought, for trickery. He skied away from the reindeer sleigh they had brought up to carry off their dead, broke off a branch with leaves still on it, waved it in token of parley, alert all the time for any sign of one of the strange weapons being brought to bear on him.

Shef saw the man in the skin coat and trousers waving a bough, noting with envy even at that moment the beautifully supple leather—Piruusi's wives had spent many a day chewing the skin to that grade of softness. He saw his alert readiness to dodge, pushed aside Fritha's crossbow, broke off a bough himself and walked forward a little way.

The Finn stopped maybe ten yards off. As Shef wondered what language he might speak, the Finn solved matters for him by calling out in fair if fractured Norse.

"You," he shouted. "Why fire? Why cut down trees, take down old people? You burn them? They do you no harm."

"Why you shoot arrows at us?" retorted Shef in the same style. "We do you no harm. You kill my friends."

"You kill my friends," replied the Finn. Shef noted a flicker of motion out of the corner of one eye, something moving from tree to tree to his left. And to his right. The Finn was calling out again, trying to fix his attention —while the others came in on him from either side. He was trying to take a prisoner, not make a parley. It might be a good idea if they did try. If Shef could embroil two or three of them Cuthred would charge to his rescue. And that might frighten them enough to ensure free passage. Of course he, Shef, might not survive it.

There was something else moving in the forest. Not to either side, but behind the parleying Finn. He had left his sleigh and the two reindeer that pulled it behind him. The animals were standing quietly trying to grub lichen of some kind off the ground. But there was something definitely there behind them.

With incredulity Shef saw the towering bulk of Echegorgun step out from behind a dwarf birch tree. He could not have been behind the tree. The tree's bole was at most a foot thick, barely thicker than one of Echegorgun's arms. Yet there he was in plain sight, looking at Shef, evidently meaning to be seen. A moment before he had not been there. In any case Shef pondered, baffled, they had just spent days and weeks crossing an open moor where you could see every bird and blade of grass. How could Echegorgun have tracked them? Even the reindeer did not seem to have noticed him. They ate on, unalarmed.

The Finn had noticed Shef's fixed stare. "Ho, ho," he hooted. "That old game. 'See behind you, Piruusi, something there.' Then I look, your men shoot, shoot."

Echegorgun stepped carefully up to one of the grazing reindeer, took its head in his massive hands, turned it with a kind of delicacy. The reindeer's legs crumpled immediately, it fell forward, held up for an instant by Echegorgun. He moved to the other, still unmoving, snapped its neck with the same care and lack of haste.

And then he had gone, faded into the birch-shade as if he had never been, leaving only two dead animals to mark his passing.

Piruusi realized suddenly that Shef was ignoring him, whipped round like an adder. Saw his dead beasts unmoving on the ground. His eyes widened, his jaw dropped, he turned back to Shef with fear and disbelief on his face.

Shef turned and looked deliberately at the Finns creeping up from each side, yelled back to Fritha and his mates to mark them. Pointed warningly at the crossbows coming up. Then walked over to where Piruusi now stood by his dead reindeer.

"How you do that?" asked Piruusi. Could Pehto have been right, old fraud or no? Was there some kind of power in this odd man with the one eye and the old spear?

He felt the broken necks of his darlings, his treasured speed beasts, and asked again, "How you do that?"

"I did not do that," said Shef. "But you see, I have friends in these woods. Friends you cannot see, friends you do not want to meet. Have you heard of such things?"

Evidently the Finn had, for he was looking round nervously now as if at any moment some creature might appear behind him and put fingers round his neck. Shef reached over and tapped him with the butt of his lance.

"No more shooting," he said. "No more tricks. We want fire, food. Give gold, silver. Go on to Jarnberaland. You know Jarnberaland?"

There was recognition in the man's eyes, as well as doubt. "I show you Jarnberaland," he agreed. "First we drink together. Drink of . . ." he seemed to have trouble finding a word. "Drink seeing-drink together. You, me, Pehto."

Not understanding, Shef nodded agreement.

CHAPTER TWENTY-SIX

On the evening of the next day, Piruusi took to Pehto the traditional offerings: the block of salt, the sack of strong-smelling half-rancid butter made from reindeer milk, the blood sausage stuffed with lumps of thick fat, the chewed and dressed reindeer hide. As the traditional extra gift he added a pair of soft boots with red thread to draw the tops tight. Pehto inspected the gifts with the expected lack of interest, and refused them twice. The third time he swept them to the side of his tent and called to his aged crone of a wife, more than forty years old already, to come and take them.

"For how many?" he asked.

"For myself and for you. For the stranger with the one eye, and for his companion."

Pehto considered. It was a brief moment for him, not of power—for there could be no question of refusal—but at least of attention. He decided not to make the most of it. The gifts Piruusi had brought were in fact generous—so generous Pehto knew something must have made him so.

"Come when the sky is dark," said the shaman.

Piruusi left without further ceremony. What he knew, and what the shaman did not, for all his claims of being able to look far afield and see what was hidden, was that the one-eye, when Piruusi had claimed compensation for his slaughtered reindeer, had stripped a gold ring from his arm and handed it over without further ado. It was true he had taken the reindeer, but he had returned the valuable hides again without argument. Piruusi had hardly ever seen gold before, the yellow iron as his tribe called it, but he was well aware of the value placed on it by the Norse-folk with whom he sometimes traded. For a ring of that weight he could buy everything the tribe owned, except for their reindeer herds.

Yet the stranger was not completely insane. When Piruusi had demanded further compensation for the two men killed by crossbow bolts, the stranger had waved at his own dead and said no more. Piruusi had noticed, too, the savage glare on the face of the very big man with the spiked shield and sword. Wiser not to provoke such, touched by the spirits. In any case, there was the matter of the dead reindeer. Piruusi had decided, tentatively, that the stranger was a mighty shaman of the Norsemen, of a kind he had not met before. He must be able to send himself out in a different shape, and that shape, probably a bear, had killed the reindeer while the man-shape stood in front of him.

They would know more after the seeing-drink. Eagerly, Piruusi went to his tent, called in the youngest of his wives, prepared to pass the time as well as possible till dark.

Shef was making a tour of their makeshift camp, with Hund. The two dead reindeer had vanished within a few hours as the starving men and women first built a fire, then eagerly began to toast strips of the fresh meat over it. Then they recovered themselves enough to heat stones, place them in their wooden pans and start more of the meat stewing its way towards tenderness. In the beginning they had been devouring the meat all but raw. Shef remembered the first rush of intoxication, almost like the effect of the winter wine, as he gulped down the first slice of fresh liver. But then, he reflected, not only had he been dreaming of thick bread and butter the day before, he had begun to wonder why he had not taken the chance of rotten shark while it was on offer.

"How do you think the people are?" asked Shef.

"It is surprising how quickly they recover," Hund said. "A day and a half ago I was afraid for Udd. He has little strength. I thought we might lose him the way we lost Godsibb, just too weak for a cold night. Now, with three heavy meals inside him, and a night spent by a good fire, he is fit for another few days' travel. One thing I worry about, though. Some of the men are showing old cuts that are opening again—cuts that had healed years before."

"What causes that?"

"No-one knows. But it comes at the end of the spring, when people have been living on stored food for the longest. All leeches of Ithun know that if you give people fresh green stuff, cabbage or kale, they recover immediately. Garlic and onions are good too. Bread is useless."

"We are not at the end of spring now, only the start of winter, and that early."

"True. But for how long were we living on shipboard rations? And what did we eat on Hrafnsey? Much dried meat, dried fish. It is fresh stuff we must have, eaten raw. I think the raw meat, or the half-cooked meat we ate yesterday may have done good. We can try and get some more meat, till we reach the Wayman mines. They will have some store of cabbage or onions there, even if it is pickled."

Shef nodded. There was something strange in this, as if food were something more than fuel you burnt, the only concern being to get enough of it. Yet he had never heard of cows or sheep or horses, or dogs or wolves come to that, sickening because they had only one thing to eat. He changed the subject.

"Do you know what it is we are to drink with the headman of the Finns tonight?"

"I will know when we see it, or sniff it or taste it. But if it is a seeing-drink, there are not so many things it could be. It might be a weak draught of the henbane that Ragnhild used on her husband, or of the deadly nightshade berry. But I doubt they grow up here in the waste. Most likely —well, we will see. One thing I will say, Shef."

Hund turned and faced Shef with unusual gravity. "We have known each other a long time, and I know you well. You are a stiff man, who has grown stiffer. Let me tell you, you are in a strange country now, stranger than Hedeby, or Kaupang, or Hrafnsey. They may ask you to do things that you would find demeaning. They mean no harm. If the headman does it, you do it."

"How about you?"

"I am a leech. It is my place to sit and observe, and see you come to no harm. Take another man to drink with you if that is what they expect. But do what they expect."

Shef remembered a proverb from their shared youth, that Father Andreas had been accustomed to say. "If you're in Rome, do as the Romans do, you mean?"

"The other way to say it is, 'if you are with the wolves you must learn to howl.' "

* * *

A short while later Shef, lance in hand, led Hund and Karli towards the Finn encampment a short quarter-mile from their own. He felt a certain release and anticipation, as if he were going to a drinking-party in Emneth in his youth, not to some strange ritual among people who had just tried to kill him. Examining his feelings, he realized why. It was freedom from the overpowering presence of Cuthred. Obviously there could be no question of taking him among strangers who might provoke him by accident. Karli seemed relieved as well. He stared at each of the Finns who occasionally swept by over the light snow on their skis.

"Some of them must be women," he remarked finally.

Shef led them to the tent he had heard described, the tent of the sorcerer. The flap was open, a withered old man beckoned them in to where Piruusi the headman already sat. Piruusi seemed irritated at the sight of three men.

"Only two," he said, holding up two fingers. "Not enough for more."

"I shall not drink," said Hund carefully. "I watch only."

Piruusi did not seem mollified, but he remained silent as the old man waved the others to sit on the skin floor, handed each of them a birchwood frame to support their backs. He began to sing a monotonous chanting song, from time to time shaking a rattle. From somewhere outside the tent a small drum thumped in accompaniment.

"He is calling the spirits to guide us," said Piruusi. "How many reindeer do you want for that gold ring on other arm? I can give you two, fat ones, though no other man would give you more than one."

Shef grinned and made a counter-offer of three entire silver pennies for three reindeer, one penny to be returned in exchange for their hides. Realizing with some relief that his guest was not completely insane, Piruusi cackled professionally and tried again.

As they reached a final agreement—ten silver pennies and a gold finger-ring for five reindeer, hides to be returned, and twenty pounds of bird feathers for sleeping bags—Pehto ended his song. With the lack of ceremony which the Finns seemed to use, he reached out of the tent and took a large steaming vessel passed in by the unknown hands that had beat the drum. He dippered out of it in turn four large mugs of hollowed pine and handed one each to Piruusi, Karli and Shef, kept the fourth himself.

"Drink," he said, in Norse.

Shef passed his mug without words to Hund, who sniffed it carefully, dipped a finger in and licked it. As he did so Piruusi's brow cleared. At last he had realized the function of the third man. He was a taster. Certainly the one-eye was a man of great importance, to have such a functionary.

"It is water in which the fly killer mushroom has been boiled."

"Is it safe to drink?"

"Safe for you, I think. You are used to these things. I dare say it will do Karli no harm."

Shef raised the mug politely to his host, and drank deep. Round him the others did the same. Shef observed that it seemed to be the polite thing to drink a third, pause, drink some more, pause again, and finish the draught. The liquid tasted hot, musty, with a faint bitterness: not pleasant, but better than many things Hund had made him swallow. The men sat in silence for a while, drifting into their own thoughts.

Shef felt his soul rise through his mouth and out, through the tent as if it were impalpable, out into the wide air and wheeling like a bird over the dark wood and the great expanse of white moorland that lay all around it. He noted with interest the lake, part-frozen, that lay on the other side of the wood, not far away: Ceolwulf had been right. But while his mind was interested, his soul was not. It darted away, like a flash, winging westwards. As it shot across land and sea, as fast as thought, the light came back into the world. At the place where it hovered, it was still evening, not night. Still autumn, not winter.

It was Hedeby. Shef recognized the mound where he had sat outside the walls and seen the terrible defeat and sacrifice that took place long ago. But the air of peace that hung over the countryside then, when he had sat there, was gone now. No contented plowman, no smoking chimneys. Instead a great camp of tents outside the wall, and lining the walls hundreds of men. It was like the siege of York that Shef had seen, and ended, two years before.

Except for two things. The walls were wood, not the stone of the Rome-folk. And the defenders had no mind to let the walls do all the work for them. Many were outside, skirmishing with the besiegers, fighting it out with sword and spear and battle-axe, exiting from sally-ports and wickets, making their raids, and returning hastily or triumphantly to the stockade.

Yet there was a pattern to the confusion, Shef slowly saw. And as he saw it, the conviction grew on him that he was not seeing the past, or some mythical story, or something that might have been. What he saw was taking place at the same moment as he sat in the Finn's tent. It was a vision, but a vision of the real, one that needed no interpretation.

The besiegers were fighting to set up catapults, mules, by the knoll where Shef had sat. The besieged were trying to hinder them. Not successfully. But then they had only been playing for time. The skirmishers heard a horn blast, drew back. On the walls nearest to the three mules that the besiegers had set up were six, ten, a dozen of the simple stone-lobbing machines that Shef had himself in-

vented, the pull-throwers. They were set up now on platforms broadening the stockade's fighting gangways.

Pull-teams clustered round each one, eight men to a machine, holding the ropes. The long arms were lowered, the thrower-captains loaded rocks into the slings, tugged the arms down. The pullers heaved in unison—not quite in unison, Shef noted professionally, the fault of the unbiddable Norsemen—the arms swept up, the slings lashed round.

A rain of stones landing round the mules, each one ten pounds' weight, coming from the top of a two-hundred-yard arc, enough to batter a helmet in on a skull and the skull into the neck. But only landing round the mules. The trouble with the pull-throwers, as Shef remembered clearly, was that they were easy to aim for line but very hard to adjust for range. The missiles were lobbed, not flung. Fine against a static army, especially one caught in a long line. Against a point target, like trying to lob stones into a bucket thirty yards off.

Shef's vision seemed to sharpen as he watched. He recognized, on the wall, shouting exhortations, the fat but formidable figure of King Hrorik, who had sold him on to the Way. He was wearing a silver helmet and carried a painted shield. And he was shouting at—in the far-off tent in the birch-woods the Shef-body grunted with surprise—shouting at Lulla, who had deserted at the Gula-Thing. So that was who had been paying the high wages for experts.

Lulla, Shef could see, was trying to set up a mule, and Edwi, the other deserter, another one ten yards away. They were having trouble. Unlike the relatively light pull-throwers, their force given by muscle-power, the mules were made of the heaviest timber to take the shock of the throwing-arm's strike. Difficult to get up high on to a fighting-platform, and not easy once you did it. But they had swayed the machines up on sheer-legs, and both the Englishmen were running round, each one trying to do, or to check, what would normally take a full catapult-team of eight.

They were going to be too late. The besiegers . . . Who were the besiegers? With a feeling of growing doom Shef saw the Raven Banner advancing across the battle-plain, the three Ragnarssons clustered about it. Even at a distance the strange white-surrounded pupils of the Snake-eye seemed to pierce the walls and the defenses, and Shef flinched as the gaze seemed to pass through him. They were calling their men on, rallying them for a charge, because they knew . . .

Their own mules shot first. Two of them. One had taken a rock from a pull-thrower right on its retainer bolt, and the crew, casualties lying around them, were struggling frantically to free the bent metal. But two was almost enough. One shot low, sent its ball skimming along into the earth-wall at the base of the stockade, where it bounced and flew just over the stockade. The second struck square on, in an instant beat flat a gap three tree-trunks wide. The Ragnarsson stormers surged forward, were stopped and heaved back.

Lulla had got his machine ready, was yelling at King Hrorik, who shouted back and hit him over the shoulders with his sword-flat. Lulla crouched behind the machine, shrieking directions—his crew seemed baffled by them—trying to get line and elevation correct. Then, battered again by the sweating Hrorik, he pulled the release.

And a hit! Shef heard voices cheering, wondered if one was his own. One of the Ragnarsson mules had disintegrated, hit square on by the much more powerful mule-ball, its crew scattered round it, laid low by splinters or the lashing twisted ropes suddenly released.

Edwi's mule shot an instant later. For a moment Shef could not follow the flight, then he realized, seeing the Ragnarsson crews duck their heads in automatic reflex, that it had shot a foot too high, skimming over the crewmen's heads and speeding on to land half a mile over.

And now the Ragnarssons had the range, had got their third mule repaired as well. Shef saw the mule-captains glance at each other, lift arms to show they were ready, drop them together as the signal to shoot. They had learnt that well. Who had taught them? More deserters? Many men had learnt how the machines worked, in Shef's army or Ivar's, or maybe even from their first makers, the black monks of York.

Shef's soul in the sky saw the flying stones trundle through the air as if they flew through treacle. He had time to project their flight, to see where they would strike, to try to gasp out warning. Then time was at the right speed again. He saw the stones smash through the logs, hurl aside the machines they had been aimed at, sweep the whole pile of wood and rope and stones and men off the wall in a shrieking pile. There was Lulla on the ground, looking up, trying to struggle up, his arm broken, while down on top of him, brushed from its base, came the ton-and-a-quarter of his machine.

Shef flicked his gaze away as he heard the thud, the snap of shattered ribs. He could not see Edwi. The Ragnarssons were streaming straight for the gap in the wall. King Hrorik was in the center of it, sword drawn, calling to his men to come on. Behind him others tried to rig up a makeshift barricade, the battle was not yet lost . . .

Shef sprang to his feet in the tent, shouting, "The warriors round Hedeby!" Realized where he was, realized the others were all conscious and watching him. He wiped cold sweat from his brow, muttered, "I saw . . . I saw a siege. In Denmark."

Piruusi caught the word "Denmark," a place he knew was far away, and grinned. Clearly this man was a great shaman of the Norse-folk. His spirit flew wide.

"What did you see?" Shef asked Karli.

His face was full of unusual dismay. He looked down, said in a low voice, "Oh. A girl."

The Finnish headman caught the word, slapped him on the back, grinning cheerfully. He said something Shef could not catch, said it again. Shef turned inquiringly to Hund.

"He says, do you need to piss?"

Shef realized he did indeed feel a pressure from his bladder. The mug had held at least a pint of the strange drink, and he must have sat in his vision for most of an hour.

"Yes," he said. "Er, where?"

The old man had brought out another vessel, a larger one, again of hollowed pine. He put it on the ground, made inviting gestures, passed another to Piruusi, who began to struggle out of his laced breeches—no easy job, in cold-weather clothes. Shef looked round, wondered if it was not possible at least to go outside. Perhaps they didn't do that here. Perhaps you could get frostbite leaving the tent much of the year. Untroubled by inhibitions, he followed the lead of his hosts, as did Karli.

The old Finn picked up Piruusi's chamber pot and Shef's mug, dippered the steaming fluid out, held it out to Shef. He recoiled, pulling his hand away. An outburst of angry Finnish from both the Finns. Then old Pehto took Shef's pot and Piruusi's mug, and did the same action for him. Piruusi took it, held it up, and deliberately drank a third.

"Remember what I told you," said Hund quietly. "'Among the wolves . . .' I think this is to show trust. You drink what went through him, he drinks what went through you, you share your visions." Piruusi clearly caught the sense of what the little leech had said, nodded vigorously.

Shef saw Karli and Pehto exchanging mugs, realized he was committed. Deliberately, he lifted the mug, controlled a reflex to gag at the strong animal smell, drained a third of it. Sat down again, drained another third. Paused ritually, drained it to the dregs.

This time his soul left faster, as if it knew what to do. But though it sped away, the journey this time did not take it to a different climate and a higher sun. It went into the dark. The dark of some poor village; Shef had seen them many times, in Norway, in England, in the Ditmarsh. All much the same, one miry street, a huddle of buildings, houses in the center, on the outskirts, on the edge of the surrounding forest, barns and byres and sties.

He was inside a barn. People there, kneeling in a row on the bare ground. Shef realized from his own upbringing what they were doing. They were taking the Christian communion, the body and blood of their god, who had once been his god. Yet Father Andreas would never have countenanced this miserable procedure, in a barn piled with sacks, only two candles burning. Nor would Shef's stepfather Wulfgar. To him, the Mass was an occasion to count your tenants, be sure all were in place, and woe betide the villager who was not! It was public. This seemed almost secret.

The priest was a thin man whose face seemed to have known much hardship, and Shef did not recognize him. But following him, holding the vessel of wine to follow the makeshift dish of wafers—that was Erkenbert the deacon. Only a deacon, and so not fit to celebrate the Mass. Nevertheless participating. And that was wrong too, for his masters, the monks of York, would also not have let one of theirs participate in such a huddled and tawdry ceremony.

The celebrants were slaves, Shef realized. Or more strictly, thralls. They had the collars round their necks, most of them. All those who did not were women. Poor women, old women. That was the way the Christian church had begun, Shef seemed to remember. Among the slaves of Rome, and the outcasts.

Some of the communionists looked up in fear, hearing heavy feet and loud voices outside. Shef's view shifted. Out there, in the village street, a dozen angry men were approaching, talking loudly to each other. They had thick Swedish accents, like Guthmund's. True Swedes then, from the Swedish heartland.

"Taking my thralls from their work!" shouted one of them.

"Getting the women in there, and who's to know what happens next with their love-feast!"

"We'll teach them their place. And the priestling with them! He should have a collar on by rights."

The one in the lead rolled a sleeve above a brawny arm. He carried a heavy leather strap. Shef's own back twinged in memory.

As the Swedes came to the door of the temporary church, two shapes moved out from the door-posts. Armored men, with helmets, cheek-flaps. In their hands they carried short pikes, though they had swords belted on as well.

"Have you come to the church to pray?" said one of them.

"If you have, you will not need that strap," said the other.

The Swedes hesitated, began to spread out. They were not armed except for knives, obviously not expecting resistance, but they were big men, angry, used to command, twelve of them, six to one. They might just try a rush.

From somewhere in the night a voice barked an order and round the corner of the barn came a double file of armored men, marching along, to Shef's surprise, with their feet all moving at the same time, a thing he had never seen. The voice barked again and they stopped all at once, again, and they turned to face the Swedes. A pause, no further order, and the front rank stepped forward, one-two-three, halting with their pike-points almost touching the leading Swede's breast. They stood, impassive.

From the rear strolled Bruno, the German Shef had met at Hedeby. As usual he seemed amused, affable. He carried a sheathed sword in one hand, drew it out a few inches, thrust it back.

"You can come into the church, you know," he said. "We would like you to. But you have to behave, mind. And if you thought you could see who was there and maybe take it out on them later—" His voice hardened. "I wouldn't like that. Someone called Thorgisl did that, not so far away."

"He was burnt in his house," said one of the Swedes.

"Yes. Burnt to ashes. But, you know, not one of his household was harmed and all his thralls escaped. It must have been the hand of God."

Bruno's good cheer vanished suddenly. He threw the sheathed sword on the ground, stepped forward to the leading man, the one still holding the strap.

"When you go home, pig, you will say, 'Oh, they had weapons and we had not.' Well, you have a knife, pig, and I have one too." A flicker, and Bruno was holding a long straight single-edge with a brass hilt. "Oh, and look, you have a strap. So why don't we just strap our wrists together, and I'll teach you to dance!"

Bruno stared up at the big man, started to reach for his arm, face working like Cuthred's. But the big Swede had had enough. He said something no-one could catch, backed away, away down the dark street. The others trailed after him, their voices raised in defiance only at a safe distance. Behind them song pealed suddenly from the barn that was now a church. Shef did not recognize the mangled Latin words or the tune, but the German Ritters straightened even tauter, began to sing as well. Vexilla regis prodeunt . . . "The battle-standards of the King advance . . ."

And in a room, not so very far away, an earthly king, with a golden coronet on his long fair plaited hair, listening to a crew of men, richly dressed but carrying strange things, rattles and dried horse penises and polished skulls.

". . . no respect for the gods," they were shouting. "Bad luck for the country. Christians wandering free and never put down. The herring gone and a poor *harvest and now the snow earlier than any man has ever known. Act or go the way of foolish King Orm!"*

The king raised a hand. "What must I do?"

"Make the great sacrifice. The true sacrifice at Uppsala. Not nine oxen and nine horses and nine dogs, but all the worst of your realm. All the poison. Ninety men and ninety women you must hang on the sacred tree, and more to bleed on the plain outside. And not old broken slaves bought cheap, but the evildoers. Christians, and witches, and warlocks, and Finns, and the cheating priests of the Asgarth Way! Hang them high and earn the gods' favor. Leave them, and we will look again along the Eiriksgata." The Way of the One King, Shef remembered from Hagbarth. The road every would-be king of the Swedes had to travel, to expose himself to challenge. This one must have traveled it.

"Very well," the king's voice rumbled. "Now here is what I will do . . ."

Outside his palace again, Shef saw the bulk of the great heathen temple at Uppsala, rising in jagged layer above layer, dragon-heads at every corner, fantastic carvings from the age of the mythic kings on its door. And outside that, the holy oak tree where the Swedes had come to sacrifice for a thousand years. Things swayed creaking on the branches. Men, women, dogs, even horses. They hung there till they rotted and dropped, eye-sockets empty, bared teeth grinning. Over the whole place lay the holy stench.

And Shef was back in the tent, eye clearing. This time he did not jump up, for the weariness and horror on him.

"What you saw?" asked Piruusi. He too looked drawn, as if he had seen something he did not want to, but he was intent as well.

"Death and danger. To me, to you. From the Swedes."

Piruusi spat on Pehto's floor. "Always danger from the Swedes. If they find us. Maybe you see that too?"

"If I see it close, I will tell you."

"You need piss again?"

"Not again."

"Yes again. You great—great *spamathr*. Drink what went through our *spamathr*."

What was that in English, Shef wondered vaguely. A man would be a *wicca*, a woman a *wicce*. A cunning one. It rhymed with pitch and flitch, a flitch of bacon. Like a halved human hanging in a smokehouse.

He struggled to his feet again, stood over the bowl.

* * *

The last two things he had seen had been "now," he knew. Not "here" in the sense of by the Finnish wizard's tent, but "here" in the world. His spirit had traveled only in place.

Where he was this time was neither "here" nor "now," not in the same way. He was in a different world. It felt as if he was underground in some lightless place, but there was glimmering light from somewhere. He seemed to be walking over an immense arching bridge, with a noisy river running below. Walking down the arch now, to something blocking the way. Not a wall. A lattice, really. It was the Grind-wall that blocked the road to Hel. Strange, that "grind" should mean that and also the death of the whales.

There were faces pushed up against the lattice, watching him, faces he did not wish to see. He walked on. As he had feared, the first one was Ragnhild's, twisted and hating, spitting out bitter words at him, shaking the lattice as if to get at him. That lattice would not be moved by any human hand, of dead person or alive. Her breast dripped thick blood.

Beside her was the little boy, eyes wondering. He did not seem to hate or to recognize Shef. He twisted away suddenly from a third figure, reaching out to grasp him, hold him to a skinny bosom. The old queen Asa, a rope round her neck.

What have these to tell me, Shef wondered. That I killed them? I know that.

The ghosts were backing away from the grille, reluctantly and angrily, as if compelled. Someone else was coming, another woman. Shef recognized a worn face from which he had brushed snow two mornings before, Godsibb, who had died unnoticed. Her face was tired still, but less lined than he remembered, more peaceful. She wanted to speak. Her voice was like a bat's squeak, and he bent forward to listen.

"Go on," it said. "Go on. I am here, in Hel, from following you. I would have been anyway. If I had not followed you I would have been a slave here—a slave to those." She nodded at the retreating ghosts of the two queens. "I am spared that."

The voice faded, and the wall, and the bridge, and the darkness. Shef found himself once more sitting in the tent, tears rolling down his cheeks. Though the vision had seemed to take no time to him, he was the last to wake again. The others looked at him, Hund with concern and Karli with fellow-feeling. The two Finns seemed pleased, satisfied, as if his emotion proved him human, of the same flesh as themselves.

Slowly Shef rose, muttered a few words, picked up his lance from by the tent-flap. Frost glinted on its tip, yet the weight of it seemed to steady his nerves. The three walked out into the freezing night and the dark birchwoods.

As they crunched through the snow towards the fire and the sentry's challenge, Shef said to the others, "We must bury Godsibb and the others properly, not burn them or hang them in a tree. We will dig beneath the fires where the ground has been warmed. Take stones from the stream-bed and make a cairn."

"Does that do the dead any good?" asked Hund.

"I think so."

CHAPTER TWENTY-SEVEN

Two nights and a day later, the party stood ready to move on, on a bright windless day, in light snow. Shef would willingly have assembled them all and set off the day before, but Hund had vetoed it.

"Some of us are too weak," he said sharply. "Hurry them on and you will find more of them not waking up in the morning, like Godsibb."

Shef, haunted by the memory of her peering through the lattice of Helgate, gave way unwillingly. Yet even as he hauled stones out of the freezing stream-bed for her cairn, watched by interested but disbelieving Finns, he thought to himself, she said "Go on."

"I have to get out of this wasteland," he had told Hund, trying to get some urgency into him. "I told you, I saw the warriors round Hedeby. It may have fallen by now, and the Ragnarssons will be richer and stronger. At the rate we're going, Sigurth will be King of all Denmark by the time we are there."

"And is it your duty to stop him?" Hund looked at his friend and reconsidered. "Well, maybe it is. But you cannot stop him from here. We will just have to move on as fast as we can."

"Do you think these visions of mine are true?" Shef asked him. "Or is it just the drink that does it, as beer and mead make men think they are mightier than they are? Maybe all my visions—maybe Vigleik's visions and all the things the Way sees, maybe they are just some kind of delusion, some kind of drunkenness."

Hund hesitated for a while before replying. "That could be," he admitted. "I will tell you one thing, Shef. That fly killer mushroom, the red one with the white spots on it, that men crush and put on the walls to keep insects off, you would not eat that by accident. But there are other things like it that sometimes grow in the corn, get reaped with it. Maybe find their way into the bread. Or the porridge. Especially if the corn has been left damp in store."

"It's always damp in store in England," said Shef. "So why doesn't everybody have these visions all the time?"

"Maybe they do, but dare not speak. But more likely you are especially sensitive to such things. You drank no more than Karli or the Finns last night, but it seemed to affect you for much longer. And then, maybe because you are affected by such things, the gods send themselves to you. Or maybe the gods have given you this weakness for their own purpose."

Shef, always impatient with speculation which could not be settled one way or the other, shook the thought off. Concentrated on hustling everyone into action, even on the rest day Hund had decreed.

So, their dead buried, a supply of cooked meat in every pack, they mustered to travel onwards. Remembering what he had seen on his soul-flight, Shef led them confidently to the lake through the birches. It was where he thought, stretching away as far as the eye could see, long and narrow, a natural water-road. Still unfrozen—but not for long as the chill of autumn gave way to winter.

Yet they had no boats. Shef had had the idea of making light boats from bark, as Brand had said the Finns did. A little experiment proved that none of Shef's party had the faintest idea how it was done. The Finns who sometimes skied by, keeping an eye on the visitors, shrugged uncomprehendingly if appealed to. Many in Shef's party were skilled craftsmen, who could—given time—have built anything up to a complete ship from trunks and planks. By the time that was done, they would all have starved.

They plodded on on foot, keeping to the birches as long as they could, for shelter from the wind and the drifting snow. Another day's travel and the wood came to an end with the lake, leaving only the immense level moor stretching out before them, now covered in snow. Nineteen pairs of eyes turned to Shef as he contemplated the prospect. All but Cuthred's showed doubt and hesitation.

Silently Shef gave orders to camp again in the kindly woods, light fires and cook their already-dwindled supplies. He waved at the Finn who seemed never to be too far away, like the wolves, and said to him firmly, "Piruusi. Bring Piruusi."

The headman skied eventually out of the dark, as untroubled by the snow and wind as if it had been a spring day in Hampshire, and settled down enjoyably to a long night of bargaining.

The real solution was to turn everyone in Shef's party into expert skiers, make skis, and set off to the Way-College mining station which, if Piruusi could be trusted—and on this he probably could—was maybe sixty, maybe a hundred miles downstream. Again, they would all have starved long before that could be achieved. In the end, and after arguing himself hoarse, Shef settled for as many pairs of spare skis as the Finn camp could provide, together with four reindeer sleighs and their drivers to take the rest. It cost Shef his second gold arm-ring, another twenty silver pennies, and four good iron wood-axes. It might have cost more if not for an intervention from Cuthred.

"Make iron yourself?" Shef asked, as they haggled over axes.

Piruusi signed a vehement no.

"What you cut with before the Norse-folk come, then?" Shef went on.

"They cut with these," said Cuthred from his place by the fire. From inside his jacket he produced a stone axe, a worked flint too big even for Cuthred's powerful hands. An axe to be used by a giant, a gift, seemingly, from Echegorgun.

Fear showed in Piruusi's eyes as he looked at it, and remembered the strange powers these pathetic foreigners were in league with. He ceased to haggle, came quickly to an agreement. The next morning, sleighs and skis arrived, and Shef began the still-laborious process of deciding who should do what, who was the strongest, the likeliest to learn. He was careful not to let only his weakest ride in the sleighs, for those carried his reserves of cash, gold and silver. He had been careful also never to let the Finns see how much he had. Drink-brother he might be to Piruusi, even piss-brother if there were such a term: none of that, he was sure, would shield Piruusi from giving in to temptation.

The early coming of winter had surprised but not particularly alarmed the Way-College's mining station deep inside Swedish Finnmark. There were a dozen men there and half that number of women, four priests of the Way, apprentices and hired workers. They had good supplies and plenty to keep them occupied. During the summer they dug the ore, during the winter smelted it and made it into trade products, pigs of iron or such things as half-finished axe-heads, which could be threaded on bars and moved in bulk. They had built their work-station at a point where they had good communications at all times, by water down the river when it was unfrozen. After that they shipped metal down, by ski and sleigh over a plain road once the ice came. They were well-stocked for the winter in food and fuel. Indeed, they spent much of their time in winter burning charcoal in the birch and pinewoods that began to grow out of the moor as it sloped down towards the sea.

When apprentice Egil first called out to him that strangers were coming from the west, Herjolf the senior of the priests was, again, surprised but not alarmed. They must be Finns, he assumed. There was no-one else there. He would soon find out what they wanted. Meanwhile he ordered work to cease and the men to arm themselves quietly, many with the new crossbows that had come out of England the year before. The Swedish steel made these, he was sure, the best weapons known in the world. Far better than the English example his friend Hagbarth priest of Njörth had given him as a model.

His men covered him, most of them keeping out of sight, as he watched the black dots sweeping across the snow. Not Finns, after all. Some of the skiers were passable, some astonishingly inept, but even the best of them did not have the easy grace of the Finns. Yet the sleighs must belong to Finns, and they were being driven well, if as sedately as if they were taking a crowd of old grandmothers to a funeral.

Herjolf's expression of doubt turned to incredulity as the leading skier put on speed, away from the others, and hissed up to him. Eyes red-rimmed from the snow glare looked at him out of a wilderness of untrimmed beard.

"Good day, Herjolf," said the apparition. "We have met. I am Thorvin priest of Thor, like yourself. I would show you my pendant if I could get it out, and my white tunic if it were not deep under my skins. But I call on you as a Way-fellow to help us. We have done the Way good service, and come a hard journey to find you."

As the sleighs and the slower skiers swept in, or crept in, Herjolf called to his men to put their weapons down and come to help. The wayfarers climbed stiffly out of the sledges where they had been loaded, took out packs, looked round in relief. One of the skiers seemed to chaffer with the Finnish sleigh-drivers, in the end paid them off and walked hobbling over as they swung away, cracking their whips and racing off in the wild style Shef had forbidden for the last three vexing days of travel.

"This is Shef Sigvarthsson," said Thorvin, introducing the one-eyed man. "You have heard many stories of him."

"Indeed I have. Now tell me, Thorvin. What are you all doing here? And where have you come from? And what do you expect me to do now?"

"We have come from the coast of Norway," said Shef. "We are going down to the coast of Sweden, where we mean to take ship for England. Or, it may be, for Denmark. It depends on what news you can give us."

Hagbarth the Njörth priest appeared at Herjolf's elbow. Shef looked at him with weary surprise. They had not met since Shef had fled from Kaupang. Yet if Hagbarth could appear at Hedeby on the business of the Way, it was natural to find him somewhere else, even here a hundred miles inland. Njörth-priests were favoured errand-runners. Shef wondered what had happened to Hagbarth's ship, the Aurvendill which had carried him from Hedeby to Kaupang.

"There is no shortage of news," he said. "Whether you will want to go on to Denmark, or to England, once you have heard it is another matter. It seems to me that your arriving in Hedeby, and then in Kaupang, started a turmoil that has never ceased since. I hope you have not brought more with you."

"We will go on as soon as we can," said Shef. "And you will remember, Hagbarth, that it was not my wish to go to Kaupang, turmoil or no. It was you who took me there. If you had followed my wishes you would have let me take passage home."

Hagbarth nodded in acknowledgement of the truth of what Shef said, and Thorvin spoke up again. "You will give us shelter for a while, then, Herjolf? We are all followers of the Way, as you will see when we are indoors."

Herjolf nodded also. "One or two of you I could have recognized under any circumstances." He pointed a finger at Udd, who had crawled out of a sledge, looked around him, recognized the chimneys of the iron-working shop and was now standing entranced, staring in at the red glow of the banked fires in the biggest forge he had ever seen.

"That is the one who invented those crossbows you are carrying," said Shef. "A *Skraeling,* he seems, yet some would say he is the man who defeated the king of the Franks and all his lancers."

Herjolf looked at Udd's unimpressive form with a new surprise and respect. "Be welcome, then," he said. "But from the look of you I doubt whether many of you will be fit to travel on soon. Here, look at that one!"

Cuthred, who had skied awkwardly but uncomplainingly for the last three days, was tugging at his woollen breeches and leggings, trying to roll them down. As he did so he swayed, holding himself up only by the effort of his will. Moving to help him Shef suddenly saw a splotch of dark blood soaking through the thick layers of wool.

"It is the disease I told you of," said Hund, stripping away the wool as Shef and Thorvin held the big man up. "See, the cut he got from Vigdjarf. It healed as if it were magic, but now it has broken out again. Come, get him indoors. He will not be fit to move for many days. Not ever, if this place has no store of greenstuffs."

The poor condition Shef's people were in became obvious once they had been taken indoors and the clothes they had worn for weeks on end stripped from them. It was the disease a later age would call scurvy: a disease of long voyages and dried food. The symptoms were obvious. Long-healed wounds opening of their own accord, teeth loosening in the jaws, fetid breath, and over it all a general weakness, lassitude and gloom. It was not unfamiliar to anyone in the North, but they expected to find it in the late spring, when folk had been cooped up in their cabins for months, eating salt herring and stored grain. The cure was light and sun, some said. Fresh food, said others. The two went together, usually. This time, Hund pointed out, there was a chance to know for sure, since there was no chance of light and sun—but leeks, onions, garlic, peas and beans to hand. If the sufferers improved, then food was the cure. Which showed, reasonably enough, that there was something in some kinds of food that there was not in others. One day a true priest of the Way might be able to extract it, dry it and store it, for the benefit of all.

But not this year, as Herjolf pointed out. There was no chance of moving on. When Herjolf, Hagbarth, Thorvin and Hund came to Shef in a body to confront him with the fact, he sat silent for a while. Ever since the first meeting with Echegorgun he had felt a fierce urge to turn, to attack his pursuers, to act instead of reacting. For weeks he had been driven on by desire to get back to the main cogwheels of the action, instead of lurking out on the edges. The desire had been sharpened by the vision he had seen in the shaman's tent, of the Ragnarssons round Hedeby and King Hrorik in the breach of the stockade.

Yet at the same time there was something very tempting in the idea of staying where they were, in the wilds yet under cover, unknown yet not lost. Patiently the priests explained things to him. They had supplies, they could get more. The road was easy to drive in any but the worst weather, or one could take sleigh down the river, once it was firmly frozen. Cultivated farmlands lay not impossibly far away, with surplus of grain and meat and all kinds of stores. No great suspicion would be aroused by the priests of the Way buying more. It might be thought they had miscalculated, or needed the food to trade with the Finns.

"And you can make yourselves useful," added Herjolf. "Your little man Udd is never out of the forge even now, and he knows a great deal. Has learnt it for himself too. Have you seen how he has found to harden steel? He should be a priest of the Way—" Herjolf barked with amusement at the thought of the scrawny Englishman reaching that dignity, then said more soberly, "No, if he were to think of that I would be willing to stand his sponsor. He is talking already of millwheels and devices, of great hammers to pound out the iron by machinery rather than by muscle. If a tenth of what he says is true, his stay will be worth all the supplies it costs us. So stay. Thorvin tells me you are a smith too, and a seeker of new knowledge. You and Udd can think, the rest can burn charcoal or blow the bellows. In the spring, then you can seek your destiny. Hagbarth's ship is laid up here in the boathouse till spring. It will take you on your way faster than any other."

Shef nodded. Beneath the relief, a kind of excitement was growing. Time to think. Time to try things out without the frantic, driving, battle-in-the-morning haste that had always been his fate so far. Time to plan. A chance to move when he was ready and the other side was not, instead of the other way round. Of course they would have a winter to prepare and grow strong too. But then they might not know he was coming.

He remembered the words of Svipdag the prisoner. What were they? "The only man who could get through what waits for you would need an iron skin." They had been spoken in malice and to frighten him, he knew, but there was a proverb in Norse that Thorvin often quoted. "The words of fate will be spoken by someone." Maybe Svipdag had been the emissary of fate. An iron skin. He would see.

Chewing carefully with loose teeth on the whole green pea-pods that Hund had forced upon him, Shef swallowed, nodded again. "We will stay, Herjolf, and I thank you for your offer. And I promise you, no-one here will be idle. Many things will be different in the spring."

Soon chimneys smoked, clangor rang out over the snow, men skied out to cut wood and raise new huts, sledged out iron to pay for food and beer. The passing Finns, wondering, saw unceasing activity when the Norse-folk usually slept.

Far in the south the Ragnarssons, with the head of King Hrorik on a pole as a reminder, marched their army from kingdom to kingdom, demanding the surrender of all the little kings of Denmark, Gamli of Fyn and Arnodd of Aalborg, Kolfinn of Sjaelland and Kari of Skaane.

In Sweden King Kjallak the Strong, brought to the throne by discontent with his peaceful predecessor Orm, consulted with his priests and heard continual reports of the insolence of the German missionaries and their protectors. We cannot defeat them, said village after village. What do we pay our herring-tax for? Come and defend us! And Kjallak agreed, but found it hard to pick a champion who was prepared to meet the Germans' awe-inspiring leader. The time would come to crush them in battle, and also in the spirit, so he told the impatient priests of the great temple at Uppsala.

And in Hamburg the fierce and saintly Archbishop Rimbert heard the same reports with pleasure, and circulated them to his brother prelates, the archbishops of the German lands, sure that destiny lay in the West, not as the fool Pope Adrian thought through some accommodation with the Greekling Emperor and his Popelet. In all the German lands the stories of the bold *Ritters* of the *Lanzenorden* spread among the landless younger sons of aristocratic families, and the recruiting tables were never free of applicants.

In Norway King Olaf Elf-of-Geirstath, whom men were now beginning to call "the Victorious," as they had never done all the days his brother was alive, looked at his retinue of under-kings, of Ringeriki and Ranriki, Hedemark and Uppland and Agdir, and at the newly-cautious embassies from the West, the fierce Rogalanders and the men of the fjords, and wondered where the man was whose luck had so changed his own.

And Godive, now swollen with child, wondered occasionally what had become of the boy she had once known, her first man and her foster-brother.

But far in the North the land lay hidden and peaceful under snow.

CHAPTER TWENTY-EIGHT

The scurvy lifted quickly as Hund forced his patients to eat onions and leeks, peas and beans, some dried, some still relatively fresh from the recent harvest. Hund made careful notes in runic script, saying that he would give the answers to other Ithun-priests. Certainly the answer to this disease lay in food, not in air or light.

With the disappearance of the scurvy went the feelings of gloom and weariness which had beset so many of the party, replaced as if by contrast by a mood of energy and excitement: all necessarily turned inwards, for the wind and the cold increasingly contrived to isolate the little community, except for the muffled sleigh-drivers trading for supplies or bringing back wood from the forest.

When he looked back on the events and the progress of that winter, Shef sometimes found it hard to believe. Sometimes easy. He had noticed already during his brief term of office as jarl of Norfolk, and even briefer term as co-king with Alfred, how little of a busy person's time was spent doing what that person wanted to do. Most time, for most people, was wasted on irrelevancies, on trivialities, on confusion and conflict, all seemingly inseparable from daily life. "It is like," Shef had said to Hagbarth the seaman-priest, "it is like sailing along with a sail tied to the back of the boat, in the water, dragging you back."

"You mean a sea-anchor," said Hagbarth. "Very useful sometimes. In a storm at night when you fear you may be running on shore."

"I dare say," said Shef impatiently. "But think, Hagbarth, think what it's like when you cast the drag off!"

In the little community of perhaps forty souls, the drag was removed. Many of them were simply glad to be alive. Those who had once lived as slaves were disinclined to quarreling or self-assertion. And of the forty a high proportion—perhaps the highest proportion ever assembled in the history of the world under such circumstances—were curious, inquisitive and skilled. The forty included seven priests of the Way, all committed by faith and temperament to the quest for new knowledge. They had ten apprentices between them, all eager young men with their way to make, a way that would be much eased if they could show contributions to new knowledge. There was Shef himself, inventor and builder of the machines that had set the Northern world on a new course. And there was Udd, perhaps the most creative and persistent of all, in spite of his shyness and life's history of low regard.

Even the others made a contribution, Cwicca and Osmod, Fritha, Hama and Wilfi. What they all shared, Shef eventually realized, was belief. They were men who had been raised from the dirt by machinery, who owed everything they had to it. Furthermore, they had seen the pride of the Vikings and of the Frankish lancers fall before them. One might almost say they did not have belief, or faith, but something even stronger, impossible for any skeptic to argue with. They knew new machines could be made for new purposes, they were certain that novelty would work. It was impossible in their presence to shrug one's shoulders and say, "that's how it's always been done."

Yet it was something like that which triggered the first major project and innovation of the winter. Large supplies of grain had been brought back from the farms towards the coast, and the bread-starved travelers were eager to have it baked. First it had to be ground. The task was handed over without thought and as a matter of course to the women in the community. Women ground flour. Many slave-women did nothing else.

However, in the spirit of fellowship which joint travel had brought, it was argued that men should take their turn too. In the end Udd was given a pestle, mortar and sack of grain, and told to take his turn at grinding. He ground ineffectively for half an hour, stared at the sack remaining, put his pestle down and went to find Shef.

"Why isn't there a mill to do this?" he protested.

Shef jerked a thumb out at the frozen ground beyond the wooden shutters. "Because the river's frozen, Udd."

"There are other ways to run a mill."

"I know," said Shef carefully, "but are you going to suggest it to Cuthred? Maybe he'd like to take a turn at his old trade? If we had an ox I'd say we could use that for power, but we only have the cows for milking, and no-one will let you use those."

"I told you," said Udd. "We could make a wind-mill."

In other circumstances a busy ruler would have been distracted from the detailed consideration needed by some task or other. In the winter waste, there was nothing else to do. Shef and Udd walked across to the water-mill which the Way-priests had set up, and which they used for half the year, to see what could be done.

Much of what was needed was there already: the two great stone wheels that did the grinding. The thick axle that turned the upper stone and the system of cog-wheels that transmitted power from the river to the wheels. That changed it from horizontal to vertical rotation, following the very latest developments. All that was needed was a new motive force. "Like a big sail, on four arms," said Udd. "There's sail-cloth in the boat-house."

"It won't work," said Herjolf, listening. "The river always flows in the same place. Wind can come from anywhere. I grant you, here it comes mostly from the mountains, the north-west. But if you set it up and the wind changed, it could tear your wheel off its supports."

"I know how to fix that," said Udd with the confidence that came to him when faced with a technical problem. "Think of the way we made the catapults rotate. We put them on small wheels and turned those on a larger wheel. We can do the same thing here. Make the whole mill rotate. It can be trained round by a beam, as we turn the trail of the new mules."

In other circumstances, again, some scoffer would have laughed the matter off. There were no scoffers here. Herjolf hesitated, then said, "Well, let's try it."

Soon most of the community was outside, dismantling the old mill, helping to build the shell of the new one, sent off to the main forge to make the heavy nails and bolts that were needed. Shef, thinking back over the event in later times, noted again how many valuable skills were present among the people there. Many were perfectly familiar with heavy weights, not daunted at all by the process of lifting the mill-wheels and taking them to the new site. Hagbarth, who had lifted and laid many a ship's keel made all of one timber, directed operations. For several days all energies were directed to the mill, even the grinding of the grain put aside by common consent till there was a better way of doing it.

Finally all was in place, and Udd was allowed to slip the retainer catch that had held the wheels from turning. He did so. The wind blew, filled the sails, they turned the vertical wheel that was to turn the horizontal one that was to turn the mill-wheel. Nothing happened except a great straining of timber. Udd slipped the catch back again.

"We need bigger sails," he said.

A day later the process was in full stream, Herjolf rubbing his hands as he thought of the profits that might be made by setting up mills of this kind all over Scandinavia. Nearly all of it country unsuited to water-power, but a ready market for a mill that would grind all year. Priests of the Way, it was their boast, supported themselves by working rather than by claiming tithes and landholdings like the priests and monks of the Christians. There was no objection, furthermore, to priests becoming rich by their knowledge—as long as they shared it.

Yet the success of the first windmill seemed only to whet Udd's appetite. As soon as the first one was working, he was at Herjolf's ear with plans for another: this time, to drive the trip-hammer that he had sketched out for Shef the year before in Kaupang. Herjolf listened dubiously, at first, not hostile, but not able to understand what Udd was proposing.

The appeal was clear enough. Iron, though well-known and well understood everywhere in the Western world, remained if not a precious metal, a valuable one. One reason for the dominance of the Franks' and Germans' armored lancers was the weight of metal they carried. This was a great investment in a world where the peasant's spade characteristically had only an iron tip over a wooden blade, and where many plows as well were little more than iron-shod scratching-sticks. Iron was expensive not because it was hard to find, like gold or silver, but because it took so many man-hours to work. The ore had to be heated again and again and beaten by hand with hammers until the slag was worked out of it, then being smelted in the crude charcoal-burning ovens. The iron of Jarnberaland was the best in the world. Still, it needed working, as did every grade of iron except the very rare pieces taken from fallen thunder-stones. Herjolf had fuel, he had ore. If the hammering time could be cut he would have the more trade-goods in the spring. But how could a turning wheel make a hammer go up and down?

Udd drew his pictures in the snow again, while Shef, called into service as the argument grew heated, translated from English to Norse—Udd's Norse had never reached the technical stage. Finally Herjolf sighed, and agreed to let Udd try. "It's a blessing," he remarked, "that this time he only wants something half the size of the last one."

"A hammer is easier to lift than a mill-wheel," Shef explained. "Udd says he is willing to start with only a light hammer."

"How light?"

"A hundredweight."

Herjolf shook his head and turned away. "Tell him to see Narfi Tyr's priest, the chronicler, and ask him for vellum and a pen. His sketches will be easier to follow if they are in pen and ink, not drawn in the snow. Besides, if what he says is true, in time to come men will fight for a page of them."

Soon, when the wind blew, the trip-hammer pounded, beating out metal at unheard of rates like the never-ceasing hammer of Völund, the lame smith of the gods.

It was Cwicca who was responsible for the next step. Not having a skilled trade, other than playing on the bagpipe and shooting a catapult, he was usually assigned to some repetitive task. One day, struggling with the leather bellows which provided forced draught to the forge, yelled at continually by the smiths not to stop or everything would be ruined, he stepped off the upper handle he had been working with his leg and shouted, "We need a machine to do this as well!"

Converting a trip-hammer to pump a bellows was almost easy. And yet the alteration brought about more change, as if one change was feeding off another. The very much improved flow of air through the ovens which smelted the finished ore raised the temperature very markedly. The smiths said iron went first blue-hot, when it was dangerous because you might put a hand on it without realizing, to red-hot, when it was soft enough to work. Only rarely had they seen iron white-hot, beginning to melt. Though cast-iron had been made, usually by accident and under especially lucky circumstances, the forced-draught bellows made molten iron for castings a possibility.

Underlying all the activity was the threat and fear, or certainty, of war. Shef had consulted Hagbarth and Narfi the priest of Tyr, and following his custom, tried to make a map of where he and his fellows had been. From all that they said, and from his own experience, he was in what looked very much like a trap, more of a trap even than the coast of Norway. From there, if he had had a ship, he could have sailed out into the open sea and tried to make the long passage to the Scottish shore, and then down the east coast to England. Where he was, even if he had free passage in Hagbarth's *Aurvendill*, he would have to make his way out of the gulf between Sweden and the far shore of the Eastern Sea, where the Balts lived, then round Skaane and through the narrows between it and Danish Sjaelland to make his way home.

"How wide is the gap there?" he asked.

"Three miles," said Hagbarth. "That's how old King Kolfinn got rich. Levying tolls. Last I heard, he wasn't likely to be there much longer. If you're right about the Ragnarssons getting rid of Hrorik, there wouldn't be too much left to stop them."

"And where is their famous Braethraborg, the Stronghold of the Brothers?"

"There," said Hagbarth, tapping the map at a spot on the north shore of Sjaelland maybe fifty miles from the narrows. Half a day's sail.

The only other way back to England that Shef could see was to go back to Hedeby and walk across the marshes to the Ditmarsh, and so be back where he started. He would be once more without a ship. And anyway, if his vision was true, and it was confirmed by Hagbarth's definite knowledge that the siege had started, then Hedeby was in enemy hands. Ragnarsson hands. Nothing anyone could imagine was worse than falling into Sigurth Ragnarsson's hands. Shef would rather have died and been hung up in Echegorgun's smokehouse.

So the iron-workers made not only ingots of pig-iron and easily-traded goods like axe-heads. They also, following Udd's direction, made bow after bow of spring-steel, cocking-handles, iron quarrels. Men and women carved wooden parts, set them in piles. Every few days they would turn from that task and assemble them. Shef noted how much quicker it was, say, to make a dozen sets of parts and then assemble them all the same way, instead of following the time-honored procedure of working on one implement till it was done, and then starting the next one. The pile of crossbows grew, well beyond the numbers they had to use them.

"We can always sell them," said Herjolf cheerfully.

"That is looking on the bright side," said Shef.

Of all the innovations Udd had brought, though, none interested Thorvin and the other smiths more than the case-hardened steel. They had borrowed Cuthred's shield repeatedly, testing its powers, and been amazed. Ideas sprang up quickly. Make mail of the strange hard metal. It proved impossible to work, too hard to bend, too hard to fit together. An attempt to take a mail-shirt and case-harden it as one unit produced only an extremely expensive lump of rings half-welded together, the waste of a month's work for a skilled smith, as Herjolf pointed out. Flat plates were relatively easy to make, but useless once made. People did not have flat surfaces to fit them over. The metal seemed to have no use in war except for shields, and even then it had disadvantages. Shields were convex both because missiles tended to fly off such a surface, and—no trivial consideration—because a rounded shield could be carried on the shoulder. No-one, not even Brand or Cuthred, could march all day holding a shield up on his arm alone. Most deaths in battle went to the side whose shield-arms tired first.

The hardened metal, while fascinating, seemed to be practically useless in war. Yet Shef could not shake off the words that Svipdag the prisoner had hurled at him. "The only man who could get through what waits for you would need an iron skin." He knew who would be waiting for him at the Braethraborg. Where was his iron skin? And how to carry it?

Shef found himself talking, often, to Hagbarth. Hagbarth was interested especially in the details of the various new types of ship that Shef had sailed or had encountered. He had nodded consideringly over Ordlaf's design for the English mule-armed "battleships," and pressed Shef again and again for details of the short action with the *Frani Ormr,* a famous craft in her own right, the greatest warship of the North, of the traditional ocean-going type.

"It's no wonder you were outsailed by her," he remarked. "I am not sure even my own *Aurvendill* would have done better. Faster by sail, I dare say. But the more oars you have for foot of keel, the faster you are rowing. In enclosed waters, *Frani Ormr* might be better."

He was interested also in the design of the two-masted *Crane,* about which Shef could tell him a good deal, having helped to dismantle her for planks and parts. King Halvdan's coastal patrol ships were familiar to Hagbarth in any event. He could make a good guess at how one would have been strengthened to take catapult shock. It was the sailing qualities of the two masts that puzzled him. Yet, Shef assured him, the *Crane* had sailed, and sailed well. The *Norfolk,* on the other hand, had been something of a tub.

"Now we've got the idea of putting the mules on wheels, to rotate them," Cwicca said one meal-time. "What we'd really like would be a mule at each end, front and back, high up. But I suppose all that weight high up would make the boat tip over, like, if the wind came from one side. Even the *Norfolk* wasn't very high out of the water."

Hagbarth, listening, snorted beer through his nostrils. " 'Make the boat tip over, like,' " he gasped. " 'Each end, front and back.' It's well for you you're not at sea and the sea-trolls listening. They punish sailors who do not use the proper *haf* words, the words to be said at sea."

"So how would you make a boat like Cwicca said?" asked Shef, ignoring the complaint about sea-language.

"I've been thinking," said Hagbarth, scratching lines in the table with his dagger. "What you want, I think—it's what they did with the *Crane,* but they only did it half way—is a rigid frame for the ship, much more solid than the way we build."

Remembering the way the *Aurvendill* had flexed on her passage from Hedeby to Kaupang, both Shef and Karli nodded.

"Then you would want to build up the sides, like this." Hagbarth drew on.

Studying the plan on the table, Shef said thoughtfully, "What you have there looks to me, in a way, like one of your own ships with a second one built over it."

Hagbarth nodded. "Yes, you could do that. A conversion."

"So we could convert, for instance, your *Aurvendill,* out there in the boathouse. Extend the keel and rivet it—we have plenty of hard steel—put in a frame, build up the freeboard, as you call it, ballast her heavy and put mules on fighting platforms bow and stern."

Hagbarth cried out in honest pain. "Not the *Aurvendill!* The most beautiful sailer in the north!"

"Though not as fast as the *Frani Ormr,"* Shef pointed out.

"If you did all that," said the unnoticed Edtheow, who had been staring grimly at Hagbarth's dagger marks on the polished table, "you could put iron plates all over it and really weigh it down."

Shef stared at her open-mouthed.

"The words of fate will be spoken by someone," remarked Thorvin, yet again.

In the end Hagbarth was sent out on skis while work started on *Aurvendill.* He had been reconciled to the idea, and confessed that he would have been fascinated to see it tried on anyone else's ship. He could not bear, though, to watch them slice into his own. After the main sawing was done, he promised, he would watch and assist. Till then, he would stay away.

Cuthred volunteered to escort him. Of all the men and women there he had played least part: refusing even to look at the mills being erected, taking little interest in the forge. He lay abed a long time with his leg-wound open, as if his body were taking revenge for the way he had overridden its demands during the berserk fit. When it healed, he took to skiing alone, quickly becoming expert, often staying out all day. When Shef asked him once whether he felt hungry or thirsty out in the waste, he replied, "There is food out there, if you know how to get it."

Shef wondered. Echegorgun had trailed them across the mountains to Piruusi's camp. Could he have followed further? The Hidden Folk seemed to be able to go where they pleased in the wastelands. Cuthred had said once that there were more of them than true people realized. Maybe he was meeting Echegorgun, or even Miltastaray, in the wasteland. The Hidden Folk liked him. Hardly anyone else did, though some among the women were sorry for him. At least he was a good protector for Hagbarth, and Hagbarth was not one of the men who were likeliest to offend him, unlike Karli, now paired with Edith, or Ceolwulf, who seemed to remind Cuthred of what he had once been.

Yule came, with roast pork and blood sausage to add to their usual fare, with tale-telling and songs from the Way-priests of their mythical stories. The deep winter came after it, with such howling winds that the mill-sails had to be taken down and stored for a while, and thick snow drifting. The small community, with ample food and fuel, blankets and down-lined bags, ignored it. Shef wondered again at the good cheer on every face, but not for long.

"It's cold up here, right enough," said Cwicca. "But if you think what it was like back in Crowland in the fens, slaving for the black monks! Lucky to have a blanket at all, no food but porridge and not much of that, living in a hut with an earth floor and that soaked through from Michaelmas to Easter. And nothing to look forward to but Lent! No, I've never passed a happier winter."

One thing that added to the gaiety was yet another of Udd's experiments. He had never forgotten the total failure of his attempt to make winter ale by steaming water off rather than freezing it off. Winter ale could be had now for the trouble of putting a bucket outside, but Udd persevered. If the strength in the drink was not left in the heated ale, he reasoned, it must have flown off with the steam. Slowly he experimented. Catching the steam. Enclosing the heated pot. Running a pipe, a copper pipe for its ductility, out from the heat into the cold, to liquefy the steam more quickly. Catching the end product. Repeating the process with ever tighter seals and more careful catchment. In the end, Udd had something which he was prepared to offer to the others. They tasted gingerly, curiously, appreciatively.

"A good drink for a cold day," said Osmod. "Not as good as mulled winter ale, I reckon, but that's more natural, isn't it. This has still some of the reek of the forge about it. 'Burnt ale,' we'll call it."

"It might be better to use wine," said Udd, though he had tasted wine no more than twice in his life.

Cuthred said nothing, but took a flask with him next time he skied alone into the snow.

* * *

The day came at last when they were ready to roll the remade *Aurvendill* out of the boathouse into a backwater of the river, now beginning to flow stronger under the ice, and to show signs of break-up.

"Should we not put something on the rollers, for luck?" asked Shef.

Hagbarth looked at him sharply. "There are some who do that," he said. "Blood usually, a sacrifice to Ran, the troll-goddess in the deeps."

"I don't mean that. Udd, have you a small keg of burnt ale? Put that under the keel. As she rolls forward, she'll crush it."

Hagbarth nodded. "And then you must give her a new name." He patted the stem-post. "She is my *Aurvendill* no longer. That is a star, you know. Made from the frostbitten toe of a giant which Thor flung into the sky. A good name for a fast ship. She is that no more. What will you call her?"

Shef said nothing till the men were at the drag-ropes, ready to pull her out of the shed in which they had worked for so long. Then, as they heaved together and the strong brown liquid splashed on the keel, he called out, "I name you *Fearnought!*"

Fearnought slid slowly down the runway and crunched through the thinning ice, to lie at rest on her ropes.

She seemed a strange craft. They had cut, spliced and riveted her keel with the stoutest wood and steel they could contrive. On the extended keel they had fitted frames every few yards, and to these frames, against the usual practice, which was to use sinew, they had nailed the planking. The *Aurvendill's* original planks now formed only the upper part of her sides. Stouter ones, split from pine-trunks, held her lower down. At prow and stern fighting platforms disfigured her previously clean lines, copies of the ones Shef had seen on Hedeby walls. Two new-built mules squatted on each. To balance their cumbrous weight the *Fearnought* was built deep and round, with heavy ballast in what was now a capacious hold. The fighting platforms had been extended to half-decking, giving some shelter for the crew underneath them, more than the skin awnings which were all Viking crews normally had, even for the Atlantic.

On two matters Hagbarth had had his way. The *Fearnought* remained a one-master, though with her greater bulk the sail had been extended outwards, though not upwards, giving her almost half as much sail area again. And the iron plates that were to armor her sides and the rotating mules were stored in the hold, to be fitted only as needed.

"I wouldn't like to try the long open-sea passage to England in her," said Hagbarth, careful to speak well away from the ship in case his words brought bad luck. "She makes the tubbiest knorr look graceful, and once you put the plates on she's worse."

"She's not designed to reach England," said Shef. "If she gets us through the narrows and round to the Frisian shore, she'll have done her job."

Just past the Braethraborg will do, thought Hagbarth, but did not say the words. He himself had no intention of risking that dangerous passage. He had a draft on Shef and Alfred's treasury for the price of the *Aurvendill,* and hoped only to collect it.

Shef wondered, indeed, who he had the right to ask to share his dangers. The English men and women who had come so far with him would continue, hoping to reach home, as would Karli, eager to tell his tales of travel in the Ditmarsh. So would Hund. Thorvin too insisted on going. Hagbarth and his small crew would travel as far as Smaaland in the south of Sweden, showing the landlubbers how to sail the boat as they did so.

As the snow melted and people thought of departure, Cuthred came to see his master.

"Do you want me to travel south with you?" he asked.

Shef stared at him. "I thought we would take you home. To Northumbria."

"There's no-one in Northumbria for me. My king is dead. I do not know if my wife is alive, but even if she is—I am no good to her now. I would rather live here in the waste. There are people here who would take me as I am. People who do not measure a man in only one way."

The terrible bitterness was in his voice again, Shef heard. And yet—he did not dare to let Cuthred go. He was worth a catapult on his own, or a case-hardened breastplate. He would be needed before they won south, of that Shef was sure.

"Do you remember the mill?" he asked. "When I released you from that, you said you were my man."

Cuthred had been a king's champion for much of his life. He understood loyalty and service, and accepted both as lasting to the death.

"See me through the Skagerrak and I will free you to return, to live in the waste, however you wish," said Shef.

Cuthred stared down at the slush. "I will see you through the Skagerrak," he agreed. "And past the Braethraborg. There will be someone waiting for me here."

CHAPTER TWENTY-NINE

The new king of the Swedes, Kjallak, knew well that he had been chosen to succeed his murdered predecessor Orm for one thing only: to cope with the menace of the German Christians, and to a lesser degree the Way-folk now spreading through the country. To return the land of the Swedes, Sveariki, to the old ways and the old customs of the priests. Failure, and the priests of Uppsala-temple would choose again.

He laid his plans carefully. A sacrifice had been demanded. A sacrifice he would give them. And it would consist of men and women from all the groups that the Swedes hated and feared: Christians, Wayfolk, Finns and even the *skogarmenn*, the small scattered communities of borderers who lived in the forests or on the moors and paid no taxes.

Chasing Finns in the winter was useless. In the summer it was hard also, because they retired with their reindeer to the deep tundra. There was a time to strike, a time when the Swedes had a natural advantage. In the deep mud of the melting season, when no-one moved if they could avoid it, but when the matchless horses of the Swedish horse-breeders could make their way. Kjallak sent sleigh-loads of forage during the winter to selected places. Picked his men and instructed them carefully. Sent them out, a week before the equinox, in wind and driving sleet.

Shef too had laid his plans. At the equinox, he thought, the ice might have gone from the fast-running river, and conditions would be good to take the *Fearnought* down-stream, on the first stage of the voyage home. His men were arming the ship carefully, stowing her dragon-plates of steel in the hold where they could be unshipped quickly, fitting beckets to the gunwales to hold crossbows and quarrels, chipping rocks for the mules.

As he watched, Shef realized that a group of Finns was heading towards them. They moved clumsily without their skis. There was still some snow on the ground, but much of it had churned to slush or mud. The Finns looked graceless, like birds with clipped wings. Yet they were often enough about the station, coming in to trade or to examine what went on. One of Herjolf's priest-companions was a devotee of the goddess Skathi, the ski-goddess of the mountains. He spoke the Finnish tongue and often traveled with them, learning their lore. Shef saw him go to meet them and turned back to the loading.

A while later, he found Ottar, Skathi's-priest, at his shoulder, and with him the Finn, Piruusi, a look of sullen anger on his face. Shef looked from face to face, wondering.

"He says the Swedes attacked his encampment two days ago," said Ottar. "Many men on horses. They had not seen them come because the snow was melting. Many Finns were killed. Some taken."

"Taken," repeated Piruusi. "One Swede got drunk, fell from horse. We catch him. He tell us, Finns to go to the temple. Temple at Uppsala. Hang there on a tree in honor of Swedish gods."

Shef nodded, still wondering why he was being told. "He wants you to rescue them," said Ottar.

"Me! I know nothing of Uppsala." But then Shef fell silent. He remembered the three visions he had had in Piruusi's tent. Of them all, he had thought most about the first, his old enemies the Ragnarssons seizing power and blocking his path. Yet he had seen the king too, the new king, threatened by his priests into promising a proper sacrifice, not the cheap disposal of surplus slaves that the Swedes had carried out for many years. And the Christians, they had been in it too.

"Did he say anything about Christians, your Swede?"

Piruusi's face lightened, he said something in Finnish. "He says he knew you were led by the spirits," said Ottar, translating. "Christians too are to go to the great oak. And the men of the Way, or so Piruusi says."

"We've had no trouble," said Shef.

"We live far up-stream. And in any case, we aren't all here."

Shef felt his heart lurch at the correction. Thorvin had gone to the farm-town thirty miles off, while the snow was still good for sleighs, taking with him Cwicca, Hama and Udd, to trade iron for food. They had not returned. If they had been taken too . . . Shef realized with surprise that of them all, Cwicca who had saved his life by pulling him from Ivar's drowning embrace, Thorvin who had taken him in as a wandering nobody, of them all, the one whose fate most concerned him was Udd. If he went, no-one could replace him. Many plans would die at birth without his inspiration.

"Do you think the Swedes might have got them?" he asked.

Ottar waved at the road from the east, from downstream. Riders were visible on it, spurring as fast as they could through the heavy mud. "I think someone is coming to tell us," he said grimly.

The news was as they had expected. The town lay in ashes, surprised at dawn and burnt to the ground. The raiders had killed every man, woman or child they met, but seized some to herd away with them on spare horses. For capture they had selected those with the pendants of the Way, or youths, or maidens. In the confusion little had been made out as to why the Swedes had attacked the town. But some said they had called out *"skogarmenn! skogarmenn!"* as they had killed. Wood-men, men of the forest, outlaws. All the same thing. Thorvin the priest had certainly been taken, been seen led away. A gap-toothed man had also been recognized, who must be Cwicca. No-one could remember seeing anyone who might have been Udd. But that was entirely probable, Shef reflected. Even people in the same room as Udd often did not see him. Till it came to iron and steel, to metal and contrivances, the little man was made to be ignored.

"What is the day of the sacrifice?" Shef asked.

Gnawing his beard, Herjolf replied, "The day the Holy Oak, the Kingdom Oak as they call it, the day its buds first show green. In ten days. Maybe twelve."

"Well," said Shef, "we shall have to get our men back. Or try at least."

"I agree with you," said Herjolf. "And so would every priest of the way, even Valgrim, if he were still alive! What the Swedes have sent us is a challenge. If they hang up our priests in their sacred clothes, with the rowan-berries at their belts and the pendants round their necks, then we will lose every convert we have ever made among the Swedes. And further afield, when the news spreads."

"Ask Piruusi what he will do," Shef said to Ottar. All that a man can, came the reply. The Swedes had taken his youngest and favorite wife. Piruusi's account of her charms was vivid, made it plain that he found her, like Udd, irreplaceable.

"Good. I need Hagbarth too. Tell him, Herjolf. This is Way business now. And another thing. I am going to fly a banner."

"With what device?"

Shef hesitated. He had seen many banners now, and knew the power they had on the imagination. There was the dreaded Raven Banner of the Ragnarssons, had been the Coiling Worm of Ivar. Alfred flew the Gold Dragon of Wessex, left over from the Rome-folk. Ragnhild's device had been the Gripping Beast. He himself had marched to Hastings under the Hammer and Cross, to unite Way-folk and English Christians against the army of the Pope. What should he choose this time? The device of Rig, the ladder he wore round his neck? No-one would recognize it. A hammer and a broken shackle, for freedom? This time he was not coming to free slaves, but to rally border-people and outlaws.

"You will fly the Hammer, surely," pressed Herjolf. "Not the Hammer and Cross, as you once did. There are no Christians here. Only the Germans and their converts, no friends of ours."

Shef decided. He still held the lance he had taken from Echegorgun, the lance that the troll-man had taken from Jarl Bolli of the Tronds. "I will have an upright lance as my own device," he said. "With a hammer across it, for the Way."

Herjolf pursed his lips. "That will look too much like a cross, for my liking."

Shef stared at him. "If I am to fight a king," he said, "I will be a king. You heard the king's order. Send me all our needlewomen, and do it at once."

As Herjolf walked away, Shef spoke quietly to Cuthred. "We will not leave till tomorrow morning. Go out tonight. No chance of help from the Huldu-folk at Uppsala, I suppose? Too far from the moors and mountains. Just the same, word can be passed. Maybe there are other half-troll families in the north besides Brand's. See to it. Make your farewells."

Shef thought to add, "and see you return," but curbed the words. If Cuthred wanted to desert, he would. All that held him now was pride, and that was not to be insulted.

Cuthred stood unspeaking in the prow of the *Fearnought* next morning, in full mail, with sword, shield, spear and helmet. He looked like a king's champion again, except for his eyes, weary, red-rimmed.

The ship was crowded with men, and women too. Only half a dozen had been left at the mining station. Priests, apprentices, Englishmen, Englishwomen and Finns were all crowded in together, fifty and more. They could never have managed to do so if the ship had needed to be rowed or sailed. But the snow-melt whirled her away without human effort, fast as a racing horse. Hagbarth at the tiller had only a lookout on the yard for ice, and men at the prow with oars to boom off floating debris.

All the way down the stream they saw the signs of devastation, burnt farms, burnt villages. Men called from the banks as they saw the standard flying, were hailed, told to rig their boats and follow. By the time the *Fearnought* reached the sea, a small armada of four- and six-oared boats trailed in her wake. At the sea itself, the fishing villages of Finnmark yielded larger craft. Shef reorganized, commandeering the largest boats, filling them with men from the smallest.

"You can't take them very far like this," protested Hagbarth. "They can't carry enough water for one thing. No, don't tell me, I know. Obey orders. You have a plan."

As the *Fearnought* and her tail of small craft nosed down the Finnish Bight, as the Swedes called the deep gulf between Swedish Finnmark and the land opposite, they sighted a cluster of small islands. Piruusi, hitherto silent, came to Shef and pointed.

"Finns on those islands," he said. "I cross sometimes, on ice. Sea-Finns."

Shef motioned to Ottar, put him, Piruusi and a clutch of his Finnish followers into a boat, told them to bring on every boat and man they could. They pressed on under light sail, waiting for the challenge that must come from King Kjallak's coastguards.

Ali the Red, skipper of the *Sea-bear,* patrolling the seas towards the Finnish Aland Isles, saw the strange sail bearing down on him, and approached cautiously. He had heard tales of strange and strangely-armed vessels, and had no mind to take needless risks. The rag-tag of sails behind, he scanned and dismissed. Fishing boats of the broken men, scavengers only. In any case, as they saw his striped sail and that of his consort, he saw them wear in unison and scud away. But what were they doing on the strange ship? The knorr miscegenated with a Frankish cog? Trying to flee as well?

"She's in range for a long shot," snarled Osmod. The former captain of halberdiers was in a state of barely-controlled rage, had been ever since he realized his long-time friend and comrade Cwicca was facing a Swedish noose, as sacrifice to Frey and Othin.

"Stand away from the mule," Shef ordered. "Get down in the hold, all of you. Hagbarth, you too. Now, Osmod, you're in charge. Turn this ship around and sail away, in flight."

Osmod gaped. "But I can't sail a ship."

"Yes you can, you've seen them do it often enough. Now you do it. Karli, Wilfi, and me, we're your sail-crew. Cuthred, take the steering oar."

"Well," said Osmod uncertainly. "Which way's the wind. Cuthred, turn the front bit away from the wind, um, to the left. Karli, you take that end of the yard, and Wilfi, that end, and turn it round so the wind is behind it. Christ, Thor, I mean, what happens next?"

While Hagbarth held his hands over his eyes, the *Fearnought* lumbered into flight, the very image of an undermanned trader on a maiden voyage. Watching, Ali grinned into his red beard and brought his two ships slanting expertly across to intercept.

"Get your heads down," ordered Shef. "Forget the mules. One crossbow each and another to hand."

He waited till the *Sea-bear* was almost alongside, her gunwales lined with fierce bearded faces, spears poised to board, before he gave the word to rise. Anyone can wind a crossbow, as Udd had said two years before. Even easier when they had only to be cocked. At ten yards' range even the most inexpert could not miss, and at ten yards' range the stout iron quarrels went through wood and mail, flesh and bone as if they were so much canvas. As Shef's archers dropped their first crossbows and reached for the second, it was already clear there would be no need for another volley.

Hagbarth stepped from ship to ship trailing a rope, looked at the few instantly demoralized survivors and ordered them to make fast alongside.

"Now the mule," said Shef, looking at the desperately turning consort vessel. "One rock over their heads, Osmod, and tell them to throw their weapons overboard."

A short time later, his fleet now consisting of three strongly manned large craft with dinghies and pinnaces in tow, Shef's armada moved on for the Swedish shore. Behind them, in small boats so loaded their gunwales were within inches of the water, the disconsolate coastguards surviving argued whether to try for the Aland Islands and the Finns, or the Swedish shore, to face their king's vengeance.

The men of the *Lanzenorden,* for all their prowess, had made few converts among the Swedes, at least among the men and the native-born. The congregations they protected had mostly been drawn from the slaves, Christians when they were brought to the land. Some were Germans, some Frisians or Franks, the majority English and Irish. The *Ritters* felt little kinship with them. They enjoyed the experience of imposing their will on the Norse who had persecuted them for so long, enjoyed realizing that power was largely a matter of concentration. When a Viking army thousands strong came down on some town or village in the West, of course they seemed superior. When fifty armed and trained Germans appeared in the middle of a Swedish village with a population of two hundred, it was the same story. If the natives ever concentrated against them, it would be a different matter. But there was no loot to be won, it was no-one's responsibility. The *Lanzenorden* wintered in peace, but not in content. The rank and file were bored, forbidden to get drunk or lord it over the handsome Swedish women. Erkenbert the deacon feared his chances of promotion were vanishing, stuck here far from the center of affairs. Bruno the leader fretted alone in his quarters. He had not found the lance of Charlemagne. If it was anywhere it was far away in the north in another country. The God in whom he trusted seemed to have deserted him.

When the frantic knocking sounded on the door of the knights' quarters, they sprang out of their torpor, chessboards flung to the ground. Weapons were seized from walls, men struggled into their armor. Someone opened the door cautiously. A thin shabby figure scrambled in.

"They've taken them," he babbled.

"Taken who?" snapped Bruno, alerted by the uproar. "Who's taken who?"

The fugitive's wits seemed to desert him, faced by hostile looks and bared weapons. Erkenbert stepped forward, spoke in English to the frightened man.

"He is from Hadding," he reported. "The town ten miles off, where we have held Mass. He says that this morning soldiers of King Kjallak came, rounded up all the Christians who have attended our services—they had a list—and took them away under guard. It is said by the Swedes, with great satisfaction, that they are to be sacrificed to pagan idols at the great temple, maybe in five days' time."

"A challenge for us," said Bruno, looking round and grinning. "Isn't that right, boys?"

"A challenge to the holy God," said Erkenbert. "We shall meet it as did the holy Boniface, who smote the great pillar Irminsul of the Saxons unharmed, and converted the pagan Saxons from their unbelief."

"I heard a different story," muttered one of the knights. "I'm a Saxon myself. But anyway, how are fifty of us going to get a bunch of sacrifices away from the whole assembly of the Swedes? There'll be thousands of them there. And the king, with his housecarls."

Bruno slapped him violently across the back. "That's why it's a challenge," he shouted. More soberly, he added, "And don't forget, they believe that things must be done in certain ways. A challenge must be answered. If

I challenge the king, he'll have to fight, or put in a champion. This isn't going to be a battle. It will be a show of our strength—of God's will. We'll face them down. Like we've done before."

His men looked uncertain, but discipline was strong, and faith in their leader even stronger. They began to collect their weapons, packs and bed-rolls and horses, working out the march in their heads. Five days. Fifty miles to pagan Uppsala. No trouble, even over muddy roads. But it would be difficult to come at the assembly of the Swedes with any element of surprise. Suspicious, too, that they had been left unharmed, when one might have expected firebrands in the thatch and men outside at dawn. Maybe King Kjallak of the Swedes had thought ahead of them. Was expecting their coming. Had prepared a welcome. The two priests of the mission found a queue at their doors of men waiting to make a confession, and ask for shrift.

CHAPTER THIRTY

As they drew nearer and nearer to Uppsala, Shef felt a mood of foreboding come over him. It should not have. Everything was going as well as anyone could possibly have expected. No resistance on the shore, the fighting men of the Swedes already marched for the assembly and the sacrifice, or so they were told. Guided by boats with lanterns sent out off shore, Piruusi had appeared with a heavy reinforcement of Finns, eager to strike a blow for once at the stronghold of their hereditary enemies. Scores of spare crossbows had been distributed and every man who received one given a short course of instruction and five practice shots—all that were needed to enable a man to load and fire a crossbow of the newest pattern, and hit his target at fifty yards' range. With the Finnish bowmen as a screen and two hundred crossbows behind them, Shef knew he had a force which was at least to be reckoned with, one that would defeat any casual or careless attack. He had had to detach only a dozen men and women to guard the boats and moor the *Fearnought* especially beyond casual reach.

Morale was high, too, borne up by resentment. Also by the cautious welcome they received as they pressed forward—too much of a straggle to be called a march—through the villages of heathen Sweden. Those who were left behind in the villages were women and slaves and the low-born. Many of those, seeing the banner with lance and hammer, took it for some kind of a cross, as Herjolf had feared, and if they were of Christian origin saw it as a liberation. Others saw the Wayman pendants and cautiously joined the party, or volunteered information. Yet others had had friends or relatives snatched for the great sacrifice, and willingly asked for weapons, to help free them. There was a sense of support, of the army growing, not shrinking as so many did on approach to battle.

So why did he feel the foreboding, Shef asked himself. It was because of Cuthred. Shef had some inner presentiment that this matter was not to be decided by pitched battle: that in the end it would come down to a test of champions. Till this time he had relied implicitly on Cuthred, on his strength and skill, but most especially on his uncompromising spirit. Cuthred never had to be encouraged, always restrained. Never till now. But now he was silent, gloomy, without the aura of lurking menace that had always surrounded him.

Jogging along on a commandeered pony, Shef found Hund riding alongside him. As usual, he did not bother to speak, merely waited for Shef's opening.

Speaking quietly, Shef glanced at Cuthred's back ten yards away and muttered, "I fear I have lost my berserk."

Hund nodded. "I had thought so too. Do you think you will have need of one?"

"Yes."

"I remember Brand talking of what makes a berserk. He said they were not men possessed by other spirits, but men who hated themselves. Maybe our berserk—" Hund avoided using his name in case Cuthred heard it "—maybe he has been given some reason not to hate himself."

Shef thought of Miltastaray and the strange remarks Echegorgun had made about the Hidden Folk, their disabilities, and their rare matings. He could see that Cuthred, if he did not think himself a man again, might have been able to think himself a troll.

"I don't want to give him that reason back," he said, "but I would prefer him a bit more like his older self."

Hund produced something from under the long cloak most of the men were now wearing, against the wind and squalls of rain. "It came to me that there might be another thing that makes the berserk. Just as your visions might be caused by something in you, or something in the grain, or something in the Finn's drink, so the berserkergang could be caused by something in the soul—or something in the body. I have talked to the Finns, with Ottar's help. The fly-killer mushroom is not the only one they use. There is this potion too." He showed Shef a flask.

"What is in it?"

"A decoction. Boiling water poured onto another mushroom. Not the red one with the white spots this time, the one that makes the seeing-drink. Nor the other one I know of, the death-cap mushroom, the one—" Hund lowered his voice again "—that looks like a prick.

"There is a third. The Finns call it the tuft-ear mushroom, after the big cat that lives in the forests. It sends men into frenzy, makes berserkers of the mildest." He handed over the flask. "If you need it, take it. Give it to Cuth—to our friend."

Shef took it thoughtfully.

Outside the great temple at Uppsala was a yard, roofed over with thatch but earth-floored, wattle-walled, the rain driving in through every chink. Nine score men and women crowded into it, hands tied into iron rings set into long bars. Given time and effort, a man could break free, untie others. But guards patrolled up and down, clubbing savagely at anyone who shifted, made anything that looked like an attempt at escape. The guards were having more trouble than usual, as they remarked to each other. Not only were there far more for the sacrifice than in living memory. They were not the usual bone-bags, dying by noose or blade only days ahead of death from cold or starvation. That was as it should be, the guards said, aiming blows to break fingers or collar-bones. The gods would have fresh meat for a change. Perhaps the Swedes' ill-luck was caused by the gods having to boil their victims down for soup.

Cwicca, nursing a fractured arm gained when a guard saw him trying to pull the iron ring out of its bar, whispered out of the corner of his mouth to Thorvin next to him. "I don't like the look of Udd."

The little man indeed seemed almost on the point of tears: natural enough, but neither Englishman nor Wayman wanted to give their enemies a chance to mock. He was staring at one of the Swedes, a priest, who had come into the slave pen. It was the custom of the Swedish priests of the temple, of the Kingdom Oak, to taunt and jeer at their captives, believing that their fear and despair were acceptable to the gods. Some said it was a custom set by their ancient king Angantyr. Others said the bastards enjoyed it. Udd's lower lip was trembling as he listened to the Swede's shouts.

"Don't think it will be quick! Don't think you'll get off easy. I have made the sacrifice at this assembly for twenty years. When I was young, then I made mistakes. I let men slide to the gods not knowing they'd gone. Not now! Those I hang, they'll still be awake with their eyes open when the ravens of Othin come to peck them out. How will you feel then, when the raven sits on your head and reaches out its beak. I've seen them! You'll try to lift your hands, won't you? But I'll have tied them down.

"And that's not all. Even after you've gone to death, gone to the gods, what do you think will happen then. You'll sit on clouds with harps in your hands, you Christians, eh? No! You are slaves here and you'll be slaves there."

The priest began to sing a sacred song, his voice and rhythm strangely like Thorvin's. This was where the Way had come from, Cwicca realized with a flash of insight. From beliefs like this one. But changed, not made gentle exactly—the Way-followers were as fierce as any—but without the undercurrent of desperate anxiety that made the true pagans, the hard-core, so addicted to pain.

"The thurs who shall have thee is called Hrimgrimnir,
    Behind Hel's gate your home;
There the wretched slaves beneath roots of trees
    Get dogs' piss for drink.
No other draught shalt thou ever drain . . ."

Udd's head dropped, his face twisted, the pagan priest saw and broke off his chant with a crow of victorious laughter. As he did so Thorvin too began to sing, his deep voice carrying on the very tune of the pagan's, but to a different rhythm:

"I saw a hall standing, sun-bright it shone,
Thatched with gold, on Gimli plain,
There shall the trusty dwell in troops,
Live for ever in love unfading . . ."

The pagan shrieked with fury, ran down the rows of chained prisoners towards his rival, shouting curses, a weighted club in his hand. As he raced past Hama, chained with the others, stuck out a foot. The priest tripped over it, landed sprawling almost at Thorvin's feet. Thorvin eyed the club regretfully, his hands chained above his shoulders. He stepped forward at full stretch, brought a booted heel down. A crunch, a snoring sound from the pagan, deep in his throat, then a choking.

"Snapped windpipe," remarked the guards, removing the body and clubbing Thorvin dispassionately senseless.

"In Thruthvangar, when we reach it," Thorvin gasped between the blows, "he will be my servant. Our servant. And we are not dead yet, though he is."

Unnoticed now, Udd began to weep again. He had traveled far, endured much, done his best to counterfeit the warrior. Now his nerve had gone, his reserve of courage drained empty.

As Shef's army closed on Uppsala, the last night before their informers insisted the sacrifice was due, the rain came down harder. The muddy tracks began to be thronged with worshipers, sightseers, adherents of King Kjallak and devotees of Othin and Frey, all mixed in hopeless confusion. Rather than trying to fight a way through all at once, Shef simply told his men to put their unfamiliar weapons under their cloaks and press on as if they were just another group, an unusually large one, heading for the ritual. In better weather the Finns, at least, would have been recognized. With all heads bent in the streaming rain, and the Finns kept in the center, no remark was made, no opposition organized. Shef heard many voices say that the gods had not relented. They would demand blood in torrents before the Swedes would see good harvests again.

In the dark hour before dawn, Shef saw the dragon-gables of the temple rear against the clouds. Even more unmistakable, the great bulk of the oak-tree itself, the Kingdom Oak, around which the Swedes had worshiped their gods and elected their kings since before they were a nation. Forty men with hands outstretched would not span the trunk, it was said. Even in the growing crowds, no-one ventured under its branches. Some of the offerings of last year still swung there, human and animal. A charnel of uncleared bones lay beneath it.

As they halted Shef sent word along to Herjolf, Osmod and the others, to try to get the men into a deep line unblocked by Swedes, and prepare them for whatever might come. He himself moved up to Cuthred's shoulder. The big man stood unspeaking, weapons hidden.

"I may need you at my shoulder soon," said Shef.

Cuthred nodded. "I will be there when you need me, lord."

"Maybe you should drink this. It—it makes a man readier, or so Hund tells me."

Cuthred took the flask, unstoppered it, and sniffed it gingerly. He snorted with sudden contempt, threw it onto the sodden ground. "I know what that is. They give it to the striplings they do not trust before battle. Offer it to me, Ella's champion! I am your man. I would have killed any man else who gave me that."

Cuthred turned his back, stood angrily aside. Shef looked at him, bent

and picked the flask up, sniffed it himself. Perhaps a third of the draught remained. They gave it to the striplings before battle? He was a stripling, or so people kept telling him. On impulse he lifted the flask, drained it, threw it back to the ground. Karli, a few feet away—he took care not to get too close to Cuthred—watched anxiously.

Horns had started to blow somewhere, low and heavy in the damp. Was it dawn? Hard to tell. Hard to tell, too, whether the Kingdom Oak was budding. But the priests of the temple seemed to have decided to begin. Doors opened as the sky slowly paled, priests filed out chanting, circled the oak. Another blare of horns, and a gate swung slowly open. Guards began to herd a double line of shuffling figures out into the chill. Shef undid his cloak, let it fall into the mud, stood breathing heavily and deeply. He was ready now to act. He waited only for his target.

*   *   *

Not very far away, behind a low ridge that fringed the temple-plain, Bruno had mustered his riders. He had decided to keep his men mounted, for the shock effect. It was true that the mounts were only Swedish horses, not the highly-trained chargers of Frankland or Germany, but his men were all horsemen, true *Ritters*. They would squeeze a charge out of any animal.

"I think they're getting ready to start," said Bruno to Erkenbert. The little deacon could hardly ride at all, but refused like the mission's priests to be left behind. Bruno had swung him up onto his own saddle-bow. Erkenbert was shivering with cold. Bruno refused to consider that it might be fear. Perhaps it was excitement at the thought of striking a blow for the faith. Erkenbert had read to them all, the day before, the legends of the holy saints, the holy *English* saints Willebald and Wynfrith, who had taken the name Boniface. They had attacked the pagan Saxons in their own sanctuaries, cut down their holy pillars, gained eternal salvation in Heaven and also everlasting glory among men. Martyrdom, Erkenbert had said, was nothing in comparison. It was certainly true that the little Englishman was eager himself to be the hero of story. Bruno had other intentions, not involving martyrdom.

"There!" said the deacon. "They are leading out the martyrs to their doom. When will you strike? Ride forward now in the strength of the Lord."

Bruno tensed, rose in his stirrups to give the order, settled slowly back. "I think someone is there before us," he said in surprise.

As the captives were led slowly forward, Shef realized that someone had come to take charge. The growing light revealed a block of gray stone in the center of the plain between the temple and the oak, a flat square platform maybe four feet high and ten across. A man stepped out from the group near the temple doors, swinging a spear. He vaulted suddenly and powerfully onto the platform, heaving himself up on the spear, and raised his hands high. A concerted shout came from his supporters, drowning out the buzz of comment from the rest of the crowd. "Kjallak!" they shouted. "Kjallak king, favored of the gods!"

Shef began to walk forward, lance in hand. He knew, but did not care, that Cuthred was behind him. His body seemed buoyed up on a cushion of air, as if something inside him were lifting him, as if his breath were too great for his lungs.

"Kjallak!" he called out harshly. "You have my men there. I want them back."

The king stared down at him, a warrior in his prime, thirty-five years old, veteran of many wars and many single combats.

"Who are you, manling, that disturbs the assembly of the Swedes?" he asked.

Shef, within range, swung the lance-butt at his legs. Kjallak leapt nimbly over it, came down on wet stone, slipped and fell. Shef vaulted onto the stone to stand over him. His voice lifted and rang across the plain, shouting out words he had never thought to say.

"You are no king! A king is to guard his people. Not hang them on trees for a crowd of old tricksters. Get off the stone! I am the king of the Swedes."

Weapons clashed in the background, but Shef ignored them. Half a dozen of Kjallak's men had run forward as soon as their king was threatened. Three met crossbow quarrels humming from the crowd. Cuthred, stepping forward, coldly cut the legs from under one, slashed furiously at the others, driving them back.

"Is this a challenge?" called Kjallak. "This is not the place or the time for it."

Shef responded with a kick that caught Kjallak rising to his feet, tumbled him off the stone. A groan rose from the watchers. Kjallak got to his feet again, face paling.

"Whatever place or time, I will kill you for that," he said. "I will make a *heimnar* of you and give what is left to the priests. You are the first sacrifice to the gods this day. But you have neither sword nor shield. How can you fight me with that old pigsticker?"

Shef looked round. He had not planned this. It was the recklessness born from Hund's potion that had done this: left him facing a fully-armed hero himself, instead of sending forward his champion Cuthred. Impossible to ask for a substitution. The day was up now, he saw, and by some chance the rain had stopped. All eyes were on him, up there on the stone, at the center of a natural amphitheater. The priests of the temple had ceased their chanting, stood there in a grisly group, next to their herded captives. Round him in a great ring of spears stood the assembly of the Swedish nation. But they made no move to interfere. They stood, waiting for the judgment of the gods. He could never expect a better chance than this. And the potion was still strong within him.

Shef threw his head back and laughed, lifted the lance and threw it point-first into the wet turf. He raised his voice so that it would carry not to Kjallak but to the rearmost row of the spectators.

"I have no sword and shield," he shouted. "But I have this!" He pulled from his belt the long single-edged knife he carried. "I will fight you Rogaland style! We need no bull's hide. We have the holy stone. I will fight you here, wrist tied to wrist, and he who steps down from the stone, he is king of the Swedes."

A slow rumble came from the crowd as they caught the words, and Kjallak, hearing it, tightened his lips. He had seen duels like that before. They took away the advantage of skill. But the crowd would not let anyone back out now. He still had strength and reach. He reached down, unbuckled his sword-belt, threw it from the stone, hearing the Swedes begin to cheer and clash spear on shield as they realized he had taken the dare.

"Dunghill cock!" he said, keeping his voice low. "You should have stuck to your own midden."

Cwicca, holding his broken arm up by the sleeve, muttered to the battered and bleeding Thorvin, "There's something funny going on. He would never have planned this. Nor he hasn't been levered into it either. This isn't like him."

"Maybe the gods have taken control of him," said Thorvin.

"Let's hope they keep it up," said Hama.

Bruno, still watching the arrangements being made from his unnoticed vantage-point, looked round thoughtfully. All eyes were on the center, where men were helping Kjallak out of his mail as Shef stripped to his tunic as well. A rope had appeared, cut from the hangman's coil, and they were preparing to lash the two men together, each man with two seconds now to see fair play. One of the temple priests had insisted on singing an invocation to Othin, and Herjolf, pushing out of the crowd, had begun a counter to it.

"We can't even get at them now," said Bruno. "The crowd's too close-packed. See here, what we'll do is this." He pointed out to his men a circuit they could make. To the right, round behind the temple and the slave-yard, to appear between the temple and the oak, where a gap had been left for the prisoners. "Come out there behind them," he concluded. "Ride forward and make a wedge. That way we'll get our people away at least."

"What's that banner they've broken out down there?" asked one of his men.

"It is a cross," cried the weak-eyed Erkenbert. "God has sent a sign!"

"Not a cross," said Bruno slowly. "It is a lance. Like the one the young man just threw down. A lance with something I can't see across it. I don't deny it may be a sign for all that."

Breathing deeply and slowly, Shef waited for the signal to begin. He wore only his breeches, shoes kicked off as well for a surer grip on the wet stone. He had no idea what to do. It did not seem to matter. Hund's potion filled him with rage and ecstasy. The calculating part of him that lived on somewhere below the potion had given up its protests, was telling him instead to keep his eye on his enemy, not just luxuriate in feelings of power.

A sudden silence as the rival chantings stopped, a blare of horns, and Kjallak stepped forward over the stone platform like a panther and slashed. Shef leapt away almost too late, felt a line of fire across his ribs, heard from some far distance the roar of acclaim. He began to move, pulling with one hand on the rope both men held, feinting to thrust with the other. Kjallak ignored the feints, waited for the real stab. When it came, the one-eye would have to step close. When he missed, Kjallak would strike again for the body. He circled always to the right, crowding the knife-hand, making his opponent back away to keep him off his blind side. Every few seconds he slashed quickly, professionally, at Shef's exposed left arm, enough to make the blood run, the strength go.

"How's it going?" asked Thorvin, his left eye swollen shut.

"He's cutting our man to bits," answered Cwicca.

He's cutting me to bits, thought Shef. He felt no pain, no physical fear, but there was an undercurrent of panic rising, as if he were out on a stage in front of thousands of people, and had forgotten what he was supposed to say. He tried a sudden sweep with one leg, a wrestling trick. Kjallak evaded it economically, and sliced him across the knee. Shef slashed back at Kjallak's rope-arm, drawing blood for the first time. Kjallak grinned and thrust suddenly over their joined arms, forcing Shef to jerk his head aside and leap back, dropping the rope, to avoid the instant second thrust for the heart.

"Learning, eh?" panted Kjallak. "But not fast enough. You should have stayed with your mother."

The thought of his mother, her life destroyed by the Vikings, stabbed Shef into a flurry of thrusts, coming forward recklessly. Kjallak dodged them, caught a couple with his own knife in a clang of metal, waited for the surge to die down. Like a berserker, he thought. Don't take them head on. Keep out of their way and wait for them to tire. He could feel it already, the spasmodic strength draining.

"Stayed with your mother," he repeated. "Maybe had a nice game of knucklebones."

Knucklebones, thought Shef. He remembered the lessons from Karli in the marsh, remembered Hedeby market. Seizing the trailing rope again, he jerked it taut, slashed it suddenly through. A groan from the crowd, a look of surprise, disgust in Kjallak's eyes.

Shef threw his knife high in the air, spinning end over end. Kjallak, whose eyes had never left it, looked up, followed it automatically for an instant, his head rising.

Shef stepped forward, pivoting from the waist as Karli had taught him, and threw a clenched left fist in a sweeping hook. He felt the blow run up his arm, felt the crunch of fist on beard and bone. Kjallak staggered. But he was a man with a neck like a bull's, knocked off balance but not down.

The spinning knife came down. As if he had practiced the catch for a dozen years, Shef caught it left-handed by the hilt, thrust upwards at the raised chin. The blade skewered through beard and chin, mouth and palate, drove on till the point wedged hard in the roof of the skull.

Shef felt the dead weight fall forward, twisted the blade, jerked it free. He turned in a slow semi-circle towards the crowd, raising the bloody knife. A roar of applause from his own men, confused cries from the rest.

"Foul!" cried one of Kjallak's seconds, stepping towards the stone. "He cut the rope! That's against the rules."

"What rules?" said Cuthred. Without further words he slashed at the second, half-severing his head. From the stone Shef saw spears poised, crossbows leveled.

A ray of sunshine broke through the clouds, fell on the bloody stone. This time a groan from the crowd, of awe. And in the same moment, a clash of metal. Shef looked up, saw between the oak and the temple a solid line of armored horsemen, driving between the prisoners and their guards, hustling the temple priests towards him. He did not know who they were, but they gave him a chance. The potion filled him with one more inspiration, a surge of fury.

"Swedes!" he called out. "You are here for good harvests and prosperity. They grow from blood. I have given you blood already, king's blood. Follow me and I will give you more."

Voices from the crowd, shouting about the oak and the sacrifices.

"You have sacrificed for years and what good has it done? You sacrificed the wrong things. You must sacrifice what is dearest to you. Start again. I will give you a better sacrifice."

Shef pointed across the clearing. "Sacrifice your oak. Cut it down now, and set free the souls that hang from it. And if the gods want blood, send it to them. Send the gods their servants, the priests of the temple."

Across the clearing, a small black-clad figure had scrambled from a horse, was running under the ghastly swaying boughs. He had an axe in his hand, snatched from a gaping priest. He reached the oak, raised the axe and swung. A groan again from the crowd at the sacrilege. Chips flew, men stared upwards for the avenging thunder. Nothing. Just the hard noise of metal on wood as Erkenbert swung like a man possessed. Slowly eyes turned towards the priests. Bruno's men rode forward, herding them towards the stone. Herjolf turned towards Shef's followers, seizing the moment.

"Right," he shouted. "Crossbows, down here and make a ring. Ottar, get your Finns organized. The rest of you, seize those men. And you," he called to Bruno, "stop your little fellow before he does himself an injury. Make a ring round the oak and get four men at it who know their business."

The Swedes watched in amazement and acquiescence as Herjolf made his grisly preparations. Before the morning was over the Kingdom Oak would be in flames, and tossed onto it as a pyre, the bodies of its servants.

"Does that make the one-eye king of the Swedes?" they asked each other.

"Who knows?" went the answers. "But he has brought back the sun."

CHAPTER THIRTY-ONE

The Ragnarsson brothers heard the news in their quarters at the Braethraborg, the Stronghold of the Brothers, their city-barracks on the island of Sjaelland in the heart of Denmark. After they had rewarded and dismissed the messenger—it was a settled policy with them always to pay for news, however unwelcome—they sat alone to consider it. Wine was on the table between them, wine from the south in a jar. It had been a profitable year for them, after a poor start. Ever since they took Hedeby they had marched or sailed from one small kingdom to another, forcing submission on the petty kings, each victory bringing them allies and troops for the next. The trade between north and south was now entirely in their hands, every load of furs or amber from the north paying toll to them, every load of wine or slaves from the south. Yet they had not succeeded in one thing, were left uneasy in their minds.

"Killed Kjallak," ruminated Halvdan Ragnarsson. "I always said he was a good boy. We should have kept him on our side. It was that business with Ivar's girl that spoiled it. Pity we couldn't get Ivar to see sense." Halvdan felt the most strongly of the brothers about the code of *drengskapr*, had taken a liking to Shef ever since his victory over the Hebrideans at the holmgang outside York. His feelings, as his brothers knew, made no difference to his loyalty. He was merely expressing an opinion.

"And now they say he's rowing south. There's only one place he could be aiming at," said Ubbi Ragnarsson. "That's here. I wonder what force he can raise."

"The reports say he has not raised anything like the full force of the Swedes," said their brother Sigurth, the Snake-eye. "That's a good thing. I know we laugh at the Swedes, they're old-fashioned, haven't had the campaigning in the West to teach them their trade. But there's a lot of them, if they got themselves together.

"Still, they haven't. Volunteers, they say, and a force he brought with him from the far North, Finns and *skogarmenn*. I doubt there's much to worry about there. What makes me think a bit harder are the Norwegians."

Olaf Elf-of-Geirstath, once he heard from the emissaries of the Way what had happened at Uppsala, had responded by calling out his full levies from all the kingdoms he had dominated since the death of his brother, and rowing south as soon as the ice would let him, to meet the man he considered to be his over-king.

"Norwegians!" said Ubbi. "And led by that fool Olaf. They'll start to fight among themselves before long, and he has sat at home for forty years. He is no threat."

"He was no threat," said Sigurth. "What bothers me is the way he's changed. Or been changed."

He sat silent, sipping the wine and pondering. His brothers exchanged glances, sat silent also. Of them all, Sigurth was the one who best read the future. He was sensitive to every change of fortune, every shift of luck and reputation.

What Sigurth was thinking was that he smelled trouble. In his experience, trouble came always from the quarter least expected, and was worst when you had had a chance to settle it and had failed to take it. He and his brothers had neglected this man Skjef, or Shef to begin with. He himself had let him off with the loss of one eye when he was entirely in his power. Then, alerted to his ability to make trouble for them, they had tried once and twice to deal with him. The first attempt had cost them their brother. The second had almost cost him and his two remaining brothers their reputation. And the man had got away from them again. Maybe he should not have restrained Halvdan when he wanted to plunge through the water and attack him. He might have lost another brother. If it had finished their enemy off once and for all, it might have been worth it.

Behind it all, Sigurth wondered, was there some suggestion, some hint, of a shift of favor from the gods? Sigurth was a skeptic in most ways, not above frightening priests or buying good omens. Yet beneath it all there had always been a bedrock certainty that the old gods did exist, and that he was their favorite, the favorite of Othin especially. Had he not sent him thousands of victims? Yet Othin might turn against a favorite in the end.

"We will send out the war-arrow," he said. "To every land we control. To turn out with full force or feel our retribution.

"You know what else worries me?" he went on. "Think of this table as the Scandinavian lands, Denmark here, Norway here, Sweden here." With flasks and mugs he began to trace a primitive map on the table. "Look at the way he's been traveling round. Here in the south, where we met his fleet at sea. Then up at Hedeby. Then off to Kaupang. Then up to the far North. And then he reappears where no-one would expect him, on the other side of the Keel mountains. He's making a circle. Or should I say a circuit?"

The circuit was the road the king rode on, to collect his taxes, expose himself to challenge, impose his authority. The *Eiriksgata* in Sweden was one. Shef's road could be seen as a greater one, a circuit of all the circuits.

"Well," said Halvdan, looking at the pattern of the mugs. "He has one step yet to take before he has completed the circuit. Or the circle. And that is here, at the Braethraborg."

Very far away, four others met in conclave. Not three brothers this time, but three brothers and their father. If he was their father, if they were really brothers. Such things become uncertain among the gods.

They stood at the Hlithskjalf, the lookout place of Asgarth, stronghold of the gods. To their eyes nothing was invisible, nothing at least on Middle-earth, centermost of the nine worlds. They saw the fleets crawling across the sea, the fish swarming beneath it, saw the corn growing and the seed springing.

"I have held him in my hand," said Othin All-father, "and let him go. And he has denied me, refused me sacrifice, slain my followers. I sent the snow and the Finns to kill him, and he escaped me. And what saved him? A troll, a iötunn, one of the brood of Loki the accursed."

The others exchanged looks. Heimdall, watchman of the gods, his great horn slung round his neck, ready to blow on the day that the iötnar should rise to bring Ragnarök to gods and men, spoke carefully. "One of the Huldu-folk saved him, All-Father. We do not know that such are the brood of Loki. But something stirred up the whales, the killers who obey nothing but their sport and their hunger. It was not I, it was not you. If it was the Chained One, as I believe, then he is the Chained One's enemy. And the enemy of our enemy is our friend."

"He burned the great oak. He burned the temple. He released those dedicated to me and to your brother Frey. Even now he sails with Christians at his side."

This time Thor tried his skills of persuasion, never very great. "The ones dedicated to you were a poor lot. He sent you others—your own priests. They were a poor lot too, but it was a fair exchange. He has Christians with him, but he has done more to weaken them than any of your favorites. What did Hermoth do against them, or Ivar whom this man killed? Kill a few, I dare say, but that only encourages the rest. This one has taken kingdoms away from them. They fear him more than you do."

A careless word, and the glare of Othin's one eye shot like a dagger at the red-bearded god, who looked down and fingered his hammer awkwardly.

"Not fear, of course," he went on. "He is a smith, though, and a friend of smiths. He is that first and last. I am for him."

"If what you say is true," said Othin eventually, "then maybe I could find a place for him in my army at Valhalla, place him among the Einheriar. Is that not reward and honor enough for any mortal?"

Only for the crazy ones, thought the god who had not spoken. Heimdall looked at him in warning, for Heimdall could hear the thoughts in a man's head, or a god's. It was true, though. Only the crazy ones saw reward in fighting to the death every day and then coming to life to talk it over every evening.

"The Einheriar are there," said the silent god, "to win the day at Ragnarök."

"Of course," said Othin. He glared at Rig with his one eye. Rig was crafty, skilled with words beyond any of his other sons. Sometimes wondered if Rig might not be a son. Certainly Rig had cuckolded many husbands, made many men bring up cuckoos. Could he do the same to gods?

"And the purpose of Ragnarök is to destroy evil and make the world anew? To repair the great maim that we and it suffered when Balder died? When the Accursed One did his greatest evil, and became for us the Chained One."

The other gods stiffened a little. The name of Balder was no longer spoken among them, or not in Othin's hearing. It was ill to stir old wounds.

Rig went on, his voice cool and ironic, as always. "But are we sure that Ragnarök will be a victory? No. That is why Othin strengthens always his army in Valhalla. If it is a victory, are we sure that there will be a better world on the other side? No. For there are prophecies to say that all of us—or all of you—will perish on that day. You, Thor, from the poison of Iörmungand the World-Serpent. You, Heimdall, facing your brother Loki. For me I have heard no prophecy. But Othin All-father—it is said that for him the jaws of Fenris-Wolf lie ever in wait.

"So why are we so eager to run to Ragnarök? Why has none of us asked himself: what if the world could be made anew without the destruction?"

Othin's fingers tightened on the shaft of his spear, and the knuckles showed white.

"One last question. We know that we tried to have Balder return from the dead, and Othin sent his hero Hermoth to try to bring him back. It failed. Yet there are stories that men have been released from Hel, though not by us."

"Christian stories," growled Thor.

"Even they may bring some hope. I know All-father shares that hope. Those who were there, they may remember. When Balder lay on his pyre, and we prepared to light it, to push it out onto the Shoreless Sea to send him down to Hel, then at that last moment Othin All-father bent and whispered words in Balder's ear. Words none heard, not even you, Heimdall. What did Othin whisper in dead Balder's ear?"

"It comes to me that I know. May I speak those words, All-father?"

"If you have thought them, Heimdall has heard them now. Two may keep a secret, but not once it is known to three. Speak, then. What did I whisper in my dead son's ear?"

"You whispered: 'Would that some god would send you back to me, my son.' "

After a long silence, Othin spoke again. "It is true. I confessed my own weakness then, as I have never done before or since."

"Confess it again. Let this play itself out without your intervention. Let my son have his chance. Let me see if I can use him to bring about a better world without the fire of Ragnarök. To cure the maim of Balder dead."

Othin stared once more at the crawling fleets below. "Very well," he said in the end. "But I will find recruits still for my Einheriar. Soon my daughters will be busy, the Valkyriar, Choosers of the Slain."

Rig made no answer, his thoughts veiled even from Heimdall.

The battle council Shef called on the deck of the *Fearnought* looked as if the battle had already taken place. Cwicca, there as captain of the catapult squads, had an arm splinted and bandaged. Thorvin's face was still covered in bruises, one eye swollen shut and just beginning to work its way open. Shef himself looked white, propped up with cushions in a chair: the gashes on his arm and leg had received more than a hundred stitches from Hund, and according to the leech what blood he had left at the end of the duel would barely have filled a wine-glass.

Others looked more warlike. At the foot of the long table Shef had commissioned sat Olaf Elf-of-Geirstath, newly and respectfully called by his Norwegian subjects, "the Victorious." Flanking him was Brand, who had made his way south at the end of the winter to buy a new Walrus. Looking at him, Shef thought the troll blood more and more obvious. His eyebrows beetled out like ledges over a cliff, his hands and knuckles seemed even too large for the rest of him. Guthmund sat next to him,

newly named on Shef's authority jarl of Sodermanland, in succession to
the dead Kjallak. The other Swedish jarls had taken the designation better
on learning that the new jarl was indeed a countryman and even a kins-
man. They had also listened with deep interest to Guthmund's emphatic
opinions on the potential wealth to be gained in the new king's service.

Herjolf too was at the council, and Ottar to carry its decisions to Piruusi
and the Finns. So too, lounging back in his seat with an air of unconcern,
was the broad-shouldered figure of the German Bruno. His men's intervention at Uppsala had won him a place at the table. There was no doubt, at
least, of his opposition to the Ragnarssons, now that they controlled
Hedeby and had abandoned Hrorik's trade-for-all policy, a standing threat
to the northern borders of Germany.

Brand, who three years ago had carried the news of Ragnar Lothbrok's
death into the Braethraborg itself—a story now continually retold—had
been asked to describe its defenses to the commanders of Shef's allied
fleet, more than a hundred warships. He had drawn the shape of the bay it
stood in, in a great tray of sand on the table, and was now sticking pieces
of wood into the sand to show the position of the main buildings.

"A tough nut to crack," he concluded. "When I went in there was a
standing patrol of half-a-dozen warships of the largest size. We hear that
has been doubled, since the Ragnarssons know we are close. Each ship
must hold at least a long hundred of men, six score, proven champions,
and they stand higher out of the water than any of our vessels—except for
the coastal patrol ships brought down by King Olaf, of which we have only
four. Of course, since the Ragnarssons' ships never leave the bay, they have
no problems with water storage and can remain fully-manned at all times,
returning for rest and food one at a time.

"And then there are the catapults. Everyone agrees that the first success
of the Ragnarssons against Hedeby was caused by their use of the new
machines. Since then they have continued to build them and train men in
their use, all directed, so they say, by a renegade monk or lay-brother from
the Minster at York."

Eyes turned with a certain reproach to the small black figure of
Erkenbert sitting at Bruno's side. Erkenbert took no notice. Since his attack on the Kingdom Oak he had lived in a perpetual daydream, in which
he continually rewrote the *legendum* of Erkenbert *arithmeticus*, smiter of the
pagans, in the form of a saint's life. He was unsure still about the role that
should be given in it to the one-eyed apostate who had smitten the pagan
king: perhaps it would be best to omit all mention of him, to ascribe the

victory to a Christian champion. In the Christian world only the Church recorded history.

"The catapults are here," Brand went on, driving a handful of pegs into the promontory that guarded access to the inner bay. "They can wreck any ships that approach and get past the standing patrol, at a range of close on a mile.

"And finally, there is the Ragnarsson main force. Armed longships, beached here—" another handful of pegs, "—at least as many of them as we have, and again without problems of water storage or provisioning."

"Tell us, Brand," said Shef. "Is there any good news?"

Brand grinned. "Well, lord, I could say 'it isn't raining,' but it probably will be soon. But yes, there is. When it comes to it, many of the Ragnarsson allies are there under coercion. They're there because the Ragnarssons came against them one at a time and forced them to surrender and contribute forces. But if they thought they could get away with it they'd desert like a shot. If the Ragnarssons are winning, they'll fight for them. If it once looks as if they're losing . . . Support will crumble very fast. To be honest, I think we would stand a good chance—if, if we could get past the hard core. But the catapults are a problem, and so are the big ships."

Brand hesitated, unsure whether he was explaining the obvious. But the council contained so many non-Norsemen it was best to be explicit. "You see, in a sea-fight the size of your ship is like, like being behind stone walls. These big ships would go to the bottom in an hour in an Atlantic storm, and their keels are always weak. But if one of them comes alongside you in enclosed water, all they have to do is throw a couple of rocks down from behind their scantlings, and you'll be swimming. They're feet higher than an ordinary ship. The men in it are protected from anything you can do, but your decks are wide open to their bows or spears. If they board you they're coming downhill. You'd have to climb a rope on a grapnel to board them, and as long as there's anyone alive on board them, that's impossible. One of King Olaf's ships could fight one of them on even terms, but they outnumber us three to one in that class. And they'll be manned, I repeat, by the Ragnarssons' best. Only Danes, I dare say, not Norwegians," Brand added with a bristle of national pride. "But not beardless boys for all that."

"Alas," said Bruno in the silence, his Norse strongly accented. "I fear we shall all have to go home."

Brand flushed angrily and started to reach over the table to grip Bruno's hand in his own, meaning to crush it till he screamed for release. Bruno evaded the grasp easily, the smile never leaving his face.

Shef rapped the table. "Enough. Thank you, Brand, for your report. Count Bruno, if you wish to go home we will continue without you." Shef held Bruno's gaze for a moment, forcing him to drop his eyes. "The Count intended a mere pleasantry. He is as determined as the rest of us to put an end to these mad dogs and restore law to the Northlands."

"Yes," said Herjolf, "but how are we to do it?"

Shef held a hand out, palm flat. "That is paper." He made it into a fist. "That is stone." He extended two fingers only. "Those are scissors. Now, who will play this game with me? Count Bruno, you."

Shef's voice was strong and certain, coming strangely from the pallid face. He was sure that he could carry them with him, sure even that he could read his man's mind well enough to win the game. What would Bruno do? He would not choose paper, that was sure. Stone or scissors? His own nature would be for the sharp cut. So he would choose stone, thinking others like himself.

"One, two, three," Shef counted. Both men thrust their hands out together, Bruno's a fist, Shef's a flat palm. "Paper wraps stone, I win."

Again, and this time Bruno would reject the scissors, which would have won last time, reject the stone which he had tried last. "One, two, three." Bruno's flat palm met Shef's two fingers. "Scissors cut paper, I win again. But enough—" Bruno's face was beginning to darken at the guffaws from Brand. "You see my point. They have big ships, and catapults, and ordinary ships. And big ships beat ordinary ships, as Brand has told us. Now what beats big ships? Catapults. And what beats catapults? Our plan must be always to oppose our strength to their weakness. Listen while I explain . . ."

As the council broke up, Shef sat back, hoarse from talking and tired still from loss of blood. Bruno, rising, performed a courteous bow in the direction of the scowling Brand, and then made his way to the head of the table.

"You have come a long way since they tried to sell you as a slave in Hedeby," he remarked. He nodded to Karli behind Shef's chair. "I see you still have your young Ditmarsher with you. But the weapon you have, that is not the one you were carrying then. May I examine it?"

Oddly reluctant, Shef reached behind him, took the lance from its place against the gunwale, passed it over. Bruno turned it over in his hands, examining its head.

"May I ask where you found this strange piece."

Shef laughed. "It would take too long to tell the full story. In a smokehouse. I am told it belonged once to a jarl of the Tronds, one Bolli. But I never met him. Or not to speak to," he added, remembering the long row of swinging carcasses. "You can see that at one time it was in the hands of Christians. Look, there are crosses on the cheek-pieces, inlaid once with gold. But that had been scraped out long before I came by it."

Bruno turned the weapon in his hands, staring at the cross-marks on the blade. He handled it gently, reverently. After a moment he said, his voice quiet, "May I ask how the weapon came to you, if you never met its owner? This jarl Bolli of the Tronds. You found it somewhere? You took it from someone?"

Shef remembered the scene in Echegorgun's smokehouse: how he had laid the weapon down, how Cuthred had picked it up and pressed it on him. There was something odd in the way Bruno was pursuing this. He was reluctant to tell him the full story.

"Let's say it passed into my hands. It belonged to no-one at the time."

"Some man had kept it, though? Some man gave it to you?"

Echegorgun kept it, thought Shef. A marbendill, not a man. And it was Cuthred who handed it to me. "Not exactly a man," he replied.

Archbishop Rimbert's words had been reported to Bruno: how he had said that the Holy Lance of Longinus and of Charlemagne would not come to light through the hand of man. His doubts vanished. He held the holy relic of Empire, at long last, in his hands. God had favored him for all his trials. Yet he was on the deck of a heathen warship, surrounded by potential foes. What was it the little deacon had said to him? "He who perseveres to the end, he shall be saved." To the end. Not just to near the end.

His voice as casual as he could make it, Bruno grounded the lance-butt gently on the deck. "It is clearly a Christian weapon," he said. "No offense, but I would rather not leave it in the hands of one who is no longer a Christian. Perhaps I can ransom it from you, as we ransom Christian slaves."

Brand tried to persuade me to get rid of it too, thought Shef. Strange. "No," he said, repeating what he had said to Brand. "I call it a good weapon that conquers, and it has brought me good luck. I have taken a fancy to it. I will keep it."

Bruno handed it back, straightened and bowed in the stiff German fashion. *"Uf widersehn, herra, bis uf die schlacht.* Farewell, lord. Till we meet in the battle."

"Awkward bastard," muttered Cuthred to Cwicca in English, watching him go.

CHAPTER THIRTY-TWO

S hef lay in sleep, conscious at some level of his mind that tomorrow would be the day of battle. The fleet lay beached some dozen miles from the entry to the bay of the Braethraborg, strongly guarded against any surprise sortie.

In his sleep he was in the bay of the Braethraborg itself, down at the far end, looking out in the direction that he knew he, Shef, must come in the morning. And indeed it was morning, and the man looking out of a just-unshuttered window could see ships creeping down the fjord towards him. Those ships, he knew, would bring his death.

The man watching swung the shutters fully open, stood facing the oncoming navy, and began to sing. The song he sang was one Shef had heard often before, a famous song among the Vikings, a favorite of Brand's. It was called "The Song of Bjarki," or "The Old Song of Bjarki." But this man was not repeating it. he was making it up for the first time. He sang:

"The day is come up, the cocks whir their wings.
Time for the wretches, to rise to their work.
Wake now, awake, you warriors, my friends,
All the best of you, beaters of Athils,
Har with the hard grip, Hrolf the archer,
Men of good stock, who scorn to flee.

*I do not wake you to wine nor whispers of women,
I wake you for the sharp showers of battle."*

*The voice of Shef's frequent mentor cut in above the voice of the singing man,
amused and ironic as usual.*

*"Now you will not fight like that," it said. "You want to win, not to gain glory.
Remember though: I have done my best for you, but you must take every
advantage you can. There is no room for weakness . . ."*

The voices faded, both the impassioned singer and the cold voice of the
god. As he woke—or perhaps they were what woke him—Shef heard the
horns of the sentries blowing to signal dawn and battle-morning. Shef lay
where he was, aware that now he was a king he could at least wait for
someone else to light the fires and make the breakfast. No question of
fighting on an empty stomach, not in the heavy manual labor of hand-to-
hand battle. He was reflecting on the vision, and on the song.

"Men of good stock," the singer had said, "who scorn to flee." Was he a
man of good stock? He supposed so. Whether his father was a god or a
jarl, or even if he had been Wulfgar the thane, there was no churl-blood
there. Did that mean that he, Shef, would scorn to flee? That those who
fled were always of bad stock? Perhaps the singer thought that not fleeing
and being noble were always the same thing. If he did, he was wrong.

And the god had said he must take every advantage. Something told
Shef that was wrong too. That was it, there was something that had been
bothering him. He sat up, called to his attendant. "Pass the word for the
Englishman Udd."

By the time Shef had his shoes on, Udd was there. Shef looked at him
critically. He was trying to hold himself together, but his face was white
and strained. He had been looking like that for days. No wonder. He had
spent weeks waiting for a painful death, and been rescued only at the last
moment. Before that he had gone through more danger and hardship than
he would have done in six lifetimes as a smith's helper, which is what he
had been once. He had been overtaxed. Yet he would not wish to desert
now.

"Udd," Shef said, "I have a special assignment for you."

Udd's lower lip quivered, the look of fear became more pronounced.

"I want you to leave the *Fearnought* and stay with the rearguard."

"Why, lord?"

Shef thought quickly. "So you can pass a message for me, if—if the day
goes badly. Here, take this money. It will buy you a passage back to

England one day, if that is what it comes to. If that happens, you are to greet King Alfred for me, and say I am sorry we could not work together for longer. And greet his queen from me as well."

Udd was looking surprised, relieved, slightly ashamed. "And what is the message for her, lord?"

"Nothing. Nothing. Just greetings, and the memory of old times. And listen, Udd. I wouldn't trust anyone to do this for me. I'm relying on you. Don't let me down."

The little man went out, still looking relieved. But less ashamed. Pointless, thought Shef. And directly against what the god said. We might need Udd during the day. But I could not bear to see those terrified eyes any more. Taking Udd out of the battle was an act of kindness. Also of defiance against the cynic-god Rig, his father and mentor.

Shef came out of the tent whistling, startling the sentries, who were used at least to reflective silence on mornings like this one. He hailed Cwicca, listening to Udd's explanation a few feet away. "Have you got that bagpipe you made over the winter, Cwicca? Well, play it today. If that doesn't scare the Ragnarssons, nothing will."

Hours later, on a calm sea, the fleet crawled towards the bay behind which lay the long-inviolate Braethraborg. To the left of it, as the fleet approached from the north, a spit of land jutted out. On it, just visible, the hulks of the Ragnarssons' four-mule catapult battery, flanked by the twist-shooters or torsion dart-throwers, and flanked again by the cheap, simple, inaccurate stone-lobbers. Out from the spit, almost blocking the entrance to the bay, lay the dozen shapes of the Ragnarssons' largest warships, the coastal patrol that never put out to sea. Behind them clustered the mass of conventional longships, the main body of their fleet, headed by Shef's old enemy, the *Frani Ormr.*

In the *Fearnought* Shef could hear the rowers grunting as they heaved on the oars—less oars now than sweeps. They were twice the size of ordinary oars and manned by two men each, the strongest in the fleet, carefully selected by Brand and Hagbarth. They had made their approach under sail, to save the rowers' strength, but now the time had come to strike the mast and yard. Close by, on the same course as the *Fearnought,* King Olaf's four large craft, each the size of the wrecked *Crane,* kept pace. Kept pace easily, at a paddling stroke, the rowers looking sideways at the strange ship they convoyed.

Shef had finally given orders to fit the plates of case-hardened steel. The two fighting platforms with the rotating mules on them were armored up

to waist height, the plates slanting outwards. It would have been impossible to armor the rest of the ship and still have her float and move, but Shef had rigged a frame that bolted onto each gunwale. On this plates were fitted, overlapping like the shingles on a roof, or like dragon-scales. They too sloped from bottom to top, beginning just above the height of the oarsmen's heads and running up till they almost met six feet above.

"You keep your shield up in battle," Shef had explained to a doubtful Hagbarth. "At least if you're expecting spears and arrows from a distance. And you keep it slanted so they'll skid off. That's what we're going to try."

Behind the laboring *Fearnought* and the large ships, as with the Ragnarsson fleet, came the mass of the attackers in the eighteen-oar-a-side craft that were the backbone of all Viking navies. Each towed behind it, hard to see in the sun-dazzle off the water, a smaller boat, fishermen's skiffs like the grind-boats of the far north, all that the local fishing villages could raise. Each held four to eight rowers and two pairs of extra men jammed in. The rowers had again been carefully selected from the best of the Swedes and Norwegians. In each boat two men clutched crossbows, two more were Bruno's German *Ritters*.

Watching from his place in the center, Sigurth Ragnarsson remarked, "Masts stepped, I see."

"Does that mean there'll be no funny business this time?" asked Ubbi. "I doubt it very much," answered Sigurth. "But we know some tricks ourselves now. Let's hope they're good ones."

Shef stood on top of the forward mule, almost the only place left on the *Fearnought* from which one could now see anything. With his one eye he watched the Ragnarsson catapult battery. He was sharp-sighted, but not enough to see what he needed to. There had to be a way to look closer! He needed to know if they were ready to shoot. If they were cunning, they might hold their first volley till Olaf's ships were in range, conceivably sink all four of them with their first rocks. If that happened the battle would be lost before it started, Shef's "scissors"—for so he had mentally labeled the big vessels in his plan—blunted by the catapults' "stone." Yet he did not want to stop the ships too far out. The less distance that had to be covered by the small boats, the "paper" in his plan, the better.

They were close to being in range, he decided. He turned and waved to King Olaf, standing next to Brand on the forecastle of his heavy ship fifty yards off, three sweeps from side to side. Olaf waved in reply, called an order. As the rowers tossed their oars and the ship lost way, a thirty-pound boulder came sighing out of the sky, at extreme range. It plumped into the water ten feet from the prow of Olaf's *Heron*, the splash throwing spray over the king. Shef grimaced. A little too closely calculated. Would they try again?

The four big ships had lost way, were being left behind as the *Fearnought* ground slowly on into catapult range. Behind them the mass of the fleet had tossed oars as well, were drifting gently forward. As they did so they dropped their tows. The dead silence of the approach was broken suddenly by harsh cheering. The skiffs had cast off, their fresh rowers straining at their oars, each boat making the best pace it could, treating the last mile as a race. As they swept past first their tow-ships and then the leading line of large craft, the oarsmen lined the side, cheering in unison as their boatswains called the time.

The first of the skiffs shot past the *Fearnought*, its helmsman one of Brand's Halogalanders. Shef could hear him shouting, "Put your backs into it, will you, before some Swedish prick gets past us." Shef waved to him, to the two *skogarmenn* crossbows crouched on the rear thwart, to Bruno in one of the pursuing boats, and to the rest of them pouring past, sixty of them spread out like hounds on the scent of a stag. His oarsmen were breathing too deep to cheer, driving their immensely heavy ship on at a quarter the speed of the racing skiffs.

How would the catapults take that? Shef saw spouts of water rise suddenly, two of them, then a third, and felt his heart leap. Every plume was a miss, every miss was one fewer chance to shoot, and a minute gained before they could rewind their clumsy machines. Yet there must have been a hit, yes, there, near the leading skiffs, men struggling in the water by shattered planks. No-one was stopping or slowing to pick them up. Shef had rubbed that in hard. No survivors will be rescued. Keep rowing and leave them. Some of the mailed men would drown, some, he hoped, keep themselves afloat on planks and swim to the nearer shore. The skiffs swept on like so many water-beetles, oars skimming. The *Fearnought* was perhaps a furlong closer to the grim, banner-waving line of the Ragnarsson fleet.

"Give me a hundred strokes," shouted Shef to the rowers. "A hundred strokes and you can rest easy. Hagbarth, call the time. Cwicca, play them along."

The big men began to heave harder, using up the last of their hoarded strength, something they would never do at the start of a normal battle, to be decided by hard hand-strokes. The screeching music urged them on. Cuthred, grinning sourly, looked up from the shadow of the armor plating. "Ogvind here says he'll row harder without the bagpipe, can you shut him up?" Shef waved back and shouted something no-one heard. As the count ran down, Shef looked again at the scene in front of him, estimating distances, looking at the enemy catapults, the racing skiffs, the Ragnarsson front line, suddenly seeming much nearer. Lucky that that at least had not moved. If they had broken their formation instantly, their "scissors" might have cut his "paper," large ships riding down small ones. But now his "paper" would wrap their "stone," his "stone" blunt their "scissors."

"Ten last strokes," Shef shouted, "and steer to starboard. Put us broadside on. Cwicca, shoot for the one with the Raven Banner. Osmod—" he raised his voice even more to reach the aft catapult, "—shoot for the one to the left of the Raven and then work left, *left,* you hear?"

The ship swung, with a final gasp the rowers completed the stroke, slumped sweating over their oars. Shef jumped from his place and ran to another vantage-point clear of the catapults. As the *Fearnought* drifted to a stop, Cwicca and Osmod stared along the trails of their mules, through the gaps left in the plating.

Cwicca dropped his hand, Hama pulled the retainer bolt, the whole ship shuddered to the thwack of the throwing arm striking its padded bar. Shuddered again a moment later as Osmod followed suit. Shef watched the skimming black dots of boulders tensely. Cwicca and Osmod had had to train most of their crews. They had missed the *Crane* at a critical moment. Would they do better this time?

Both dots came to an abrupt end in the center of the Ragnarsson line, Shef was almost sure he could see splinters fly. He waited for the sudden collapse, the disappearance of a ship opened up like a flower, as he had seen happen at the battle off the Elbe. Nothing. The line was still there, dragon-heads glaring. What had the Ragnarssons done? Had they armored their ships?

"Two hits," Shef shouted. "Work out to left and right, as ordered." He did not know what was happening. But in machine-war, as in the old kind, once battle was joined you just had to put your head down and keep doing your job.

The winders whirled their levers, the oarsmen backed water gently to Hagbarth's directions, trying to keep the ship broadside onto the enemy line. Again the double shudder as the stones released, again the black streaks of boulders flying into the line of ships. Still no gaps, no sagging prows. But he could see men running, leaping from ship to ship. Something was taking effect.

As he stared out, the *Fearnought* was suddenly battered down in the water. A great clang made Shef cringe, something whirred over his head in pieces. He looked round, realized that the catapults up on the spit of land had changed their aim, were shooting now not at the skiffs closing on them, but at the ship destroying their battle-line. If the *Fearnought* had not been armored she would have sunk then and there. The boulder had hit dead center, in line with the stepped mast, had shattered on impact with the case-hardened plates, the fragments whistling overhead. Shef stepped through the rowers to join Hagbarth looking at the damage. The plates were unharmed, but the wooden frame that held them had cracked clean through, leaving the outer shell sagging.

Again the *Fearnought* quivered to her own discharges, and again and again came the violent clangs of boulders striking. One struck forward of center, again shattering the frame, the other on the aft catapult platform. Osmod stepped up, pushing sagging plates out of the way, shoving winders back to their places. "Some rope," he called, "tie these timbers back, we can shoot again." The whole platform was out of line, Shef saw, something broken deep in its mounting. They could not take very much more of this battering. A steel plate slid free of its broken frame, fell into the sea, leaving a gap of sunlight.

"Turn the ship while they're winding," Shef shouted. "Turn the undamaged side towards them. Three more volleys and we're done."

* * *

The leading skiffs had reached the shore, on the spit a hundred yards short of the battery. As they closed they had been engaged first by the dart-shooters, then the quick-shooting stone lobbing devices Shef's men called pull-throwers. The former were no danger to boats, but demoralizing as they drove their huge darts through man and mail. The latter could sink a boat, but only by random shooting, unaimable. The boats pressed on, clumping at the last moment to make a concerted charge onto the shore.

Two hundred picked men faced them, knee-deep in the water, ready to beat them back, protect their own catapults, give them more time to destroy the ship that was destroying their own front line. In the boats the crossbowmen cocked their weapons, prepared to shoot them down. In machine-war all the parts had to fit together, each part doing its job. If the parts separated, they were useless. If they fitted together, battle turned into butchery. The air filled with the zip of crossbow quarrels shot at short range through shield and mail. As the Ragnarsson champions fell, shot down by unarmored *skogarmenn*, the heavily-armed Germans stumbled from the boats, formed a line in the water, locked shields and marched forward, Bruno in the center. The Swedish and Norwegian oarsmen grabbed swords and axes and followed. For a few moments there was the traditional melee of battle, the clang of blade on blade. Then the Ragnarsson line, already shot full of holes, disintegrated completely, became a scatter of men fighting back to back or trying to struggle to safety. Bruno called his men together, dressed their ranks, took them up the slope at a steady trot. Some catapulteers ran at once, others tried for a last shot or groped for sword and shield.

How the Ragnarsson ships stayed afloat Shef could not tell, but someone seemed to have had enough. Behind the front line he could see their smaller craft beginning to sweep out, to come forward in a charge. And the front line might not be sinking, but they were lower in the water, he could see a dragon-head tip sideways. The *Fearnought* had almost done her duty. She had battered the Ragnarssons' twelve largest into unmaneuverable hulks, though they were grapneled together so that the one held the other up. Now the smaller craft would have to take over.

But as they swept forward King Olaf, also reading the battle from half a mile behind, ordered his horns to blow and his rowers to pull. The *Heron* and her three consorts drove forward to engage the enemy, horns blaring relentlessly across the shivering water. Paper had wrapped stone—small boats against catapults. Stone had blunted scissors—the *Fearnought's* catapults against the large craft. Now, as King Olaf's giant warships swept towards the Ragnarssons' conventional longships, it was scissors to cut paper.

Shef watched as the *Heron* swept past, seeing Olaf and Brand on the forecastle directing the course, watching the two leading Ragnarsson ships boldly steer to take her on each side, like mastiffs trying to pull down a bull. They were met by a volley of crossbows, a shower of javelins hurled downwards, great rocks as heavy as a man could lift flung over the side to shatter the bottom-boards. One smaller ship hurled grapnels, managed to pull herself alongside though already starting to sink. Her crew scrambled up the sides of the larger ship, met spear-thrusts and sword-blows before they could free a hand. The *Heron* brushed them aside, steered to run down another. Behind her and her consorts the main body of Shef's fleet poured on, aiming for gaps in the enemy ranks, picking their targets.

Shef leaned on the gunwale, looking round. That was it, he thought. The battle was over, except for finishing off. He could see the Ragnarsson catapults had been captured, could see the row of abandoned skiffs drawn up on the shore. King Olaf's late but well-timed charge had broken the back of the enemy fleet. The biggest Ragnarsson ships had never come into action at all, been battered down by the *Fearnought*.

How easily it could have gone the other way! Without the crossbows the skiffs might not have made their landing. Then the *Fearnought* would have been battered to pieces, and King Olaf's ships as soon as they moved forward. If the *Fearnought* had not been there, then even if the Ragnarsson catapults had not done the business, their twelve great dragon-boats would have come out and engaged Olaf three to one. But paper wraps stone, stone blunts scissors, scissors cut paper. Every time. That is how it is with machine-war.

"She's going to the bottom," Hagbarth said briefly. "I think one of those boulders broke her back, finally. Look." He pointed to the water swilling round the open hold.

"Cwicca, Osmod," shouted Shef. "Get your crews bailing. All right, Hagbarth, see if you can beach her. Over there, on the spit below the catapults."

The crippled *Fearnought* crept across the water, while the battle both in the bay and on land moved rapidly away from her, leaving her limping across an empty sea dotted with wreckage and the heads of exhausted swimmers.

CHAPTER THIRTY-THREE

The *Fearnought* beached, or sank, but either way touched bottom a few yards from the sandy shore. Dead and wounded men lay stretched out in a scatter not far away. Here and there in the water, hands waved feebly for rescue. Shef pointed them out to Hagbarth. "Get a couple of men into the row-boat and pick up as many as you can. Send some more along the shore to do what they can for the wounded. Hund will direct them."

Hagbarth nodded. "I'll get the rest working to shed the plates and lighten the ship. I think we can refloat her in the end."

"All right." Shef looked up the slope to where the Ragnarssons had mounted their catapults. No-one there. The battle had moved on, the catapulteers fled, the men from Shef's small-boat flotilla pursuing them and heading for the loot to be found in the now-undefended Braethraborg itself. Shef felt weariness descending on him with the relief of tension, felt he could bear to make no more decisions. Now that the noise of battle had gone by, a lark was singing, high in the air above the grassy slope, reminding him of days in the Emneth meadows years ago. Maybe those days would come back. Days of peace.

He decided to walk up the gentle slope to look over the other side into the bay, see the end of the battle and what must follow it, the sack of the Braethraborg. As he started off up the slope, lance in hand, Cuthred followed him. Karli followed also, a few paces behind. Hagbarth watched them go, felt a moment's concern. On any battlefield there were likely to be men who had feigned death, enemies who might suddenly get to their feet again. It was Viking routine to police a battlefield before ceasing precautions, going over it in teams to strip bodies, finish enemy wounded and look for those worth ransom. This time it had not been done. Still, the king had two bodyguards with him, and there was much to be done on shore. Hagbarth put aside his concern, began to detail the others to their tasks.

At the top of the slope Shef saw again the scattering of dead, not many of them—the catapulteers had mostly run as they saw the drilled German line come up the hill at them. From the highest point he looked out over the scene he had seen in his vision, from the other end of the fjord. A long, green, peaceful bay. Clustered together maybe a mile off, the row on row of longhouses, barracks, shipyards, slipways, slave-pens that had been for so long the center of the Ragnarssons' power, the most feared place in the north. Now the core of that power was sinking in the bay, smashed by King Olaf's ships now making their stately way towards the main dock. The survivors were being hunted down by the smaller craft following up. Some ships, manned by Sigurth's reluctant levies, were steering widely round in an attempt to make their escape. At the center of the whole scene, battered into hulks by the *Fearnought*'s artillery, the twelve great dragon-boats lay holed, awash, their crews clinging to timbers, waiting to be rescued or to drown. All over the bay small boats, makeshift rafts or strong swimmers made for the shore.

"Not much for me to do today," said Cuthred behind Shef. "I might as well have stayed behind."

Shef did not reply. His eye had been caught by three bedraggled warriors beaching a small boat below him, on the side of the spit away from the grounded *Fearnought*. They had seen him too, were walking briskly up the slope.

"Maybe this could be a good day after all," said Sigurth Ragnarsson, in the lead. He had begun the battle in the center ship of the line of the great warships. It had been struck and all but split open by the first stone that came flying from the strange metal-plated boat the Sigvarthsson had deployed. The grapnels which held ship to ship all along the line had kept his own afloat. But still the stones had come flying, flying, while he waited in a fury of impatience for his own artillery to find the range, smash the interloper. In the end he had torn the Raven Banner from the mast, and transferred it, himself and his brothers to his beloved *Frani Ormr,* leading the main fleet behind the shelter of the great patrol craft. Then, with the metal boat at last sinking and out of action, he had led the charge of the smaller ships against King Olaf's *Heron*.

That had failed too, the *Frani Ormr* sunk under him, her bottom smashed open by a boulder heaved from a higher deck. He and his brothers had had to kill several of their own men in the melee that followed to get off the sinking ship. His fleet and army had disintegrated behind him. In a bare hour, without the chance to strike a blow, he had been cast down from power and kingship to being once again a mere warrior, owning only his clothes and his weapons and what he carried on his person. Sigurth had heard that Othin betrayed his followers. But only, so the stories said, to glorious death, sword in hand. Not to ignominious defeat without a chance to strike.

Yet now, Sigurth thought, it might be that Othin stood his friend after all. For there, in front of him, was the source of all their troubles. With two men only by him, to match Sigurth and his two mighty brothers. Three against three.

Shef looked round, recognizing from fifty yards the strange eyes of the Snake-eye. Sigurth, Halvdan and Ubbi, every one of them a champion, and all of them fully armed for the hand-to-hand battle that had not taken place. Against them himself, carrying only his old and fragile lance, with neither armor nor shield, Karli, still clutching his cheap sword, and Cuthred. Could even Cuthred fight three champions at once, with only the doubtful help Shef and Karli could give him? This was what Shef had always hoped and schemed to avoid: the fair fight on even ground against better and more experienced men. The sensible thing to do was run at once, down to the shore and the cover of the *Fearnought's* crossbows. Shef turned to the others, starting to signal to them, point the way back over the little hill.

Too late. Cuthred's eyes had gone wide, he was breathing in with great gasps, slaver beginning to run from the corners of his mouth. He too had recognized the Snake-eye.

Shef shook him by the arm, was shrugged aside with a careless sweep from the shield, its spike missing his face by a fraction. "Cuthred," he shouted. "We must run, for now. Kill them later."

"Kill them now," came a hoarse inhuman answer.

"Remember, you are my man! I released you from the mill. You swore allegiance."

Cuthred turned to look Shef full in the eye, some fragment of intelligence still under his control despite the coming berserkergang. "I was someone's man before you, king. Those are the men who killed King Ella."

He struggled to form words, his face twisting. Shef thought he caught the word "sorry." And then the berserk had thrust past him, running gleefully over the grass at the oncoming trio.

He stopped feet short of them, called out tauntingly, his voice clear and high, full of delight.

"Sons of Ragnar," he shouted. "I killed your father. I tore out his finger-nails to make him talk. Then I bound him and put him in the snake-pit, the *ormgarthr*. He died blue in the face with his hands tied. You will not meet him in Valhalla."

He threw his head back, with a crow of triumphant laughter. Quick as a snake came the javelin from Sigurth. As quick the parry from the hardened shield that sent it flying high overhead. Then Cuthred had charged.

Sigurth stepped deftly away from him, dodging the first slash and duck-ing the back-stroke. Then Ubbi and Halvdan closed in, one from each side, swords swinging. The air was full of the clang of metal as Cuthred beat blows aside, swung and stabbed himself, pressing both men instantly back.

Yet he could not pursue three at once. Sigurth looked for a moment at the melee he had evaded, then turned from it, came on, sword drawn, shield up. Shef looked round. Karli stood by him, face pale, still clutching the reforged sword Shef had given him, taken from the unlucky Hrani. Shef had his lance. Neither had shields. Sigurth outnumbered them one to two. Yet he could not run now and leave Cuthred alone.

"No water between us this time, clever boy," said Sigurth. As he jumped forward Shef stabbed at him with the lance, the first time he had ever tried to wield it in earnest. Sigurth slashed head from wooden shaft with one forehand blow, swung the backhand instantly at Shef's neck. He ducked, sprang back, dropping the useless shaft and pulling out the belt-knife with which he had killed Kjallak. He still felt numb, useless, unprepared. Now was the time he needed Hund's potion. But Hund was on the other side of the hill.

Karli stepped forward to protect his master, swung with the sword he had carried proudly since the day Shef gave it to him. With sick recogni-tion Shef saw that he had forgotten once more everything that had ever been told him about how to wield it. He struck like a plowboy, like a churl, like a webfoot from the fen. Sigurth took the first blow easily on his blade, waited with something like disbelief for the slow second, caught it on his shield and swung with an adder's speed before Karli could recover. Karli had no shield, no helmet. Shef heard the butcher's chunk of cleaver into bone as sword bit deep into skull. The stocky man from the Ditmarsh dropped his weapon, sprawled at the Snake-eye's feet.

Downslope Cuthred was beating Halvdan to his knees with a furious assault. Ubbi, head slashed from shoulders, lay a few yards from him. Sigurth saw the scene out of the corner of his eye and turned again to Shef.

"I'd better make sure of you, then," he said, stepping round Karli's body. Shef faced the veteran warrior with knife alone, too close to turn his back and run.

From far above Othin the one-eyed god looked down on his devotee, Sigurth son of Ragnar. "He is a great warrior," he said ruefully.

"But he has lost the battle," came the reply from the clever-faced god beside him.

"If it had been a fair match he would have won."

"Take him for your Einheriar then."

Othin paused in thought. Should he allow his worshiper one last victory? The words of his son Rig came back to him, and his own words too, the words he had whispered in the ear of his beloved son Balder on the funeral pyre. "Would that some god would bring you back to me, my son." No god had, no hero had, not even his trusted Hermoth. Maybe they were right. Blood was not the cure, but tears. He would never draw tears from the Snake-eye. Regretfully, he made his decision. "Not for nothing do they call me Botlverk, doer of evil, betrayer of warriors," he muttered, heard only by Rig and the all-hearing ears of Heimdall.

He whistled a call to his Valkyriar, who fly unseen over every battlefield, choosing the slain and throwing over them their nets of weakness, paralysis, making weapons turn in the hand and eyes miss the flight of spear or arrow. With his great spear he pointed out the Snake-eye.

Sigurth came up the slight slope like a hunting beast, sword-point low, shield high, his white-rimmed eyes never leaving Shef's face. Shef backed away from him, short knife in hand, open to slash or thrust as soon as Sigurth could close the six bare feet between them. As he backed he felt, suddenly, the ground beneath him at a different angle. They had reached the top of the slope, were starting to cross it. In a few moments they would be among the abandoned catapults, in sight from the *Fearnought*. If he could delay a hundred heartbeats longer . . . The same thought came to Sigurth. He came on faster, determined to make sure work before anyone could intervene.

All day the lace on his rawhide shoe had worked looser and looser. Now it trailed in the short grass. As he took the pace forward that would set up the killing thrust, Sigurth trod on the lace, tried to step forward with the foot that was trapped, slipped and stumbled off balance. He dropped his shield-arm, bracing himself for a moment with his left hand on the grass.

Shef, backing away, stepped forward on pure reflex and stabbed forward with the Rogaland knife. It drove home through the beard and under the chin, exactly as it had done with Kjallak. For an instant Sigurth stared up at him, the strange eyes widening in shock. Then they seemed to see something behind Shef's back, a look of mingled recognition and disgust crossed the dying face. The sword lifted as if to stab at some shape, some betrayer in the sky.

Shef twisted the knife savagely once and leaped back, as Sigurth fell face down.

Cuthred was limping up the slope towards him. His face was gashed open, a long unbleeding split, like the wound a butcher makes in long-dead meat. His mail was hacked and torn in a dozen places. It seemed impossible that he could walk, one thigh seemingly half-severed again, the one slashed open by Vigdjarf.

"You got one, I got two," he remarked. "I avenged King Ella. I will speak well of you to him." As he stood swaying the crazy light died in his eyes. In a more normal voice he added, "I wish you could bury me whole. Send word to the trolls for me, to Miltastaray. I would have been her man."

Suddenly blood began to flow from his wounds, as the strange auto-control of berserkergang left him. He sank down, rolled on to his back. When Shef felt for a pulse, there was none. He walked across the blood-stained grass to look to Karli, but without hope. Warriors like the Snake-eye did not miss their stroke. Not unless they were prevented. His guess was right. Karli was stone-dead as well, brains mixed with the blood around him, his cheerful expression faded for ever to one of surprise and dismay. Bad news for Edith, and a score of others. Bad news for Miltas-taray.

Shef mechanically retrieved Cuthred's sword, started to trudge back to the ship, shoulders bowed. As he reached the abandoned catapults, to his surprise he saw Bruno the German standing in front of him. Behind him, Shef saw that Hagbarth had noticed as well, was calling men from their work on the *Fearnought* and directing them over the side. But for the moment they were alone.

"I saw your duel," said Bruno. "Now you have killed two Ragnarssons. But I don't know how you do it. It seemed that he should kill you easily. Any one of my men could have done it. I doubt you would be any match for me."

"Why should we be a match?"

"You have something I want. Where is your lance?"

Shef waved over one shoulder. "Back there. What is it to you?"

As if in answer Bruno aimed a blow at him with his long horseman's sword. Shef parried automatically with the sword he had taken from Cuthred, parried again and again, found the sword spinning from his hand and the point of Bruno's resting in the hollow of his throat, exactly where he had stabbed Sigurth the Snake-eye.

"What is it to me?" repeated Bruno. "It is the Holy Lance with which Jesus Christ was slain. By a German centurion. The Lance that shed the Holy Blood."

Shef remembered the vision he had seen of a crucifixion, the man in the red-crested helmet speaking German words. "Yes," he said, speaking carefully with the cold point pricking his skin. "I believe you."

"He who holds it will be the Emperor. True Emperor of the West, successor of Charlemagne, uniter once more of the Roman Empire. The German Roman Empire."

Shef felt immense pressure bearing down on him, pressure greater than the fear of the sharp steel point at his throat. Twice men had tried to make him release the lance, twice he had resisted them. If he handed it over now he might be condemning the whole world to a new domination, a new tyranny from a new Rome, stronger than the old Rome and the old Pope. If he refused he would die. Had he the right to save his life at such a price? With Karli and Cuthred dead in the grass beside him?

And yet the Lance was not his. So much was clear. It belonged to the Christians. What they would do with it, only their God knew. But they had the right to follow their vision, as he and the Way, he and Thorvin and Vigleik and all the others had the right to follow theirs. Remembering his own vision of the dying Christ, remembering King Edmund of the East Angles and the old woman he and Alfred had met lamenting in the forest-clearing, he felt there was something yet to come from the Cross. If not from the Church. Yet Bruno was no Churchman.

"If the Lance is to make a German Empire," said Shef stiffly, "it had better be a German who holds it, then. You will find the lance-head by my companion's body there, where Sigurth cut it from its shaft. Only the head is ancient work. The shaft has been many times renewed."

Bruno seemed, for a moment, nonplused. "You are prepared to give it up? I would not do so, even with a point at my throat." He thought a moment longer, ignoring the men now running up the hill towards them. "It is true. Your emblem is not the spear, whether of Othin or of the centurion Longinus. What you wear round your neck, as I have told you, is the *graduale*. It is your destiny to pursue that, as mine was to retrieve the Lance."

He twitched his blade back, raised it in salute. "I ought to kill you just the same," he said. "I fear you are a dangerous man, though no swordsman. But it would not be knightly, in cold blood. Farewell, then, King of the North. Remember I was the first to hail you so."

He ran down the slope, picked something from the bloody grass, kissed it, and sped away towards a line of horses being led towards him from the Braethraborg corrals.

Shef took a crossbow from one of the lightly-armed *skogarmenn* who came panting up the hill, cocked it, dropped in a quarrel, looked at the broad back running away sixty, eighty, a hundred yards off.

I ought to kill you too, he reflected. But it would not be knightly, in cold blood, to return ill for good. Farewell, then, Emperor-to-be. Or as you say, *auf wiedersehen.*